THE
PUSHCART PRIZE, XXXI

2007
PUSHCART PRIZE XXXI
BEST OF THE
SMALL PRESSES

EDITED BY BILL HENDERSON
WITH THE PUSHCART PRIZE EDITORS

I.C.C. LIBRARY

Acknowledgments

Selections for The Pushcart Prize are reprinted with the permission of authors and presses cited. Copyright reverts to authors and presses immediately after publication.

Distributed by W. W. Norton & Co.
500 Fifth Ave., New York, N.Y. 10110

Library of Congress Card Number: 76–58675
ISBN (hardcover): 13: 978-1-888889-43-7
                  10: 1-88888-9-43-8
ISBN (paperback): 13: 978-1-888889-44-4
                  10:1-88888-9-44-6
ISSN: 0149–7863

For Genie

INTRODUCTION

by BILL HENDERSON

"WRITERS BLOCK" is the common term. Despair another. I know many of the writers and readers of this series have been there.

Last year was my turn. I received a diagnosis of cancer—since purged—and worse, for me, I witnessed the slow death of my dog Lulu from the same disease. Lulu was a shaggy mutt I adopted from the local animal shelter. A committee might have dreamed her up—a German shepherd head with a dash of Airedale around the ears and the body of a golden Retriever, plus a constantly thumping floppy tail. She was my every day, every minute companion for ten years, loving without conditions, filled with peace. Our simple daily joy was a run on the ocean beach. And that was plenty for me.

When cancer killed her, I drifted into a sorrow deeper than any worries about my own health. I simply couldn't see the future. I didn't know how to get there or why I should bother. The future was a blank. The labor of the press became too much to contemplate. After 30 years of publishing, I was exhausted.

I mention my own private sorrow only to record for you what happened next.

A phone call. Cedering Fox, the dynamo producer of literary readings by renowned actors in Los Angeles, New York and London, telephoned. Could she do a Pushcart Prize event in East Hampton to benefit our endowment, The Pushcart Prize Fellowships? Of course, I said, wondering if we could fill the hall. In mid-summer it happened. Oscar-winner Marsha Gay Hardin, Peter Boyle of "Young Frankenstein" fame and the wonderful David Strathairn (lead in "Goodnight and Good Luck") and others read stories by Ray Carver, Joyce Carol Oates, Russell Banks, Pamela Painter and Mark Halliday. The place was packed. The actors told the audience, and me, how terribly important the Pushcart Prize series is to our literary culture, particularly for young writers and all those not enamored of the dollar as the only hallmark of value. The prolonged applause was very heartening.

Then another phone call. Elliot Figman, head of Poets & Writers, called to announce that Pushcart had been picked for their annual "Writers For Writers" award. And right behind that, a call from Geeta Jensen of the National Book Critics Circle with news that I had won the Ivan Sandrof Lifetime Achievement Award. At gatherings in New York I accepted both honors for all of our contributing editors and writers over three decades.

With such an outpouring of thanks and affection it was hard to stay depressed. I fell in love with the future all over again.

My wife Genie and I started a radio program, Radio Pushcart. We broadcast from WERU in East Orland, Maine and can be heard via the web worldwide. We also opened the "smallest bookstore in the world" near Maine's Acadia National Park dedicated to small press titles.

So off we dance into the next thirty years.

A few observations: this edition includes more presses than any other recent Pushcart—fifty-one presses are reprinted and many more listed, including nine presses that are new to the series: Tupelo Press, *Runes*, *Ninth Letter*, Hollyridge Press, *Pebble Lake Review*, *Crowd*, *Cue*, *Oregon Humanities* and *New Issues*.

My continuing gratitude for the financial contributions of the members of the Pushcart Prize Fellowships—their names are listed later in the book. If you wish to join them, please contact us. This endowment insures the future of the Pushcart Prize series.

One of the truly impossible jobs of this project is selecting poetry from the thousands of nominations each year. For PPXXXI guest co-editors Eleanor Wilner and Linda Bierds did the impossible.

Eleanor Wilner has published six books of poetry, most recently *The Girl with Bees in Her Hair* (2004) and *Reversing the Spell: New and Selected Poems* (1998) Copper Canyon Press, and *Otherwise* (1993) from The University of Chicago Press; a translation of Euripides' *Medea* in *Euripides I*, The University of Pennsylvania Press; and a book on visionary imagination, *Gathering the Winds*, Johns Hopkins

University Press. Her work appears in over thirty anthologies, including *The Norton Anthology of Poetry* (Fourth Edition).

Her awards include a MacArthur Foundation Fellowship, the Juniper Prize, two Pushcart Prizes, and grants from the National Endowment for the Arts and Pennsylvania Council on the Arts. A former Editor of *The American Poetry Review*, she is currently an Advisory Editor of *Calyx: A Journal of Art and Literature by Women*. She holds a Ph.D. from Johns Hopkins University, has taught at many colleges and universities, most recently at the University of Chicago, Northwestern University, and Smith College. She currently teaches in the MFA Program for Writers at Warren Wilson College, Asheville, NC, and lives in Philadelphia.

Linda Bierds' seventh book of poetry, *First Hand*, was published in April 2005 by Putnam. Her prizes include the PEN/West Poetry Award and the Washington State Governor's Writers Award, two grants from the National Endowment for the Arts, four Pushcart Prizes, the Consuelo Ford Award from the Poetry Society of America, a 1995 Notable Book Selection from the American Library Association (for *The Ghost Trio*) and fellowships from the Ingram Merrill Foundation, the Artist Trust Foundation of Washington, and the Guggenheim Memorial Foundation.. In 1998 she was named a Fellow of the John D. and Catherine T. MacArthur Foundation. She is a professor of English at the University of Washington and lives on Bainbridge Island, just west of Seattle.

Thank you Eleanor and Linda.

And my profound thanks to the hundreds of presses and staff contributing editors, and to our readers Carolyn Waite, Angela Park, Jack Driscoll, Joe Hurka and David Means, and to Hannah Turner, our manager.

Without you all I couldn't begin to continue this celebration.

Goodbye Lulu. Thank you too.

THE PEOPLE WHO HELPED

FOUNDING EDITORS—*Anaïs Nin (1903–1977), Buckminster Fuller (1895–1983), Charles Newman (1938–2006), Daniel Halpern, Gordon Lish, Harry Smith, Hugh Fox, Ishmael Reed, Joyce Carol Oates, Len Fulton, Leonard Randolph, Leslie Fiedler (1917–2003), Nona Balakian (1918–1991), Paul Bowles (1910–1999), Paul Engle (1908–1991), Ralph Ellison (1914–1994), Reynolds Price, Rhoda Schwartz, Richard Morris, Ted Wilentz (1915–2001), Tom Montag, William Phillips (1907–2002), Poetry editor: H. L. Van Brunt:*

CONTRIBUTING EDITORS FOR THIS EDITION—
Alice Schell, Kenneth Gangemi, Jeffrey Hammond, Marie Sheppard Williams, Deb Olin Unferth, John Kister, M.D. Elevitch, Rebecca McClanahan, Cynthia Weiner, Jim Simmerman, Joe Ashby Porter, Pat Strachan, Ben Fountain, Robert Boyers, Jack Pendarvis, Daniel Orozco, Donald Revell, George Keithley, H.E. Francis, Alice Mattison, Daniel Henry, Jessica Roeder, John Fulton, Tracy Mayor, Stephen Dunn, George Gessert, Karen Bender, Robert Wrigley, Dick Allen, Rosellen Brown, Edward Hoagland, DeWitt Henry, R.C. Hildebrandt, Philip Levine, Kim Addonizio, Beth Ann Fennelly, Dana Levin, Karl Elder, Rachel Loden, Wally Lamb, Robert McBrearty, Nancy Richard, Mike Newirth, Valerie Laken, Stacey Richter, Elizabeth McKenzie, Katherine Taylor, Marianna Cherry, Kristin King, Richard Garcia, Lucia Perillo, Maura Stanton, Suzanne Cleary, Lee Upton, Dara Wier, Thomas E. Kennedy, Edward Hirsch, Fred Leebron, Jana Harris, Martha Collins, Nance Van Winckel, Nadine Meyer, Michael Waters, Andrea Hollander Budy, Gerald

Shapiro, John Allman, Dana Levin, David St. John, Margaret Luongo, Sherod Santos, Jeffrey Harrison, Bob Hicok, Joan Murray, Valerie Sayers, Steve Kowit, Wesley McNair, David Jauss, Atsuro Riley, Jim Moore, Ed Falco, Judith Kitchen, Robert Thomas, Philip Dacey, Grace Schulman, David Baker, Alice Fulton, Tony Ardizzone, Jane Hirshfield, Ed Ochester, Rita Dove, Carl Phillips, Lysley Tenorio, Joseph Hurka, Carolyn Alessio, Kirk Nesset, Dorianne Laux, Reginald Shepherd, Paul Maliszewski, Brenda Miller, Renée Ashley Joyce Carol Oates, Joshua Mehigan, Tony Hoagland, Mark Irwin, Claire Bateman, Sharon Dilworth, Catherine Barnett, Lia Purpura, Reginald Gibbons, Jane Brox, Salvatore Scibona, Katrina Roberts, Dan Masterson, Rosanna Warren, Sharon Solwitz, Brigit Pegeen Kelly, Josip Novakovich, Tony Quagliano, Christina Zawadiwsky, Gerry Locklin, Joan Connor, Jack Marshall, Rachel Hadas, Emily Fox Gordon, Daniel Anderson, Robert Cording, Michael Collier, Ralph Angel, Angie Estes, Richard Burgin, Nancy McCabe, Ron Tanner, John Drury, Michael Dennis Browne, David Wojahn, Linda Bierds, Michael Heffernan, Marianne Boruch, Kathy Callaway, Kim Barnes, Claire Davis, Jim Barnes, Stuart Dischell, Christopher Howell, Jean Thompson, S.L. Wisenberg, Ted Deppe, Judith Hall, Ellen Bass, BJ Ward, Robin Hemley, Len Roberts, Paul Zimmer, Dennis Vannatta, Carol Dennis, Charles Harper Webb, Pinckney Benedict, Daniel Hoffman, Lance Olsen, Vern Rutsala, James Reiss, Susan Hahn, Elizabeth Spires, Melanie Rae Thon, Colette Inez, Floyd Skloot, Gary Gildner, Laura Kasischke, William Olsen, Roger Weingarten, Alan Michael Parker, Tom Filer, Kay Ryan, Donald Platt, Bruce Beasley, Lloyd Schwartz, Joan Swift, Kathleen Hill, Gibbons Ruark, Eric Puchner, Elizabeth Graver, Gary Fincke, Marilyn Hacker, Stephen Corey, Nicola Mason, Daisy Fried, Antler, Erin McGraw, Frederick Busch, Philip Appleman, Billy Collins, Timothy Geiger, Marvin Bell, Kevin Prufer, Kathy Fagan, Christopher Buckley, Sydney Lea, Debra Spark, Arthur Smith, Richard Jackson, Diann Blakely, Michael Marton, Rick Bass, Caroline Langston, Pamela Stewart. Richard Kostelanetz, Mark Wisniewski, Patricia Henley, David Gessner, Henry Carlile, Siv Cedering, Karen Bender, Mike Newirth, Sylvia Watanabe

PAST POETRY EDITORS—H. L. Van Brunt, Naomi Lazard, Lynne Spaulding, Herb Leibowitz, Jon Galassi, Grace Schulman, Carolyn Forché, Gerald Stern, Stanley Plumly, William Stafford,

CONTENTS

15

THE
PUSHCART PRIZE, XXXI

REFRESH, REFRESH

fiction by BENJAMIN PERCY

from THE PARIS REVIEW

W HEN SCHOOL LET OUT the two of us went to my backyard to fight. We were trying to make each other tougher. So in the grass, in the shade of the pines and junipers, Gordon and I slung off our back-packs and laid down a pale-green garden hose, tip to tip, making a ring. Then we stripped off our shirts and put on our gold-colored boxing gloves and fought.

Every round went two minutes. If you stepped out of the ring, you lost. If you cried, you lost. If you got knocked out or if you yelled stop, you lost. Afterwards we drank Coca-Colas and smoked Marlboros, our chests heaving, our faces all different shades of blacks and reds and yellows.

We began fighting after Seth Johnson—a no-neck linebacker with teeth like corn kernels and hands like T-bone steaks—beat Gordon until his face swelled and split open and purpled around the edges. Eventually he healed, the rough husks of scabs peeling away to reveal a different face than the one I remembered—older, squarer, fiercer, his left eyebrow separated by a gummy white scar. It was his idea that we should fight each other. He wanted to be ready. He wanted to hurt those who hurt him. And if he went down, he would go down swinging as he was sure his father would. This is what we all wanted: to please our fathers, to make them proud, even though they had left us.

This was in Crow, Oregon, a high desert town in the foothills of the Cascade Mountains. In Crow we have fifteen hundred people, a

Dairy Queen, a BP gas station, a Food-4-Less, a meatpacking plant, a bright-green football field irrigated by canal water, and your standard assortment of taverns and churches. Nothing distinguishes us from Bend or Redmond or La Pine or any of the other nowhere towns off Route 97, except for this: we are home to the 2nd Battalion, 34th Marines.

The marines live on a fifty-acre base in the hills just outside of town, a collection of one-story cinder-block buildings interrupted by cheat grass and sagebrush. Throughout my childhood I could hear, if I cupped a hand to my ear, the lowing of bulls, the bleating of sheep, and the report of assault rifles shouting from the hilltops. It's said that conditions here in Oregon's ranch country closely match the mountainous terrain of Afghanistan and northern Iraq.

Our fathers—Gordon's and mine—were like the other fathers in Crow. All of them, just about, had enlisted as part-time soldiers, as reservists, for drill pay: several thousand a year for a private and several thousand more for a sergeant. Beer pay, they called it, and for two weeks every year plus one weekend a month, they trained. They threw on their cammies and filled their rucksacks and kissed us goodbye and the gates of the 2nd Battalion drew closed behind them.

Our fathers would vanish into the pine-studded hills, returning to us Sunday night with their faces reddened from weather, their biceps trembling from fatigue, and their hands smelling of rifle grease. They would talk about ECPs and PRPs and MEUs and WMDs and they would do push-ups in the middle of the living room and they would call six o'clock "eighteen hundred hours" and they would high-five and yell, "Semper fi." Then a few days would pass and they would go back to the way they were, to the men we knew: Coors-drinking, baseball-throwing, crotch-scratching, Aqua Velva-smelling fathers.

No longer. In January the battalion was activated and in March they shipped off for Iraq. Our fathers—our coaches, our teachers, our barbers, our cooks, our gas-station attendants and UPS deliverymen and deputies and firemen and mechanics—our fathers, so many of them, climbed onto the olive-green school buses and pressed their palms to the windows and gave us the bravest, most hopeful smiles you can imagine and vanished. Just like that.

Nights, I sometimes got on my Honda dirt bike and rode through the hills and canyons of Deschutes County. Beneath me the engine growled and shuddered, while all around me the wind, like something alive, bullied me, tried to drag me from my bike. A dark world slipped past as I downshifted, leaning into a turn, and accelerated on a straightaway—my speed seventy, then eighty—concentrating only on the twenty yards of road glowing ahead of me.

On this bike I could ride and ride and ride, away from here, up and over the Cascades, through the Willamette Valley, until I reached the ocean, where the broad black backs of whales regularly broke the surface of the water, and even further—further still—until I caught up with the horizon, where my father would be waiting. Inevitably, I ended up at Hole in the Ground.

A long time ago a meteor came screeching down from space and left behind a crater five thousand feet wide and three hundred feet deep. Hole in the Ground is frequented during the winter by the daredevil sledders among us and during the summer by bearded geologists interested in the metal fragments strewn across its bottom. I dangled my feet over the edge of the crater and leaned back on my elbows and took in the black sky—no moon, only stars—just a little lighter than a raven. Every few minutes a star seemed to come unstuck, streaking through the night in a bright flash that burned into nothingness.

In the near distance Crow glowed grayish green against the darkness—a reminder of how close to oblivion we lived. A chunk of space ice or a solar wind could have jogged the meteor sideways and rather than landing here it could have landed there at the intersection of Main and Farwell. No Dairy Queen, no Crow High, no 2nd Battalion. It didn't take much imagination to realize how something can drop out of the sky and change everything.

This was in October, when Gordon and I circled each other in the backyard after school. We wore our golden boxing gloves, cracked with age and flaking when we pounded them together. Browned grass crunched beneath our sneakers and dust rose in little puffs like distress signals.

Gordon was thin to the point of being scrawny. His collarbone poked against his skin like a swallowed coat hanger. His head was too big for his body and his eyes were too big for his head and football players—Seth Johnson among them—regularly tossed him into garbage cans and called him E.T.

He had had a bad day. And I could tell from the look on his face—the watery eyes, the trembling lips that revealed in quick flashes his buckteeth—that he wanted, he *needed*, to hit me. So I let him. I

21

raised my gloves to my face and pulled my elbows against my ribs and Gordon lunged forward, his arms snapping like rubber bands. I stood still, allowing his fists to work up and down my body, allowing him to throw the weight of his anger on me, until eventually he grew too tired to hit anymore and I opened up my stance and floored him with a right cross to the temple. He lay there, sprawled out in the grass with a small smile on his E.T. face. "Damn," he said in a dreamy voice. A drop of blood gathered along the corner of his eye and streaked down his temple into his hair.

My father wore steel-toed boots, Carhartt jeans, and a T-shirt advertising some place he had traveled, maybe Yellowstone or Seattle. He looked like someone you might see shopping for motor oil at Bi-Mart. To hide his receding hairline he wore a John Deere cap that laid a shadow across his face. His brown eyes blinked above a considerable nose underlined by a gray mustache. Like me, my father was short and squat, a bulldog. His belly was a swollen bag and his shoulders were broad, good for carrying me during parades and at fairs when I was younger. He laughed a lot. He liked game shows. He drank too much beer and smoked too many cigarettes and spent too much time with his buddies, fishing, hunting, bullshitting, which probably had something to do with why my mother divorced him and moved to Boise with a hairdresser and triathlete named Chuck.

At first, after my father left, like all of the other fathers, he would e-mail whenever he could. He would tell me about the heat, the gallons of water he drank every day, the sand that got into everything, the baths he took with baby wipes. He would tell me how safe he was, how very safe. This was when he was stationed in Turkey. Then the reservists shipped for Kirkuk, where insurgents and sandstorms attacked almost daily. The e-mails came less frequently. Weeks of silence passed between them.

Sometimes, on the computer, I would hit refresh, refresh, *refresh*, hoping. In October I received an e-mail that read: "Hi Josh. I'm OK. Don't worry. Do your homework. Love, Dad." I printed it up and hung it on my door with a piece of Scotch tape.

For twenty years my father worked at Nosler, Inc.—the bullet manufacturer based out of Bend—and the Marines trained him as an ammunition technician. Gordon liked to say his father was a gunnery sergeant and he was, but we all knew he was also the battalion mess-manager, a cook, which was how he made his living in Crow, tending the grill at Hamburger Patty's. We knew their titles but we didn't know, not really, what their titles meant, what our fathers *did* over there. We imagined them doing heroic things: rescuing Iraqi babies from burning huts, sniping suicide bombers before they could detonate on a crowded city street. We drew on Hollywood and TV news to develop elaborate scenarios where maybe, at twilight, during a trek through the mountains of northern Iraq, bearded insurgents ambushed our fathers with rocket launchers. We imagined them silhouetted by a fiery explosion. We imagined them burrowing into the sand like lizards and firing their M-16s, their bullets streaking through the darkness like the meteorites I observed on sleepless nights.

When Gordon and I fought we painted our faces—black and green and brown—with the camo-grease our fathers left behind. It made our eyes and teeth appear startlingly white. And it smeared away against our gloves just as the grass smeared away beneath our sneakers—and the ring became a circle of dirt, the dirt a reddish color that looked a lot like scabbed flesh. One time Gordon hammered my shoulder so hard I couldn't lift my arm for a week. Another time I elbowed one of his kidneys and he peed blood. We struck each other with such force and frequency the golden gloves crumbled and our knuckles showed through the sweat-soaked, blood-soaked foam like teeth through a busted lip. So we bought another set of gloves, and as the air grew steadily colder we fought with steam blasting from our mouths.

Our fathers had left us, but men remained in Crow. There were old men, like my grandfather, whom I lived with—men who had paid their dues, who had worked their jobs and fought their wars and now spent their days at the gas station, drinking bad coffee from Styrofoam cups, complaining about the weather, arguing about the best months to reap alfalfa. And there were incapable men. Men who rarely shaved and watched daytime television in their once-white underpants. Men who lived in trailers and filled their shopping carts with Busch Light, summer sausage, Oreo cookies.

And then there were vulturous men like Dave Lightener—men who scavenged whatever our fathers had left behind. Dave Lightener worked as a recruitment officer. I'm guessing he was the only recruitment officer in world history who drove a Vespa scooter with a Support Our Troops ribbon magnet on its rear. We sometimes saw it parked outside the homes of young women whose husbands had gone to war. Dave had big ears and small eyes and wore his hair in your standard-issue high-and-tight buzz. He often spoke in a too-loud voice about all the insurgents he gunned down when working a Falluja patrol unit. He lived with his mother in Crow, but spent his days in Bend and Redmond trolling the parking lots of Best Buy, ShopKo, K-Mart, Wal-Mart, Mountain View Mall. He was looking for people like us, people who were angry and dissatisfied and poor.

But Dave Lightener knew better than to bother us. On duty he stayed away from Crow entirely. Recruiting there would be too much like poaching the burned section of forest where deer, rib-slatted and wobbly-legged, nosed through the ash, seeking something green.

We didn't fully understand the reason our fathers were fighting. We only understood that they *had* to fight. The necessity of it made the reason irrelevant. "It's all part of the game," my grandfather said. "It's just the way it is." We could only cross our fingers and wish on stars and hit refresh, *refresh*, hoping they would return to us, praying we would never find Dave Lightener on our porch uttering the words *I regret to inform you . . .*

One time, my grandfather dropped Gordon and me off at Mountain View Mall and there, near the glass-doored entrance, stood Dave Lightener. He wore his creased khaki uniform and spoke with a group of Mexican teenagers. They were laughing, shaking their heads and walking away from him as we approached. We had our hats pulled low and he didn't recognize us.

"Question for you, gentlemen," he said in the voice of telemarketers and door-to-door Jehovah's Witnesses. "What do you plan on doing with your lives?"

Gordon pulled off his hat with a flourish, as if he were part of some *ta-da!* magic act and his face was the trick. "I plan on killing some crazy-ass Muslims," he said and forced a smile. "How about you, Josh?"

"Yeah," I said. "Kill some people then get myself killed." I grimaced even as I played along. "That sounds like a good plan."

Dave Lightener's lips tightened into a thin line, his posture straightened, and he asked us what we thought our fathers would think, hearing us right now. "They're out there risking their lives, defending our freedom, and you're cracking sick jokes," he said. "I think that's sick."

We hated him for his soft hands and clean uniform. We hated him because he sent people like us off to die. Because at twenty-three he had attained a higher rank than our fathers. Because he slept with the lonely wives of soldiers. And now we hated him even more for making us feel ashamed. I wanted to say something sarcastic but Gordon was quicker. His hand was out before him, his fingers gripping an imaginary bottle. "Here's your maple syrup," he said.

Dave said, "And what is that for?"

"To eat my ass with," Gordon said.

Right then a skateboarder-type with green hair and a nose ring walked from the mall, a bagful of DVDs swinging from his fist, and Dave Lightener forgot us. "Hey, friend," he was saying. "Let me ask you something. Do you like war movies?"

In November we drove our dirt bikes deep into the woods to hunt. Sunlight fell through tall pines and birch clusters and lay in puddles along the logging roads that wound past the hillsides packed with huckleberries and on the moraines where coyotes scurried, trying to flee from us and slipping, causing tiny avalanches of loose rock. It hadn't rained in nearly a month, so the crabgrass and the cheat grass and the pine needles had lost their color, dry and blond as cornhusks, crackling beneath my boots when the road we followed petered out into nothing and I stepped off my bike. In this waterless stillness, it seemed you could hear every chipmunk within a square acre rustling for pine nuts, and when the breeze rose into a cold wind the forest became a giant whisper.

We dumped our tent and our sleeping bags near a basalt grotto with a spring bubbling from it and Gordon said, "Let's go, troops," holding his rifle before his chest diagonally, as a soldier would. He dressed as a soldier would too, wearing his father's over-large cammies rather than the mandatory blaze-orange gear. Fifty feet apart, we worked our way downhill through the forest, through a huckleberry thicket, through a clear-cut crowded with stumps, taking care not to make much noise or slip on the pine needles carpeting the ground. A chipmunk worrying at a pinecone screeched its astonishment when a peregrine falcon swooped down and seized it, carrying it off between the trees to some secret place. Its wings made no sound, and neither did the blaze-orange-clad hunter when he appeared in a clearing several hundred yards below us.

Gordon made some sort of SWAT-team gesture—meant, I think, to say, stay low—and I made my way carefully toward him. From behind a boulder we peered through our scopes, tracking the hunter, who looked, in his vest and ear-flapped hat, like a monstrous pumpkin. "That cock-sucker," Gordon said in a harsh whisper. The hunter was Seth Johnson. His rifle was strapped to his back and his mouth was moving—he was talking to someone. At the corner of the meadow he joined four members of the varsity football squad, who sat on logs around a smoldering campfire, their arms bobbing like oil pump jacks as they brought their beers to their mouths.

I took my eye from my scope and noticed Gordon fingering the trigger of his 30.06. I told him to quit fooling around and he pulled his hand suddenly away from the stock and smiled guiltily and said he just wanted to know what it felt like having that power over someone. Then his trigger finger rose up and touched the gummy white scar that split his eyebrow. "I say we fuck with them a little."

I shook my head no.

Gordon said, "Just a little—to scare them."

"They've got guns," I said, and he said, "So we'll come back tonight."

Later, after an early dinner of beef jerky and trail mix and Gatorade, I happened upon a four-point stag nibbling on some bear grass, and I rested my rifle on a stump and shot it, and it stumbled backwards and collapsed with a rose blooming from behind its shoulder where the heart was hidden. Gordon came running and we stood around the deer and smoked a few cigarettes, watching the thick arterial blood run from its mouth. Then we took out our knives and got to work. I cut around the anus, cutting away the penis and testes, and then ran the knife along the belly, unzipping the hide to reveal the delicate pink flesh and greenish vessels into which our hands disappeared.

The blood steamed in the cold mountain air, and when we finished—when we'd skinned the deer and hacked at its joints and cut out its back strap and boned out its shoulders and hips, its neck and ribs, making chops, roasts, steaks, quartering the meat so we could bundle it into our insulated saddle-bags—Gordon picked up the deer head by the antlers and held it before his own. Blood from its neck made a pattering sound on the ground, and in the half-light of early evening Gordon began to do a little dance, bending his knees and stomping his feet.

"I think I've got an idea," he said and pretended to charge at me with the antlers. I pushed him away and he said, "Don't pussy out on me, Josh." I was exhausted and reeked of gore, but I could appreciate the need for revenge. "Just to scare them, right, Gordo?" I said.

26

"Right."

We lugged our meat back to camp and Gordon brought the deer hide. He slit a hole in its middle and poked his head through so the hide hung off him loosely, a hairy sack, and I helped him smear mud and blood across his face. Then, with his Leatherman, he sawed off the antlers and held them in each hand and slashed at the air as if they were claws.

Night had come on and the moon hung over the Cascades, grayly lighting our way as we crept through the forest imagining ourselves in enemy territory, with trip wires and guard towers and snarling dogs around every corner. From behind the boulder that overlooked their campsite, we observed our enemies as they swapped hunting stories and joked about Jessica Robertson's big-ass titties and passed around a bottle of whiskey and drank to excess and finally pissed on the fire to extinguish it. When they retired to their tents we waited an hour before making our way down the hill with such care that it took us another hour before we were upon them. Somewhere an owl hooted, its noise barely noticeable over the chorus of snores that rose from their tents. Seth's Bronco was parked nearby—the license plate read SMAN—and all their rifles lay in its cab. I collected the guns, slinging them over my shoulder, then I eased my knife into each of Seth's tires.

I still had my knife out when we were standing beside Seth's tent, and when a cloud scudded over the moon and made the meadow fully dark I stabbed the nylon and in one quick jerk opened up a slit. Gordon rushed in, his antler-claws slashing. I could see nothing but shadows but I could hear Seth scream the scream of a little girl as Gordon raked at him with the antlers and hissed and howled like some cave-creature hungry for man-flesh. When the tents around us came alive with confused voices, Gordon reemerged with a horrible smile on his face and I followed him up the hillside, crashing through the undergrowth, leaving Seth to make sense of the nightmare that had descended upon him without warning.

Winter came. Snow fell, and we threw on our coveralls and wrenched on our studded tires and drove our dirt bikes to Hole in the Ground, dragging our sleds behind us with towropes. Our engines filled the white silence of the afternoon. Our back tires kicked up plumes of powder and on sharp turns slipped out beneath us, and we lay there in the middle of the road, bleeding, laughing, unafraid.

Earlier, for lunch, we had cooked a pound of bacon with a stick of

27

butter. The grease, which hardened into a white waxy pool, we used as polish, buffing it into the bottoms of our sleds. Speed was what we wanted at Hole in the Ground. We descended the steepest section of the crater into its heart, three hundred feet below us. We followed each other in the same track, ironing down the snow to create a chute, blue-hued and frictionless, that would allow us to travel at a speed equivalent to freefall. Our eyeballs glazed with frost, our ears roared with wind, and our stomachs rose into our throats as we rocketed down and felt like we were five again—and then we began the slow climb back the way we came and felt fifty.

We wore crampons and ascended in a zigzagging series of switchbacks. It took nearly an hour. The air had begun to go purple with evening when we stood again at the lip of the crater, sweating in our coveralls, taking in the view through the fog of our breath. Gordon packed a snowball. I said, "You better not hit me with that." He cocked his arm threateningly and smiled, then dropped to his knees to roll the snowball into something bigger. He rolled it until it grew to the size of a large man curled into the fetal position. From the back of his bike he took the piece of garden hose he used to siphon gas from fancy foreign cars and he worked it into his tank, sucking at its end until gas flowed.

He doused the giant snowball as if he hoped it would sprout. It didn't melt—he'd packed it tight enough—but it puckered slightly and appeared leaden, and when Gordon withdrew his Zippo, sparked it, and held it toward the ball, the fumes caught flame and the whole thing erupted with a gasping noise that sent me staggering back a few steps.

Gordon rushed forward and kicked the ball of fire, sending it rolling, tumbling down the crater, down our chute like a meteor, and the snow beneath it instantly melted only to freeze again a moment later, making a slick blue ribbon. When we sledded it, we went so fast our minds emptied and we felt a sensation at once like flying and falling.

On the news Iraqi insurgents fired their assault rifles. On the news a car bomb in Baghdad blew up seven American soldiers at a traffic checkpoint. On the news the president said he did not think it was wise to provide a time frame for troop withdrawal. I checked my e-mail before breakfast and found nothing but spam.

Gordon and I fought in the snow wearing snow boots. We fought so much our wounds never got a chance to heal and our faces took on a permanent look of decay. Our wrists felt swollen, our knees ached, our joints felt full of tiny dry wasps. We fought until fighting hurt too much and we took up drinking instead. Weekends, we drove our dirt bikes to Bend, twenty miles away, and bought beer and took it to Hole in the Ground and drank there until a bright line of sunlight appeared on the horizon and illuminated the snow-blanketed desert. Nobody asked for our IDs and when we held up our empty bottles and stared at our reflections in the glass, warped and ghostly, we knew why. And we weren't alone. Black bags grew beneath the eyes of the sons and daughters and wives of Crow, their shoulders stooped, wrinkles enclosing their mouths like parentheses.

Our fathers haunted us. They were everywhere: in the grocery store when we spotted a thirty-pack of Coors on sale for ten bucks; on the highway when we passed a jacked-up Dodge with a dozen hay bales stacked in its bed; in the sky when a jet roared by, reminding us of faraway places. And now, as our bodies thickened with muscle, as we stopped shaving and grew patchy beards, we saw our fathers even in the mirror. We began to look like them. Our fathers, who had been taken from us, were everywhere, at every turn, imprisoning us.

Seth Johnson's father was a staff sergeant. Like his son, he was a big man but not big enough. Just before Christmas he stepped on a cluster bomb. A U.S. warplane dropped it and the sand camouflaged it and he stepped on it and it tore him into many meaty pieces. When Dave Lightener climbed up the front porch with a black armband and a somber expression, Mrs. Johnson, who was cooking a honeyed ham at the time, collapsed on the kitchen floor. Seth pushed his way out the door and punched Dave in the face, breaking his nose before he could utter the words *I regret to inform you* . . .

Hearing about this, we felt bad for all of ten seconds. Then we felt good because it was his father and not ours. And then we felt bad again and on Christmas Eve we drove to Seth's house and laid down on his porch the rifles we had stolen, along with a six-pack of Coors, and then, just as we were about to leave, Gordon dug in his back pocket and removed his wallet and placed under the six-pack all the money he had—a few fives, some ones. "Fucking Christmas," he said.

We got braver and went to the bars—The Golden Nugget, The Weary Traveler, The Pine Tavern—where we square-danced with older women wearing purple eye shadow and sparkly dreamcatcher earrings and push-up bras and clattery high heels. We told them we were Marines back from a six-month deployment and they said, "Re-

29

ally?" and we said, "Yes, ma'am," and when they asked for our names we gave them the names of our fathers. Then we bought them drinks and they drank them in a gulping way and breathed hotly in our faces and we brought our mouths against theirs and they tasted like menthol cigarettes, like burnt detergent. And then we went home with them, to their trailers, to their waterbeds, where among their stuffed animals we fucked them.

Mid-afternoon and it was already full dark. On our way to The Weary Traveler we stopped by my house to bum some money off my grandfather, only to find Dave Lightener waiting for us. He must have just gotten there—he was halfway up the porch steps—when our headlights cast an anemic glow over him and he turned to face us with a scrunched-up expression, as if trying to figure out who we were. He wore the black band around his arm and, over his nose, a white-bandaged splint.

We did not turn off our engines. Instead we sat in the driveway, idling, the exhaust from our bikes and the breath from our mouths clouding the air. Above us a star hissed across the moonlit sky, vaguely bright like a light turned on in a day-lit room. Then Dave began down the steps and we leapt off our bikes to meet him. Before he could speak I brought my fist to his diaphragm, knocking the breath from his body. He looked like a gun-shot actor in a Western, clutching his belly with both hands, doubled over, his face making a nice target for Gordon's knee. A snap sound preceded Dave falling on his back with blood coming from his already broken nose.

He put up his hands and we hit our way through them. I punched him once, twice, in the ribs while Gordon kicked him in the spine and stomach and then we stood around gulping air and allowed him to struggle to his feet. When he righted himself, he wiped his face with his hand and blood dripped from his fingers. I moved in and roundhoused with my right and then my left, my fists knocking his head loose on its hinges. Again he collapsed, a bloody bag of a man. His eyes walled and turned up, trying to see the animal bodies looming over him. He opened his mouth to speak and I pointed a finger at him and said, with enough hatred in my voice to break a back, "*Don't* say a word. Don't you dare. Not one word."

He closed his mouth and tried to crawl away and I brought a boot down on the back of his skull and left it there a moment, grinding his face into the ground so that when he lifted his head the snow held a red impression of his face. Gordon went inside and returned a moment later with a roll of duct tape and we held Dave down and bound his wrists and ankles and threw him on a sled and taped him to it many times over and then tied the sled to the back of Gordon's bike and drove at a perilous speed to Hole in the Ground.

The moon shone down and the snow glowed with pale blue light as we smoked cigarettes, looking down into the crater, with Dave at our feet. There was something childish about the way our breath puffed from our mouths in tiny clouds. It was as if we were imitating choo-choo trains. And for a moment, just a moment, we were kids again. Just a couple of stupid kids. Gordon must have felt this, too, because he said, "My mom wouldn't even let me play with toy guns when I was little." And he sighed heavily as if he couldn't understand how he, how we, had ended up here.

Then, with a sudden lurch, Dave began struggling and yelling at us in a slurred voice and my face hardened with anger and I put my hands on him and pushed him slowly to the lip of the crater and he grew silent. For a moment I forgot myself, staring off into the dark oblivion. It was beautiful and horrifying. "I could shove you right now," I said. "And if I did, you'd be dead."

"Please don't," he said, his voice cracking. He began to cry. "Oh fuck. Don't. Please." Hearing his great shuddering sobs didn't bring me the satisfaction I had hoped for. If anything, I felt as I did that day, so long ago, when we taunted him in the Mountain View Mall parking lot—shameful, false.

"Ready?" I said. "One!" I inched him a little closer to the edge. "Two!" I moved him a little closer still and as I did felt unwieldy, at once wild and exhausted, my body seeming to take on another twenty, thirty, forty years. When I finally said, "Three," my voice was barely a whisper.

We left Dave there, sobbing at the brink of the crater. We got on our bikes and we drove to Bend and we drove so fast I imagined catching fire like a meteor, burning up in a flash, howling as my heat consumed me, as we made our way to the U.S. Marine Recruiting Office where we would at last answer the fierce alarm of war and put our pens to paper and make our fathers proud.

Nominated by The Paris Review

LAUNDRY

by MAUREEN STANTON

from THE IOWA REVIEW

> *There is a mystical rite under the material act of cleaning and tidying, for what
> is done with love is always more than itself and partakes of the celestial orders.*
> —May Sarton

My GRANDMOTHER, MADELINE JULIANO, grew up in a shack in a place called Stoney Lonesome. Long since condemned and the land reclaimed by West Point Military Academy in the Hudson River Valley of New York, the house was set in the woods among rolling hills strewn with glacial erratics, large boulders pulled along by the mile-thick tongue of ice as it retreated north. At nearby Long Pond, at a small mouth where the spring-fed lake pours itself out, in the stream that flows over these rocks, my grandmother scrubbed clothes. She was taken out of school in sixth grade to care for her three younger brothers who remained in school, and was hired out to keep house in nearby Highland Falls for the wives of doctors and lawyers and officers from West Point.

Every morning, in spring and summer and fall and winter, before she walked six miles to her job as a maid, my grandmother scoured her family's clothes in a trickle of water that remained fluid when the lake froze. She spread the clothes on the rocks to dry like skins. I imagine her hands, chapped and raw from washing other people's clothes and linens for years.

At nineteen, Madeline married Clarence Starr, a groundskeeper at West Point, and they lived in a caretaker's residence for fourteen years, with their three children, Barbara, Clarissa (my mother), and Skeeter. The house was set on several rural acres with peach and apple orchards, and through the woods was Round Pond, where my mother swam, and in the winter, ice-fished with her father. The house was large and elegant, with French doors leading to a flagstone patio, and a massive fireplace in the living room. They had no electricity even though it was the early forties, but the house and land were paradise and they were happy there.

My grandmother and her two daughters, Barbara and Clarissa, washed clothes with a tub and washboard, using a hard chunk of Fels Naphtha soap or lye soap my grandmother poured into pans and sliced into irregular rectangles. They cranked the wet clothes through a wringer, careful not to catch their fingers between the rollers, then hung the laundry outside. In the winter, when the pants froze solid on the line, they'd bring them inside to finish drying, the frozen trousers standing upright as if embodied, as if they'd walk around the kitchen, collapsing as they warmed.

• • •

Etymologically speaking, laundry was not always women's work. In the 1300s, the word *lavender*, deriving from Old French and meaning "to wash," was equally gendered: *lavandier*, the masculine, or *lavandiere*, feminine. But over time *lavender* slipped to mean "washerwoman" or "laundress." *Launder*, the later form of lavender, referred to a person of either sex who washed linen, though in literature and common usage it rarely meant washerman, or a man who washes clothes (and if so, referred to a Chinese man). Since the chore of laundry was relegated to women, the word itself became imbued with gender, signified a sex.

Feminists tried to sunder the chore from the sex. In 1975, the *London Times* reports, the Greater London Council changed the post of "laundry woman" to "laundry worker." Still, on the website for the Maytag Corporation, the tiny cartoon people worshiping the appliances—washer, dryer, vacuum cleaner—are women; the only male figure is the lonely Maytag repairman, introduced in 1967, a domestic hero always available to fix the broken washing machines of troubled homemakers while the husband is at work and the children at school, just the two of them, the forlorn repairman and the lonely housewife.

33

In television commercials for laundry detergent, the housewife sensually presses her face into a soft, warm, fragrant, fluffy towel which, along with a tidy bowl, signifies her success as a wife and mother, as a woman, her love for her family. Laundry signifies love.

•••

When my mother was ten, officials at West Point decided that the caretaker house at Round Pond deserved to be an officer's home. My grandfather and grandmother bought a tiny house in Highland Falls. My mother loved the house at Round Pond and didn't want to move. When the big truck came, she ran into the woods and hid behind a boulder, where her father found her hours later, asleep. She hated the smaller village house even though it had electricity, which meant they had a tub with an electric agitator to wash the clothes.

Needing to help pay a mortgage, and closer to town, my grandmother returned to housekeeping part-time. She worked for Sadie Schwarz whose family owned Schwarz's Men's Clothing, and the Chirellis who owned the Chevrolet dealership, and one day a week for the Kopalds, who owned the boutique where my mother bought the Ship 'N Shore blouses she ironed crisply and hung in her closet. My mother visited her mother at work sometimes. Once she found her at the Kopalds' on her knees, scrubbing three rooms of wall-to-wall carpet with a hand-brush. My mother disregarded my grandmother's worried scolding and opened the Kopalds' refrigerator, where she discovered a leftover shriveled hot dog and crackers, the lunch Mrs. Kopald had left for my grandmother.

In 1954, six years after they bought the house, my grandfather, Clarence, died of cancer, and so my grandmother, widowed at thirty-nine, began to keep house full-time. My mother was sixteen then, old enough to ignore the pleas from her mother not to phone Mrs. Schwarz, Mrs. Chirelli, and Mrs. Kopald. "With my father gone, my mother needs seventy-five cents an hour now," my mother told them. This was a ten-cent raise, which the women agreed to, except for Mrs. Schwarz who called my mother "fresh."

After her husband died, after she returned to work full-time, my grandmother bought a fancy new electric washing machine and hooked it up in the kitchen, the only place it fit in their tiny house.

•••

In colonial Massachusetts, laundry day was called Blue Monday, blue for the labor it involved—boiling kettles of water, stirring a soup of laundry, rinsing, wringing, hanging: an all-day task—and blue for the bluing women used to brighten garments. In the tomb of Beni Hasson, an Egyptian who lived in the 18th century B.C., there is a picture of two figures washing clothes much the same way as the Pilgrims did, as my grandmother did: by hand. The first patent for a machine that washed clothes was filed by Rodger Rodgerson in 1780, an Englishman. Why did it take thirty-six centuries to discover a labor-saving device for cleaning clothes?

Washing machines were considered "lifesavers" for women, and early models were called "The Housewife's Darling" and "Hired Girl," though they still required hand cranking. The first "automatic" washers debuted in 1937. Whirlpool's version was imprinted with the slogan: "Saves Women's Lives," and an ad for Horton Washers promised its machine would "keep wrinkles out of your face—keep you youthful." A washing machine is a vast improvement over a stick, a rock and a stream, but women are not yet saved. According to Linda Eggerss, a spokeswoman for Maytag Corporation, women still handle laundry chores in 93 percent of American families, with only about a third getting help from a husband or child.

•••

At eighteen, my mother transferred from her job at the Grand Union grocery store in Highland Falls to a position with an affiliate, The Blue Stamp Company of New Jersey. There she met Sylvia Buglino, the wildest, most foul-mouthed girl she ever encountered. It was with Sylvia, and her friend Violet Trappani, that my mother first said "fuck."

My mother lived in Sylvia's brother's bedroom; he was in the service, so came home only occasionally. When he did, my mother rode the train and bus to Highland Falls and slept at home for the weekend. When she noticed more and more often how arthritis pained her mother's hands and feet, she moved back home to help care for her younger brother, Skeeter. My mother found a job at Stewart Air Force Base in Newburgh, and with her increased pay, bought herself a used upright piano for thirty-five dollars, which she dreamed of playing. She moved the piano into the kitchen, right next to the washing machine.

At Stewart Air Force Base in 1956, my mother met my father, Patrick—tall, black-haired, Irish. He was working on a top-secret project, something to do with computer programming and missile launches. My mother invited him for dinner and after dinner he played the piano in the kitchen and there she fell in love with him and gave up her dream of playing the piano for the man who could. They married, moved to Massachusetts where my father found a better job, and soon after, my sister Susan was born.

When my mother moved out of the house in Highland Falls, my grandmother's brother—my great Uncle Vince—chopped up the piano, which was the best way to get it through the low thresholds and narrow doors of the house. In the space where the piano was, right next to the washing machine, my grandmother installed her first dryer.

• • •

I'm not surprised that the first clothes dryer was invented in England, which I think of as perpetually damp. Called a ventilator, it was a cylindrical drum with holes punched in the surface, which you turned by hand over a fire, like roasting a chicken over a spit. The clothes dried, but often smelled of smoke and were covered with soot.

The introduction of automatic dryers to the market around 1946 worried consumers, who feared their garments would be scorched or shrunk, and so in 1950, Elaine K. Weaver, a Research Associate at the Ohio Agricultural Experiment Station, conducted the first comprehensive, scientific study. She published her findings in a bulletin called "Automatic Drying versus Out-of-Door Drying," in which she determined, among other results, through the analysis of Micromation films, that line drying required an average of 625 steps and 57.5 minutes, while using an automatic dryer required only 3 steps and 9 minutes. "Less than 1/6 of the time was required for the operations of the worker," Weaver wrote. "Walking was almost completely eliminated as were stooping, bending, reaching and lifting."

• • •

In 1960, when my mother was twenty-one, she pushed me out of her body and into the world. "When I had you, I said to your father, 'That's it, I want a dryer.' The third one will put you over." My sister Susan was two, Sally was one. My mother had three babies in diapers. By the time I turned one, Sue was toilet trained, but then my mother bore Joanne and so she still had three babies in diapers: heavy wet stinking shitty ammonia-smelling cloth diapers that she washed in her washer and dried in her new dryer. One baby will soil over 5,000 diapers before being potty-trained. If the third one will put you over, what will the seventh do? After Joanne there came Patrick and Barbie. Even by the time Mikey was born in 1970 when I was ten, my mother was still using cloth diapers. Which means that she washed over 35,000 diapers in her life.

• • •

My mother ordered paper dresses once, from an ad in the back of a magazine. Disposable clothing promised relief from the endless loads of laundry. The day the dresses were delivered, she put one on immediately. The material was not much thicker than a sturdy paper towel, plain blue, sleeveless, the hem just above her knees. She looked like an inmate, a paper doll prisoner. Wearing the paper dress, she set about her regular routine of chores, bending, picking up, stretching to make eight beds, for we were slothful children who did not put away our toys or clothes or make our beds unless scolded and punished, and even then fell quickly back to indolence. The paper dress slowly tore and ripped and shredded until my mother's bra and patches of her underwear were exposed and she trailed ribbons of parchment, and then finally the dress slipped right off her. It didn't last until dinner. I remember her disappointment.

• • •

My mother moved quickly around the house doing chores, a cleaning dervish.

"Ma!" we'd yell up the stairs if we needed her.

"MA!" we'd scream out the back door.

Down in the cellar was a good bet, one of the few places she stood still for any length of time: washing, folding, ironing. "Why didn't you answer?" I'd ask when I found her there, quiet, hiding, a cool sanctuary on a summer day, sorting a mound of dirty laundry nearly as tall as she, which fell from the chute two floors above.

"What do you want?" she'd ask. "I'm busy."

You got the idea that whatever you had to say had better be good and not whiny.

There in the basement, over laundry, my mother imparted to me womanly knowledge—menstruation, reproduction, body parts— while she folded and ironed my father's shirts. I sat in an old inflated tire tube on the cellar floor and impatiently listened to her speech. I was more fascinated watching her sprinkle water over the shirts on the ironing board from a glass bottle fitted with a metal spout, like a garden watering can, an antique implement that had belonged to her mother, Madeline Juliano Starr.

This was just before my parents divorced and my mother went to nursing school for a year and then back to work, and then all of us, except for Mikey who was two, were suddenly responsible for our own laundry, even Barbie, and she was only eight. That's when it became fine to use a towel five or six times. Before, when my mother washed the laundry, we'd take two towels to shower, one for our hair only, and throw them both down the chute, away and out of sight, not to be regarded again until they were plump and folded and magically restored to the linen closet.

When we became responsible for our own wash, laundry wars commenced. We'd remove each other's still-wet clothes from the dryer and leave them in a damp pile, usurping the machine for our own loads. I pilfered clean bikinis from my sisters' drawers. We hoarded towels, hiding them in our closets and dressers. Most often, I'd have to fish around in the damp heap of dirty laundry under the chute in the basement for a towel that did not smell too mildewy and might be used one more time. That's when I learned how to do laundry, just after my parents separated, just after my mother told me the facts of life, just after I started my period.

• • •

Cleanliness is next to godliness. Ancient Egyptians laundered not only their own clothes, but those of idols representing *ka*, a spirit they believed resided in the body and survived after death. The *Vedas*, sacred Hindu books, decreed the washing of clothes essential to physical and moral well being. Muhammad commanded Muslims to keep their clothes clean, and Moses furnished the Israelites with detailed laundering instructions:

> Where there is a stain of mould, whether in a garment of wool or linen, or in the warp or weft of linen or wool, or in a skin or anything made of skin; if the stain is greenish or reddish in the garment or skin or in the warp or weft, or in anything made of skin, it is a stain of mould which must be shown to the priest.
>
> The priest shall examine it and put the stained material aside for seven days. On the seventh day he shall examine it again. If the stain has spread in the garment, warp, weft, or skin, whatever the use of the skin, the stain is a rotting mould: it is ritually unclean.
>
> He shall burn the garment or the warp or weft, whether wool or linen, or anything of skin which is stained; because it is a rotting mould, it must be destroyed by fire. But if the priest sees that the stain has not spread in the garment, warp or weft, or anything made of skin, he shall give orders for the stained material to be washed, and then he shall put it aside for another seven days.
>
> After it has been washed the priest shall examine the stain; if it has not changed its appearance, although it has not spread, it is unclean and you shall destroy it by fire, whether the rot is on the right side or the wrong. If the priest examines it and finds the stain faded after being washed, he shall tear it out of the garment, skin, warp, or weft.
>
> If, however, the stain reappears in the garment, warp, or weft, or in anything of skin, it is breaking out afresh and you shall destroy by fire whatever is stained. If you wash the garment, warp, weft, or anything of skin and the stain disappears, it shall be washed a second time and then it shall be ritually clean.—Leviticus 13 (Laws of Purification and Atonement), *New English Bible*. Oxford University Press, 1970.

• • •

The King James Bible (Old and New Testaments) contains the word "wash" 161 times and "clean" 245 times, referring to souls and hands

and feet and bodies and "inwards" (private parts too sinful to iden-
tify) and garments and vestments and clothes. In the Bible, people
are washed in butter, in wine, in blood, in milk, in tears. In water.

Once when I was in college at the University of Massachusetts, I
saw a group of students from the Campus Crusade for Christ being
holobaptized in Puffers Pond in Amherst. As my friends and I
slothed around on blankets, getting drunk on cheap beer, inductees
walked fully clothed into the pond, and waist deep, as the preacher
blessed them, fell backwards in the water and emerged reborn,
swaddled in towels on the shore.

•••

In 1984, a year after I graduated college, I met Steve, an electrician,
and moved from Massachusetts to Michigan with him. Steve was re-
sponsible and mature, unlike my previous boyfriends. He carried a
handkerchief in his back pocket like my father had, which made him
seem like a man and not a boy. I loved that Steve was domestic, that
he washed dishes and vacuumed and was in many ways more fastidi-
ous than I. Steve separated whites from colors, folded towels in a
precise and uniform manner, and there was comfort in this routine,
in this domestic partnership with Steve, the man I was sure I would
marry.

We did our laundry together every other Saturday at the laundro-
mat in Saline, a block from our apartment, and in the quiet time
while we waited for our clothes to dry, I wrote in my journal.

> *January, 1985.* Saline Coin-Op Laundry. Two small boys
> are zooming around the laundromat on invisible motorcy-
> cles, revving, and gripping imaginary handlebars, running
> in short little steps with their miniature legs. The two kids
> are going brrrm brrrm and doing wrist motions. Now one
> kid is going brrrm brrrm and spitting on me.
>
> The motorcyclists' younger brother keeps popping his
> head around the Ms. Pac-man machine and sticking his
> tongue out at me. I admire his courage. I would never
> dare approach a complete stranger and stick my tongue
> out. Now he has just opened up his mouth really wide and
> showed me his little piece of chewed-up pink gum. Now

he just walked right up to me and touched me, as if I were a movie star.

One of the little boys tries to lift a box of detergent that weighs as much as himself. He sees me watching him and thrusts his middle finger at me vehemently. When I don't respond, he looks at his finger to see if it's the right one, and satisfied that it is, shakes the finger at me again. I continue staring at him and he stares at me until his mother comes in and picks up her basket and off they go.

I love to watch mothers and their children in laundromats. It makes me wish that I had children, and glad that I don't.

● ● ●

Laundromat is one of those proper nouns turned common, as common as the people who use them (renters mostly, about 89 million in the U.S.). Formerly, Laundromat was the brand name of an automatic washing machine sold in 1943 by Westinghouse: like Kleenex for tissue. The proper term for a public laundry facility was launderette, *ette* designating the noun as feminine or diminutive (kitchenette, bachelorette, brunette, coquette, suffragette). It's not so simple to extract the feminine from laundry.

My mother has never washed clothes in a laundromat. A washer and a clothesline or a dryer have followed her throughout her life: marriage at nineteen, divorce at thirty-four, remarriage at sixty after a twenty-five year relationship, widowed at sixty-one. In her second marriage, as in her first, she performed most of the domestic chores. She washed and ironed Ed's shirts for work, as she had my father's, and she even ironed his jeans as he was a meticulous man who liked a crease in his pants. In forty years of being a wife, a mother, a nurse, my mother never learned to play the piano. I told her when she was widowed that she should take piano lessons.

● ● ●

Eighteen months after I moved to Michigan to live with Steve, he was diagnosed with terminal cancer. The oncologist prognosed that Steve wouldn't live more than two months, so advanced was his dis-

41

ease, which had started in his liver and spread along his spinal column, which caused him excruciating pain. The domestic chores we'd shared fell to me: cooking, cleaning, shopping, laundry.

One Saturday, a year after the oncologist predicted Steve would be dead, my coworker, Vicki Norfleet, called me and said, "Can I borrow your dirty laundry for the afternoon?" I was touched by her generous offer, and would have appreciated her help as I was exhausted from my job and from taking care of Steve, who'd grown increasingly weak and sick. But I declined Vicki's offer because I was too embarrassed to let her handle each piece of my laundry. I did not know her that well.

There was another reason I declined Vicki's offer, which I did not admit back then. Going to the laundromat was an excuse, a legitimate, guilt-free reason to escape Steve's and my tiny apartment for a few hours. Washing laundry was simple, a chore I could handle, a relief from taking care of Steve who was dying swiftly for a thirty-year-old, though it was also a slow, lingering death. Doing laundry was repetitive and mindless, purposeful and perpetual; clothes would always need laundering, now and forever.

• • •

A week before Steve died, we moved from our little apartment to his parents' home, the house in which he was born, and had left at eighteen. Michigan was enduring a month-long heat wave in August 1987, and so for the last several weeks of Steve's life, he wore only a pair of yellow, red, and blue polka-dot boxer shorts. The morning he died, reclined in his La-Z-Boy, in a bedroom of his parents house, his bowel ruptured, and so I removed the boxer shorts to clean him. At six a.m., when the funeral home people took his body away on a stretcher, he was naked.

The next day, I picked out a shirt and pants for him to wear to his funeral. (Steve never wore underwear, and what would it matter anyway? Socks, too, were unnecessary.) After, I moved in with my sister in Ann Arbor, and went back to work full-time. Some weeks later, when I was forced by a lack of clean underwear to schlep my clothes to the laundromat, I came across the yellow, red, and blue polka-dot boxer shorts, which looked so tiny in my hands. A joke gift from Steve's cousin after he'd first entered the hospital, the boxers were 100% cotton and had shrunk, so Steve did not fit into them until the end of his life when he carried only a hundred pounds on his six-one frame. I washed the boxer shorts, and a handkerchief, the last two pieces of Steve's laundry, which I still have.

• • •

April, 1988. I am sitting in the Super Suds Laundry in Ann Arbor, Michigan. This laundromat is clean, has a non-smoking section, Christmas decorations year round, candy machine, soap machine, sink with paper towels, and a four-foot long taxidermied swordfish mounted on the wall. Wednesday is Senior Citizen day at the Super Suds, twenty-five cents off each wash. Laundromats should have Singles Nights, wash your laundry, drink wine and eat cheese, meet other desperately lonely souls. When Steve was alive, I dined alone in restaurants often, thought nothing of it. After he died, when I ate in a restaurant alone, I felt as if LONELY were stamped across my forehead in large red letters.

Some people dress up for the laundromat. Will they meet their lover here? Are they hoping this will be the day, the moment, the cosmic second when their soul mates, like lost socks, will enter their lives mysteriously? Will they converse with their future mate while folding intimate articles of clothing, trying to hide the girdles, the ripped, holey women's briefs? There was a shift in my life that I can't pinpoint exactly, but is evident when my laundry is accumulated before me: the transition from bikini underwear to briefs. I don't remember consciously making this decision, but it seems to have occurred around the same time that store clerks began to call me Ma'am.

• • •

Nine months after Steve died, I bought my first house, in which I lived for five years before I moved back east. My house came with a washer and dryer, but in spite of the convenience, I missed the regular trips to the laundromat. I still went sometimes, especially when too many clothes piled up and I wanted them washed all at once, instantly, a baptism. I'd hog two Texas Jumbo Washers. (Do they have more laundry in Texas, bigger pants, towels the size of blankets for which they need six-load washers?) And then I'd dry everything miraculously in twelve minutes by hogging seven or eight dryers. I'd watch my clothes tumble around in an endless relay race, socks handing off to shirts or pants. It was relaxing, like watching a fish tank.

Laundromats are pure efficiency, lovely spiro-gyro machines at your disposal. I love the machines that dispense miniature boxes of soap, which remind me of the individual cereal boxes my mother rarely purchased for me and my six siblings. It was truly a special occasion when she did indulge in the variety pack of twelve tiny cereal boxes—the kind whose bellies you slice open as if performing surgery, a cesarean section, then pour milk in and transform the box into a bowl: ergonomic, economic, thrilling. The same sense of pleasure blooms in me if I've forgotten my economy-size laundry soap and I get to pay fifty cents or a dollar for a box of mini-Tide or mini-Cheer or mini-Bounce, identical to the huge supermarket-size boxes, an offspring.

• • •

Women, according to Roman legend, discovered soap around 200 A.D. Washing clothes in the Tiber River at the foot of Sapo Hill, rubbing the fabric with clay from the river's banks, they noticed their garments became cleaner in that location. They deduced that ashes and animal fats were responsible, remains from sacrificial ceremonies atop Sapo Hill, which were washed by rain into the river and clay bank. Saponification, the chemical process for soap making, is named after Sapo Hill.

As a nation, we wash about thirty-five billion loads of laundry per year, spending five billion dollars on detergent, which ranks fifth in sales of mass market household products, after carbonated beverages, salty snacks, beer, and cold cereal. Soap is big business, which is probably how the Soap and Detergent Association landed Jack Kemp as a keynote speaker for its 75th annual meeting in Boca Raton.

New Yorkers purchase the most laundry detergent, perhaps because New York City is a "veritable fantasia of filth," as Eliza Truitt wrote in *Slate*. She tested the efficacy of laundry detergents by hurling underwear into Second Avenue, dragging them through gutters, smearing them with barbecue sauce from a restaurant called the Cowgirl Hall of Fame, squirting them with raspberry jelly from Krispy Kreme doughnuts, and finally sticking them in a plastic bag for a few days before laundering them. Unlike the folks at *Consumer*

44

Reports, Ms. Truitt did not have a radiation spectrometer to gauge the whiteness and brightness of laundered fabrics, which is perhaps why she found the differences among the detergents to be "negligible," and concluded that "it doesn't really matter which one you choose: It'll all come out in the wash."

•••

The only time since I was twelve that I did not wash my own laundry was a two-year stint when I was thirty-three to thirty-five and my job and commute kept me so exhausted that I was loath to spend Saturdays washing laundry, so instead I dropped my heaping baskets of soiled clothes at Lilliana's Laundromat on Munjoy Hill in Portland, Maine, and paid seventy-five cents a pound, about twenty-five dollars every other week. The man who worked Saturdays at Lilliana's was an Italian with milky white skin, black hair and eyes, hirsute, in his late twenties, the son of the owner, Lilliana.

At first, I withheld my underwear. The son, the monochromatic young man, was a student at the Bangor Theological Seminary. How could I have allowed him to see my accursed, blood-stained underthings? Eventually I grew tired of washing my own underwear when I was paying fifty dollars a month for someone else to deal with my dirty laundry, so I'd push the underwear to the bottom of the basket. At least I'd be long gone when he discovered them. I figured: he's a divinity student; he'll forgive me.

Shoving my laundry off to someone else was a pleasure, but not without guilt. Toil and scut work and labor are my heritage: my maternal grandmother, Madeline, the maid; her husband, Clarence, the groundskeeper; my paternal grandmother, Margaret, a cafeteria lady; my grandfather, Patrick, a forklift driver. My father was the first in a couple hundred years of ancestors on both sides of my family to employ brain instead of brawn.

Service is in my genealogy.

Perhaps that's why I like going to laundromats, the venue of the poor and the working class, the unpropertied, because toil and labor are somehow pure and good for the soul, or at least are penance, thus promise redemption or absolution: cleansing. Laundromats remind me of from whence I came, allow me to honor the labor of my grandmothers, humble me. In first grade, my sister told my mother that I'd boasted to our neighbor, Mrs. Hobaica, about receiving straight A's on my report card. I was scolded for bragging. In my family, pride was a sin, especially for girls.

•••

Since the first launderettes (a.k.a. washaterias, laundreezes) appeared in the United States in the late 1940s, people have long wanted to make them into something more than what they are. Enterprising proprietors (there are some 35,000 coin laundries in the United States) have offered ancillary services such as tanning beds, shoe repair, and mailboxes. Mobil of Japan has recently launched a gas station that offers one-hour laundry services; they plan to open twenty such facilities over the next five years. Laundry Lounge, Inc. in Canada is a laundromat *et* coffee house. Dirty Dungarees in Columbus, Ohio is a laundromat and bar. I lived in Columbus for three years during graduate school, but I never washed my clothes at Dirty Dungarees. A laundromat with "dirty" in its name did not seem promising, and I imagined my clothes would smell of cigarettes and beer, or that I'd have to fend off inebriated men lewdly eyeing my delicates.

In the late '70s and early '80s, Helpy-Selfy, a laundromat in Fort Lauderdale, offered topless dancers in its rear lounge. Helpy-Selfy went under, and today a conservative morality has crept into laundromats. Lucy's Laundry in Torrance, California (whose top executives do not include anyone named Lucy), wants to be "a gathering place for the family," says Simon Smith, senior vice president. They aim to "keep the entire family entertained" by offering play areas for children and convenience stores in every unit. (Convenience stores are entertaining?) They vow to keep the "wrong element" from loitering, and won't stock violent video games.

I've patronized laundromats for seventeen of my twenty-two adult years. I'm a laundromat purist. There's not much more I'd add to the basic set-up of washers and dryers and carts and tables. But going to the laundromat could become obsolete in the future. SpinCycle, Inc., the nation's leading chain in the five billion dollar coin-operated laundromat industry (five billion dollars: 20,000,000,000 quarters) has recently introduced *Total Laundry Care*. A customer dials a toll-free number or logs onto a website to place an order for laundry pick-up. SpinCycle's *Total Laundry Care* personnel (eight to ten

46

"well-trained" attendants at each facility) arrive at your home, pick up your dirty clothes, then sort, wash, dry, fold, and deliver your clean laundry to your doorstep.

•••

Laundry is deeply private, which is why doing laundry in public is intimate, almost shameful, a form of public atonement. Most people arrive in laundromats dirty. They have worn all of their nice clean clothes and so arrive wearing holey, stretched-out sweat pants. Occupied in the task of laundering, people shed their carefully constructed personas and masks. They are honest. Vulnerable. Once I saw a biker folding clothes. He did not look so tough handling undershirts and socks. When the ritual is over, our clothes are clean and folded, and a kind of lesser order is restored. Dirt is gone; life starts anew. The bodies we put into these fresh clothes may do something different this time around. I've had a fantasy of taking home someone else's load of clean clothes and wearing them all week, exchanging lives in a way, for what are clothes but costumes?

Laundry reveals who you are: Were you kneeling in the garden? Eating barbecue? Painting? Do you wear synthetics or natural fibers? Do you have a baby, a husband? Does he work in a gas station, in construction? Does he wear boxers or briefs? Are you gentle-cycling your lingerie? Is there romance in your life? Are you airing your dirty laundry? It will all come out in the wash.

What does my laundry disclose?

Towels, far too many towels. Most I inherited from Steve who always liked a plump, absorbent, freshly laundered towel which he used once then threw in the hamper. Gluttony. Some were gifts. A towel as a gift. Steve's sister gave me a huge navy blue towel for Christmas once. I thought it was a strange present, but then realizing how poor and utilitarian she and her husband were (hunting frogs, squirrels, duck, muskrat, deer, rabbit, to stretch the food budget), I understood it was a luxury item to them, this oversized, plush, brand new towel.

I have a small white towel indelibly stamped "American International Hospital," where Steve was treated for cancer. I don't remember taking the towel.

My mother bought me a set of red and black towels after I bought

47

my house. The house came with a red toilet seat and that became the theme for the bathroom: shower curtain, area rug, toothbrush and soap holder, black and red, the color scheme of a bordello.

I confess to hoarding towels. I can't resist a sale, a deliciously low price on stacks and stacks of thick-pile, almost moist, teal or pink or lavender towels that promise warmth and sensuality. The last time I moved, while unpacking boxes, I counted: I own over twenty-five bath towels, not hand towels, washcloths, or kitchen towels, which I'm sure would bring the total to over fifty. I've thought of having a cocktail party after which everyone leaves with (or in) a towel.

•••

February, 2000. I am at the Summit Street Laundromat in Columbus, Ohio. This laundromat has bright blue walls—a color that can turn you crazy—with wrought iron fencing over the windows for security. During the week, in the middle of the day, it's nearly empty. The manager is a man with no incisors, only canine teeth, so he looks like a vampire, a shriveled, short, drunk and feckless throat-sucker. He sits at the picnic table in the laundromat and every minute or so spits great greenish gobs into the waste basket, drinks can after can of Budweiser, and smokes.

The drunken manager approaches me as I pull sheets out of the dryer. He talks to me, pressing himself close, with cloying, sweet alcohol breath. His face is so near mine that I imagine kissing him, and then I am repulsed. (I call this Opposite Reaction Syndrome, which I suffer from: when the thing you least want to think or do is exactly what you think of doing: laughing at a funeral, thrusting your hand down a churning garbage disposal.)

"The people in Boston are more prejudiced than in the south, but they pretend they aren't," he says.

Why has he deemed me to hear this message at this time?

Sometimes I wonder what all the people in the world are doing at a particular moment: how many people are sitting on the toilet right now, are eating potato chips, are being born, are dying? Are doing laundry like me? How many people are fucking right now?

I sometimes wonder that.

What is going on in the universe the moment the drunk laundromat manager delivers his wisdom: volcanos erupting, regimes being toppled, infectious disease breaking out, new mathematical formulas being discovered, stars dying, casting out their final light.

A crazy man comes into the laundromat to get warm. He holds up a dirty dime. "Want to taste this?" he asks.

"No," I reply, as if his offer is utterly sane.

"My mother wants me to taste it," he says, puts the dirty dime in his mouth.

I wonder what it tastes like.

A disheveled woman comes in with her short-haired terrier on a leash. She lights a cigarette, stares out the window, and says, "So many people driving by on Summit. All those people—I'm glad I'm not them. God made all those jillions of people and he has to take care of them. He is guilty in a way. I don't know what's going to happen to them, all their pain. It bothers me, but I guess he must know." She finishes her cigarette and walks out.

A couple comes in dragging four huge garbage bags of clothes. The woman smiles apologetically, says to me, "We just moved here. After paying first and last month's rent, $500, we had to wait two weeks to have enough money to do our laundry."

I hear her confession. Go forth and launder.

•••

Thus spake Moses when he came down from Mt. Sinai. In Exodus 19 he gave the Israelites the Ten Commandments and the people said, "Whatever the Lord has said we will do." Moses returned to speak with God, and God said, "Go to the people and hallow them today and tomorrow make them wash their clothes." They had to prepare for the Lord to descend upon them, and so Moses hallowed the people, and the people washed their clothes.

•••

In 1582, Pope Gregory XIII and his astronomer, Clavius, calculated that the calendar they'd been using (the Julian calendar, after Julius Caesar in 46 B.C.) was eleven minutes and four seconds longer than the solar year, and so by then the calendar was ten days out of sync. The pope and his astronomer solved the problem by producing the first Gregorian calendar, to which they made an initial adjustment;

49

they omitted ten days. In 1582, the date following October 4 was October 15th. Just like that: time lost.

I've spent approximately 576 hours attending Mass, which I ceased in my early teens after my parents divorced: twenty-four days of my life from which I gained very little. Since I began washing my clothes at the age of twelve, around the time I quit attending church, I've logged an estimated 2,016 hours doing laundry, 84 days of my life so far. The laundromat, for me, has become a kind of sanctuary. I put my quarters in the dryer and buy time in twelve-minute increments and life is slowed and altered by the simplicity and singularity of the task.

The laundromat is one of the few places in which I allow my mind to wander. I sometimes feel like crying in laundromats. In laundromats, I am sometimes moved. In the laundromat, as I conduct the most ignoble chore, I find myself pondering the cycles of life, the structure of time, the nature of humanity: how we all need clean garments, clean sheets to sleep on, how we are all alike ultimately, walking around in our clothes, covering our bodies with fabric, as if that could protect us from anything.

Nominated by Sherod Santos, Iowa Review

THE INNOCENT

by JEAN NORDHAUS

from WEST BRANCH

Alone and together, we stand on the platform
a mob of strangers awaiting a train. There may be
among us a wifebeater; surely, a thief. That man
in the blue dolphin tie; that frazzled woman,
gathering in her scattered girls; each of us caught
in the swill of our being; none of us blameless,
not one of us pure. Greedy, covetous,
selfish, vain, we have trafficked in lies; we
have practiced small cruelties. Even the baby,
asleep in a sling on his mother's breast,
has been willful, has shaken with rage.

Yet, if fate arrives, as a wind, in a bullet,
a bomb, at the instant of shock, in the silent
heart of conflagration, we will all
be transformed into innocents, cleansed
in the fires of violence, punished not for any sins
committed—but for standing where we stand,
together in the soft, the vulnerable flesh.

Nominated by John Kistner

COCKTAIL HOUR

fiction by KATE BRAVERMAN

from MISSISSIPPI REVIEW

Bᴇʀɴɪᴇ Rᴏᴛʜ ɪs ɴᴏᴛ ɢᴏɪɴɢ to get his twenty-year service plaque in the lobby. The hospital he founded has been purchased by Westec Medical Division. Bernie Roth is merely the former figurehead of an ad hoc insurrection that has no meaning in the realm of litigation. The project coordinator makes it clear that his presence is unnecessary, in fact, it's intolerable.

He leaves the merger meeting three days early. Bernie Roth takes a midnight flight, and his green-tinted contact lenses sting as he drives from the airport directly home. The house is perched on a cliff of purple succulents above the ocean that is, today, a dark blue like certain fabrics in which you see the grain and stitches.

Chloe designed their house with an architect from Milan. It's a two-story Mediterranean villa with arches, balconies, a turret, orange tiles on the roof, and graceful windows of leaded glass that face interior courtyards enclosed by bougainvillea draped walls. And it's not painted pink, Chloe has meticulously explained. It's a salmon terra cotta.

Chloe's car is in the driveway. It's a weekday and she should be out. He notices her car with surprise and relief, realizing that if she hadn't been home, he would have called her and asked her to return immediately.

He finds Chloe in the bedroom, standing inside her closet, apparently arranging clothing. She is wearing a silk kimono imprinted with red peonies, her blond hair is tied back in a ponytail and she seems startled to see him. She actually touches two fingers to her throat in a gesture of surprise when she looks up, and her mouth is momentarily wide. He starts to embrace her but, for some reason, stops, and lays down on the bed instead.

"You're three days early," Chloe says. There's something accusatory in her tone.

"I was invited to leave," Bernie explains, prone. "I'm not getting my plaque."

"Why not?" Chloe asks. She glances at him, briefly, then continues moving clothing through the one hundred twenty square feet of her cedar closet.

Spring-cleaning is inappropriate, he decides. Insulting and dismissive. Bernie wants a scotch and he wants her to lay down with him, in that order, now.

"Their focus groups don't like plaques. It reminds the consumer of death. Their lobbies are strictly ferns with central gravel fountains. They're identical, like McDonald's." He closes his eyes.

Bernie waits for Chloe to offer him consolation. A drink and a quick tennis game, perhaps. It's still early. They could have lunch, walk on the beach. Then he could tell her his joke. Westec Medical Division. WMD. See, there are weapons of mass destruction, after all. They're just not in Baghdad. They're in La Jolla.

Bernie Roth is aware of an agitating interference in the room. He must remove his contacts. His vision is blurred and scratchy, as if his eyes are being clawed. "What are you doing?" he asks.

"I'm packing, Bernie. I'm not getting my plaque, either. I intended to be gone before you got back." Chloe resumes her closet activities. He sees now, the selected dresses and suits and skirts hanging in one area, an assembly of shoes and purses already on the bedroom floor below the French windows leading to the mahogany bedroom terrace. Her entire set of luggage is in the corner, garment bags, cosmetic cases and assorted carry ons. The suitcases are open and most of them are nearly filled.

"Where are you going?" Bernie sits up. Is this an unscheduled Book Club related journey? A prize-winning poet must be fetched at an airport and properly entertained? Is there a problem with the children? Maybe he needs a scotch and a cup of coffee.

"I'm just going, Bernie. That's the point. Not where." Chloe pauses. "I'm leaving you. This. Us. La Jolla. I'm through."

"You're leaving me? As in a separation? A divorce?" Bernie stares at her. "Now?"

"Affirmative. Sorry about the scheduling. But it's always something. The siege of festivities. Christmas. Birthdays. Valentine's Day. Our anniversary. Departures tend to be awkward." Chloe looks directly at him. "Can you give me an hour or so to wrap it up here?"

"Wrap it up here? What is this? A movie set? You're divorcing me and you want me to leave our bedroom now?" Bernie repeats.

He examines the bedroom as if he's never quite seen it before. Their bed has four oak posts supporting a yellow brocade canopy. The walls are an ochre intended to suggest aged stucco. Ochre, not yellow. A stone kiva fireplace is dead center across from the bed. Navajo rugs lay over glazed orange Spanish tiles. The ceiling is a sequence of Douglas fir beams somehow procured from a derelict church in New Mexico. Bernie assumes her decorator hires bandits. An elaborate copper and glass chandelier with a history involving Gold Rush opera theaters and saloons hangs suspended from the middle of the beams. Chloe insisted it was necessary, despite the earthquake hazard. It was essential for what did she call it? The hybrid Pueblo Revival style?

"I have a list and this is confusing. Yes. Why don't you make yourself a drink? I'll join you downstairs in a bit, OK?" It's not a question.

"Isn't this sudden? I've been preoccupied with the merger, but—" he begins.

"Actually, it's a coincidence. It doesn't really have to do with you," Chloe says, over her shoulder. She extracts a pair of fire-engine red high-heeled shoes. She holds them in her hands, as if determining their possible flammability. Or is she weighing them? Is she taking a special flight? Are there baggage limitations? Is she going on safari?

"We've been married twenty-four years. I must have some involvement." Bernie entertains the notion that this is a ghastly practical joke, or the consequence of an anomalous miscommunication. A faulty computer transmitting a garbled fax designed for someone else entirely, perhaps.

Chloe is within her fortress of closet, on her knees, nonchalantly evaluating pocketbooks and shoes with both hands. She does have a list, he notices that now, and a pen where she checks off and crosses out items. She's also listening to music. Bob Dylan live, he decides. It's her favorite, the *Rolling Thunder* tour. Or the other one she plays incessantly, *Blood on the Tracks*. They made a pact when Irving and Natalie went to college. She would not play Bob Dylan in his pres-

54

ence. In return, he would not subject her to John Coltrane or Monk. No Dizzy Gillespie or Charlie Parker, either. Chloe deems his music agitating. In fact, his entire jazz collection is, by agreement, kept in his study, as if they were vials of pathogens. Or slides of children with pre-op facial deformities.

Bernie stares at her back for an arrested moment, in which time simultaneously elongates and compresses. Then he pushes himself up from the embroidered damask pillows with their intimidating wavy rims of thick silk ribbons requiring handling so specialized he fears them, stands unsteadily, and walks down stairs to the kitchen. He pours scotch into a water glass.

Outside is a tiled courtyard with a marble statue of what he assumes is a woman rendered in an abstract manner embedded in the center of a round shallow pool with a fountain. Flowers that resemble lotuses but aren't drift slowly across the surface like small abandoned boats. He realizes the petals form a further layer of mosaic. So this is how his wife makes stone breathe. Then he reads the Sunday *New York Times* front page twice. The script is glutinous, indecipherable. He pours another scotch and dials Sam Goldberg's private emergency cell line.

"The WMD negotiations? You're still there?" Sam doesn't wait for a response. "I'm at lunch with a client, Bernie. Can I get back to you?"

"Chloe says she's divorcing me," Bernie begins.

"I'm representing her, yes." Sam sounds equitable, even expansive.

"You're my best friend," Bernie reminds him.

"I love you both. She came to me first. I'll call you back." The phone goes still in his hand, which feels suddenly numb. He remembers that his hospital is now simply part of two hundred fifty small medical facilities owned by a corporation based in Baltimore. He is merely one of 12,500 doctors they choose to employ.

Bernie climbs the wooden stairs to their bedroom. Chloe is placing shoes in an enormous cardboard box. "Imelda Marcos had fewer shoes," he notes. He's wondered about her shoe accumulation, the pumps and stilettos and platforms, how odd for a woman who habitually wears sandals or is barefoot. "Won't you need a porter or two?"

"My job is over. The chauffeuring. The scheduling. Tennis lessons and matches. Music classes. Not to mention the soccer practices and interminable playoffs. The surfboard transportation logistics. Piano recitals. Ballet productions. The play dates," Chloe pauses. She reaches for something in a drawer on the far side of the closet. She withdraws a package of cigarettes. She lights one and faces him.

"Listen. It begins in preschool. These kids don't play. They have auditions. If they pass, if they get a call back, a sort of nanny-chaperoned courtship ensues. It's loathsome." She expels smoke. "Later, it's worse."

He hasn't seen her with a cigarette since Ion and Gnat first went to nursery school. The fumes are infiltrating the room, further irritating his contacts. Bob Dylan is whining off key and out of time, contaminating the air, now on an auditory level. It should be labeled a posthumous rather than live performance, he decides. He shuts off the switch.

"I didn't know you still smoked," Bernie said. "Or that you hated the children's activities."

"Soccer did me in. Soccer, for Christ's sake. How does soccer figure? When did that make your short list? How many professional soccer stars has La Jolla produced? It's just crap." Chloe is vehement.

"We accepted division of labor as a viable vestigial tradition. But you could have refused," Bernie counters.

"You can't say no to soccer. It's the new measure of motherhood. It's the fucking gold standard. I sat in parking lots between chauffering, feeling like Shiva with her arms amputated." Chloe finishes her cigarette. She uses a yellow shoe with a red flower at the toe for an ashtray.

"Let's have a drink downstairs," Bernie suggests. His voice is reasonable. He is able to produce this effect by pretending he is someone else entirely, a concierge or a waiter. "I'm finishing the Laphroaig."

Chloe consults her watch. It's the Piaget he gave her when their son entered college. His wife shrugs, the kimono sleeves drift briefly from her sides like twin crane skimming an inlet, hunting. "One drink," she assents.

They sit in the kitchen. He considers the Westec buy-out. For two decades, he entered the hospital each morning and paused in a gesture of respect near walls engraved with the names of doctors who had achieved their twenty, twenty-five and thirty year status. Next year, he would have had his own twenty-year service plaque installed. Chloe has already arranged the catering. He would be permanently mounted beside Milstein and Kim, McKenzie, Fuentes and Weintraub. They were there when Northern San Diego Children's Clinic was built, the landscaping just put in, the first bougainvillea and hibiscus bushes growing against still dusty cinder blocks. Chloe planted pink and white camellias the next year. Then wisteria and roses.

Bernie realizes the kitchen floor is actually a composition of hand-painted tiles, purple and blue irises and violets. The stems and leaves are a raised green enamel suggesting channels and veins. So this is how she prepares their meals, barefoot, standing on a version of cool garden. He finds cheese and fruit in the refrigerator and bagels in the cabinet. A china platter with ornate silver handles he vividly recalls packing in plastic wrap and hauling in a special crate on a plane sits between them. Where were they returning from? Portugal? Prague? Chloe averts her eyes.

"I love California Lent. It comes the spring you're fifteen and lasts the rest of your life." She looks tired.

"Just gain a few pounds and let's stay married." Bernie spreads cream cheese on a bagel. It's stale. Chloe smokes another cigarette.

"I'm leaving a few pounds early. I'm one of the last original wives. Do you realize that?" Chloe asks. "I'm forty-six. Let's just skip menopause and the obligatory trophy wife syndrome. We did our jobs. Now the task is finished."

"We had a deal. We agreed to be postmodern," Bernie points out. "No empires with historically disastrous ends. No mistresses with unnecessary dangerous complications. No tax fraud. No start-ups or IPO's. Just us, with plausible defendable borders."

"We did that. You built the clinic. I did this." Chloe indicates the formal dining room with her fingers, and by extension, he surmises, the entire house and grounds, courtyards, swimming pool and tennis court, gazebos and rose gardens.

"You saw it as a job?" Bernie is amazed.

"It was a performance art piece. Remember when Book Club discovered one-man shows? Spalding Gray. Reno. Sandra Bernhard. Laurie Anderson. We went with the Weintraubs on opening night, remember?"

Bernie Roth thinks for a moment. Then he says, "No."

"It was the hospital benefit that year. A bit arty for you. We went back stage. Elaine had Laurie Anderson's entire tour profile. We realized we were earning more than she was. We had our own multi-million dollar a year performance art pieces. We just had smaller venues and a limited audience. Elaine Weintraub, the original wife. Before the current version. The ex-TV late night weather girl? The anorexic redhead with the room temperature IQ? Jesus. Elaine Weintraub was my best friend. You don't even remember her." Chloe finishes her scotch.

"Our marriage was an art piece, a performance?" Bernie is incredulous.

"The four piece choreography. The music lessons. Sports and tutors. Surfing and swim meets. The theme birthday party extravaganzas. Christ. Not to mention the gardeners I bailed out of jail. The maids with alcoholic boyfriends. Their secret abortions. The relentless complications. The emergency loans. It was 24/7 for twenty years. And I'm not getting a plaque either." Chloe stares at the table. Bernie pours more scotch.

Outside is sunlight that surprises him with its nuances, its fluid avenues of yellows that are not solid at all, but tentative and in curious transition. Streaks like gold threads waver across the surface of the fountain, a filigree embossing the koi. Bernie thinks of brass bells and abruptly senses a clash in the air. So this is the sound of a day being sliced in half.

"I walk through this house and it's like being trapped in a postcard," Chloe indicates the living room table, a square of inlaid mahogany completely covered with framed photographs. She picks them up, one by one. "Agra. Bali. Rome. Luxor. Maui. Everyone holding hands and smiling. It's a laminated version of reality."

"But this was our life," Bernie realizes. He stands near her. "You wanted Thanksgiving in a Beirut back alley? Easter in a Turkish tenement? That wasn't our experience. What's encased in glass is, in point of fact, the truth."

"Really?" Chloe sounds bitter and combative. She is still wearing the kimono with the extravagant sleeves that seem to suggest intention. But she has put on pink lipstick and diamond earrings. She has brushed her hair. Perhaps she sprayed her wrists with perfume. Then her skin would be a distillation of all things floral and vanilla. "This isn't truth," Chloe said. "It's an advertisement for consumption."

For a moment, Bernie thinks she is alluding to tuberculosis. TB is rebounding globally. Half of Europe tests positive. Studies suggest nearly forty percent of New York City college students have indications of exposure. Malaria is also making a spectacular come back. Polio is a possibility, too. Its crossover potential is seriously underrated. A major influenza epidemic is inevitable, actually statistically overdue. Of course, smallpox could be the defining epidemic of the millennium. Then he realizes his wife is not talking about infections. He holds a silver framed photograph selected at random. "You don't appear to be suffering in Tahiti," Bernie observes.

"I didn't suffer. I just wasn't engaged. It was like filling stamps in a geography game. More accumulation. Just like the grotesque children's activities." Chloe seems to be considering another drink.

"Grotesque?" Bernie repeats.

"Piano. Cello. Guitar. Ballet. Gymnastics. Basketball. Karate. Theater arts. Choral group. Ceramics. Mime. What kid has that plethora of aptitudes?" Chloe demands.

He is apparently meant to say something. "I have no idea," he admits.

"They don't have affinities or longings. Every stray spasm of temporary enthusiasm gets an immediate new uniform. They lack affection and discipline. Activities are another form of consumption. Now a video. Now a violin. Now Chinese. Now a chainsaw." Chloe sighs.

Bernie considers the possibility that he may pass out. He barely slept at the negotiations, which were not mediations, but rather the inordinately slow unraveling of a *fait accompli*. His hotel room was curiously uncomfortable, the sheets and towels abrasively starched, the walls a deliberately muted blue reminiscent of an interminable depression. The sense of transience in carpet and upholstery stains disturbed him. There were lingering odors he couldn't identify. Perhaps it was perfume, insect repellant, spilled wine, suntan lotion and something intangible that leaked from a stranger writing a postcard. He had insomnia for the first time since he was an intern and nightmares about his father.

"What are you going to tell Ion and Gnat?" Bernie tries.

"I've taken care of that." Chloe almost smiles. There is strain around her mouth. It's as close to a sneer as she can permit herself. Her genetic code doesn't allow her to further distort her face.

"You've talked to them?" Bernie is tentative and afraid. He needs to establish coordinates. He must assemble reliable data.

"Ion and Gnat. How chic we thought their nicknames were. How millennial. Naturally I've spoken with them." Chloe stares at him. "Natalie used to tell me what a great mother I was. I had my standard line. I'd say—"

"I'm compensated. I've got my CEO salary, yearly incentive

bonuses, stock options and pension plan," Bernie supplies. "Of course I remember."

"I wasn't kidding," Chloe states.

After a moment, in which he feels dazed and incoherent, and thinks oddly and wildly of hummingbirds and lizards, and how patterns on reptiles resemble certain common skin disorders, he asks, "What did the children say?"

"They're a monolith of narcissism and indifference. They want assurances there's no hostility and the finances are secure. If separate doesn't intrude on their scant psychological resources, it's fine. They require known quantities. If it arrives from two locations, that's irrelevant. Just so we don't necessitate their engagement."

"Is that it?" Bernie senses there is considerably more. His best skill has always been diagnostic.

"Not quite. They both have messages for you," Chloe pauses. She takes a breath. "And this is the last act of translation I'm going to engage in. After this, you'll have to gather and distill your own information."

"Shoot." Bernie is dizzy. He doesn't want to flinch.

"Ion quit the tennis team." Chloe actually laughs.

"He won the Desert Classic as a sophomore. He's ranked number three in California, for Christ's sake. He has a full scholarship." Bernie realizes he is yelling.

"He knows we can afford it, without his playing. He hates tennis. Thinks it's decadent, imperialistic and retrograde. He quit last year. I've been paying his tuition. Quietly. Part of my job. The choreography, mediation and scheduling aspect."

"What about his major?" Bernie insists.

"He hasn't been pre-med since freshman midterms." Chloe avoids his eyes.

"What is his major, precisely?" Bernie is more alert. He understands rage is a form of fuel.

"Urban Design. It's like modern history but with community projects."

"Community projects?" Bernie puts his glass down. "Like Houses for Habitats?" He has a vague recognition of this organization. Perhaps he's seen it listed on intern resumes.

"He's specializing in athletics for the handicapped. Creating playgrounds with wheelchair ramps in barrios. Also, he isn't Ion anymore. He's Grivin," Chloe informs him. "He plays drums in a band. He says it's a good drummer's name."

"Grivin?" Bernie repeats.

"An anagram of his wretched birth name. Irving. I should never have agreed to that." Chloe lights another cigarette. She shakes her head from side to side. "But you were having that affair with the nurse. And I was on the verge of suicide. Guess I just lost that one in the sun."

There is a pause during which Bernie considers the delicacy of the respiratory system and the necessity to gather filaments of air into his body, and keep his lungs oxygenated. "What about Gnat? What about Natalie?"

"No pre-med there, either. Sorry. She's in Women's Studies." Chloe examines her hands. Her fingernails are translucent with pearl white slivers at their tips. Or perhaps they are arcs of silver, permanently engraved by some new cosmetic process.

"And? Come on. I feel it, Chloe. I'm down. Kick me hard." The scotch is making him nauseous. He decides to make a pot of coffee and take a Dexedrine.

"She's calling herself Nat and living with a woman," Chloe reveals.

"She's a lesbian?" Bernie tries to concentrate on Gnat, on Natalie. She was an excellent camper. When they rafted the Grand Canyon, it was Gnat who helped him erect the tents, identify the correct poles and how to position them. Her natural ability to recognize constellations was exceptional. She rarely tangled a fishing line. Was this unusual? Was her spatial aptitude an indication of abnormality? Had he failed to diagnosis a monumental malfunction?

"Fifty-six percent of her entering class listed their orientation as bisexual." Chloe finishes examining her fingernails. Then she drinks her third scotch. "I suggest we adopt a neutral position."

Events are accelerating in a frantic progression, each revelation is increasingly surreal. Day is assuming hallucinatory proportions. He concludes that his present condition resembles severe jetlag combined with sixth round chemotherapy. And there is, of course, the matter of the luggage. The suitcases packed in the bedroom. She must have arranged for someone to carry them down the stairs and load them into her car.

"Do you care about that?" Bernie manages. "Our daughter is gay."

"Why would I care?" Chloe seems surprised.

"What will happen to the Christmas decorations?" Bernie asks. He considers their holiday ritual. Chloe and Gnat selected new ornaments for their permanent tree legacy, one for each family member, one each December. The two hundred year-old brocade angels with twelve-carat gold threads around their wings from Belgium. The gingham elves with pewter crowns. The silver maple leaves. The glass snowflakes, each with intricate individual facets and panels.

"Nat will take them no matter what. If she goes butch. If she opts for artificial insemination. She'll take the ornaments. And she knew you'd ask that." Chloe is leaning against the wall, her eyes partially closed.

Bernie pours coffee. He removes a bottle of amphetamines from his suit jacket pocket. He takes three tablets and offers the bottle to Chloe. She moves toward it with such unexpected rapidity, he can't determine how many pills she extracts. Bernie watches her hands, following her fingers to where they terminate in glazed nails translucent like the undersides of certain tropical seashells.

"Remember the glass snowflakes?" Bernie asks.

"From Tibet? With triangular amber panels like medieval cathedral windows?" Chloe recalls. "I thought they'd look good as earrings. I imagined them on a young wife on a pyre. Of course, that wouldn't work for me anymore."

"That's what you were thinking? In front of the goddamned pedigreed twenty-two foot Colorado blue spruce? Ritual incineration?" Bernie places his hands over his eyes. There are numerous anecdotally reported cases of sudden stress induced blindness. He puts on his sunglasses.

Chloe pours herself a cup of black coffee. Her movements are slow, listless, stalled. The room is a series of sea swells. He realizes they are floating like the petals of the flowers that are not lotuses just above the koi.

"And you're putting the fucking suitcases in your car and driving away?" Bernie is incensed. "Sam Goldberg is your lawyer?"

"He can represent both of us. Or I'll take Leonard and you can have Sam," Chloe offers. She drinks a second cup of coffee.

"Leonard is my golf partner," Bernie says.

"We know where all the bodies are buried. It's a cemetery. There's enough to go around. When in doubt, just keep it, Bernie." She studies the interior of her porcelain cup.

Then Chloe goes upstairs. She returns, slowly and methodically, with suitcases. He's surprised by her muscular arms. She knows instinctively how to balance her torso, shift her weight, and bend her knees. She is barely sweating. She has replaced the kimono with a short beige linen dress with spaghetti straps that accentuate her tanned shoulders. Twenty years of yoga and tennis. Then the bags of groceries when the maids disappeared, were picked up by immigration, or beaten up by boyfriends. In between, they had babies and abortions. They visited relatives in their home villages and often didn't return for months. Then the gardeners vanished. Chloe spent days in the garden with a shovel. Yes, she could easily load the baggage into her car. Even the inexplicable cardboard box of shoes. And that is the next step. Bernie considers the heavy carved oak front door that leads to the circular cobblestone driveway.

"What about the jewelry?" Bernie inquires. He always gave her a necklace on her birthday. Rubies in Katmandu. Pearls in Shanghai. Silver and turquoise in Santa Fe. Gold in Greece. He can remember each separate composition of stones and the rooms above plazas and rivers and lagoons where he unwrapped his offering and fastened the clasp around her throat. Sometimes there were cathedral bells and foghorns, drums from carnivals and parades, waves and sea birds.

"I took the diamonds. I left you the rest. They're in my safe. The key is on my pillow." Chloe pours another cup of black coffee.

"Why leave me any?" Bernie wonders.

"You may need them for bartering purposes later. Sometimes a strand of Colombian emeralds really hits the spot." Chloe lights another cigarette. This is not the behavior of a novice. This is no small stray gesture of recidivism. Does her yoga instructor know? Her aroma therapist? Book Club and the hospital board? And what does she mean by barter. That's a curious concept.

"Wait a minute. Look. This is for your birthday. I got it early." Bernie is excited. It's the amphetamines, cutting through his fatigue, his heavy and unnatural disorientation. Airports are terminals of contagion. A maximum exposure situation. He might be incubating a malevolent viral mutation. Still, he is clarifying his thinking.

"I can't wait." Chloe gazes at her watch.

Bernie walks into his study, the only room Chloe permitted him to decorate, and returns with a small wooden box. "Here," he said. He feels wildly triumphant.

"I'm not interested," Chloe informs him.

Her voice has more energy now. The amphetamines. Perhaps they should take two more. Bernie produces the bottle. Chloe allows her fingers to reach into the pills. She stands near him while he opens the box. A single grayish stone.

"I'm going to have it set," Bernie explains. "It's an agate from the beach in Chile. From Isla Negra where Neruda lived. I went there. I skipped Rio. Didn't you wonder why I went to a river parasite conference in Brazil? I needed an excuse. I changed planes for Chile at the airport. Then I drove. I walked beaches for miles. I found it for you. I pulled it out of the water." Bernie holds the pebble in his palm between them. His hands are shaking. "Now you can tell me what the stones know."

"Bernie, you're a lovely man." Chloe touches his cheek. "You've made it a wonderful job."

"I want to know what the stones know," Bernie says. "That was your goddamned dissertation. Your personal grail. You were going to decode Neruda's stones and explain them to me."

"That's prehistory, Bernie. You'd need an archeologist to dig back that far. A paleontologist." Chloe turns away from the agate. It looks lonely and ashen. It knows it is an orphan.

"What about the house? The furniture? The paintings? The sculpture? Each sofa a distillation of your personal evolution? That's what you said," Bernie remembers.

"I tried to amuse myself. Forget it. The house is too big for you," Chloe determines. "The kids are never coming back."

"They're never coming back?" Bernie finds himself repeating. The afternoon is a kind of three-dimensional mantra. Phrases are recited, but they are like howls people make on roller coasters, ludicrous vows and confessions. Words came from their mouths, but they are sacraments in reverse, staining the air. They are curses.

"Not for more than a day here and there. Now there won't be the plague of holidays to entice them." Chloe glances around the downstairs rooms, detached and calculating. "Unload it. The market is good now."

"Chloe," Bernie takes a breath. "I love you."

"It's been terrific, really. This is my terminal performance of prophecy on command. My final act of analysis and emergency emotional counsel. OK. I'm gazing into my crystal ball for the last time. It's the goddess of real estate. She says sell."

"Chloe. Let's talk this out. There's more to say. I can say more." Bernie tastes the amphetamines now, an unmistakable metallic sting between his lips. It's spreading through his body; microscopic steel chips, hard-wiring his muscles, his reflexes and agility. She can load the suitcases into her car. But he outweighs her by seventy pounds, and he is wearing leather shoes. One must not discount the element of surprise. Chloe can do head and shoulder stands, she has mastered all the strength and flexibility postures, but she has never been in a street fight.

"OK." Chloe is suddenly unexpectedly agreeable. "One final note. That stricture I gave you about only wearing black and gray Armani?"

"Yes?" Bernie closes his eyes.

"I remove it. You should do jeans for a while, T-shirts. Downscale. Lose the Porsche." Chloe takes a silver sandaled step toward the front door.

"You don't love me?" Bernie is confused and chaotic and finds the combination not entirely unpleasant. His trepidation has been replaced by an erratic turbulent energy. He is blocking the door, with its thick carved oak panels and intricate squares of stained glass implanted in the center and along the edges. Her decorator no doubt looted that from a church, too. And he is not going to let her walk out to the driveway.

"Love you? I'm all dried up in that department. One marriage, two children, and the full liturgy of soccer. The one hundred unique ornaments I was designated curator for. The secret acts of mediation. Messenger services. Currency exchange. Frankly, specific love isn't even on my radar screen." Chloe seems resigned.

"What do you want? I can give it to you." Bernie is desperate.

"Solitude. Drift. I'll travel. Maybe pen a mediocre verse here or there. It requires a climate you can't provide. You can't survive the altitude I'm looking for, believe me," Chloe says. "And no more question and answer quizzes. No more multiple-choice tests. No more essays."

"Will you take this?" He extends the agate. "You said swallows and constellations of stars were inside. The mysteries of oceans. Metamorphosis and mythology. Take it."

"No more homework. School's out, Bernie. School's out forever." Chloe sings the phrase, twice.

He thinks it might be an Aerosmith song. Or, perhaps and worse, Alice Cooper.

Once he settles the suitcase problem, he's going to play Coltrane on the house speakers at full volume. Dizzy and Monk. Parker and Miles. It's going to be jazz week. Jazz month.

Bernie stands directly in front of his wife. Her suitcases are near the door. She is holding her car keys. Still, Bernie is beginning to get his bearings. There is a machinery in the periphery. He is starting to hear it hum and pump. There are mechanisms. Barter? Deduction is a gift. It becomes a skill experience polishes into a tool. The most fiercely reckless intuitions often prove accurate. And he can see the schematics now. There are blueprints and diagrams and there is nothing subtle about them.

"You don't visit the hospital anymore," Bernie notes. "You used to come for lunch. We had our special noon appointment."

"I couldn't stand all the doors opening to those discreet pastel alcoves. The rooms where women who still have eggs sit. Women with babies in their wombs. I could hear them devising names for infants. They do it alphabetically. Amy. Beatrice. Clarissa. Devra. Erica. Francine. Gabrielle." Chloe glares at him.

"That's a lie," Bernie says, shocked. He wants to slap her across the face.

"Back away," Chloe orders. Her voice is high and thin. It wavers, hangs in the air and loses its sense of direction and purpose. He considers fireworks, how they explode, tattooing the sky with a passionate conviction that quickly dissipates. Then she says, "Do you want the police here?"

Bernie Roth envisions the La Jolla police; two or three freshly painted vehicles parked in the circular cobblestone driveway, each officer tanned and uncertain. He imagines them standing in the marble entranceway below the oasis of stately sixty-foot palm trees. The fronds cast unusually vertical shadows like arrows and darts. From certain angles, the house looks like Malta. He'd once suggested mounting an antique cannon in the turret. And domestic complaints are a gray area. He is, after all, the senior doctor at the hospital. Alternatively, he imagines chasing her car, positioning himself at the end of the driveway, his back against the wrought iron gate, his arms spread wide. She might impale him.

What are his options, precisely? He can shut off the master switch on his computer, of course, locking the garage and gates. Chloe refused to learn how to manipulate the systems. She said she wasn't intelligent enough for such smart appliances. He often worried what she would do in an emergency power failure. Or he could call Ron

Klein. Ron is running the psychiatric unit now. A wife with a menopausal psychotic break requiring hospitalization. It happens all the time. Ron owes him a few favors. But favors are a limited resource and he needs to ration them.

"I'm delirious," Bernie realizes. "I need to take something."

The green in his wife's eyes intensifies. It is like observing a river coming out of a mist. Or emeralds just professionally cleaned by sonic wave devices in a jewelry store.

"You're going to open the cookie jar?" Chloe asks. "But you're under suspicion. You swore no more until Christmas."

"That's nine months away. Isn't that unnecessarily punitive and arbitrary?" Bernie wanders into his study.

This is the only area of the house he has been allotted. He designed it himself in one weekend. He didn't need a decorator. He ordered over the Internet. The walls are mahogany and the bookshelves contain his medical library, computer files and jazz discs. The lamps are solid brass. The sofa is brown leather like oak leaves in mid-October. The floor is red maple. Chloe disparaged his aesthetics and dismissed his study as aggressively masculine. But she is following him now.

Bernie Roth has always possessed the capacity for strategic action. It might be time to retire now, after all. Empty nest syndrome demands attention. Menopause is problematic. They can build something new, on a beach in Costa Rica or Mexico, perhaps. Grivin can help with the construction. Maybe he can get extra credit course points. And Nat. She can bring her girlfriend. They're probably both good with hammers.

Bernie walks directly to the wall safe and unlocks it. The safe contains one blue canvas duffle all-purpose sports bag wedged against the metal. It fills the entire safe and Bernie has to yank it out. Chloe watches him unzip the bag. Bernie extracts a handful of glass vials. He removes a box of syringes.

The agate from Isla Negra is in his pocket. Later, Chloe will tell him about Neruda, the poet she was enthralled with when they first met. When she recited stanzas about volcanoes and poppies, he didn't hear the words precisely, but rather followed the narrative through her mouth and eyes. It was medical school and he was stupefied with exhaustion. He heard the phrases she offered as a music that was visual. It was a sequence of facial expressions, a tapestry of geometries composed from flesh. Trajectories formed on her lips, which were rivers and bays with bridges, and exited through her eyes, which were green wells and portals that could foretell the future.

Tell me what the stones know, he will command later. I want to be initiated into the language of agates. Show me how they form bodies like infants and feed themselves from stars. And Chloe will comply. She will find the capacity for jazz. It's simple. Saxophones mean spread your legs. Later, she'll laugh at his WMD joke. Her throat will emit sounds that look like strings of rubies and sapphires. She will fall down on her knees and explain everything. She will invent and improvise. He'll help her remember why she has a mouth.

"The usual?" Bernie asks, glass vials in his hand. He prepares a mixture that is two parts morphine, one part cocaine. He prefers the reverse. He taps the air bubbles out of the two syringes. "We'll celebrate the birth of God early this year. Take a few weeks off. Reassess our position."

Chloe apparently agrees. She has removed her beige dress with the thin shoulder straps. She isn't wearing underwear. She curls on her side on the leather sofa like a fawn at dusk. Bernie Roth reaches for his wife. She extends her right arm, the one with the good veins. He injects her first. Then he injects himself.

Nominated by Mississippi Review, Kirk Nesset

DOUBLE ABECEDARIAN: 1963

by JULIE LARIOS

from THE GEORGIA REVIEW

Alleycat year, 1963: B.B.'s jazz
Bells out a backstage door—sly,
Cool (the sax always about sex),
Drugged (the horn hollow),
Edgy. Sure, it hurts, it's a sharp shiv
For the Generation Post-Perdu,
Gone on The Bomb and pot.
Hootches on fire somewhere: Les Français
In Saigon, trying to get out, remember?
Jive, Chicken Little—le crazy coq
Killed when the sky falls (drop by drop,
L'amour as napalm, melting bamboo
Mostly but men and women, too, and children.
Nothing wrong with that yet). Mom
Opens the oven door—sure, it's still
Pie, still apple, Dad's tie still has a tie tack,
Queer only means odd, and everyone's straight, O.J.
Runs drills into the twilight zone, Di
Sleeps clueless in a crib, Mario Savio gets high,
Thinking speech could be free. We're smug
Undergraduates, we listen and sway to any riff
Veering out at us through a bullhorn—Gee,

We begin to say, give peace a chance. But *thud*.
Xanadu, I guess, will have to wait, peace isn't PC
Yet, and MLK's still Junior. Meanwhile, B.B.
Zeroes in. He's the black King, and JFK is DOA.

Nominated by Richard Garcia

VOICES

by JOHN CLAYTON

from THE MISSOURI REVIEW

Words come to him at the edge of sleep. Hebrew. Bits of daily prayers, of daily blessings. Fragments in English, voices, many voices, no one he knows: *inasmuch as . . . the forlorn ones . . . adversary song.* A sign of sleep to come. But it's not his own sleep he's entering. It's somebody else's dream. He's listening in. Whose dream is this? And in the daytime: gliding down the mile-long hill on his drive to the clinic, voices in his ears, obscure gestures, pure lilt and syntax. He invents a political thriller: a receiver has been sewn into a subcutaneous pouch of a spy. Then who's on the other end of the line, whispering mischief? He's had schizophrenic patients who firmly believed such things. Or maybe messenger angels—*malachai*—with words of prophecy? Sam Krassner has a costly investment in the dynamics of individual unconscious processes—a Ph.D. in psychology and years of clinical training. This training says, you may not know what's happening, but you can bet a soul struggle is going on. Something worked on, worked out; it's residue of battle he's hearing at a distance. But suppose the voices are nothing personal. Think of all the griefs he's privy to every day. In his private practice in Northampton, Massachusetts, he hears subtle suffering like his own: spouse, sibling, parents; guilt, grief, rage. At the clinic, the same, but compounded with the intermeshed griefs of class and race he resists taking inside. Or perhaps they are inside, the words duplicating themselves in him like a virus—sorrowing, raging words no longer tied to particular voices.

And they *are* waves, for they can't be distinguished. Look. One client at the clinic, Barbara Hammond, yes, sure she's neurotic, enacts "narcissistic injury," but mixed up with so many other troubles—she's obese and diabetic, ashamed of herself as a physical being, she can't get a decent job, doesn't believe she could be trained for anything even if she had money for training, and this assumption that she's a dead-end person humiliates her further, so that, as she expects, she is demeaned by her out-of-work husband, who debases her when he bothers coming home; and in turn she demeans her children, who enact their humiliation by doing dismally in school, continuing the pattern. A circle of pain. Circles overlap circles. And it's not just personal. Powerless, does Barbara even care that she is represented in the state legislature by a guy who consistently votes against funding the social services that might help her change her life?

Sam wonders. Maybe the words he hears are of love needing to be expressed. Isn't it true he has to keep his clients' suffering at bay? You might call it a sensible professional attitude, but that's not it. After all, he can effect so little change; he resists feeling for Barbara or, say, the enraged counterman, or the mother of a boy with terminal cancer. He stays outside the poverty and chaos of these lives. What good would it do to open his heart? But maybe his heart has a different opinion.

Sam's life is stuck. Is that why the voices have been busy? He makes this discovery: if on his noontime walk he sits on a bench and, closing his eyes, holds his cell to his ear and pretends to be on the phone, he can listen to voices under voices. Like in a busy restaurant. Sometimes a phrase from a news report, sometimes "Blessed Are You O Lord," or murmurs so ambiguous he doesn't know in what language. The quieter he gets, the deeper the place from which the voices seem to come. It's as if he had a surveillance microphone and could keep extending its focus further and further through crowds of talk—fifty feet, a hundred, a hundred fifty.

It's after a certain therapy session with Barbara Hammond that the words seem to tell him that he should do something. What happens is this:

Hot September day. Barbara comes in, heaving as always her 250 pounds side to side, falling forward hip to hip. A beauty about her in spite of the weight; she reminds him of an enormous blues singer. Today on one hip she hefts a three-year-old, her youngest, and sits in the upholstered chair, child in her lap. Yards and yards of material in that flowered summer dress; the child floats in it. Barbara says sorry, sorry, sorry, last minute my neighbor called, she's sick, can't take Alicia, so you mind? We went over this when you first came in, Dr. Krassner says. But . . . you're here, and at least—he laughs—your other two children *aren't*. Sure. It'll be all right this time, Barbara.

Sweet child, sweet little girl, hiding her face in her mother's great breasts, beautiful child, much darker than Barbara, almost pure African. He listens to Barbara, humiliation upon humiliation, her husband staying out for days, comes home to *use her like a toilet*; and the caseworker you sent me, that spy, his eyes so suspicious I'm getting away with something.

"Barbara—do you really think *I* sent you that caseworker?"

"What do I get away with? You tell me. What?" Barbara has a powerful sense of drama. *"Why am I supposed to keep on going? You tell me."* Even when she's demeaned, neglected, bruised, she's the star of her sad show; there's a certain glory in that, and power. How, Sam wonders, do you interrupt her performance to get at the real grief that fuels it? His attention wanders to the child, who peeks at him from time to time, hiding in the dress, popping out to grin, and then becomes absorbed in folding the flowered cloth of her mother's lap into a soft-sculpture flower.

Does Barbara feel his attention float away? When he asks her, So, Barbara, let's put things together. How do you see your options? She says, "Well, Doctor, I'll tell you." And doesn't tell him. "It's hard to figure out your choices?" he probes. "Oh, no. My 'options'? Well, we've got a friendly little gas pipe in the apartment. We cook with gas. You ever hear that, Doctor? Cooking with gas? How about *not*-cooking with gas? Course, when the kids are out. What d'you think of my option, Doctor?"

"Barbara, don't you even play with that idea. If I think you really mean it, you know I'm going to have to do something about it."

"You scare the shit out of me. I'm scared this Ph.D. white guy going to lock me away someplace where they feed me and dope me up and I watch the television all day." Her face softens. At times she looks like a big teenager. So odd, this mix of relaxation and despair! She slumps in her chair. Rivers of the big summer flowers in her dress flow over the arms of her chair. He imagines her flowing over the room, drowning him.

"Barbara, when you have children, you lose your right to kill yourself."

"Nice to know I used to have rights."

"They're your riches, those three kids. You understand me?"

"Riches! Well, sure, I do see your point. Thanks for the warning, Dr. Krassner. Don't you worry. I'm just messing with you, Dr. Krassner. I'm gonna become a great writer."

"A writer?"

"I told you I'm in a writing class, a workshop, uh-huh—and teacher thinks I'm good."

"If you told me, it didn't register. Tell me about it."

She tells. Her eyes get swallowed by all that fat; made tiny. Perception = interpretation: the way you see contains within it the meaning for you. For instance, her eyes. Isn't he saying she can't see, can't see or be seen? That she's hiding? And her beauty—for he thinks of her as *beauty buried in fat*. Barbara is only thirty for godsakes! He peels away the layers of fat and imagines her ten years ago, before the children. Her skin soft as the skin of her child. Wanting to touch Barbara, wanting to soothe her, he reaches out to her little girl. As if *there's* the full beauty, undisguised. The child shrinks away, but Barbara sweet-talks her, "You go right ahead now, honey. The doctor means to be nice," and says to Krassner, "Her name is Alicia."

"Hi, Alicia."

Now he has a problem: he's made himself vulnerable. Alicia lets him take her hand, and, still shrinking into her mother's breasts, she grins at him. He says, "Your riches, Barbara."

"Yeah? And I guess I'm too stupid to figure that out?"

Embarrassed, he says, "What a lovely little girl." He'd take her home in a minute, begin the whole process of parenting all over. He wants to make sure this child is safe, whole. His own children are grown, one in college, one in Boston. So that's the session. She tells him pieces of her story: a neighbor who makes the building shake with heavy bass from his stereo and sells stuff out of his apartment—drugs, computers, TVs. Scares her, kind of people come around. Next time I'll come alone, Doc. It's okay, he says. Alicia makes me understand what it's like for you. He asks himself: Does Barbara get anything out of these sessions except to tell stories, to vent griefs? It lets her get other help—day care, help with her diabetes, food stamps, maybe training. Barbara hauls herself to her feet. The office is air conditioned, but there are quarter-moons of sweat at the armpits of her flowered dress. It's a nice dress, picked up, she told him, at a survival center. But those big flowers!—wrong costume for a big woman. She kisses Alicia, and Sam Krassner imagines she's kissing him good-bye.

After she's gone, he stands at the mirror in the men's room, staring at his own creaturely self. It's not to contrast himself—healthy, thank God, slim except for an insignificant pound or three of thickness at his waist from too much sitting, his mustache and sideburns beginning to gray; why, if he removes his rimless glasses he looks almost handsome in his own eyes—it's not to contrast himself with Barbara. Rather, what he feels is their common physical being: his flesh, hers. It's as if they're both standing in front of the mirror in odd communion.

It's after that session, on the way home, Springfield to Amherst, he hears words in a sentence. You know how you turn around in the street at the thump of a bass and an angry voice coming from somewhere—oh, from *there*, you say, open convertible, two guys with stocking caps and an attitude, sound system meant as a weapon against the world. It's that much not-in-his-head. The words clear enough but meaning what? STRICT PROCEDURE. Or maybe it's CONSTRICTED PROCEDURE or STRICTLY PROCEED. If these words are coming from an angel, he wishes the angel would be less mumbly. But still, doesn't he know? Oh, he *knows*.

Barbara. He takes the next exit, drives under the highway and enters heading south. He's sweating with anxiety—that he's onto something/that he's a little crazy. He calls the clinic, gets Barbara's phone number, her address, directions. He calls his wife's voice mail at her office. "Sheryl, it's four-thirty. I've got a problem with a patient. I may be late getting home. Sorry."

This is against all the rules, strictures about professional distance. It's not as if he's never heard gestures of suicide, mostly a way of saying, listen, I'm in that much desperation. You don't go running to a patient's house. But he's in the middle of a fairy tale. He saves, heals, transforms.

It's a run-down neighborhood but not as damaged as he'd imagined. Some houses are boarded up, their front yards littered, and most freestanding houses are in need of paint and upkeep. But there are renovated apartment buildings and quite a few places attended to with care and work. It looks like a neighborhood coming back. Critics say "gentrified," but what's happening—his patients tell him—is that some young family is struggling to make payments and have enough left over for repairs and paint; husband, wife, kids

75

spend their weekends fixing up the place. He admires the little trees held straight by wire on the front lawns. Look at them leafing in sweet, young green as if they were champions of the forest. He feels the beauty and dignity of these loved houses.

But Barbara Hammond lives in an old red brick apartment building, not renovated, four floors high, next door to a one-story flat-roofed building, a bar. Barbara's mentioned the place; it's one of the bars where her husband goes to liquor up before he can get himself to go home for a conjugal visit. Nice life. He's scared for her—but scared, too, for himself. It's like visiting hell. No voices now. He's on his own. Mission or mishegos? There's no need for the buzzers just inside the big front glass door cracked corner to corner, because the inside door, bulwark against invasion, is askew, won't close, as if someone strong got real mad one night. But he pushes Barbara's buzzer, expects no answer. His heart is thumping. It's all he can do to push the front door open and walk into the dimly lit foyer and up the dimmer stairs. A smell of clammy walls. Graffiti on the ceiling over the stairs; highly stylized, unreadable. One word, *F U C K*, clear enough. Music thumps from somewhere. From somewhere, a talk-show voice. From somewhere, a hip-hop beat. Up to the second floor and up again. He walks softly as he can. Barbara's on the third floor. At her door he smells for gas. But suppose she's sealed the crack under the door.

He knocks. "Barbara?" Louder. "BARBARA?"

"And who the fuck are you?" A slow voice from the stairwell behind him.

He speaks back into the semidark. "She's my client. I'm a little worried about her."

"Yeah? And just what you worried about?" It's a wiry black man in overalls over a Red Sox sweatshirt, inspecting, glowering, long pry bar in hand. Reasonable suspicion, Krassner thinks—but feels interrogated, threatened.

"I'm not even sure she's home. I saw her at my office a couple of hours ago—just want to make sure she's okay. I guess she's probably not home."

"She's home. I saw her come in." The man sucks at his lower lip. "I'll go get us a key. You stay cool." He hurries off. Krassner keeps on knocking till he's back. "I'm kind of a superintendent," the man says. "I keep my eye on things. I got a key just in case."

"I'm Sam Krassner."

"Uh-huh. I'm Emet Brock. What? You a social worker?" But he doesn't wait for an answer. He uses the key. Door's on a chain. "Ah, hell." In a minute he's back again with a bolt cutter, and in another minute, Krassner holding it taut, Brock has broken the chain, and they're in.

Clothes clutter, toy clutter, food clutter, a smell, not gas. Brock takes the lead. No one in the living room, no one in the first bedroom. In the second, half off the bed, there she is, knocked out, puke all over her flowered dress and on the bedside table three plastic vials from the pharmacy, empty. An intense, sour smell fills the room.

"Oh, God!" Krassner gets close, puts his fingers to Barbara's throat. Brock is already at the phone. Krassner opens a window, realizes he hasn't been breathing, finds towels, wipes up the worst of the mess. The thing is to get her moving. He's not so strong, and Brock is a small man. They have to lift 250 pounds. "Give me a hand," he calls.

The woman is dead weight. I mean, put her on her feet, she'd collapse into a lump on the floor. Brock on one side, Krassner the other, they each wrap an arm over their shoulders and heave her to a sitting position. "Maybe if she gets vertical," Krassner says, "she'll throw up some more. More she throws up the better. You know where her kids are?"

Krassner starts down the stairs after the attendants, meaning to follow the ambulance to Bay State Medical—but what good? It's the kids he has to think about. He yells down the stairwell, "If she wakes up, tell her I'm checking on her kids!" He turns back; from her apartment calls the hospital to let them know what's going on, calls Marty Shire, her caseworker from DSS. This is her caseworker's job—to follow up, to take care of the kids. By now it's after six. But he doesn't leave. He pokes through the living room. A giant TV-stereo commands the room like an altar—or the Ark of the Covenant. With the rack of music and videos, it takes up a wall. Above it, a framed poster of Martin Luther King. He's afraid he'll find drugs, afraid because she's told him she'd stopped using and he believed. But all over the room he sees books. Books from the Springfield Public Library, from used bookstores. Novels, books of self-help. She hadn't told him she was reading.

He gets a pail from the kitchen closet, fills it full of hot, soapy water and, best he can, scrubs up. He feels like an idiot. What's he doing it for? Well, for the kids, so they don't come back to a stink. When he's dumped the pail into the toilet, cleaned his hands, is about to go home, a girl walks in, eleven, twelve, must be Barbara's oldest. Pail in his hand, he's got to be the one to tell her. And at this point he doesn't even know if her mother's alive. He thumbs his mental Rolodex for her name. "I'm Sam Krassner. I've been trying to help your mother. Your mother's sick right now."

The girl's in jeans and a T-shirt, name of some band splashed in red across her skinny chest. She backs toward the door. Sam Krassner puts down the pail and holds out his hands, palms up, mudra of innocence. "Hey, you don't have to be scared. I'm your mother's friend. Your mother is in the hospital."

"Mr. Emet?" she calls, and Brock, behind her by the door, says, "I take it from here, Doc."

"I *told* you I heard someone in here," she says to Brock.

And Krassner explains, as if he were doing something wrong—I'm just trying to help, keep you kids out of foster care, because that's what'll happen, and—honey, you're Denise, right?—Do you have a grandma or an aunt you can stay with a few days? Emet Brock is shaking his head. "You don't know their daddy," he says. Sitting on the sagging sofa, he folds his arms. "Their daddy comes back here to check on the kids, well you better run, mister, or you be on the evening news. You just try telling him you're a *social worker*—" These last words he says in parody of a school principal or a pastor or a professor.

"I'm not a social worker, I'm a psychologist, a therapist."

"You a white man around his family. No offense. You want to help, better help by *phone*."

Denise is trying to get words in—My mother's in the hospital? What hospital? What happened? Brock stands up, puts a hand on her shoulder. "What's your auntie's name, you know, lady comes see you a lot? Where she live?"

"My mother do something to herself? She try something? She always talking."

"Your mother took too many pills. We'll call the hospital, find out what's going on. But we need to get hold of your auntie," Sam Krassner says. "And your brother and your little sister. Can you help? Your brother's in day care, right? Where's day care? And Alicia—where's Alicia?"

He goes with Brock—they follow Denise to day care to pick up

Mickey, then to the neighbor's to collect Alicia. (*Remember me, Alicia? You came to my office?*) Denise becomes transformed from little kid to family leader. She's up front, holding both kids' hands as they go around the corner to Jackie, who's an aunt, it turns out, only by love. At the corner near the bar, three young men watch them pass. Krassner, a little frightened, keeps his eyes on the kids. Looking at the kids from behind, he feels hopeful; if they're this beautiful . . .

He's saved a life. Mazeltov! The rabbis tell us in *Pirke Avot* that to save a single life, it's as if you saved a whole world. Not bad work for a hot September day. But now he feels responsible for her in a new way. Well, of course. He is. Tendrils have grown between them.

Driving back to Amherst at dusk, he's sure what Sheryl will say. *If I were you, I'd stay out of it now.* But when he gets home and microwaves his dinner and tells her his story, she sits by him and runs her fingers through his hair and says, "Well, my big old hero, Superdoc. You must feel terrific. So will she be all right, this Barbara?"

"Oh, yes. We got to her in time, thank God. But will the *kids* be all right is another question. Can Barbara be a real mother? I don't know what to make of her."

"So tell me—this Barbara, she's beautiful?"

"Not the way you mean. There's something about her. But only thirty and so damaged."

"How did you know in the first place?" she asks. "Something she said in the session?"

"Well, she played with the romance of killing herself, but she's done that before." He smiles at Sheryl, a smile he knows she'll know is phony, and he imagines coming clean, telling her about the voices. *Your husband's hearing angels.* "It's your husband's therapeutic intuition."

"Oh, bullshit, my darling. I think I'll decide to be jealous. She must be breathtaking."

"Right." She's kidding and not kidding. He knows where it's coming from: their old friends, maybe closest friends, the man, a psychiatrist, six months ago he ran off with his patient, broke apart their lives—his daughters', his wife's, his own. They haven't even heard from him.

"Well, you stay out of it now," she says, as if summarizing a long discussion they never had.

He answers with the Jewish *mudra* of acquiescence: lower lip out, shoulders up to ears, neck retrenched turtle-like, hands open. See? No weapons. But by not answering in words, he hasn't committed himself. And how can he stay out? The kids, those kids. And what about the protocols of maintaining a professional attitude toward the sufferer whose suffering he professes to assuage?—those protocols were developed partly to protect healers from their own need to res- cue, the need that got them into the profession in the first place. They make sense. You can't help people when you bring your own noise into the room. Then, too, you need to be a model of calm, of shalom, for people who are not calm, whose lives feel like chaos. It's not bad, this professional style. But sometimes he feels its cost and burden. Now he's not thinking of Barbara the patient but of Barbara the sufferer and Barbara's kids, and the community that needs to hold those kids.

The voice he heard in his car today doesn't care a damn for pro- fessional detachment.

Between private patients from his office in Northampton, he helps the way Emet Brock suggested: by phone, checking with Barbara's social worker, talking to the aunt, finally talking over the phone to Barbara herself, who, still under "observation," stoned on tranquiliz- ers, speaks in the language of irony: it's ironic she's alive, ironic he wants her to live. *You like my life so much, why don't you take it up and live it for me, just let me alone, Dr. Krassner?* Selfish! So unbe- lievably selfish, he thinks. He has to remind himself: even the outra- geous selfishness is a masochistic gesture, like twisting a knife into her own flesh—*see how worthless I am?* Hard not to condemn her.

It's under the engine noise on his drive over the Connecticut to Amherst and his health club that he hears a voice again. But all it says is LISTEN. To what? He pulls over by a farm stand, buys some corn, sits in his car waiting. Listens, he listens, Shema, and nothing comes, and it doesn't matter. Because he knows damned well what it wants him to do. "Listen" can mean "obey." *You listen to me.* Listen- ing, he turns the Subaru around and recrosses the river, heads down 91 toward Springfield. *Holy One, protect us all.* On the cell he calls Barbara—no answer; calls Jackie Chambers, the "aunt." She works till five at the desk of a hotel in West Springfield. To her voice mail: "Listen. Are the kids okay? Are they with you? I've got a little time— think I'll drop in. If it's not a good time, call my cell." And his num- ber.

Five o'clock. Driving to Springfield he gets an idea: pizza for the kids! He imagines the three of them gobbling a pizza. From the road he calls the only pizza place he knows in Springfield, just a few blocks out of his way, and drives to Barbara's with a big white box. No answer to his ring, so he tries Brock, who comes out to the vestibule, holds the crooked inner door open. Late-afternoon sun floods the little space between inner and outer doors, lights them both up. Krassner holds the white box on his palm like an offering. "Pizza's for the kids. They here?"

"Well, well. You the pizza man."

"That's it. Barbara been back?"

"Not so I seen. Maybe the kids are with that aunt. I thought I warn you to stay off. Look—it don't matter to *me* you come around here, but that husband of hers, well, he's a crazy fucker. Just I don't feel like cleaning up your blood off these stairs," he says, pointing over his shoulder.

"Thanks." Brock smiles a funny, crooked smile. Is Brock razzing him, ragging him? "I'll try not to drip."

"Man thinks I'm kidding. You'll see. No pizza for me?"

"Afraid not. Got to go find the kids."

"So long, Pizza Man."

Same three young guys standing on the corner near the bar. They stop talking as he passes. They stare. In the infinite depth of a single instant he wants to smile a big fake smile their way but keeps his face blank. It would be saying, *There's no such thing as racism in your lives, or if there is, please recognize that I'm not any part of it. Don't think of me as white. Don't take out your anger on me.* But he's got a couple of patients at the clinic in their midtwenties. He knows too much about their anger to pull off that smile of innocence. The whole story of race relations is present at this almost-interaction. He avoids eye contact, but one of the young men says in high tenor, almost falsetto, "That pizza for me?"

Now he can smile. Passing them, he heaves a breath, feels their eyes on his back as he comes to Jackie's building. It's been renovated with federal funds—new windows, new doors, new sheetrock, new plumbing and electricity. He buzzes, gets buzzed in. Jackie's apartment is on the third floor; as he climbs he can hear Alicia's laugh. Jackie's standing outside her half-open door with her arms folded. This is a real good-looking woman, about Barbara's age, maybe thirty, but lean, athletic, clear-eyed. Her hair is set in cornrows, the cornrows lifted into a crown—no, a tiara, a black tiara. Just home from work, she's still in a suit, gray polyester, and a white blouse. When she remembers him her eyes soften, she steps inside and opens the door all the way. Denise comes out to stand at Jackie's shoulder, and Mickey and Alicia peek from the living room. Krassner calls out, "It's just the Pizza Man!" Then, to Jackie, "I hope you don't mind if they eat a snack."

"Mind! Think I feel like cooking?"

They clear the table in the kitchen where Mickey and Alicia were drawing. Jackie takes out plates. "How about for you?"

"No, thanks. How's Barbara?"

She stops, silverware in her hand, and meets his eyes. He's not expecting so direct a look; he's the one who glances away. "You stick around, you see for yourself," she says. "You understand, there's a lot to that woman, Dr. Krassner. She's so smart, you wouldn't believe."

Krassner nods; his eyes well up—not professional at all. He asks the kids, "Pizza okay?"

"Great," Mickey says, hunched over his eating.

"Who am I?" he asks Alicia.

"The Pizza Man!"

And the Pizza Man sits at the feast, pulling at his mustache, resting his bifocals on the tip of his nose to look at them—a guest, not partaking. He wishes he'd bought two pies. Mickey is making a jet plane out of his slice, then crashing the plane into his mouth.

Just for this crazy moment Krassner's got a second family.

Rap at the door, Barbara's here. She looks doughy, dowdy, glazed. It doesn't take her half a minute to put down a plastic bag she's brought from the hospital, to take off her man's windbreaker and play the role she's scripted for today. In this role, she's very calm; she draws out her words, pitch rising and falling as if she were singing. "My baby's eatin' pizza," (or is it "My babies eatin' pizza"?) To most people walking into Jackie's kitchen, Barbara would appear a happy, loving mother. Krassner hears it as role, opera, tragedy, *Madame Butterfly, Medea*; it scares him, his heart gets pumping, and Jackie knows, too—she puts her arm around as much of Barbara as she can manage, kisses her cheek and steers her toward a chair. Barbara isn't having any of it. She shakes Jackie off. Her head's waving, rocking, she's using the rocking to build up whatever internal energy she can muster for an explosion, Krassner's sure. He's seeing *crazy*. No—

gestures of crazy. "Barbara, we're all here. Your beautiful children and Jackie and me, we're all here, dear."

Dear! So intimate, so outside permissible language for therapy. It's as if one of his disowned voices broke into his own speech. He flushes; Barbara doesn't seem to have heard. She's on stage, mad tragedy-queen. *Watch out.* Denise stops eating and stands behind her mother, rubs her shoulders, her neck, says, "Still a slice left, Mama." Barbara's rocking. "But what" she asks, "are we doing here? What we doing in my good friend's house? Beautiful Jackie. Finish up, children. I'm your mother come back from the dead to bring you up best I can. I know what *you* doing here, Dr. Krassner. You think you gonna take these children away from their mother?"

"The opposite, Barbara. I'm trying to keep you together."

"We just goin' home," she says in almost a drawl, not her own urban, Northern speech.

Jackie says "Barb, honey? Why don't you stay a while? Dr. Krassner's just leaving."

"I am leaving," he says. "But talk to me, Barbara. Will you be able to handle things? Are you taking medication? What did they prescribe? Please. Can you just talk to me so I'm not uneasy?" He's lying. If he wants information, he can call her social worker, the hospital, the admitting physician. What he wants is to see, can she be here in the room with him, talk coherently?

Barbara says, sings, "You got a kitchen knife, Jackie honey?"

"What you need a kitchen knife for?"

"That's right. Maybe I don't." She lifts Alicia from her chair and plants kisses over her neck, her cheeks; she takes Mickey by the shoulder, and when he finishes his slice and gets up, she buries his face in her belly. Denise is talking with her eyes to Jackie, and Krassner doesn't know the language. But talk of knives and her textbook gestures of decompensating, of a psychotic break he reads in her eyes—don't they mean he needs to hospitalize this patient, get in touch with Barbara's social worker and with Crisis Services? Of course—except these *aren't* gestures of real madness; they're gestures meant to indicate madness.

"I'll walk you home."

"What a gentleman my doctor is!" Barbara says to Jackie. "You want to come along, too? Or you think I can get around the fuckin' corner in one piece?"

"You know I believe in you, sweetie. Stop messing around, will you? You scaring your kids, honey. Just remember what you showed me."

"What?"

"Your writing, your journal. You know."

"Good days and bad days, baby. This definitely not one of my good days." But Barbara laughs, thank God, a full-lung laugh, the real thing.

All at once, Denise shepherds her mother and the kids toward the door. Mickey leans down to the kitchen table to grab Alicia's crusts in one hand, then takes his mother's arm with the other. Alicia burrows against her mother; Krassner says, "Home, home, home," as if a celebration were going on, and since it's anything but a celebration, he feels false as hell, weighed down with sadness he can't show. No need for voices to tell him anything; no need to be a prophet: he knows in his own bones the way this will play out.

The three young men are gone as they turn the corner, but in front of Barbara's building one man is waiting, leaning against the pilaster to one side of the door, and right away Krassner sees it's not Brock and he knows who it must be. He's in for it. *You damned fool*, he says to himself.

Eugene Hammond hovers tall above Barbara. Krassner's nightmare, hulking, thick-necked, his eyes bloodshot, his skull shaved bald, his clothes stained, sloppy.

"Daddy!" Alicia yells. Mickey goes, "Hi, Daddy," but without enthusiasm. Denise doesn't say hello. Barbara says, "My Eugene!"— which she pronounces *YOU-gene*. So much going on in this moment. If he could tease it apart, Krassner thinks as he snatches the looks in their eyes, it would contain a bitter history of whites and blacks, a history of power and powerlessness, of men and women. *Maybe I'll die here*. He's silent; he knows the last thing he should do is speak.

Eugene Hammond speaks. "They told me you were hanging out with this white guy." Very calm—the calm spooks Krassner, and at once Denise is weeping. Hammond says, "What *you* cryin' for? What's this got to do with you, girl?" Then, to Barbara—"Told me you messing around, and it does look like."

"This is my *doctor*, Eugene. You get the fuck away. You the last thing I need just now."

"Maybe I'm the last thing you gonna see. Look at this doctor of yours. He's pissing in his pants, your Jew doctor."

84

Krassner says in a gentle voice, "Mr. Hammond, Mr. Hammond, here's the story. I'm trying to keep your family in one piece. All right? Your wife's been in the hospital. You know that?"

"DID YOU HEAR ME TALK TO YOU?" Hammond points his finger into the air between them, rap, rap, rap. Krassner is silent. Now, almost a whisper: "I didn't say shit to you, Mister. You lucky if I don't kill you with my hands. And you, crazy woman. You pill woman. Oh. You *some* kind of mother."

Barbara makes a fist and thump, thump, thumps hard at the side of her head. Denise tugs her arm and holds it against her own chest as if holding a lover. She hasn't looked at her father. Hammond gestures to them like a contemptuous traffic cop waving along a line of cars, and one by one they pass by and into the building. Suddenly Brock's there in the vestibule. "Eugene, m'man, you just let the good man go home now."

Hammond stands at the cracked glass door and stares Krassner down. "Go home? He damn lucky if he gets home tonight. Why he here? Fuck he want here?" Turning, pressing his chest up against Krassner, he whispers, "When you be come and hearing me invite you to my house?"

Brock laughs. "C'mon, man. Your point's made, Eugene."

Hammond steps back; Krassner stumbles back; now Hammond turns and, brushing past Brock, disappears into the dark foyer. Brock comes out onto the stoop and shakes his head. "I know," Krassner says. "You told me."

Sheryl, home just before Sam, assumes he's been at the club and has had a different sort of workout. He kisses her in passing, retreats to his study with a mumble, "Something I got to do . . ." and there is something: he calls Marty Shire, Barbara's caseworker, writes notes about Eugene Hammond for a report to the Massachusetts DSS. He's legally, of course, a "mandated reporter" of abuse, of neglect. But it's not a clear case. Barbara's been shoved against the wall a couple of times, or so she tells him, but mostly she's been terrorized. The children, she says, Hammond hasn't touched. Neglect he surely can report, must report. But how do you report chaos, terror, whispers of the makings of a tragedy?

Now, while Sheryl clatters in the kitchen, he sits, his office a synagogue, his laptop a prayer book, and stares into the pixels and the cloudy white of the screen. He's hungry for a voice not his own. All at once his heart softens, breath comes easy, and a voice does come, barely audible, more a keening like the song of blood in his ears. Now a word, COMMENCE, but the voice neglects to tell him what he's to commence. What good is such a voice? Now again, a word, all by itself, TENDER. To *be* tender? To *tender* his resignation? To resign himself? To soften?

At dinner he tells Sheryl about Hammond. She presses her fingers to her lips. She looks down at the food. It disturbs him: she doesn't even tell him to back off, to be careful. Her silence scares him. He clears the dishes, rolls up his sleeves, stacks the dishwasher.

His hands are still damp when he hears yelling outside—someone yelling. At once he knows it's Eugene Hammond. He opens the window to hear. "Krassner. You! *Doctor* Krassner!" Hammond stands in the driveway, T-shirt over baggy jeans. "I'll be right there, *Eu*-gene!" he calls, pronouncing the name Barbara's way, then shuts the window and goes into Sheryl's study. She's looking out through the slats of the blinds. He lays his hand on her nape, soothes, soothes. "Don't worry. Don't get frightened."

Her fingers at her lips. "You're going to call the police, aren't you? You want me to call?"

"Wait. Sheryl. I call the police and there's no stopping it, like a roller coaster it'll just go down, down into tragedy. The poor man's in agony."

"Don't try to be such a saint, Sam. I'm calling 911." But she just sits there in the mauve yoga pants she always wears at home, fingers rubbing her cheek. He feels a surge of anger against her for her fear and helplessness.

Sam is at the door. He's in slacks and an open shirt. The night spring air is sweet from someone's garden. Hammond stands under a tree, washed in the glare of a security light. The light distorts his features into a monster mask. As Krassner steps outside, Hammond yells, "What's the matter? You think you come to my house I can't come to yours? You address in the phone book, Krassner. So? YOU FUCKING MY WIFE, DOCTOR KRASSNER?" This he bellows so the neighborhood can hear. But it's not that kind of neighborhood. Even Hammond's bull voice won't carry through the trees of these two-acre lots. However . . . it will carry clearly enough to Sheryl.

His own voice Krassner can't find. What's he to say? *No, no, I'm not messing with your wife?* Bad idea—just get him started. Maybe

86

Hammond's brought a gun, a knife. God knows, fists would be sufficient. Hammond has him by thirty pounds and twenty years, and to say that's a joke—even as a young man he'd have stood no chance. He can't speak. But a muscle lets go. Maybe it's his very helplessness that eases him. He knows—knows—he won't need to think about it; *words will be available.* They may not change anything, but they'll be there. Krassner can breathe. Grateful, he plunks himself down on the brick steps leading to his front door. "Want to sit and talk, Eugene? You want a soda?"

"Too damn late to talk. Think you talk your way outta this, Doctor?" But they're in dialogue. Hammond moves no closer. "She tell you all about me, she tell you what a bastard I am?" Not waiting for an answer—"You tell her to leave me? That what you tell her? She say you do."

"She'll say things. She's full of pain. You are, too."

Hammond peers across the lawn. "You crying? Look like you crying."

Krassner hadn't been aware. "Well? It gets me."

"What kind of motherfuckin' doctor cries?"

Krassner ignores him. "And your kids, Eugene—what about them?"

"Crazy woman, what she gonna do to my kids?"

"Both of you, Eugene. What's all this battling going to do to your kids? You've got beautiful kids. Look, you want to split a soda?"

"She gets me crazy. I go crazy. I can do things." So peculiar!—like an old Jewish mourner, he shuts his eyes and rocks his head side to side.

"Why don't you come to my office tomorrow and talk? I bet we can bypass the usual bureaucracy. You know? Maybe we can change things. I'd like to try."

"Can't change shit. Can't. Change. Shit."

Here's this powerful man standing by the maple tree, looking as if he could make a world with his big hands, and he says this. He's trapped in his story. Trapped in his words. And they're not even his. *They've been whispered to him the way words were whispered to me.* Sam Krassner wants to give him new words. "Can't change a lot of things," Krassner says. "Might change some. Beautiful kids. It's worth trying."

But Hammond shakes his head. "Too *late* for that shit. See, you don't know." And he turns away, picks up the baseball bat he's stowed by a tree on the front lawn, and goes back to his rusting Camaro. He doesn't look back. He opens the trunk, puts away the bat, he's gone.

At once Sheryl comes out onto the front steps. "Thank God," she says. "You did well."

He's feeling a little sick. Heart pounding, he takes Sheryl's arm and they walk back into the house; without asking, she pours him a shot of bourbon. "You did really well," she says.

Her eyes are shining; kind, quiet eyes—they're why he first loved her. Still, he's irritated; she makes him feel he simply manipulated the man. "We'll see." He shrugs. "He says it's too late. Maybe it's not." He doesn't tell her that the words came to him, weren't really his, weren't tools of manipulation. An angel's words, an offering. "Did you call 911?"

"I was afraid what could happen if he heard a siren."

The bourbon helps. In Krassner's inner eyes this angry man comes in and talks, and through the words they come to know one another, Krassner no longer white repressor, Hammond no longer the latest incarnation of drunken Cossacks who made Krassner's ancestors flee the Pale. Back at his desk, not knowing he's going to call, he picks up the phone and dials Barbara. No answer and no answer. He calls her friend. Jackie's at home, her voice flat. "Just wanted to touch base," he says.

"Barbara's still at the hospital. At Bay State. They're doing okay."

"What? The hospital? I don't know anything, Jackie. What? She try to kill herself again?"

"*No.* I was sure you must know. Right after you left their place, they went upstairs, and that Eugene, he picked up a baseball bat and came after her. The kids were screaming, and Denise, poor baby, she tried to protect her mama, she hugged her so Eugene couldn't get at her."

"Oh, my God. Oh, my God."

"The bastard kept swinging his bat. If he hit Denise on the head, she be dead now. Broke her collarbone, broke her wrist, maybe some ribs. Man there, superintendent, he saved her life."

The police are out looking for Hammond. Krassner calls to let them know Hammond came to his house; then he sits. What good are those damn words? An angel's voice? What good? Is he really puppet to an angel? Maybe it's the other way around—he's got this angel puppet on his lap and pretends the words are coming from a holy place.

Next evening he visits Denise in the hospital. Her father didn't hit her head, but her face looks swollen, puffy. He won't embarrass her by staring. He tells Denise how brave she was.

She cries, "Mister. You get out! Please! You made enough trouble." She won't look at him. She curls away into a small thing, faces the white curtain separating beds.

Saturday, after Shabbat services, he visits Hammond in j ail in Springfield. "You minded your business," Hammond says, "I wouldn't be here now. You lucky I don't kill you. You got cigarettes for me?"

"You want me to get you cigarettes?"

"I won't smoke your cigarettes."

Barbara he can't find at all. She's not with Denise; she doesn't come to the clinic. More grief: the caseworker's report—Barbara went after Hammond with a knife—went for him *first*. This blurs the story. His eyes blur when he reads the report. A knife. He thinks: failure; total defeat. If she's lucky, Denise will live with Jackie; the little kids will end up in foster care. He thinks about taking Alicia and Mickey into his own home, but Sheryl would be furious if he asked.

He can't sleep; exhausted, at eleven he crashes as if drunk—into darkness, random language, but, wide awake at midnight, he can't remember what he dreamed, makes himself a snack and reads. At work, snippets of voice; he shoves them away.

"What happened to that poor woman?" Sheryl asks. He shrugs. He knows Barbara's out of his program, can imagine the rest. He'd like to blame Sheryl—but for what? Lack of faith, he supposes, now that he himself has none. He thinks about those kids in foster care. Mickey, Alicia. He sees a tunnel of dark air, a dark wind spout, carry them away as shadows. Finally—two weeks later—he asks Sheryl, "What about taking those kids? Temporarily. If DSS allows."

"That's so generous," she says. "Really, Sam. But impossible. Anyway, that man scares me too much. When he gets out, a few months, maybe just a few weeks, you don't think he'd come after you? If you've got his kids? A white doctor taking his kids away?"

So he stays in touch with Jackie Chambers. She's his only source. "Barbara? She's living with her mother. She's . . . not in great condition."

"Look. Jackie. The younger kids. You think there's any way they could stay with you for a while? Suppose I sent you a small check every month?"

"You saw my place, Dr. Krassner. Real nice of you, though."

Words come at the edge of sleep. *Genuflect . . . Cognizance.* He's wide awake, hunting for meanings. Suppose after all an angel—so what? What good are an angel's words when someone takes a baseball bat to a child? Midnight, but he calls Barbara's number. The phone's disconnected, and when he calls Emet Brock next day he finds out she doesn't live there anymore. "You were right," he says to Brock.

Brock soothes. "You tried. This not about *you,* Doctor."

All day these are the words he hears. *This not about you.* He protests to Brock in his head, I didn't think it was about me. But on the way home from the clinic he turns off public radio, pulls into a Wal-Mart parking lot. *Or did I? Think it was about me? How I failed. My story.*

Everybody's got their story. Eugene has his, Barbara hers; this is Sam's story—blabber to wrap the heart in. He blurts a sad laugh, and it comes to him what he's been hearing all these weeks. It's like half-hearing a television play from the next room and only a few of the words slip through. That's what he's been hearing—fragments of a story, a word here and there. Whose story? At just this moment, with a gasp in his belly as if a rollercoaster were starting down, down, he slips through a crack between stories. In this gap the words fly like eagles below you in a canyon, floating, far beyond your willing, on the thermals. They're not his, the words; it's not his story.

A few weeks later he finds on his list of appointments at the clinic: *4 p.m.—Barbara Hammond.*

A couple of minutes late, she enters in a flurry; late, he surmises, so she could enter in a flurry and get through embarrassment. A pulse in his temple beats. "Good to see you," he says.

She wears the same floral dress; she sure doesn't look like spring, but she's fixed her hair like Jackie's, in a braided tiara—maybe, he thinks, it was Jackie fixed it for her. She's living with her mother and her stepfather. It's not the ideal situation, but she's got a job. Her caseworker came through for a change. "Nothing great. Doing home care for a couple of old women."

He holds back his questions: *The knife, what about that knife?* He says, "That's wonderful."

"Try it."

"And the kids?"

Denise is still with Jackie, she says; the others are kind of with Barbara. "Actually, they're with my mother till I show I'm okay."

"Are you okay?"

"If I were okay—" She leans forward till he can feel the warmth of her breath. "—you think I'd be here looking at *you*?"

In the place between stories, they lean back and have a laugh together.

Nominated by The Missouri Review

FACING ALTARS: POETRY AND PRAYER

by MARY KARR

from POETRY

To CONFESS MY UNLIKELY CATHOLICISM in *Poetry*—a journal founded in part on and for the godless, twentieth-century disillusionaries of J. Alfred Prufrock and his pals—feels like an act of perversion kinkier than any dildo-wielding dominatrix could manage on HBO's "Real Sex Extra." I can't even blame it on my being a cradle Catholic, some brainwashed escapee of the pleated skirt and communion veil who—after a misspent youth and facing an Eleanor Rigby-like dotage—plodded back into the confession booth some rainy Saturday.

Not victim but volunteer, I converted in 1996 after a lifetime of undiluted agnosticism. Hearing about my baptism, a pal sent me a postcard that read, "Not you on the Pope's team. Say it ain't so!" Well, while probably not the late Pope's favorite Catholic (nor he my favorite pope), I took the blessing and ate the broken bread. And just as I continue to live in America and vote despite my revulsion for many US policies, I continue to enjoy the sacraments despite my fervent aversion to certain doctrines. Call me a cafeteria Catholic if you like, but to that I'd say, Who isn't?

Perversely enough, the request for this confession showed up last winter during one of my lowest spiritual gullies. A blizzard's dive-bombing winds had kept all the bodegas locked for the second day running (thus depriving New Yorkers of newspapers and orange juice), and I found—in my otherwise bare mailbox—a letter asking me to write about my allegedly deep and abiding faith. That very morning, I'd confessed to my spiritual advisor that while I still believed in God, he had come to seem like Miles Davis, some nasty genius scowling out from under his hat, scornful of my mere being and on the verge of waving me off the stage for the crap job I was doing. The late William Matthews has a great line about Mingus, who "flurried" a musician from the stand by saying, "We've suffered a diminuendo in personnel . . ." I felt doomed to be that diminuendo, an erasure mark that matched the erasure mark I saw in the grayed-out heavens.

Any attempt at prayer in this state is a slow spin on a hot spit, but poetry is still healing balm, partly because it's always helped me feel less alone, even in earliest childhood. Poets were my first priests, and poetry itself my first altar. It was a lot of other firsts too, of course: first classroom/chat room/confessional. But it was most crucially the first source of awe for me, because it eased a nagging isolation: it was a line thrown to my drear-minded self from seemingly glorious Others.

From a very early age, when I read a poem, it was as if the poet's burning taper touched some charred filament in my rib cage to set me alight. Somehow—long before I'd published—that connection even extended from me outward. Lifting my face from the page, I often faced my fellow creatures with less dread. Maybe secreted in one of them was an ache or tenderness similar to the one I'd just eaten of. As that conduit into a community, poetry never failed me, even if the poet reaching me was some poor wretch even more abject than myself. Poetry never left me stranded, and as an atheist most of my life, I presumed its mojo was a highbrow, intellectual version of what religion did for those more gullible believers in my midst—dumb bunnies to a one, the faithful seemed to me, till I became one.

In the Texas oil town where I grew up, fierceness won fights, but I was thin-skinned—an unfashionably bookish kid whose brain wattage was sapped by a consuming inner life others didn't seem to bear the burden of. I just seemed to have more frames per second than other kids. Plus, early on, I twigged to the fact that my clan differed from our neighbors. Partly because of my family's entrenched atheism, kids weren't allowed to enter my yard—also since my artist mother was known to paint "nekked" women and guzzle vodka straight out of the bottle. She was seductive and mercurial and given to deep doldrums and mysterious vanishings, and I sought nothing so much as her favor. Poetry was my first lure. Even as a preschooler, I could sometimes draw her out of a sulk by reciting the works of e.e. cummings and A.A. Milne.

In my godless household, poems were the only prayers that got said—the closest thing to sacred speech at all. I remember mother bringing me Eliot's poems from the library, and she not only swooned over them, she swooned over my swooning over them, which felt as close as she came to swooning over me. Even my large-breasted and socially adroit older sister *got* Eliot—though Lecia warned me off telling kids at school that I read that kind of stuff. At about age twelve, I remember sitting on our flowered bedspread reading him to Lecia while she primped for a date. *Read it again, the whole thing.* She was a fourteen-year-old leaning into the mirror with a Maybelline wand, saying, *Goddamn that's great . . .* Poetry was the family's religion. Beauty bonded us.

Church language works that way among believers, I would wager— whether prayer or hymn. Uttering the same noises in unison is part of what consolidates a congregation (along with shared rituals like baptisms and weddings, which are mostly words). Like poetry, prayer often begins in torment, until the intensity of language forges a shape worthy of both labels: "true" and "beautiful." (Only in my deepest prayers does language evaporate, and a wide and wordless silence takes over.) But if you're in a frame of mind dark enough to refuse prayer, nothing can ease the ache like a dark poem. Wrestling with gnarled or engrossing language may not bring peace per se, but it can occupy a brain pumping out bad news like ticker tape and thus bring you back to the alleged rationality associated with the human phylum.

So it was for me last winter—my most recent dark night of the soul—when my faith got sandblasted away for some weeks. Part of this was due to circumstances. Right after a move to New York, fortune delivered a triple whammy: my kid off to college, a live-in love ending volcanically, then medical maladies that kept me laid up for weeks alone. In a state of scalding hurt—sleepless and unable to conjure hope at some future prospects—suddenly (it felt sudden, as if a pall descended over me one day) God seemed vaporous as any perfume.

To kneel and pray in this state is almost physically painful. At best, it's like talking into a bucket. At worst, you feel like a chump, some heartsick fool still sending valentines to a cad. With my friends away for the holidays, poetry seemed my only solace for more than a month. Maybe a few times I dipped into the Psalms or the book of Job. But more often I bent over the "terrible sonnets" of Gerard Manley Hopkins to find shape for my desolation:

> I am gall, I am heartburn. God's most deep decree
> Bitter would have me taste: my taste was me;
> Bones built in me, flesh filled, blood brimmed the curse.
> Self yeast of spirit a dull dough sours. I see
> The lost are like this, and their scourge to be
> As I am mine, their sweating selves, but worse.

I was also reading that bleak scribbler Bill Knott, to find a bitter companion to sip my own gall with. He'd aptly captured my spiritual state in "Brighton Rock by Graham Greene," where he imagines a sequel for Greene's book: the offspring that criminal sociopath Pinky Brown conceived in the body of pitiful Rose Wilson before he died becomes a teenager in a skiffle band called Brighton Rockers. This kid's inborn anguish resounds in the grotesque Mass his mom sits through:

> Every Sunday now in church Rose slices
>
> her ring-finger off, onto the collection-plate;
> once the sextons have gathered enough
> bodily parts from the congregation, enough
>
> to add up to an entire being, the priest sub-
> stitutes that entire being for the one
> on the cross: they bring Him down in the name
>
> of brown and rose and pink, sadness
> and shame. His body, remade, is yelled at
> and made to get a haircut, go to school,
>
> study, to do each day like the rest
> of us crawling through this igloo of hell
> and laugh it up, show pain a good time,
>
> and read Brighton Rock by Graham Greene.

This winter, I felt yelled at by the world at large and God in particular. The rhythm of Knott's final sentence says it all—"to DO each DAY like the REST/of us"—the first phrase is a stair plod, with an extra stumble step to line's end, where it becomes a cliff you fall off (no REST here)—"CRAWling through this IGloo of HELL."

People usually (always?) come to church as they do to prayer and poetry—through suffering and terror. Need and fear. In some Edenic past, our ancestors began to evolve hard-wiring that actually requires us (so I believe) to make a noise beautiful enough to lay on the altar of the Creator/Rain God/Fertility Queen. With both prayer and poetry, we use elegance to exalt, but we also beg and grieve and tremble. We suffer with prayer and poetry alike. Boy, do we suffer.

The faithless contenders for prayer's relief who sometimes ask me for help praying (still a comic notion) often say it seems hypocritical to turn to God only now during whatever crisis is forcing them toward it—kid with leukemia, say, husband lost in the World Trade Center. But no one I know has ever turned to God any other way. As the adage says, there are no atheists in foxholes. Maybe saints turn to God to exalt him. The rest of us tend to show up holding out a tin cup. Put the penny of your prayer in this slot and pull the handle—that's how I thought of it at first, and I think that's typical. The Catholic church I attended in Syracuse, New York (St. Lucy's) said it best on the banner stretched across its front: SINNERS WELCOME.

That's how I came to prayer nearly fifteen years back, through what James Laughlin (via *Pilgrim's Progress*) used to call the "Slough of Despond," and over the years prayer led me to God, and God led me to church—a journey fueled by gradually accruing comforts and some massively freakish coincidences.

Okay, I couldn't stop drinking. I'd tried everything *but* prayer. And somebody suggested to me that I kneel every morning and ask God for help not picking up a cocktail, then kneel at night to say thanks. "But I don't believe in God," I said. Again Bill Knott came to mind:

> People who get down
> on their knees to me
> are the answers to my prayers.
> —*Credo*

The very idea of prostrating myself brought up the old Marxist saw about religion being the opiate for the masses and congregations dumb as cows. God as Nazi? I wouldn't have it. My spiritual advisor at the time was an ex-heroin addict who radiated vigor. Janice had enough street cred for me to say to her, "Fuck that god. Any god who'd want people kneeling and sniveling—"

Janice cut me off. "You don't do it for God, you asshole," she said. She told me to try it like an experiment: pray for thirty days, and see if I stayed sober and my life got better.

Franz Wright states my position vis-à-vis my earliest prayers in "Request," here in its entirety:

> Please love me
> and I will play for you
> this poem
> upon the guitar
> I myself made
> out of cardboard and black threads
> when I was ten years old.
> Love me or else.
> —*Request*

I started kneeling to pray morning and night—spitefully at first, in a bitter pout. The truth is, I still fancied the idea that glugging down Jack Daniels would stay my turmoil, but doing so had resulted in my car hurtling into stuff. I had a baby to whom I had made many vows, and—whatever whiskey's virtues—it had gotten hard to maintain my initial argument that it made me a calmer mom to a colicky infant.

So I prayed—not with the misty-eyed glee I'd seen in *The Song of Bernadette*, nor with the butch conviction of Charlton Heston playing Moses in *The Ten Commandments*. I prayed with belligerence, at least once with a middle finger aimed at the light fixture—my own small unloaded bazooka pointed at the Almighty. I said, *Keep me sober*, in the morning. I said, *Thanks*, at night.

And I didn't get drunk (though before I started praying, I'd been bouncing on and off the wagon for a few years, with and without the help of others). This new sobriety seemed—to one who'd studied positivism and philosophy of science in college—a psychological pay-off for the dumb process of getting on my knees twice a day to talk to myself. One MIT-trained scientist told me she prayed to her "sober self"—a palatable concept for this agnostic.

Poet Thomas Lux was somebody I saw a lot those days around Cambridge, since our babies were a year apart in age. One day after I'd been doing these perfunctory prayers for a while, I asked Lux—himself off the sauce for some years—if he'd ever prayed. He was barbecuing by a swimming pool for a gaggle of poets (Allen Grossman in a three-piece suit and watch fob was there that day, God love him). The scene comes back to me with Lux poking at meat splayed on the grill while I swirled my naked son around the swimming pool. Did he actually *pray*? I couldn't imagine it—Lux, that dismal sucker.

Ever taciturn, Lux told me: I say thanks.

For what? I wanted to know. Robert Hass's *Praise* was a cult favorite at that time, but despite its title the poems mostly dealt with failures in devotion to beauty or the disappointments endemic to both pleasure and marriage. Its epigraph had a man facing down a huge and ominous monster and saying—from futility and blind fear—"I think I shall praise it." Hass had been my teacher when he was writing those poems, and though he instilled in me reverence for poetry, his own pantheistic ardor for trees and birds mystified me. My once alcohol-soaked life had convinced me that everything was too much, and nothing was enough (it's a depressant drug, after all). In my twisted cosmology (not yet articulated to myself), the ominous monster Hass "praised" was God.

Back in Lux's pool, I honestly couldn't think of anything to be grateful for. I told him something like I was glad I still had all my limbs. That's what I mean about how my mind didn't take in reality before I began to pray. I couldn't register the privilege of holding my blond and ringleted boy, who chortled and bubbled and splashed on my lap.

It was a clear day, and Lux was standing in his Speedo suit at the barbecue turning sausages and chicken with one of those diabolical-looking forks. Say thanks for the sky, Lux said, say it to the floorboards. This isn't hard, Mare.

At some point, I also said to him, What kind of god would permit the Holocaust?

To which Lux said, You're not in the Holocaust.

In other words, what is the Holocaust my business?

No one ever had an odder guru than the uber-ironic Thomas Lux, but I started following his advice by mouthing rote thank-you's to the air, and, right off, I discovered something. There was an entire aspect to my life that I had been blind to—the small, good things that came in abundance. A religious friend once told me of his own faith, "I've memorized the bad news." Suddenly, the world view to which I'd clung so desperately as realistic—we die, worms eat us, there is no God—was not so much realistic as the focal expression of my own grief-sodden inwardness. Like Hawthorne's reverend in "The Minister's Black Veil," I could only interpret the world through some dark screen of grief or self-absorbed fear.

Not too long after this talk with Lux (in a time of crisis—the end of my marriage), someone gave me the prayer allegedly from St. Francis of Assisi. It's one of those rote prayers that cradle-Catholics can resent having drilled into them, but I started saying it with my five-year-old son every night:

> Lord, make me an instrument of Thy peace.
> Where there is hatred, let me sow love;
> where there is conflict, pardon;
> where there is doubt, faith;
> where there is despair, hope;
> where there is sadness, joy;
> where there is darkness, light.
>
> O Divine Master, ask that I not so much seek
> to be consoled as to console;
> to be understood as to understand;
> to be loved as to love.
>
> For it is in giving that we receive.
> It is in pardoning that we are pardoned,
> and it is in dying that we are reborn
> to eternal life.

Even for the blithely godless, these wishes are pretty easy to choke down. I mean, it's not hard to believe that, if you can become an instrument for love and pardon rather than wallowing in self-pity, then your life will improve. The only parts of the prayer I initially bridled against were the phrase "O Divine Master" and the last two lines about eternal life, which I thought were horseshit. Something of it bored into my thick head, though, for reciting it began to enact some powerful calm in me.

Within a year of starting the prayer, my son told me he wanted to go to church "to see if God's there"—perhaps the only reason that could have roused my lazy ass from the Sunday *Times*. Thus we embarked on what I called God-a-rama—a search entirely for my son's benefit; despite my consistent prayer life, I still had small use for organized religion. I ferried Dev to various temples and mosques and zendos (any place a friend would bring us) with no more curiosity than I brought to soccer (a sport I loathe) when he took that up. If anything, the Catholic Church one pal took us to was repugnant, ideologically speaking. It set my feminist spikes prickling.

But the Church's carnality, which seemed crude at the outset—people lighting candles and talking to dolls—worked its voodoo on me. The very word *incarnation* derives from the Latin *in carne*: in meat. There is a *body* on the cross in my church. (Which made me think at first that the people worshipped the suffering, till my teenage son told me one day at Mass: "What else would get everybody's attention but something really grisly? It's like *Pulp Fiction*." In other words, we wouldn't have it any other way.)

Through the simple physical motions I followed during Mass (me, *following* something!), our bodies standing and sitting and kneeling in concert, I often felt my mind grow quiet, and my surface differences from others began to be obliterated. The poet William Matthews once noted that when his sons drew everyone as a stick figure, they evoked Shakespeare's "poor, bare, forked animal," which was—spiritually speaking—accurate:

> they were powerless enough to know
>
> the radical equality of human
> souls, but too coddled to know they knew it.
> They could only draw it, and they blamed
> their limited techniques for the great truth
> that they showed, that we're made in the image
> of each other and don't know it.
> —*The Generations*

So the bovine exercises during Mass made me feel like part of a tribe, in a way, and the effect carried over in me even after church.

Poetry had worked the same way. I've written elsewhere of its Eucharistic qualities—something else Hass taught me. In memorizing the poems I loved, I "ate" them in a way. I breathed as the poet breathed to recite the words: someone else's suffering and passion enters your body to transform you, partly by joining you to others in a saving circle.

Prayer had been the first cornerstone. How could it not be? In language (poetry) I'd found a way out of myself—to my mother, then to a wider community (the poets I imagined for years), then to a poetry audience for which I wrote, then to the Lord, who (paradoxically) speaks most powerfully to me through quiet. People will think I'm nuts when I say I prayed about whether to take a job and end my marriage and switch my son's day care. I prayed about what to write and wrote a bestseller that dug me out of my single mom's financial hole. Of course, I also pray to write like Wallace Stevens and don't. I pray to be five-ten and remain five inches short. Doubt still plagues me. As Zola once noted vis-à-vis his trip back from Lourdes, he saw crutches and wheelchairs thrown out, but not artificial legs. Milosz is more articulate about it in "Veni Creator":

I am only a man: I need visible signs.
I tire easily, building the stairway of abstraction.
Many a time I asked, you know it well, that the statue in church
lift its hand, only once, just once, for me.

Prayer has yielded comfort and direction—all well and good. But imagine my horror when I began to have experiences of joy. For me, joy arrives in the body (where else would it find me?), yet doesn't originate there. Nature never drew me into joy as it does others, but my fellow creatures as the crown of creation often spark joy in me: kids on a Little League diamond in full summer—even idly tossing their mitts into the air; the visual burst of a painted Basquiat angel in Everlast boxing shorts at the Brooklyn Museum last week (can't stop thinking about it); my teenage son at night in the dead of winter burying our kitten in a shoebox so I wouldn't have to see her ruined by the car that hit her—his flushed face later breaking the news to me—a grief countered by my radical joy at his sudden maturity. In the right mind-set, the faces that come at me on the New York street are like Pound's apparitions, "petals on a wet, black bough." Inherent in joy is always a sense of *joining* with others (and/or God). The spirit I breathe in at such times (inspiration) always moves through others.

But nothing can maim a poet's practice like joy. As Henri de Montherlant says, "Happiness writes white." What poet—in this century or any other—has founded her work on happiness? We can all drum up a few happy poems here and there, but from Symbolism and the High Moderns forward, poetry has often spread the virus of morbidity. It's been shared comfort for the dispossessed. Yes, we have Whitman opening his arms to "the blab of the pave." We have James Wright breaking into blossom, but he has to step out of his body to do so. We have the revelatory moments of Tranströmer and the guilty pleasure and religious striving of Milosz. W.H. Auden captured the ethos when he wrote, "The purpose of poetry is disenchantment." Poetry in the recent past hasn't allowed us much joy.

My own efforts to lighten my otherwise dour opus seem watered down. I thought of calling my latest collection of poems *Coathanger Bent Into Halo* (too clunky, I decided, but I was thinking how the wire hanger used for an illegal abortion could also be twisted into an angel's crown for a child's pageant). Still, the poems about Christ salted through the book spend way more time on crucifixion than resurrection. I've written elegies galore, love poems bitter as those of Catullus. I've written from scorched-earth terror and longing out the wazoo. My new aesthetic struggle is to accommodate joy as part of my literary enterprise, but I still tend to be a gloomy and serotonin-challenged bitch.

But doesn't dark poetry gather us together in a way that would meet the Holy Spirit's approval?

Rewind to last winter: my spiritual wasteland, when I received a request from *Poetry* to write about my faith. It was the third such request I'd gotten in a little more than a week, and it came from an editor I "owed" in some ways. How many times did Peter deny knowing Christ? I know, I know, my skeptical reader. It's only my naive, magical thinking that makes such a simple request (times three) seem like a tap on the shoulder from the Almighty, but for one whose experience of joy has come in middle age on the rent and tattered wings of disbelief, it suffices. Having devoted the first half of my life to the dark, I feel obliged to revere any pinpoint of light now. And writing this essay did fling open windows in me so the sun shone down again. I hit my knees, and felt God's sturdy presence, and knew it wasn't God who'd vanished in the first place.

Milosz, who dubbed himself the "least normal person in Father Chomski's class," describes the sense of alert presence from prayer or the wisdom of age in "Late Ripeness"—a lit-up poem of the type I aspire to write:

> Not soon, as late as the approach of my ninetieth year,
> I felt a door opening in me and I entered
> the clarity of early morning.
>
> One after another my former lives were departing,
> like ships, together with their sorrow.
>
> And the countries, cities, gardens, the bays of seas
> assigned to my brush came closer,
> ready now to be described better than they were before.
> I was not separated from people, grief and pity joined us.
> We forget—I kept saying—that we are all children of the King.

That's why I pray and poetize: to be able to see my brothers and sisters despite my own (often petty) agonies, to partake of the majesty that's every Judas's birthright.

Nominated by Joan Murray, Atsuro Riley, Poetry

HWY 1

by BRIAN TURNER

from THE GEORGIA REVIEW

> *I see a horizon lit with blood,*
> *And many a starless night.*
> *A generation comes and another goes*
> *And the fire keeps burning.*
> —*Al-Jawahiri*

It begins as the Highway of Death.
It begins with an untold number of ghosts
searching the road at night
for the way home, to Najaf, Kirkuk,
Mosul, and Kanni al Saad. It begins here
with a shuffling of feet on the long road north.

This is the spice road of old, the caravan trail
of camel dust and heat, where Egyptian limes
and sultani lemons swayed in crates
strapped down by leather, where merchants
traded privet flowers and musk, aloes,
honeycombs, and silk brought from the Orient.

And the convoy pushes on, past Marsh Arabs
and the Euphrates wheel, past wild camels
and waving children who marvel at the painted guns,
past the ruins of Babylon and Sumer,

through the land of Gilgamesh where the minarets
sound the muezzin's prayer, resonant and deep.

Cranes roost atop the power lines
in huge bowl-shaped nests of sticks and twigs,
and when a sergeant shoots one from the highway
it pauses, as if amazed that death has found it
here, at 7:00 A.M. on such a beautiful morning,
before pitching over the side and falling
in a slow unraveling of feathers and wings.

Nominated by Judith Kitchen, Philip Levine, Robert Wrigley

IF A STRANGER APPROACHES YOU ABOUT CARRYING A FOREIGN OBJECT WITH YOU ONTO THE PLANE . . .

fiction by LAURA KASISCHKE

from PLOUGHSHARES

ONCE THERE WAS A WOMAN who was asked by a stranger to carry a foreign object with her onto a plane:

When the stranger approached her, the woman was sitting at the edge of her chair a few feet from the gate out of which her plane was scheduled to leave. Her legs were crossed. She was wearing a black turtleneck and slim black pants. Black boots. Pearl studs in her ears. She was swinging the loose leg, the one that was tossed over the knee of the other—swinging it slowly and rhythmically, like a pendulum, as she tried to drink her latte in burning sips.

By the time the stranger approached her and asked her to carry the foreign object with her onto the plane, the woman had already owned that latte for at least twenty minutes, but it hadn't cooled a single degree. It was as if there were a thermonuclear process at work inside her cup—the steamed milk and espresso somehow generating together their own heat—and the tip of her tongue had been stung numb from trying to drink it, and the plastic nipple of the cup's white lid was smeared with her lipstick.

Her name was Kathy Bliss. She was anxious. At home, her two-year-old was sick, but she'd had to go to Maine, anyway, because she'd been asked to speak on behalf of the nonprofit for which she worked, and possibly thousands upon thousands of dollars would be gifted to it by her hosts if she were able to conjure the right combination of passion and desperation with which she was sometimes able to speak on behalf of her nonprofit. She didn't much believe in what they were doing, which was, to her mind, mostly justifying the spending of their donations on computers and letterhead and lunches with donors, but she had her eye on another nonprofit, one devoted to curing a disease (or at least *publicizing* a disease) which no one knew about until it was contracted, at which time the body attacked itself, turning the skin into a suit of armor, petrifying the internal organs one by one. The vice president of this nonprofit had his eye on the regional directorship of the American Cancer Society, she knew, and with some luck his position would be open, and she would be ready to move into it.

Still, she'd always understood that you have to put your energy into the place you are if you want to move on to another place; and, on occasion, she could be convincing—something about the podium, a bottle of water, a few notes, and all eyes on her—and there was clearly no one else at her nonprofit who could even remotely have been considered for this engagement. (Jen, with her multiple piercings? Rob, with his speech impediment?) She had to go.

The baby was sick, but the baby would be fine. Kathy Bliss had a husband, after all, who would take care of their baby. He was the baby's father, for God's sake. This wasn't 1952. The man had a Ph.D. in compassion; who was she to think the baby would be any better off with her there just because she was *of a certain gender?* And if she hadn't had to go to Maine, Garrett would have gone to work himself, which would have left only one parent at home, anyway, doing the same thing either way—cuddling, cleaning up puke, taking the temp, filling the sippy cup with cold water.

Still, Kathy Bliss felt a pain, which she knew, intellectually, was imaginary, but nonetheless was excruciating, hovering around a few inches above her breasts, as if only moments ago something adhesive—a bandage, duct tape, a baby—had been ripped away from her bare flesh and taken a top layer of cellular material with it.

The latte had scalded her tongue (just the tip) to the point that she could feel, when she moved it across the ridge behind teeth, the rough little bumps of it gone completely dead—just a prickling dullness. Without the taste buds to interfere, Kathy Bliss could really feel the ridge behind the back of her teeth, the place where the bone smoothed into flesh, the difference between what was there for now and what, when she was dead, would be left. She took another sip. Better. Maybe it had cooled down a bit, or maybe her tongue couldn't register the heat of it anymore. That was probably dangerous, she thought. The way people got scalded. Their nerve endings dulled, and they stepped into the tub without knowing it would cook them.

"Sorry," the stranger said after his pant leg brushed her knee, but she didn't really look at him, not yet. His tan belt was at eye level, nothing remarkable about it, and then he was gone.

As was always the case in airports, there was a small crowd of confused people (the elderly, the poor, some foreigners) standing patiently in a line they didn't need to stand in, and a woman behind a counter who was waving them away one by one as they approached her with their fully sufficient pieces of paper.

"We'll be boarding in forty minutes," the woman said over and over, refusing to smile, make eye contact, or answer questions. The woman had a spectacular hairpiece on top of her head. A kind of beehive with fronds. When she waved, the fronds shivered, caught the light, looking fountain-like, or like incandescent antennae. Although the woman had dark skin (tanning booth?), her real hair was a pale pink-blond beneath the hairpiece, which was the synthetic blond of a Barbie doll. What had the woman been thinking, Kathy Bliss wondered, that morning at the mirror, placing it atop her head. What had she believed she would look like with that thing on her head? Had she *wanted* to look the way she did—shocking, alien, a creature out of an illustrated Hans Christian Andersen?

Many years before, when Kathy Bliss was a college student, in an incident that had, she believed, changed and defined her forever, she'd come across a dead body in the Arboretum. A woman. Stabbed. Mostly bones and some scraps of clothing—and she (Kathy Bliss, not the dead woman) had run screaming.

It had been a very quick glimpse, so of course she hadn't known at the time that the body was that of a woman, or that the woman had been stabbed, knew nothing of the details until she was given them

108

later by the police. Still, she knew that she must have stood there open-mouthed for at least a second or two (she had been running on a trail but gone off of it to pee) because she clearly saw, or *remembered* seeing, that there were bees in that dead woman's hair.

When a few people left the line, a few more entered it. All over the airport, there were such sad, small crowds. They hesitated together at every counter, not ready to believe that all was well, not able to so easily accept the assurance that they already had what they needed, that they had found their proper places so quickly and had only now to wait. Kathy Bliss herself had forced one such crowd to part for her when she entered the terminal, pulling her luggage on wheels behind her as she made her way to security. She could feel their eyes on her back as she passed, knew they were probably loathing and admiring in equal measure her swift professional purposefulness. *She* knew where she was going. *She'd* done this a million times.

But, to her ears, anyway, the wheels of her luggage made the sound of a spit turning quickly (but with some effort) over a burning pit, as she dragged it behind her. She had no idea why. They weren't rusty. It was a fairly new bag. It had never been left out in the rain or pulled through the mud. But there it was, the sound of a spit, turning. A pig on that spit. An apple in its mouth. That final humiliation: *We shall eat you, Pig.*

She couldn't believe it when, at the SAVe a LIFe! picnic that summer, that they'd actually *done* that, actually roasted a pig on a spit with an apple crammed into its mouth.

At first, she hadn't noticed it because she'd been busy meeting and greeting. ("Yes, yes, of course I remember. Nice to see you again. Thank you for coming.")

But after she'd filled her glass with punch and had just tipped the glass to her lips, she'd seen it out of the corner of her eye, taken one step toward it, seen it fully then, and reeled—literally reeled—and splashed pink punch onto her chest, where it trickled down in a sweet zigzagging rivulet between her breasts.

Luckily, she'd been wearing a low-cut dress, also pink.

"Whoa," the college president she'd been standing next to said when she reeled. "Friend of yours or something? Are you a vegetarian?"

"Jesus," she'd said, "I am now," turning her back to the spit, trying to smile. But there was a cool film of sweat all over her body, as if

109

each pore had opened in a moment, coating her with dew. "What a spectacle."

"Isn't that the point?" the college president had said.

"Because of heightened security measures," the ceiling droned, *"we ask that you report any unattended luggage. If a stranger should approach you and ask you to carry a foreign object with you onto a plane, please contact a member of security personnel immediately."*

"Excuse me?" the stranger said, taking a seat beside her.

Kathy Bliss turned, swinging her leg off her knee, placing both black boots beside one another on the floor.

"Yes?"

The stranger was young and handsome. He had dark hair and tan skin and large brown eyes. Slender fingers. What appeared to be an actual gold Rolex on his wrist. He was wearing a white shirt with a red tie and a black leather jacket. An Arab, she thought right away, and then felt bad for thinking it. He had no accent; she could tell that already from the two words he'd spoken. He was an American, not an "Arab." He was probably more American than she was, her mother's parents having stumbled into this country from Liverpool, broke, in the twenties, her paternal grandparents having dashed across the Canadian border in the thirties in search of higher-paying employment with the US Postal Service.

Still, it must be awful, she thought, to *look* like an Arab in an airport these days. It must have felt, she supposed, like wearing a scarlet A. Everyone staring, either wondering suspiciously about you and feeling guilty about wondering, or feeling suspicious and self-righteous about staring and wondering. "I'm sorry to bother you," the stranger said. "Are you, by any chance, going to Portland?"

"Yes," Kathy Bliss said.

"Well—" he smiled, and then his breast pocket began to play the theme from *The Lone Ranger* loudly and digitally, and he reached into it and fumbled around for a moment until it stopped and he said, "Sorry," shaking his head. For a crazy second Kathy Bliss thought of asking him to check the caller ID, to make sure her husband wasn't trying to reach her with some news about the baby (she'd turned her own cell off to conserve the battery, and would check it just before she got on the plane)—but, of course, this stranger had nothing to do with her baby.

"Can I help you?" she asked.

The man had a tiny gold cross in his left earlobe. It was really very beautiful—and strange, too, how masculine that little earring made him look with the dark shadow of beard on his chiseled jawline, and how masculine he made that earring by wearing it in his ear, with its foiled brilliance. A small, bold statement. It might have been a religious statement or a fashion statement, what difference did it make?

"Yes, but please," he said, "if this sounds strange to you, just send me away."

"Okay?" she said. A question.

"Okay," he said. "I'm supposed to be going to Portland for my mother's seventieth birthday, but I just got a call from my girlfriend telling me"—he smiled ruefully, rolled his eyes to the ceiling—"I'm sorry, I should make something up here, but I'll just tell you the truth: she's pregnant. And she's flipping out. And I feel like"—he tossed some emptiness into the air with his palms, making a gesture she'd seen men make many times in response to women's emotional states—"honestly—I think I ought to go buy her an engagement ring *today*, and get my butt back to our apartment. I mean, this isn't a disaster. Or it doesn't *have* to be. We were getting married, anyway, and we knew we might get pregnant. We weren't even using any—" He shook his head. "I'm sorry, *really* sorry, to be filling you in on all these details. I'd made it through security, I was planning to just go and come back maybe even tonight, and then I realized—I just realized I shouldn't go at all. That I should go straight back to my girlfriend right now." He inhaled, looked at Kathy Bliss as if trying to gauge her reaction. "I'm sorry," he said, "to fill you, a complete stranger, in on these sordid details."

Kathy Bliss tried to laugh sympathetically. She shook her head a little. Shrugged. "It's okay," she said. "Been there, done that!"

The stranger laughed pretty hard at this. His teeth were very straight and white, although one of the front ones had what looked to be a hairline crack in it. A very thin gray crack. Her two-year-old, Connor, had just recently gotten so many new teeth that it surprised her every time he opened his mouth. The teeth were like little dabs of meringue. Clean and white and peaked. She liked to smell his breath. It was as if there were a pure little spring in there. His mouth smelled like mineral water.

"Well, there you have it," the stranger said. "I guess, if nothing else, we're all here because *somebody'd* been there and done that."

"That, too," Kathy Bliss said. "But, I mean, I have a child. It's a great thing."

"Yeah," he said. "I'm starting to forget, in all this hysteria, the great fact that I'm going to be a dad—"

"Well, congratulations from me," Kathy Bliss said. She felt the warm implication of tears starting somewhere around her sinuses, and swallowed. She changed her latte cup from her right hand to her left, reached over the metal armrest, and offered her hand to him. He shook it, smiling. Then he shook his own hand as if it had been burned. "Jeez," he said, "that's one burning handshake."

"My latte," she said. "It's like molten lava."

"I guess so," he said.

The stranger was wearing khaki pants with very precisely ironed creases. For a quick second Kathy Bliss wondered if his girlfriend was also an Arab, and then she remembered that she had no way of knowing that *he* was an Arab, and far more evidence, anyway, that he *wasn't*—and reminded herself that it didn't matter, anyway. So, maybe his parents had been born in Egypt, or Iran. The color of his skin was beautiful! A warm milky brown. She felt a pang of jealousy about the girlfriend, lying on their bed at home, not knowing that this beautiful stranger was making desperate plans to buy her a diamond that day. What a thing, this life. Love. God, when it worked, it really worked! She had, herself, fallen in love with her husband upon first sight. She'd been given his name as the best shrink in town for the kind of problem she was having—which was spending every minute of her day trying not to think about the dead body in the Arboretum for two solid years after she'd seen it—and she had no sooner settled herself in the chair across from his, and he'd crossed his legs, looking more anxious and frightened than she, herself, the *patient*, felt, that she knew she wanted to marry him. And he'd cured her, too. Without drugs. A few behavior modifications. A rubber band around her wrist, a mantra, a series of self-punishments and rewards.

"Well, to make a long story short," the stranger said, "my girlfriend's freaking out back at our apartment, and my mother's turning seventy in Portland, and I'm her only son, who's such a scoundrel and an ingrate, not to mention morally reprehensible for impregnating someone he's not married to, *yet*, that he's not even showing up for her party, so"—and here he shook his head and looked directly into Kathy Bliss's eyes—"I wonder if I, a stranger, could ask you, a passenger, to carry a foreign object with you onto the plane?"

"Oh my God," Kathy Bliss said. "All these years I was wondering if anyone was ever going to ask me that."

"I think," the stranger said, "now is the point at which you ought to contact security personnel—like, right away."

"Yes," she said, "I think I may have heard an announcement pertaining to that. And I've always wondered to myself what kind of idiot would actually do such a thing, like carry a foreign object onto a plane."

"Well," the stranger said, "here's the object you've been waiting your whole life to carry with you onto the plane."

Out of a pocket in the inner lining of his coat, the stranger produced a narrow rectangular box wrapped in gold paper. He sighed. "It's a gold necklace, and if you'd be so foolhardy as to carry it with you onto the plane, I'd call my brother and have him meet you at baggage claim and get it to the party this evening. *But*"—he waved his slender fingers around over the box—"I totally understand if you think that's nuts."

"I have no problem with it," she said. "Don't worry, I won't contact security personnel."

"Let me open it for you, at least," he said, "so you know you're not carrying a bomb—"

"If you managed to get a bomb in that little package," she said, "you deserve to have it carried by a passenger onto the plane."

She regretted the joke even as she said it, saw the Towers dissolving into dust on her television again. It had been on the floor because the entertainment center had not yet arrived (it was being custom-built somewhere in Illinois) and there was no table or counter big enough to put the television on. The baby was crying (eight weeks old), so she'd had to stand and pace with his hot little face leaking tears onto her shoulders as those Towers collapsed at her feet. The front door had been open, and it had smelled to her as if the stone-blue perfect sky out there were dissolving in talcumish particles of dried flowers—such a beautiful day it horrified her. An illusion dipped in blue. She could have walked with her baby straight out the front door or right into the big-screen TV of it, and they might have turned themselves into nothing but subatomic particles, blue light, perfume.

There was nothing funny about terrorism. Nothing even remotely funny about terrorism. Still, she was from the Midwest, and it

113

seemed like a long time ago already. No more National Guard in the airport—those boys with their big weapons trying not to look bored and out of place around every corner. She had, herself, only been to New York a few times, and never to those Towers, having only glimpsed them from her plane as it banked into LaGuardia. From the plane, they'd looked like Legos, and no matter how real she knew it all was, on the television, on the floor, it had not looked real. And the least likely plane a terrorist would want to blow up or hijack was one traveling from Grand Rapids, Michigan, to Portland, Maine. Right? "Don't unwrap that," she said. "It's exquisite. I trust you."

"I insist," he said. "This is too weird and too much of a . . . cliché! I have my dignity!" He laughed. "And in any case, I will doubt your sanity if you don't let me open it. I can't have a crazy woman delivering my mother's birthday present—"

"No," Kathy Bliss said, snatching the little present off his lap. "You'll never get it wrapped like this again. It's like a little dream. I'd be insane if I thought you could get anything *but* a necklace in that box."

He made his mouth into a zero, and sighed, loosened his tie a little by inserting his index finger between the knot and his collar. From somewhere on the other side of the wall of screens that listed arrivals and departures, a baby began to cry, and the feeling came back to her—the ripping, intensely, as if yet another layer of skin, or whatever was underneath her skin, were being pulled off her torso in one quick yank. The stranger took the cellphone out of his pocket and said, "I'll call my brother. Can I tell him your name? I'll have him at baggage claim—I mean—" He interrupted himself here. "I'm assuming that's where you'll be going—" He looked at the black bag at her feet. "Did you check luggage?"

"Yes," she said. "I mean no, but I can go to baggage claim, no problem. Tell him—"

"I'll have him carry a sign, with your name on it, okay?"

"Yes. Kathy Bliss."

"Bliss?" He smiled. "Like, 'bliss'?"

"Yes," she said. "Like the Joseph Campbell thing. 'Follow your bliss.' "

He smiled, but she could tell he hadn't heard of Joseph Campbell, or the advice of Joseph Campbell. She had, herself, been in graduate school when the PBS series with Bill Moyers had aired, and gotten together every Tuesday night with a group of women from her Mind,

114

Brain, and Violence Seminar to watch it. A lot of joking about Bliss, and following it, had been made. When she'd get up to go to the bathroom or to get a beer out of the refrigerator, someone always pretended to follow her.

"We would like to begin boarding passengers on Flight 5236 to Portland, Maine. Passengers traveling with small children or needing special assistance . . ."

"That's me," she said.

"Yes," he said. "Of course. I'll make the call after you board. But let me tell you, my brother—he's twenty-two, but he looks a lot like me. I haven't seen him in a year, and sometimes he has long hair and sometimes he shaves his head, so"—he shrugged—"who knows. But he's about five-nine, one hundred sixty pounds—"

Kathy Bliss slipped the gold-wrapped box into her black bag carefully, so he could see that he could trust her with it. "Well," she said, "he'll have my name on a piece of paper, right? It'll be simple."

"Am I right, the plane's supposed to land at 12:51?" the stranger asked, peeking into the inner lining of his suit coat again, as if to look at his own unnecessary itinerary.

"Yep," she said. "12:51, assuming we're on time."

"Here," he said, hurrying with a piece of paper and a pen he'd taken from the pocket of his suit coat, "my brother's name is Mack Kaloustian. He'll be there. Or I'll kill him, and he knows it."

Kaloustian. Armenian. Kathy Bliss blinked and saw a spray of bullets raking through a family in a stand of trees on a mountain-top, a mother shielding her child, collapsing onto him: That child might have been this stranger's grandmother. And then they were boarding her row—12. Kathy Bliss stood up and extended her hand to the stranger. "Good luck to you," she said with all the warmth she could generate with only four words. The second word, *luck*, caught in her throat—a little emotional fishhook made out of consonants—because it was all so lovely, and simple, and lucky. Nothing but goodness in it for anyone. And her part in this sweet small drama moved her deeply, too—this gesture she was making of pure human cama-raderie, this nonprofit venture, this small recognition of the cliché *We're all in this together*. That it mattered. Love. Family. The stranger. The favor. The bond of trust between them. He knew she wouldn't disappear into Portland with his gold necklace. She knew he wouldn't—what? Send her onto a plane with an explosive? He shook her hand so warmly it was like a hug. He said, "I can't tell you

115

how much I appreciate this," and she said, "Of course. I'm happy to be able to help," and then she walked backwards so she could extend the moment of their smiling and parting, and then turned, inhaling, and began the dull and claustrophobic process of boarding her plane.

Kathy Bliss had been born and raised in a little stone house at the edge of a deep forest. "Honest to God," she always had to say after giving someone this piece of information about herself for the first time. "But it was nothing like you're imagining."

Her father had worked for a minimum-security prison, and the prison had been the thing her bedroom window faced, its high cyclone fencing topped by hundreds of yards of coiled barbed wire. In the summer, the sun rising in the east over the prison turned that barbed wire into a blinding fretwork, all spun-sugar and baroque and glitter, as if the air had been embroidered with silver thread by a gifted witch. She'd squint at it pretending that what her bedroom faced was an enchanted castle, as if the little stone house at the edge of the dark forest really were something from a fairy tale. But it was a sedentary childhood. Her parents wouldn't let her play in the yard or wait outside for the bus because, if there were an escape, she would make too good a hostage, being the prison director's daughter. For this reason, Kathy Bliss rarely had the chance to see the prisoners milling around behind that barbed wire, wearing their orange jumpsuits, and was able, therefore, to imagine them handsome and gallant as knights.

She and her mother had moved, when Kathy was nine, after her father died from an illness that announced itself first as bleeding gums, and then paralysis, and then he was just gone. She was thinking about this blip in her first years—the stone house, the barbed-wire castle—and watching the other passengers struggle onto the plane, shoving their heavy luggage into overhead compartments, the fat ones sweating, the thin ones trembling, the mothers with babies and little children looking blissfully burdened, when a voice came over the plane's intercom and said, "If there is a Katherine Bliss onboard, could she please press the flight attendant call button now?"

"Oh my God," Kathy Bliss said so loudly that an old woman standing in the aisle next to her whirled around and hit the call button for her. "Is that you?" the old woman said, as if she knew what they were calling Kathy Bliss about, as if everyone knew. "Yes," she said. "I forgot to check my messages." "Oh dear," the old woman said. The skin hung off her face in gray rags, and yet she'd made herself up care-fully that morning, with tastefully understated foundation and blush, the kind of replica of life that would cause all gathered around her casket to say, "She just looks as if she's sleeping." There began a cold trickling at the tip of Kathy Bliss's spine, and then it turned into a fine mist, coating every inch of her. She could not close her mouth. She tried to stand, but there were so many people in the aisle she couldn't get out of her seat, although the old woman had turned to face the strangers surging forward and put a bony arm in front of her as if to try to block their passage. "Ma'am," a flight attendant said from ten feet behind that line, looking at the old woman. "Are you Mrs. Bliss?"

"No," the old woman said, and pointed to Kathy. "This is Mrs. Bliss."

"We have a message for you, Mrs. Bliss," the flight attendant called over the shoulders of the passengers in the aisle. She was a huge blond beauty, a Norse goddess. Someone who might stand on a mountain peak with a bolt of lightning in her fist. The crowd in the aisle dissolved to make way for her, and she pressed a folded piece of paper into Kathy Bliss's shaking hand: *Baby in hospital. Call home now. Husband.*

It was a week later—after the long pale nights at his crib-side in the hospital, taking turns pretending to sleep as the other paced, the tests, and the antibiotics, and the failure of the first ones to fight off the infection, and the terrifying night when the baby didn't wake during his injection, and they could clearly see the residency doctor's hand shaking as he punched the emergency button. It was after they'd begun a whole new life on the children's floor. *Sesame Street* in the lounge all day, as if the world were being run by benevolent toys, and then CNN scrolling its silent, redundant messages to them all night below images of the cynical and maimed. After they'd got-ten to know the nurses. It was after Kathy Bliss had fallen in love, madly, with one doctor after another—not a sexual love, but a deep wild worship of the archetype, a reverent adulation of the Healer—and then grown to despise them one by one, and then to see them merely as human beings. It was after she'd spent some self-conscious moments on her knees in the hospital chapel, which turned into deep semi-conscious communions with the Almighty as the hospital intercom called out its mundane codes and locations in the hallway

117

behind her—and the baby was taking fluids, and then solids, and then given a signature of release, and the nurses hugged Kathy Bliss and her husband, and let their hands wave magically, baptismally, over the head of the baby, who laughed, sputtered, still a little weak, scarlet-cheeked, but very much of this world, and cured for the next leg of the journey into the future, when they packed up the stuffed animals and picture books and headed for home—it was after all these events had come to an end that Kathy Bliss remembered the foreign object, given to her by the stranger, which had stayed where she'd tucked it into her carry-on luggage, where she'd left it in the hallway of her house, tossed under a table, in a panic, on her brief stop there between the airport and the hospital.

Garrett had gone to work, and the baby was napping in a patch of sunlight that poured green and gold through the front door onto the living room floor. It was a warm late-summer day. The phone had been unplugged the night before, and stayed that way. She hadn't turned the television on once since they'd come home. The silence swelled and receded in a manner that would have been imperceivable to her only two weeks before, but which now seemed sacred, full of implication, a kind of immaculate tableau rolled out over the neighborhood in the middle of the day when no one was anywhere, and only the cats crossed the streets, padding in considerate quiet on their starry little paws. She glanced at the black bag.

She got down on her knees and pulled the bag to her, and removed the umbrella, and the pink makeup bag, and the folded black sweater, the brother's name, *Mack Kaloustian* (but hadn't the stranger said he was his mother's only son?), and saw it there, the box, in its gold paper, and recognized it only vaguely, as neither a gift nor a recrimination, a threat, or a blessing.

She didn't open it, but imagined herself opening it. Imagined herself as a passenger on that plane, unable to resist it. Holding it to her ear. Shaking it, maybe. Lifting the edge of the gold paper, tearing it away from the box. And then, the certain, brilliant cataclysm that would follow. The lurching of unsteady weight in the sky, and then the inertia, followed by tumbling. The numbing sensation of great speed and realization in your face. She'd been a fool to take it with her onto the plane. It could have killed them all.

Or, the simple gold braid of it.

Tasteful. Elegant. A thoughtful gift chosen by a devoted son for his beloved mother. And she imagined taking the necklace out of the

118

box, holding it up to her own neck at the mirror, admiring the glint of it around her neck—this bit of love and brevity snatched from the throat of a stranger—wearing it with an evening gown, passing it down as an heirloom to her children:

Who was to say, she thought to herself as she began to peel the gold paper away, that something stolen, without malice or intent, is any less yours than something you've been given?

Nominated by Kristin King, Valerie Laken, Pinckney Benedict,
Sydney Lea, Debra Spark, Diann Blakely, Ploughshares

HARD RAIN

by TONY HOAGLAND

from HARD RAIN (HOLLYRIDGE PRESS)

After I heard *It's a Hard Rain's A-Gonna Fall*
played softly by an accordion quartet
through the ceiling speakers at the Springdale Shopping Mall,
I understood: there's nothing
we can't pluck the stinger from,

nothing we can't turn into a soft drink flavor or a t-shirt.
Even serenity can become something horrible
if you make a commercial about it
using smiling, white-haired people

quoting Thoreau to sell retirement homes
in the Everglades, where the swamp has been
drained and bulldozed into a nineteen-hole golf course
with electrified alligator barriers.

You can't keep beating yourself up, Billy
I heard the therapist say on television
       to the teenage murderer,
About all those people you killed—
You just have to be the best person you can be,

one day at a time—

and everybody in the audience claps and weeps a little,
because the level of deep feeling has been touched,
and they want to believe that
that the power of Forgiveness is greater
than the power of Consequence, or History.

Dear Abby:
My father is a businessman who travels.
Each time he returns from one of his trips,
his shoes and trousers
                    are covered with blood—
but he never forgets to bring me a nice present;
Should I say something?
                            Signed, America.

I used to think I was not part of this,
that I could mind my own business and get along,

but that was just another song
that had been taught to me since birth—

whose words I was humming under my breath,
as I was walking thorough the Springdale Mall.

Nominated by Marianne Boruch, B. J. Ward, Wesley McNair, Charles Harper Webb

EXTRAORDINARY RENDITION

by MAXINE KUMIN

from THE AMERICAN POETRY REVIEW

Only the oak and the beech hang onto their leaves
at the end, the oak leaves bruised the color of those
insurgent boys Iraqi policemen captured

purpling their eyes and cheekbones before
lining them up to testify to the Americans
that, no, no, they had not been beaten . . .

The beech leaves dry to brown, a palette of cinnamon.
They curl undefended, they have no stake in the outcome.
Art redeems us from time, it has been written.

Meanwhile we've exported stress positions, shackles,
dog attacks, sleep deprivation, waterboarding.
To rend: *to tear (one's garments or hair)*

in anguish or rage. To render: *to give what is due
or owed.* The Pope's message
this Sunday is the spiritual value of suffering.

Extraordinary how the sun comes up
with its rendition of daybreak,
staining the sky with indifference.

Nominated by Michael Waters, Wesley McNair, Jane Hirshfield

THE FRANK ORISON

fiction by SCOTT GEIGER

from CONJUNCTIONS

MAX ORISON EMERGES from the garage pulling the type of red wagon forever popular with children his age. Frank Orison, his father, rides squarely in the wagon's bed, mute as a chessman. A primitive daylight shines low in the sky. Morning comes slowly up this way, climbing the broad pine trees along the drive. Through patches of sunshine and over long shadows cast by the trees, Max and his father go. At the drive's end, they turn to make their way through the neighborhood. The wagon wheels clatter over broken slabs of sidewalk. They pass houses set back behind yards of low shrubbery and maples. Two familiar shapes stir in their windows. They keep pace with the Orisons, leaping from one window to the next. The figures reappear in the windows of each house as Max and his father pass. But Max doesn't notice. He whistles an improvised tune for happy Saturday adventures with his father.

It's either up to the airfield or down to the jetties.

This Saturday morning custom defines the Orisons. Without it, could it be Saturday? Could Max still be Max? Could Frank Orison still be his father? How Max loves to watch the jets and the biplanes pull themselves off the earth and over the horizon. He thinks of a windy Saturday last summer at the airfield, the morning they saw men use cables to pull a red-and-white dirigible down out of the sky. This scene reminded Max of the fishermen on the jetties, of their excitement, their pointy smiles, and their shouts as they reel in their perch. The dirigible lay down gleaming against the black tarmac in the end, and men wove cables along its belly to fasten it down. The "when-I's" and "if-I's" conventional to boys' talk played out of Max's mouth for hours afterward. Max would have a jet and if not a jet, a biplane; if not a biplane, a blimp; and if not a blimp, a fishing rod would do for now, though he would fish only in the spring since the sea lions nap on the jetties on summer afternoons. Max thinks of them as halfway dogs, and dogs scare him.

It's down to the beach and the jetties, Max decides. The year's too young for sea lions. But not for blue jays. One lands on a crab apple tree nearby and chirps inquisitively. Max grins at the bird with a dreamy, feline smile. Everything tries its best to come to life for the summertime, to attend a warm, green world.

A silver sedan drives by doing the speed limit. For an instant, the Orisons and the wagon are reversed on the side of the car. The name on the wagon flips like a sock turned inside out. When it comes to mirrors, Max knows how they pervert details. Still he cannot help but stare. He's the sad story dog, the one holding a bone between its teeth as it stares down the well. Mirrors remind Max of how things fall short, how the world performs below expectations. Could this be because the world is very old? Each time the Griers' station wagon struggles down the block, fuming blackly, he's sure that that will be its last voyage. But inside the jalopy, Mr. Grier seems to know better. He holds the steering wheel with his fingertips and looks resolutely out at the road ahead of him, while lower on his face, his lips sculpt words. Is it prayer, Max wonders, that keeps the station wagon moving? Max's mother has said the Griers are ruined. So isn't it likely then that the present imperfection of mirrors, like today's sputtering engine, is only an early symptom of worse things to come?

Max wishes his father had something reassuring to say.

They travel through the morning down the boulevard and out of town to the beach and the jetties. Below a landscaped park, the beach begins amid rolling dunes seeded with finger grass and sleeping plant. The wagon performs poorly in the sand, but in the end Max and Frank Orison arrive at their destination: the last stone block of the farthest jetty. At high tide the waves will break against the stones where Max now spreads a blue-checked beach towel. The last tide left a dark green vein of seaweed in a crevice. Max is leaning down to stroke it with the back of his fingers when the sound of wings surprises him. He stands up to find a fat gray gull preening itself on his father.

Shoo!

Frank Orison remains calm, absolutely still.

Shoo, stupid bird! Max says.

He swipes at the gull and it flitters off into the breeze above the gray-green water. The same breeze plasters Max's hair over his eyes. He removes his shoes and socks, and sits facing his father. He lets his right leg dangle over the side and his left foot rest on the edge, his left knee raised; his left elbow rests on the knee so his left fist can prop up his tilted head. Fishermen cast silently against the offing. He takes in the pale blue sky and the freighters out at sea. But just then there's a blinding bit of the sun bouncing off his father's face, straight into Max's eyes. He winces and, shielding his eyes with his left hand, uses the big toe of his left foot to turn his father just enough.

Were any evil to befall Frank Orison—theft, for example, or the ever-present threat of discovery by his mother—Max will rely on replicas. One rainy day, he found that sugar cubes could be carved in his father's image. He took an emery board to a cube and shaved one corner flat. This became his steady base, his foot. With the cube standing upright, he drew the emery board over what was now the topmost corner, pulling it lightly toward his chest and downward at an acute angle. He worked gingerly, and in time the pentagonal asymmetry of his father's face revealed itself. Max keeps dozens of such miniature fathers in his dresser drawer. Most he shaved from sugar cubes before his mother had the chance to plop them in her tea. A few he cut from cork, four he molded from white beeswax; one is balsa wood, one is a fragment of cinder block he ground for weeks against a piece of callous steel. Many of the replicas fathered poorly. The sugar dads proved especially defective: they crumbled too easily in his palm or out-of-doors on humid April days. They tempted the birds and the squirrels and the ants. Ants captured two, a fly licked another, and there was one Max ate in a moment of doubt. Others fell to everyday hazards and carelessness: one wax father was smooshed in the back pocket of his blue trousers, and he lost a balsa wood replica somewhere in his desk at school.

Max has learned over the course of months how to protect his Frank Orisons. Errands with his mother, for example, call for either a balsa wood or a cork father. But Saturday adventures require *the* Frank Orison, the original, which he found at the airfield on that Saturday morning he left the house alone. His father was too heavy to carry, so he went home and got his red wagon. Max has not been able to create a replica on that scale, nor one so strong and resilient, so confident and handsome. He's lucky to have found such a worldly father, too, who so brightly reflects everything around him. But his attempt to make a backup miniature from one of his mother's hand mirrors failed. The blood ran in threads between his fingers down onto the Oriental rug. Should evil befall the Frank Orison, Max knows he will never be able to replace him. Should the worst happen, he will make do with his pocket Frank Orisons until at last he's too old for fathers.

At a sleepy corner where two streets merge into a third, Max Orison passes the Griers' house on his return from the jetties. It's a shabby dark place with a yard of willows and sprawling rhododendron. Max sees Edgar Grier and his twin, Sly, loitering between weedy flower beds with Sam Treble and his fearsome dalmatian. The handle of the wagon dampens inside Max's grip. These older boys and the dalmatian preside over the neighborhood. Edgar, Sly, and Sam weave in and out of yards as they please, picking this way and that, throwing off their teenage noise. Their oily skins and disproportionate limbs make the boys a tribe unto themselves. The dalmatian is probably their leader. Wherever the Griers and Treble go, they slink doggishly in imitation. Whenever they stand still, their shoulders droop like the dalmatian paused in a prowl. And sure enough, the dalmatian notices Max first. The boys follow the barking.

The three saunter up to Max and surround him. Sam looms in the shade of a willow bough.

Jamie Tyson's older sister jogs on Saturdays at noon sharp, says Edgar. We saw her in a sports bra.

It was black, adds Sly Grier. His eyes, expectant, pendulum from Sam to Edgar.

Max's feet spread apart and his arms cross.

What's that in the wagon? asks Sam.

My father, Max says.

The boys chortle.

You idiot! Sly says. The joke is "Your mamma," not "My father"!

The same silver sedan drives by doing the speed limit. A tableau peels off its side: four boys, a dog, leaves, grass, a red wagon with a shining metal polyhedron on board.

Your dad left to be on television, says Edgar.

No.

No, what? Edgar asks.

Max shakes his head. The palms of his hands turned upward, he says, No, he's right here in my wagon.

The boys step closer. Even Sly Grier, whose language is always on the tip of his tongue, has nothing to say about the polyhedron. The Frank Orison stands two smooth and metallic feet tall. There are eight sides to him. The largest is defined by five edges, a pentagonal diamond-shaped slope almost half his total height. This could be his face, and this is where Max looks for the sort of help sons seek from their fathers. But the Frank Orison isn't that kind of father. He rests squarely in the wagon, rigid as an urn. Max sees instead his own head framed between the five edges. Reflections move vaguely all along the Frank Orison's skin: the new leaves swaying slowly overhead, the dappled coat of the dalmatian. The boys' faces appear, too, though weakly, as if faded in memory.

Max knows that there is a man called Frank Orison. Max uses memories of him all the time. But memory fathers cannot go up to the airfield or down to the jetties.

A garage door opens across the street.

Edgar, impatient, flicks the Frank Orison on the side. A low bell chime echoes through him. The dalmatian cocks his head.

You've got to be kidding, says Edgar. He does it again, the dalmatian barks.

Sly cannot be contained. Mr. Orison is hollow! he says.

Max's arms unfold, his hands drop into his pockets. He wants to laugh.

Then something new arises or intervenes in Sam Treble.

Where are you going? he asks.

Home.

Where were you?

The beach.

Why?

To watch birds and ore freighters and the fishermen, says Max. To look at the sky and water. Don't you do that sort of thing with your dad?

So what, says Sam Treble. You don't either.

The afternoon is soundless in the moment before Max takes his first step. He pulls the wagon around Sam Treble and past the Griers.

Edgar takes one last flick at the Frank Orison but misses inexplicably. He begins to follow the wagon, to try again, but Sam Treble calls him back into the willow shade. Max and his wagon go off down the street, the Frank Orison glinting all the while in the afternoon light.

Max is reckless: he takes his father to Dads-in-Class Day and pastes on his side a red-and-white label that reads HELLO, MY NAME IS . . . MR. FRANK ORISON. The other fathers are ordinary sorts. Wrinkled men in cardigans and ties, bearded ones in T-shirts under flannel, the young and fighting kind in olive green uniforms, and suited elites with clear complexions and compelling smiles—they all disbelieve. Max hoists his father onto the corner of his desk. Murmurs rise and beady looks are brought to bear. Someone laughs once and others follow. Melodramatic Emma Friese throws her hands toward the ceiling. She slouches down in her chair and lets her forearms tumble back onto her head as it shakes from side to side in exasperation.

When will it end? says Emma. Where will it end?

Max slides the Frank Orison into the middle of the desk. Max hides.

When Miss Jupiter comes in, she thinks the Frank Orison is a kind of prank.

She calls Mrs. Orison. There's a meeting at four o'clock. The Frank Orison sits alone in a brown paper bag beside Miss Jupiter's desk. Max rolls and unrolls the cuffs of his pale blue sweater while his mother and teacher talk as if he weren't there.

A cry for help, Natalie, if you ask my opinion, Miss Jupiter says. Stunts like this always are. It will necessitate a memorandum in his permanent record, I'm afraid. But no larger conclusions will be drawn. I know you're concerned about that, naturally. Nothing that could become public. You have my assurance. The entire staff here is just so proud of Max's father and we all wish him the best.

Yes, says Mrs. Orison. Thank you.

Max's mother confiscates the Frank Orison. She bags him up with the asparagus stumps and a green-glass chardonnay bottle.

After dinner, Max poses the Question to his mother.

Don't torture me again, sweetie, she says without looking up from her paperwork and calculator. I've already told you that he's away, traveling all over the country. He wants a new and very important job, but to get it he has to be away almost all the time. Sometimes he comes home while you're asleep and leaves before you wake up. But I can't say when he'll be home next. I just don't know.

Max says, I could swear—

Pranks in school reflect poorly on me, Max. Remember that hurts my business reputation and your father's reputation in the community. If people see you playing with *that* and calling *that* your father, he may come home without getting his new and very important job.

All of his traveling would be for naught.

Max uses his silence.

His mother looks at Max over her glasses. Her skin is soft and creased around the mouth, and the shape of her hair is failing late at night like a spent candle. Her lips are very red and her sharp teeth show as she starts to speak.

Please try to understand, she says. Please.

She touches Max's hand, the one with the bandage. She kisses it.

Come nightfall, Max cannot help but retrieve him from the garbage can. He tiptoes back through the house and in the bathroom spritzes him with blue window cleaner. He wipes down the Frank Orison, the original and still the best, until he can see himself in his father. Once he's finished, Max quietly carries him into the bedroom and locks the door. No one knows more about the world than Max's mother, but still he cannot bring himself to accept what she says. Max does not necessarily believe the Frank Orison to be his father, not in the conventional sense. But he has come to admire and value him in ways different from the father seen in his memories. The Frank Orison sparkles expertly in sunshine. He warms in the afternoons and cools in the evenings, like the wind and the water. His faces are smooth, his corners crisp. There is no scarring nor any outward indication, like soldering, for instance, that his father is in any way provisional or contrived. Nothing on him droops or sags. There are no wrinkles or smells or softness to him. The Frank Orison is pure as a wheel on the wagon in which he rides when they go down to the jetties or up to the airfield on their Saturday voyages.

Max speaks soft words to the Frank Orison by the nightlight's butter yellow glow.

Halfway off to sleep, however, a yearning for a more permanent father begins in Max. Such a father would be wrought from huge stone blocks or erected like skyscrapers out of steel and glass, titanium and bronze. He imagines a city rising up around such a patrimony. How silent it would be. How weather would pass over and around him. There would be no stores nor trades to speak of, so no coins to jingle nor currency to fold, no street names, no signs. No one would go to such a city, except Max Orison, to play alone in his father's compassing shadow.

Nominated by Alan Michael Parker

A SHORT HISTORY OF MY BREATH

by KRISTIN KOVACIC

from THE JOURNAL

My DAUGHTER, my second child, was born on January 12, 1995. It was a long labor, twenty-four hours or so, and a "natural" birth—that is, I labored without medication, my steady husband at my side, and the doctor caught the baby, sweet Rosalie. This had not been the plan.

Veterans of my son's birth sixteen months earlier, we knew just how to do it. We knew which Lamaze exercises worked (mostly slow breathing) which music to bring (slow R&B to hook the slow breathing to). We knew how important it was to stay calm and focused: because panic, even nervous laughter, interrupts your breathing and brings its own, separate pain. And most important, we knew which pain medications to ask for and when. I faced my second labor with fewer illusions and more strategy, and was prepared for the satisfactions of doing something a second time.

What I wasn't prepared for was a disappearing obstetrician. From the morning we entered the hospital, to the time of Rosalie's birth that night, he did not visit us. Though everyone assured us he was in the hospital and could be paged, we were led to believe that the criterion for "paging" him was some kind of emergency. Jim and I, champions of calm, could not bring ourselves to cry wolf. We figured the doctor was busy with hysterical laboring couples and that he would eventually stop by and see me, as my former OB had done, to help me time my medication. But the doctor did not come, and so we breathed, to stay focused and calm, hour after hour. Still he did not come, and we breathed and we waited, like shy customers dining at a busy restaurant, waited for the overworked doctor to come and offer us a cocktail, while the pain mounted and my stamina flagged, and the nurses mostly ignored us, we seemed so in control. And the doctor did not come, and we breathed and held on, to the voices of Sam Cooke and Aaron Neville, and I worked myself into a kind of furious calm, which Jim later described as a coma, but which I experienced as an intense duet with Sam Cooke on "Change Gonna Come"—until the pain was so great that I lost my focus, and cried out, "PAGE the doctor."

But it was too late, the baby was coming, and the cocktail hour had passed, the bar closed, and I pushed through a pain so beyond what I had known that I screamed in surprise—It hurts! It really hurts!—dismayed that no one, not the lazy doctor, who'd apparently been sleeping while I labored, and now fumbled with his gloves, not the nurses, who were so distant before and who were now yelling at me, and not by a mile my husband, fellow soldier of the breath, who looked, bizarrely, happy—no one would catch my alarm. I knew then that I was alone with the pain, there was no sharing or translating it or singing it away. I was certain I would die from it. I have never been so frightened.

Later, after the pain stopped, after the shakes and warm blankets and the first real meal in days, after a day or three spent gazing at Rosalie's lovely, wizened face, I started to wonder what all that pain had been for. What *good* had it done? I raged, anew, at my incompetent doctor and my own passivity in the face of what clearly *was* an emergency. Would any less pain and fear have made her less perfect? Her birth less joyful and miraculous? The experience of natural childbirth is supposed to be an empowering one, I know, connecting women to our awesome mythic strength, but I did not feel like a goddess. A mother already, I knew how quickly the high drama of birth dissolves into the more ordinary work of care. I was not a goddess; I was a chump, a weak consumer—satisfied with the product, but disgusted by the service in that joint. Pinned to a nursing infant while my toddler tore books into bits at my feet, I fantasized about demanding my money back, about suing the bastard, but of course I was too exhausted to pursue this.

Flash forward almost seven years, September 28, 2001, and I am

132

in the hospital again. My son Ramsey, just eight, is having a Nissen fundoplication—a last-resort surgery to abate his chronic gastro-intestinal reflux disease. In short, everything he eats comes back up into his mouth, and no drug in any quantity will stop it. He is fragile and anemic and flops around like a marionette after he eats. There may be a name for his problem, Sandifer's Syndrome, but not a clear treatment. It's taken us four years of medical specialty care to get to this moment, and what the surgeon will do today is detach his stomach from the abdomen wall, lift it from the top, and wrap it around the bottom of his esophagus. Then he will stitch it there, his stomach like a cravat that with luck will create just enough pressure to keep his food in, yet still allow him to swallow. It is this part that still gets to me—the not swallowing, a side-effect called disphagia. I can't dislodge the lump in my throat.

I ask my son if it tickles when the surgeon marks, with a pen, blue X's on his abdomen. I force myself not to remember how tender his skin is, there and everywhere. I look straight into his eyes and nowhere else, not his wrists, braceleted and taped, and surely not his neck, where he is most a child. He tells me that now he knows for sure he'll be a professional hockey player like Mario Lemieux when he grows up, because he will *already* have had surgery.

He is brave, which is to say he trusts us. I think about how bad he's going to feel before he can possibly feel good again.

But I am clear-eyed, all business, with a few more questions for the doctor as they wheel him off. In the wake of my hospital labors, and the years spent diagnosing and treating his condition, I've transformed myself into a militant medical consumer. No more waiting to be served. I ask questions, get second opinions. I challenge doctors and keep detailed notes. I read everything I can and show what I know. I am probably obnoxious. But I've learned the hard way to do this, to keep everyone around my son awake and concentrating, and I think this is what will save him—this vigilance, and the best procedure at the best children's hospital with the best surgeon in the region.

When the swinging doors close behind him, I start to cry into my husband's shirt, but the tears feel dangerous. The last tears I shed were just two weeks ago, in my classroom full of high school students, all of us crying silently from our desks as we watched television, the tiny people and their tiny, futile banners, waving from the top of the World Trade Center. If I begin to cry now, I feel I will weep without stopping, everyone will begin to weep, and we will all stop being vigilant, now when it seems most necessary.

When they bring him back to us, the surgeon tells us he is pleased, but of course we won't know for some time. He explains how his stomach has been filled with air, and that now, with a fresh suture at the top of it, his stomach has to release the air, and he will feel pain when it does. "How much pain?" I ask, but of course I know the answer—pain is untranslatable, unquantifiable. The surgeon prescribes morphine at six-hour intervals. I look at the clock and note the dose.

Informed as I am, I am unprepared for the pain when it arrives. First he calls my name, *Mom?*, like the prelude to a question from the back seat of the car. Then he calls more plaintively, like a request for some help in the bathroom. Then he calls my name in the voice all parents know is hurt for real, and which is received by your entire body. His eyes have closed, and his head is thrashing from side to side exactly like an epileptic in seizure. His face, sweet and soft, and which I have adored for eight years, contorts into a silent, grotesque scream. Jim and I, helpless, watch our son drown in his pain, and then we watch him emerge, maybe half a minute later, panting, an exhausted swimmer. We are all terrified.

But when the next wave comes, the soft call, my body, as if of its own accord, knows what to do. I climb into his bed. I touch him everywhere I can, my skin on his skin; I touch my face to his; I put my mouth in his ear. My body knows to go down there with him, to let him feel me there. And somehow I know, like in dreams where you speak a new language, exactly which words to say. I tell him I am with him, and that we will breathe together, slow and steady, to blow the pain away. I tell him that I know it hurts, but that it will not last forever. I tell him that what he's doing is amazing; he's the bravest boy in the world, braver than Mario Lemieux.

I feel his eyelash flutter on my cheek when it is over. He pushes out one more slow breath, laced with morphine I can taste. "Thank you," he says, and his politeness at such a moment makes me laugh. Until I realize that he means it, that he felt my presence in his pain, and that it felt like a gift. I tell him we will handle this together; he will not be alone, not for a single second.

The doctors we summon have nothing more to give us. The morphine cannot ease the pressure that has built up within him. They are mystified and alarmed about why he thrashes so. It's either a childish reaction to pain, or he's developed another, more serious problem—dysphagia or something neurologic. The doctors leave us to "see what develops," to wait for the waves to come, and to face them down together, all the while wondering whether something worse is lurking. This, I understand, will be our labor.

Through the night, and the following day, my son and I row the sea of pain, becoming an efficient crew. He calls, I come, we breathe, and the dark wave washes over us. Occasionally he naps, and I stare at the dear face of memory—my perfect, sleeping child—but I don't sleep and I don't dream. I am vigilant. In the middle of the night, I prevent a sleepy resident from triple-dosing his meds. In the morning, the toilet breaks, flooding his room, and I make the nurses move him to another. I am difficult to everyone but him. I lose track of time and forget to eat and suddenly it's night again. Jim comes to force me home to bed, and while Ramsey naps, I show him the ship of our rituals—where to touch, how to breathe, what to say. As I leave I make a wifely prayer that he will perform this routine exactly as I described, without any masculine variation. But as I watch him settle next to our son, I can see in his face how much he too is suffering, and I understand he will find his own way. I remember our own long night together, laboring to bring forth this very child. It is, coincidentally, the anniversary of our marriage, though neither of us can mention it.

The garage beneath the hospital is empty; it's a long walk through black space to our car. I sit behind the wheel and stare out into it, the threatening dark, and it surprises me to notice that I don't feel afraid. I imagine Ramsey waking above me, and I will him to remember how to breathe. I swallow the stale air of the car. I am not afraid and not merely exhausted, though I haven't slept in days. I am something else—another feeling, deep and new. And though a name for it doesn't arrive (and perhaps doesn't exist), it has something to do with use. I feel I have been used. Every part of me, every molecule concentrated to ease his suffering. I am a worrier by nature, a temperament now pathologized as "anxious," and which my own doctor helpfully described as "unconsciously holding your breath." And so it startles me that here, at the darkest hour, is where anxiety dies, where I breathe without thinking.

I don't know if my son will be okay. But I feel, at this moment, elated, or rather, entirely alive and on the verge of disappearing. I know now, of course, what the pain of childbirth had been for, what *good* it was. It was for this work I have to do now, and this pure feeling of purpose. Perhaps I am finally, entirely, a mother.

Strangely, it occurs to me that it may have been this feeling—not pleasure, or pain, but this strange state of grace—that was perverted to make men fly planes into buildings. Suddenly I can imagine it, can feel their deadly calm. We all want to be used, the body cries for it, though we don't often listen to its call. And it is perhaps a kind of holding in—of our astonishing usefulness—that makes everybody I know seem a little anxious.

Two years later, I will watch our president, in response to the bombers, deliberately ratchet up everyone's anxiety, creating a need for crisis—something as dark and heavy as war—to stop the worry. In the young men and women called up, the parents wrapping yellow ribbons around trees, I would see the strange elation that comes with knowing exactly what you're supposed to do, the paradoxical relief in facing down a big, bad thing. They would seem imperturbable, undismayed, unlike the rest of us on the margins of the action—or perhaps this is merely what's visible through the lens of our nationalistic media.

Now that I'm a mother, and the mother of a child in pain, I see through pain. It is perhaps no more accurate a view than any other. But I would like to believe that my son, too, sees differently, now that he is completely, perfectly well. His teacher has reported a new confidence at school, building upon the glory he received eating cheeseburgers with a straw, flashing the constellation of tiny scars on his belly. Mainly, he feels better; he can eat normally, voraciously.

But I secretly believe that he felt it, too, the grace of suffering. That he remembers being on the other side, inside pain, connected to the outside world only by the tether of his breath, and his mother's voice. And I believe that he knows, if only in the body's memory, which is incorruptible, that it was enough to pull him through.

Nominated by The Journal

MOONSNAIL

by CLEOPATRA MATHIS

from THE GEORGIA REVIEW

I killed it for its shell, its design and shape,
not caring about the animal coiled inside, faceless
mudworm, intestinal, with its amorphous foot
fixed like a door to repel crabs or gulls.
I thought I'd see some taut muscle, not that oozing,
the giving over of a thick pulsing jelly
wound and wound to its end. I didn't think of it
answering to a clock, hurling forward as the waves

shoved onto sand, waiting to open and burrow,
to feed before the water dragged it back.
Traffic of the tides, that ugly life
filled a house which took on hues of blue and rose,
some pretty moss as it aged, perfect form
spiraling to the innermost point
marked by a round black eye.

Five shells now, lined up by size,
but not like Russian dolls, an amusing emptiness
to fit a pattern. These are freed from their true selves—
the disgusting, the lax—though, I admit, not evil,
not what my grandmother warned against: the devil
waiting for the opening praise provides.
Spit, she said, in the face of beauty or truth
to chase harm away.

It's useless to spit in this ocean,
always the churning surface and everything underneath
riding in. Polished by the sea's punishing thrust,
empty shells survive. But I didn't want those—
I chose the inhabited, the *something there*,
and removed it. It's simple: I laid each one out
in the blinding day, the sun did its work, the ants came,
then I shook it hard.

Nominated by Sydney Lea, Grace Schulman, Richard Jackson

THE LION'S MOUTH

fiction by BEN FOUNTAIN

from THE PARIS REVIEW

J ILL ARRIVED AT THE ROYAL SIERRA every evening around six, took a stool in front of the TV at the open-air bar, and passed the time watching the news and quietly drinking herself stupid while Starkey did deals out on the terrace. The Royal sat on one of the peninsula's remotest points, a cheap concrete shell with a nice beach and a crumbling veneer of tropical luxury. No one touched the pool for fear of cholera; weeds and debris were overtaking the neglected grounds, and mold billowed over the walls in complex swirls like countries on a sprawling fantasy map. The Royal was, however, possibly the safest place in Freetown, and certainly, to Jill's mind, the most degenerate, the hotel of choice for the louche community of foreigners who viewed Sierra Leone as an opportunity. A clutch of coal-black whores sat on a couch near the bar, boldly eyeing every white man who walked through the door, while a few more girls were trolling the tables on the terrace. Last year the front line had been a few miles south, and though the rebels had been driven out months ago, shooting could still be heard at night, the U.N. skirmishing with the holdouts or freelance gangs. In the mornings bodies occasionally washed up on the Royal's postcard-perfect beach.

"Another rum cola, miss?" asked the barman.

"Thanks, padi."

The news segued from the American presidential campaign into a story on the wealth effect, the triumphant affluence that the U.S. was enjoying thanks to its high-tech genius and the long bull market. Jill felt discouraged, if only briefly; she'd let the greatest money-grab in history pass her by, though even if she'd been living in the States all this time she would have done her best to ignore it. She had a congenital distrust of money and luxury, her militant asceticism further aggravated by a very low tolerance for boredom. How did you get the money from there to here? First of all you had to care, and caring, as far as Jill could see, was an accident of birth, just as her own predilection was an accident, a random number that came up. Her father cared about money, very much so; she'd grown up more than comfortably on Connecticut's gold coast. She had a brother at Salomon Brothers who apparently cared, and an entrepreneur sister who was getting rich off the software she cooked up in a Tribeca loft. So much on the one hand, so little on the other; often she wondered what kept the world from going up in flames. *Do you think they'd cut my funding if white people were dropping dead?* She'd written that to her mother, who'd written back: *Come home. We have hungry people in America too.*

She turned on her stool and caught Starkey's eye; he was deep in conversation with a glistening black man, but not so deep that he couldn't manage a little irony for Jill, a smug shadowing around the corners of his lips. They were talking diamonds, probably, though it could be anything, palm oil, bauxite, shrimp, titanium, rubber—for a country with a ruined economy there were an awful lot of deals around, and Starkey, who'd lived here on and off for years, seemed to have a paying role in most of them. And he made it look so easy, which was a revelation for Jill, who'd always viewed the getting of money in terms of hassle and guilt. "Don't work hard, work smart," he told her in his plummy English voice, and that was part of it, the mellow, cheerful voice that made the things he said sound so reasonable. He gave people hope, he made them feel close to something real, this in a place that kept threatening to slide past zero.

Presently he excused himself and came over to the bar. Physically he wasn't much, a short, thick-legged man with a blunt, fleshy face and thinning hair dyed an improbable midnight-black. He had an embarrassing taste for gold accessories, and most days dressed for business in shorts, espadrilles, Hugo Boss golf shirts—resort-wear, here in one of the world's genuine hellholes. Shed of his clothes he was worse than she'd expected, his body pale and soft as a mitt of dough, shot through with a vestigial stringiness. What had surprised Jill as much as anything was how little all of this mattered to her.

140

He brushed her hand, a gesture that managed to be both casual and intimate. "So what's the news at home, love?"

This was a running tease, his insistence on seeing her devotion to the news as a bright girl's interest in current events. They both understood she watched mainly for the sedative effect.

"Oh, they're still getting rich," she said. "And wondering which third-world country they need to bomb next. Being an American these days, that's sort of like being a walking joke, right?"

"Come now, no one holds you responsible. Have you had anything to eat?"

She shook her head.

"Then join us. Come have dinner and forget the news."

"I would," she said in mock distress, "but I never know what to say to your friends."

"Nonsense, you're perfectly charming. All of my friends adore you."

Adored, sure; white women of any description were in short supply. "Who's that black man you were talking to?"

Starkey accepted a fresh drink from the barman; his hands around the glass were like plump beef filets. "That's Kamora. The diamond officer at the heliport."

"I knew I'd seen him somewhere. So he's a friend too?"

"After a fashion. He dropped by with a bit of news."

"Good or bad?"

"Well, you'll probably be pleased. Though it's not so nice for me." Starkey cut her a look; in the dim light of the bar his eyes were wine-dark. "They arrested a man in Antwerp today, someone from Ferrin's outfit. Trying to pass a batch of Salone diamonds, apparently."

"You're kidding."

"I am not." Starkey's face was grave. "Rather a shock, isn't it? Everyone knew the ban was good p.r., but nobody thought they'd actually try to enforce the damn thing."

For months pressure had been building for an industry embargo on unregistered diamonds out of Sierra Leone, the "blood diamonds" that kept the rebels in operation. Years ago the RUF had charged out of Liberia pushing some vague Marxist rhetoric about liberating the country, their rationale for an agenda that mainly involved robbing, raping, and murdering every peasant they could get their hands on. They kept their columns well-stocked with ganja and coke, and it was the rebel foot soldiers—most of them teenagers, some no older than ten or twelve—who'd filled the DP camps with amputees. "Chopping," they called it, their signature practice of hacking off one or both of their victims' arms. "Short sleeves or long?" they were said to taunt as they raised their machetes.

"Go on, Jill. I give you permission to gloat."

Jill was staring stonefaced at the TV. To feel conflicted at this point was impossible—there was no conflict, not when she thought about the suffering she'd seen.

"I'm not gloating. I just don't see how they can do it."

"They can't," Starkey agreed, "but they could definitely slow it down. And trade's been sketchy enough as it is the last few months."

Jill sipped her rum. "So what are you going to do?"

"Oh," he said easily, "no sense running off in a panic. I'll stick around a bit, see if they're serious."

"And if they are?"

He consulted his drink. "Suppose I'd have to follow the trade in that case. Mono or Guinea, that's where you'll see the stones turning up."

"Gee, Starkey, you'd actually cut out on us? Think of all the great fun you'd miss around here."

His laugh was phlegmy, coarse, as raw as the blender at the end of the bar pulverizing ice. "Well yes, I really should think about that. All the fun one might miss in dear old Salone." He turned fond as his laughter trailed off, his eyes tender, fixed on hers as if he meant to coax out some sort of therapeutic truth. Jill turned back to the TV— she felt, rather than heard, the faint break of his sigh, his feathery chuckle as he leaned in close.

"Do you know how good you look right now? You're a gift, Jill, that's what you are to me. You're just amazing, love."

She felt warm, slack; her eyes went slightly out of focus. Was this what it felt like to be loved? Before Starkey she'd never let anyone talk to her this way, and lately she had trouble remembering why.

I want the hardest place—she'd actually said that when she signed her contract. She'd spent two years in Guatemala with the Peace Corps, then three years in Haiti with Save The Children, and after that she wouldn't be satisfied with anything but the very worst. *I want the hardest place*—on any given day that was usually Sierra Leone, "the mountain of the lion," a small, obscure West African country known mainly for its top-quality kimberlite diamonds and the breathtaking cruelty of its civil war. She'd signed on as country project director for World Aid Ministries, a Protestant umbrella group that specialized in long-term food relief; a religious vocation wasn't necessary for the job, only a tolerance for what might be charitably called spartan living and a masochistic attitude toward work. So here was the joke: She'd come to Salone determined to lead an authentic life and instead had discovered all the clichés in herself. She wanted to be stupid. She wanted to be rich. She wanted to be lazy, kept, indulged—this was where her fantasies took her lately, mental explorations of the guiltless life. Starkey was rich, and old enough to be her father, a package of clichés that neatly fit her own. She'd tried to pick a fight with him at the Embassy party where they met; anyone in diamonds should have been her natural enemy, but something benign in his eyes, the patient sag of his face, seemed to express a basic decency. She felt calm in his presence, she felt safe; without much fuss she'd gone back to the Royal Sierra with him that night, and it had quickly developed into a standing thing, Jill driving over every evening and staying the night. Her friends in the NGO community thought she'd lost her mind. Maybe I have, she told herself, maybe that's what crazy is. Despising precisely those things you're most attracted to.

"So Jill, you really like this guy?"

She was sitting on the cinderblock porch outside her office, skimming the registration binder that Dennis Hatch had brought over from U.S. AID. Sometime in the next few weeks she would be leading a small convoy through the southeast, delivering resettlement packages in advance of the planned repatriation of refugees. That is if the situation held—if the RUF honored the Lomé Accords, if the U.N. peacekeepers could hang onto their weapons, if the rainy season held off and her drivers stayed sober. If a hundred different things she couldn't control came together at a single moment in time.

"I suppose," she said absently, flipping pages. Each sheet contained the vital statistics for a single family. Age, height, weight, arm circumference—numerical stick figures.

"He sure must like you." Dennis was looking through the door to her office, admiring the electrical inverter that Starkey had donated. "Is it possible the word 'whipped' could apply here?"

"I'm not clear how much seed rice is going into the package."

"Well, we're still elaborating our information on that." After ten years in the development field Dennis had mastered a sardonic form of bureaucratese that Jill found alternately funny and maddening.

"Can you even give me a definite date?"

"Negative."

Dennis folded himself into the straw-bottomed chair beside Jill's. He had the lean, near-haggard body of a fanatic runner, and was good-looking in a nerdy sort of way, which was more or less Jill's type. His intelligence and contempt for authority made him her natural ally inside the system, and since he'd arrived in-country a year ago their friendship kept threatening to be something more. But their timing was off, their rhythm, the intangible whatever; all those late nights they'd sat up talking and drinking, and he could never bring himself to make a pass at her. She knew he wasn't gay, so what did that make him? Barely relevant, that's how it struck her lately.

She turned to the budget at the front of the binder. "One-forty per ton for transport."

"Can you live with that?"

"You offering better?"

"Nah."

Jill shut the binder. "Then I guess I'll have to live with it."

Several women from the sewing co-op passed by with snacks they'd bought from the street vendors outside, the women greeting Jill and Dennis with shy hellos. The co-op was housed in a building at the back of the compound, a sideline to the project's core food-relief mission. A year ago, in an absurd expense of time and energy, Jill had followed an inspiration and put the co-op together, converting the warehouse space, cadging basic supplies, plucking forty women from the refugee camps and putting them to work making skirt-like *lapas*. The project's main warehouse faced the office, a large cinderblock structure with a sheet-metal roof and rolling metal doors at either end. Everything in sight reflected Jill's rage for order: the stone paths, the neatly thatched *baffas* and sheds, the flame trees she'd planted about the grounds for shade. Beyond the walls lay a world of squalor and chaos, but here she'd managed to carve out a small island of control.

"So how's your beau these days?" Dennis asked in a chipper voice.

"He's fine."

"What's he say about the embargo?"

"It's bad for business."

144

Dennis laughed. "Duh, Jill. But good for the country. Hopefully."

"He doesn't deny it."

"You know the U.N.'s set up checkpoints on all the roads out of Kono. And anybody flying in from the interior is basically subject to a strip search."

"It's still a joke, there's no way they can stop it. You can hide a million dollars' worth of stones in a tube of toothpaste and still have room for most of the toothpaste."

"Well, I guess you'd be the expert now."

"That's just common sense, Dennis, it doesn't take any expertise."

He flashed her a vicious look, out of all proportion to what she'd said. She had to check an impulse to apologize.

"Christ, Jill, what do you see in this guy? I'm saying this as a friend—"

She turned away.

"—somebody who really cares about you. These are not good people you're hanging around with, okay? They're into a lot of nasty stuff, they're basically bleeding the country dry and that's against everything we're working for. It just makes me wonder where your head is at."

Jill was calm; she felt as if she was floating above the argument. "So who do you want me to hang around?"

"Look, all I'm saying is I'm worried about you. It doesn't fit, you and this guy, every time I try to picture it I come up blank. I just think your being with him is a symptom of something."

"Well, yes. Sex is usually a symptom of something."

Dennis winced. "All right, okay, I'll shut up now. I know I'm way out of line." He ran a hand through his hair. "Not that anything I've said matters anyway."

Jill acknowledged this with a half-smile; she realized that Dennis mostly made her sad these days.

"You know," he said, "as long as you've got this guy wrapped around your little finger, you might hit him up for a contribution to the co-op."

"Nope. It just doesn't work that way."

"Has anything come through?"

"Handicap International turned us down last week—I guess they don't believe there's such a thing as one-armed seamstresses. CRS said no, Global Relief, everybody. They're sending all their money to Kosovo now."

"Well, Kosovo's hot these days. And a lot of people have pretty much written off Salone." He stretched a leg, gingerly popped the knee. "How much longer can you keep it going?"

"A couple of weeks. Maybe a month if we really string it out."

"If you give me the numbers I'll try to get something for you. Enough to keep it going till some real money comes through."

"Aisha's got the books," Jill said, rising at once. "Come on."

The co-op was housed in a narrow concrete building with barred windows along one side and rough wooden tables arranged in rows. Wicker baskets full of country cloth and *gara* were placed at each row, and the women worked in teams of two, one woman stitching while the other held the cloth; in a matter of weeks they'd grown so proficient that each team could sew as fast as any able-bodied seamstress. On a good day the co-op turned out over two hundred garments, but the stuff sold too slowly piecemeal, and the Lebanese traders wouldn't buy in bulk until they were satisfied the peace was going to hold.

Jill always felt a kind of compression when she stepped into the co-op, a crowding of awareness that made her hushed and anxious while at the same time lifting her out of herself. How believers might feel when they entered a church—it had something to do with suffering, she suspected, but beyond that she lacked the energy to analyze it. While Dennis and Aisha went through the books Jill tallied and stacked the morning's output of clothes, looking over the room while she worked. Her eye inevitably lingered on the women's stumps; on some level she never really stopped thinking about that, though for a long time she'd tried to deny her obsession, this thing she had—which seemed shameful, vaguely pornographic—for visualizing her own mutilation. "It go red when you chopped," one of the women had told her. "Everyt'ing go red, red, like your mind on fire." Jill was sure she would die of horror if it happened to her; most did, ostensibly from shock or loss of blood, and how these women had survived was beyond her comprehension. Not just survived—how they seemed capable at times of quite genuine joy. Lately Jill had seen them laughing and chatting as they worked, edging back toward something like normal life. They had no idea that she was a couple of weeks away from shutting them down.

"I can't make any promises," Dennis said as she walked him across the compound to his jeep. The street noise beyond the walls roared like a slow avalanche.

"You know I appreciate it," she said, and felt hopeful enough to try a joke: "Feel free to puff up the numbers all you want."

"Well, you know that's never a good idea." He didn't smile—did he think she was serious? At the jeep he turned and studied her so intently that she feared some sort of ridiculous scene.

"Jill."

"What." She avoided his eye.

"Are you sure you're okay?"

"I'm fine, Dennis."

"I don't know, you just seem awfully tired lately. Frankly I think you're kind of depressed, not that it's any of my business. But a lot of us are concerned."

This affected her more than she might have expected. She had to swallow, then consciously smooth out her breathing, but even so the irony didn't sound quite right. "Well, I may be having a normal reaction to this place."

"It's still depression, Jill. If I were you I'd be putting some thought into that."

Sometimes at night, when they were alone in his room, Starkey would take out a batch of diamonds and instruct her on the finer points of valuation. He seemed to enjoy the ego-boost of mentoring her, the *noblesse* and not-so-subtle sexual subtext, and Jill went along with it, amused, not uninterested, though the diamonds themselves were disappointing. In their rough state they were such chalky little nubs, airy nothings that rattled around your palm like baby teeth, and yet they put him at the center of something vital. At night she watched him empty his pockets as he undressed, spilling out scraps of paper, cocktail napkins, matchbook covers, all with names and phone numbers scribbled on them. By eight the next morning his cell phone was going, by nine he was meeting people downstairs, receiving them on the terrace like a little king. She was starting to see the point of it, how making money might actually be interesting, and how the more you made the more interesting it could be. And lately another revelation had come to her: Starkey was responsible only for himself. This was, she thought, the great luxury of business, of a life devoted solely to making money; it seemed strange to her, exotic in the way of forbidden things, until she remembered that this was how most people lived.

Yet in his way he took care of so many people—or was that just

147

part of his practice of working smart? He was extravagant with gifts and favors, a soft touch for beggars, and he tipped as if bent on keeping the whole staff afloat. He had a trade-school education—mechanical drafting, he'd confessed with a dry laugh—and talked enough about his past for Jill to get the sense of a hardscrabble childhood, so different from her own. He wasn't at all touchy or bitter about it; he seemed to take real pleasure in the narrative of what he called her "American" life, the big house, the horse stables, good schools, college. In bed he had definite ideas about what he wanted, though he never pressed, never insisted. He didn't have to, Jill reflected, laughing to herself, feeling the heat rising into her neck and face. She supposed that's what a nice man did for you.

"Look at those bastards."

She was at the bar, sipping her third drink of the evening. Dennis Hatch slid onto the stool next to her, jutting his chin at the TV; CNN was running a story on the latest crop of tech billionaires.

"What are you doing here?"

"Meeting." His eyes stayed fixed on the TV. "Kind of makes you want to puke, doesn't it."

"In a way you've got to hand it to them. They had the energy, they went for it. They pulled it off."

"You got any money in the market?"

"Not a cent."

"Me either." He laughed. "I can't wait for the damn thing to crash."

Jill supposed she sympathized; supposed she even agreed. "So who are you meeting?"

"Some WFP honchos from Conakry, we're tightening up the strategic stocks plan. Just in case."

"Could be a good move."

"Star beer," Dennis said to the barman, then he turned on his stool to look over the terrace. The tables were packed with an ecumenical mix of whites and Africans. Thrashing, bass-heavy music played on the sound system, while waiters hustled up and down the steps with drinks. A stunning hooker with blond cornrows passed two feet in front of Dennis, raking him out of the corner of her eye. He turned to Jill with a smirk.

"Always a party at the Royal."

"Somebody's gotta do it."

"How come you're sitting up here?"

148

She followed the line of his gaze to Starkey's table, where the people and chairs were stacked three deep. "He's having office hours."

"So?"

So—she felt like a whore when she sat at his table? "I'd just rather sit up here."

Dennis turned back to the bar; they talked shop, traded gossip about their fellow expats, speculated on the political situation. Jill didn't mention the co-op; she made herself wait for Dennis to bring it up, and when he didn't she was gradually given to understand that there would be no money from the government. Despairing as she nodded and sipped her drink, maintaining, minimizing the personal side; by now it was second nature. Presently Starkey walked over to the bar, giving Dennis a bland smile as he ordered a Sassman's. Jill introduced the two men.

"Ah, U.S. AID," said Starkey. They shook hands around Jill. "Still a growth industry, what?"

"Unfortunately yes."

"I should think the only one in Salone at the moment."

"I don't know, I understand you diamond guys are doing pretty well."

"On the contrary, they've put a ban on our product. Or haven't you heard."

"I didn't think a little thing like the law slowed you guys down."

Jill kept her eyes on the television, one hand on her drink. She wasn't especially shocked that they'd gotten into it, just surprised that it happened so quickly.

"Please," said Starkey, "let me enlighten you. My man's sitting up in Koidu with six months' worth of stones and I can't get to him even if I wanted to. And everyone here is in the same boat, we're all slowly bleeding to death. Another month or two of this and we'll be closing up shop."

"Cry me a river," Dennis said through his teeth.

"Beg your pardon?"

"Cry me a river, it's an expression. Basically it means all you guys can go fuck yourselves."

"Oh. Well. That's awfully sentimental of you."

Dennis snorted into his beer.

"You think I'm being facetious? I'm quite serious actually, the whole embargo concept is a sentimental crock. It gets the human-rights chaps all warm and fuzzy, but what it's really about is DeBeers

149

keeping a lock on the market. Seems so righteous of them, lobbying for the ban and all that—they'll shut down the juniors in the name of good citizenship, then they'll move in and open up the tap again. It's all a farce, son, it's a sham. I shouldn't think a smart fella like you would need me to explain."

"It's never clean," Dennis said. "I sure as hell don't need the likes of you to tell me that."

"Yes, well said, it's never clean. But you're wrong if you think things are actually going to change. People will buy and sell diamonds as always, my friend. They'll just be different people. Well," he hoisted his drink at Dennis, "cheers."

Starkey turned to leave, but Jill caught him by the arm.

"Stay," she murmured, tightening her grip. "Don't mind him. Just stay."

Dennis blanched; Jill wondered what it meant that for once she felt no pity for him. He turned away, then looked back as if he couldn't help himself. "Screw you guys," he finally muttered, and left.

"Oh dear," Starkey fretted, watching Dennis make his way across the terrace. "I do hope I didn't spoil anything for you."

"It doesn't matter." Jill smiled and pulled him onto the stool next to her. She almost laughed; for the first time in months she felt clear about things.

"If you can get your guy down to Bomi," she said, "I'll bring those diamonds in for you."

"Get out. How would you manage that?"

"We've got some trucks going upline next week, we'll be in Bomi one of those days. If your guy can meet me there I'll get your diamonds."

"Really, Jill, you have no idea—how would you get past the checkpoints?"

"You think they ever mess with me?"

He acknowledged this with a thoughtful nod. "You know the U.N.'s not the only risk."

"So pay me. Pay me for my trouble."

He looked at his drink.

"This is business, just treat it like a business deal. What's the going rate for something like this?"

Starkey hesitated. "Three percent."

"Which comes to?"

150

"Quite a bit, if Petrik's got what he says he's got." He looked up from his drink. "This is for your project, isn't it, your sewing shop. For Christ's sake, just let me give you the money."

"If you had it to spare, but you don't. And I wouldn't take it anyway."

"Say I agreed to let you go—what would you do for security?"

"I'll have the trucks and crews, just like always. Anything else I'd just draw attention to myself."

Starkey looked bleak, like a man imagining his own funeral. "What about your moral objection to all this?"

"Like the man said, it's never clean."

Starkey chewed the inside of his cheek for a moment. It occurred to her that he must be desperate to consider this; either that, or the challenge appealed to him, the sheer balls it would take to let her go alone.

"I'll need to hop down to Jo-burg for the cash, which you'd have to ferry in. So you see, you'd be on the spot both ways. With no security to speak of."

"I'll be under the radar, look at it that way." She laughed and squeezed his hand, wondering how much the rum had stoked her mood. "I can handle it, okay? I've done lots and lots of really hard things in my life, I don't see why I can't do this too."

"Well," he said a bit sadly, lifting the glass to his lips, "no one ever said you lacked potential."

It began, as it always did, with rumors—they started several days before she left Freetown, hints of movement, something stirring up-country, the stories rippling through the capital in barely perceptible waves. The rumors swelled and took shape as the trucks began their swing through the southeast, and soon she was hearing it on the radio news: the RUF had surrounded peacekeepers in Magburaka and Makeni, effectively holding the towns hostage, and more peacekeepers were turned back on the road to Bendu, faced down by a bunch of kids with automatic weapons. Testing, prodding, seeing how far they could push before the U.N. pushed back—that was Jill's rationalist take on the situation, though at the depot in Kabili the Irish priest's explanation was like a slap in the face: "The devil is hungry again." The devil, or whatever psychopathic gods lived out there—Jill was beginning to hate them all. The news became something else she was responsible for, along with her drivers' morale, the insane lo-

151

gistics, the neverending drama of flats and breakdowns. The strategy she'd developed over dozens of these trips was simply to keep going until something made her stop, and when the Ghanian officer confronted her at the Falla depot she thought that perhaps the time had come. She thought she was busted—he was that formal, that menacing with his small squad in tow, and Jill was spacey from the heat and four nights of short sleep. He got off on a tangent about rogue kammajohs and disarmament centers and reports of "demonstrations" in the area, and it took her a while to realize that he was talking about the rebels. She almost laughed—oh, them? In that same formal shout he asked if she would accept an armed escort to Makela.

By then she already had the diamonds. They were in a cloth pouch stuffed at the bottom of her daypack; she'd gotten them the day before, while the trucks were unloading at the Bomi depot. She'd slipped away on the pretext of delivering some letters, crossed the square by a small cinderblock mosque and followed the street past rows of mud-brick houses and sludgy garden plots. Except for a few pot-bellied children she was alone on the street—people, dogs, goats, every other living thing had sought shelter from the sun, and peering out from under the bill of her baseball cap Jill watched the street vibrate under the onslaught of light, its outlines shimmering like a half-formed mirage. In two minutes her blouse was soaked through with sweat. No one could handle sun like this for long, and she concentrated on her breathing and the motion of her legs, pulling awareness into herself as a way of saving strength. She was not, she noticed with some satisfaction, very afraid; the dense bricks of cash in the daypack gave her a sense of purpose, their heaviness pleasant on her shoulder, somehow steadying. Presently she saw what she was looking for, a hand-painted sign announcing the CHAZ-3 BAR wired to a tamarind tree by the street. She passed through a gap in the palm-thatch fence and followed the path up to the bar, a small wood-frame structure with a rusting metal roof and bushpoles supporting the porch overhang. The door stood open, the interior a bruise of shadows; she didn't falter until she heard voices inside, and then she was scared in spite of all the guarantees, in spite of Starkey's calm coaching and her own resolve. Afraid, and suddenly weary to the point of despair; this was part of the deal now, the drag-weight of fear. Another thing she'd have to carry for the rest of the trip.

She kept going because she couldn't think of anything else to do.

Petrik was there, a wild-haired Russian for whom the payoff seemed to be a mere sideline, a distraction from the main business of the day, which was convincing Jill to go back to Koidu with him. "I'm rich," he declared, slouching against her—they were sitting thigh-to-thigh on a plank bench. Four Leonean soldiers sat at the table with them, dark, strapping men in camouflage fatigues who fell out laughing at everything Petrik said. His security, Jill guessed, the hired help; Petrik scowled but otherwise ignored their hazing.

"I'm rich," he insisted as the soldiers cracked up. "I know it looks not possible but is true, seven years I do nothing but work! Seven years in this shithole, one more year I take my money and I go home."

"Good," said Jill. She'd accepted a warm orange Fanta. The soldiers and Petrik were pouring gin from a filthy plastic jug, everyone sluggish and greasy-looking in the heat. The old lady who ran the place sat at the next table over, a tiny, frizzle-headed woman with immense earlobes. From time to time she reached for the jug and poured herself a drink.

"You tell Starkey I do one more year for him."

"I'll tell him," Jill said.

"Stay with me," the Russian said, begging her with puppy eyes. "I go crazy for you baby, I take care of you. When you with me you don't worry for nothing, okay?"

"I have to go back. I'm sorry."

"I give you everything baby, you know it's true!"

"I'm sorry. I promised Starkey I'd be back in two days."

"Fuck Starkey, he's not the boss around here!" The Africans howled and slapped the table. "Me! Only Petrik is the boss in Kono! Just stay one night baby, I go nuts for you. Only one night Petrik asks you for."

"I can't," Jill said, wondering how much choice she had in the matter.

"Just one night. Please baby."

"I'm sorry. I have people waiting for me."

To Jill's horror he slumped over and started sobbing, which inspired a fresh surge of laughter from the Africans. The old lady chattered happily in Sherbro; she and the soldiers regarded Petrik with the dull satisfaction of people staring at an animal in the zoo. When it became clear that nothing was going to happen soon, Jill turned to the soldier with the most stripes.

"Please," she said, "talk to him. Tell him I need to go."

The soldier eyed her a moment, then leaned over and thrust his hand into the white man's pocket with a brusque, almost sexual familiarity. He pulled out a blue cloth pouch and handed it to Jill over Petrik's head; she pulled out the shrink-wrapped bricks of American currency and passed them back, then stuffed the pouch into the bottom of her daypack. She started to rise but the Russian grabbed her arm.

"Please baby." His face wrecked, pathetic; strings of cottony spittle stuck to his lips. "Give me one kiss and I let you go. Just one kiss baby, it's not so much."

It seemed the fastest, easiest way to go, but when she bent to kiss him it wasn't without some shading of mercy. As her lips met his she reflected that she'd never kissed a crying man before. She shuddered, but didn't rush; the Africans hooted and clapped. They were still laughing when she started down the path.

They left Falla at two in the afternoon, traveling west through a lush, monotonous country of remnant rain forest and abandoned rice paddies. Jill rode in the Mazda doublecab with Pa Conteh, while Pa's son Edmund followed in an ancient Mercedes flatbed. Jill had left Freetown with nine trucks, sending them back to the capital on successive days as their loads were delivered. After Falla the Mercedes and Mazda were empty as well; this was the first leg of the homeward trip, and as the potholes and gullies slung her around Jill considered the crude irony of the situation. Up ahead, the U.N. escort; down by her feet, blood diamonds. To gloat on it, even to think it, seemed like bad luck, though she knew that Starkey, a fearless collector of Third World ironies, would relish the story. In this she supposed she would always fail him as a student.

Pa kept riding the bumper of the U.N. jeep, trying to hurry it along. The Ghanian soldiers stared back with scathing indolence.

"These guys," Pa said in a disgusted voice, "what's the problem with these guys?"

"Take it easy, Pa. We don't want to run over the U.N."

Pa grunted; like most Leoneans he was scared of the dark and loathed the prospect of traveling at night. He was a small, wiry man with a flat-nosed Mende face, easily the best in Jill's spotty talent pool of drivers. A good mechanic, fluent in Mende and English, and so ferociously loyal that he embarrassed her at times; if Pa had a fault it was his tendency toward pessimism, though Jill reasoned that in most situations he was merely advocating the realist point of view.

"We going to Makela?" he asked for the third time.

"That's the plan."

"Lots of soldiers in Makela."

"According to the officer."

"We stay the night."

"I think that would be the smart thing to do."

He eased off the accelerator, momentarily reassured. Jill kept the daypack on the floor, half-consciously nudging it with her shoe from time to time. They gradually passed into a series of gently rolling hills, the peaks as round and mossy-green as turtles' backs. The rich mineral smell of wet earth filled the cab; dense stands of fetid jungle alternated with grassy fields, the country almost oppressive in its luxuriance. Clusters of mud-wattle huts punctuated the route, their roofs freshly thatched, with staked fields beyond, but Jill could count the human beings she saw on one hand. They'd heard about the trouble and taken off, either to the towns or deep bush; the loneliness of the country, its still, desolate air, set off a hum in her head like a blank tape, and she was glad when the Ghanians passed them off to a detachment of Indian peacekeepers. There were two jeeps now, eight soldiers in all, and the Indians were considered the most professional contingent in the U.N. force. The lead jeep swung around and pulled even with the Mazda, the heat rising off their engines in cellophane waves.

"You are going to Makela?" the officer called up to Pa. He was fit, in early middle age, with alert, hawkish features and a trim mustache. His face and khakis were powdered with rose-colored dust.

"That's right."

The officer smiled when he spotted Jill in the cab; his next words seemed directed at her. "We're going to pull over for a bit, there's some business near Makela we need to sort out." His starched, precise English made her think of Starkey. "Nothing to worry about. I shouldn't think we'll be long."

They followed the jeep off the road and parked under a stand of locust trees. So here you are, Jill thought, slowly jamming the daypack under the seat with her feet. Stuck here with your head in the lion's mouth, and nothing to do but sit still and wait. Edmund walked up to bum a cigarette and get the news; they passed the water jug around, then he went back to his truck to nap. Jill settled her head against the seat and tried to relax. A dull, dry ache had taken root behind her eyes, and amid the full-body throb of general soreness there were pockets of quite specific pain, as if she'd been struck here and there with a baseball bat. She wanted to sleep but her eyes kept flipping open, gazing past the umbrella of trees to the field beyond, then the low forested hills in the distance. The arc of the horizon, the glaring, empty sky, gave her the sense of being trapped in a vast bowl of light.

"Eh, Miss Jill, how long we going to sit?" Pa was fingering the juju bundle around his neck and staring at the soldiers, who didn't seem to be in any rush. The officer and sergeant were looking through a stack of maps, the officer speaking occasionally into the jeep radio. The other soldiers stood around with their helmets off, smoking and slapping at flies.

"No idea, Pa. It's their call."

"What they doing?"

"Scoping out the situation, I guess."

"Time to go," Pa muttered gloomily, squinting at the sun. "Too many rebel man out here. You just sit, after a while they gonna find you for sure."

Jill reflected that riding with her number-one driver could be downright depressing sometimes. She rested her head against the seat and watched a flock of herons turning loops above the field, their bodies startling white against the background of green. Their elegance, the serene, fluent curves of their flight, seemed to merge into the ongoing stream of her longing, the desire—only lately admitted—that she very much wanted to go home. She'd chosen this life because she couldn't imagine any other way, but over time, without her strictly being aware of it, the dead stares of the thousands of amputees had served to drain all the purpose out of her work. Those stares, the aura of hopelessness that always settled over the camps, implied that they knew something Jill didn't, a basic fact that had taken her years to understand. They were finished, their lives were over—if not now, then soon, and this applied to virtually every other Leonean as well. Her work was a delaying action at best, a brief comfort and hope to a very small few—she was handing them a drink of water through the window while the house burned down around their heads. She couldn't save them, she couldn't save anyone but herself, which made her presence here the worst sort of self-indulgence, her mission a long-running fantasy. In this light Starkey began to seem pure to her, his career an ideal she might aspire to. There was truth in that kind of life, a black-edged clarity; more than anyone else she'd ever met, he seemed to operate from a firm understanding of what was and was not possible. Such knowledge seemed to her the key to happiness, or failing that, a way of being that might be plausible, and for a time, sitting there in the sweltering truck, Jill felt as if this version was within her reach.

She could have it, but she would have to quit this kind of life, and the co-op was the deal that would let her walk away. That was the sequence she worked out sitting there in the truck, as if one couldn't happen without the other—as if the whole moral concept could be bought off with a bribe. She'd take her payoff from Starkey and turn it over to the co-op, and only then would she be allowed to leave.

She had no memory of dozing off; there was only a blank, then the thing that shouldered her out of sleep, wakefulness a half-beat behind the fear. She opened her eyes to see the herons flapping toward the treeline.

"Shhh!" hissed Pa Conteh. "You hear that?"

A faint clattering in the distance, bursts of automatic fire like nails raining down on a metal roof. With a word from their sergeant the soldiers pulled their rifles from the jeeps and formed a loose perimeter around the stand of trees. The officer was talking steadily into the radio now, taking notes, shuffling through his stack of maps. No one seemed rattled or panicked, Jill noticed; they'd simply gotten extremely efficient in their movements.

"Rocket," Pa murmured when the explosions started. RPG's, standard with the rebels—Jill had learned about rockets the year before, while she sat out the fighting in the basement of the Cape Hotel.

"It's getting closer?" Pa asked.

"I think it is."

For the next twenty minutes they sat and listened while the gunfire grew more distinct, an excruciating exercise in self-control. Pa groaned and shook his head; Jill jammed the daypack farther underneath the seat and made herself sit completely still. Finally the officer climbed out of his jeep and walked toward the truck. His name was stenciled over his right breast pocket, *Sawhey*; he was folding a map as he came, bending it back along the creases as he approached Jill's door.

"So sorry for the delay." His voice was calm, matter-of-fact; Jill felt herself release a breath.

"That's all right."

"Apparently the situation is quite serious," he continued in the same conversational tone. "I'm afraid that Makela is out of the question today. We have a sizeable garrison in Guendu, however," he laid the map on her windowsill and pointed to a town, "and we believe the roads are clear. I strongly recommend that we proceed there."

"Could we just go back to Falla?"

"No. Apparently the situation has deteriorated there as well."

"Wow." Jill laughed without exactly meaning to. "That was fast."

"Yes," Sawhey said briskly. "So it's Guendu, then?"

"Guendu's fine. Whatever you say."

"We would like to make a detour, here," he went back to the map, "we've been asked to evacuate a small NGO group in this location. Would you be willing to carry them in your lorries?"

"Of course."

"That would be most helpful. Let's proceed then."

They followed Sawhey's jeep as it turned and headed east, back the way they'd come; as the Mazda made its lumbering u-turn Jill could see columns of smoke rising to the west. They drove for several miles, then turned south and took a trail through the deserted countryside, their route little more than a confluence of dry streambeds and overlapping ruts. After an hour of crawling along in low gear they came to a highway, the roadbed littered with chunks of macadam and broken rock. They turned west, the low sun blinding them now, an orange ball raging just above the horizon; after several miles they followed Sawhey's jeep onto a dirt road marked by crumbling stone gates. The road wound through a narrow belt of grassland, the jungle framing the margins like sheer canyon walls. Ahead Jill could see a set of smaller stone portals with a cyclone fence stretching to either side, then a surreal cluster of ranch-style homes. Tennis courts, a basketball hoop, the angled stanchion of a high-dive—she'd seen such places before, self-contained bits of suburbia plopped down in the bush to house foreign logging or mining engineers. She started to ask Pa if he knew this place when a flash of movement caught her eye. A man, shirtless, in torn camouflage pants, had stepped from the trees, then fifteen, twenty, thirty wild-looking men were strung along the edge of the bush, waving rifles and machetes and screaming at the trucks.

"Shit," said Jill. Pa Conteh was grimly muttering to himself. Not just her mind but her whole being seemed to spool down—as if watching from some far remove, Jill saw one of the rebels lift his gun and fire into the air. Pa, Jill, the soldiers in the jeeps, everyone flinched, raising a howl of laughter from the rebels. In the jeeps the soldiers swung their rifles toward the rebels, barrels held at forty-five degrees. Jill braced for more shots but no one fired.

"Jesus, Pa."

He was muttering something over and over, shaking his head as if resigned to the dreadful worst. They passed through the stone portals and followed Sawhey's jeep toward the houses. Jill could see people huddled in the interior courtyard, a crowd of Africans sitting or crouching low. Something was off, she could feel it as the truck approached—the place was shabby, barely holding together, and that glimpse of the crowd had left her strangely unnerved. Pa parked in such a way that her view was blocked.

"Do you know this place?"

He shook his head, unable to speak just then. They glanced back and saw the rebels sauntering toward the fence, laughing and jeering as they crossed the field.

"I don't think I'm gonna see my wife again," Pa said.

Jill felt so wretched that she wanted to hug the old man. Sawhey and two of his men disappeared between the houses; the other soldiers formed a line among the jeeps and trucks. Soon Sawhey reappeared leading an older, heavy white woman by the arm, the woman sobbing, pleading with him in a guttural smear. She was a nun: bareheaded, dressed in men's work clothes, but a nun nevertheless—after years in the relief business Jill could spot them at a glance. The other soldiers came behind with two more nuns, both of them weeping as messily as the first. A handful of black women followed with quick, controlled steps, looking neither left nor right as they hurried toward the truck.

The first nun stumbled and fell to her knees. Sawhey launched into a complicated slapstick routine, pulling here, gathering there, straining to manage it all; after several seconds of this Jill jumped out of the truck and jogged toward them. As she cleared the corner of the nearest house the courtyard was gradually revealed to her, the crowd seething, roiling in place like a termite mound. Some were weeping, some babbling or laughing to themselves, others rocking back and forth or wringing their hands—the process of understand-

159

ing was like a slow electric shock, a gathering jolt that finally brought her up short. She had the nun under the arm by then, but she wavered, undone by all those lunatic faces.

"Come on," Sawhey gasped, "help me."

Jill heaved, the nun lurched to her feet. The three of them staggered toward the truck.

"Do you speak Dutch?" Sawhey panted. Jill shook her head.

"They're Dutch," he managed between breaths, "there were supposed to be more." The other women were climbing into the back of the Mazda. "I think everyone bolted but these." With Pa pulling from inside they managed to hoist the nun into the Mazda's cab. Jill turned and started back toward the courtyard.

"Get in the lorry," Sawhey told her.

"What?"

"Get in the lorry," Sawhey repeated.

"What about them?" Jill motioned toward the courtyard.

"Our orders are to evacuate staff."

Jill took a step toward Sawhey. "You're going to *leave* them?"

"Our orders are to evacuate staff."

"Good God." Jill looked past the trucks—the rebels were strung along the fence like outraged crows, cawing, bending over to show their asses, rattling the steel mesh with their machetes. They knew the soldiers wouldn't shoot unless attacked.

"Don't you know what they'll do to these people?"

"It's out of my hands. Get in the lorry, please."

Jill turned and ran back to the courtyard. She stopped at the edge of the crowd and went through the motions of making a count, though she knew there were far too many for the trucks. Physically they looked fit enough—they were well-fed, and most of them had decent clothes and shoes, but below that line of thought she was struggling, unsure what kind of claim they had on her. How flawed were they, how deficient; how deep their lack of essential human stuff, and could she live with herself if she walked away and left them to this lavish butchery. There would be no limits here, she knew that in her bones. Here it would be a pure Brueghel vision of hell, cretins and lunatics left in the care of compulsive torturers. They didn't even have their reason to protect them, the scant, maybe infinitesimal shield of being able to meet their tormentor with a sane eye. Better to go ahead and shoot them, she thought. Better to have the soldiers machine-gun the lot than leave them for the rebels to carve up.

"Miss." Sawhey had appeared at her side with an enlisted man—did they mean to drag her off too? "Please, Miss, we need to leave at once."

"How far is it to Guendu?" she asked sharply.

"Fourteen kilometers," he answered with supreme patience. "Please, I insist that you come with us at once."

"We'll walk them out. We'll put as many on the trucks as we can and the rest will have to walk."

Sawhey blinked; it was as if she'd jabbed him with a pin. "My orders are to evacuate staff."

"And you'll evacuate staff, nobody's telling you not to evacuate staff. But you can bring out everybody else too."

He seemed to hold his breath as he glanced over the crowd. "It can't be done."

"Of course it can. We'll make a column, we'll put the jeeps and trucks at the front and the back and everybody else will be in the middle. It'll be slow but we can make it."

For a split-second his discipline cracked, his face collapsing as if punched from inside. "Don't you think I would save them if I could?" he cried. "I can't handle these people, I don't have the men. Even if we try that mob will fire before we reach the first gate."

"They won't if they know you'll fire back."

He seemed to plead with her now. "I don't have enough men, can't you see that? Perhaps they'd wait until dark, perhaps we'd get that far. But as soon as night falls we'll be slaughtered."

It surpassed her, simply carried her along—in some clenched part of herself she registered surprise, a faint grace-note of wonder as it happened.

"No," she told Sawhey, "I can fix that. Those people aren't going to touch us."

Later, playing it back in her mind, she found that whole blocks of memory had been lost to her. She couldn't recall getting her daypack from the Mazda, nor stepping into the open away from trucks, away from the thin, sheltering line of soldiers. There must have been an exchange, an understanding of sorts, because she started down the road with a vague sense of assurance, a mental imprint of their rifles coming to bear. Then it was all jump-cuts and pieces of things, fragments spliced one after another—the awful heat, the scything bird-song in the bush, her nausea and a sharp copper taste in her mouth. How the sun threw orange shafts of light across the road, shadow and

161

light alternating like flattened stairs, and how the rebels fell silent when they saw her coming. Like a switch had been thrown, that sudden, then her despair when they rallied and started in again, howling, obscenely urging her on.

At a certain point she lost the sense of her feet touching the ground. Things went away, spinning off as if gravity had lost its hold—mainly it was about not showing fear at precisely those moments when you were most afraid. Eyes, mouth, voice, strict control of the pressure points, because fear was a tacit form of consent. She was close enough now to see the lumps in their skin, the juju bundles they'd sewn into themselves. They wore rags and tatters of clothes but fairly bristled with weapons; they were boys, teenagers most of them, red-eyed, heads swiveling as they drifted toward the gate. Giggling, clearly messed up on something. Several pointed their guns at her and laughed.

She stopped on a line even with the two stone portals. "Who's the head man," she called in a neutral voice, pitching it between request and command.

There was more laughter. "You a long way from home," a voice answered.

"Sure, padi. But don't you know I'm trying hard to get back there."

The youth who'd spoken waved down the road with his gun. He was tall and gaunt, bare-chested, his thin Fullah face edged with decorative scars. Bandoliers wreathed his body like a fashion statement—*gangsta*, that was the style they aspired to. Tupac Shakur was their Haile Selassie.

"Walk on," he said in a jeering voice. "Nobody stopping you."

"Yeah, that would be fine, I appreciate that. But what I'm asking is you let my friends come with me, saby? Let them pass, all these people good people here. Nobody here you need be making trouble with."

The youth laughed; she watched his eyes range past her shoulder, scanning the soldiers at her back. The rest of the mob stood slack-jawed and goggling, their stares like cigarette burns on her skin.

"You and de soldiers, I leave you go outta de goodness a my heart. Everybody else got to stay, das de order. We in charge of security in all dis place now."

"Come on padi, these people sick. Let these people go to Guendu for the doctor."

"We got doctor," he said, raising a laugh from his friends.

"Let them go, nobody but simple people here. Nobody here going to make any trouble for you." When the youth just stared, Jill added: "I'll pay."

He wasn't impressed. "What you pay," he snapped.

She pulled the cloth pouch out of her daypack, loosened the drawstring, and poured a spoonful of diamonds into her hand. "This now," she said, showing him her hand. "And this later," she lifted the pouch, "when we get to Guendu."

The youth came forward several steps, close enough for Jill to hear the asthma in his chest. When he saw what she had he seemed to blank out for a moment.

"Yah." He swallowed, came a few steps closer. "You give me everyt'ing now, you free to go. Give me everyt'ing now and all dese people free to go." When she refused he made a childish swipe at her hand, then played it for a joke when she pulled back. He was laughing, trembling slightly as he glanced from her to the soldiers, trying to solve the hard calculation they presented. The cost of taking them, and his own chances in a fight. Whether he'd be among the lucky when it was all said and done.

"Do the trade," Jill said quietly. "You're a very rich man if you do the trade."

His eyes got busy—diamonds, soldiers, then back to the diamonds. Working the numbers so hard she could hear them squeal. He licked his lips, took one last look at the soldiers, and carefully held out his hand.

Most were manageable. The nuns told them to walk and so they walked, lapsing into a one-track catatonic state in which the next step forward was the only thing. Others, though docile enough, were prone to wandering off or sitting down in the road, and it was a struggle to keep them focused and moving with the group. Those who couldn't be managed at all—the violent, the contrary, the overwrought—had to be bound and secured in the trucks, where they passed the night howling like kenneled dogs. What the column must have looked like to someone watching from the bush, Jill could only imagine—like a nightmare, an apparition some sorcerer had conjured up, a shambling caravan of demons and freaks. The rebels bought into the spirit of the thing, buzzing up and down the line in their junkheap technicals and yowling like angels of the apocalypse, singing songs, urging the walkers on, doing note-perfect imitations of the lunatics. Toward Jill and the others they assumed a pose of bluff camaraderie, shouting advice and officiously pointing out the stragglers.

The engulfing dark, the fragile beam-shafts of the trucks' headlights, made it seem as if she was walking down a tunnel or chute, a low, dust-choked space of jagged shadows and light. From time to time Sawhey would leave his jeep and drop back through the column to find her. He'd give her a drink from his canteen and they would walk together, herding the people at the rear of the column along. The nuns and their staff were farther ahead, spaced at intervals to keep the column intact.

"They just keep going," Sawhey said during one visit.

"Yes," said Jill. Everything hurt, legs, lungs, feet. She welcomed the pain; she hoped it would fill all her interior space.

"Do you think they understand what's happening to them?"

"No."

"That's what I think too," he replied. "None of us does, not really. That's the conclusion I've come to lately." They walked in silence for a time. "Wouldn't you care to ride in the jeep?"

"No."

"You're planning to walk all the way to Guendu."

"Yes, that's what I'm planning to do."

"You know," he said after a moment, "you make me ashamed of myself. I don't think I'm a particularly bad man, but you make me ashamed of myself."

She wanted to hit him then. By now she was convinced that something was wrong with her, and that was what she planned to say to Starkey: I'm sick, I'm mentally disturbed. That's why I gave away your diamonds, I'm fucked up in the head. To the women of the co-op she couldn't imagine what she'd say—nothing, hopefully, if she could manage it. If she could resist the idiot urge to explain herself. At dawn a detachment of peacekeepers met them at the outskirts of Guendu, and as the column filed into the waking town Jill pulled the daypack out from under Pa Conteh's seat and threw it to the Fullah youth. Tossed it carelessly, like so much dirty laundry, glad that she couldn't do any more damage with it. After that things ran together in an ugly blur—the walk into town, the peacekeepers herding them along, everyone collapsing finally in the dusty square. Pa Conteh found Jill propped against a concrete wall; he led her back to the Mazda, got her settled in the cab and went to find them something to eat. She was still there, dozing with the door swung open, when she heard someone approach.

"Miss. Excuse me, Miss."

She opened her eyes. Sawhey was standing there with a group of officers. Jill let her head fall back against the seat. Smoke from a hundred cooking fires was rising over the town, spindly columns drifting past the thatch and sheet-metal roofs, delicately twisting into nothing as they rose past the palms. For several moments she followed the smoke with her eyes, trying to find the exact point where it dissolved into air—there, that's where she existed, where she'd lived her whole life. Turning back to the soldiers felt like the hardest thing she would ever do.

"Please, Miss," Sawhey said. "We need to know what to do with these people now."

Nominated by Katherine Taylor

A HISTORY OF THE AMERICAN WEST

by KEVIN PRUFER

from LYRIC

The American West slept on an open raft. His chest
was brown and flecked with hair. Hat tipped forward
to cover the eyes, one hand limp,
                            cutting the water,
the other draped over the thigh, touching the thigh—
Skin like tobacco,
                    skin gone coarse and dry,
and like John Brown the sun rose and rose, then died
in the empty sky.

                            ✿ ✿ ✿

                    An eyelash twitched,
the eyeball rolled beneath the lid. Purse of lips,
the tongue that played behind the teeth in sleep.
The West
            was dreaming about fields, about a clutter
of rising birds, how they lift from the waving grass
like nets into the sky.
                            The raft turned in the current,
nudged the shore.
                            The West licked his drying lips,
dreamed now of a boy—himself—

on a horse,
looking over a field of singing birds,
off to the desert's edge, a clot of buildings, a shadow
on the sand around it.
From far away, the voices of girls
say, *Yes.* Say, *Come from the horse with your hat
and your leather.* Say, *How beautiful,*
your hair blown back
and filled with sand, cheeks red where the weather
bit them.
The West smiled in sleep,
ran his tongue over sharpened teeth.

∘ ∘ ∘

Years later, of course, our bombs disturbed the desert,
blooming like orchids.
Years later, we watered the sand:
fallout, cancer, birds caught in the cloud and down
to the dunes with them,
the thud of breaking bodies,
wings torn back and rustling in the grass.
One day,
the sky was blue as an eye pinned open. Then the flash
and rush of wind, the stalk that rose and split,
and petals, gray and black.
And lush.

∘ ∘ ∘

In the dream, the girls say, *Lush.* Say, *Lips,*
wet where the dew has kissed them.
And, *Sand*
caressing the hair blown back.
Girls in the cluster
of a desert town,
girls in the schoolyard
holding out their arms to him,
and the West,
on his raft, dreams of ribbons, sunburnt legs, the West,

who has no family he remembers, the West,
raised on a raft or a plow,
                        who cannot recall,
but in the dream pushes westward on his horse,
into the sand.

✿ ✿ ✿

He slept and slept, stalled in the brush
                                at the river bank.
Water lapped against the raft. The smooth chest
rose and fell. Gorgeous in his jeans and sunburnt arms,
gone
        to the bomb blast and the gasp of time,
to Brigham Young and his wagonload of wives,
the heel and rein of men on horseback. The railroad,
the churn of every train.
                        Cather, Crane, and dustclouds
when, for weeks, the farms burned under rainless skies.

✿ ✿ ✿

The West content and tan, because that is his history,
caught in an eddy,
                    gone to everything but the gentle dream
in which the West rides westward, toward the desert town,
into the girls who crowd around,
                                who touch the horse's
sweat-damp coat, who stroke the shank, the saddle,
and his thigh—
            lush, lush, they say, then smile
and haul him down.

Nominated by Martha Collins, Richard Burgin, Alan Michael Parker, David Baker, Lyric

ELEGY (WITH ADVERTISEMENT) STRUGGLING TO FIND ITS HERO

by MARK IRWIN

from KENYON REVIEW

It was a century in which we touched ourselves in mirrors
over and over. It was a decade of fast yet permanent
memories. The kaleidoscope of pain

some inflicted on others seemed inexhaustible
as the positions of *sex*, a term
whose meaning is as hybridized as the latest orchid. Terrorism

had reached a new peak, and we gradually
didn't give a shit which airline we got on, as long as the pilot
was sober, and the stash of pretzels, beer, and soft drinks

remained intact. On TV, a teenage idol has just crawled, dripping
wet,
from the top of a giant Pepsi can, or maybe I imagined it,
flicking through channels where the panoply

of *reality shows* has begun to exorcise
the very notion of reality, for both the scrutinized actor
and the debilitated viewer who becomes confused and often reaches

into the pastel screen for his glass, while down Broadway
sirens provide a kind of glamorous chorus
for this script of history where everything is so neatly measured

in miles, pounds, or megabits. How nice it would be
to drowse in the immeasurable. How nice
it would be to escape.

> *And there's a wobbly marble bench*
> *beneath an out-of-focus tree on the Web*
> *I like to occasion my body with.*

How brief we've become in our speed
I think How fast the eternal.
How desperately

we need a clearing, a place
beyond, but not necessarily
of nature. *And the rain*

was so deep the entire forest smelled of stone, then the sun
broke, burying the long shadows
in gold. And the wounded

king woke in a book long since closed, and the princess
came to in a bed so large
she could never leave. How desperately

we need a new legend, one with a hero, tired
though he may be. One who has used
business to give up

business, one who has bought
with his heart what we
sold with ours.

Nominated by Angie Estes, Ralph Angel

DOGGED

fiction by RISTEARD O'KEITINN

from ANTIOCH REVIEW

THE DOG WAS UNPREDICTABLE, mean. Ken Furlch had given it to Colby one day while he was in Furlch's Texaco station, servicing one of his cigarette venders. The dog had just taken a bite out of Ken's daughter's Shetland pony. They'd heard the pony kicking up a ruckus tethered behind the tire shed, found the dog hanging from its side, like some kind of giant leech, legs dangling, teeth buried in its flanks. Wouldn't let go, neck muscles bulging, jaws clamped down tight as a lock-wrench. Ken finally had to pry it loose with a broom handle, all the while his brother, Odell, beating on it with a piece of muffler pipe.

Mostly mutt, maybe some pit bull, bowlegged, one ear chewed off to a nub and no tail to speak of; from behind, the dog appeared almost runty. Up front, though, it had a barrel-chest and a thick neck, an oversized head shaped like a maul, little beady eyes the color of drained motor oil. Its coat was short and drab, faintly skewbald with patches of dingy gray. Not much to look at, Colby thought, but then neither was he. Be good to have a dog, a mean one at that, and he took it home with him to the farm that same day.

Both Colby and his father, Earl, had been born on the farm, but neither one had much interest in farming. After Colby's grandfather, Otho, had died back in the fifties, Earl had kept the house—a substantial, prairie clapboard with all new plumbing—but leased out the land to a tenant farmer and gone to work with the Hanford Tobacco Company, traveling around the Midwest, selling wholesale bulk tobacco, cigars and chew. During this time he also began buying

171

vending machines—mostly cigarette venders but a few candy too—setting them out on various locations along his sales beat. Ten years later his venders were doing so well he quit his job with Hanford to concentrate full-time on them.

Colby had grown up in the business, first learning how to fix and refurbish old equipment, then, when he could drive, helping his father service the routes, refilling merchandise and collecting money. Then in the early seventies, Earl came down with emphysema—he was a two-pack-a-day man and Colby ended up taking over more and more of the operation. The disease progressed rapidly, Earl cutting back on his smoking but refusing to quit altogether, and it wasn't long before all he could do was ride along in the pickup and keep Colby company, that and inhale forlornly through a tube attached to a big, green, oxygen tank resting in his lap. He finally died in the fall of '75. By then he was totally bedridden, couldn't suck enough wind into his lungs to blow out a match.

Colby had lost his mother, Stella, years earlier when she'd driven into town to go shopping one sunny spring day and never returned. Two weeks later her green Rambler was found abandoned at a strip mall three states away in Raleigh, North Carolina. There the trail dead-ended, however, and as months turned into years, little hope remained of finding her or even learning what had happened—whether she'd been abducted or simply run off on her own. In any event she was gone and Colby, who was barely four at the time, came away with few lasting memories of her.

The dog had no trouble adjusting to its new surroundings, acted as though it had been on the farm all its life. It ate and slept hog-healthy, never wandered off, was always there waiting for Colby when he returned, waiting and keeping an eye on things. For better than a year, the two of them got along fairly well together—mainly keeping to themselves, staying out of each other's way.

"That's some watchdog you got there," said Phil Hatcher one afternoon. Colby had just returned home from servicing a string of truck stops east of Belle Rive on Interstate 64. Phil was a county supervisor, had dropped by to discuss blacktopping a nearby access road. Right then, though, he was wearing only one shoe and standing on top of his Buick Regal, midnight blue, the dog circling it, growling and staring up at him like he was a treed coon.

172

"Faster'n he looks," he said climbing down after Colby had chained up the dog. "Got a serious set of jaws on him, too."

Colby handed him his other shoe, badly chewed and sopping with strings of white drool. He offered to pay for it.

"Comes with the territory," the supervisor said, shaking his head. He wiped the shoe on a clump of timothy and put it back on. "Dog's only doing his job."

After that Colby started taking the dog with him sometimes, letting it ride in the back of the pickup when he went into town. The dog was good about not jumping out and pretty soon he was taking it along most everywhere he went. One thing for sure with the dog in back, growling and glaring at passersby, he felt a whole lot more at ease leaving the truck unattended. He didn't like leaving the house unattended, though, particularly at night, so when it came to servicing distant routes like along Interstate 57, north to Decatur or clear down to the state's southernmost tip at Cairo—treks where he had to spend several days on the road—he still left the dog at home, watching after things.

Then Colby got married. It was the middle of July and her name was Ray Jeana Voyles. She was an Effingham girl, had been married twice before. (Both to real losers, she was quick to confide: one a gambler and a drunk—he'd wound up going bankrupt; the other a felon, now serving time in Danville for stealing cars and writing bad checks.) She'd moved to Mill Shoals after her last divorce three years ago, had been living there ever since. With a blowtorch of upswept red hair and skin that glowed pure and white as polished meerschaum, she was also not a long way off from pretty, fifteen years younger than him, and he had no idea what he'd done to fool her.

For Colby the marriage was his first. In his mid-forties, going a little slag-bellied from a taste for beer, he'd never had much confidence with the ladies, had lost most of his hair by the time he was twenty, at least on top where it counted, and he'd always felt it gave his face the appearance of not quite fitting his head. He'd stare at himself in the mirror one day and see his brow rising up and up till it was almost overlapping his crown, as though he were all face. Later he'd look again and see just the reverse—like one of those trick cubes—he'd be all head, all pate crushing down on the lower features of his face, making them look squinched together, small and inconsequential. Eventually, he took to wearing glasses—no vision

173

problem, just felt they helped break up that vast expanse of fore-head.

Colby had met Ray Jeana when she was bartending at Lucky's, a tavern he frequented just outside town on the road to Burnt Prairie. He also operated a cigarette vender there, one of his father's origi-nals, an old National single tier, push-pull, a real antique, but still a workhorse, death on slugs—even with its old-fashioned mechanical rejecter—and Lucky'd let him set the unit right out there next to the jukebox where it did a bang-up business, particularly on weekends.

When he'd get done restocking the columns with packs of Camel, Winston, Marlboro, Viceroy, Kool, Pall Mall, he'd take the coin box and empty it on the bar, count out Lucky's six percent in front of Ray-J—that's what everybody called her. He'd also toss her an occa-sional leftover pack of smokes. Marlboro Lights was her brand, but she wasn't picky—not about cigarettes, anyway. (Now men, she'd joke—don't even ask.) After that he'd hang around and have a couple of beers with her, shoot the breeze.

One time when she had no customers, he'd brought in the rest of his week's take, plugged in his coin-sorter and let her help him stack-wrap the profits. She really seemed to like it, just made her eyes light up his whole afternoon. When they were done, had all the coins rolled up neat and tidy, ready to deposit in the county bank down in Carmi, she slipped a hand over his and gave it a squeeze.

Next thing he was bragging about how business was booming, how for the last decade or so, sales had been pretty puny and getting punier every day what with more and more people quitting smoking or never even getting started. A few years back, though, it'd all turned around. Why was that? she asked, her hand still resting on his. All he could think to tell her was teenage smoking, or more accurately—be-cause teenagers had always been smoking—it had to do with the gov-ernment and its growing campaign against teenage smoking.

"Don't take a six-pack of smarts to figure that out," she said grin-ning. "I expect your vending machines they ain't all that particular who's sticking money in them."

"Hey, I'm legal," he said with a wink. "Warning placards on every last one of them."

She laughed, then asked how come she'd never seen him light up. She was drinking Jack and Coke, had just lit up a Camel herself from a pack he'd tossed her way. He told her about his dad, watching him slowly die day by day, gasping away like a carp on a stringer, drowning pretty much in his own rancid air. He said he'd tried to smoke once after that, back in his mid-twenties. He'd taken one drag and that had been the end of it, felt as if he'd stuffed his chest full of hot cinders, scorched his brain.

Ray-J told him she'd quit once, gained about twenty pounds in three weeks. So much for good intentions, she announced, sliding over a coaster and stubbing out the butt of her cigarette. But not before she was puffing away on a new one she'd lit off it.

Surprised, Colby found himself recalling a distant, early memory: his mother standing in a doorway, lighting one cigarette off another, her hair, he could still see it, long and straight, dark as raw Onarga honey pouring warmly to her shoulders, back-lit from the hall. He was standing there, too, on bathroom tile, had just slid off the big toilet—proud he could use it without falling in—waiting to bend over and be wiped. And she was looking down at him with the kindest eyes in all the world.

He told Ray-J about his mother, how she'd run off when he was little, never did find her way back home.

"Sounds like my old man," she said. "Long gone before I was even born."

Though pleased to be sharing common ground, Colby puzzled over what he'd just said, knew it wasn't altogether true. Authorities tended to believe his mother had met with foul play, probably been raped and murdered, then dumped in a shallow grave somewhere. Most people—including his father—were of a similar mind, preferring to view Stella as an innocent victim rather than a woman who'd desert her own family. Not him, though. Not when he was growing up, anyway. He didn't want her dead and buried—even if it meant she'd run off. Never mind placing blame, he just wanted her back, to see her and hear her voice again, the way it made him feel inside, like there was a caring, a softness and calm, holding everything together.

Of course, that was back when it still seemed to matter, before he'd learned how not to cry anymore, his sense of loss gradually becoming lost itself. By now she might be dead anyway, even if she'd never left the farm. Just like Earl. From natural causes.

"And wouldn't you know, he'd turn up again," Ray-J was saying. "Five or six years ago . . . an old, burned-out hippie. Every time I see his sorry ass around town, I'm wishing just why the Christ he couldn't stay gone."

Later, she walked out with Colby to his pickup and gave him a kiss. While they stood there for a few moments grappling one another in the parking lot, she noticed the dog watching from the back of the truck, wanted to know its name. Didn't have one, he told her. Always came running, though, when he whistled. She tried whistling, but the dog didn't come running, lifted a leg over its ear, ignoring her, began chewing at its hind-end.

Two days after she'd moved in, she told him she didn't like the dog, wanted him to get rid of it. He asked her why. It was the way it looked at her, she said—like it wanted to hump her leg or worse. It smelled bad, too. They were lying in bed after a conjugal partaking. She'd just lit up a Marlboro Light. Colby said he'd see what he could do about it, then asked her if she was "up for seconds." She started to decline, then told him that depends. Depends on what? he asked. "On whether you meant what you said about the dog, you know, doing something about it." He said, of course he meant it. She seemed pleased and told him to "hold on a sec," while she grabbed an ashtray off the nightstand, set it next to her on the bed. Then lying back, still holding her cigarette off to one side, she motioned for him to once more climb on.

Before they really got going, she pulled away, asked if he'd mind maybe trying it this time, you know, wearing his glasses.

A week later she was after him again. He'd let things slide, hoping she'd get used to the dog and change her mind. Now she claimed it had growled at her, that it was just plain mean. "That's how a watch-dog's supposed to be," he told her. She told him she didn't need a watchdog, that she couldn't relax at night, couldn't even think of having kids, for instance, with an animal like that running around. Colby wanted kids, but the one time he'd brought up the subject, she'd called him "mister," said he'd better cool down on that notion real quick, as she had no intentions of getting all stretched out of shape till she was good and ready.

Another week went by; then another after that. She'd spend her days hardly even speaking to him. Colby decided letting things slide was not working out nearly soon enough to suit her. Himself either, for that matter.

"I'm going to get rid of it," he announced one night, reaching across the bed, rubbing her shoulder, thinking of how much he missed the touch of that creamy-white skin. "We'll see," she said, lighting up a Virginia Slim. "Talk's cheap. In the meantime don't expect to find me relaxing any. Don't expect any favors of an exciting nature coming your way."

At first he tried finding a home for the dog. He got no takers. He thought about just turning it loose somewhere, but he'd heard too many stories about abandoned dogs: starving, running wild in packs, killing livestock, attacking children. . . . Instead he called the vet over in Carmi to see about putting it to sleep. When he found out how much it cost, he tried the Humane Society up in Benton. They'd do it for less, but it was a long drive; time you got through figuring time and gas, going and coming, it wasn't all that much of a saving.

A month went by and Ray-J told him she sure wasn't getting any younger, that it wouldn't surprise her one little bit if she just up and forgot how to relax altogether. Colby told her the dog would be gone tomorrow, that he'd take care of the matter once and for all on his three-day run down to Cairo.

The next morning he woke up bright and purposeful. He downed two cups of coffee, stuck the cup in a sink full of last night's dirty dishes—he'd get to them later—then went out and fed the dog a last meal. Which seemed only fair.

He'd decided to put off the trip to Cairo another day. That meant—after getting rid of the dog—he'd have the night to spend with Ray-J. All that nagging, he figured she'd be more than ready to celebrate, most certainly be up for some serious relaxation.

He hoped other things would improve between them, too, get back to the way they'd been earlier, those first few weeks of their marriage before she'd got so uptight about the dog. She'd been so different then, laughing and joking around, enjoying his company just like when she was back working at Lucky's. Now it seemed she was always sore at him, always sulking, avoiding him every chance she got. She was drinking more, too, and sleeping in late, sometimes past noon.

While the dog was eating its Gravy Train, he went into the house and began rummaging through a closet for his gun. The search took awhile. He couldn't remember the last time he'd used it, an old .22 rifle he'd had since boyhood. The storage space was also cluttered with an overflow from Ray-J's closet upstairs. He finally found the rifle buried under a stack of her shoeboxes—wondered how any one person could own so many shoes. It was his own fault, he supposed: Sick of traveling, he'd given her a credit card instead of a honeymoon. "It's everywhere you want to be," he'd told her. But he hadn't counted on the Effingham Mall.

Outside again he lowered the tailgate to his pickup and whistled. He didn't have to whistle twice. The dog came running, leapt into the truck-bed, took its favorite position directly behind the cab, leaning out, waiting for the wind.

Colby drove a couple of miles over to Baxter Road and the old material service pit, a makeshift dumpsite that had sprung up since the township landfill had raised its rates. He drove on down into the pit, ignoring a bullet-riddled no-trespassing sign, parked at the bottom by a shallow drainage pond.

Gun in hand he climbed down from the truck, gave the dog a nod and it leaped out, all excited, huffing and snorting, immediately trotted over to the pond. Colby watched it take a few spirited steps into the orange, scum-crusted water, splashing and biting at the surface before settling down for a drink.

Yesterday had been in the high nineties, and the sun was already starting to heat up. Dog'd be cooling off soon enough, he thought.

He picked his way through piles of trash, a couple of junked refrigerators, some rusted-out heater coils. When he came to an old, shredded mattress lying on the ground by some charred furniture, he stopped. As good a spot as any.

The dog was off sniffing in a mound of garbage. Colby whistled. It straightened up, looked at him, its good ear perked. When he didn't whistle again, it took a few more sniffs, then a piss. A moment later it sauntered over, bounded up onto the mattress, unsteadily stepping across some exposed springs toward him.

"Sit!" said Colby, pumping a round into the rifle's breech. The dog sat. A couple of feet away, panting now, whining in the heat, looking around, looking back at the garbage it had just left, looking at Colby, then scratching itself, snapping at flies.

He raised the rifle to his shoulder, gave one last whistle to get the dog's attention, get it looking at him and holding its head still. It was almost like taking a picture. *Say cheese*, he thought, thinking it was funny, but he didn't say it, sensed it would become something a lot less than funny if he actually did.

Then, dotting the rifle's open V-sight, he shot the dog between the eyes.

The dog dropped to the mattress, collapsed instantly, as if life had never even been a consideration. Colby grabbed a hind leg and dragged it off the mattress, covered it with some corrugated cardboard he found scattered nearby.

Back in the truck heading home, he decided he could use a cold beer, swung into town.

"How're things working out between you and Ray Jeana?" Lucky asked, tending bar himself. He brought over a Bud and a glass.

"Okay." Colby was the only customer. He debated telling Lucky about shooting the dog, elected to keep it to himself.

"I've seen it happen before. Women like her, wild and all, settling down like a potted plant. You know, their past no more an indication of the future than your last hand of poker."

Colby knew the gay divorcee stories—everybody in town did. Nothing he couldn't live with, though. He poured his beer into the glass. He drank it halfway down in two big swallows, finished it off with two more.

Lucky ran a hand through his silvering yellow hair. "Hot out," he said.

When Colby pulled into the drive, the dog was sitting there waiting for him. It was over by the stoop, right where it always sat, resting in the shade. The two of them stared at each other.

"What're you doing home?" asked Ray-J stepping out onto the front porch. "I thought you were heading down to Cairo today."

"I told you I was getting rid of the dog," he told her. "I just took it out to the dump and shot it."

"He don't look very shot to me."

Colby didn't answer. He walked over to the stoop for a closer look. The dog seemed glad to see him, was doing its best to wag its stub tail. The hole was there all right—right between the eyes where he'd aimed. Not much blood, though. He could see a thin web of it beneath the wound; a few trickles that had run down its muzzle were already dried and turning brown in the hot sun. The hole itself had stopped bleeding, looked dark and crusted with dust. Around its edge he could make out tiny splinters of bone.

He walked back to the truck and whistled. The dog got up and came over, not exactly running but not limping either. When it tried to jump up into the bed, though, it couldn't seem to get set, its legs moving one way then another, leaving it stumbling about, whining. Colby finally picked it up. He started to put it into the back, changed his mind and carried it around to the cab, set it on the seat next to him. He'd never let it ride up front before, guessed today he'd make an exception.

On the way back to the dump, he looked over at the dog and wondered what it must be thinking. He wondered if it remembered him shooting it—remembered even getting shot. When they swung off Baxter Road and headed down to the pond, he expected the dog to start getting antsy, show some signs of old déjà vu how-do-you-do. Maybe start pacing, hot stepping it around the front seat, maybe growling. It did neither, just sat there panting, matter-of-factly staring out the window, not even perking up its good ear.

Grabbing his gun again and climbing out of the truck, Colby made his way through the trash to the old mattress. He didn't bother whistling, didn't have to. There was no wandering off now—no wading into the pond or rooting through garbage—the dog followed him obediently, seemed almost afraid to let him out of its sight.

When they reached the mattress, it was unable to climb onto it, couldn't quite lift its front paws over the springs. Colby told it to never mind, that it was doing just fine, just sitting there on the ground where it was sitting. He pumped a new round into the chamber and once more took aim. No need whistling to get its attention now either: It had its eyes on him, hawking every move he made, as if this time around it didn't want to miss a trick.

He felt like offering it a blindfold, then, more to the truth, wanted one for himself. Staring into those beady eyes was definitely making him uncomfortable. It's not that they were so fearful or pleading— not all that trusting either, he thought. They were just so goddamn alert, so intensely interested in what was going on, like it was just on the verge of making sense of things—what had already happened and what was going to happen.

Get on with it, Colby heard himself whisper. He was thinking way too much, giving himself a headache. He broke gaze with the dog's eyes, aiming at the hole between them. That made things a lot easier. Just a target, nothing personal. He'd shoot it right where he'd shot it before, right where the first bullet had already tunneled a path through that bony ridge of forehead. No way would this bullet fail to get the job done.

———

180

On the way home he stopped off again at Lucky's. Almost noon, there were a number of cars in the lot. Climbing out of the truck, he noted Wade Enis's Malibu parked nearby, its right front fender crumpled, starting to rust out from a two-year-old collision with a telephone pole. The wreck had taken place after closing hours out on the old Wabash turnoff. Enis hadn't been hurt. Neither had Carl Holcumb. Ray-J, however, sitting between the two of them, got her head gashed open by the rearview mirror. What she was doing on a dead-end road that time of night, particularly with those two hellers, was—as the saying went back then—*everybody's guess*. Course, it all happened before he knew her; still, he wished Enis'd get that damn fender fixed.

Walking inside he could smell the cooking grease from the lunch grill and saw several people sitting at the bar, washing down burgers and fries with beer. He also saw Enis swaggering around by the pool table, heard his loud mouth, his grating laugh, and kept right on walking to the other end of the bar. There he pulled up a stool next to Bub Thompson, waved off a menu—he wasn't hungry—ordered a beer.

Thompson, a lineman for ComEd, glanced over and nodded, then went back to watching a ball game on the overhead TV. He was doing shots with a beer chaser. Colby knew he'd been laid off, had been drinking heavy for several months now.

"Had to shoot my dog today," Colby said when Lucky brought his beer.

"Get old on you, did he?"

"Nope—wouldn't believe what happened, though."

"How's that?"

"Shot it out Baxter Road at the pit. That was earlier this morning. Drove on home, the damn thing's waiting for me there in the yard. Calm as you please like nothing ever happened."

"I'd say time to get your sights aligned," said Lucky with a laugh.

Colby laughed too but he shook his head. "Shot it right between the eyes. Bullet hole staring back at me to prove it. Just got done shooting it again."

"I heard once of a dude getting shot five times in the head," said Slater Hoge. He was standing nearby washing glasses, worked at Lucky's only when he wasn't busy roofing. "Over in East St. Louis. Some mugger stuck a pistol in his mouth and emptied the clip, robbed him and left him for dead. A week later the dude's up and out of the hospital, walking around. Slurred his words some and, you know, had trouble remembering things, but otherwise good as new."

"Hard to believe," said Colby.

"I don't believe it," said Lucky.

"No, it was on the news and everything," insisted Slater. "The way the doctors explained it, it's like the first couple of bullets they weren't fatal—but not only that, they ended up blocking the other bullets, you know, acting like a shield."

"I'll tell you, that's a hell of a thing," said Bub Thompson, slowly turning away from the TV, staring bleary-eyed at Colby, "having to shoot your dog. . . . Old Spitzy, I had to put her down winter before last. Raised her from a pup. Fifteen years old. Hindquarters went ka-put. Couldn't do nothing . . . just lying around in her shit all day. Took her to the vet, though. I'll tell you, no ways in hell could I a done her myself."

Colby nodded.

"Hey, Colby, you and me, what's say we drink us a little toast to our dogs? Old Spitzy, long gone now, and yours, recently departed, old—what'dya say his name was?"

Colby was silent, holding his glass.

"Your dog—what'dya call him?"

"Didn't really have a name," said Colby.

Bub stared at him, his shot glass already hoisted. "What does that mean, didn't really have a name?"

Colby shrugged, felt his grip tighten on his glass. He knew Bub had a surly streak in him once he got to drinking.

Bub continued staring at him. "What kind of man don't give his dog a name? I never heard of such a thing. Hey, Lucky, you hear that?"

Lucky made no comment, was busy pouring refills.

"Didn't need a name. It always come when I whistled."

"*It* always come when you whistled? It's an *it*?" Bub snorted disbelief, contempt. "Well, I just don't know about you, Colby . . . but I'll tell you this: I'll be goddamned if I'm going to drink to an *it* and I mean that. You want me to drink to your dog you can goddamn well name him here and now. Call him dog or motherfucker or shit-for-brains, but call him by goddamn something. And I mean that. Don't I, Lucky? Don't I mean that?"

"In Vietnam they eat dogs," said Lucky, back with the cook now, putting tomatoes and lettuce on a bun.

182

"Well, fuck you, Luckster, this ain't Vietnam!"

"Watch your mouth, Bub. There's ladies present." Lucky nodded toward a table where Lynn Gable and her sister, Amy, who worked across the road at Ace Hardware, had just sat down.

Bub gave another snort, this one of dismissal, downed his shot, and went back to watching the ballgame.

Feeling both dogged and dogged, Colby sat there for a moment, still squeezing his glass. Then he took a drink. "Lassie," he finally said, more to himself than anybody. "How about I call him Lassie?"

Bub wasn't listening. The Cards had just tied up the game, had a runner on third with no outs.

Driving back to the farm, Colby wondered if the dog would be there waiting for him again. Lassie. It had just sort of popped into his head at the bar—a pretty dumb-ass name for a dick-swinger. Must have been thinking about the old movie, *Lassie Come Home*. He'd seen it years ago as a kid, had never forgotten it. He could still see the dog whining at the front door, back from climbing mountains, swimming rivers—even getting shot at—half dead, battered and bloody, but come hell or high water, wanting to be let in.

Colby made up his mind right then and there, swinging off the county blacktop, if he *did* find the dog at home again, that would be the end of it. No more trips to the dump. He didn't care what Ray-J said. Far as he was concerned the dog could stay on the farm and outlive the both of them.

The more he thought about the guy in East St. Louis getting shot five times in the head, the more he got to thinking about shooting the dog: how being at such close range, he'd actually managed to fire the bullet that second time into the earlier wound. It now occurred to him that the second bullet might very well have slammed smack into the other one—just like in Slater's story. Meaning the first bullet just may have stopped that second bullet dead in its tracks. Instead of the dog.

And the closer he got to the farm, the more he found himself believing that's exactly what happened. Hell, that dog was just too mean to die. He'd be there all right, waiting in his favorite spot by the stoop just like before. Colby, he'd climb out of the truck and call his name—he wouldn't whistle—he'd call "Lassie! Lassie!" over and over as he walked right up to him and gave him a pat. He'd pour him a bowl of cold milk to drink—no, for all his troubles, he'd, by god, cook him a steak! Bandage up that hole in his head too. Maybe later they'd take a drive over to the vet, see about extracting the bullets.

When he pulled into the drive, the dog was nowhere to be seen. Colby supposed he shouldn't be surprised, but he was. He'd wanted him to be there so badly, never mind the colliding bullet theory, had so convinced himself of the dog's toughness, his invincibility. . . .

He got out of the truck and walked around the house, whistling— no sense calling out the name Lassie, the dog wouldn't know it— even searched the barn, the old crib and silo. When he finally brought himself to realize the dog wasn't there, he had a feeling so heavy in his chest it seemed about as far from surprise as he could ever get.

"Took you long enough," said Ray-J when he told her the deed was done. He shrugged and stood there waiting for her to say something else, but she turned and walked out of the room without another word.

In the kitchen he reminded her that he'd done exactly what she'd asked him to do, that she ought to be happy. "Oh, I'm jumping for joy," she said. Then she pointed to the sink full of dishes and thanked him for leaving them there for her to stare at all day, accused him of doing it just to piss her off. He couldn't believe how she was acting. If anything she was even more sour-tempered than before, seemed particularly upset that he hadn't gone on the Cairo run.

"You said you were going today. You told me you were going," she kept harping over a dinner of Kentucky Fried, extra crispy, he'd picked up in town. As though he were guilty of breaking some sort of promise. When he asked her what all the fuss was about, why it made any difference whether he left today or tomorrow, she got angry. She lit up a cigarette, took several puffs, stuffed it out, lit up another and went on how she needed a break every now and then, how much she was counting on it, time by herself. . . .

Colby wanted to tell her about stopping off at Lucky's, giving the dog a name. Instead he forked in a mouthful of slaw, continued for the rest of the meal, eating in silence.

Later that night, unable to fall asleep, he got out of bed—Ray-J was snoring away all full of Jack and spite—went downstairs to make a ham sandwich and pour himself a beer.

While he sat at the kitchen table eating his sandwich, he noticed through the hallway a ring of light moving across a wall in the darkness of the dining room. He got up and walked over to a window.

He could see a car creeping partway up the drive, wondered who that could be this time of night. When it came to a stop near his truck, one headlight cockeyed, shining off into the trees, he had no doubts. Wade Enis's Malibu. A moment later it was slowly backing out. He watched it swing around onto the country road and speed off, stood there watching till its red taillights disappeared behind a field of high corn, the darkness like a wave of gloom, filling in silently behind it.

He sat back down, didn't touch his sandwich, finished his beer. There was one more beer in the fridge and he finished that one too. Then he just sat for awhile trying not to think.

Finally he got up, turned off the lights, and headed upstairs.

Ray-J had rolled over, was no longer snoring, though appeared to be asleep. Kicking off his slippers, about to climb back into bed, he felt for one caught moment like shaking her awake, getting in her ear; next thing he was remembering the rifle still out in the pickup, that he'd forgotten to bring it in. As he stood there staring down at her, she began to blur, grow fainter and fainter before his eyes until he was gazing right on through her to the coldest ashes of his own desire.

Of a sudden he inhaled fear, choked on it, looked quickly away, trembling, as if searching the room for something long missing within himself . . . a vague memory, a distant, forgotten notion— everything somehow fitting together differently.

He was still standing there trembling when he thought he heard a noise—the sound of scratching at the back door. Without stopping to put on his slippers, he hurried downstairs again.

He unlocked the back door and opened it. Nothing was there. He even stepped out on the porch barefoot and stood for awhile searching the yard, moonlit and swollen with shadows. There was little wind, nothing moving that he could see. He gave a whistle, whistled again. Nothing. He started to go back inside, then spun around.

"Lassie . . ." he called out—feeling silly as he did—did it anyway. "Lassie, you out there, boy?"

Nominated by Antioch Review

A DAY IN MAY: LOS ANGELES, 1960

by PHILIP LEVINE

from THE GEORGIA REVIEW

A FEW DAYS AGO I got a call from a reporter from the San Francisco *Chronicle* informing me that my old friend, the poet Thom Gunn, had died in his sleep, probably of a heart attack. This fellow had the task of writing his obituary, and somehow he'd gotten my name. I was stunned into silence for a time. I couldn't believe it: the Thom I saw in my mind's eye was so young, and energetic, surrounded by an aura of mystery I'd never penetrated—and also so generous and loving. The guy in the motorcycle jacket and jeans I'd met in 1957 at Stanford was tall and slender, a few years younger than I but so much more a man of the world, moving with the very grace of his marvelous poems which I knew before I knew him and which had made me want to know him. I began to answer the reporter's questions—how had I met him, what had he meant to me, to American poetry. The more I talked about him the more I wanted to talk about him, for he had been such a fixed star in my poetry world, someone I learned from—not only how to write poems about the world I'd lived in but also how to face rejection. After thirty minutes the reporter seemed to awaken and said he had to go off to write this article, time was getting short; then he was gone and I was alone with my remembrances.

My mind drifted to the day I first got to know Gunn well, the first day I truly shared with him, a day I hadn't mentioned to the reporter. For me it was an unusually long and rich day in Los Angeles, involving three other writers. Now all of them are dead and I'm the only one left to tell the story—perhaps I should say tell my version of the story of that day, tailored and trimmed by imagination and memory.

For me the day began at 5:00 A.M., for I had to drive from Fresno, California, to Los Angeles to collect Thom and John Berryman at the LA airport. They were flying down from Berkeley where Thom was a regular at the university and where John was teaching for the spring semester. The three of us were scheduled to read at Los Angeles State College (as it was then called) that day in the early afternoon. At the time I'd given only a few public readings, and I found the prospect of this day both daunting and exciting. Their plane was scheduled to arrive at 10:15, and much to my surprise I made it on time, driving a terrible Chevy I'd requisitioned from Fresno State, where I was completing my second year of teaching. (I had serious doubts my old Ford would have made it at all.)

I hadn't seen John Berryman since I'd said goodbye to him at the Iowa City airport six years before in the spring of 1954, and much had happened since. For one thing, we'd each married for the second time, but now I had three sons. John's second marriage was to a woman named Levine with whom he'd fathered his only son. He had also published his breakthrough volume, *Homage to Mistress Bradstreet*, which had received some of the acclaim it deserved.

In other ways, nothing had changed. John was still cleanshaven, dressed in a semi-Brooks Brothers style which failed to hide his gangly build and terrible posture. Thom, incredibly handsome—dark haired, hawk nosed in a forties British film star manner—was doing his best to look American, sporting a baseball cap and wearing a red jacket, the lettering of which spelled Forty Niners in the appropriate script. When the two poets emerged from the plane and saw me waiting, Thom—flashing a huge smile—yelled, "See, what did I tell you!"

John looked stunned. "Levine," he shouted at me, "what have you done to yourself? You've shrunk!"

It seems that on the plane the two poets had argued over my size, John insisting I was enormous, the size of a Chicago Bears linebacker, and Thom just as certain I was a relatively small man, shorter than either of them—which I was—and no heavier than Thom. (At the time I was five feet ten inches tall and weighed around one hundred sixty-five pounds, pretty much what I am now, only the pounds

187

are in different places; just why John remembered me as a brute is another story I'd just as soon not tell.)

In the years I'd known John, he'd never taken being wrong very well, and this occasion was no exception. He needed something quickly to recover from the shock of my shrinkage, which he feared was related to some life-threatening medical problem. "Does this airport have a bar," he said, "or have we burrowed further into incivility than even Berkeley?"

Fortunately I knew the location of a bar in the airport near where I was parked, a towerlike structure the top of which turned slowly to reveal clouds of collecting pollution through which the airplanes rising and descending broke every few minutes. Thom—never much of a drinker—ordered a glass of orange juice; I went for seltzer on the rocks. Unfazed, John asked for a double martini and then began to explain his new theory of drink.

"When last I saw you, Levine, my drinking was not in hand, for which I'm sorry, but since then I've mastered the art." He went on to explain the cardinal points of this new approach. "To begin with, you never *never* drink in bars; it's a huge waste of money, and one is liable to meet all sorts of unsavory characters while inebriated and possibly defenseless." Ordering a second martini, he seemed perfectly apt at ignoring where he was. "I went to the master drinker, William Empson," he said, "and he explained that it is all quite simple: one discovers what is ideal for one and drinks that and only that. Quite simple. In the morning one fills a carafe with one's chosen spirits, and when the day wears on and it's empty, one's drinking for that day is over. *Over* completely," he shouted in that strange high voice of his that dogs could barely hear.

"How large a carafe?" I inquired.

"In my case, one *litre*." In his crazy accent you could hear the British spelling.

Our host for the day was the poet Henri Coulette, and so we drove to his apartment in South Pasadena. Henri had met John when I did, when we studied with John in a wonderful poetry writing class he taught at the University of Iowa back in 1954, the only class of its kind he ever taught, and certainly one of the finest anyone ever taught. John had a yen to see Forest Lawn cemetery, and Henri—a native Angeleno and the only one of us who'd ever visited it—took us to the place. Upon entering the grounds, we found a man busily whitewashing an enormous reproduction of Michelangelo's *David*. "The perfect piece of art for a cemetery," remarked John. "Being dead isn't bad enough—they have to remind you of what life looked like at its most glorious."

The place was enormous and confusing, so Henri went off to find some sort of map or guide and returned with a young man dressed in funereal black who pretended to be familiar with the name of John Berryman, the eminent American poet.

"You may visit any part of the park," he told us; "merely remember to be respectful of the graves. Picnicking is not allowed."

John wanted to know where the most famous of the old-time film stars were buried.

"Up there," the young man said, pointing to a hilltop, "where the views are most spectacular."

"Do you expect the deceased to enjoy the view?" John asked.

No, that luxury was there for the mourners.

It turned out there was a poets' corner in the cemetery, to which we immediately headed, but among the gravestones was not a single name any of us had ever encountered before. John was disgusted and wanted out immediately. He wanted to know where they'd found these "women of both sexes with three names" and how they had dubbed them poets. Thom patiently talked him out of returning to the young man and challenging him to present us with their credentials as poets. "John, the guy is just doing his job."

"When your countrymen have a poets' corner, as they do in Westminster Abbey," John railed, "they put Milton and Dryden in it. Can't we do better than these nonentities who never published in anything but local newspapers? I'm forgetting vanity presses. One mustn't forget vanity presses."

Thom then recalled asking to see the tomb of Andrew Marvell—an early hero of his—in the great cathedral of York. "It took me almost an hour to find anyone who'd heard the name." It turned out this old cleric for whom the name had resonance told him with disgust how Marvell's remains had long ago been stolen for Westminster Abbey.

Henri, who had raised the money for today's reading as well as organized the program, explained how it would work. Thom and I would share the first forty minutes, and then Berryman would read for forty minutes. Christopher Isherwood, who was a screenwriter at a major

Hollywood studio and was that term teaching a course at LA State entitled "Auden and Others"—"Mainly a few hours of fascinating chat," said Henri—had asked to introduce Thom, who appeared very touched by this information. He said he'd met Isherwood and presented him with his most recent book, but had no idea he'd read it. Henri would do the honors for John and me. Being the least experienced reader and certainly the least known of the group—I hadn't yet published a book—I asked to go first. The event would take place in the college theater for an audience that Coulette estimated at five hundred or more: Isherwood had asked to be allowed to take us all to a late lunch at some swanky place in Hollywood once the reading was over.

While I paced nervously backstage, a little, tanned, muscular man in short sleeves—no doubt a stagehand, I thought—with the most gorgeous smile in the world wished me luck in what I took to be an Italian accent. I was too distracted to hear any of Coulette's introduction. The lighting was dramatic: the audience in darkness, a single spot on the reader, who stood behind a podium. The sound system was superb, and within a single poem I warmed to the task and didn't do badly (my previous reading, with Gary Snyder in North Beach, had been a disaster: for me, not for Gary, who'd read splendidly). I then took Thom's seat in the front row, to watch the Italian stagehand introduce him. The man had donned a blue double-breasted blazer and was none other than Christopher Isherwood.

Thom had then and for the rest of his career a very modest style of reading; he read with enough emotion to demonstrate his seriousness, but he never went over the top. He spoke little between poems —just enough to mark a pause between one poem and another; he clarified whatever references required clarification, but unlike many readers today he never spoke so much that the poem itself came as an anticlimax since you'd already learned what was coming. That day I was still too far into my own reading to catch the first few poems; besides, I knew the poems so well I could have recited them, for most of what he read was from a book that had deeply influenced me, *The Sense of Movement*, his second book. When he came to the poem "My Sad Captains" and several others from a volume-to-be, I suddenly awoke, for these were some of the most accomplished syllabic poems ever written, and marked a new departure in his work. Thom had already found a style that perfectly suited his nature, and he never let his private life intrude on his readings. He fulfilled my notion of what a poet's stage presence ought to be. Years later I heard him laugh over a long-remembered reading by Marianne Moore; he claimed he didn't know when she was explaining the poem, examining her life, gossiping, or simply reading what was on the page. After a while he thought her explanations—which often came in the middle of the poem—were merely portions of the poem she'd neglected to write.

That day, Thom was very much at ease, very much the same man on stage as the one offstage. He put the audience at ease.

An audience at ease was exactly what Berryman did not want. It's hard to say just what he did want besides their full attention. After Coulette's lavish introduction, John came out slowly, stared at the audience, and murmured "My heavings" into the microphone. He seemed genuinely moved to be standing before such a large and totally silent audience, and he began with an anecdote.

"The last reading I gave," he said, "was in a basement classroom on the campus at UC Berkeley, no doubt arranged by either the Dean of Death or my first wife. There was not a shred of publicity, though all the readers—Thom, Louis Simpson, and I—are currently on the faculty. As I told the audience of twelve—which included the readers— I had no idea why I was so nervous since there were more students in my 9:00 A.M. class when the girls showed up." Pause. "But then the girls never showed up." All this was delivered in that strange, breathless voice that hovered between a tenor and an alto in his Ivy League-fraudulent English accent. At any moment he seemed on the verge of collapse from the burden of so much emotion. The audience roared, and without further comment he launched into the recitation of a Chinese poem in Chinese, which he did not bother to translate, then to Jon Silkin's little-known, extraordinary poem "Death of a Son (who died in a mental hospital age one)," and from there to one of Blake's less known songs, "To Night."

As Coulette later remarked, John had a way of reading that made you think you were encountering the poem for the first time. The audience was utterly silent, hypnotized or awed. Then he presented a group of poems from his recently published pamphlet, "His thoughts made pockets & the plane buckt." These were the first composed poems of what would later be called *The Dream Songs*, and we—the

191

poets in the audience, perhaps the entire audience—were stunned by the originality, the combination of wit and seriousness, and the sheer vitality and resourcefulness of the writing.

Before he read them he gave us a short explanation. "I want this to be clear. What you are about to hear is not autobiography. This fellow Henry, who occupies center stage in many of these poems, is not to be confused with me or Mr. Coulette or any other Henry you may happen to know. He is a poetic invention not of the stature of Hamlet or Lear, but unlike those inventions he is both contemporary and entirely mine." Then John threw himself into the poems totally. It was obvious that he believed they were what he was meant to write, what he had been preparing for all his poetic life. When he finished to tumultuous applause he seemed completely spent.

Before the lights came on, Isherwood, who was seated behind me, tapped me on the shoulder and informed me that my mother was in the audience. "Charming woman," he said. He seemed to think this was amazing, as if she'd come all the way from Detroit to hear me, and not from Culver City, five miles away. Or perhaps he thought it was ordinary—he had a way of saying things that made them sound very special.

And then the lights did come on. As I made my way out of the theater I was assailed by an enormous black man who had in tow a gorgeous tall woman of uncertain ethnicity; she could easily have been a Samoan princess out of a Jon Hall movie. Once she opened her mouth, it was clear she was an American and, I would guess, a theater major. The man and woman had made a wager on which of the other two readers was English. The man—who was actually the poet Michael Harper, then a student of Coulette's—insisted it was Gunn who was English; the woman was just as sure it was Berryman. I wanted to side with her, but it was my sad duty to inform her that Gunn was the only true Englishman. She was stymied. Where had he gotten that accent? "He was born in Oklahoma," I said, which though true explained nothing. At the time, I was as puzzled as she.

We were then taken outside in a group, the three readers and two introducers, and photographed for the college publicity department against the backdrop of one of the more hideous state buildings. (The various branches of the California State University system look designed by some architect who'd apprenticed under Mussolini's cultural minister and failed. I have since tried without success to obtain

192

a copy of one of the photographs, but they seem to have vanished.) From there we were whisked to a tony Hollywood restaurant of Isherwood's choosing. Berryman immediately ordered another martini while ogling the voluptuous woman who had seated us. She seemed to have a particular affection for Isherwood, addressing him as Christopher.

The contrast between Christopher and John was severe. John was all motion: tall, badly coordinated, he seemed to be moving in several directions at the same time, always with a cigarette in one hand and demanding attention. I would not say he was singularly ugly—he was funny looking; there was too much unaccounted-for space between his upper lip and his nose and, since he rarely stopped talking, one's eyes were drawn to that spot. Isherwood, on the other hand, was short, compactly built, and incredibly handsome, the sort of looks one associates with an Olympic oarsman; and though he was lined around the eyes, which were wide and beautiful, he was one of those men who look young until they are suddenly truly old (the British film actor Tom Courtney is another example of the type). He was also deeply tanned from his morning ocean swims; he had the aura of true health, inner and outer. In a word he was beautiful. Furthermore, unlike Berryman, he seemed to have no particular need to talk.

Once he got a martini and then a second one, John seemed to have no particular interest in eating. Thom and I ripped into a seafood platter that was the specialty of the house. Christopher was sorry that nothing of interest was going on at the studio or he would have gladly taken us on a tour. He then told a story of the last time he'd taken a poet on a tour of the studio, the poet being a young Robert Lowell. They happened upon the set of a Jayne Mansfield movie in which she was receiving a back massage clad only in a towel that covered her from the waist down. For some reason the filming was interrupted and Miss Mansfield sat up, revealing her breasts, which Isherwood then described as large, and he said, holding both hands high above his chest, "I suppose the way men like them." Within less than a minute a wardrobe mistress covered her with a bathrobe. Christopher then took Lowell on the sets of several other films, and then to lunch at the studio dining room, which was packed with film stars. Lowell seemed curiously distracted and finally asked, "You don't suppose we could return to the Mansfield set?" Isherwood assured him that in all his years in Hollywood he'd never seen anything quite like what they'd observed that morning. Lowell still insisted. When they returned to the set, they were in the process of filming another scene in which Miss Mansfield was fully clothed. Lowell called it quits.

Berryman was curiously silent during the telling of this tale. I thought he was simply worn out from the reading, which had been incredibly intense. Soon the beautiful hostess who had first directed us to our table appeared at Christopher's side to inform him that a car was waiting for him from the studio. He was being summoned back to work.

"I should be grateful," he said; "they gave me half of the day off, but I feel I would like to stay with all of you. Please, stay as long as you like, and eat and drink whatever you like. It's all on me, or rather the studio." He assured us that we were in the capable hands of the hostess, who would see to all our needs within reason. And he was gone.

No sooner had he left than Berryman announced, "It's not fair."

Thom asked him what wasn't fair.

"Did you see," John said, "how that gorgeous woman couldn't take her hands off him, and he couldn't give a fig for any woman. Here I am, totally enthralled with her, and she doesn't know I'm alive. He has it all and I have nothing."

Thom tried to talk him out of it. "John," he said, "Christopher is a name in Hollywood. He comes here frequently; he comes here with celebrities from the studio. Of course they pay special attention to him. It means nothing about you; it means he's Christopher Isherwood." But Berryman clung to his funk, insisting that life wasn't fair, especially to him. Finally Coulette suggested we visit a particular bar in downtown LA that would be full of attractive women who would fall all over John, so off we went in Coulette's Jaguar sedan. Unfortunately, when we arrived at the bar it was almost empty; still, somehow Berryman's mood shifted upward noticeably when a tall blond woman came to our booth to take our orders.

"You could make me very happy," said John. "Do you know how?"

The woman had the good sense to say nothing.

"All you have to do is tell me that man"—and he pointed at the bartender, who seemed half asleep beneath the silent television screen—"tell me he knows how to fix a proper double martini."

That she could do, she assured him, and the rest of us breathed a sigh of relief.

It must have been in the hilarity that followed John's first taste of his martini, which he claimed was, though not perfect, by far the best he'd encountered west of the Hudson, and he had encountered numberless examples—it must have been in that moment that I agreed to do something remarkably stupid, something I should never have done.

Thom had told Berryman that I could do an imitation of him that was almost perfect. Berryman said, "I've heard you've been passing yourself off as me, Levine. It won't do; any fool can tell a Berryman from a Levine. For one thing, since you've shrunk you're too short to be a Berryman, though I must admit you've done a credible job of foisting off your terrible poems on the even more terrible editors of literary magazines."

When dealing with individual poems of mine, John could say remarkably useful and insightful things—he was an absolutely superb practical critic, the best I had then encountered. But he took pleasure in referring to my work as a whole as my "terrible poems." Perhaps hearing that remark for the twentieth time I was more than a little peeved; in any case, I launched my voice into that particularly hysterical style that marked his reading and gave him back one of his favorite passages from "Song of Myself."

Thom exploded with laughter. "Perfect, Phil. You've got him perfectly."

Berryman simply rose from the booth and left the bar, though where he might go in downtown Los Angeles, a city he did not know, was anyone's guess. "That was a mistake," Coulette said, and I knew he was right. Thom wondered if we ought to go looking for John, certain that he could be lost in five minutes. Coulette was more sanguine. "Stay right here," he said, "He'll be back in no time."

Of course he was right. In less than ten minutes John was back. He'd purchased a box of Band-Aids at a drugstore and was determined to plaster one across my mouth, something I was not about to let him do. I apologized for what I'd done and claimed it was not meant as an imitation but rather as a cruel parody, which only demonstrated the weakness of my character.

"You did not sound like me, not for a second!" John snapped. "Your mouth should be sewn shut forever for taking your master in vain."

I assured him I'd learned my lesson and henceforth I would never take his name or his voice in vain.

By this time we'd tired of the empty bar, and the rest of us were more than a little exhausted by John. It was now late afternoon, and John wondered if it were possible to visit one of the storied hangouts of the Beats, who were known to "infest the city." He was immensely curious about these characters who'd seized so much attention and had managed to pass themselves off as artists and poets, although as far as he could tell none of them could write anything worth reading.

"They don't understand Whitman, they imitate his worst mannerisms. They don't understand Buddhism, but they have mastered the art of self-promotion," he said. He was reminded of a remark F. R. Leavis had made regarding the Sitwells, which he quoted: "Theirs is not a chapter in the history of literature but one in the history of public relations." Ginsberg he especially belittled, and I wondered if he weren't a little jealous of someone who was quickly becoming the spokesperson for an entire generation.

Coulette knew exactly the place where John could view the Beats in their native habitat. It was in Venice, by the sea. As we left, Thom asked to be dropped off. I wasn't sure whether it was because he was worn out by John's shenanigans or whether he simply had better things to do. I also knew that Thom had great regard for some of the so-called Beat writers, whom he knew personally in San Francisco, especially Robert Duncan. In any event we dropped him off in Santa Monica and headed south to Venice.

The place we arrived at was a huge barnlike structure only a few hundred yards from the Pacific. It looked as though it had been furnished from a Salvation Army warehouse. Beer, wine, and soft drinks were all they served, although the place reeked of pot. Fortunately they carried Ballantine ale, one of John's favorites, and we went off to inspect the premises.

What we first stumbled into was a huge, sparsely furnished post-Victorian living room with several large chairs from which the stuffing was leaking, and two old couches that faced each other at a distance of six feet or so. On one sat a cleanshaven, quite presentable young man, and on the other, facing him, a woman of about his age wearing Levis and a white blouse. Neither was reading, although between them was a low table stacked with books. In fact, they didn't seem to be doing anything at all; and it seemed unlikely that they'd been speaking to each other or ever intended to do so.

"Have you two been introduced?" John said. "If not, I would be more than glad to do the honors."

The woman, who was extremely attractive even without a touch of makeup on, said nothing; she neither looked away nor looked at any of us, but merely continued to stare off at nothing we could see. The young man finally said, "Thanks, but don't bother."

The place was quite warm. John removed his jacket, rolled up his sleeves over his slender forearms, and pacing back and forth between the two young people, he began to lecture the air. "This is what is meant by being 'Beat.' One is reduced to complete passivity, to accepting as little as possible. While this man in any other circumstances would make some sort of overture to this very handsome woman, or this woman might acknowledge his presence, or ours, or even flirt a teeny bit—even though that is a practice banished to the previous century—these two do nothing at all. And they do it with great determination, and I suppose skill. They are about the work of being 'Beat,' and the poetry written by them or about them or for them will do exactly as much as they are presently doing, which is to say *nothing*."

At last the young man looked up at John and said, "Yup, you got it."

Berryman soon ran out of patience with these two. He was also sure the beer had been watered—or, worse, was not what it was advertised to be. "Beer is at best not much," he said, "but I think this was brewed in Munich in 1944 and the Bavarians used sawdust instead of grain." He wanted whiskey; it seemed to him years since he'd had a real glass of whiskey. Coulette said he had an unopened bottle of Chivas at his place, and John thought that might just hold him until dinner.

At the time Coulette was living in a second floor apartment in South Pasadena with his wife Jackie, a public school teacher. Just as we were about to turn down his street, the police pulled over the car ahead of us, a convertible carrying two suntanned young surfer types in the front seats. We stopped behind the two cars. Shirtless, the blond driver leaped out to face one of the cops, who immediately pushed a revolver into his bare belly and forced him to bend over the hood of his car.

197

John, who was sitting next to Coulette in the front seat, shouted, "Stop it! He's going to kill that man for driving without his shirt on!" He seemed perfectly serious and enraged. "These are storm troopers! They should wear black shirts like the SS!" He'd never seen anything like it in America, but he'd heard all about the incredible brutality of LA cops, and now he could see that what he'd heard was true. Coulette assured him that he'd lived in the Los Angeles area most of his life and he'd never seen anything like this either. "It's exactly like what Isherwood told us about taking Lowell through the studio," he said. "Once in his life he sees a naked woman on the set, but Lowell thinks it's a daily occurrence. The visitor comes to Los Angeles, and the city does its worst to be LA."

Berryman was unconvinced. "Levine, you saw it. You're from Detroit, a place notorious for brutality. Did you ever see anything like this?"

No, I hadn't, but then men didn't go around half-naked in Detroit. I'd seen police brutality, it just looked different when it wasn't out in this dazzling sunshine. I told him I'd seen a cop beating a man while another cop held a gun on him, but that was in jail. It wasn't out for the whole world to see.

Berryman was shaken, and claimed he needed a drink badly; the Chivas would do although he'd switched to bourbon as a regular drink.

How did the day end? I too began drinking and, as I lacked the capacity of either Berryman or Henri Coulette, my memory of events from here on gets hazy. I know the three of us and Coulette's wife Jackie went out to a steakhouse for dinner. Feeling sick from a sudden attack of tachycardia (something I've lived with since I was a child); I went out into the alley behind the restaurant and threw up. Later Henri came out to check on me, and I told him the worst was over, which was true; my heartbeat had returned to normal.

Someone picked up the check, probably Henri. We stopped off at his apartment, which was near John's hotel. Jackie, who operated as Henri's publicist, wanted him to show John a poem he'd recently published in *The Paris Review*, a superb poem about a loner who lives in a huge park in LA. Berryman misread the poem; he seemed to think it was written in syllabics. Henri and I had both been experimenting with syllabics for some years, but this poem was not one of those experiments. We endured a drunken lecture on the proper use

198

of syllabics, though the poem in question was clearly written in rhymed tetrameter, and though as far as I could tell John—who'd never written in syllabics—knew nothing about the form.

Jackie excused herself, sensibly, and went to bed. An hour later we wound up at the hotel where John was staying, the Green Hotel in Pasadena, now no longer extant. When we arrived the revelers from a high school graduation dance were leaving. Most of the men looked as drunk as John, while the women were lovely in their satiny gowns that revealed their tan shoulders and a good measure of their young bosoms. John simply stood and stared until the last of them left. Once again he cursed his rotten luck for being so ugly and so old. It was impossible to know if he was serious. At the time, though badly used he didn't look any older than he was—forty-six; he was in possession of his hair and still quite slender and wiry. He had once congratulated himself for not being handsome, and assured me that beautiful people did not write memorable poetry, but that I should not despair for, like him, I was ugly enough to be a great poet.

I know the night ended, but I'm not completely sure how. Once we got to John's room, he pleaded for a bottle of bourbon. Room service was out of the question. "They rob you," he announced, no doubt from considerable experience. He gave me a short list of his favorites and I left him with Henri in attendance while he stretched out on his bed berating Coulette for letting him devour so many martinis and so much poisonous Scotch. "If my wife had been here she would have managed me better."

I know I went out in search of a liquor store. Henri had drawn me a map and assured me it was only a few blocks away. Not trusting myself to drive, I decided to walk, but the streets curved and often suddenly ended, and before long I was completely lost. I searched my pockets but the map was gone. I know I wandered helplessly for what seemed like hours and had no idea where I was. At one point I caught up with a woman carrying a small suitcase, which gave me hope that she could point me the way to the Green Hotel. By this time the sky was turning gray and I knew the dawn couldn't be far off. Unfortunately, she spoke no English, and at the time I knew no Spanish. We stood side by side at a traffic light at one of those wide boulevards with no traffic, I helpless and she on her way somewhere, perhaps to a job or a waiting family. She seemed for no reason I could fathom more than a little scared of me.

I know by this time I was sober, and that somehow an hour or so later—certainly by accident—I stumbled on the way to the Coulettes' apartment building; there I found the state car where I'd left it the day before. It seemed pointless to awaken the Coulettes at 5:00 A.M. I chose to leave LA before the traffic got going and the freeways jammed up, and was back in Fresno in four hours. More than a little wrecked, I slept for much of that Saturday. I know that when I recovered I didn't care whether I ever saw John Berryman again, which was awful since he was the finest teacher I'd ever had. I knew then a terrible truth that has remained with me to this day: love can die within me. The most brilliant man I'd ever known was both going mad and killing himself, and I was shocked into an emotional silence. He was simply no longer the John Berryman I'd known, the generous teacher whose friendship I once valued as much as any I'd ever made; and I was no longer the young man who had adored him. My Berryman was gone, and so was the Levine of 1954, and there was nothing I could think of to do about it.

I began this remembrance with the hope of presenting the Thom Gunn I knew for forty-five years, but having chosen to write about that particular day, I let Berryman dominate the narrative just as he'd dominated the day. His demand for attention was epic, whereas Thom, who was so much less needy, could simply let the world come to him. John, when I knew him earlier, had his good days, but I had already seen him behave just as irrationally when drinking. He could be generous, kindly toward others, gentle, and in class was always both brilliant and candid. Somehow he seemed able to leave behind his madness. I believe he regarded teaching as a high calling, and he gave it his all, never compromising his beliefs to win the popularity or affection of his poetry students.

Thom was something else. Without the least effort on his part, he seemed larger than life. He was one of the half dozen or so people I've known who had what I'll call an "aura," a sort of inner beauty that was manifest in all his actions. I doubt he was aware of how beautiful he was. Over the years he grew more noble; I know that's a ridiculous word to use in a contemporary context, but it seems right. His sweetness was overwhelming; each time I saw him over the years it was evident.

I remember once in particular in a restaurant in Berkeley, as I approached he got up, walked over to me, and said "Phil," as though it were a charmed name; he put his hands on my shoulders and kissed me. He seemed totally unafraid to display his feelings. The first time he visited me in Fresno, I came back from some domestic chore to discover him in a rapt conversation with my three sons, the oldest of whom was twelve at the time. They were utterly relaxed in his presence and he in theirs, talking—of course—about contemporary pop music, which they were just discovering and about which Thom knew a surprising amount. No sooner had he left than they wanted to know when he was coming back. If Thom Gunn was who poets were, they were all for poets. Unfortunately for poets, but fortunately for him, he was not; never once in all the years did I ever hear him make a single reference to what we could call "a career," or complain that his work was not anthologized or revered. A much more typical remark from him was the following, made when he had just returned to California from England in the late 1960s: "You won't believe this, Phil," he said. "They've discovered fun in England."

We took to exchanging books over the years, and we would comment on each other's work. I'll never forget one remark he made in a letter he sent me in 1974 after he read my book *1933*. "Be careful, Phil," he wrote; "you are in danger of sentimentalizing the child you were." Such tact. I reread the book with his warning in mind and saw that I had already done what I was in danger of doing.

He also had a marvelous sense of humor and perfect timing. In the early 1960s an editor at McGraw-Hill brought us together with the poet William Stafford to put together a freshman reader by poets for the enormous audience that hungered for it; we were promised a large advance and the certainty of a huge success. The meeting took place in a hotel suite in Berkeley after a huge, mediocre meal in the hotel dining room. The editor—a big, sympathetic man you knew immediately had failed at everything he'd ever tried—acted as though he knew everything about selling books. He wanted each of us to name pieces—essays, stories, poems—we thought essential. Gunn and I seemed in accord; together we agreed on a list that included Sartre's essays on American cities, "America" by Allen Ginsberg, work by Henry Miller, Jean Genet, Pierre Gascar, A. J. Liebling, William Blake, James Baldwin, George Orwell, Rebecca West, Elizabeth Bishop, Paul Goodman, Gary Snyder—writers we felt young people wouldn't otherwise encounter and needed to read. We both wanted a reader like no other. After enduring our proposals in silence for twenty minutes, Stafford made it clear that he could not put his name on a reader that lacked Milton's "Areopagitica." I re-

201

marked that the freshman students I taught at Fresno State could never stay awake through the entire essay. The editor had a great fondness for Stafford, but he saw immediately that we were not the right mix. Conversation flagged, and soon Thom and I decided it was time to get back to San Francisco—Thom to his apartment, I to the digs of friends. As we stood waiting for the elevator, I said, "I really like his poems"—meaning Stafford's, of course. "So do I," said Thom, and then after a brief pause, "I wonder who writes them."

A few years back, he hosted two readings by August Kleinzahler and me, the first on the campus of UC Berkeley, the second at Berkeley High. At the second, which took place on a beautiful late morning in spring, we read to a small audience that was enclosed inside a much larger audience made up of students who had no interest in poetry. I was amazed by Thom's tact; he bargained with a group of large, tough-looking young women—if they would sit quietly in a corner at the back of this vast room and speak softly and not giggle loudly as they removed their nail polish, he would not bring the wrath of their teachers and counselors down on them. As he arranged it, the event was a delight; we had about twenty-five kids directly in front of us who were taken with poetry, and in the background a sort of low tidal sound that disturbed no one. The hour ended with all of us satisfied.

I thought then: Gunn is some sort of angel sent to earth to make us all feel better, and sometimes—when he was Thom Gunn the magnificent poet—to feel very deeply about our lives as well as the lives we didn't live or didn't comprehend until we lived inside his poems. I can't believe how much we've lost.

Nominated by Lucia Perillo, David St. John; Len Roberts; Charles Harper Webb; Christopher Buckley, Wesley McNair

A THOUGHT, FOR EXAMPLE, IS A FORM

by MARY ANN SAMYN

from NEW ISSUES POETRY AND PROSE

—Of light. And at the center, light. And at the edges,
more light. This is you, all the way through. You turn

your arm—say *arm*, think it, even—but
the thinking's light too, that's the rub.

Arm light, ear light, chin light. Head to—
Can you travel this way? Can you be your own lantern?

One of the difficulties is that I love what's special.
Mine Mine Mine. Glorious.

Got it? It almost works too well: the darkness,
the shaft and going down and *hand me that lamp*,

will you? So that when I asked the question,
I was hoping for a better answer, i.e. clarity.

But once you've coaxed *that* out, then what?
A path of fieldstones and each one more blank—

more *cleared*—than the last? Oh, terrific.
And have you looked it up in the dictionary?

Unbelievable: *electromagnetic radiation* something
or other, ellipses mine, *perceived by the unaided,*

normal human eye. Or I. You know: who you are.
It doesn't get anymore complicated than this,

and yet it does. Not simply daybreak, wake up,
rise and shine, but worse, as in *can you throw some light*

on the question—you—curled there on the bed?
The point being that you can't see it. The point.

Of light. Where it enters. The top of your head:
tousled hair, too too sleepy. How can this be

and does anyone want to take this shift while I
clean up a bit? Or is this the way a fire cleans?

You know: first the light and then the hurt
and then the new shoots and how the deer love it.

Nominated by New Issues Poetry & Prose, Kathy Fagan

PERSEPHONE THE WANDERER

by LOUISE GLÜCK

from TRIQUARTERLY

In the first version, Persephone
is taken from her mother
and the goddess of the earth
punishes the earth—this is
consistent with what we know of human behavior,

that human beings take profound satisfaction
in doing harm, particularly
unconscious harm:

we may call this
negative creation.

Persephone's initial
sojourn in hell continues to be
pawed over by scholars who dispute
the sensations of the virgin:

did she cooperate in her rape,
or was she drugged, violated against her will,
as happens so often now to modern girls.

As is well known, the return of the beloved
does not correct
the loss of the beloved: Persephone

returns home
stained with red juice like
a character in Hawthorne—

I am not certain I will
keep this word: is earth
"home" to Persephone? Is she at home, conceivably,
in the bed of the god? Is she
at home nowhere? Is she
a born wanderer, in other words
an existential
replica of her own mother, less
hamstrung by ideas of causality?

You are allowed to like
no one, you know. The characters
are not people.
They are aspects of a dilemma or conflict.

Three parts: just as the soul is divided,
ego, superego, id. Likewise

the three levels of the known world,
a kind of diagram that separates
heaven from earth from hell.

You must ask yourself:
where is it snowing?

White of forgetfulness,
of desecration—

It is snowing on earth; the cold wind says

Persephone is having sex in hell.
Unlike the rest of us, she doesn't know

what winter is, only that
she is what causes it.

She is lying in the bed of Hades.
What is in her mind?
Is she afraid? Has something
blotted out the idea
of mind?

She does know the earth
is run by mothers, this much
is certain. She also knows
she is not what is called
a girl any longer. Regarding
incarceration, she believes

she has been a prisoner since she has been a daughter.

The terrible reunions in store for her
will take up the rest of her life.
When the passion for expiation
is chronic, fierce, you do not choose
the way you live. You do not live;
you are not allowed to die.

You drift between earth and death
which seem, finally,
strangely alike. Scholars tell us

that there is no point in knowing what you want
when the forces contending over you
could kill you.

White of forgetfulness,
white of safety—

They say
there is a rift in the human soul
which was not constructed to belong
entirely to life. Earth

asks us to deny this rift, a threat
disguised as suggestion—
as we have seen
in the tale of Persephone
which should be read

as an argument between the mother and the lover—
the daughter is just meat.

When death confronts her, she has never seen
the meadow without the daisies.
Suddenly she is no longer
singing her maidenly songs
about her mother's
beauty and fecundity. Where
the rift is, the break is.

Song of the earth,
song of the mythic vision of eternal life—

My soul
shattered with the strain
of trying to belong to earth—

What will you do,
when it is your turn in the field with the god?

Nominated by Rosanna Warren, Jane Hirshfield, TriQuarterly

THE ODDS IT WOULD BE YOU

fiction by ALICE MATTISON

from THE THREEPENNY REVIEW

IN 1976, WHEN BRADLEY KAPLOWITZ was twenty-eight, he took lessons and learned to drive. A New Yorker with a pocket full of subway tokens costing fifty cents each, he rented a Dodge Dart so he could take his bald mother, Bobbie, on vacation. Bradley worked at a downtown bookstore, where a regular customer had mentioned an old-fashioned resort in the Adirondacks, at which he'd spent a week or two each summer since childhood. "Loons!" said the man. Though Bradley was hoping to be a writer, he didn't know what kind of birds loons were. The man described cabins at the edge of a lake. The dining room served three meals a day, he said, but the place wasn't fancy. "Nothing dressy," Bobbie had said.

With many miles still to drive on Route 28, Bradley and his mother turned off the Northway, which they had never seen before, at Warrensburg. Bobbie remembered long-ago trips on Route 9 to Lake George—the Burma Shave signs, the motor courts with their tiny separate houses. When Bradley was a baby, he and Bobbie—his father had already departed—were brought along on a vacation by Bobbie's sister Sylvia and her husband, Lou.

"Are you tired? Do you want to stop?" Bradley asked, as they drove into Warrensburg. His mother sat trustingly beside him in her orange-pink turban, a color too harsh for her skin. He wanted to stop. As soon as he had a license, she was sure they could drive anywhere.

"I should take my pills," she said. He found a little lunch counter. They'd had lunch outside of Albany, but now they ordered pie and coffee. The waitress brought water. "In New York these days, you have to ask for water," Bobbie said.

Bradley hated watching her take the array of pills. She did it with abandon, like a starlet in a movie tossing down barbiturates after being left by her lover. Bobbie tipped her head back to gulp the water, but ate little of her lemon meringue pie.

They traveled west. They were going to a big lake, the site of the crime in the real story behind *An American Tragedy*. Bradley had read it at City College but he barely remembered it, yet it was still vivid for Bobbie, who said she'd read it in high school. "He rows her out onto the lake—" she said. "You know he's going to do it, but you're begging him, 'Don't!' "

After a while she slept, her lipsticked mouth open, her head tilted back. The turban was askew when Bradley glanced at her. When she awoke she resettled it, telling him, her voice a little groggy, "Want to hear something funny? When I first bought it and put it on, I thought, This isn't going to stay. Then I thought, I know what I need, a hatpin! Picture it, honey, picture it."

Bradley didn't want to picture it, but couldn't help it: as he steered around curves, his hands tight on the wheel, he imagined the fake pearl at one end, the sharp point at the other, not sliding harmlessly through tangled hair but straight into his mother's skull. "Horrible," he said. "Hush."

"Edwin didn't want to hear about it either." Edwin Friend was his mother's boyfriend. If they'd married, Bradley considered, would Edwin have been braver? He and Bobbie were the same age, but now he looked older than she did, old from fear, though he was well. Edwin drove Bobbie to doctors' appointments, waiting in his big car outside. "I don't like it when they call me Mr. Kaplowitz," he told Bradley. If his mother had become Bobbie Friend—such a lighthearted name—would she have gotten well, gotten her hair back: a tentative fuzz, then a soft crewcut, then thickening curls?

They reached the resort after five. When Bradley opened the car door, the air was pungent with the smell of the woods. His legs trembled as he walked to the office to check in, while Bobbie waited in the car. He put from his mind the knowledge that he'd have to drive as far again in only a week.

"The wood boy will come to your cabin every morning at 6:30," the woman in the office told him placidly.

"The what?" It sounded like an animal. Bradley looked past her as she sat in front of a window. The lake glittered in the late afternoon sun. He heard the whirr of a motorboat, then saw it pulling a water-skier, who fell. The boat circled round for her.

"The wood boy. He's quiet." Water in the cabin, she said, was heated by the fireplace. The wood boy would start a fire each morning, so Bradley and his mother could take hot showers.

He got back into the car and described this arrangement to his mother, afraid she'd scold or grow petulant, feeling guilty for luring her here. The man in the bookstore hadn't mentioned the wood boy. But Bobbie laughed. "I wonder if the water really gets hot," she said. "Well, we can bathe in the lake." Bradley turned the key in the ignition one last time, and followed the instructions the woman had given him, driving slowly along a rutted road behind several widely separated log cabins, and at last parking the car. He turned off the engine and now let himself take in the silence, which was broken only by the light sound of the lake and the hum of the motorboat that pulled the water-skiers. He didn't bother with the suitcases, but helped his mother out, and they walked up some rough steps cut into the hill. His pants clung to his legs, but a breeze was already drying the sweat and making him cool.

The cabin had two bedrooms and a living room. In the bathroom, a tank for hot water felt cold to Bradley's touch. His mother hadn't followed him inside. She sank into an Adirondack chair on the porch, facing the lake. "Oh, honey, *look*," she called. He knew what she meant: it was what they had imagined: birch trees, evergreens, the lake, and dense woods beyond it. He was giddy with relief, carrying in their suitcases. Then he took her arm, and they walked on the lakeside path to dinner. That night they heard the reckless laughter of a loon.

Next day it rained. Sure enough, the wood boy was quiet, but Bradley awoke and listened. He waited in bed until he heard the boy leave, listening to the thump of logs being lowered to the floor and the sound of rain right above his head. Then he went into the living room, where a fire blazed from tinder.

After breakfast, Bobbie sat in her Adirondack chair on the porch, knitting a little sweater of fine yellow wool. One of Bradley's cousins was pregnant. Bradley sat in the other chair, looking at the gray lake and misty woods, digesting the unaccustomed breakfast—he'd had eggs and toast and potatoes. He was sleepy and bored, but content. It seemed that all he needed to do was keep Bobbie where she was, sitting back with her elbows close to her body, as the silvery blue knitting needles, with sixes on their bottoms, made their way, forward and back, through the looped and twisted yarn. She came to the end of a ball, which had slowly unraveled at her feet. She took another skein from her old pink quilted knitting bag, which Bradley had known most of his life. Now Bradley hitched his chair closer to his mother's so he could hold the skein on his outstretched wrists. As Bobbie wound her ball, Bradley tried to be even more helpful, tilting the skein this way and that by raising one arm slightly, then the other, his palms up. Without the yarn, he would have looked like someone *beseeching*. His mother's face looked young and enterprising as she worked, biting her lip slightly, concentrating. Finally the new ball—perfectly round, like something from a photograph on a calendar, including a kitten—was done.

"You're a good son," she said. "A better son than a mother."

"No," said Bradley. "A wonderful mother."

She was silent. With the ball in her lap, she tied its end to the short end of yarn coming off the yellow scrap that hung from the needles. Beginning to knit again, she said, "I'm sorry, honey."

"For what, what's wrong?" he said.

"Oh, nothing's wrong *here*, it's lovely," she said, as if he'd been the one who'd apologized. She glanced toward the lake, where mist rose in curls and streaks. "I mean—"

He knew now what she meant. "Hush," he said.

She was apologizing for what was going to happen. A good mother does not leave her son.

At lunch, Bradley ate onion soup for the first time. As he ate, he felt something alien in his mouth, and before he could decide not to, he'd swallowed it. It stuck, neither up nor down. Bobbie was talking about Edwin. "We could have married," she said. "We always meant to." Edwin had had a wife, a secret wife whom Bobbie somehow knew about. Then Edwin had divorced his wife. In the days when he'd claimed to be a bachelor, he said he couldn't marry because of his old, frail mother, and maybe that had been the truth all along, wife or no. His mother was still alive, managing alone in a smelly apartment in Red Hook, in her nineties. "But I'm not sorry!" Bobbie now said brightly.

Bradley didn't want to frighten her. He cleared his throat. Then, feeling self-conscious, he used his finger, but of course he couldn't reach whatever it was. At last he said, "I've got something caught in my throat," and his mother stiffened with alarm, her eyes wide open. "I can talk, it's all right," Bradley said, but he couldn't endure the sensation, the sense of something caught. "Excuse me." He left the dining room. It was still raining lightly. Outside the building, he leaned over, panicky now, pressing his hands on his knees. He didn't care if he vomited, even if everyone in the dining room saw. He coughed and retched, but nothing came. Had the object moved? Was it blocking his windpipe? At last, as his eyes teared, he strained and brought up saliva, and something. He drew it out: a woody brown piece of the skin of an onion. His throat was swollen from his straining. He dropped the onionskin, wiped his eyes on his sleeve, and returned to the dining room. All the children in the room looked up as he entered. The waitress, a college girl, approached him. "Are you all right?"

"I'm fine," Bradley said. "I had a piece of onionskin lodged in my throat, but I coughed it up."

Outside, the rain seemed to be stopping, and blue areas appeared in the sky. Bradley gingerly ate a little more soup. "You're sure you're okay, honey?" Bobbie said.

"I'm sure."

While they ate dessert, the chef came out of the kitchen and walked over to their table. He was a skinny man in an apron and a chef's hat. "I just want to apologize," he said.

"Oh, it's nothing," Bradley said, wishing the incident would end.

"I saw the onionskin fall into the pot, but I just couldn't find it," the chef said. "I was afraid somebody would get it. Now, what were the odds it would be you?"

Puzzled, Bradley calculated the odds—one in about forty, except that not everyone had had soup. The chef's question seemed like one only Bradley could ask, but it pleased him.

Afterwards, the weather cleared, but it was too cool to swim. Bradley had been adding logs to the fire all day, and for the first time since their arrival, the water tank was hot, so they both took showers. Then he proposed that they take out a canoe.

"I won't be much help," his mother said.

He had been to Boy Scout camp. "I think I can do it," he said.

The placid woman in the office was on the phone, so while he waited Bradley looked at a map of the lake that hung near her desk. Then she helped him carry a wooden canoe out of a shed and along the dock, dropping two life jackets into the bottom. No one was on the dock. The water-skiers, who had appeared as soon as the rain stopped, were gone. Bradley and the woman lowered the canoe into the water, while Bobbie stood by, her hand on the turban. There was a breeze. Then the woman held the rim of the canoe, kneeling on the dock in her blue jeans and leaning forward, while Bradley helped his mother into the bow, and settled himself in the stern with his paddle. The woman gave a brief underhand wave and turned back to the office.

Bradley remembered the stroke. Soon he found a rhythm, and in a short time he'd brought them a little distance from the dock, with the shore on his right. He struck out for deeper water, afraid of running aground.

As if continuing the conversation that had been interrupted at lunch, his mother said, "It's not always a bad thing, not to marry. At least I was married long enough to have you!"

"Yes," Bradley said to her back, not sure where this was going.

"Something I think about," she said. "You know, honey. The way you are. Now, I don't think there's anything wrong with it, you know. But not to marry, have children . . ."

"Yes," Bradley said, stroking hard. He steered past an inlet that looked narrow and shallow. The shore beyond it curved out, then in. He saw only a few houses in the dense evergreen woods.

"I think—if your father had stayed, if I'd been different, a different sort of mother. Maybe it wouldn't have happened."

Bradley was silent, considering what to say. He felt angry, and paddled hard but didn't speak until the feeling passed. "I can't imagine being different," he said then. "I was meant to be gay."

"Then it's all right?" she said, her back in a white sweater in front of him, her head looking ahead of her in its foolish turban.

"It's all right," he said.

They kept on, moving swiftly. Bobbie studied the lake shore. "Maybe we'll see a deer coming to drink," she said. But a short time later she said, "Shall we go back, honey?"

He'd tired her. He turned the canoe. Now the shore was on his left. The resort was a long way off, past a peninsula he'd need to steer around. In front of him, his mother had folded her arms against the wind, which was now in their faces. It was hard to paddle, and he was tired. They'd gone too far.

"Are you cold?" he said.

"A little." He insisted on giving her his sweater, a woolen pullover. He took it off and held it out to her, but she wouldn't put it on over her white nylon cardigan. She took that off and handed it back to him. "Around your shoulders, at least. It will make a little difference." To please her, Bradley tied the white sleeves around his neck. The sweater did give him a little warmth. "Now, you wouldn't drown a girl in the lake," his mother said, and it took him a minute to remember *An American Tragedy*.

The lake looked entirely different from the other direction. Bradley remembered a brown boat house, but he didn't see it. He came to the entrance to an inlet. Could the resort be in it? Had he come out into the wider lake, not realizing because the curve was gentle on that side? This inlet seemed too wide to be the one he'd bypassed, but he didn't enter it. Now and then they passed a dock, but never one that looked familiar. Children he'd seen swimming had disappeared. Bradley realized that he had no idea how their resort would look from the water. He couldn't remember how close to the shore the office was, whether the shed from which they'd taken the canoe would protrude from the trees. Maybe they'd already passed the resort. He paddled, rested, paddled. They made slow progress against the wind. Bradley looked at his mother, bulkier than she really was in the brown sweater, like a sturdier, more practical mother. She'd never wear brown. His throat was sore from the mishap at lunch. It felt as if he'd been crying, or as if he was getting a sore throat, the cozy kind that makes it permissible to shed responsibility and go to bed with tea and books. He'd liked that kind of illness as a child. Bobbie would bring him alphabet soup and chocolate pudding.

In his mind, Bradley again stood in the office, idly waiting for the woman who owned the resort to end her telephone call, staring at the map. Looking at the now cloudy lake, he struggled to form the map again in his mind, the kidney shape of the lake, with an extra lobe. He pictured the smudged black print, the lake's firm outline. The resort was marked with a star, closer to the western than the eastern end. It was on a wide, gently curved bay. Then came the inlet, then another bay, and then a peninsula.

215

"Someone will come along," his mother said, and he knew she knew they were lost.

"That's right," said Bradley, but he saw no boats. The tangled woods came down to the lake, and it seemed that nobody lived in them. Stroking and stroking, his tired hands gripping the paddle, his throat aching, Bradley brought his mother a little farther, then again a little farther, over the water.

Nominated by Lloyd Schwartz, Jane Hirshfield, Threepenny Review

DEAD BOYS CLUB

by REGINALD SHEPHERD

from FIVE FINGERS REVIEW

Gods and demigods are disasters:
kingship without kingdom,
his summer is war

Fleet Achilles refuses to outrun death,
his thighs white with dust
as if he were already ash
and burned bone: a lesser deity
failed into flesh, his solitude
ratified by slaughter

He is the thing that happens
only once, repeated
in blind effigy, the acrid smoke
of praise-song epithets: all glory
and catastrophe, he carries his grace
like a wound

His war burns like summer,
Troy's beach is singed gold,
the sea is not in his keeping

o

He is a beautiful killing machine,
and he is dead:

217

One boy kissed into bliss
by myth, who can't remember
his own name, can't hear
the fatal fact of him
echoing down the busy centuries
he has no time for anymore

*(But if you do not go
you will be loved and forgotten)*

He can't feel his fame
kissing men's throats
that he would cut if he were here:
Achilles is wind
held in the mouth,
a breeze parting the lips

These are not words
and will not last

Nominated by Marilyn Hacker

SALVATION

by STEPHEN DUNN

from POETRY

Finally, I gave up on obeisance,
and refused to welcome
either retribution or the tease

of sunny days. As for the can't-be-
seen, the sum-of-all-details,
the One—oh, when it came

to salvation I was only sure
I needed to be spared
someone else's version of it.

The small prayers I devised
had in them the hard sounds
of *split* and *frost*.

I wanted them to speak
as if it made sense to speak
to what isn't there

in the beaconless dark.
I wanted them to startle
by how little they asked.

Nominated by B.J. Ward, Poetry

REFUND

fiction by KAREN E. BENDER

from PLOUGHSHARES

THEY HAD NO CONTRACT. It would be a simple transaction. A sublet in Tribeca for the month of September. Two bedrooms and a terrace: $3,000.

They were almost forty years old, children of responsible, middle-class parents, and had created this mess out of their own sordid desires. Josh and Clarissa had lived for twelve years in a dingy brick high-rise in the Manhattan neighborhood of Tribeca. They had been lonely, met, married, worked at their art for years, presented their work to a world that was shockingly indifferent, floundered in debt, defaulted on student loans, began to lie to their parents about their financial status, and lived in a constant state of fear. They were afraid of what they might say when friends told them gleefully about their vacations; they were afraid of opening another magazine to find another grad school colleague profiled and beautifully photographed, modest, bemused; they were afraid of each other, disappointed that each could not rescue the other from this predicament of debt and bitterness. They lay in bed at 5:30 in the morning, listening to their three-year-old son, Sammy, hurtling toward the first sunbeam with the call: "More fun. More fun." The wistful, hopeful cry made their blood go cold. One of them stumbled towards the relentless dawn, inevitably tripping over the trucks that Sammy had lined up in hopeful parades, as though he still had the conviction that there was somewhere wonderful to go.

Their rent-subsidized apartment was located in a dull seventies high-rise, where, at first, they braved the abandoned, crumbling warehouses and hefty rats for a rent so cheap they could not afford to live anywhere else. But then the neighborhood changed. They were on the strip of land known as Tribeca, their building a few blocks south of Canal, six blocks north of the World Trade Center, and now there were lofts selling for twenty million dollars, new restaurants with glossy, slim customers posed as though in liquor ads, movie star neighbors moving in such rarified circles they were never actually seen. Walking into their own building, they heard shrill hallway arguments about the misbehavior of companion animals, feuds about laundry hoisted prematurely out of the dryer. The residents were on edge because they were doomed; the building would soon be privatized, rents hiked, and they would all end up on the street. Josh and Clarissa now skulked through their neighborhood with the cowed posture of trespassers.

Their son was almost three years old. Soon it would be time to send him to a preschool. In the park sandbox, mothers talked about Rainbows, the most expensive preschool in the area. Those who had been turned down or could not afford the school spoke of it with a strangled passion. One mother claimed she had stormed out when the director had asked to see her income tax statement during an interview. But another mother, whose son was a student there, leaned toward Clarissa one day after admiring Sammy's exuberant personality, and said, "That's the only place where they truly treat the children like human beings."

This statement had propelled Clarissa through the doors of Rainbows to observe a class. The director, dressed in flowing, silk robes, and with large, lidded eyes that made her resemble a woodlands creature from a fairy tale, walked Clarissa through the airy rooms. The director said that the children particularly enjoyed "Medieval Studies," which apparently meant that the children dressed up as kings and queens. Clarissa watched the children of successful lawyers, doctors, executives, and various moguls stack blocks, roll trucks, and cry. One child had tried to hand her a block. When she had smiled at him, a teacher gave her a laminated list of rules for class observation. Number 5 was: *Do not engage with a child who tries to talk to you. It interferes with their work.* She was ashamed that she had smiled at the child, and that shame convinced her that the school was the only place for Sammy to go.

"Ten thousand dollars," said Josh, "so that he can scribble? No. No. No." She mailed in the application, anyway—and when she received the acceptance she felt it was a sign of some greater good fortune. Their son gazed at them with his beautiful, pure brown eyes, his future gleaming, unsullied, new.

"At least visit the other schools," pleaded Josh, and she tried. At one, she peered through a square window in a door to see a crowd of children screaming to be let out. One child punched in a security code, a red light flashed, the door opened, and he shot out, to the roaring approval of the others. That was it. They had enough room on their Visa for the first tuition installment; they loaded it on.

Then Josh heard about a job for the two of them teaching art at a small university in Virginia, three weeks paid in September, accommodations for all of them in a hotel. They could hurl money toward Sammy's tuition. Their apartment would be empty for a month. It occurred to them they could sublet their apartment and pay off part of their substantial debt load. "Let's charge a fortune," said Josh.

Josh's college friend, Gary, an investment banker, delivered the subletter to them. "I think you can get three thousand," he said. Their rent was five hundred and fifty a month. Josh wrote the ad: *Fabulous Tribeca apartment. Two bedrooms, terrace. Three thousand for September.* Gary sent his friends a mass e-mail, and the call came the next day.

"My name is Kim. Gary gave me your name. He says you have apartment to let. I live in Montreal, and I am looking for accommodations in the city for September."

"Right," Clarissa said. "Thanks for calling. Well, we're by the Hudson, beautiful views, wood floors . . . uh . . . we have a dishwasher." She paused. "Down the block," she said carefully, "is Nobu."

"No-*bu*," said Kim, solemnly. There was silence. "I've known Gary for three years," Kim said. "We met in the south of France with his friends Janna from Paris and Juan from Brazil . . . we were in town for the day for the Beaujolais festival. We became friends. Now we follow the Michelin guide all over Europe together. We have a race to see who has the most frequent flyer miles . . . I have 67,000 but he has more." She paused. "I want to go to Nobu. I want to go with my friend Darla. She is my best friend. I want to walk there!"

"Now, it's not fancy," Clarissa said, alarmed.

"I want to walk to Montrachet!"

Kim wanted to send the money immediately; she magically wired $3,000 into their checking account, and that was that.

It was September 1. Kim held the keys to their apartment. They checked their ATM as they headed out of town. The three thousand dollars registered on their account. Josh whistled when he saw it. They drove toward a month's employment, a couple in front, a child in the car seat, across the bridges, out of the city. She and Josh held hands. Clarissa turned once to look back at the city, the skyline rising, glittering, frozen and grand in the clear autumn light.

She had dropped Josh off to look at televisions at a department store when she heard the news on the car radio. Her body startled. Howard Stern's show came on the air, and the tone of the hosts was terrifying: lost and humorless. "We know who did it," said a caller, "and we need to go kill them."

Her hands were trembling so it was difficult to grip the wheel. She raced to the store, where the staff and customers had abandoned their personas and stood, statues, in front of the television screens.

She stood with the group in the electronics section, in front of dozens of screens. They saw the Towers on fire. A giant tower buckled on the screen in front of them, frail as a sandcastle. Grown men around her yelled, No! in shocked, womanly voices. Sammy was immediately attracted to the picture. "Booming sound," said their son. She let him watch. "Booming!" he yelled.

The fact that they lived by the Trade Center made them objects of concern. "I'm so sorry," said strangers. They stood, awkward, marked with an awful, bewildering luck. "Where would you have been?" asked someone eagerly, as though they had been potential victims and they craved an intimacy with the disaster. "We would have been one block away," Clarissa said. Her arms became cold. This admission felt strangely like bragging. It occurred to her that others thought that they could have been dead. Around nine o'clock they would have been steps away, bringing Sammy to his first day of school.

The chair of the art department told them to take the day off, and they spent it in the hotel. It was stale and hot, full of a thousand strangers' breaths. She was not supposed to be here, and did not know what to do with herself, grubby, ashamed, alive. She felt fat and sickened by her own flesh. The TV droned casualty estimates into the room. The curtains were drawn, and the room was dark. They tried all day to get Sammy to nap. He popped out of his room, awake, excited by their fear. He imitated them, shouting into the phone. "Hello!" he called gaily. "Hello."

Somehow, the day ended. They drove down the dark streets, Sammy screaming with exhaustion, until he fell asleep. A student had said to them: Providence had brought them here. "You have been blessed," the student said in a respectful tone, before inviting them to church. Clarissa declined, though she kept thinking about this. She asked Josh, "Do you think we were blessed?"

"We're not special," he said. "Don't feel special. It could be us next time. It could be us any minute."

She looked out the window. This was not the answer she wanted. "Why do you say that?" she said. "How do you wake up in the morning? How are you going to walk Sammy across the street—"

He reached for her hand. They were ridiculous with unexpected luck. His fingers felt strange, rubbery; she clung to them, bewildered by the raw facts of their fingers, their hair.

"Hello," said the voice, aggrieved, three days later. "Hello, Clarissa. It's me."

"Hello?" asked Clarissa. "Who is this?"

"I was on my way there. I wanted to go to the observation deck. I went the wrong way on the subway, or I would be dead. I got out, and there were all these people running. Then I saw the second plane. I started running, and then I couldn't get the windows closed because I've never seen windows like yours—"

"I'm sorry," Clarissa whispered, "I'm sorry—"

"They said there's a bomb under the George Washington Bridge!" Kim shouted. "I can't get the ferry to New Jersey, it's closed. Is there a heliport in Manhattan? I'll pay anything to get to a heliport. Can you tell me?"

"I don't know," said Clarissa. "I don't know where one is—"

There was a pause. "I'm leaving town," said Kim. "I can't stay here. And I want a refund. I want it all back."

One day before they left Virginia to return to New York, Clarissa received an e-mail: IN REGARDS TO REFUND

I have not heard from you in regards to the status of my refund. Perhaps you are too busy to think about me

224

now. All the hotels are giving refunds. Also free rooms in the future, suite upgrades. My pet peeves are injustice and dishonesty. I know when I am being treated fairly. You did not tell me certain facts about the apartment, which was, I am sorry to say, filthy. Black goo all over the refrigerator. I had to wear plastic gloves to keep my hands clean.

Darla and I planned our vacation for a long time. We are best friends. We were going to buy the same clothes, go to the newest restaurants. People would admire us and say who are those glamour girls. Her hair is red and more beautiful, but I will admit I have nicer legs, we wanted to start a commotion.

I expect to receive payment of US $3000 within a week.

When they got out of their cab at Canal Street, the border between civilian New York and the war zone, they unloaded their luggage by the rows of blue police barricades. "Let's see your ID," said the state trooper, standing, trim and noble in his brown uniform, surrounded by pans of homemade cookies. "Do you live here, or do you have reservations?"

They looked at him.

"The restaurants gave us lists of people who have reservations," he said, pulling out a piece of paper. They offered their driver's license, and the officer agreed: this was where they lived.

He offered to give them a ride to their building. The car floated by the gray, scrolled buildings, the streets deserted as though the neighborhood had simply been a stage set, built quickly, then abandoned. The sky had become a pale, sickly orange and gray. There were too many police cars posed at corners; sirens pierced the warm air. There were American flags everywhere, as though everyone was desperate to have the same thought. People hurried down the streets, carrying groceries, pushing strollers; some were wearing surgical masks. She was suddenly leaden with sadness, a feeling that was precious in its simplicity.

Kim had left in great haste, sheets piled in the living room, a pale lipstick in the bathroom sink. Clarissa picked up the lipstick and touched the tip; the color was an unearthly pink. Sammy ran ahead of them. She thought that they should make some grand entrance, that they should say something profound to each other, but she

225

merely listened to their presence ring through the apartment; the sound was perplexingly beautiful.

They were home. There was the smell, unlike anything she had smelled before. Burning concrete and computers and office carpets and jets and steel girders and people. There was nothing natural about the smell, it tasted bitter and metal in her mouth, and blew through their neighborhood at variable times; the mornings began, sweet and deceptive, the afternoons became heavy with it. She began to get a sore throat, and her tongue became numb. The girls at the American Lung Association table gave her a white paper mask and told her that there was nothing to worry about, but to keep her windows closed and stay inside. She walked against the small stream of people wearing paper masks. The streets were dark and shiny, the sanitation trucks spraying down the street to keep the dust from lifting into the air. A man walked the streets in a suit and a gas mask. Did he know something they did not? Where did he get the gas mask? People used to strut in their neighborhood, but now everyone was simply moving forward, in dull impersonations of themselves.

She went out to the market the first morning after they returned. She pushed Sammy in his stroller downtown, heading straight toward the empty sky. In the market, she picked out cereal, detergent, apples to the pop soundtrack in the supermarket, the cheerful music that usually made her feel as though she were part of some drama greater than herself. Now it floated around her, impossible, but the supermarket did not shut it off.

When she ran into neighbors, anyone: Modesto, the maintenance men in the building, the counter man at the bodega, mothers from the playground, she moved toward them, the fact of their existence, her fingers like talons. It did not matter that she did not know their names. How are you, they asked each other, and it seemed like they were saying I love you.

"How are you?" Modesto asked.

"Where were you?" she asked.

"How is your apartment?"

"I'm glad to see you."

The meetings were hushed and tender, and then, with further discussion, she found that the neighbors had become deformed by a part of their personalities. The mothers who had been angry now were enormous, stiff-shouldered with anger, the mothers who were

226

fearful were feathery, barely rooted to the ground. "Why do they close the park for asbestos," said one angrily, "when before it was just full of piss and shit."

She stood with Josh, that first week, looking out their closed window at the lines of dump trucks taking the rubble to the barge. They sat, sweaty, greasy, in their living room, listening to the crash of the crumbled buildings as they fell into the steel barge. The swerve of the cranes sounded like huge, screaming cats, and when the heavy debris crashed into the barge, the sound was so loud they could feel it in their jaws.

They drifted quickly from their damp new gratitude for their lives to the fact that they had to live them. One week after their return, they sat beside the pile of bills that had accumulated. They sat before the pile as though before a dozen accusations; then Josh got up from the pile of bills that they could not pay. He went to his closet and brought out suits that she had not seen since he was in his twenties. She was startled when she saw him, the same slim figure, but now with gray hair. This sudden aging seemed a terrible betrayal. Suddenly, she realized that she had stopped looking closely at herself in the mirror. She dragged out some of the dresses she had worn fifteen years ago: stretchy Lycra dresses that clung to her skin. Now she looked like a sausage exploding from its casing. She had been hostage to the absurd notion that by acting young, you will not age. The part-time jobs, the haphazard routine, had kept them mired in a state of hope, preserved at the crest of some wonderful transformation.

"We were fools," he said.

Clarissa looked at herself in the mirror. She tried to hold her stomach in.

"We have to get real jobs. We should have had them fifteen years ago. What are we doing?"

"What about your art?" she asked. "We can cut back. We can eat beans more." He stared at her. "We can get another gallery, you're doing great work—"

She hated the tinny, rotting optimism in her voice. It had pushed them forward blindly, roughly, toward an imagined place where they would be seen for who they really were. She had wanted to walk through museums to see her work displayed on the walls. That sort of presence would, she had thought, cure her sorrow for her own death. But of course, it would not.

227

"We were idiots," he said.

They looked out the window at the smoke rising. His eyelashes were dark and beautiful. She remembered how when she married him, she hoped that their children would have those eyelashes, believed that loveliness would be protection against some cruelty. She rubbed her face, which was damp with sweat. Her mind seemed to have stopped. There was a short pause outside; the crane operators stopped for a moment of silence whenever they found part of a body. She looked out and saw one of the workers holding his hat. She opened one of the windows. The sickening, metallic smell entered the apartment.

"Kim wants all her money back," she said.

He lifted his hands in bewilderment.

"I'd give it back," she said. "Of course I would. But the way she yelled at me, and how she said this place was dirty where I know it was clean—"

"How can we pay her?" he laughed bitterly. "We can't pay anyone."

> Dear Kim:
>
> We are so sorry for your terrible experience. We are so glad you were not harmed. This is indeed a terrible time for the world. You did stay in our apartment for ten nights, and I have calculated this stay, at current hotel rates, at $150 a night. We are also deducting a fee for cleaning the apartment, as you did leave a window open letting some contaminated dust inside. This leaves you with a refund of $1,000. The first installment of this, in $20, will arrive in a week. Peace be with you.

She took a deep breath and pressed "Send."

She took Sammy to his first day of school. She walked down the street, past the taped fliers. The local day spa was offering free massages for firemen and policemen. A neighborhood restaurant offered a $25 Prix Fixe, Macaroni and Roast Beef, Eat American. Donations to Ladder 8 for Missing Fireman accepted. Dozens of Xeroxed faces of the missing clung to lampposts, wrapped with tape; they stared into the street. Loving husband and father. Our dear daughter. Worked on the 87th floor. Worked at Windows on the World. Please call. She walked by them slowly, and suddenly she could not breathe. The missing people were on every corner. They were smiling and happy in the photos, and many were younger than her.

The preschool was a block north of the wooden blue police barricades that separated regular life from the crumbled heap of buildings, the endless black smoke. Her stroller rattled past them and through the doors of the preschool. The school staff floated around, greeting everyone, with an unnerving intimacy, by their first names. Sammy darted into his classroom, and she stood with a cloud of mothers. They had walked to school under the smoky, foul skies, wearing leather coats in blue and orange. It seemed a paltry, mean decision, deciding what to wear, waking up and hearing the broken buildings falling into the boats. They had decided to dress up. Their hair was frosted golden and brown, and they were beautiful, and when they left, they cupped hands over their mouths.

"Have you gone out to dinner yet?" she heard one mother ask another. "You wouldn't believe the good deals down here, plus you can get reservations. Prix fixe at Chanterelle, thirty-five bucks, incredible, plus you have money for a good bottle of wine."

"The Independence has a special, Eat American," said another. "The wait staff is fast and gracious. They have the most exquisite apple pie."

Clarissa closed her eyes and rubbed her face, wondering whether she should admire these mothers' resilience or be appalled.

"We were refugees at the Plaza," she heard another mother say. "They had a special for everyone living below Canal. We had to go. They were generous. Our place was covered in that dust. We started throwing up, and I knew we had to get out. It cost a ton to get it cleaned. Should we stay or go? Can someone just tell me?" She whirled around, looking.

The teacher came over. "The children are doing well," he said. "Do you want to say bye before you go?"

Now Clarissa swerved through the room like a drunken person. Your child was not in the world, and then he was, suddenly, part of it. She crouched and breathed his clean, heartbreaking smell. "I'm going bye," she said.

Her child ignored her. Slowly, she stood up.

In the office off the main hallway, the in-house psychologist was holding a drop-in support session in which parents could talk about their feelings about sending their children to preschool three blocks from the site. Clarissa stood with the group clustered around the psychologist. One mother said, "My child screamed the whole way here, saying she was scared and didn't want to go, and I dropped her off, but then, well, I wonder, is she right to be scared?"

"Why is she right?" asked the psychologist.

"Well, because," called Clarissa, from the back.

"You have to believe it is safe," said the psychologist. "You tell them a kid's job is to go to school, and a parent's job is to keep you safe."

"But what if we don't know if it's safe?" Clarissa asked.

"Where is it safe?" the psychologist said. "Here? Brooklyn? Vermont? Milwaukee?"

The parents leaned toward her, awaiting an answer.

"You have to tell them a little lie," the psychologist said.

Later that day she received an e-mail with the heading: STUNNED.

> I don't know how you decided on this number as a refund. It is very unfair. Who are you to decide how much money to refund me? You were lucky; I was the one who suffered. I was on my way there!
>
> You did not tell me about the low water pressure or the scribbled crayon on the walls. Those facts would have made me not rent the apartment, and then I would NOT have been there. I thought you were my friend. Some friend. Do you even know what a friend is? Darla, my best friend, is kind to everyone, especially kittens. She once went to the animal shelter and brought her old Gucci towels to make the kittens more comfortable. I could see the fat attendants eyeing them! She told them to make sure the kittens took their towels with them to their new home.
>
> You left oily hairs in your hairbrush. I have your hairbrush. I have your Maybelline mascara. It is a horrid color. Who would put Maybelline on her eyelashes? Who would look good in navy blue? Are you trying to be younger than your age? You do not look so youthful in the snapshots on your refrigerator. You dress as though you think you are. You should not wear jeans when you are in your late thir-

ties. I don't care if it is a bohemian sort of thing, it is just sad.

I am requesting $3000 plus $1000 for every nightmare I have had since the attack, which currently totals 24. You owe me US $27000, payable now.

Josh found a job as an illustrator at an advertising firm, and each morning, he sprinted down their hallway toward the office that gave him a new life. Sammy would not say goodbye without giving his father one of his toys to keep during the day. "Take one toy," Sammy said, thrusting a tiny plastic dinosaur or little truck into the pocket of his father's suit. Sammy could not decide which toy he wanted his father to have to remember him, and when Josh finally had to leave, Sammy began to wail. He began to race after his father, and she had to grab him. "Daddy will be back," she said in a strained, cooing voice. "We'll see him later—"

He looked at her as though she were a fool.

One morning she tried to distract him by walking up to SoHo to see which artists had shown up. She peered at one, where one member of the staff had expressed interest in her work, but had then vanished in an abrupt, unexplained departure. Another young woman, perhaps ten feet tall, wearing the monochrome dark outfits all the gallery staff wore, came over. Sammy was butting his head against the doorway, like a small bull.

"I'm sorry, but he can't come in," she said.

Her face was perfectly blank, which Clarissa wanted to see as a personality deficiency, but was instead an adaptive expression to New York and the desperate artists that banged on this gallery's door. Sammy lurched forward. The girl blocked the door. "Sorry," she said, sounding strained, "ma'am—"

Clarissa grabbed Sammy. She bumped into the American flag that was hanging from the gallery's door.

"God bless America," said the girl, quickly. They loved all of America, but they were afraid of her.

"Come on," she said to Sammy. "I'll get you a ball."

She bought him a small red ball, and they passed the local park where they had spent much of their time before the attack. It had been beautiful, children playing under large green trees, honeyed patches of sunlight. Now the plants in the garden had been flattened when people raced, terrified, out of the park. The park had been closed briefly to clean up asbestos contamination. Sammy hurled his new ball into the park and darted in, chortling with joy. His ball was rolling to a garbage bin that said, NO PLAYING ON OR AROUND THIS CONTAINER. On the trees were fliers: EPA IS LYING. TOXIC DUST EVERYWHERE. UNITE!

"No!" she yelled. "No more ball."

She grabbed him by the waist and lifted him. He scratched her, leaving two red lines on her arms. He kicked. She struggled to find a way to hold him so that he would not hurt her, but he was wild. She wanted to scream at him, but instead whispered shut up into the air. She was not a good mother, she was afraid. "Come on," she yelled, and swung him up on the shoulder. His scream vibrated through his Elmo shirt. She hated him for revealing to her what a terrible mother she was. She did not know how to protect him from the world. When he was older, he would not remember the Towers. She envied his ignorance, longed for it.

"Hey!" someone called. It was a kindly park janitor. "I got your ball for you," she said.

"It was by that bin, you're not supposed to touch it—"

The janitor looked at her. "You can just wipe it off." She took a Kleenex from her pocket and wiped the ball. Clarissa wondered what sort of person would live with their child by a toxic zone, beside police barricades encircling targets of violence. She shuddered, for that sort of person was herself.

"That's just where they keep the rat poison," said the janitor, cheerfully.

"The rat poison," said Clarissa, numbly. She had never thought the term rat poison would sound nostalgic, but she was strangely calmed.

Dear Clarissa:

You have forgotten about me. I have not forgotten about you. You were lucky. You were out of town. I had to endure your apartment. I can still feel the dirt on my skin. I cannot believe that you keep a child in that filthy apartment. You cannot control him from drawing on the walls. Furthermore, his drawings do not even show any artistic merit.

This is a pathetic way for someone who is 38 to live. I figured it out. I have ten more years of life to live over

232

you. Ha ha! This is how I wanted to spend it: wake up, go to the top of the building, look out and take pictures with my new camera, come down, go to lunch at Nobu, walk around SoHo, buy something for my husband, go look at the shoes at Prada, have tea at the Plaza, jet off to Zermatt, stop in London. I want it all. I have the good taste to appreciate what is worthy in life.

My refund is US $29,000, payable now.

Dear Kim:

Don't try to pass the buck to me. You lived. You were lucky. Do you know what we were doing when you were here trying all the restaurants? Working. We are always working. We never rest. Do you know how many jobs I've had in the last year, trying to make money and make time for my art? Twelve. Do you know how close I came to getting a review in the Times? The guy came and loved my work. The words he used were "ground-breaking." Then along came this woman who videoed her own vagina and played the video to the soundtrack of The Sound of Music. There was room for just one review and she got it. It was a good one.

I am considering the refund and the appropriate amount considering the fact that we should all rise above ourselves during this terrible time. Peace be with you.

Each morning, when she walked Sammy into Rainbows, she felt first a sweet, exquisite rush of relief. Sammy jumped out of the stroller to a cream-colored room scented like oranges, inconceivably sweet. "Hello, Sammy," the teachers said, as though he was a visiting dignitary. "Sammy's here. Hello, Sammy. Hello."

They allowed him into this beautiful room, and waved at her, expecting her to walk out to continue her own life. She looked at the street, and she did not know where she could go. The hallway was mostly empty. She sat and watched the children play.

The mother who had been a refugee at the Plaza was heading a committee to raise money for tuition lost when parents withdrew their children. She was taking a poll in the hallway regarding how much to charge for the tickets. "I'm thinking something spectacular. A French theme," she told Clarissa. "Dinner, casino, a silent auction.

Do you think people would pay fifty, one hundred, or two hundred per ticket?"

"I would pay one thousand," Clarissa said.

The woman looked right at her. It was as though Clarissa had told her something wonderful about herself. "Yes," she said, softly.

Dear Clarissa:

It is not my concern that you never rest. You cannot get the money from me. It was your choice to pursue this "job" of artist. Why would I owe you anything? You were not honest with me. Honesty is the best policy. When Darla left her husband, she told him that she could not stand his skinny legs. That was just something she felt he should know. We all have our tolerances. The knowledge might have helped him in his later dating life. You should have told me about the water pressure, scribbled crayon, hallway odor, broken TV, useless air conditioner. Why didn't you? I expect US $31,000 payable now.

Dear Kim:

You idiot. You have been spared. Other people died who were nicer than you. Do you even know how to love?

Dear Clarissa:

How dare you. I was there. You were not. I ran. I almost lost my life, so you have lost your right to harass me. How dare you ask if I can love. I love many people. I love friends. I love good service in restaurants. I love people who bring me delicious things. I love the crème brûlée at the Four Seasons. I love the shoe salesgirl at Bendel's. So you see I have a great ability for love. Maybe you could learn something about it. Love! Love! Love!

You owe me US $31,000, payable now.

There were no more e-mails. At night, Clarissa lay beside Josh, awake, listening to the wild screaming of the cranes.

On October 30, she sat down and wrote a check for two hundred and sixty-three dollars and seventy-five cents. There was no reason for this amount except that it was what they had left in the bank ac-

234

count that month. She did not know what to write on the note, so she scribbled, quickly: *Here is your refund. God Bless.*

Halloween would be Sammy's last day at the school. The bad tuition check for $2,000 had been sent a week before, and she wanted to stop showing up before they could ask her about it. Sammy dressed as a lion. All the children were in costume. A few mothers were loitering in the lobby, captivated by the sight of their children pretending to be something else. Sammy's class was populated with two miniature Annies, a Superman, a ballerina, three princesses, some indeterminate sparkly beings, a dog, and Sammy, the lion. The teacher read them a Halloween story, speaking to them as though she believed they would live forever. The children listened as though they believed this, too. Clarissa pressed her hands to the glass window that separated the parents from their children; she wanted to fall into the classroom and join them.

After school, she wanted to buy Sammy a special treat. She bought him a blue helium balloon at a party store. He marched down the street, grinning; she lumbered after him, this tiny being with a golden mane and tail. Suddenly, Sammy stopped and handed her the balloon. "Let it fly away," he said.

"I'm not getting you another," she said.

"Let it fly away!" he shouted. "Let it!"

She took the balloon and released it. The wind pushed it roughly into the air. Her son laughed, an impossibly bright, flute-like sound. Other people stopped and watched the balloon jab into the air. They laughed at Sammy's amusement, as though captivated by some tender memory of themselves. Then the balloon was gone.

"Where is it?" he asked.

"I don't know," she said.

Her child looked at her.

"Get it," he said.

A week later, she picked up the phone. "Two hundred and sixty-three? How did you come up with this number? You owe me $54,200, why don't you give me my money?"

"Look!" said Clarissa. "You went the wrong way on the subway. Why do you keep bothering us?"

"You were lucky," said Kim. "You weren't where you were supposed to be."

"You weren't, either," said Clarissa. "You went the wrong way—"

"Maybe it wasn't the wrong way. Maybe the Towers were the mistake. Why would I have wanted to go there, anyway? Maybe I was supposed to meet someone there, and they never showed up. What do you think of that?"

Clarissa felt cold. "Were you supposed to meet someone there?"

"Would I get my $54,200?"

"Were you meeting someone there?" asked Clarissa. "Were you?"

"She is named Darla," said Kim.

"Why didn't you say this?" asked Clarissa.

"Will you pay me my money?"

Clarissa's throat felt hot.

"I was talking to her on my cellphone," said Kim. "She was on the elevator to the observation deck." She paused. "She wanted to go to the Empire State Building, but I thought at the Towers we would get a better view."

What did one owe for being alive? What was the right way to breathe, to taste a strawberry, to love?

"Kim," said Clarissa, "I—"

"Do you know how long I'm going to charge you?" Kim said, her voice rising.

Clarissa closed her eyes.

"Do you know?" asked Kim.

Nominated by Lucia Perillo, Joyce Carol Oates

VEXING PRAXIS/HOCUS NEXUS

by MARK HALLIDAY

from PLEIADES

THERE IS A COUNTERPROGRESSIVE, dysfunctionalizing rupture in the assertive assurance of antibourgeois vigilant outraged experimentalism in the United States of Megacapitalism today. This rupture is the result of a rampant and repugnantly energetic opportunistic imitation of outraged antibourgeois experimentalism, whereby persons who don't reelyreely care about opposing the Texan depredations of the billionaire corporate power megastructure have entrepreneurially managed to purvey types of poetry not based in authentic radical engagedness as if these productions were contributions to the honorable resistance. The counterfeiting is in countless instances so insidiously meticulous—like the productions of megabudget corporate advertising firms—that it becomes torturously difficult to distinguish real resistant radicality (RRR) from mere ersatz showbiz arriviste aestheticism. This is a crisis to which I do not as yet have a solution, but I will set forth its stark parameters here so that those of us who reelyreely detest the greed-grid of commodificationist co-optation can "circle our laptops" and collectively adumbrate the outlines of a truly grimly serious antibourgeois response.

It was as long ago as 1998 when several of my friends and I first noticed the crisis looming. We were reading the latest issues of *Edge*, *Contra*, and *Post-Post* in our local organic alternative to Starbucks, when we began to realize a pervasive dismay crawling across our skins like commando teams of polluted spiders. Instead of the righteous satisfaction we usually felt at participating in RRR and

237

supporting the courageously marginalized shadow-community of authentic outraged experimentalists, we discovered we were starting to feel as if some uninvited guests were quaffing the wine at our party, wearing black clothes newer than our own and tacky in some as-yet-undefined ways. To be sure, the journals in front of us contained poems of RRR, written by our email correspondents and friends and ourselves, poems deconstructively constructed via experimentalist defamiliarizing hyperfracture (EDH), whereby the hegemony of the corporate greed-grid is radically undermined for the sake of a future undoing of global capitalism to be achieved by terrifically "messed-up" language—good!—but these EDH poems animated by RRR were printed *side by side* with some poems by poets whose RRR credentials seemed dubious at best, poets five or even ten years younger than ourselves, too young to have credibly inhabited a maturely serious radical engagedness. What we sensed, though, that day in 1998, was not just a matter of the immaturity of these newly appearing poets, but a matter of the creepy insidious imitation of serious EDH, a mimicking of stylistic features so slickly skillful—on the technical level—as to produce poems outwardly extremely similar to poems of RRR. Turning the pages of *Edge, Contra* and *Post-Post* that day, we became so uneasy that poetry of RRR began to look like mere shallow opportunist aping of RRR, and vice versa! Suddenly it was all too possible to imagine a reader to whom *all* outraged antibourgeois language-inquisitional experimentalism might seem only trendy theatrical gamesmanship! What a disgusting vision!

And the danger we glimpsed that day in 1998 has mushroomed into the pervasive crisis of avant-garde culture that has incised the dysfunctionalizing rupture I began by noting. Serious poets of real resistant radicality today are under threat. We are in danger of disappearing amid waves of copycat pseudo-rebels who blithely co-opt our EDH poetics for the sake of careerist self-advancement. We can detect—in a kind of olfactory way—that such co-opters are not reelyreely against the appropriative insatiability of imperialism and the lobotomizing deceit of megacapitalism's airbrushing of reality into sellability. But how can we prove it?

The problem is exacerbated by our awareness that "critical demonstration" and evidentiary "proof" are *a priori* reifying hegemonic repressions. Nevertheless, it may be significant, and strategically progressive, if I here give an example of the insidious non-serious counterfeiting that has attained such nauseating kudzu dissemination among ostensibly RRR journals and presses. Therefore, though nothing could be more repugnant to me than capitalist "self"-promotion, here is a passage from my long poem "Whir of Blips (Repudiate)":

> (eyeballs) (windshields) limited access
> nerves in contact
> energy untabulated
> roomfuls of goofballs
> my blip de-interlocks
> quilted braids kaput
>
> asseverated flaneur—dejecta and relic—
> triumphalist afloat the grim prospect
> in the desert with no phone
>
> the taxi is accidental
> no trace of my passage
> illusion of depth (Felicia's crackers with no cheese)
>
> that prefab Kansas goodness
> sugar to defenestrate
> but there is a waffling
>
> but to whir toward light

I must place faith in the serious RRR reader, whose training in the struggles of avant- and post-avant refusal of imperialist commodificationist conventionality enables her or him to perceive the painfully engaged quality which animates the above passage. And I can confidently testify that this passage, and all of "Whir of Blips (Repudiate)," was written in an agonized fever of reelyreely grim resistance to the corporate greedgrid as it distorts the daily experience of individuals who fail to recognize their own co-optation. But of course, my certainty that the poem expresses authentic outraged antibourgeois resistance is based partly on my "insider" status as the author (insofar as we still use that very last-century term) of the poem. I know what the poem strives for; and my closest comrades know it. But what of a reader new to EDH, and new to the struggle against corporate global glutinous Halliburton imperialist capitalism (CGGHIC), who encounters my poem in the *same journal* with

239

"Mineral Dry Heave (Ho You)" by Darnelle Smankey—how can we be sure that such a reader will detect the vast difference between the two texts? Here is a passage from the Smankey poem:

exhaustion yields recognition—electrical snaps
here is the soiled couch the professional sewage
Superbowl commentators fester
                                        jetsam of objectification
we recede
beneath the creamed repetitions (Alonzo scarfs the dip)
blocked from
walled from
                        on the tundra with no cell service
dis- non- irr-
                        mutated to mute on the bus

that brickbat Missouri smileage
flail
toward apartments of contact
lineaments immediated
                        yet there is a succumbing to reference

but to ravish you "you" yo

Admittedly the passage from "Mineral Dry Heave (Ho You)" displays a kind of surface glitter, and offers perhaps some initial pleasure in its fielding of implications. But we need to remember that pleasure is not the point in the RRR struggle against CGGHIC. Moreover, the pleasure arguably offered by the Smankey passage is surely only initial pleasure, momentary, dissolving as soon as the reader ponders this production with the eyes and nose of someone reelyreely alert to the sly disguises adopted by co-opted consumerist language. I will not fall prey to the temptation of "demonstrating" the essential shallowness of the Smankey passage (surely the utterly predigested reference to "Superbowl commentators" does that work for me!). The point here is to realize the extreme danger created by Smankey-like texts, the danger that the unsuspecting reader—and this consumerist pleasure-addled info-flooded nation is full of unsuspecting readers including increasing numbers of those who in fact do read journals such as *Edge, Contra,* and *Post-Post*—will fail to detect that the Smankey is nothing but a cheap, easy, glib aping of a passionate outraged antibourgeois EDH text such as my "Whirl of Blips (Repudiate)." I don't suggest that Darnelle Smankey has specifically ripped off my particular poem—no, my point is much larger, deeper, more pervasive and disinterested than that! My point is that readers can be fooled. If real resistant radicality is to survive and even, with tremendous courage, thrive, we must find some way to prevent readers from embracing (and then perhaps imitating!) such copycat happy-golucky opportunist pseudo-indeterminate dishings as "Mineral Dry Heave (Ho You)" as if such texts had *anything* to do with serious violation of corporate greedgrid hegemony.

Smankeyism is the ragweed of the avant garde. It is spreading at an astounding rate. I cannot name a single journal which I can now pick up with confidence that all the poems in it will embody RRR, though EDH mannerisms may appear throughout. (If there is one exception, it would be the journal which Ruth Whack and I have just started, *Renegade Unsucker*, the trial first issue of which is as yet available only by sending $12 to me at an address to be announced elsewhere.) As I have indicated, there is a strangely bilious disorientation that results from reading dozens and dozens of poems and *sensing* that only very few of them reflect bona fide rad-avant resistant engagedness (RARE) yet being unable to *point out* the substantive difference between those few and the many poems exploiting EDH as a merely aesthetic kind of play or entertainment. Aestheticism is collaborationist. Aestheticism derives from the notion that the "work of art" must be "pleasing" to an "audience" irrespective of its essential political vector. Where linguistic features of a poem are generated to satisfy aesthetic criteria, those features become nothing deeper than a marketing ploy *even if* we can't readily tell them apart from the disjunctive antibourgeois praxis of RRR poetry.

Needless to say, the healthy progressive response to this crisis is not an "openminded" picnic-spirited tolerance of all experimentalist hyperfractured work. That would be the slippery-sloped path to granola-and-strawberries bourgeois "I'm okay You're okay" paralyzing Prozac centrism. That must not be the fate of the avant (or post-avant) garde!

This crisis fertilizes bizarre thoughts. It is so hyperextensive that at some after-midnight moments I begin to envisage a future in which openly "saying" what you "mean" in a poem might become, by the kind of inversion or "emergency flipping" theorized by Belneuve-Farfelu-Crasse, the truly radical shucking of the chains of linguistic

241

convention! I realize how crazy that sounds. I have not been sleeping a lot. Around 3 a.m. you can feel the city swarming with Smankeys, you feel they are awake at their computers, you feel they will become 90% or even 96% of the avant garde of tomorrow—opportunist interlopers whose writing, you suspect, ultimately accomplishes nothing (apart from their own ephemeral glorification) except for the amusement of a few people who refine upon their feelings till anything in the ununderstandable way will go down with them.

But those thoughts are poison and must be spat out. I spit them out. I am going to survive as an authentic unco-opted radical experimentalist. I am going to keep writing poems that evince a *stance* rather than a *pose*. What will this mean for my writing, exactly? I don't know. I feel a headache clamping down when I wonder, how much more *can* I disrupt the syntax which is (we know) the dominant Texan mega-capitalist culture's crucial weapon? What have I not yet tried? Somehow, somehow I will dobisrobupt sobyntobax to a degree that says No to, and potentially terrifies, all the imperialist controllers in their power-lunch suits.

Meanwhile, the crisis I've identified persists. I have acknowledged that there does not exist, yet, a reliable litmus test to confirm a poem's engagedness in RRR. Until such a subtle test can be developed, we are left with the archaic concept of intentionality. That is, our response to a poem must, for now, come down to the question of whether we know for sure that the motive, the originating impetus for a given poem consists in the poet's desire to use EDH in the desperate struggle against CGGHIC. And the judging of this seems to be (as I have painfully admitted), for now, not a rational inductive rule-governed procedure, but a matter of smelling. Antibourgeois radical experimentalism today needs some extremely sensitive smellers. And frankly, the only ones I can recommend with confidence are myself and my friend Ruth Whack. (Ruth's nose occasionally misses a significant odor, but not often.) Thus I can make this provisional offer to the reader of this essay: When you want to find out whether a particular poem is reelyreely engaged, radical, and resistant (rather than chickenshittingly fecklessly playing around with the methods of radicality), send the poem to me and Ruth, c/o this journal, with $3 (cash only), and we will reply within three weeks. Take courage! We will never desert the cause.

Nominated by William Olsen, Daniel Hoffman, Carl Dennis, Lucia Perillo, Pleiades

RADIO CRACKLING, RADIO GONE

by LISA OLSTEIN

from CROWD

Thousands of planes were flying and then
they stopped. We spend days moving our eyes

across makeshift desks, we sit on a makeshift floor;
we prepare for almost nothing that might happen.

Early on, distant relations kept calling.
Now, nothing: sound of water

tippling a seawall. Nothing: sparks
lighting the brush, sparks polishing the hail,

the flotsam of cars left standing perfectly still.
Thud of night bird against night air,

there you are on the porch, swath
of feathers visible through the glass,

there you are on the stairs where the cat fell
like a stone because her heart stopped.

What have you found in the wind above town square?
Is it true that even the statues have gone?

Is there really a hush over everything as there used to be
in morning when one by one we took off our veils?

Nominated by Dara Wier, Crowd

BYE-BYE LARRY

fiction by KATHERINE KARLIN

from ZYZZYVA

LARRY MICHALIK did not die a glorious refinery death. He did not explode in a fireball as the spark of a welder's torch ignited methane fumes. He was not sheared by the claws of rail cars coupling in the yard. He did not dive into the mouth of a flare stack, leaving behind his work boots on the diamond-plate catwalk. He did not wander into an empty tank, purged with nitrogen, and drown in the oxygen-free air.

Larry Michalik merely lowered his union coffee mug one morning, dropped his head, and went out like a flame.

We thought he had dozed off. For the rest of the shift, we prodded him with the eraser end of a pencil, jotted down his readings, and silenced the alarms buzzing on his control board. Only when his relief showed up did we realize Larry was dead.

Here's where I should deliver a eulogy. For the most part, oil men are easy to like. When I started this job, they all looked the same to me, but I made a point of drawing a story from each of them. On the evening shift, in spring, when the refinery lights twinkle against the darkening sky and we fish plastic bottles out of the sludge pond, I get them to reveal something personal. One keeps a girlfriend and a whole secret family in Florida. Another committed acts of sabotage before the '83 strike. A third has a brother serving time.

You never know what a man will tell a young woman, warm and receptive, who is not his wife. I don't care if the stories are true; the moment is full and tender. Days later, I will pass the same man on the hot tarmac or in the bright light of the control room, and electricity crackles in the air between us. We don't even have to look at each other.

But strip away Larry Michalik's blandness and there was more blandness. The closest thing he had to a hobby was Ann-Margret. He taped in his locker a life-sized poster of young Ann-Margret in a mini-dress and go-go boots, her chin tucked coquettishly and her hair blown into an after-sex tangle.

"I tell you what, Gina," Larry said to me once. "She looks better at 60 than you do in your twenties. Better than you ever will."

I dug my fists into the pockets of my coveralls. "I like the movie she made with Bette Davis," I said. "You know. The one where Bette Davis is a drunk old beggar-woman and Ann-Margret's her daughter being raised in a convent overseas, who thinks her mother is some fancy society lady. Then Ann-Margret brings home her fiancé, who's, like, the prince of Spain, and Bette Davis has to get Glenn Ford to help her clean up and pretend she's rich." My voice cranked up a notch with excitement. "Right up to the end of the movie you expect her to admit that she's just an old drunk, so the daughter can tell her she loves her for who she is. But what's cool is that Bette Davis pulls it off. It's the only movie I ever saw that says lying is the best policy."

I watched Larry's face for a sign of recognition. He simply looked into the distance and said, "She was just a young filly in that one. What a beautiful girl."

The fact is, I didn't care much for the deceased.

Before the wake, we stumble off the midnight shift and gather at Stan's taproom. The wives will meet us at the widow's house, bringing tuna casseroles and Jell-O molds. Stan's is nothing more than a room with a long counter and a single neon Rolling Rock ad and a mirror so corroded it reflects nothing. I sip a beer and roll cork coasters down the length of the bar; dressed in my girl clothes—a denim jacket frayed at the collar and a short denim skirt—I feel bare.

Franny Sadlowski and Chessie Cesare sit on the next barstools. Chessie, our shop steward, has the *Philadelphia Inquirer* open to the business page. Franny reads aloud a quiz from a copy of his girlfriend's *Cosmo* called "Are You *Truly* Honest With Him?"

Here's what I know about Franny: He has a round little pot belly like a piglet. He's 39, and his girlfriend is 17.

About Chessie I know this: He's 43 and has a long, sad Sicilian face. After his divorce, he moved in with a real estate agent, ten years his senior. In the mornings, he takes his coffee and newspaper out on the balcony of their condo and props his feet on the railing, and he watches his real estate agent go off to work in her mint-colored suit, her hair a shimmery blond helmet, joining the other attractive divorcees who stream out of the building every morning—a river of travel agents, executive assistants, event planners. Chessie has come a long way from his South Philly days.

Besides that, I know little about Chessie's private life. Because we're both Italian, I thought he'd extend a little old-fashioned *paisano* camaraderie. But when I angle for stories, his face slams shut like a check valve.

Franny asks, "You're away on a business trip, and carry on a flirtation with a handsome co-worker. Do you tell your significant other?"

Chessie looks glumly into his beer. "I don't carry on flirtations."

"You don't go on business trips," I say.

"The hell I don't. I was in Alaska." That's another thing about Chessie: He did a stint on an icebreaker in the Coast Guard. "And even there I never had to flirt. I've never had trouble nailing a woman. What girls there were up there, I banged them."

"Inuit chicks?" Franny looks up from his magazine.

"Nah, man. These were American girls. Cheerleaders."

"Oh," Franny says.

The other mourners are paying their tabs and flapping the front panels of their jackets, birds about to take flight. My tongue feels swollen to twice its size, and I pull it out of my mouth with my fingers.

"Put that thing away," Chessie says.

"It feels weird," I say. "Does it look too big?"

Franny peers into my mouth. "You'll make some guy very happy."

"Look, don't point that at me," Chessie says. He thinks I want him. In fact, Chessie lacks the imagination necessary to conjure up a world in which not every woman wants him. But it would be accurate to say I want to *be* him. Or at least, I want to have his swagger, his confidence, his ability to divine the cool from the uncool by the grace of his presence. I want to unlock that strongbox, his mind.

There on the business page is a three-column picture of our current plant manager, Margo Allshouse. The photo was snapped from a low angle to make her look tall against a distillation tower. Her arms are folded, her mouth set with determination. She is wearing a tailored suit and a hardhat. She's our first woman plant manager, and came to us fresh off a lockout she'd engineered downriver.

Famously, during a recent grievance procedure, Chessie jumped to his feet and said, "Lady, we make gasoline. What the hell do you do?" For weeks it was a mantra around the plant. The guys at the catalytic cracker embellished the story by having Chessie grab his crotch. On the docks, they were saying he had unzipped his fly and freed his penis, flexible as a chicken's neck, to waggle at Margo Allshouse. By the time the story hit the distillation units, Margo Allshouse had yawned and said, "If you had *two* dicks I could still outfuck you, Chessie."

Now, most of us think Chessie's vendetta is getting a little old, and, as he starts to read aloud from the business page, more of the men slap money on the bar and head for the widow's house. " 'The brawny Delaware Valley oil worker is becoming a thing of the past.' " He swallows some beer. "That's a quote. Fucking Margo Allshouse."

I pull some crumpled dollars from my skirt pocket and smooth them out on the countertop. "She assumes we don't read the business pages," I say.

"Tell me something I don't know," Chessie says.

"Okay," I say. I handle my tongue again, considering his challenge. "I'll try to think of something you don't know."

I could tell him that I've seen Margo Allshouse around town, at Miss Kitty's and at Patsy's, cozying up to the bar with the other corporate dykes, wearing silk blouses and drinking ice-clear martinis. These are the women who laugh too loud and look around to make sure we're watching. I've always resented them encroaching on my territory, and wished they would crawl back to the B-schools they crawled out of.

Still, I once tapped on our lesbians-in-arms connection to my advantage, on a particular evening shift when I got my period and didn't have a single tampon in my locker. A few years earlier, some of us had petitioned for a Tampax dispenser in the women's change room, but as soon as we got it we busted the lock and stole all the goods, and they never restocked it. A janitor had told me that the executive women's room had tampons for free, baskets full of them, wrapped in pink wrappers and rose-scented like bouquets. They were there for the taking.

This was around the holidays, and I'd been eating a lot of fatty foods, butter cookies, and bundt cakes. My flow was as thick and clotted as the grease from a Christmas duck. So I put on my coat and walked down River Drive, between the noisy cat crackers and the hissing steam lines and the jungles of dense pipe, careful to skirt the icy puddles, until the road opened to the low brick buildings of the executive offices. It was easy to break in; after big office parties, we used to help ourselves to the leftover cake and punch, once all the managers and secretaries were gone. Because I was the skinniest, the men usually hoisted me to a second-floor window that had been left open a crack; I could slither in and run downstairs to admit the others. On this night I was alone, but I was able to scale up the drainpipe and work my way into a conference room.

The women's bathroom was everything I dreamed it would be. A fantasy of feminine hygiene. I struggled out of my coat and dropped my coveralls to insert a tampon. Then I suited myself up again and stuffed every pocket with extras. I put tampons in the hip pockets and back pockets of my coveralls, in the thigh pockets where I usually carry a pair of channel locks, in the deep, wide pockets of my Carhart jacket. I tucked some in the sweatband of my hardhat.

The hallway smelled of disinfectant, and the exit lights shone on the waxed floor. In my work clothes, I felt like a dirty blight. Tampon paper rustled with every step I took. Behind me I heard a door opening, and the crustacean click of a woman's heels. I froze. The clicks came closer and I turned slowly. Because I was so stuffed with tampons, my arms were bowed like a gunslinger's. And there was Margo Allshouse.

Of course, she didn't know me from Adam. She might not have recognized that I was a woman. She saw the Carhart, the steel-toes, the coveralls. She saw the hardhat. She saw I didn't belong there. And I suddenly remembered a story about a guy who was fired for driving out of the refinery gate with a carton of toilet paper he'd lifted from the supply shed. The men shook their heads in wonder. "Guy gave up a $50,000-a-year job for 30 bucks worth of toilet paper."

This would be my legacy. Fired for stealing tampons.

So when I saw Margo Allshouse, I panicked. I figured the only chance I had was to appeal to a sense of solidarity; if I was lucky enough, she had one.

"We know each other," I said.

"Excuse me?" Her beady eyes stared a hole into me.

"You know. Like, Miss Kitty's."

I waited for a flicker of recognition, but this encounter was too far out of context for her to digest. I could see Margo Allshouse was flipping through her mental files, probably figuring out how to fire me. And I remembered the last time I had seen her: Someone had put that old song on the jukebox, "How Lovely to Be a Woman," and she and her friends were singing along, guffawing. So I started singing it, making up the words I didn't know.

"*How lovely to be a woman*—remember?" I rolled my hips a little. "*And have one job to do, to pick out a boy and train him, and tell him what to do.*" As I sang, I backed toward the stairwell. At least I had the presence of mind not to sing a Janis Ian song, which, even facing joblessness, was more of a cliché than I could stand. Before Margo Allshouse could collect her thoughts, I was out of the building.

I told the men that story, about how I climbed in and stole tampons. I told them about seeing Margo Allshouse and my escape. But I didn't go into Miss Kitty or the song. Too much back-information can kill the anecdote.

We step from the dark of the bar into the morning. It is one of those foggy cool days of a Delaware Valley autumn. Across the street, there's a Wawa that sells wrinkled old hot dogs and slushy drinks; next to that is the Iron Age shoe store, now closed, and a beauty supply shop next to that. Only hookers, gimps, and bikers live in the refinery town, where the tap water tastes like diesel and the rumble from the units rattles the frame houses. My co-workers drive ten, twenty miles to treeless subdivisions where they can escape the fumes. From the plant chimneys down the hill, steam rises in parallel stripes, slanting across the sky toward Wilmington. The flare burns low and blue and barely visible against the mist hanging over the river. The gasoline tanks sit like fat white buttons on gray gabardine.

Franny lays a hand on my shoulder and leans heavily against me. "I have a rock in my shoe." He slips off his Florsheim and tips it; a clear tiny pebble falls to the ground. "Well, it *felt* like a rock."

I drive. Franny and Chessie climb in the back seat of my Saturn and fall asleep—Franny wheezing slightly, Chessie wagging his head back and forth as I round corners. I take River Road, past the locked-out plant Margo Allshouse left behind. The parking lot is empty except for a lone security guard. A cooling tower faces the street and the cedar louvers, once alive and springy with algae, are splintered and bleached like bones in the desert.

Larry Michalik lived on a wide flat macadam street with wide flat homes. Pickups and SUVs are parked in the driveway and along the curb outside his house. By the time we arrive, the wake is in full swing.

Larry's widow sits in a folding chair drinking a tumbler of bourbon and holding a cigarette. She has short red hair and wide-set eyes. She looks like a woodpecker. Most of the co-workers gather by the server where the drinks are kept, in front of a mirror with a braided gold frame.

Chessie and Franny vanish into the crowd, while I pay my respects. "I'm sorry about Larry," I say.

The widow eyes me.

"I worked on his shift," I add. Her mouth twists up at one corner in kind of a grimace. She waits for me to say something kind.

"He loved Ann-Margret," I say.

"That's the best you can do?" she says. She has a whiskey voice, like a lot of these wives. I take my leave of the widow and go over to get a Coke.

A knot of men are standing near the liquor. Franny is telling the story of how he tried to fax his dick, back when we still faxed things. We'd read about a couple of women in Seattle who Xeroxed their asses and faxed them around, and Franny got inspired. Standing on tiptoe, he laid his penis on the glass top of the copier, and gently, gently lowered the rubber lid. Problem was, Franny had chosen the older Xerox machine, with the mechanism that glided back and forth as it exposed the image, and Franny had to dance a dainty sidestep to keep up.

I wander away. Some of the wives who know me tousle my hair and tell me not to take any shit.

Then a ripple runs through the room like a breeze scuttling litter. I look over some of the men's shoulders and see that Margo Allshouse herself has arrived, an unusual thing for a manager to do. Often, they'll send flowers to the funeral home, but a personal appearance is rare. Chessie turns his back to her, and as he does he happens to face me, blocking my view. "Ain't this some shit," he says, not to me in particular.

Margo Allshouse wears what she probably calls casual wear—a maroon silk blouse and wool skirt and low heels. She looks great. At once, I feel ashamed of my denim skirt. Margo, of course, knows exactly the right thing for a wake—attractive, but not too sexy—and it occurs to me that if I were taller, smarter, and had paid more attention in school, I might have been a power lesbian, too. My bare legs glow like milk.

Everyone quiets down as Margo takes the widow's hand in hers and shakes it firmly, like a man. "Mrs. Michalik, we're so sorry about Larry. He went like a soldier."

Larry's widow examines Margo Allshouse with eyes spaced so far apart she has to turn her face one way and then the other. She says, "One crack about Ann-Margret, and I'll knock you from here to Christmas."

There's no way Margo can understand the reference—it's not as if she has any idea who Larry Michalik was or what he looked like—but she turns her wrist in a gesture of complicity and says, "I couldn't agree more. I hated *Grumpy Old Men*."

The widow says, "You and me both, sweetheart. Have some cake."

Margo Allshouse is magnificent.

Some of the wives bring her cake, and the men flirt with her a little. Chessie looks over his shoulder and then smirks in my direction. When he grows angry, his eyes get narrower and narrower. I've seen it happen in the plant. One time, he nearly socked a pipefitter for spreading out his tools before Chessie signed a work permit. He's prickly like that.

"Let's give her some shit," he says, over my head.

I get the feeling Chessie thinks he can handle Margo Allshouse because he lives with a divorced real estate agent, a class act. He knows women. But he's got it all wrong. Margo Allshouse is in a different league.

"Hey, Margo," he calls to her. "Have a drink. Here's one more pension you won't have to worry about stealing."

Margo turns to look at him. She's walking into an ambush, and I have a sisterly instinct to warn her. But Margo cocks her head and smiles and says, "Oh, hello, Chess. I would have a drink, but apparently you've gotten a head start."

Chessie elbows aside some of the wake-goers to approach her. "Damn straight. I've been drinking all morning. I've been drinking since I read the morning paper. Seen it yet?"

Franny steps between them and spreads his pudgy fingers. "Come on, Chess. It's a wake. We're all here to have a good time."

"The Delaware Valley oil worker is becoming a thing of the past," Chessie quotes.

Margo laughs. "That isn't exactly a secret, Chess. Our future is in development and research. The oil worker is disappearing from the valley."

Chessie lifts his glass, as though he were toasting her. "You know what? That's where you're wrong. The jobs may be gone. We're still here."

"O.K.," Franny says, clapping his hands together. "Let's sing a song for Larry. We could sing an Ann-Margret song. How about 'Viva Las Vegas'?" Franny moves his hips Elvis-style, twirling an imaginary hula hoop around his middle. "Huh-huh-huh," he sings. "How does it go? *I wish there were more than 24 hours each day.*"

"That's the second verse, dickhead," someone says.

Chessie turns his back to Margo, his shoulders hunched forward. He emits anger, like a dog with its ears flat on its head. And Margo, Margo hunches her shoulders forward, too. Even though they're ten feet apart on the living room floor, with a half dozen people singing "Viva Las Vegas" between them, they're dancing, her body responding sympathetically to his.

Then it's clear to me. Somewhere, some time, they did fuck.

Chessie and Margo Allshouse. How did it happen? How did they make initial contact, that glancing exchange of word or gesture that establishes what each of them wants. Was it angry? Was it tender? Did he brush his hand against hers as they both reached for a doughnut in the negotiating room? Did their eruption over dental benefits and retirement plans refuse to subside until they had driven, in separate cars, to the No-Tell on Route 9? Or did they plan their tryst in crisp, contractual language?

And when they got there, did they take off their clothes in silence or was there groping and grunting? And those clothes! Margo's businesswoman suit, impossible to penetrate: zippers and hooks and eyelets and a double strand of pearls, support-top hose that snaps like a rubber band. Once Chessie navigated all that, did she look naked and vulnerable, or, with her make-up and hairdo, did she maintain her polished enamel glaze? There's a whole grown-up world out there I know nothing about, where people have sex for reasons other than desire—for power and vengeance. I have a lot to learn.

Chessie marches out of the living room and out the front door. I think he means to slam it, but it eases shut against its hydraulic piston. No one marches out after him. The men are busy singing "How Lovely to be a Woman," and Franny has a napkin tucked into his belt like a skirt and his hands cupped over his nipples. Margo Allshouse stares at me from across the room. Finally she recognizes me.

"How lovely to have a figure that's round instead of flat. Whenever you hear boys whistle, you're what they're whistling at." Everyone whistles, and some of the wives stick dollar bills down Franny's pants. One of the men shouts, "You make a pretty good faggot, Fran," and, as always, my stomach convulses, a little more violently because Margo is looking at me, her eyebrow raised.

I know that look. It's the look, sympathetic and reproachful, that my friends give me when they ask, "Still not out at work, Gina?" And as I stammer that it hasn't come up, really, or that I haven't found the right time, the perfect opening, the look gets more impatient. I'm not kidding anyone.

But it's easy for them. They all work in offices or schools, places where a certain decorum is expected. They don't have to listen to the sick jokes. They don't have to stand in the snow all night steaming down propane lines to keep them from freezing, hoping to get spelled for a lunch break. They don't climb tank cars or handle explosives. They don't have so much fun on the job, and they don't have as much to lose.

Margo has made her appearance. It's time for her to leave. This is her first misstep, as far as I can tell: overstaying. But she makes her way toward me, still with that cocked eyebrow, until she is standing next to me and murmurs in my ear: "You're looking at a dying breed."

I jerk my head back to look at her. With all the gaiety in the room, it's hard to hear, but I'm pretty sure I got her right. I put my mouth by her ear, close enough to smell her perfume and feel her hair on my forehead, and say, "What is?"

"These men. Oil workers."

I step back and laugh. Anyone watching would think we were sharing a good joke. *"I'm* an oil worker."

Margo looks into the plastic cup she's holding and taps a fingernail against it. So she thinks we're in the same club, she and I; that's my fault. But some of the men are watching, and I don't want to stand next to her anymore. Everyone is treating Margo with courtesy, because that's the way they are, but no one's forgotten that she's the enemy.

Through the Michaliks' picture window I can see Chessie lurching about from parked car to parked car. He stands before a BMW, apparently studying the front grill, but then I realize he's pissing.

"Is that your car?" I ask Margo.

She follows my gaze. "Son of a bitch," she says.

She puts her cup, half-empty, on the server with the other litter and goes out the door. No one stops singing to say good-bye. I watch through the window as she confronts Chessie. They both hang their heads as they speak, their necks like stalks bearing heavy fruit. Chessie removes a hand from his back pocket to point a finger at her. Then she does something that surprises me—she laughs—and climbs into her BMW. As she pulls away, Chessie manages a half-hearted wave.

The men start singing "Bye Bye Birdie," and as I head outside, Franny throws his arms around me. "Dance with me, Gina." Then he takes my hand and spins me around. Franny dances pretty well for a fat guy. When he's done spinning, he presents me to the crowd, and they clap and laugh, and someone says, "Careful, Franny, she's old enough to drive."

Chessie sits on the grass, his legs straight out in front of him. As I approach him, he says, "What do you do when you're not at work?"

"Me?" Chessie never lobs questions my way. I look around to see if someone's behind me.

"No, not you. Madonna."

"I don't know. Hang out." I fall on the lawn and sit beside him.

"I think you got something you're not telling us."

I jerk my head toward the spot where the Beamer was parked. "What did Margo Allshouse say to you?"

"Is that your fucking business?"

"As much as what I do in my off-time is yours."

Chessie laughs. "Two points." He pulls a blade of grass from the Michaliks' lawn and sticks it between his teeth. "I know exactly what that woman needs."

So I'm wrong. They haven't fucked, and for some reason I'm a little disappointed. "Perhaps you're right," I say.

"Trust me."

Poor Chessie. All his illusions about the world are coming to an end.

It's close to noon. The street is flat and shadowless, not a living thing in sight. Only the sound of the men singing "Bye Bye Birdie," their voices rising drunkenly on "Birdie," interrupts the stillness. In a few years, after they close down the refinery and bring in the big cranes and dismantle the units and sell them for scrap, our spot along the river will be as silent and odorless as this one.

"My old man worked in the shipyard," he says.

"Mine, too."

"Back then, every week someone got killed. The refinery was considered the *good* job. And it was, once. Before the strike. We could do anything we wanted. Brought hookers into the plant, cooled cans of beer in the propane chiller. As long as the product was flowing, they looked the other way. Our baseball team was the best in the valley, and if a shift interfered with a game, they let us play the game. Fuck the shift."

Some of the men spill out of the house and onto the street. One of them opens the trunk of his Chrysler New Yorker and others group around. He hands out counterfeit Hummel figurines.

"You should have been there," Chessie says.

The men examine the statuettes and heft them, testing their weight. Some of them get out their wallets and hand bills to the Chrysler man. Franny starts tossing a figurine in the air, and the others follow his lead.

"Margo Allshouse is a dyke," I tell Chessie.

He snatches the blade of grass from his mouth. "Get out of here."

"Seriously."

"Well, that explains a lot." His eyes narrow. "How the hell do you know?"

"I just know."

Now all the men are throwing figurines in the air, each trying to hit the other's. I hear the Chrysler man say, "You break it, you pay for it."

Forgotten, Larry Michalik's widow staggers out of her house with a cardboard cylinder in her hand. She steps out of her mules and, barefoot, crosses the lawn in front of us toward the hedge dividing her yard from her neighbor's. "Jesus. Weeds," she says.

She keeps walking and disappears between two boxwoods. The shrubbery quakes as her hoarse deep voice emerges: "Give me a hand, will you?"

Chessie and I look at each other and laugh. We climb to our feet, and, curious, go help her disperse the dead.

Nominated by ZYZZYVA

MASTERING THE ART OF FRENCH COOKING

by E.J. LEVY

from SALMAGUNDI

I HAVE NO PHOTOGRAPH of my mother cooking, but when I recall my childhood this is how I picture her: standing in the kitchen of our suburban ranch house, a blue-and-white-checked terry cloth apron tied at her waist, her lovely head bent over a recipe, a hiss of frying butter, a smell of onions and broth, and open like a hymnal on the counter beside her, a copy of Julia Child's *Mastering the Art of French Cooking*.

The book's cover is delicately patterned like wallpaper—white with miniature red fleurs-de-lis and tiny teal stars—the title and authors' names modestly scripted in a rectangular frame no larger than a recipe card: a model of feminine self-effacement.

This unassuming book was my mother's most reliable companion throughout my childhood, and from the table laid with a blue cotton cloth, not yet set with flatware and plates and glasses of ice water, not yet laid with bowls of broccoli spears, *boeuf bourguignon*, potatoes sautéed in butter, I observed her as she sought in its pages an elusive balance between the bitter and sweet.

It is a scene less remembered than invoked, an amalgam of the many evenings when I sat and watched my mother cook at the copper gas stove whose handles glowed a soft burnished too-human pink. Tall and remote as statuary, dressed stylishly in cashmere and pumps, a chestnut bouffant framing her face and its high cheekbones, her pale-blue eyes cast down, my mother consulted her

257

recipes night after night. It is a scene suffused in memory with a diffuse golden light and a sense of enormous safety and an awareness that beyond that radiant kitchen lay the shadow-draped lawn, the cold, starry night of another Midwestern autumn.

My mother had few pleasures when I was growing up. She liked to read. She liked to play the piano. She liked to cook. Of these, she did a good deal of the first, very little of the second, and a great deal of the third. She was of that generation of women caught in the sexual crossfire of women's liberation, who knew enough to probe for their desires, but not enough to practice them.

Born into the permissive Sixties, raised in the disillusioned Seventies, the third of three children, I came of age in a world where few rules were trusted, few applied. Of those that did, the rules contained in my mother's cookbooks were paramount.

The foods of my childhood were romantic. *Boeuf bourguignon. Vichyssoise. Salade Niçoise. Bouillabaisse. Béarnaise. Mousseline au Chocolat.* Years before I could spell these foods, I learned their names from my mother's lips, their smells by heart.

At the time I took no notice of the gustatory schizophrenia that governed our meals: the extravagant French cuisine prepared on the nights my father dined with us; the Swanson TV dinners on the nights we ate alone, we three kids and my mother, nights that came more frequently as the Sixties ebbed into the Seventies. On those nights we ate our dinners in silence and watched the Vietnam war on television, and I took a childish proprietary delight in having a dinner of my own, served in its aluminum tray, with each portion precisely fitted to its geometrical place. These dinners were heated under thin tin foil and served on plates, and we ate directly from the metal trays our meals of soft whipped potatoes, brown gravy, sliced turkey, cubed carrots and military-green peas.

Had I noticed these culinary cycles, I doubt that I would have recognized them for the strategic maneuvers they seem to me in retrospect. Precisely what my parents were warring over I'm not sure, but it seems clear to me now that in the intricate territorial maneuvers that for years defined their marriage, cooking was my mother's principal weapon. Proof of her superiority. My father might not feel tenderness, but he would have to admire her. My mother cooked with a vengeance in those years, or perhaps I should say she cooked for revenge. In her hands, cuisine became a martial art.

My mother spent herself in cooking. Whipping egg whites by hand with her muscular forearm, rubbing down a turkey with garlic and butter and rosemary and thyme, she sublimated her enormous unfeminine ambition in extravagant hubristic cuisine. Disdainful of the Sisyphean chores of house cleaning, she threw herself into the task of feeding us in style. If we were what we ate, she was hell bent on making her brood singular, Continental, and I knew throughout my childhood that I would disappoint her.

In the kitchen, my mother could invent for herself a coterie of scent and flavor, a retinue of exquisite associates, even though she would later have to eat them. What she craved in those years was a companion, not children, but my father was often gone, and I was ill suited to the role.

I lacked utterly the romance my mother craved. Indifferent to books, unsociable, I could not master French. Though I would study the language for five years in high school I would never get beyond the rudiments of ordering in restaurants and asking directions to the municipal pool (*Je voudrais un bifteck, s'il vous plaît. Oú est la piscine?*). In the face of my mother's yearning, I became a spectator of desire, passive, watchful, wary. Well into my twenties I remained innocent of my tastes, caught up in observing my mother's passions and fearful too that I might betray her, call into question her unswerving desires with desires of my own.

Julia Child was the only reliable companion my mother had in those years, other than the woman who came once a week to clean the house. Across the street the Segals had a "live-in girl," a local college student who came in to watch the children in the afternoons, while Mrs. Segal nursed a nervous breakdown. Each year these live-in girls changed: now blond, now brunette, with names like Stacy and Joanne. They taught us how to shoot hoops, how to ride bikes, how to appreciate soap operas. In our house there was no "live-in girl," there was only Mrs. Williams, the "cleaning lady."

I was quiet on the days when Mrs. Williams came to clean, embarrassed that we needed someone to help us keep our lives in order, embarrassed too by the fact that she was black and we were white. On the afternoons she came to clean I could not help but see my family as White People, part of a pattern of white folks who hired black folks to pick up after them. I felt ashamed when I saw my

259

mother and Mrs. Williams chatting over coffee at our kitchen table. I saw their silhouettes against history and they made an ugly broken line. I read in it patronage, condescension, exploitation, thwarted rage.

I thought at the time that it was misapplied gentility that prompted my mother to sit with Mrs. Williams while she ate lunch. Their conversations seemed to me a matter of polite routine. They spoke generally. Of the latest space launch. Watergate, the price of oil. The conversation was not intimate. But they shared it. Later, when Mrs. Williams was dying of breast cancer, she told my mother that my mother had been her best friend. Her *best*friend. My mother told me this with wonder, as if she were amazed that anyone had ever considered her a friend. Now I wonder if the declaration moved her too because she understood its corollary: that Mrs. Williams had been her best, perhaps her only, friend.

Cooking was not the only medium in which my mother excelled. She organized birthday parties on an epic scale—fashioning piñatas out of crepe paper and papier-mâché, organizing haunted houses, and games of smell and memory—and she made us prize-winning costumes well beyond the point at which we should rightly have given up masquerading.

I was 15 when I won the final prize in a series of prizes won for her costumes, for a banana suit she'd made me, a full-length, four-paneled yellow cotton shift worn over a conical cardboard cap to shape the crown, and yellow tights. My mother had ingeniously designed the suit with a triangular front panel that could be secured with Velcro to the crown or "peeled" down to reveal—through a round hole in the cloth—my face.

The prize for this costume, my father reminds me, was a radio designed to look like a box of frozen niblet corn—a square, yellow plastic radio with an authentic Green Giant label. This was the late Seventies and in America you could buy a lot of things that looked like food but weren't. You could buy a scented candle in the shape of a chocolate sundae, sculpted in a tulip glass with piles of frothy false whipped cream and a perfect wax cherry. You could buy a soda glass tipped on its side out of which a carbonated cola-colored liquid spilled into a puddle of clear plastic. There was shampoo that smelled of herbs or lemons; tiny soaps in the shape of peaches and green apples; paperweights shaped like giant aspirin, four inches in diameter, cast in plaster; the plastic simulacrum of a slice of pineapple or a fried egg dangling at the end of a key chain.

It was an era of food impersonation. A cultural critic might dismiss this as conspicuous consumption: possessed of abundance, we could mock necessity. Food, for us, could be a plaything—revenge for all those childhood admonitions not to play with your food. But I think that there was in this as well a sign of political disaffection—an ironic commentary on the unreliability of appearances in the wake of Watergate and Vietnam (in South Africa such objects were also popular at the time, a Fulbright scholar from Zimbabwe will tell me years later)—and a measure of spiritual dislocation. As if, glutted with comfort and suspicious of appearances, we had lost touch with what sustains us and had relinquished faith in even the most elementary source of life. Food.

Mixed marriage. The phrase itself recalls cuisine: mixed greens, mixed vegetables, "mix carefully two cups sifted flour with. . . ." As if marriage were a form of sentimental cookery, a blending of disparate ingredients—man and woman—to produce a new and delectable whole. "She's my honey bun, my sweet pea, my cookie, sugar"; "You can't make an omelet without breaking a few eggs."

English is spiced with phrases that attest to our enduring attachment to food as metaphor, and point to our abiding faith in affection's ability to sustain us as vitally as food. But the phrase mixed marriage suggests as well the limits of love, its inability to transform difference, and is a warning. In the mythic goulash of American culture, the melting pot is supposed to inspire amity, not love. One should melt, it seems, not mix. Marriage, of the kind my parents ventured to embrace—between gentile and Jew—went, according to the conventions of the time, too far.

It was in part because of their differences that my mother married my father. He must have seemed to her exotic, with his dark skin, jet eyes, his full sensuous mouth; at 70 he will look like Rossano Brazzi, but at age 31, when my parents meet at the University of Minnesota on the stairs of Eddy Hall as my beautiful mother descends from a library in the tower where she has finished her day's research and my father ascends to his office where he is a young professor of psychology, he is more handsome even than a movie star—I can see this in photos from the time—because his face is radiant with expectation for his future.

For my father, son of Russian and Latvian immigrants, marrying my mother must have seemed like marrying America itself. Her ancestors had come over in 1620 on that first and famous boat and though my mother's family was of modest means, her speech and gestures bespeak gentility. Her English is precise, peppered with Latinate words and French phrases, her pronunciations are distinctive and slightly Anglicized (not cer-EE-bral, she corrects me, CER-eh-bral). She possesses all the Victorian virtues: widely read, she is an accomplished pianist and a gifted painter; she speaks French and Czech, is knowledgeable in art and history, physics, physiology, and philosophy. Although she is a passionate conversationalist, she has a habit of concluding her sentences on a slight descending note as if she has discovered part way through speech that it is too wearying to converse after all, and so gives up. My mother's verbal inflections are the telltale signs of class in classless America and marrying her, my father crossed the tracks. He could not know how he would resent the crossing; she could not know how she would resent the role of wife.

My mother's enormous ambitions were channeled by her marriage into a narrow course—like a great roaring river forced against its nature to straighten and be dammed, resulting in floods, lost canyons—and her desires became more powerful for having been restrained. It seemed to me only a matter of time before she'd reassert her claim to wilder, broader terrain. Throughout my childhood, I waited for my mother to leave.

Given the centrality of culinary concerns in my childhood, it is unsurprising perhaps that my first act on leaving home was to codify my eating. My first term at college, I eschewed the freshman ritual of room decoration—the requisite Monet prints, the tacky O'Keeffe's—in favor of regulations: I tacked a single notice to the bulletin board beside my desk specifying what I could and could not eat. My schema was simple: 1,000 calories each day, plus, if absolutely necessary, a pack of sugarless gum and as much as a pound of carrots (my skin, in certain photos from the period, is tinted orange from excess carotene). I swam my meals off each morning with a two-mile swim at dawn, and a cold shower.

My saporous palette was unimaginative and highly unesthetic and varied little from an essentially white and brown motif: poached white fish, bran cereal, skim milk, egg whites, with the occasional splash out into carrots. I practiced a sort of secular asceticism, in which repression of desire was for its own sake deemed a virtue.

In time, I grew thin, then I grew fat. My senior year, by an inverse of my earlier illogic, I ate almost without cessation: lacking authentic desire to guide me, I consumed indiscriminately. Unpracticed in the exercise of tastes, I lumbered insensibly from one meal to the next. I often ate dinner twice, followed up by a pound bag of M & M's or a slice of pizza. The pop psychology of the day informed me that my eating habits were an effort to "stuff rage," but it seemed to me that I was after ballast. Something to weight me to the world, as love was said to do. Despite my heft, I felt insubstantial as steam, airy and faint as an echo.

Therapy was merely insulting. One waif-like counselor, who had herself been anorectic and spoke in a breathy, childlike voice, insisted earnestly and frequently, whenever I confessed to a thought, "That it is your bulimia speaking." She said this irrespective of my statements, like a spiritualist warning of demons in the ether. I raged, I wept, I reasoned. But it was not me, she averred, but my bulimia—*speaking*. She made it sound as if I had a troll living inside me. And I knew it was a lie. I told her I thought this whole thing, my eating and all, was about desire, about being attracted to women. But she set me straight.

In the space of two years I would pass through half a dozen women's hands (none of them a lover's)—therapists, social workers, Ph.D. candidates, even a stern Irish psychiatrist, who looked unnervingly like the actress Colleen Dewhurst—and all of them in short order would assure me that I was not desirous of women. As if it were unthinkable, a thing scripted on the body at birth, a thing you could read in the face, the hands; as if sexual desire were not after all an acquired taste.

I was twenty-five before I went to bed with a woman and when I did I found that all along I had been right. Though it strains credulity, the following morning I woke and found that I had lost ten pounds in the night and had recovered my sense of taste. I never again had trouble with food, though my tastes surprised me. Things I never knew I liked suddenly glowed on the gustatory horizon like beacons. Plump oily avocados. The dainty lavender-sheathed teeth of garlic. Ginger. Tonic and Tanqueray gin. Green olives. Blood oranges. Pungent Italian cheese.

If education is ultimately the fashioning of a self through the cultivation of discernment and taste, this was my education, and with it came an acute craving for books and music and film. I discovered in that summer the writings of Virginia Woolf and the films of Ingmar Bergman, the paintings of Jasper Johns and Gertrude Stein's prose and John Cage's symphonies, Italian wines and sex. And I began, tentatively, fearfully, to write (though even the effort to keep a journal was an ordeal; I was tortured by doubt: How could I know what was worthy of recording, what I liked enough, what mattered enough to note and keep?).

"Do you love him?" I once asked my mother, when I was 13 and still young enough to think that was a simple question, a thing one had or didn't have, the thing that mattered; when I did not yet understand all the other painful, difficult things that bind people more surely than love ever will.

"I like your father," she said. "That is more important."

I do not misremember this. It remains with me like a recipe I follow scrupulously, an old family recipe. And when in my first year of graduate school my lover asks me if I love her, I try to form an answer as precise as my mother's before me; I say "I am very fond of you, I like and respect you," and watch as pain rises in her face like a leavening loaf. I have learned from my mother and Julia Child how to master French cooking, but I have no mastery when it comes to love. It will take me a long time to get the hang of this; it will take practice.

In my second year of graduate school, I enroll in an introductory French class. The instructor is a handsome man from Haiti, and the whole class is a little in love with him. In Minneapolis, the home of the sartorially challenged, where a prominent Uptown billboard exhorts passersby to "Dress like you're not from around here," he is a fashion oasis. An anomaly in these rooms of unmodulated beige, he is dressed this drear January morning in a black turtleneck, chinos, belt, heavy gold chain, ring, watch. He looks like he might go straight from this 11:15 a.m. class to a nightclub—or as if he has just come from one.

Born thirty miles east of Cap Haitien, the second largest city in

Haiti, he is an unlikely figure in these rooms filled with privileged white kids from the suburbs. His own education, he recalls, was "sketchy," snatched from stints in lycée (the equivalent of an American secondary school) in Cap-Haitien. His parents did not live together and life under Duvalier was difficult; he did, he says, what was necessary to survive.

All my adult life I have sought out people like this, people who I sense can instruct me in how to live in the world. Who know how to survive, to hustle. How to make it from one day to the next. The things my mother and father couldn't teach me or never knew. I will spend my twenties and early thirties seeking out people like this, like a junkie; I can't get enough of certitude or attitude.

The questions you ask in an introductory language class are always the important ones, the original ones that the raw fact of language inspires, the ones we ask as children then forget when we grow up. On the first day of class I dutifully copy into my notebook the questions the instructor has written on the board: *Qui suis-je? Qui êtes-vous?* It is only later, while scanning the pages of this notebook, that I am startled to see the questions I have scribbled there, demanding an answer: Who am I? Who are you?

I had been in junior high or high school when I first began to imagine that my parents would separate as soon as their children left home. I had come to expect this, so that when my siblings and I did leave I was genuinely shocked, even disappointed, that my parents stayed together. I didn't understand that they were, after all those years, if not fond of one another, at least established, that they were afraid of loneliness, that approaching 60, approaching 70, they were too tired to fight and so perhaps could make room as they hadn't previously for tenderness. I didn't understand that it is not that time heals all, but that in time the simple fact of having survived together can come to outweigh other concerns, that if you're not careful, you can forget that you ever hoped for something more than sustenance.

"Your parents seem so comfortable," a friend of mine commented after we had dined with my parents in New York City a few years back, when my folks were visiting me. "Yes," I said, with something like regret, recognizing in that moment for the first time their surrender in a long-waged battle. "I think they are." These days my mother orders in Thanksgiving dinner from a restaurant in St. Paul. She orders unlikely foods: in place of the traditional turkey with trimmings, there is a large, squat, hatbox-shaped vegetable torte with marinara sauce, green salad, cranberries from the can. At dinner, she presides from the head of the table, opposite my father, smiling. Sedate as a pudding.

In college, I met a young woman who had corresponded throughout her childhood with Julia Child. It was from her that I first heard that Child had been an alcoholic and often was drunk on the set. My mother, if she recognized drunkenness for what it was, nevertheless cast the story differently: she laughed about how Child, having dropped a chicken on the floor during a taping, had had the aplomb to pick it up and cook it anyhow. This delighted my mother, this imperturbability, the ability in the face of disappointment to carry on.

I have asked my mother if she regrets her marriage, her choices; and she has told me it is pointless to regret. That she did what she could do. What more can we ask of ourselves? I want to tell her, but do not, that we must ask for so much more, for everything, for love and tenderness and decency and courage. That we must be much more than comfortable, that we must be better than we think we can be, so that if in some foreign tongue we are confronted with those childhood questions—"*Qui êtes-vous?*" "*Qui suis-je?*"—we will not be afraid to answer.

A few weeks ago, I came across a copy of *Mastering the Art of French Cooking* in a second-hand shop, unused, for $7.49. I bought it and took it home. Fingering its rough pulpy pages, consulting its index for names that conjured my long-ago abandoned childhood, I scanned the book as if its pages could provide an explanation, as if it were a secret record of my mother's thwarted passion. I held it in my lap, hesitant to read it, as if it were after all a private matter, a diary of those bygone days when it still seemed possible in this country, in our lives, to bring together disparate elements and mix them—artfully, beautifully—and make of them some new and marvelous whole.

Nominated by Sherod Santos, Salmagundi

SELF PORTRAIT IN INK

by BRUCE BEASLEY

from VIRGINIA QUARTERLY REVIEW

As the gone-
translucent

octopus
jet-blasts into evasion, vanishing

while its ink-sac spurts
a cloud of defensive

mucus & coagulant
azure-black pigment,

self-shaped
octopus imago in ink, so the shark

gnashes at that blobbed
sepia phantom,

pseudomorph
that disperses into black

nebulae & shreds
with each shark-strike

& the escaped
octopus throbs

beyond, see-through
in the see-through water, untouched—:

so, go
little poem, little

ink-smudge-on-fingertip
& -print, mimicker

& camouflage,
self-getaway, cloud-

scribble, write
out my dissipating

name on the water,
emptied sac of self-illusive ink . . .

Nominated by Brenda Miller, Robin Hemley, Donald Platt

THE ROLE OF A LIFETIME

by FLOYD SKLOOT

from APPROXIMATELY PARADISE (TUPELO PRESS)

I am bound upon a wheel of fire

—*King Lear*

He could not imagine himself as Lear.
He could do age. He could rage on a heath.
Wounded pride, a man gone wild: he could be clear
on those, stalking the stage, ranting beneath
a moon tinged red. Let words rather than full
throated roars carry fury while the wind
howled. He could do that. And the awful pull
of the lost daughter, the old man more sinned
against than sinning. The whole wheel of fire
thing. But not play a wayward mind! Be cut
to the brains, strange to himself, his entire
soul wrenched free, then remember his lines but
act forgetting. Understand pure nonsense
well enough to make no sense when saying
it. Wits turned was one thing; wits in absence
performed with wit was something else. Playing
Lear would force him to inhabit his fear,
fathom the future he had almost reached
already. Why, just last week, running here
and there to find lost keys, a friend's name leached

from memory. Gone. No, nor could he bring
himself to speak the plain and awful line
that shows the man within the shattered king:
I fear I am not in my perfect mind.

Nominated by Tupelo Press, Richard Burgin

WHAT FUNDAMENTALISTS NEED FOR THEIR SALVATION

by DAVID JAMES DUNCAN

from ORION

> *The question before the human race is, whether the God of nature shall govern the world by his own laws, or whether priests and kings shall rule it by fictitious miracles.*
>
> —John Adams, to Thomas Jefferson, 1815

I WAS BORN A CHOSEN PERSON, though this state of affairs was not of my choosing. My mother, grandmother, and great-grandmother were staunch Seventh Day Adventists—an Apocalypse-preaching. Saturday-worshiping fundamentalist sect that arose in the mid-nineteenth century. Our faith's founder prophesied Jesus's Second Coming and "the Rapture" in 1850. When both failed to occur, he instead formed the church into which the matriarchs of my family were later born. These strong women gave their offspring no choice but to attend the same churches and share their faith, so attend and share we did. My father and grandfather, however, did not attend church, and none of my friends at public school were SDAs either. I, in other words was "saved"—no plagues of boils and frogs or eternal hellfire for me—whereas my father, grandfather, and school friends were, according to our preachers, impending toast. Sound suspicious to you? It sure did to me.

My earliest memory of Adventist faith-training is of being four years old in Sabbath School and having to sing "Jesus Wants Me for a Sunbeam" while making our fingers extend out around our faces like "sunbeams." I felt nothing for Jesus as we did this—and I loved Jesus, found him heroic from earliest memory. All I can recall feeling during the sunbeam song was bafflement that our teachers would make us do such silly things.

Similar confusion invaded my attempts to recite "Now I Lay Me Down to Sleep" at bedtime. Not only did this prayer not give me courage to face the night, it felt unfair to say it. To expect God to listen to a rote ditty, then protect us in response, seemed like offering Him almost nothing but asking Him for a lot. As for the time I asked Jesus for a base hit at a ballgame, when I stepped to the plate and struck out on three pitches I was relieved: if every kid in America could get a hit just by asking Jesus, we'd all bat a thousand and ruin baseball in a day.

Intense spiritual feelings were frequent visitors during my boyhood, but they did not come from churchgoing or from bargaining with God through prayer. The connection I felt to the Creator came, unmediated, from Creation itself. The spontaneous gratitude I felt for birds and birdsong, tree-covered and snowcapped mountains, rivers and their trout, moon- and starlight, summer winds on wilderness lakes, the same lakes silenced by winter snows, spring resurrections after autumn's mass deaths—the intimacy, intricacy, and interwovenness of these things—became the spiritual instructors of my boyhood. In even the smallest suburban wilds I felt linked to powers and mysteries I could imagine calling the Presence of God.

In fifteen years of churchgoing I did not once feel this same sense of Presence. What I felt instead was a lot of heavily agendaed, fear-based information being shoved at me by men on the church payroll. Though these men claimed to speak for God, I was never convinced.

On the day I was granted the option of what our preachers called "leaving the faith," I did, and increased my faith by so doing. Following intuition and love with all the sincerity and attentiveness I could muster, I consciously chose to spend my life in the company of rivers, wilderness, wisdom literature, like-minded friends, and quiet contemplation. And as it's turned out, this life, though dirt-poor in church pews, has enriched me with a sense of the holy, and left me far more grateful than I'll ever be able to say.

Three decades of intimacy with some of the world's greatest wisdom texts and some of the West's most beautiful rivers led me to assume I'd escaped the orbit of organized religion entirely. Then came a night in Medford, Oregon. After giving a literary reading to a warm, sometimes raucous, not-at-all-churchlike crowd, I was walking to the car when one of the most astute men I know—my good friend Sam Alvord—clapped me on the back and amiably remarked, "I enjoy your evangelism."

The last word in Sam's sentence flabbergasted me. *Evangelism?* I was a storyteller, not one of those dang proselytizers! The evangelists I'd known since childhood thought the supposed "inerrancy" of the Bible magically neutralized their own flaming errancy and gave them an apostolic right to judge humanity and bilk it at the same time. The evangelists I'd known proclaimed themselves saved, the rest of us damned, and swore that only by shouting *"John 3:16! John 3:16!"* at others, as if selling Redemption Peanuts at a ballgame, could we avoid an Eternal State of Ouch. Evangelists, as I saw 'em, were a self-enlisted army of Cousin Sydneys from Mark Twain's *Tom Sawyer*, preaching a tattletale religiosity that boiled down to the cry. *If you don't believe what the Bible and me say, and pay me for saying it, I'm gonna tell God on you and you're gonna get in Big Trouble!*

Then clear-eyed, honest Sam says, "I enjoy your evangelism"?

Shit O. Deer.

My first response to Sam's remark was to repress the living be-jeezus out of it. Ten years passed before I dared look up the "e-word" in the *Oxford English Dictionary*. What I finally found there was, well . . . I guess the word pretty much has to be, *damning*. Though the range of meanings surrounding the root-word "evangel" is broad, a whole raft of definitions tied my public readings, literary writings, and me to Sam's characterization. Insofar as I believe Jesus is the bee's knees, and insofar as I speak words that could be seen as spreading the spiritual intent of the gospels, I must admit, with "fear and trembling," that I am (gulp!) *evangelical*.

Now, having damned myself in what we might call "anti-evangelical circles," I'd like to qualify my confession by stating what the word "evangelical" suggests to me.

Religious laws, in all the major traditions, have both a letter and a spirit. As I understand the words and example of Jesus, the spirit of a law is all-important, whereas the letter, while useful in conjunction with spirit, becomes lifeless and deadly without it. In accord with this distinction, a yearning to worship on wilderness ridges or beside rivers, rather than in churches, could legitimately be called *evangelical*. Jesus himself began his mission after forty days and nights in wilderness. According to the same letter-versus-spirit distinction, the law-heavy literalism of many so-called evangelicals is not evangelical at all: "evangel" means "the gospels," the essence of the gospels is Jesus, and literalism is not something that Jesus personified or taught.

I would also propose that one needn't be a Christian for the word to apply; if your words or deeds harmonize with the example of Jesus, you are evangelical in spirit whether you claim to be or not. When the non-Christian Ambrose Bierce, for instance, wrote, "War is the means by which Americans learn geography," there was acid dripping almost visibly from his pen. His words, however, are aimed at the same antiwar end as the gospel statements "Love thine enemies" and "Love thy neighbor as thyself." And "Blessed are the peacemakers." Bierce's wit is in this sense evangelical whether he likes it or not.

Evangelism was never intended to mean the missionary zeal of self-righteous proselytizers claiming that their narrow interpretation of scripture will prevent eternal punishments and pay eternal rewards. Evangelism implies, on the contrary, the kind of all-embracing universality evident in Mother Teresa's prayer, "May God break my heart so completely that the whole world falls in." Not just fellow nuns, Catholics, Calcuttans, Indians. *The whole world*. It gives me pause to realize that, were such a prayer said by me and answered by God, I would afterward possess a heart so open that even hate-driven zealots would fall inside. There is a self-righteous knot in me that finds zealotry so repugnant it wants to sit on the sidelines with the like-minded, plaster our cars with bumper stickers that say MEAN PEOPLE SUCK AND NO BILLIONAIRE LEFT BEHIND and WHO WOULD JESUS BOMB?, and leave it at that. But I can't. My sense of the world as a gift, my sense of a grace operative in this world despite its terrors, propels me to allow the world to open my heart still wider, even if the openness comes by breaking, for I have seen the whole world fall into a few hearts, and nothing has ever struck me as more beautiful.

The whole world, for example, seemed to fall into the heart of Mahatma Gandhi, not only on the day he said, "I am a Christian, I am a Hindu, I am a Muslim, I am a Jew," but on the day he proved the depth of his declaration when, after receiving two fatal bullets from a fundamentalist zealot, he blessed that zealot with a *namasté* before dying. For the fundamentalists of each tradition he names, Gandhi's four-fold profession of faith is three-fourths heresy. But it is also a statement that makes livable sense of Jesus's "love thy neighbor as thyself" and, for me personally, a description of spiritual terrain in which I yearn to take up residence. If, because of this yearning, these pages are found offensive by some, how can I not feel honored by that very offense?

The world's great religions, though far from identical, are close enough in ultimate aim that huge-hearted individuals within each faith have shown themselves able to love and serve their neighbors regardless of their neighbors' various faiths. I consider it evangelical, in the Jesus-loving sense of the word, to serve followers of Abraham, Mohammed, Shakyamuni, Rama, and Jesus, or nonfollowers of the same, without discrimination or distinction.

The gulf between this open-hearted evangelism and the aims of modern fundamentalism is vast. Most of the famed leaders of the new "Bible-based" American political alliances share a conviction that their causes and agendas are approved of and directly inspired by no less a being than God. This enviable conviction is less enviably arrived at by accepting on faith, hence as fact, that the Christian Bible pared down to American TV English is God's "word" to humankind, that this same Bible is His only word to humankind, and that the politicized apocalyptic fundamentalist's unprecedentedly selective slant on this Bible is the one true slant.

The position is remarkably self-insulating. Possessing little knowledge of or regard for the world's wealth of religious, literary, spiritual, and cultural traditions, fundamentalist leaders accept no concept of love or compassion but their own. They can therefore honestly, and even cheerfully, say that it is out of Christian compassion and a sort of tough love for others that they seek to impose on all others their tendentiously literalized God, Bible, and slant. But how "tough" can love be before it ceases to be love at all? Well-known variations on the theme include the various Inquisitions' murderously tough love for "heretics" who for centuries were defined as merely defiant of the Inquisition itself; the European Catholic and American Puritan tough love for "witches" who for centuries were defined as virtually any sexually active or humanitarian or unusually skilled single woman whose healing herbs or independence from men defied a male church hierarchy's claim to be the source of all healing; the Conquistadors' genocidally tough love for the Incas, Aztecs, and Mayans whose gold they stole for the glory of a church meant to honor the perfect poverty of a life begun in a manager and ended on a cross; the missionaries' and U.S. Cavalry's genocidally tough love for land-rich indigenous peoples whose crime was merely to exist; and, today, the Bush team's murderously tough love for an oil-rich Muslim world as likely to convert to Texas neocon values as Bush himself is likely to convert to Islam.

Each of these crusader groups has seen itself as fighting to make its own or some other culture more Christian even as it tramples the teachings of Christ into a blood-soaked earth. The result, among millions of nonfundamentalists, has been revulsion toward anything that chooses to call itself Christian. But I see no more crucial tool for defusing fundamentalist aggression than the four books of the gospels, and can think of no more crucial question to keep asking our crusaders than whether there is anything truly imitative of Jesus—that is, anything compassionate, self-abnegating, empathetic, forgiving, and enemy-loving—in their assaults on those they have determined to be "evil."

The appropriation of Christian terminology by the American political movement known as neoconservative has resulted in a breed of believer I'm tempted to call "avengelical," but in the interests of diplomacy will simply call right-wing. The fusion of right-wing politics and religiosity has changed America's leadership, altered our identity in the eyes of the world, and created a mood of close-minded vehemence in millions. Critics of the right-wing/fundamentalist conflation are now often demonized not just as traitors to America, but as enemies of a new kind of Americanized God. A growing number of people of faith, however, believe that Americans are being asked to worship a bogus image of God. Though examples of the deception are numerous, I'll describe two which came to my attention through the writings of the evangelical Christian Jim Wallis.

On the first anniversary of the destruction of the World Trade Center, President Bush gave a speech in New York in which he said that the "ideal of America is the hope of all mankind." Six billion people on Earth are not Americans; to call America their hope is, to put it mildly, hubristic. What's more, all those who place their hope not in nations but in God are obligated by their faith to find Bush's statement untrue. But Bush's speechwriters ratchet the rhetoric up even further. After calling America the world's hope, Bush added, "That hope still lights our way. And the light shines in the darkness. And the darkness has not overcome it." As Wallis points out in "Dangerous Religion" (*Mississippi Review*, Vol. 10, No. 1), these last sentences are lifted straight out of the Gospel of John, where they refer not to America or any nation, but to the word of God and the light of Christ.

Second example: in his 2003 State of the Union address, the president said that there is "power, wonder-working power in the goodness and idealism and faith of the American people"—words stolen from a hymn that in fact says there is "power, wonder-working power in the blood of the Lamb." This thievery is breathtaking, and leaves me wondering what Bush's speechwritters might steal next. John I:I perhaps? *In the beginning was America, and America was with God, and America was God. . . .*

"The real theological problem in America today," writes Wallis, is "the nationalist religion . . . that confuses the identity of the nation with the church, and God's purposes with the mission of American empire. America's foreign policy is more than preemptive, it is theologically presumptuous; not only unilateral, but dangerously messianic; not just arrogant, but . . . blasphemous."

I would add the Bush administration's notion of stewardship to Wallis's list of blasphemies. To describe the current war on nature as stewardship is to forsake the very teachings of the Bible. In Genesis, men and women are made in the image of the God who just created and blessed all creatures and their ability to multiply, and Adam is placed in Eden merely "to dress it and keep it." In Exodus, the Sabbath rest is given to animals as well as humans. In Leviticus, humans are told by God to tend the land carefully and not treat it as a possession, because "the land is mine, and you are but aliens who have become my tenants." And again in the psalms: "The Earth is the Lord's, and the fullness thereof." Then in the gospels we meet, in Jesus, a leader who refuses political power and defines dominion as "Thy will be done, on earth as it is in heaven," a king of kings whose life is characterized throughout by sensitivity to the meek, the weak, the poor, the voiceless, field lilies, the fowls of the air, and all other forms of life.

American fundamentalists, despite avowed love for this same Jesus, predominately support an administration that has worked to weaken the Clean Air and Clean Water acts and gut the Endangered Species and Environmental Policy acts; this administration has stopped fining air and water polluters, dropped all suits against coal-fired power, weakened limits on pollutants that destroy ozone, increased the amount of mercury in the air and water, vowed to drill in the Arctic wildlife sanctuary, stopped citizen review of logging proposals in the people's own forests—the list goes on and on. I wish that none of it were true. I wish that devastation, extinctions, ever-more-powerful hurricanes, epidemic diseases, and cancers were not raining down upon us as I write. But since they are, I must ask: how righteous, how truthful, how *Christian* is the cunning of speechwriters who place words meant to praise God, or even Christ's spilled blood, in the mouth of a man who instead uses them to exalt an empire born of the destruction of America's own ecosystems, civility, diplomacy, and honesty?

The manipulators who convert the very "blood of the Lamb" into the phrase "the American people" force those of faith to make a call. To treat the Earth as disposable and the Bible as God, turn that God into a political action committee, equate arrogance and effrontery with evangelism, right-wing politics with worship, aggression with compassion, devastation with stewardship, disingenuous televised prattle with prayer, and call the result Christianity, is, according to the teachings of Jesus, not an enviable position, but a fatal one.

Those of us struggling to defend ravaged landscapes, demonized Muslims, ecologically disinherited children, vanished compassion, and every other casualty of neocon-fundamentalist rhetoric are dealing with end results, not the primary cause. We might do better to shift our attention to the fundamentalist machinery itself.

Contemporary American fundamentalism is more a manufactured product, or even an industrial byproduct, than a result of careful reflection. The "Christian" Right's fully-automated evangelical machinery runs twenty-four hours a day—like McDonald's, Coca-Cola's, and ExxonMobil's—making converts globally. But to what? The conversion industry's notion of the word "Christian" has substituted a "Rapture Index" and Armageddon fantasy for Christ's interior kingdom of heaven and love of neighbor; it is funded by donors lured by a tele-vangelical "guarantee" of "a hundredfold increase on all financial donations," as if Mark 10:30 were an ad for a financial pyramid scheme and Jesus never said, "Sell all thou hast and distribute unto the poor"; it has replaced once-personal relationships between parishioners and priests or preachers with radio and TV bombast, sham healings, and congregation-fleecing scams performed by televangelical rock stars; it has trumped worship characterized by contemplative music, reflective thought, and silent prayer with three-ring media-circuses and "victory campaigns"; it inserts lobbyists in its pulpits and political brochures in its pews, claims that both speak for Jesus, and raises millions for this Jesus though its version of him preaches neo-con policies straight out of Washington think tanks and spends most of "His" money on war, it quotes Mark 10:15 and Matthew 5:44 and Matthew 6:6 and Luke 18:9–14 a grand total of never; it revels in its election of a violent, historically ignorant, science-flaunting, carcinogenic-policied president who goads us toward theocracy at home even as he decries theocracies overseas; it defies cooperation and reason in governance, exults in division, and hastens the degeneration of a democracy built upon cooperation and reason; it claims an exclusive monopoly on truth ("America is the hope of all mankind . . .") yet trivializes truth globally by evincing ignorance of Christianity's historic essence and disrespect toward the world's ethnic and religious diversity and astonishingly rich cultural present and past.

To refer to peregrinating Celtic monks and fundamentalist lobbyists, Origen and Oral Roberts, the Desert Fathers and Jerry Falwell, Dante and Pat Robertson, St. Francis and the TV "prosperity gospel" hucksters, Lady Julian of Norwich and Tim LaHaye, or John of the Cross and George W. Bush all as Christian stretches the word so thin its meaning vanishes. The term "carbon-based life-form" is as informative.

Though it may shock those who equate fundamentalism and Christianity, ninety years ago the word "fundamentalist" did not exist. The term was coined by an American Protestant splinter-group, which in 1920 proclaimed that adhering to "the literal inerrancy of the Bible" was the true Christian faith. The current size of this group does not change the aberrance of its stance: deification of the mere words of the Bible, in light of every scripture-based wisdom tradition *including Christianity's two-thousand-year-old own,* is not just naïveté, it is idolatry.

This, in all sincerity, is why fundamentalists need to honor, respect, even love those who are no such thing. How can those lost in literalism save one another? As Max Weber once put it: "We [Christians] are building an iron cage, and we're inside of it, and we're closing the door. And the handle is on the outside."

The protagonist of my first novel, *The River Why*, was a fly fisher and spiritual seeker named Gus. In that book Gus voices serious reservations about the Being some believers so possessively refer to as God. But a problem that Gus and I ran into in telling his story was that, after a climatic all-night adventure with a river and a huge chinook salmon, he had a sudden, transrational (or, in the old Christian lexicon, mystical) experience that left him too overwhelmed to speak with accuracy, yet too grateful to remain mute. This paradox is autobiographical. As the recipient of several such detonations, I felt bound by gratitude to let my protagonist speak. But as a lifelong witness of the fundamentalist assault on the Christian lexicon, I felt compelled to speak in non-Christian terms. Though Gus spoke of a presence so God-like that in the end he dubbed it "the Ancient One," his account of his experience did not once invoke the word "God."

Reader reactions to this climax have been neatly divided. Those who have experienced similar detonations have sometimes been so moved by the scene that their eyes filled as they thanked me for writing it—and those who've experienced no such detonation have asked why I ruined a dang good fishin' yarn with woo-woo. I admire both reactions. Both are constitutionally correct. Both are perfectly honest. What more should a writer want from his reader? What more, for that matter, can a mortal, be they skeptic or mystic, offer the Absolute?

The French novelist and philosopher Rene Daumal describes the paradox I faced perfectly. He wrote: "I swear to you that I have to force myself to write or to pronounce this word: God. It is a noise I make with my mouth or a movement of the fingers that hold my pen. To pronounce or to write this word makes me ashamed. What is real here is that shame. . . . Must I never speak of the Unknowable because it would be a lie? Must I speak of the Unknowable because I know that I proceed from it and am bound to bear witness to it? This contradiction is the prime mover of my best thoughts."

Another word for this shame, in my view, is *reverence*. And fundamentalism, speaking of the Unknowable, too often lacks this essential quality. The kind of fundamentalism that now more or less governs our country does not just proudly pronounce the word "God," it defines and Americanizes God, worships its own definition, and aims to impose that definition on all. What an abyss between this effrontery and the Christ-inspired self-giving of a St. Francis, Mother Teresa, or Martin Luther King! What a contrast, too, between this kind of Christianity and that of the Amish, who practice no evangelism, who tease those who quote the Bible too often (calling them "scripture smart"), and who consider it laughable to pronounce oneself "saved," since God alone is capable of such almighty judgments.

God is unlimited. Thought and language are limited. God is the fathomless but beautiful Mystery Who creates the universe and you and me, and sustains it and us every instant, and always shall. The instant we define fathomless Mystery It is no longer fathomless. To define is to limit. The greater a person's confidence in their definition of God, the more sure I feel that their worship of Him has become the worship of their own definition.

The word "God," looked at not as a Being but as a word, is very simple. Three letters. "Dog" backwards. And the word is English, mind you. Three letters of a language invented just a thousand years ago, by Norman conquerors trying to work out a way to command their Anglo-Saxon chattel. To kill or condemn others in the name of a three-letter mongrel Norman/Anglo-Saxon word is tragically absurd. A mortal being who presumes, via the study of Holy Writ, to know the will of Absolute Being and kill in accord with that "knowledge" is, I think you could say, Absolutely mistaken.

If America's literature has arrived at any theological consensus concerning what humans owe the Divine, it might be this: better to be honest to God, even if that means stating one's complete lack of belief in any such Being, than to allow one's mind and imagination to be processed by an ideology factory. In literature as in life, there are ways of disbelieving in God that are more loving, and in this sense more imitative of Jesus, than some forms of orthodox belief. There are agnostic and atheist humanitarians, for example, who believe as they do, and love their neighbors as they do, because the cruelty of humanity makes it impossible for them to conceive of a God who is anything but remiss or cruel. Rather than consider God cruel, they choose doubt or disbelief, and serve others anyway. This is a back-handed form of reverence, a beautiful kind of shame.

It seems to upset some fundamentalists that literature's answer to "the God question" is as open-minded as the Constitution's. There is also no doubt that the openness our literature and Constitution encourage results in a theological cacophony and mood of irritable interdependence that bear little or no resemblance to the self-righteousness now reigning in the average conservative church. But America remains a country that stakes its life and literature on the belief that this cacophony and interdependence are not only legal, but essential to our health.

Edward Abbey remains welcome to say, "God is Love? Not bloody likely!" Goethe remains welcome to reply, "As a man is, so is his God; therefore God is often an object of mockery." And readers of both remain free to draw their own intelligent conclusions.

If my tone here has been sharp, it's because I don't see a way to engage in peaceable exchange on faith matters with those so full of certainties that they only preach, never listen. Every fundamentalist who believes there is just one Holy Book is ignoring the fact that the Christian Bible, Koran, Torah, and Vedas are each considered to be that one book, and the God of each faith has become the empowerer of millions of potentially violent literalists. The proponents of all four faiths consider themselves chosen, they are all now armed with nuclear weapons, and the zealots of each faith are prepared to kill in defense of their chosenness. This is why each faith stands in need not of a turning away from tradition, but of a compassion rebellion against the presumptuous "certainties" of the zealots within each tradition, and a universal recognition that the sigh within the prayer is the same in the heart of the Christian, the Muslim, the Hindu, and the Jew.

Far from feeling dismayed by the differences between these faiths, I am haunted and heartened that Christians sigh for the One called *Jesus*; Muslims for the One named *Allah*; Jews for *YHWH*, "He who causes to be"; Hindus for *Brahmin*, "the Big," who speaks the beginning-middle-end word, *AUM*—and all four traditions hold that these Names cannot be properly said lest we first garb ourselves in utmost humility and surround our naming with silence.

All faiths call humanity to love, service, and stewardship, and all acts of love, service, and stewardship are holy. To put the call in Christian terms: it is this world, not the next, that God loved so much that He bequeathed it His Son. In response to the Armageddon fantasies of his day, the Son himself said, "The kingdom of God cometh not with observation . . . for behold, the kingdom of God is within you."

There is one irreplaceable Earth, and she is finite. She can absorb just so many wounds or poisons before she ceases to support life. Millions of us have recognized that in wounding the Earth for centuries we have been wounding ourselves.

There is likewise, for most humans on Earth, just one mother tongue, and it is less widely recognized that a given tongue at a given time consists of only so many words, and that these words can absorb only so many abuses before they cease to mean. America's spiritual vocabulary—with its huge defining terms such as "God," "soul," "sacrifice," "mysticism," "faith," "salvation," "grace," "redemption"—has been enduring a series of abuses so constricting that the damage may last for centuries. Too many of us (myself included) have tried to sidestep this damage by simply rejecting the terminology. But the defamation of a religious vocabulary cannot be undone by turning away; the harm is undone when we work to reopen each word's true history, nuance, and depth. Holy words need stewardship as surely as do gardens, orchards, or ecosystems. When lovingly tended, such words surround us with spaciousness and mystery the way a sacred grove surrounds us with peace and oxygenated air. But when we abandon our holy words and fail to replace them, we end up living in a spiritual clearcut.

If Americans of European descent are to understand and honor the legacy of Celtic, European, Middle Eastern, and other Christian traditions and pass our literature, music, art, monasticism, and mysticism on intact, the right-wing hijacking of Christianity must be defined as the reductionist rip-off that it is. To allow televangelists or pulpit neocons to claim exclusive ownership of Jesus is to hand that incomparable lover of enemies, prostitutes, foreigners, children, and fishermen over to those who evince no such love. And to cede the word "Christian" to Earth-trashing literalists who say "the end is nigh" feels rather like ceding my backyard henhouse to weasels. For my hens (and morning omelettes) such a concession would sure enough bring on "the end of the world." But neither my chickens nor I consider the end of our world something to yearn for or work toward.

The God of politically organized fundamentalism, as advertised daily by a wide array of media, is a Supramundane Caucasian Male as furious with humanity's failure to live by the prohibitions of Leviticus as He is oblivious to the "Christian" Right's failure to live the compassion of the gospels and stewardship of both testaments. As surely as I feel love and need for food and water, I feel love and need for God. But these feelings have nothing to do with Supramundane Males planning torments for those who don't abide by neocon "moral values." If the "Christian" Right's God is indeed God, then all my spiritual heroes from Valmiki and Laotze, Bodhidharma and Socrates, Kabir and Mira Bai, Rumi and Hafiz, Dogen and Dante, Teresa of Avila and Julian of Norwich, Eckhart and the Beguines, Aquinas and Sankaracharya, Black Elk and Chief Joseph, Tolstoy and Dostoyevsky, Thoreau and Muir, Shunryu and D. T. Suzuki, Gandhi and the Dalai Lama, to Merton and Snyder, will be consigned to perdition with me—for the One we all worship is an infinitely more loving, infinitely less fathomable Being.

Based on the lives and words of the preceding heroes and on the Person and gospels of Jesus himself, I believe humanity's situation to be rather different. I hold the evangelical truth of the matter to be that contemporary fundamentalists, especially those aimed at empire and Armageddon, need us nonfundamentalists, mystics, ecosystem activists, unprogrammable artists, agnostic humanitarians, incorrigible writers, truth-telling musicians, incorruptible scientists, organic gardeners, slow-food farmers, gay restaurateurs, wilderness visionaries, pagan preachers of sustainability, compassion-driven entrepreneurs, heartbroken Muslims, grief-stricken children, loving believers, loving disbelievers, peace-marching millions, and the One who loves us all in such a huge way that it is not going too far to say *they need us for their salvation.*

As Mark Twain pointed out more than a century ago, the only truly prominent community that fundamentalists have so far established in any world, real or imaginary, is hell.

Nominated by Daniel Henry

THE LAND OF PAIN

fiction by STACEY RICHTER

from WILLOW SPRINGS

YOU GO FOR A WALK and during the walk something happens: you trip, you fall, you dive off a cliff; you crash, you twist, you type, you age. When you get home you notice that your house looks slightly different than when you left—mushier, if that's possible, with misaligned corners. You open the door and are surprised to find a foil banner hanging over the mantle.

It says: *Welcome to the Land of Pain.*

So you go to the doctor and the doctor has you follow the standard management protocol (ice/rest/exercise/pills/ignore). When that doesn't work you go for the aggressive therapy intervention (surgery/pills/rest/ignore). Unfortunately that doesn't work either, and one bright afternoon the doctor and her entire staff sit you down and explain that you've basically reached the end of the line. Your options are these: 1) nothing, or 2) the brainless clone.

You're trying to be jaunty about this, upbeat and optimistic, and so opt for the brainless clone. Oh, they just call her that—she's not really brainless. She has a wee, reptilian brainstem that attends to her motor skills, her bodily functions, her ambulation and self-care and whatnot. She can be trained to do tricks and loves chocolate. When they pull her out of the vat she is well-formed and healthy and everybody is exceedingly pleased with her, though personally you're freaked out to see this little you, this exact genetic replica of yourself (only much younger, of course, and with no brain save a reptilian brainstem). But you're also excited, trembling with hope, because these brainless clones are state-of-the-art and the next big thing and like a miracle and for the good of mankind and a leap forward for science and all that.

You take her home and put her on accelerator, a clear goo that comes in a green squeeze bottle and is, they've told you, sort of like plant food. With this stuff dripped into her food she grows at a brisk pace. You ignore her for a while, but as she starts to enter various awkward stages which you recognize from your own girlhood, you haul her out of the cage and cart her off to lessons. You make her study ballet. You force her to do yoga. You have her practice in padded rooms, far from any of the known entrances, pitfalls, chutes or trapdoors that lead to the Land of Pain. You want her graceful. You want her flexible and strong.

Because she's your ticket out, sweetheart. She's your luxury cruise to a tropical island.

Sometimes you sit and watch her to see if you can catch her growing. You drip extra gobs of accelerator into her food (though this is not recommended). Her routine goes: in the cage, eat, sleep, defecate, stare blankly. Out of the cage: *plié, relevé*, sun salute, headstand, stare blankly. The legality of the deal is that she needs to grow to adulthood before you can have the operation. This is the operation where they take out your big, thinking-and-feeling brain that possesses humanity and patch it into the smooth cavity inside her head, into that flesh-lined bucket (thwack!), so that from that moment on your consciousness exists inside a pain-free, healthy, twirling and leaping body, identical to your own (except younger, and not in pain). What do they do with your old body? They use it for experiments.

As of yet, no one has successfully undergone the brain transfer operation.

But, they assure you, it's only a matter of time.

Anyway, you enjoy just hanging out and watching your clone practice. She's got those buck teeth and short little legs you had at her age. You cut her hair so she has the dorky bangs you once had. If you toss her a chocolate kiss she'll do a pirouette. For a whole candy bar, she'll attempt a solo from *Swan Lake*.

In the meantime, you undergo a series of medical tests in an attempt to better understand the painful region. The painful region is explored with needles in an effort to isolate the painful spot. If they can pinpoint the painful spot, say the doctors, then they will be able to discuss treatment strategies with you. And if they cannot reach it with the needles they have tried so far, they will just have to try some longer ones.

You say: Any luck yet with the old brain switcheroo, doc?

Doc says: We're close, very close.

The brainless clone continues to ripen. Though the process is accelerated, it nevertheless takes several years, years you spend languishing in the Land of Pain: eating grapes, watching movies, popping pills, worsening, enduring therapies, pretending you are not in the Land, etc. The brainless clone barrels into adolescence, a time you spent slumping through the halls of junior high with a book clasped before your breasts. She looks better than you ever did, clear-skinned and white-toothed, and in her own way she's clever too. She's figured out how to open her cage with her feet. You wonder: Why not with her hands? Ah, well, they don't call them brainless for nothing! You try to get her to stay in her cage but you're not much of a disciplinarian. You're supposed to squirt her with water when she's bad, but she looks so bewildered when you do, so wounded and damp, that you give it up. You're also supposed to be able to direct her movements by shining a flashlight in her face (this is also the way you wrangle Sea Monkeys, they inform you) but this only makes her fold into a weeping ball, presenting such a startling replica of your own miserable adolescence that you toss the flashlight in the trash and give her a cookie, vaguely wondering exactly who is training whom.

The result of this is that the brainless clone gains the run of the house. She twirls around all the time. If she walks, she walks on her tiptoes. She takes up more space than you ever imagined possible. It's as though a tiny, wind-up jewelry box dancer has been turned into a giant adolescent monster through the ingestion of radioactive produce. You dodge around her swanlike arms and contemplate how you were never that graceful or slender or pretty. Complex feelings ensue.

You and the other members of the study have been advised not to give names to your brainless clones. Researchers come to the house every couple of months to check up on her progress, her care and feeding, your compliance and mental health. As soon as they leave, you take off her scrub suit and dress her in a silk tutu. You've named her Princess Fifi.

At home, your answering machine says: Hello, you have reached THE LAND OF PAIN, over a background of thundering organ music. None of your callers finds this funny or even particularly comprehensible. It looks like you've failed at the long tradition of cracking jokes in the face of adversity and thus signaling that you're a tough cookie and a brave little bumblebee and a trooper and all that. The truth is you're getting sick of pretending like the Land of Pain is not a sad and lonely place. You're sick of pretending that losing the full use of your body—a pain-free body similar to the brainless clone's—has been anything less than entirely heartbreaking.

Things could be worse, the doctors are fond of reminding you. Chin up! It's just pain, it won't kill you. You decide this is typical of the kind of thoughts people have when they do not live in the Land of Pain. Your thoughts run more along the lines of: Why not do a few good deeds to boost your karma, then throw in the towel? Maybe in the next life, you'd get a better body. Unfortunately, things look bad all around out there: war, genocide, children with machine guns, rape and plunder and tyranny and epidemics. You don't want to be reincarnated into one of those bodies.

Anyway, you don't believe in reincarnation.

The brainless clone keeps twirling between you and the TV when you're trying to watch the horrible news programs that remind you how much worse things could be. You try to kick her out of the way and get mud all over your socks. Ever since she learned how to crawl through the doggy door, she's been ripping her tutus and dragging them in the dirt. She's been climbing trees and running through the sprinklers, getting sunburned and collecting scars that you'll eventually have to explain, once you inhabit her body. What's more, your assistive animal (which you obtained after watching a videotape of a sweet, serious collie picking up coins with her mouth) considers your leather armchair a chew-toy and has reduced half of it to pulp. Somehow you had the idea that the assistive animal was going to be a terrific help. You had a whole fantasy scenario built up in your mind in which this wonderful assistive animal would do all the things you found difficult—organizing your shoes, picking up coins off the floor, making the bed with its little teeth and paws, dragging the sheets up carefully over the mattress (good dog!), stuffing a pillow into a clean pillowcase with her snout. Then she'd curl up at your feet while you relaxed in a specially designed, inexpensive contraption that suspended you in a warm soothing fluid, relaxed and completely pain-free.

When you try to scoot the chair away, the dog sinks her teeth into the other side, growling happily, proposing a superfun game of tug-of-war. You muse on the fact that something like twenty-three muscles govern the frolicsomeness of that wagging tail. And it's obvious none of them hurt.

You take your medication and sack out in front of the television (which you can only really watch when you manage to nudge the pirouetting brainless clone into a corner). Now is the hour when citizens on talk shows tell their tragic stories in the second person, saying *you you you* about all the bad, traumatic, unfortunate experiences in their lives ("You just feel so betrayed when you see that little panda pulling a gun") as though they have a genetic defect that prevents them from using the pronoun "I." This is sloppy and angers the grammar and usage thug in you. You've concluded that citizens telling their tales of adversity find the second person compelling because "you" is impersonal and removed, yet somehow includes everyone in its scope ("It could be you staring down the barrel at that panda bear next, sweetheart!") whereas "I" is an orphaned baby doe blinking in a dark forest.

"You are always in pain," for example, is a more manageable utterance than the direct, final: "I am always in pain."

At nightfall, you can't find the assistive animal anywhere. Finally, you locate her curled up in the cage with the brainless clone, nose tucked under her tail. They adore each other. And you, you, my friend, are filled with jealousy.

You go to the doctor and the doctor says: Rate your pain on a scale of one to ten, with one being negligible and ten being the worst pain you can possibly imagine—you brace yourself here—*like surgery on your internal organs without anesthesia!* The doctor asks this every time you visit, and every time it horrifies you. You imagine an awful knoll in the Land of Pain where doctors remove livers and kidneys without the benefit of anesthesia while brainless clones dance to the soothing strains of waiting room music. In the foreground, assistive animals grab twitching organs in their mouths and run off to bury them.

You are not being a brave little bumblebee.

What's more, a few minutes later you start crying there on the greenish exam table because the doctor is telling you they have completed the brainless clone study and have concluded that, unfortunately, they cannot, at this time, transfer human brains from one body to another. And there is very little else they can do to help you. When you start to cry the doctor takes a deep breath, and, with a kind of angry glee (similar to when the assistive animal picks up a coin and runs around the house, while you attempt to chase), starts to recite, in detail, a list of all her patients who are worse off than you are. She describes neighborhoods in the Land of Pain more burned out and dangerous than you ever dreamed of, hellish vistas where the afflicted and wracked limp through the streets in hailstorms while gobbling more Oxycontin and forgetting who the president is. Phantom Limb Pain. Fibromyalgia. Double Carpal Tunnel (with a cherry on top), Stiff Person Syndrome. You sniffle contritely and feel a weird, toxic gratitude that goes: Thank God. Thank God I'm only as fucked up as I am and not as fucked up as those other people.

The doctor says: We understand you have a choice when choosing Lands, and we'd like to thank you for choosing to spend the safest part of your journey here, in the Land of Pain.

Geographically speaking, the Land of Pain is a subcontinent of the World of the Sick. The World of the Sick is a nifty, parallel universe that exists inside the World of the Well. The curious fact is that while most of the citizens of the World of the Well don't even realize that the World of the Sick exists, *all* of the inhabitants of the World of the Sick know about the World of the Well. The Sick live among the Well like spies, pod-people, or daywalking vampires: different, afraid, and isolated; and like spies, pod-people, and daywalkers, the Sick who can manage to mingle with the Well reflexively disguise their identity. And you, with your white picket fence and your neatly trimmed lawn in the Land of Pain, you are no different. There's no little chair on your license plate. You look normal, you are able to leave the house for hours at a time, you've tried to pass yourself off as hunky-dory.

But now everyone knows, because in her maturity the brainless clone follows you everywhere. She won't let you out of her sight. She bellows like a baby calf if you stray too far from her, she bellows so fiercely that you think perhaps she'll go on forever. She's inconsolable and stubborn and unpredictable and thanks to years of physical training she possesses astonishing stamina. Rather than fight it, you do what you've always done and cave in. You take her everywhere with you. She trots beside you, grunting. She won't wear anything now but soiled tutus and you have to attach her to your wrist with a tether because, well, she doesn't exactly have a brain. You find the whole spectacle humiliating: she's an idea whose time has passed, a relic of a failed era. It's like you're this weird person carrying around an eight-track player and truckin' to disco. Certain kids find this cool and follow at a distance, trying to affect her distracted, zombie stance. Far worse are the religious zealots, who bother you constantly. They know where you live. They mobilize when you go to the doctor or the supermarket. They surround your car and chant: *Even without a cerebellum/That young lady's going to heaven!* The nuts are convinced she has a soul (though she has no brain) and even though you have to get a restraining order against them, you're secretly inclined to agree.

So you walk around with this big, grunting, simple ballerina following you and everyone knows there's something so wrong with you that you once actually contemplated having your brain taken out and put into someone else's body, which in fact isn't the worst part. The worst part is when everyone goes: Oh! She's so cute! Were you ever that cute? There, tethered to you with a piece of coiled plastic, is your lost youth and vitality: a pretty ballerina, arm raised, back arched, foot aiming toward the sky. She's a poet of the body, ignited with life, and despite the fact that she has no brain you're in awe of all she has.

A friend says to you: Oh, these people take them to live on a farm. They have a farm for the brainless clones out in the country where they get to run around in the fresh air, and there are orchards and meadows and pet bunnies and they're well-cared for and all that. A group of bran-eating hippies runs it—they do it for karma credits or energy wavelengths or something weird but reputedly not-evil. A lot of the brainless clones are living there now. They have sing-alongs.

You say: Sounds fishy.

Your friend says: Yeah. Oh but wait—the thing is they grow those pears there, the ones we used to get at the corner market. Remember those pears?

You remember. You used to stop at a little market and buy the most ravishing pears, sweet and crisp, and every time you did the proprietor would roar: *You will be back for more of these pears!* They were yellow-gold. You'd eat them in the park while the juice ran off your elbow. You went back again and again, just as the man predicted. It was the longest pear-season ever. You were convinced it would never end.

But of course it did end, and you moved to another part of the city, and by chance wandered into the Land of Pain and forgot all about the pears, since you had other things on your mind.

So you take her to the farm. She wants to get off her leash and run around all the time now anyway. You bundle up her ballet slippers and her tutus and her bags of Brainless Clone Chow and push her into the backseat of the car and set off for the country. She keeps sticking her entire head out the window as you drive, making that bellowing noise, so awful and familiar and constant. My God, you think, make her stop.

When you arrive, she jumps out as soon as you open the car door. You give her a little kiss on her zombie brow and unclip the leash. She stands for a minute, sniffing the air, chest heaving, fingers trembling, then breaks into a dead run for the orchard. Her tutu is the cleanest you could find, a pink one, and the pears hang above her like yellow lanterns. Her arms unfurl as she reaches up and her fingertips graze the branches. Then she lifts a foot and begins to dance. She's a damn good dancer; breathtaking really, like a scarf drifting through the air. You watch for a while, trying not to imagine all she could have been if she'd actually had a brain.

There are a couple dozen other brainless clones romping in the orchard too. They all look alert and healthy: they are eating pears, wrestling, singing snatches of camp songs, picking their noses, doing somersaults. It's sort of beautiful but also awful. What if their owners suddenly all showed up? What if they arrived with their crutches and wheelchairs and bad eyes and frozen joints and stood around (if they could stand) and watched (if they could watch) as their clones pranced and jumped and fell down and then got back up again? It would be too much to endure.

The weird karma people appear and offer you a bowl of cereal. She's cute, they say. She'll like it here. Everything will be fine. You all stand for a while watching the clones horse around. Then they tell you that it's time to say goodbye.

Oh no, you say: No. You don't want to say goodbye.

They take away your bowl of cereal and look at you with gentle, patchouli-scented eyes. They tell you that it's good to say goodbye and that you really should.

But no, you argue. Wait. Hold it right there. Just who do they think they are, telling you to say goodbye? There are things in life you never imagined saying goodbye to. How can you say goodbye to your unbroken version? How can it be that people don't get better? How can their pretty ballerinas dance away under the pears while their owners hobble home, on their feet, on their crutches, in their wheelchairs? It's not fair! Only when they're unable to do the simplest things do they realize that the simplest things were so full of joy: taking a walk, picking a pear, picking up a child who says carry me.

So there it is. You don't want to say goodbye.

Chill out, say the weird karma people. No one is making you leave her here. It's voluntary. If you keep her she'll probably still follow you around, bellowing. But (and here they look very sinister) they believe that the universe will be far more peaceful in its vibrations if you can manage to say goodbye. They stand with their wispy ponytails and their heavy bags of granola, perhaps suitable for use as a weapon, so you decide to give it a try. You call out *Goodbye little clone* in a small voice, without much conviction. *Bye-bye Fifi.* You give your brainless princess a wave, but of course she's not looking at you. She's too busy dancing beneath the pears.

You accept a bag of cereal from the karma people and start to drive back to town. Your assistive animal sleeps in the backseat, twitching and whining, chasing rabbits or perhaps a flock of brainless clones. Somehow, though you're certain you didn't make any wrong turns, you end up on a strange, unrecognizable stretch of freeway. You realize that you're angry, very angry: wherever you are, you would like to know just how you ended up here! You'd demand to know, if only you could find someone to ask. Then a green, reflective sign rears up along the side of the road. It says: Next Exit: The Land of Pain.

You exit.

Nominated by Willow Springs

RESTORATION

by SALLY KEITH

from CUE

THE LINE IS NECK CENTERED, halving the body's weight so that her stance has no jut. It has no awkward lean. And her hands fit inside of her face, like fretting, a wall, relief. These hands that throw the axe and plumb the earth—furiously they nail the beams together. They split the cloth to wrap a wound. They nimbly thread the eye to fix a gown. They fit—almost beautiful, struck, wheezing and gray. They make a cave for the eyes, but light still slips in finger slats, unevenly, giving night a yellow-blue. But behind her hands, imagine, her eyes staying shut—the bolt then for a twice chained door.

Stay. The picket fence, even if storm blown, I'll come to do the painting, I'll come to tear the forsythia away. The bluebird house, even if the jays. I'll come. I'll stand in the field with you. See, already, I'm scaring them away. I'm waving my arms, mad, in the sky. Then the old farmhouse, because I've studied the order they fall. The window frames go out from their squares. The façade like a hand of splayed cards. The roof begins to buckle. Then the people leave. A chair gets left on the porch. Splotches of copper decay on the legs. And then begins the floor. Stay. I'll bring in a lamp and light us a corner. I'll bring in a plant and two chairs. We will live.

Light is pouring through the dust, breeding in beams, making a fugue for dark walls. I want to sit with you. Come back from the fields. Look, I'm stopped in the space of this door. It is calm here.

Even if the wind is blowing, lifting the siding up from the house, swirling the dirt to eddies and branding a silvery sheen on the soy. Even if you think you can't forget the storm. Look, now. Ignore the wind. Ignore the watery, watery road.

Nominated by Cue

HOME ON THE RAIN

fiction by JONATHAN CARROLL

from CONJUNCTIONS

I CAN'T SAY FOR SURE when it started because he never told me. And I'm not a mind reader. I'm not an exceptionally observant person and am the first to admit it. I like life the way it is. I watch the passing parade uncritically, rather than with a pair of high-powered binoculars and a scorecard so that I can identify all the players and details. I don't care how well or poorly the costumes have been sewn, so long as they look good from afar. If that clown on stilts is having an affair with his neighbor, so what? If he's fun to watch now, that's all that matters. I'm like most of the crowd—oohing and aahing at the big floats, clapping at the beauty queens and championship teams as they pass, tearing up when the brass band plays the national anthem.

So, no, I wasn't aware of anything special happening either to my husband or our life until I discovered what he was doing.

Look, we'd been married for eleven years. Live that long with someone and you just simply stop paying attention to certain things at a certain point. Isn't that what happens to most couples, no matter how much you love your partner? Their curly hairs in the sink, the stories they repeat for the hundredth time, the way they sometimes eat with their mouth open. We know all these things and either accept them, ignore them, or force ourselves to tolerate them because they're all part of the lifetime meal we chose to share with a partner. Not everything in marriage is dessert.

I found out about it because of the camera. He's not usually a sloppy guy. You should know that. He doesn't leave things lying around, especially if they're fragile or valuable, like that camera. He's not careless. His books and records are alphabetized; he likes things clean and in place. So did he leave it out like that so I'd find it? Sometimes I think so.

I'm sorry. I'm getting offtrack.

One Saturday when I was alone in the apartment I walked into the living room and on the coffee table was a small black-and-silver digital camera I'd never seen before. It was a beautiful thing. A GLIB, made in Germany. Who did that belong to? It was a point-and-shoot camera and simple to figure out how to work. So I turned it on and scrolled through the pictures that had been taken. There were about a dozen in there. All of them were either photos of different kinds of scaffolding or high views of the city. Pictures that could only have been taken from way above the ground.

Alan came in an hour later and I asked where this camera came from. Very nonchalantly he took it and said it belonged to one of his clients who'd left it at the office after a meeting. He was going to call the man later to tell him he had it. I said I'd looked at the pictures in there and Alan shrugged. He asked what they were of and what I thought of them. I said most were of scaffolding, which wasn't terribly exciting. He smiled and asked what I had expected to see. I said, Oh, I don't know—maybe a little filth?

That was the end of that. He dropped the camera into his pocket and I didn't see it again for a long time. Weeks, I guess, and by then there were a lot more pictures inside.

He didn't act strange. Once in a while he'd leave for work in the morning wearing clothes that didn't seem right. They were casual clothes, no tie or suit as usual. When I asked about them, he said he didn't have to be in court that day and was just going to the office to take care of paperwork.

Look, I know it sounds defensive, but we have our lives. We have our own concerns and schedules. So long as nothing interferes with them, we don't think much about what our partner is doing during a day. Especially after you've been together for years. Maybe when we were first married I'd stop what I was doing in the middle of the morning and wonder, What is my husband doing right now? But "husband" was the brand-new delicious word in my vocabulary back then and I couldn't get enough of saying it. Stuff like that gets sanded away over the years. I was just grateful I still really liked seeing him at the end of every day; that we still had things to share and talk about. I don't know what happy is but I think we were happy. So many of our friends had divorced or lived in the same space but didn't say two words to each other for days. It was not like that with Alan and me. It really wasn't. We still sat together most evenings and talked instead of watching television or going our separate ways after dinner. We did things together. We looked forward to weekends and holidays when it would be just the two of us. I'm not trying to sound defensive or make excuses, please know that. I loved him, but, maybe more important, I truly *liked* him and still enjoyed being around him.

Everyone has their secrets, but so long as they don't affect your partner, what's the harm?

Until he discovered the scaffolding, Alan Harris had no secrets. From time to time he masturbated, picked his nose, or told mild lies. But those things were not secrets as far as he was concerned because he assumed everyone did them. To him a secret was something you hid from the world because it was repellent and uniquely yours, thus something you really did not want people to know. At forty-two, he didn't care what people knew about him because he honestly felt he had nothing to hide. He liked his wife and didn't cheat on her. He liked his life enough so that he didn't daydream often about another one. He had enough money so that when he saw something he wanted, he bought it. But there wasn't much that he wanted. He was not a contented man so much as a comfortable one and that was sufficient for him. He was a lawyer. Lawyers are on good terms with compromise.

One morning he was looking out the window of his office while talking on the telephone. He noticed that construction was starting on the dilapidated building across the street. A large crew of workers was just beginning to sort, assemble, and erect metal scaffolding that would soon rise from the street and eventually cover the facade of the building like an exoskeleton. And when that was erected, restoration on the building itself would begin in earnest.

Two red flatbed trucks with attached cranes unloaded huge tightly wrapped piles of scaffolding segments. Once unbound, they were then handed up piece by piece to the workers on the different levels. It pleased Harris to watch the process as it always did when he saw this happening. It meant people were employed, buildings were being renovated ("healed" was the word that often came to his mind when he witnessed this), and the result was another small breath of new life was being breathed into the city he liked so much.

"What are you looking at?"

His secretary had come into the office long after he had hung up the phone but remained at the window, watching them work across the street.

"I love to watch when they put up scaffolding. Did you ever see them do it, the process?"

She joined him at the window, where they remained companionably silent a while, watching the action down below. Metal pieces changed hands. Tools were used; instructions shouted that they couldn't hear way up here through the thick double-paned glass. Eventually the secretary half-smiled, shrugged, and left. Harris felt a small pinch of anger at her indifference or insensitivity, whatever it was. How could she not be interested in this? How could she not appreciate what a cool thing it was? Men at work on something that would help lift the face of the neighborhood. Skilled at their jobs, they knew exactly what to do, what tools to carry in their wide leather belts, what section to call down for. He wondered what the names of the separate pieces were. Did they know them by number—give me a number eight? Or were there specific names—strut, crossbar, clamp?

That evening he worked till eight. He was tired and hungry and fed up with the paperwork on a case that was going nowhere but filled up too much of his time. That was one of the problems with the law—there were such a variety of twists and turns in it that you could walk through its mazes for years and still never find the exit. That was good for his law firm because they billed by the hour. But for the individual, no end in sight wasn't much of an incentive to come to work in the morning. While tiredly pulling on his overcoat he again thought of the scaffolding and the men who put it up. They knew exactly when a job would be finished. Put it up, take it down, and then move on to the next place. Their daily life was full of beginning, middle, and end. A cynic would say, Yeah, sure, but it's grunt work and any dummy could do it. Still, on nights like these Harris envied them, whether they were dummies or not. Working outside all day, they finished at five, and after washing their hands they climbed back down into the city they were helping to heal. They went with their pals into a bar where they had a few drinks and chatted, knowing they had done a good day's work and that they would be finished with it next week.

It was cold outside and he hiked up his collar. He had left his briefcase back in the office on purpose because he knew that if he brought it home, he would work there, too, and a man needs some rest. Standing on the sidewalk in front of his building, he tried to decide whether to get something to eat before going home or to pick something up on the way and eat it in the kitchen. He smiled when he thought of sitting at the kitchen table and opening a white Styrofoam container full of tasty, still-warm takeout food. He pictured his wife bringing him a bottle of cold Mexican beer from the refrigerator and then sitting down opposite him, happy that he was home and hers again. While these things filled his mind he unconsciously stared at the construction site. Without any more thought, he looked both ways, and when the coast was clear, walked across the street so that he could take a closer look at the work in progress.

Standing underneath and looking up, he couldn't see much because it was so dark, and what scaffolding had been erected cut the gloom up there with metal and wood crosshatching. Harris crossed to the nearest platform and put his hand on one of the poles. As he did, a large truck rumbled past on the street nearby and he could feel it vibrate through the metal. When the truck had passed he kept his hand where it was because it felt right there. For a few moments he felt more grounded than he had all day. Closing his eyes, he tightened his grip on the pole. Two people walked past, talking. He could hear them close by but didn't open his eyes.

Later at home, he considered telling his wife about the experience but didn't. Not because he wanted to keep it a secret. Not because he didn't want her to know. He knew she would be delighted to hear the story because it was so unlike him to do something as odd and spontaneous as that. Stand still on a sidewalk with his eyes closed holding onto a metal bar for no reason other than he felt like it? That was not her husband. She would have loved hearing the story for that very reason. But he just didn't mention it.

The next day at work was a rotten one. When he left the office even later than the night before, Harris walked straight over to the construction site and repeated the gesture. Only this time it was a conscious move and not a whim. Closing his eyes and taking hold of the same metal support pole, he silently asked for some of the energy of the men who had worked there today. He asked that it enter his body and revive his heart or wipe him clean of the sludge or . . . something.

No dice. No lightning bolts or electric currents raced up his arm and into his soul. The pole remained a cold pole in his hand until he sheepishly let go of it and smiled at his own silliness. As he was about to leave, he heard someone directly above him singing the song "Home on the Range." When he looked up, he saw a pair of big black boots descending near him. A big black man was wearing them. He wore a puffy down jacket and a yellow hard hat. He had a nice deep voice. Dropping from the scaffolding above Harris, the man stopped singing as soon as his feet touched ground.

"Hey there, how you doing?"

Alan smiled and dipped his head in a shy hello. "Fine. I'm just fine."

"I'll tell you, it's getting damned cold up there. Fall's definitely coming." The man rubbed his hands together and grinned.

Alan pointed directly up. "Is it really colder up there than it is on the ground?"

The worker considered the question before answering. "It can be. Especially when the wind is blowing. You wanna go up and see?"

"Now?"

"Sure. It's beautiful up there now. You see all the lights of the city. It looks like a chest full of golden diamonds. Come on, I'll have you up and down in half an hour."

It turned out to be the most wonderful thing he had done in ages. The worker's name was Lyle Talbot and he was simply a great guy. Alan couldn't figure out why Lyle had invited him to climb the scaffolding. But eventually as they worked their way up, talking all the way, it became perfectly clear that this man just liked showing off the view from way up high. It was that uncomplicated and generous. Let me show you something special.

Alan had no fear of heights but as they climbed and climbed, some of the pieces of the structure were wobblier or more unstable than others. Several times his stomach clenched suddenly in fear at a missed step, a loose plank, or one that felt like it was about to give way. Lyle didn't hesitate or look down once. When he wasn't talking to Alan he sang "Home on the Range" quietly under his breath.

"Stop here." They were about halfway up. Lyle reached into one of the large pockets on his coat and brought out a small silver thermos. "Let's have a little sip of hot coffee. It'll warm up our bones. You cold?"

Alan was too enthralled to be cold. From that vantage point the city was overpoweringly beautiful. It flickered, shimmered, and twinkled all at once. The noise from down on the street was a constant heartening hum of motion and electric life. The wind blew at them in cold sudden, invigorating gusts. Lyle was exactly right when he said before that all the lights looked gold. Of course many were different colors—blue, red, white. But the predominant color was gold. Gold against the black of night. And none of them stayed still—the lights constantly blinked and fluttered, they flicked on and off or moved. Alan only wished he had a camera. He would have filled it with pictures of everything.

There was only the one cup that doubled as the top of the thermos, so the men passed it back and forth between them, sharing the strong hot drink.

When it was gone, Lyle slowly screwed the top back onto the thermos and asked Alan if he was ready to go back down. It was really cold now and the wind had picked up in the last few minutes. Craning his head straight back, Alan looked toward the levels above them. Part of him wanted to keep climbing but he knew it was time to go home.

"Yes, I'm ready. And, Lyle, thank you so much for inviting me. It's been magical. Really. Looking at the city from here is so different from out the window of an office building. It's like the difference between riding on a motorcycle and in a car. Up here with nature in your face, the wind and the cold, you feel like you're flying above everything, but like a bird on your own wings. The wind's lifting and dropping you. . . . It's just great."

Lyle nodded. He reached into a different pocket and, rummaging around in there, brought out a thick metal bolt about two inches long. "Here—keep this as a souvenir of tonight."

Alan took it and closed his fingers carefully around the bolt. "I'll treasure it."

The next day at lunchtime he bought the GLIB camera. Walking into a camera shop near his office, Alan said to a salesman that he wanted a very good simple digital camera small enough to fit in a pocket. Without hesitating, the salesman took a GLIB out of the display case and placed it on the counter. It was the size of a deck of cards and had only two buttons on the top. He said it was so simple to operate that anyone could be taking pictures within fifteen minutes. But because the camera used a precision Zeiss lens, the results were outstanding.

Alan sat on a park bench and read the instructions. With some time left before he had to be back in the office, he took the first pictures of the scaffolding that he had climbed the night before.

Later he shot some pictures of the building site from his office, then some more from down on the street after work. He photographed the scaffolding first thing in the morning, in the afternoon, and at night, when it was barely visible except for some glints and glimmers off the metal here and there.

The nice thing about a digital camera was it allowed him to see the results immediately. He didn't like any of them. He took a picture, looked at it, and erased it. Again and again and again. He did not have even one saved on his camera. This went on for days. He was not a photographer, not an artist, and he knew it. But art wasn't the point. Just once he wanted to take a picture of the scaffolding that somehow caught a small part of what he had experienced up there that night with Lyle. When he had taken *that* picture he would be content.

He had no idea why he was doing this. He was not an obsessive man. Orderly and pragmatic, yes, but even the word *obsession* he used only once or twice a year and never in reference to himself. In the middle of all these goings-on he even asked his wife if she thought he had ever been obsessive about anything. Unhesitatingly she said no. Perhaps he had grown a hobby. There was nothing wrong with a hobby. Perhaps he just liked taking pictures of scaffolding and men at work on it.

One evening after dinner at their favorite restaurant the couple were strolling in a section of town that had lots of art galleries. In one of them was a photo exhibit by an artist who took only black-and-white pictures of unsharpened pencils lying alone on square white plates. There were a great many of them but none were particularly interesting. How many ways were there to arrange a pencil on a plate? But Alan pulled his wife into the gallery anyway and spent a long time looking. Amused at this, she went along until finally enough was enough. Sidling up to him, she whispered, "I'll buy you any two pencils you want if we can leave now."

He felt better after that. Seeing those photographs felt like a kind of vindication for what he was doing. There were people who took pictures of pencils, others of scaffolding.

By this time, the crew that had originally erected the scaffolding across the street was gone, and work on the facade of the building itself had begun. It was hard to clearly see what the workers were doing now. He saw some filling gaps with mortar while others scraped the surface with hand tools but not much else. Alan wanted to know more and to see things up close. One Friday afternoon he left work a little early and went across the street. A few minutes later he told his first lie about this matter.

A worker wearing a hard hat and carrying an orange chain saw walked by and saw him taking photographs. "Are you the guy from the insurance company?"

Without hesitating Alan said yes.

"Well, then, I guess you want to come up and take some pictures. Come on."

Those were the photographs Alan's wife saw when she discovered the camera in their living room. They were not good pictures but they were the first ones he had been able to take from any height so he had not erased any of them yet.

It took some time for him to realize that there was too much hustle and bustle on a construction site during the day. Initially he got to see what he wanted—men working on the renovation. In fact, he was so pleased with the other world up high on the scaffolding that he started going to other construction sites around the city. Pretending he was from "the insurance company" and emanating an authoritative air, he was allowed almost free access to all levels. He climbed, he descended, he talked to the workers, and he took pictures. It was an invigorating contrast to the staid, airless work in a law office where most days were spent pursuing the ineffable or trivial, the clever loophole or the rare kill-shot precedent buried deep in the law library.

Construction work was noisy, straightforward, tactile, and visibly productive. Alan loved to dress in casual clothes and walk out into the morning knowing that in an hour he would be high over this city, seeing it from a perspective few people were ever lucky enough to experience.

But one day he realized, after having done it six or seven times, that what he really wanted now was to somehow recapture that magical night on the building with Lyle Talbot. That experience was akin to the first time he'd ever ridden a bicycle correctly. The miraculous moment when the boy discovered his own center of gravity and pulled away from his father's guiding hand toward freedom. Seeing the city at night from on high with Lyle, drinking his coffee from a warm metal cup, and feeling fully aware and alive was one of his most memorable experiences in recent years. He wanted very much to repeat it.

Alan had not seen Lyle again after that night, although he had passed the building many times since the night they met. He carried the thick bolt in his pocket that Lyle had given him and toyed with it constantly. He was a pragmatist and did not believe in magic, luck, or religion. But the bolt was the closest thing to a talisman he had ever possessed. He would have been very disturbed if he had lost it.

The second time his wife saw the camera it was sitting on his desk. Once again she looked at the photographs inside. What caught and chilled her was two pictures of their living room that Alan had taken by mistake. The camera was obviously his, not some client's, as he had earlier said. What was going on here? Why had he lied to her? Did these pictures mean something? For two days she thought about it, trying to decide what to do. Just ask him about it? Say straight out she thought it was very strange that he had lied and now she wanted to know if he was concealing things she should know? The possibilities frightened her. What could be so bad that this kind, straightforward man felt the need to lie to his best friend and partner?

He disappeared before she had a chance to confront him.

Alan Harris did not sleep well; he never had. Four or five hours a night and then his eyes would open for good to the day even if it was still dark outside. Fully awake, he would pad around the apartment in his pajamas, sometimes reading, watching television, or making breakfast. She was used to it. If she felt him stir in the bed, she would pull a pillow over her head and go back to sleep.

He had come home from work glum and tired. They ate a quiet dinner together and then he went to bed at ten. She mentioned that if he went to sleep now he'd wake up very early but he shook his head and did it anyway.

At three he awoke and a plan jumped into his mind. Knowing he would not be able to get back to sleep, he'd put on his clothes and walk over to the Lyle site, as he called it now. Once there, he would climb the scaffolding and stand where they had stood together that night. Why not? That's what he wanted to do and that's what he would do.

While dressing he glanced out the window and saw that the streets were glistening black. Did that mean the view from high up would be obscured by this bad weather? He hoped not but the thought did not deter him. Putting on his rain jacket and cap, he slipped out the front door, closing it behind him with a quiet metallic click.

The streets were wet and empty. Occasionally a cab hissed by. He passed a couple weaving down the sidewalk arm in arm, totally oblivious to anything but each other. It was not cold for that time of year but he buttoned up his jacket anyway because it would be colder up where he was going.

On reaching the site, he looked left and right to make sure no one was watching. Then, as if to reassure himself, he touched the metal bolt in his pocket and smiled, silently greeting the absent Lyle and explaining what he was about to do.

Everything on the scaffolding was slippery this time. More than once he made a slip or slide that set his heart thumping in his chest and adrenaline racing around his body. It was a rare feeling for him and he didn't know if he liked or hated it.

Now and again he would stop to turn around and look at the view behind him. In the rain the city below appeared liquid, as if it had just been formed of meltable things like licorice or blown glass. It looked fragile, like all of it would easily break if tapped with a hammer.

When he reached the level where he had stopped with Lyle, Alan Harris turned to face the view, then squatted down on his haunches and put both hands up under his armpits for warmth. It was a favorite position that he took when he knew he was going to be somewhere for a while.

A few minutes passed and then a voice nearby said, "Hey, look, let's get back to work, huh? Hand me that mallet."

Taken completely by surprise, Alan looked to the right with very wide, startled eyes. Standing at the other end of his level was a man wearing paint-covered overalls, a loaded leather tool belt, and a yellow hard hat. It was not Lyle Talbot.

"Excuse me?"

"Hup hup—there's work to do, man. We ain't getting paid to sit around. Hand me that mallet there."

Alan looked down in the dark and shadows at his feet and, sure enough, nearby was a wooden-handled mallet with a thick rubber head. Even in the dark he could see that the tool had been well used. Hesitantly he stood, picked it up, and walked down to the end where the other was standing.

"I don't—"

The man shook his head and turned to face the building. Sliding a short steel chisel out of his loaded tool belt, he pointed it at the façade. "You see this layer here? It's gotta all be knocked off before we can reface it. This whole section has to be chiseled down to the base. You understand? Do it like this."

For the next few minutes he demonstrated what he wanted Alan to do with the mallet and chisel. The lawyer watched and remained silent. What could he say? What was this guy doing up here working in the middle of the night anyway? Alan had so many questions but he was the trespasser here; he had obviously been mistaken for one of the night work crew. He would just wait until the guy was done talking and after he'd left, Alan would sneak down to the street again and take off.

"Here, now you try it." The man stuck out both hands holding the tools.

Taking them tentatively, Alan put the chisel against the building face and gave it a good whack with the mallet.

"Harder! That stuff's been up for years. You're not gonna get any of it off by petting it."

Alan hit the chisel another shot, much harder this time. A small chuck of facade broke off.

"Harder, man. It's not a woman—it's a wall. *Hit* it."

Smiling at the image, he hit the chisel with all of his might and this time a sizable piece came off.

"Good, good—that's the way to do it. I'll be back later." Wiping his hands on his overalls, the worker walked to the edge and, swinging to the outside on one of the poles there, began to climb down the scaffolding. He jingled as he moved because he carried so many different kinds of metal on his belt.

Alan thought it best to wait a while before descending. With nothing else to do, he started back to work with the mallet and chisel on the building.

It did not happen until he had been working for another quarter hour. It was satisfying, invigorating work, and although he wondered

307

about the noise he was making, he figured that being this high up absorbed most of the sound. He was unused to hand work but it felt very good. While hammering away, he thought, I must find a hobby where I do things like this on a regular basis. Maybe take a course in furniture making or even sculpting. The tools he held were formidable and bluntly honest. What a gratifying change it was to work with his hands and a mostly empty mind.

As his thoughts wandered around in that direction, he hit the chisel a ringing blow that sent a piece flying off the face but it did not drop like the others. This white bit, about the size of a pocketknife, simply hung in the air between him and the building. It did not fall. Alan's hands holding the tools slowly dropped to his sides as he stared at it in disbelief, but the piece of building remained suspended near his chest.

"Take it. Break a little bit off and eat it." The voice came from behind. Turning, he was almost face to face with a hefty middle-aged woman in black glasses and work clothes. He had not heard her come up. He pointed to the floating piece and she nodded. Reaching out, he took it from the air and did as he was told. Breaking off a small piece, he hesitantly put it on the tip of his tongue and closed his mouth. He chewed.

His wife never saw him again. After the fear and worry, anger and utter confusion, her heart and mind were almost ruined by his disappearance.

In the end she was saved by a good man—a professor of Hebrew at the local university who lived in their building and courted her in a shy but determined way. Their relationship began by her pouring out her heart to him and his wisely saying nothing. Jews are used to mystery; often it is their third parent. They know there really is nothing one can say about it and the only response when mystery flattens others is to nod and show compassion. So many Jewish lives and frequently the way they die makes no sense at all, as history has shown. Fully aware of this, in the midst of her suffering, the professor handed her a piece of paper that began her healing. On it he had written, "The world is not yours to finish, but neither are you free to take no part in it." She read it and did not even get a chance to ask who had said this before a wave of grief swept over her and made her sob. But for the first time since her husband had gone, she was crying to cleanse rather than to hold and although it took a long time, that moment marked the beginning of her recovery.

After having eaten the piece of the building, Alan Harris was transformed. Others were not so lucky. In the months that followed, he saw many come to work on the scaffolding but they were soon sent back to their lives with no explanation as to why they had failed.

When he asked about this, he was told that people were given two days to work. If they did not discover their piece of a building to eat in that time, they were sent away, all memories of the last forty-eight hours erased from their minds. When they got back home they told their relieved families that they had no recollection of where they had been. Thank God they had found their way home again. They were welcomed and kissed and feted. They returned to their lives only grateful and happy that they had survived. These rejects still enjoyed looking at buildings that were being repaired but it never went deeper than that. They remained fans, like someone with time to kill who stops a while to look at a busy construction site.

From that point on, Alan never got tired and never was hungry again. He and the rest of the crew labored day and night until the regular restoration on the building was completed, and then their bosses moved them to another one across town that had just had scaffolding erected on its face in preparation for renovation.

Their crew always blended in with the normal ones that had been hired to restore the different facades. When you see someone on a construction site wearing the same kind of clothes as you, carrying the same tools, wearing the same hard hat, and doing the same kind of work, you don't ask, What are you doing here? You assume they belong.

But what was it exactly that Alan Harris and the others in his group were doing? In the beginning, he constantly asked that question of his fellow workers but they all had different answers. They argued about it constantly. One of them said that they were looking for something lost in the various pitted, crumbling facades they helped repair. It was like archaeology. Their supervisors knew what it was and once it had been found everyone would be told. So far, though, it had eluded them and that was why they kept being moved from building to building.

Another man, a tall Azeri-Turk with a weak jaw and ferocious brown eyes who used to run a thriving tailor shop, swore that they were rebuilding the City of God as St. Augustine had originally envisioned it. In a voice that both accused and taunted, he demanded to know if Alan had read *The City of God*. The lawyer sheepishly admitted that he had not.

"Well, find a copy and *read* it! You'll see exactly what I am talking about. We are here because we have been chosen to do God's work on earth."

Some workers laughed when they heard that, others smiled dismissively. Everyone on Alan's crew had their own idea about why they were here and what this labor meant. They unanimously agreed on only one thing and that was how lucky they were to be there. Nothing any of them had ever done in their lives had brought them so much pleasure and fulfillment.

Periodically, one or another of them disappeared and was never seen again but no one made a big deal of it. Inevitably someone would ask, "Where's Lola? I haven't seen her for a while." Those nearby would pause a moment to look left and right and then shrug. Lola (or Ron, Chris, or Dorothy) was somewhere but where wasn't their concern. Within days, a new member would replace the missing worker.

One early evening in the middle of cold winter sleet, Alan was cleaning a gargoyle high up on the face of an ornate apartment building. He used a well-worn wire brush and a bottle of bleach. Now and then he had to stop, walk to the edge of the scaffolding, and, turning away from the building, look out at the city for a while because the fumes from the bleach were overpowering.

He was thinking about the first night when he'd met Lyle Talbot. As he scrubbed decades of embedded dirt and pollution off the ugly stone face, without knowing it he began to hum "Home on the Range," which was the song Lyle had sung. When he became aware of this, the sleet was turning into hard rain. Quietly and with a smile, Alan sang, "Home, home on the rain—" Then his voice petered out into silence because that's exactly where he was—at home on the rain in the winter in the evening in the middle of the greatest mystery he had ever known but didn't need to solve because it lifted and cared for him and made his life so much better.

In a small receding part of his heart Alan Harris acknowledged that his abrupt disappearance was now likely to be the greatest mystery in his wife's life. She deserved an explanation but would never

310

get one. Anyway, what could he have said—after I ate part of a building it kidnapped me forever?

"What *would* you tell her if you had the chance?"

Alan was very high up on the scaffolding. No one else was around. The others were working on the other side of the gigantic building. When he heard the voice behind him he knew it could have come from only one place. Turning to look, he saw that the gargoyle was watching him. It blinked its blank eyes.

"Come here." The gargoyle was a grotesque mix of monkey, Fuseli dwarf, and something even the artist couldn't have described. Its face was threatening and funny at the same time. It was an "Either I'll kill you or I'll make you laugh" face.

Without hesitation Alan walked back to where he had been working. The gargoyle's face was just above eye level. "I don't know what I would tell her. I hope she's all right. That's the only reason I'd ever go down again. Just to see if she's all right."

"You *can* go down. You're finished here." Those words, even coming from a gargoyle, were like a sudden punch in the stomach.

"What do you mean?"

"We've got what we want from you. And we're grateful, so we're giving you a choice: you can go back to your life and try to work things out with your wife, or you can move along. Move up to the next level."

"And what's that?"

The gargoyle shook its head. "You wouldn't understand even if I told you. It's impossible to describe."

"Can't you give me some kind of hint or an indication?"

"No. But you'll have to choose right now."

Alan thought about his good wife and his dry life and the view of the world from behind a tenth-floor double-paned safety window. He loved the mystery of what had happened to him. That more than anything made him decide.

The gargoyle had long monkey's arms crossed so tightly over its broad chest that they were almost invisible. Those arms snapped out now and with fearsome strength shoved Alan off the scaffolding.

He did not have time to be afraid. As he was pushed, his mind was still on the enigma his life had become and how much he loved it. When he realized what had just happened to him, this expanded into a kind of all-encompassing WHAT? And as he fell backward through the rain he thought only "OK."

311

When he landed some seconds later with a flutter of wings and a nonstop burbling and cooing, he was a gray speckled pigeon with empty golden eyes and a brain the size of a sunflower seed. He strutted back and forth, trembling his wings back into comfort. Down at the other end of the windowsill he saw what looked like something to eat so he walked over to investigate.

On the other side of the window a woman sat alone at her kitchen table drinking steaming tea. She had a date tonight and was thinking about what to wear. She saw the bird on the windowsill and wondered what it was like living outside on a rainy December night like this. For one second, no more than two, the woman and the pigeon looked directly at each other. The bird's gold eye was as blank and mysterious as death. The woman's was as full and mysterious as life. The bird bobbed its head then, tapping its beak along the sill for food like a blind man tapping his way home.

Nominated by Conjunctions

CLOCKS

by PAM DURBAN

from SHENANDOAH

W<small>E</small> LIVED WITHIN WALKING DISTANCE of my father's mother. Even after they married, none of her five children moved far away, unless they had to, and if they did they came back to South Carolina as soon as they could and settled down close to her again. On Sunday afternoons we visited her. Nothing ever seemed to change in that house. Year after year, the long, dark, hall closet stayed stuffed with the same coats, dresses, shoes and hat boxes. There was always a biscuit wrapped in tinfoil on the stove in the kitchen, a pot of cold grits on a burner. Underneath the house, a cellar with a cool clay floor held boxes of swollen books, ripe with mildew, and more boxes of chipped dishes and baby carriages with broken springs. A black Buick sat in the garage under an oak tree in the side yard, its tires flat, its dusty seats littered with cracked acorns, its cream-colored steering wheel gone yellow.

Maybe that's why, in memory, those visits happen on the same unchanging Sunday afternoon, always in fall or winter, when a small fire burns in the fireplace in that faded, worn front room. An earthy dampness rises from the cellar and makes the air ancient. On this one Sunday afternoon that we walk in and out of every week, my grandmother is old and we are young. She sits beside the fireplace in a wing chair covered with a faded pink slip-cover, stroking the Chihuahua or poodle that trembles on her lap. A stack of thin silver bracelets jingles each time she lifts her hand. I look at my grandmother and try and see the girl I've heard stories about, the one who drove the family horses up to the summer cabin at Cedar Mountain,

313

a three-day ride, alone, or the young woman with soulful eyes, II've seen in a photograph, but I cannot find her except as she is now, an old woman with a narrow, fine-boned face and blue eyes so pale it seems the color has drained out of them. I am a child and time is not yet real to me; it measures only the distance between events that have to be gotten through—a school day, a doctor's appointment—or enjoyed—Christmas Day, summer vacation; it is not a force that carries and changes everything.

My father pokes up the fire and throws on another pine log. She offers coffee or Cokes, pound cake or ginger snaps that come from a tall jar on a shelf in the pantry that smells of these cookies. Once we're all settled with our snacks, the talk begins to circle the same old subjects. *Something's wrong with the furnace,* she says. *She's cold all the time. Her stomach is sour lately, food tastes like cardboard. The girl they've hired is lazy, and she may be stealing. You know the way they do.* Her voice is South Carolina soft and buttery, and as she talks to my father, my mother sighs, crosses her legs, folds her arms, stares out the front window while we lie on the rug or sit on stools in front of the fire, soaking in its warmth and eating our cookies.

My mother has no patience whatsoever for my grandmother's whining or the way she calls my father and his older brother *the boys*. *The boys* are married men now with families of their own; they support their mother like men, too, as they've done since just after World War II during which their father died suddenly, leaving his family drowning in unexpected debt. From 1943, the year of his death, until the end of the war, their mother rented out rooms to school teachers, and my father's three sisters waited on the boarders at the long table in the dining room. Since 1945, however, her sons have taken care of her. They have kept her comfortable in this big, drafty, peeling wooden house where pine seedlings sprout in the gutters, and where, all winter, a river of fuel oil pours into a rusty tank behind the house and out into the cranky furnace. They buy her groceries; they even give her what my mother calls *pin money*. And is she grateful? She is not. Her boys have let her down; that is the real source of her sorrow and of their boyhood, too. If only they would do right by her she might call them men.

My mother's mother was independent when most women were not. She had to be. Widowed in 1921, the young mother of three small children, she taught school in Macon, Georgia, and in the summers she sent my mother and her sister and brother to live with better-off relatives in Atlanta, so that she could work selling insurance or encyclopedias door to door. At 60 she went to the Belgian Congo to teach the children of the Presbyterian missionaries there. She would never have asked her *children* to carry her through life like a queen on a cushion stuffed with their sacrifices. By raising her mother above her mother-in-law, my mother nurses a sense of *her* family's superiority over my grandmother's, who has always made the superiority of her family clear, especially to her children's spouses, who married above themselves by marrying her children, as her husband had once done by marrying her.

At least once a month, my father's mother returns to the question that's troubled her since 1943. When the complaints are done, the shopping list comes out. She needs this or that, she says, and my father answers that money is tight this month. As he talks her through the numbers, she frowns, she glares. Finally, she's heard enough. "Frampton," she asks sharply, as though she *will not* be put off again, when she's been waiting all this time for her boys to give her back the life that she remembers and deserves, "what happened to the money your father made?" My mother's sigh explodes, and my father closes his eyes, grips his forehead with one hand and squeezes his temples, the way he does when he's about to blow. The way he looks when we do word problems together at the dining room table and I *do not get it*, my mind goes blank, balks, then freezes and cannot grasp the vectors of time, distance and speed that are so obvious to him. "Mother, there was no money, remember?" he says, and while she frowns into the fire and considers this, silence falls. I feel bad for him and uneasy, too, for all of us, and just when it seems that we are all sinking into the silence, that it will never end, he slaps his knees and gets up to wind the mantle clock.

It is a small black cathedral of a clock with spires and an ornate gold filigree face that marks the quarter hour with Westminster chimes. He swings open the round glass door, picks up a brass key from inside the case, inserts the key into one of the two holes in the face and begins to wind. As he winds, he leans toward the clock, feeling through the key for the mainspring's stiffening resistance. When the key no longer turns, he pulls it out, inserts it in the other hole and winds the chimes, replaces the key in the bottom of the case and shuts the door until it clicks. He always looks satisfied turning away from his mother's clock on a Sunday afternoon; it seems to cheer him up. He smiles at his mother, and she smiles back, but not for long,

315

and I am hopeful too, because now it's almost over. Of course I didn't know any of this then. I've brought the knowledge back and laid it over the past, which is memory doing its work: finding pattern, connection and meaning, weaving a story out of time.

When the first notes of the Westminster chimes ripple out across the room again, my mother stands up, ready to go. As we all stand to leave, he tells his mother that the furnace is fine. It's just been checked and serviced for winter, he says, but to reassure her, he turns up the thermostat and stands with his head bowed, listening, until the blower clicks on and warm air begins to drift up from the floor vents. At the door, he pats her on the shoulder and says what he says every week, "Don't take counsel of your fears, Mother," and then we're free.

He winds the clocks at home, too. The Seth Thomas clock on the mantle over the living room fireplace and the clock from his father's office, a tall clock in an oak case that stands on the mantle over the fireplace in the den. On its glass door, painted in gold, is my grandfather's name, G. A. Durban, and his business, Real Estate & Insurance. *Time-keeping is a serious responsibility*, this clock says with the wide sweeps of its long brass pendulum, its deep and dignified chiming. Because of its larger mainspring, my father winds it only once a month. He writes the date on a piece of paper that he stores inside the case. He enjoys all his roles: husband, father, provider, good son, and the chores that define them. He keeps notebooks. In one, he critiques each Christmas season and lists ways to make the next one better. In another, he keeps track of the dates when he fertilizes the grass, the azaleas and camellias in the yard. He's a creature of habit, which makes him easy to find. He likes his breakfast early, rolls into the driveway for lunch at one each weekday afternoon, lies down for a nap, returns to the office at three, comes home to sit down at the supper table at six, fall, winter, spring. My brother and I know the exact minute we must leave on our bicycles in order to ride to the place where we can see his car turn onto our street, so we can race him home.

Winding the clocks, fertilizing the lawn, sharpening all the pencils in the house, turning out the lights at night, adjusting the thermostat, oiling the bearings in the attic fan motor every spring, he strung his life together as a series of reliable, repetitive events. He was reliability itself. Beneath it all, steady as a heartbeat, ran a faith in time as a

316

kind of promise, as though no matter what was happening in the present, we were always on the way to someplace better. Clearing out the house after his death, I came across a box of my letters from college and a folder of carbon copies of the weekly letters he wrote to me. In my letters, I chatted about classes and dates and roommates; I confessed that I'd overdrawn my bank account; I was unhappy, I said, and disillusioned. He answered that he had deposited money in my account. As for the unhappiness, I must *take an even strain on things*. I must *have a little faith in the future. Stick to it and situation will clear up. Just do the best you can and wait for better times. Time takes care of a lot of miseries.*

Where did he get this optimism? He was mostly a moody man, disappointed and burdened by almost everything, except time, which he trusted, always to bring good out of bad. Maybe he was born with it, the way we're born with extra vertebrae at the end of our spines, vestigial tails left over from our evolutionary climb, or the impulse to flight or fight that's triggered by any threat. Maybe this faith in time is a deep instinct, too, evolved over centuries spent living through cycles of light and darkness, watching the orderly mystery of tides and seasons, into a trust in the power of cycles to soften time's irreversibly linear drive, until it became a part of our emotional anatomy, the root of religion, the biology of the metaphysics of faith. Or maybe I have seen this in him because it is what I need to believe. Or he learned it where he learned so many things: in the war.

During the three years that he served in the army in the South Pacific, my mother wrote to him every day. He wrote to her whenever he could, and the letters have all survived. What's remarkable about them, aside from the fact that my father managed to keep them as his infantry regiment moved from New Guinea up through the Philippines toward Japan, and that they survived in a leather suitcase in the attic for over fifty years, is the steadiness of their faith. His letters to her always ended with his urging her to think of the future, always the future, when they would be together and their life would begin, almost as if the war were a wall that stood between them and the life1 they would get to, eventually. They never doubted, at least to cach other, that they had a future coming to them.

I guess it's not so remarkable, really, the belief, the insistence, that they'd been promised a future. Certainly, it's not unique, given the time they lived through. What else could they have said to one another except to remember who they'd been and to count on where they were going? What else would have been safe to say? Could he have told her about the first Japanese soldier he killed? Or the first dead American he saw, rolled off a stretcher on one side of the Tor River in New Guinea where he waited with his unit to go into combat for the first time? He led his rifle company through landings against defended beaches on Noemfour Island and Luzon. He won two Purple Hearts and a Bronze Star. In New Guinea, the Japanese charged his rifle company with swords. On Luzon, he ordered men with flame throwers to roast the Japanese in their caves. His company drew their equipment for the invasion of Japan. Later, from the safety of home, he typed up those stories. But he didn't tell them in his letters; the censor wouldn't have allowed it, and even if there'd been no censor to black out sentences and paragraphs, neither of them would have allowed bad news to slip through because to do so would have broken the vow of hope they'd sworn each other to.

I read their letters, and I feel them there again, alive in those words, alive to each other and to the future they kept alive for one another. He couldn't wait to see her pout "the way you do sometimes," he wrote. *Dear Pretty*, she called him. They wrote about the children they wanted, at least a dozen. She sent pin-ups, photographs of herself in high heels and shorts, her dark, thick hair pulled back from her heart-shaped face. He sent back pictures of himself, grinning from a foxhole on Kiriwina Island. "This is me in my favorite foxhole," he wrote on the back of the photograph. "The Japs bombed us two or three times a week." She sent drawings of a new outfit she'd sewed and a swatch of the cloth, for him to feel. He sketched plans for the house they'd build when he came home, and she wrote that she'd found the lot she wanted to build it on. They counted for each other the months, then the years they'd been apart as though that widening gap were carrying them toward, not away, from each other. "Every minute that passes is a minute nearer Mariah and home," he wrote. Or maybe what they trusted was that time would stand still for them until they could catch up with it again. "I really haven't aged that much," she wrote on the back of a photograph of herself, smiling under a big white hat, a little bleak around the eyes.

Then, it happened. Hiroshima and Nagasaki and the Japanese surrender. In the fall of 1945, he went to Japan with the occupying army, and by Christmas that year he was home. They'd kept the faith, and now time returned the favor. When the train on which he'd traveled from the west coast finally reached Augusta, Georgia, seventeen miles from Aiken, across the Savannah River, he went to a hotel and called her from the lobby. Then he went upstairs to change his shirt and wash his face. He couldn't have been gone for more than five minutes, he said, and when he went back down to the lobby to wait for her, there she was, waiting for him. "She must have skimmed the tops of those hills," he always said, and she said she couldn't remember the drive. One minute, she was leaving the house, the next, she was standing in the hotel lobby looking at his face. And whatever really happened, in the story that memory and faith make of time, a miracle returned them to one another and the future they'd believed in began.

Three days after our father's funeral, my brother and I closed up the house that now belonged to us. Our mother had died two years earlier, and now, with Dad gone, it was really the end of the life we'd lived together as a family in that house. It was that strange, slack time between the time a last parent dies and when the house gets cleared out and sold, a pause, like a breath drawn in and held. When it gets breathed out, everything will change, but nobody's breathing yet. The tables and chairs, the pillows with funny sayings stitched on them ("My idea of housework is to sweep the room with a glance." "Everyone is entitled to my opinion."), the refrigerator magnets, the monthly calendar beside the phone with doctor's appointments written in the squares, the light through the windows, the birds at the feeders. The books on the living room shelves beside the fireplace. All of it was exactly as it had always been; only they were gone, and already the unstirred stillness of a closed-up house was settling over everything.

We'd taken the silver to an aunt's house, cleaned out the refrigerator and filled the bird feeders, installed timers on the lights. We were sitting in the living room with our organizers open, checking off chores and marking dates for the next time we'd come. That's when we started to try and remember the last time we'd heard the ticking and chiming of the key-wound clocks. The Seth Thomas, our grandmother's small black cathedral that we'd inherited after she died, our grandfather's office clock back in the den. All of them had stopped; only the battery operated and electronic models still ran: the clock on the microwave and the kitchen wall clock that signaled the hour with bird calls. The hoot of a Horned Owl at twelve, a Mockingbird's song at three.

We couldn't remember the last time we'd heard the older clocks chime. During the ten months when our mother was dying, winding the clocks was not at the top of anyone's list. There was help to be hired, pain to be watched for and eased as we tried to keep ahead of the steady and relentless progress of her cancer. In the last weeks of her life, time was what passed between one dose of morphine and the next. And for two years after Mother died, no one thought about the clocks while our father floundered in depression and deepening confusion. It seemed that every week he found another way to give up on something that had mattered to him. Our reliable father, who wouldn't get out of bed some days or shave or keep himself clean. After his heart attack, time became what stretched between one visit to the ICU and the next. Winding the clocks then would have been a luxury, a sign that life was normal and orderly, and so we had not, and now there was silence.

"Come look at this," my brother said, and we walked from the living room back to the den. Inside the tall clock from our grandfather's office, he'd found the piece of paper on which our father had written the dates when he wound the clock. A year's worth of dates, moving steadily from January to December 2000, the month Mother's cancer was diagnosed. After that, the record got spotty. He wound the clock in January, then in March. He wound it in June, and then in August, when hospice took over her care. After that, he either stopped winding the clock or he stopped writing down the date, and in the missing dates, the stopped clock, it seemed we read the story of his grief and hopelessness, his despair. When Mother got sick, he stopped caring, we said; that's when time stopped counting anything that mattered to him. We said he believed in a better time until he couldn't anymore, and when he lost faith in time, he lost faith in everything.

That's what we said, and the story helped us make sense of the free-fall we'd been in for the last three years, since Mother got sick, and of the terrifying fact that after she died, our father no longer wanted to live. And maybe he didn't. Maybe that is finally the truth about the end of his life, that he lost faith in everything, that he gave up. I know it felt that way to live through it. But lately, over a year past his death, I've begun to think that maybe the idea that he gave up is too neat and too simple to be true. Or maybe this belief in uncertainty has become my own faith now. Because the only certainty in our lives is death; everything else is life, and life is neither still nor certain in any way.

On the morning of the last day of his life my father was released from the hospital with his badly damaged heart pumping at a fraction of its normal urgency. But the arrhythmia was under control, his medications had been fine-tuned. He was stable, and the doctors were hopeful, guardedly hopeful, that with time and cardiac rehab his heart might get stronger. Now it seems absurd that we believed he would recover. They'd also said that his heart was failing, that failure was not something the heart recovered from, but given hope, you don't hear degrees; hope is hope and we'd absorbed it. As a nurse rolled his wheelchair down the hall toward the ambulance that would take him to the nursing home, he trailed his fingers along the tile wall and smiled, as though he'd never felt tile before. The minister from Mother's church was walking with him, and just before they lifted him into the ambulance he said to her, "You know, Martha, the hard part is over."

After he died that night, those words began to echo. *The hard part is over.* Maybe words spoken from the edge of death always do. One last chance at meaning against the silence that comes after. No wonder we believe they're deep and wise. He knew he was going to die, my brother and I said, so *life* was the hard part that was over. And maybe he did mean that. But I believe he meant it literally as well, and first. In the hospital, his heart had stopped, but they'd brought him back, and he'd spent days on a ventilator in the ICU. Conscious again, he'd been confused and belligerent, tortured by thirst and frightened. One morning after he'd been moved down to the cardiac floor, he'd gotten out of bed and yanked the needles and IV lines out of his body, laughed at the blood and the people who rushed in to stop it. Now the hard part was finished, the indignity and the fear, and if a bad time was over, that could only mean that a better time was coming. Now, a year and more beyond his death, I tell myself that he died believing he was going to live, still on the clock. As I must be as well, having come to that conclusion.

Nominated by Frederick Busch, Gary Gildner, Daniel Anderson, David Jauss, Andrea Hollander Budy, Shenandoah

MYTH

by NATASHA TRETHEWEY

from NEW ENGLAND REVIEW

I was asleep while you were dying.
It's as if you slipped through some rift, a hollow
I make between my slumber and my waking,

the Erebus I keep you in, still trying
not to let go. You'll be dead again tomorrow,
but in dreams you live. So I try taking

you back into morning. Sleep-heavy, turning,
my eyes open, I find you do not follow.
Again and again, this constant forsaking.

*

Again and again, this constant forsaking:
my eyes open, I find you do not follow.
You back into morning, sleep-heavy, turning.

But in dreams you live. So I try taking,
not to let go. You'll be dead again tomorrow.
The Erebus I keep you in—still, trying—

I make between my slumber and my waking.
It's as if you slipped through some rift, a hollow.
I was asleep while you were dying.

Nominated by Lucia Perillo, Rita Dove

THE 167TH PSALM OF ELVIS

by TONY BARNSTONE

from RUNES

Blessed are the marble breasts of Venus,
those ancient miracles, for they are upright and milk white
and they point above the heads of the crowd in the casino.
Blessed are the crowds that play, and whose reflections
sway in the polish of her eggshell eyes,
for they move in shimmers and flights of birds
as they circle the games
and they are beautiful and helpless.
Bless the fast glances that handle the waitress,
bless her miniskirt toga and the flame-gold scotch,
and bless the gamblers who gaze at the stage.
Remember also the dancer and remember her dance,
her long neck arched like a wild white goose,
the tassels on her nipples that shoot like sparks,
and bless the legs and bless the breasts
for they are fruit and honey
and they are generous to the eyes.
Have mercy on my wallet, the dollars I punch into the slot,
and grace the wheels swapping clubs and hearts.
Mercy on me too, as I stumble as if in a hashish haze
watching the reels spin away, for I am a blown fuse
and I need someone to bless me before it's too late.
Honor the chance in a million, the slot machine jolting,

the yellow light flashing, honor the voice that calls *jackpot*,
and the coins that crush into the brushed steel tray,
for there is a time for winning and a time for losing
and if you cast your bread upon the waters
you will find it again after many days.
Pity the crowd around the blessed winner
all patting his back as if it rubs off,
this juice, this force, this whatever
that might save them from their own cursed luck.
And pity the poor winner whose hand claws back
into his bucket of coins and who cannot walk away,
because he'd do anything for the feeling
he had when the great pattern rose from the chaos
of cherries and lemons and diamonds and stars
and he knew for that moment he was blessed.

Nominated by Andrea Hollander Budy

TAJ MAHAL

fiction by LINSEY ABRAMS

from MISSISSIPPI REVIEW

—for Fred Reynolds

YOU CAN BAIT WILD HOGS with Twinkies, fish heads, you name it. But spiked cobs is preferred since the aroma carries. Then it slows the bastards down. Currently, the hunters have forfeited their advantage, having just finished off the bourbon that, along with their guns and the corn, they toted into the woods around midnight. Three hours of crouching in a bush on the edge of a swamp nearly froze their asses off, though it was that or hiding in a tree. Skip was afraid of falling out from the booze or shooting too high when the pigs came . . . if they ever do . . . but anyway his cousin Tiny couldn't climb a ladder with guardrails. Not that they're feeling any pain now.

Hogs are nocturnal while attracted to light, which is why at the full moon so many hunters can be found creeping through the woods. Armed vampires. In Texas, they sell packages that include access to private land plus two nights in a motel. The state has open season on hogs, no restrictions—you can hunt them on Christmas Day or the Fourth of July, in a Humvee with a spotlight on top, with a bazooka if you want.

Skip and Tiny drove nonstop from South Carolina to Sneedsville, Texas, according to their long-planned itinerary. Skip's itinerary. If he'd had anyone else to take he would have left Tiny behind. Even if they weren't so wasted, his cousin would be useless facing the pigs. But the rates were for two.

Tiny is overweight. Actually, so are half the people they know, but Tiny is in a class by himself. Way beyond love handles or pile-driver thighs, or even the unnatural asses on some women—from hormones in the feed but don't say that in cattle country—his size seems an impossible end-product of babyhood. He's like one of the piglets people bought for house pets, unaware that an adult potbelly, at one hundred twenty pounds, can reroute a sink pipe or flip the TV . . . eat the dishtowels then the slipcovers before mowing down a china cabinet. Unlike a cat, say. Only you can't drive your son to some remote location after dark then pull over and open the car door to fate. Children aren't a craze you can declare over just because they grew up.

Skip read in a magazine that being a hundred pounds overweight takes ten years off life expectancy. It ages you like one of those diseases people in science fiction catch on Mars, where time has different rules. Well, that's *one* way to wear out your heart.

"Are you sure you soaked the corn thoroughly?" Skip says. Tiny nods morosely. "And laid the dirt back on thick but not too thick?" Another chin dip, though what kind of a question is *that*? Since community college Skip overthinks things, which is why his wife filed for divorce . . . that, and losing his hair. Lucky for him he still has Tiny to boss—with Skip's new status they've been spending time together the way they did in childhood. Skip as cowboy, Tiny as Indian. Skip as God, Tiny as man. Skip as man, Tiny as woman. But only once, a relief to both parties.

This time, among many directives, Skip insisted Tiny clear the last hunting party's bait from the hole—it smelled so bad even a pig wouldn't eat it—while Skip loaded the guns. Excuse: Tiny might stick the bullets backwards and get their heads blown off. Skip rented a .44 Magnum, and Tiny—he failed at the supervised target practice yesterday—a .270 Winchester, which was supposed to help his chances of hitting something.

"God damn, it's a miracle . . . here comes one," Skip says, raising his bald head. He elbows his cousin, who's so stiff from sitting on the ground he can barely part the bushes. Tiny sees a small pig, *ambling*—that's the only word for it—toward the corn pit. "Little porker," Skip says. His tone is creepy. He gropes frantically for the Magnum, which turns up under his thigh, itself an unattached object since going numb. Hunting is a bitch.

"Maybe we shouldn't shoot it after all," Tiny says. If he were sober he wouldn't be thinking out loud. "It's not a fair fight really."

326

Skip kneels to stick his head in Tiny's face. "What are you, fucking Wyatt Earp? That's why we came here . . . to shoot things. Remember?" This in a stage whisper before, losing his balance, he tips over. From the ground Skip commands, "Shoot the pig." He waggles the barrel of Tiny's Winchester before realizing what he's shaking hands with. In sole possession of his weapon, Tiny wipes off Skip's fingerprints with a Kleenex.

Meanwhile, the little hog feels seasick and stops eating. Pigs can't hold their liquor, though who in this crowd can? At eighty pounds it's still cute, but it's not the same potbelly that just a month ago received E-mail and was ridden around the Winn-Dixie in a shopping cart. Teetering, it starts a trot toward the hunters . . . either bad judgment or poor eyesight. In fact, its instincts, already scrambled by domestication, have completely broken down in the wild.

"But it didn't do anything," Tiny protests. He has yet to get up, and probably won't.

"It's alive, isn't it?" Skip responds.

Real life has never elicited such drama. He's like Captain Bligh in a poor man's *Mutiny on the Bounty*, Tiny and the pig his wayward crew. It's time to punish all forms of treason then . . . and on videotape, a tip from the brochure. The thrill is boundless as the sea, till it dawns on Skip, they left the camera at the motel. He ought to club Tiny with the tripod.

The hunter rises to his feet and squats, pistol in both hands, the way they taught them at target practice. It feels obscene, somewhat of a consolation.

Tiny swings around to grab one of his cousin's ankles. "No don't." Outstretched in the moonlight, he looks like a big starfish. Or might to the hog.

Cocking the chest-high Magnum, Skip tries to kick free. It looks like a hot foot that, wrenched from Tiny's grip, quickly dies out. Training a bead on the hog, Skip launches one of his elaborate daredevil theories. Courtesy of higher education.

"The thing is, it's fat," he addresses Tiny on the ground. "Realistically . . . it should go on a diet," he continues, ". . . like you should." Satisfied with his argument so far, Skip proceeds, "Only in the wild the rules are sadly different." He drills Tiny with his boot, suddenly stuck on why the pig must die. Then *Bingo!* "The fact is"—Skip glances pitifully below—"nature just can't tolerate this excessive link in the food chain. So"—he better squeeze the trigger before the

s.o.b. jumps in his lap—"in about one second there's going to be a *missing* link."
Gunshot.

❖

BB's grandmother named the little pig Taj Mahal. Now both are gone, the potbelly abandoned by the girl's father fifty miles up FM 1278 one night three weeks ago, and her grandmother deposited in the nursing home in September. Daylight hours. Before her dementia, she would call out when the two of them were alone, *"Let's get this party started."* BB in her new outlaw mentality had downloaded Pink's song from an illegal site on the Internet, and she and her grandmother would play it in the kitchen and dance. Disco mix. The girl would be half-suicidal now, shipwrecked here with her parents. Only as her grandmother would say, if she remembered to say it, *Homicide before suicide.*

It's 5:30, just after work for her mother and father, and just before for BB, the family's only overlap in the space-time continuum. Every weeknight it's like the Last Supper, starring Judas, Judas, and Judas. The girl includes herself in this—she should have resisted both betrayals to the death. After eating, BB will drive to the hospital in Amarillo, where she works graveyard while her father gets cross-eyed on beer and her mother watches *ER*, that total piece of crap.

"Pass the ketchup," BB's father says. She does, without comment. The girl's not speaking to either parent since they gave her grandmother, then Taj Mahal, the bum's rush. They may or may not be aware of this since no one talks anyway, except at the TV. The three of them are watching the Dan Rather News. Nevermind the scandal, he's from Texas.

A fancy graphic unfurls: *Are the Skies Safe?*

"Don't count on it," BB's father says. Shot of a jumbo jet, an unlikely candidate for flight, all things being even.

"I mean, who wants to fly when you can't take a nail file?" her mother adds. The father gives her a look. "It's unhygienic," she protests.

BB's got it memorized: how they cut the meals then the peanuts, and how a Bud costs $4.00 while *you're lucky if they give you a napkin.* Not that her parents should take this personally. Her grandmother is the only one of the four of them who's flown in an airplane. Dallas to Las Vegas and back. Twice . . . since the entertainment there featured "world-class acts," and the casinos and hotels were "elegant."

"I'm telling you, it's criminal," BB's father says. "They talk, they vote, they talk, they vote." He's got on his chapped look. "It's a no-brainer. Arm the pilots," he tells the TV, ". . . with *Uzis*."

"You shouldn't pay all that money to have to tackle terrorists," BB's mother agrees.

"Well, I'd like to tackle some," her father says, talking to his wife in spite of himself. "Or maybe a few Frenchmen." He never gave a rat's ass about the U.N. or the Arabs before 9/11, but now they've pissed him off.

BB is despondent. She would pretend she's adopted, only that would mean renouncing her grandmother.

When it became clear something was wrong, the family drove to the Regional Medical Center. A series of "events" had rerouted some neural pathways, apparently. The doctor, who graduated med school that spring, wouldn't even be goaded into using the word *stroke*—if she ended up in Chicago like she intended, after the six-year posting to Siberia, Texas, that ensured forgiveness of her loans, she was going to treat only healthy patients. Dermatology or something. Bottom line, no cancer. In the meantime she was rotating specialties at the only bona fide surgical facility for three counties.

BB herself is a health care practitioner. She began volunteering locally at Childress Hospital before the decline. Her ridiculous fantasy had been to develop skills to keep her grandmother home till she died. The girl had planned on physical ailments requiring, in ascending seriousness: support hose, physical therapy, nitro, diapers, bedpans with rotation against sores, oxygen, recovery from operations . . . finally and, god forbid, chemo drips. Worst case, hospice with morphine. Not that they let a volunteer, or even an aide, which she became after graduating, near the drugs. Addiction was limited to doctors and the supervising nurses . . . unless you got lucky. "Events" hadn't crossed her mind.

When the girl was young it had been tough to weather disappointment: a cute boy who mocked her, coming in second in the art show the year she should have won. Later it was the general idiocy of humankind, death as a cruel joke, the callousness of her parents. Still, because of her grandmother's attentions BB had flourished. She accepted herself, which sounds small but she came to realize was not.

In the chicken-scratch back yard BB's stored everything that ever belonged to the hog—the Alpine-flowered Swiss ribbon that baby Taj Mahal had worn for a collar, its bowl and a plastic toy mouse—plus the clothes, nail files, Epsom salts, etc. the grandmother left forever on BB's twin bed, where she'd slept since leaving her third husband during the Clinton administration. A collection of memorabilia unconnected to BB, mostly from Las Vegas, fills a shoebox in the closet. The *connected* remains in the grandmother's possession.

What's outside, all of which the girl will part with for good but not now, will last a while in the shed. Tar paper over two-by-fours, it looks like some poor man's tent on the moon. In childhood BB made pin pricks in the roof so she could sit there in daylight pretending they were the constellations. *To summon the magic and solace of the night.*

BB's heroes are Annie Sullivan, miracle worker to the deaf, dumb and blind Helen Keller; Barbara Jordan, against all odds as a black woman, the most intelligent person in Texas; and, of course, Pink. But above them all towers her grandmother, who in the last great act of her life bent to Earth and snatched BB up.

The girl pushes back her chair.

"Don't scratch the linoleum," her mother says. "And don't forget stopping by the Home." *As if*, BB smolders.

"Not that the old bat's going to remember." This from her own son. BB's parents wheeze with laughter. Smokers.

Their daughter shoots a withering look. But they're glued to the news again. On her way out she's going to slam the door to make them jump.

Slam.

*

The drive to work was BB's favorite part of the day. Now it's mixed since she scours the roadside for Taj Mahal. BB doesn't expect to find the hog, but it haunts her she might not be looking if by a miracle it did appear. The car in which the three of them tooled around is BB's exclusive property now. The grandmother wrote out a "wish list," which, notarized, entitled BB to her worldly possessions and savings passbook.

A scene from the past:

"Could you do something about that Mohawk hairdo?"

Being out of it is one thing but inaccuracies weigh on BB. "It's punk," the girl told the supervising nurse. "It's a regular haircut but the putty makes it stand up."

"Well, tell it to sit down. This is cardiac . . . you could flatline the whole floor."

"The patients love me," BB said. It just came out.

Tactical error, since the director of personnel is the supervisor's boyfriend. Naturally, he's married. The hospital is like *The Sopranos*, where the men screw all subordinates, i.e., the whole of womankind. It's enough to make someone a lesbian. Anyway, she got transferred to the Emergency Room. The patients there are in no shape to love BB or anyone.

The girl pulls off 287. She downshifts into the parking lot, then yanks the emergency brake after touch down in the closest spot to the lobby. It's for *Handicapped*, but who isn't?

It's quiet inside, all wheelchairs on blocks till tomorrow. The Home, even in cold weather, smells . . . a cliché people find funny until, in spite of their great sense of humor, they end up in one. Upstairs, BB exchanges V-signs with an aide.

"Gran?" BB sticks her head in the solarium, where her grandmother likes to sit.

"Oh, hi, chigger." She's at the window overlooking the high school, where the kids moon the old people after football games. "I wasn't expecting you just now," she ventures. Though BB visits five days a week, the grandmother is pleasantly surprised each time.

"Come here, doodle bug." She pats the straight chair beside one she took for herself. No couches for the grandmother, who sits upright for concentration. Not that it helps. "How's Taj Mahal?" she asks. Twice BB revealed the hog's fate—they're sticklers for the truth—but it slipped her grandmother's mind both times, and will again. Why break that old heart over and over?

"TJ's good," BB lies, trying to look innocent. Then, inspired, adlibs, "But he's getting fat."

"How fat?" her grandmother asks, scandalized.

"One hundred pounds!" BB reveals.

"That rascal," BB's grandmother says. Her hands keep moving to the girl's knees, to smooth the wrinkles in her uniform. She daydreams about the pig, while BB sways to the Muzak. Hardly *Get This Party Started!* How the mighty have fallen.

The grandmother looks at her watch then exclaims, "You better

skedaddle, Dr. BB." In practical terms, she has no idea of the time—
it's a show of interest in the girl's affairs.

BB just got there, but she *is* late. "OK," she says, getting up, then
pulling the grandmother to standing. They walk down the corridor to
her room.

"Listen to your replacement," the grandmother says, stopping in
the doorway to point at her snoring roommate. The woman's teeth
are out; she's the size of a small laundry bag under the covers.

It's so depressing, BB doesn't know what to say. She starts to tear
up as they cross the threshold.

"Don't cry for *me*, Argentina," the grandmother scolds. There's a
rule against shutting the door, so forget privacy. "Because *I*'ve been
around the world, and seen its wonders. That's the best comfort in
old age . . . to have done things while you could." She flattens the col-
lar of BB's jeans jacket. "I'll name my personal highlights." The
grandmother pauses then ticks off on her fingers: "Eiffel Tower,
Luxor Pyramid, Canals of Venice, French Riviera . . . and best, Taj
Mahal." Too bad she's remembering just the replicas in Las Vegas.
Or is it?

"Promise me two things," the grandmother says, poking the girl's
few droopy strands of hair. BB nods. "One, that you'll visit those
places before *you* get too old . . . though don't if you can help it . . .
get old that is." A touch of her old hokey sense of humor, causing BB
to smirk. "OK?" The girl smirks again. "And two, remember who
loves you."

Her grandmother fingers a flowery crepe paper lei at her neck,
which BB knows is from last night's fake Hawaiian Luau. The week
before it was Rodeo Party, with plastic horseshoes for door prizes.
Everything's fake in this world. Either that, or it's too sad.

❀

From Skip's viewpoint it all happened in a whirl, first the freak ac-
cident . . . then being airlifted out of the woods to Amarillo. Just like
Full Metal Jacket, the Vietnam movie . . . in a chopper. If he hadn't
been in excruciating pain, it would have been the best thing that ever
happened to him.

Still, after the liquor wore off in the emergency room, and before
they got the Demerol, he called Tiny a *dumb fuck*. Not that Tiny
cared, for once, having lost a half pint of blood himself. Anyway, he
was prepared to die, either way, until he realized that his cousin, who

332

wouldn't give him credit if Tiny was owed the Lotto jackpot, had completely missed the fact that he'd shot him on purpose. Granted, it hadn't been a total success, since Tiny shot himself, too, and almost the hog. But he'd done it with one bullet. Incredibly. Nobody ever bought the single shooter theory, only now who was to say? Tell him about crazy angles.

By tomorrow Tiny will prefer the return of Texas to Mexico over visiting there ever again. At the moment, however, he's a man without a country. Call him a citizen of Shangri-la or Prince of Hogs. Captain Winchester. It's the drugs.

"Blah . . . blah . . . blah." That's Tiny's answer to everything Skip says—perhaps it's pig Latin *ha ha*—until lack of response puts his cousin to sleep.

They've been parked for centuries on gurneys next to the AA bulletin board. The last they saw of the human race was some bitch of an intern who retightened Skip's tourniquet, causing him to curse her out. Tiny's sure they're being punished and would worry about bleeding to death, only that's why there's malpractice. Still, studying his fellow victims at the far end of the corridor he wonders if a few haven't died since he last looked.

"Jesus H. Christ."

Tiny lifts his head, takes stock of the situation then returns it to the pillow. "Hi, Skip." His cousin might have regained his faculties, in which case he wouldn't take kindly to *blah blah blah*.

"Oh god . . . did I die and go to heaven?" Skips shouts. This causes a general freak-out among the wounded. Even Tiny rolls over. She's some kind of gorgeous futuristic candy striper, Skip decides, as the girl breezes up the corridor with a basin. In his addled state, he reaches out for her hand.

"It's sterile," she says, blocking the basin with her hip. Then she's gone.

Skip's slumps back, exhausted but triumphant. "I'm in love," he says.

"Well, you're not divorced yet," Tiny pipes up, ". . . only *separated*." On his back again, hypnotized by the ceiling fan, he considers, "Plus, I don't know about her hair. . . ."

Propping himself up, Skip musters his last strength to insult his cousin. "Have you seen *your* hair recently?"

In fact, the plaid hunting hat, lost in the melee, gave Tiny a flattop. His head looks like it shrunk a size, bad news for a fat man. He

333

catches sight of it reflected off some chrome, but his self-image was already shot. So no harm done.

"At least *I* have some," Tiny replies. He knows he's digging his own grave unless his cousin stays prone for life. But shooting Skip has changed him.

°

It's a scene in the ER as usual. Plus BB's a magnet for men like that joker on the gurney. Her grandmother says they're attracted to her *vitality*. So be it. The people in here could use some.

The orderlies call it the Knife and Gun Club. Hunters keep the place in business, along with men who drink too much then go to town on anyone unluckily nearby. Recently BB had a dream set in, no kidding, the *Land of Misfortune*—there was a sign. It looked suspiciously like her place of employment, where tonight victims of asthma, rape, self-served Clorox, and worse . . . crowd the premises. On weekend nights and the full moon you see every imaginable harm. Tonight is double whammy.

Sick of stanching blood and assembling IVs, BB swings by those bozos who shot each other. They keep trying to flag her down, which is objectionable. But it's human contact as opposed to an errand or procedure. She's working on a triple shift—that's twenty-four hours—which can happen when it's this crazy and they're under-staffed. Everyone protests for the record, but it's their duty as medical providers. Also: *It's important to have a purpose in life.*

"Hi," BB says, sneaking up on the hunters, who've been moved to cots. Skip nearly flips his, but gravity is Tiny's friend. "I'm Nurse BB." Not entirely true, at least not yet. "Who are you guys?"

The irritating one's called Skip, and the fat one's name is Tiny. Oh, brother.

"Will you marry me?" Skip asks BB now that they've been introduced.

"No, but I'll be your fiancée," the girl says. She's humoring the guy, something she would never do beyond the confines of a hospital. But here it shouldn't matter if you're a loser.

"You can't be his fiancée. Skip's married," Tiny rats on his cousin. Then he goes against twenty-six years of personal experience. "But *I'm* single."

"You are too much . . . you liar," BB addresses Skip before turning

334

back to Tiny. She crouches beside his cot. "OK. I'll be engaged to you instead . . . only no sex before marriage."

"Catch-22!" Skip crows. But Tiny, who's no Don Juan, accepts the terms.

"Ahem." BB looks up. It's the doctor who diagnosed her grand-mother, on her first day of rotation in the ER.

"Pardon me?" the girl asks. They haven't said two words since rec-ognizing each other hours ago. But here they are.

"Enough chitchat," the doctor says. "Break it up." She's Tiny and Skip's age but speaks like the others are children.

"I'm performing patient care," BB enunciates. She throws a side-long glance to Tiny, who's thrilled.

"This is totally unprofessional," the woman says.

"Is it professional"—Skip half sits up—"to give someone gangrene with a tourniquet?" She grabs his leg. "Ouch!" It's quite a scream.

"Be quiet. I'm examining you."

The would-be dermatologist pulls back the cover to find blood sopped through the leg bandages and onto the pallet beneath Skip. She's losing her composure, what little she has left after sixteen hours of ear-to-ear chicken pox, run-ins with barbed wire, a no-seatbelt survivor of a car crash, and one presenting psycho. Her third pair of scrubs is blood-speckled and worse, and her feet hurt even in the ugly orthopedic shoes.

The uncovering of Skip's wound is painful, and he howls. "Stop be-ing dramatic . . . it's fine," she says without conviction.

"No thanks to you," Skip mutters.

No indeed. It doesn't take a brain surgeon—though BB has no il-lusions about *that*; it's an expression—to tell he's going to lose the leg. Dr. Know-It-All should have sent him to the OR immediately.

"I'll be right back," the intern says. She would run for help but can hardly make her legs work. Meanwhile, Skip is softly moaning. BB reaches to smooth his brow.

"You look sad," Tiny tells his fiancée. He's trying to ignore her min-istrations to his cousin.

"I am, a little," BB admits. She's starved for a good listener.

"Why?" Tiny asks. He always felt he'd be good at relationships, though it's been moot till now.

"Oh, I miss my grandmother . . . she's in a home," BB says. She wonders if this confession to a total stranger is pathetic.

"How horrible," Tiny says. He's getting winded sitting up, but he's not going to take a rest during one of the great moments of his life.

"And our pet, Taj Mahal—"

"Is Taj Mahal a hamster?" Skip asks, hovering like Tiny's smaller shadow. That's no dog or even cat name.

"My father dropped him off in the middle of nowhere," BB says, "at night." The thought knocks the stuffing out of her. "He is . . . was . . . a potbelly."

Skip has no idea what a potbelly is, and he wouldn't care if he did, he's so tired now. The hunter slumps back to the pallet, losing consciousness. It's like death only it isn't. Lucky him.

"Oh, no," Tiny says, starting to cry. They're murderers, at least they intended to be. And there are more where Skip and Tiny came from. All the cute little hogs with their nicknames and pigtails—if it wasn't the nurse's pet, it was someone else's. *Taj Mahal.*

Watching the big man weep, BB can't believe he's so sensitive . . . though they say fat people are, from being treated poorly. It's the last shameless prejudice . . . well, maybe not the last.

Tiny faints. The Triage Team comes running—though not for him—in a flash Skip's on a gurney and being wheeled top speed to the elevator. So his cousin is BB's responsibility. She dashes for the smelling salts.

"Let's get in gear here," the girl says. She waves the bottle under his nose, causing a shudder.

"Don't ever wake me," Tiny wails.

The poor guy must be hallucinating from pain. BB checks the chart and sees the Demerol. Good. The girl increases the drip flow on the IV, not technically her job.

"How's that?" BB asks. No answer from Tiny, though his eyes are open.

Maybe he should tell her. Confessing might make him feel better. But it could easily make him feel worse. Or maybe it doesn't matter, he suddenly thinks. *Sigh.*

"Have you tried MET-Rx?" The girl is staring down from above, her hair like wild grass. Tiny shakes his head, and then keeps shaking it because he likes the feeling until she grabs his ear. "Well, you should," BB says. "Nothing personal. It's my *professional* opinion."

"Maybe I *will* go on a diet," Tiny muses. But it's a pipe dream. "Good night," he says, sleepy and peaceful from the drug.

"Good night," BB says.

It's as if they really *are* married, Tiny thinks before nodding off.

The girl wanders into the main room. It's still a total zoo, too loud and the people, injured or not, look shell-shocked. There are scenes like this in all the hospitals of the world, BB thinks. Trouble is like garbage: you take it to the dump each week, but there's always more to follow.

Tomorrow BB will visit her grandmother, and for months to come. Slowly she'll slip away from the girl, from every Taj Mahal, then from life itself. Against her expectations now, BB will survive it.

Nominated by Mississippi Review

NUDE DESCENDING

by DZVINIA ORLOWSKY

from PEBBLE LAKE REVIEW

Be broken in bright light,
a drain in your back, your body
releasing its deepest red,
like a cardinal opening a wing
within. Halved, one side soft,
the other, a scar running
like a railroad track up to your underarm
where your life was spared, that open
field of broken glass and bad boys
who'd slit anyone's skin just for the thrill,
just as the doctor appeared, asked you
to count backwards. Be shattered
walking the hospital corridor, slowly,
as each nurse changes her face, her name,
smiles and pretends to know you.
Be just at the top of God knows what list,
turn toward a mirror and see all fire,
know your name spills like coal.
Be broken in your car, watch
the light snowfall gather
on the car's hood, disappear;
dream of eating only air.
Stand at the top of the stairs,

in light falling from the high window.
Be fractured, discharged, come down
lightly as the first snowfall,
white points, torches in your hands.

Nominated by Jane Brox, Pebble Lake Review

HALLEY'S COMET

fiction by LAURA KRUGHOFF

from THE THREEPENNY REVIEW

ALICE HASN'T LOOKED at her lover, Suzanne, since they climbed into bed. This seems to be acceptable since Alice is in shock. She should be trying to decide what kind of person she's going to be in the face of tragedy, but instead she's been thinking about Suzanne. Like how she still mentally refers to Suzanne as her lover. She knows this is no longer the proper nomenclature—lover. She should think of Suzanne as her partner. People are always talking about their partners these days. Even straight people. It makes Alice think of boardrooms and business lunches. Hello, yes, good to meet you. This is my partner, Suzanne. We're in bedroom real estate. No one has had a girlfriend, let alone a lover, in more than a decade. Suzanne does not seem to have these troubles. Alice has heard her use the word "partner" on numerous occasions. It doesn't bother her one bit. She is kinder than Alice in many ways, which makes it a good thing that it's Alice's parents who have been killed and not Suzanne's. There's that, at least.

If they had shared property, that would be something, Alice thinks. They really would be partners, in that case. Although what does "shared property" mean, anyway? They've shared an automobile insurance policy since 1998. They'd been getting killed on individual premiums. They invested in a set of fancy-pants copper-bottomed pots and pans when they moved in together. In a fit of consumerism, they'd also bought a set of stoneware dishes. How far is that supposed to get you, some pots and pans, a few plates, and a State Farm agent? Suzanne interrupts this line of intellectual inquiry by reaching out for Alice's hand. Her touch is so soft and familiar after all these years that it opens up a hollow ache in Alice's chest. She knows she might not have thought to take Suzanne's hand so gently if it were Suzanne who had just suffered some terrible piece of news.

"Are you going to talk to me?" Suzanne asks. Alice lies motionless on her back. Suzanne draws her lover's knuckles to her lips.

"Do I have to?" Alice asks.

"Of course not," Suzanne says. Her lips are dry and cool against Alice's fingers.

"I don't think I've got anything to say," Alice says. She works her hand free from Suzanne's grip and laces her fingers together across her chest. "I'm feeling all the wrong things."

"Tell me about it," Suzanne says. "Really, lay it on me."

"I think it's mundane and stupid that my parents flipped their big, dumb F150 on the interstate and died in some run-of-the-mill traffic accident," Alice says. "How's that?"

"Okay," Suzanne says, "it's a start." She is like that—a goddamned active listener no matter what Alice says. She is a veritable rock. They'd been making dinner together earlier that evening when Alice's sister, Sara, called with the news that their parents had both been killed. When Alice blanched white and nearly passed out, the phone pressed to the side of her head, Suzanne calmly took the knife from Alice's hand and placed a stool beneath her.

"Do you want to talk about it?" Suzanne asks.

"Are we talking already?" Alice asks.

"I think so. Yes."

"Since we're knee-deep in it already," Alice says. She puts both hands over her face, only partly because the pressure feels good on her eyes. "I think if they were going to go together, if things were going to get as dramatic as all this, then it should have been some catastrophic farm accident—some conflagration—you know what I mean?"

"No."

"Something terrible. Like my dad running my mom over with a tractor, and then the tractor bursting into flames. Wouldn't that make more sense?"

"No, it wouldn't make more sense."

"I know," Alice says. "I mean, trucks roll over all the time. Especially when the driver is losing his sight, which he won't admit, and when the wheels hit those god-awful ridges on the side of the inter-

341

state that are supposed to wake up the drunks or something, and then the driver overcorrects and yanks the whole half-ton pickup over on top of itself. That happens all the freaking time."

Suzanne waits patiently for Alice to continue. In the silence between them a cop car speeds through the alley beneath their bedroom window. Alice turns toward Suzanne for the first time since they climbed into bed.

"I knew a guy who had his arms ripped off in a combine once," Alice says.

"Okay," Suzanne says. Alice is always impressed by Suzanne's ability to roll with the punches.

"Now that should kill a man. He should have died, I'm sure. People weren't designed to be able to suffer the removal of their arms and just go on kicking as if nothing had happened. The problem is we're all so ready for trauma. We've got the paramedics, the choppers, the airlifts, the 911. Hardly anyone dies anymore. One of these days we're all going to quit. Apparently not my folks though, right?"

"How did you know him?" Suzanne asks.

"He was the dad of the guy who took my friend Wendy to the prom. Senior year. Our junior year some other guy took her."

"When?"

"I said our senior year," Alice says.

"No, I mean the man's arms. When did the thing happen with his arms?"

"Oh," Alice says. "When Wendy and I were fifteen."

Suzanne scoots herself up against Alice. Alice shifts onto her back so that Suzanne can put her cheek against the hard, flat surface of Alice's sternum. Alice rests one hand on Suzanne's head.

"He was harvesting beans. You know the combine I mean, Suz? The one with the rotating contraption up front? Not the flat kind with fingers for field corn." Suzanne nods her head against Alice's chest. "He was out in the field alone when the blades stopped turning. So this old guy, this knucklehead, shuts everything off, gets down from the combine, and decides to fix the son of a bitch himself. There's a belt off or something's jammed in there or something, because this genius shoves both arms into the front of this gigantic cutting machine—both arms, up to the shoulder sockets—and the next thing you know, those blades are turning and his arms get ripped off. Not sliced. They don't get severed by the blades. He gets his hands caught up in the works and the combine just pulls his arms right off.

He was a goddamn idiot and should have bled to death in the field all by himself in a minute, but his wife, half a mile away at the house, saw the combine stop and drove out across the field to see what was up. She drives straight up to the combine and he's standing there looking dazed with no arms on."

Suzanne slips one hand beneath Alice's shirt. She rests her fingers in the ridges of Alice's ribs.

"That's the part that fucking gets me," Alice says. "This guy's eyes are blown wide open with shock. He doesn't even know his own name he's so gone with pain, and his little housewife can either faint dead at his feet or goddamn do something. And she does something. Can you imagine, Suzanne?"

"No, I can't."

"Can you imagine if something happened like that? What would you do if you found me with my arms ripped off?"

"I don't know, Alice."

"Would you save me?"

"I'd try," Suzanne says.

"Would you save me?"

"Stop it," Suzanne says.

"I kind of feel like I'd know how to feel if it had been terrible like that," Alice says.

"It was terrible," Suzanne says.

"It was a car accident," Alice says. "It was quick. They went together. They never knew what hit them. Blah, blah, blah."

"It was terrible," Suzanne says.

"Will you come home with me?" Alice asks. "Will you do this? The coffins and the funeral parlor, and the ham-salad sandwiches the church ladies are going to try to stuff in our faces after the wake?"

"Yes, of course," Suzanne says. "You don't have to ask."

But Alice does have to ask because Suzanne has never been home with her to her parents' farm. In all the nine years they've been together, Alice has only ever mentioned Suzanne to her parents as a friend—and then as a roommate beginning four years ago. That's her story on brief trips home to the Hoosier state. She is a different person there, shucking sweet corn on the back porch with her father, for god's sake. Mostly, her father talked about funny stories he'd read in *Reader's Digest* or what book of the Bible his Sunday school class was studying. He found most of them painfully dull. Her mother, with her broad, blank moon-face hardly ever asked Alice a personal question. By the time Alice was in her twenties, her mother had become bewildered and quiet around her oldest daughter. It has not been difficult for Alice to keep herself, her life, separate from that strange place where she grew up. In many ways, the subject of Suzanne just failed to come up. But on some nights at home, after her parents had clicked off the news and ambled off to bed, Alice would sit out on the back porch with a bottle of beer watching the moon appear and disappear behind high summer clouds. On some nights, Alice would want Suzanne there with her so bad that it hurt.

Thirty-five, Alice thinks, and closeted like a kid. How ridiculously dumb. She'd always thought she'd tell her folks about Suzanne when she knew that Suzanne was the one. But earlier that evening, before the phone rang, Alice had been considering quitting Suzanne. She had been wondering how it would feel to stop chopping arugula after nine years and just say, You know, Suzanne, I'm not sure I'm still in this. I think I might look for my own place.

"I want to feel your skin," Suzanne says. There is a brief tussle as Alice and Suzanne pull off their own T-shirts and settle back into their former position, Suzanne's cheek against Alice's chest. Alice can feel Suzanne's breath on her right breast. They lie quietly in the dark, both waiting for what Alice will do next, until Suzanne's breathing evens and shallows and Alice knows her lover is asleep.

In the morning, Suzanne makes all of the arrangements for leaving town. Alice sits at the kitchen counter in a T-shirt and her underwear while Suzanne leaves a message with the chemistry department at the university that her research assistant will cover her courses for a couple of weeks. Suzanne also phones the arts foundation where Alice works as a grant writer. Alice goes to lie down on the living room floor when Suzanne begins accepting condolences on her behalf. Suzanne packs a suitcase for the both of them. Two days later, at the Earlbach Family Funeral Home, a thirteen-hour drive from Alice and Suzanne's apartment in Minneapolis, Suzanne smiles gracefully and introduces herself as Alice's roommate to the parade of family friends and acquaintances who file through. Suzanne looks stunning in her black crepe dress. Alice thinks it's inappropriate to be admiring the cut of her lover's dress here in the funeral parlor, a funeral parlor crawling with pale Protestants, but she does all the same. No one could deny that Suzanne has marvelous breasts, not even Protestants in a room crowded with reeking flowers and two closed caskets.

There is that to be thankful for, the crushing impact of the truck cab rolling over which necessitated closed caskets. Sara had tried to insist that they could hire a special mortician, someone adept at major reconstruction, but Alice had put her foot down. What a morbid practice it all was in any case, pumping bodies full of chemicals and caking makeup on every inch of exposed flesh. Who were those morticians trying to fool? Is it not enough to stand in a hot room with the bodies in caskets? Why have the whole town traipsing through to peer down into their parents' dead, stitched-together and heavily made-up faces? Paul, Sara's husband, had not exactly agreed with Alice, but he had suggested to her sister that the expense was significant. Leave it to Paul to argue economics when the real issues at hand were decency and decorum, a simple refusal to take part in the whole gaudy, macabre business of pasting over the destruction of death.

Suzanne, returning from her trip to the kitchen to fill Alice's coffee cup, stops to speak with Paul. The two seem to have developed a quick camaraderie, even though they had not previously met. When she speaks to Paul, Suzanne has to look up, and her soft, light hair falls back from her face. Sometimes, when she's nervous or when she's particularly captivated by something she's reading in the paper over breakfast, Suzanne gives in to the habit of tucking her hair behind her ears and holding it there. If she tugs so hard that her hair seems to strain against her scalp Alice says, Suzanne, and Suzanne lets go. Tonight, however, speaking with Paul, she tucks her hair behind her ears and drops her fingers back around Alice's mug of coffee. She nods and smiles and Paul laughs.

"Well, you're awfully chummy with Paul," Alice says when Suzanne hands her the coffee cup.

"Paul is nice," Suzanne says.

"He's a potato," Alice says.

Alice tries to take a sip of coffee but it burns her lips.

"Shit, this is hot," she says.

"Yes," Suzanne says. "It's coffee."

Alice can feel herself starting to sweat. Her skin is prickly and clammy beneath her suit. When she runs a hand through her short, dark hair, she catches a whiff of her armpit.

"This place makes me itch," Alice says. "It's the chemicals. The whole place is full of toxic chemicals."

"You don't look well," Suzanne says, taking Alice by the elbow like a child. "Come on. Come here. Let's sit."

They cross the room and sit on a low couch. It is a brocade piece of squat furniture that Alice's grandmother would have called a divan. It occurs to Alice, for the first time, that she and Sara are the last. Her grandparents all died by the time she was in middle school. Her father's brother died in his forties of a massive heart attack, leaving behind only his persimmony widow who faded from their lives. Her mother, too, had a single brother, but he drowned when Alice and Sara's mother was in high school.

"Are you okay?" Suzanne asks.

"No one's talking to me," Alice says. "This whole place is swarming with people and almost no one is talking to me. The entire time you were gone, I think three people came over to say they were sorry. That's what they're saying. Inane shit like that."

"That's what people say at funeral homes. Give them a break."

"I'm bereaved," Alice says. "They should be giving me a break. Am I that terrible, that people I knew as a kid can't come over and say one decent thing to me?"

"You are ferocious," Suzanne says. "You look terrifying. If I didn't know you I'd be scared to death."

They are sitting too close to each other on the couch. There is a softness, a laughing, in Suzanne's eyes. She looks at Alice as if at any moment she could raise her fingertips to Alice's cheek.

"Don't touch me," Alice says.

"I wouldn't," Suzanne says. She leans back and crosses her legs.

"I just mean you shouldn't. Not with everyone looking. That's the last thing I need."

"I said I wouldn't," Suzanne says.

Alice blows on her coffee. Across the room, Paul has guided Sara to a matching loveseat, and for one peculiar moment both couples catch each other's eyes. Sara has been quietly weeping on and off for the past three days. Her face is swollen and puffy with grief.

"She's doing it better than me," Alice says.

"What?"

"Mourning. I don't think I'm mourning yet," Alice says.

"Yes you are," Suzanne says.

On the other side of the room, a small man wearing wire spectacles and a blue suit approaches Sara and Paul. Paul stands up and shakes the man's hand. The man reaches down and takes Sara's hand in his own, which is missing its thumb. His pink scalp shows through his thin white hair.

"That guy was our Sunday school teacher," Alice says.

"He looks nice," Suzanne says.

"He was," Alice says. "He had a tendency to digress from the Bible, though. Back when Ryan White was dying of AIDS, he taught a whole Sunday school lesson on how we shouldn't sit on the toilet seats at school. Just in case the school had been infiltrated by gays. He was really worried about government plots and cover-ups. He thought the government was corrupt with closet cases."

"God," Suzanne says.

"Yeah, but he was nice anyway, though." Alice knows Suzanne is reading her for sarcasm, but she's serious. "His wife almost died of polio."

"You're kidding," Suzanne says.

"No."

"What happened to his hand?" Suzanne asks.

"He got it caught in a grain dryer a couple of years ago," Alice says.

"I'm not sure I believe you sometimes," Suzanne says.

"Oh, do," Alice says. "Extremities get lopped off left and right around here."

"We should go be with your sister," Suzanne says.

"I don't want to," Alice says.

"It doesn't always matter," Suzanne says, "what you want. Sometimes you should do things just because." She stands, drawing Alice up along with her. "Come on, I'll go with you."

Alice's legs feel weak. There seems to be ten miles of pink carpet between her and her sister, but Suzanne puts a calm, steady hand in the small of her back.

A week later, Sara and Alice sit together on the floor of their parents' home office. They have emptied out the last of the filing cabinets and shelves. Tax returns dating back decades, deeds and titles, various licenses, bank statements, and folders full of insurance information are strewn across the floor. Evidence of family life—snapshots, letters, art projects made by the girls when they were in school—is mixed in among the legal documents. Both women sit within arm's reach of a wastebasket.

"Do you want this?" Sara asks, a file folder in her outstretched hand.

Alice takes the folder and thumbs through half a dozen book reports and a number of term papers she wrote in high school English classes.

"My god," Alice says. "I had no idea they kept them." She dumps the file folder and all of its contents in the recycling box.

"They kept everything," Sara says. "Here, have a look."

Sara turns a large manila envelope upside-down, and a handful of flattened construction paper hand-puppets tumble out.

"Do you remember Queen Bee Alice and her Circus Friends?" Sara asks.

The girls had spent hours and hours cutting, pasting, and coloring puppets when they were in elementary school. At the height of their Queen Bee Alice episode, there had been a cast of characters of a dozen or more. Now, laughing, Sara unfolds Loony Linda the Lion Tamer.

"Whatever happened to Loony Linda?" Alice asks.

"She got eaten by one of her lions there toward the end. You wouldn't let me play her after that."

"I'd forgotten all about these."

"Would you like them?" Sara asks.

Alice dumps the puppets in the wastebasket.

"Don't throw them out," Sara says. "I'll keep them if you don't want them. Give them here."

Alice retrieves the puppets and hands them back to Sara. Sara smooths the construction paper and returns the puppets to their envelope. The sisters work together quietly for many minutes. Occasionally, one holds up a document or a folder for the other's appraisal, and with a silent gesture the piece is either exchanged or discarded as they both see fit. It is like imagining their parents naked, Alice thinks, to be pawing through their private things. But there is no one else, and the property will be auctioned tomorrow, so they must.

"What should we do about all these pictures?" Sara asks, opening a box of water-damaged photographs. "It seems a shame to throw away pictures, even if they aren't any good."

"We've got pictures coming out of our ears," Alice says. "If you don't want them, we should throw them away."

"What about the old ones?"

"I don't know who half these people are," Alice says. She thumbs through a stack of old snapshots.

"We could find out," Sara says.

"How? Who are we going to ask?"

"Alice," Sara says.

"What? It's true. If you don't know and I don't know, we're shit out of luck."

"Would you not swear?"

"Sara," Alice says.

"Alice," Sara says.

"I'm going outside for a cigarette," Alice says. When she stands, her knees throb from the way she's been sitting with her legs tucked under her.

"I thought you quit smoking," Sara says.

"I did. Ten years ago."

"How long did that last?"

"Ten years," Alice says.

Out on the wide back porch, she digs her pack of Camels out of the jacket's breast pocket. Still unaccustomed to nicotine, her head swims at the first drag.

"I thought you quit smoking," Alice says aloud as she exhales smoke through clenched teeth.

Suzanne had said the exact same thing to her after her parents' funeral when Alice asked her to pull over at the Crystal-Flash for cigarettes, as if for the entirety of their relationship Alice had been sneaking around smoking, like a bad girl in a high school bathroom. Alice puts her feet up on the railing. The southern breeze is chilly but smells of wet dirt and growing things. She and Sara have agreed to spend their last two nights alone together in their parents' house. Suzanne has taken a hotel room in the nearest town, and Paul has driven the two hours back down to Louisville, where he and Sara live. Sara and Alice have less than twenty-four hours to sort through the paperwork in the office, to ferret out the last remnants of value from that jumbled mess. They spent last evening reading magazines in separate rooms of the house. When Alice went to the kitchen for a glass of water, she didn't bother turning on a light. She stood in the dark looking out the window over the sink, trying not to be frightened by the once familiar sound of floorboards and foundation settling. Sara had been startled when she found her sister in the kitchen. Why are you standing here in the dark? she'd asked. I was just thinking, Alice said. You know, Sara had said, sometimes you give me the creeps.

If she gives Sara the creeps, this whole damn place gives Alice the creeps. The fields stretch out, half-bare, under the chilly, gray, too-early spring sky. The trouble with farming is all the dirt, Alice thinks.

Somebody knocked down all the trees about a hundred and fifty years ago, and ever since people have been stripping the land down to naked dirt at least once a year. In the first place it's bleak. In the second, it lets the rain wash all the topsoil into the rivers every spring. Some day someone will scrape the dirt down to the bedrock, down to the veritable bone, and that will be the end of that. She began haranguing her father about going no-till after she took a college ecology course called "Deforestation: Cross-Hemisphere Hypocrisy." But as for bleak, Alice can see that no-till is no better, not with the beleaguered remains of last year's corn crop clinging to the ground. Better for the soil, true, but no improvement on the bleak-front.

Alice is stubbing out her cigarette when Sara comes out on the porch, the cordless phone held out like an offering.

"Alice," Sara says, "it's Suzanne."

"Tell her I'll call her back."

Alice doesn't take her eyes from the southern sky, but without looking she knows her sister hasn't moved. She knows Sara is just standing there, holding the screen door open, cordless receiver stretched out in her hand.

"Fine," Alice says, "give it here."

Sara crosses the porch and puts the phone in Alice's hand. Then she rights an overturned deck chair and settles in next to Alice.

"Hey Suz," Alice says. "No, no, I'm not busy. I'm just sitting out here on the porch for a smoke. I'll call you later, okay?"

Alice listens for a moment longer and then clicks off the phone without saying anything else.

"How's Suzanne?" Sara asks.

"Fine."

"Is she coming out for the auction tomorrow?"

"No," Alice says. "I asked her not to. I just want to get all of this over with."

"It wouldn't kill you to be nice," Sara says.

"How am I not nice to you?"

"To Suzanne," Sara says. "She's worried about you. She just wants to hear your voice."

"Thanks," Alice says. "I'll take that into account."

Beyond the porch and a stretch of grass, the barn sits with its wide door yawning open. Their father must have been in the middle of many things. Two grain wagons have been pulled out of the barn, their red paint blistered by rust. They've been shoved up against the west-facing side of the barn. Alice thinks they must have been in the way of something her father was after in the back of the barn. The wagons won't be needed until harvest.

"What are those doing out?" Alice asks.

Sara seems to consider the grain wagons for nearly a minute before she furrows her brow and says, "I don't know."

When Alice was in high school, some small boy climbed into a grain wagon full of field corn and got killed in his own backyard. One of the Weston boys, Alice thinks, though she couldn't say for sure. No one knew why the child had climbed into the wagon—he had certainly been warned not to—but when the grain shifted, he must have struggled his way to the bottom. It was like drowning without water. Or perhaps the boy had been crushed before he could suffocate. Either way, it took his parents hours of searching before they thought to look where they found him, a flood of harvested corn spilled out around them on the ground.

"Was it one of the Weston boys who got killed in a grain wagon?" Alice asks.

"Yes," Sara says. "Tyler. What on earth made you think of that?"

"I've been thinking about accidents," Alice says. "I've been telling Suzanne."

"That's morbid."

"Yes, well," Alice says, "these seem like morbid times." Alice picks up her pack of cigarettes and lights another. She thinks that if she smokes long enough, her sister will have to go inside.

"How long have you and Suzanne been together?" Sara asks.

Alice nearly chokes on smoke. When she looks at her sister, Sara's head is turned, her gaze cast out past the barn to the east.

"I didn't know we were going to talk about all that," Alice says.

"It seems sort of stupid not to, don't you think?"

Alice leans back in her deck chair and closes her eyes. If she hunches her shoulders she can block most of her body from the chill in the breeze.

"Nearly nine years," Alice says.

"Oh," Sara says. "My gosh, Alice. I didn't know that. That's almost as long as Paul and I have been married."

"Yeah, I know," Alice says.

"Was she your first?" Sara asks. Her face is flushed but her expression is natural.

"Oh, for god's sake, Sara. Do we have to muck through all of this?"

"I'm just asking," Sara says. "I'd like to know."

"Not by a long shot," Alice says. She suddenly feels sick on nicotine and stubs her cigarette in the ashtray. The wind tosses the ash.

"When did you know?" Sara asks. "Did you know all the way back when we were kids, or in high school, or what?"

"I don't know, Sara," Alice says. "I don't think I knew anything back then. I don't think I was me all those years ago. I hardly remember high school." They sit in silence for a few moments before Alice asks, "Is that it? Are we finished?"

"Sure," Sara says, but she doesn't get up.

"When did that accident happen with Tyler?" Alice asks after a moment of silence. "I was still in high school. Either junior or senior year, I think."

Sara chews on her fingernail as she thinks.

"Your junior year?" she asks. "It was the fall before Halley's Comet came around."

"I'd forgotten," Alice says.

"About the comet?"

"About both, I guess."

"I couldn't," Sara says. "I mean Halley's Comet. Not that Tyler wasn't a tragedy, but seeing Halley's Comet really felt historic, you know? Like something was happening. We were really seeing something."

They had been driving home together from the mall late one night when Sara had suggested they stop the pickup and look for the comet. It was a hard, cold night in February and Alice had pulled the truck over into the frozen weeds at the side of a county road and shut off the engine and the lights. The sky was moonless, just a wash of stars across a sea of black. Alice had felt dizzy standing in the middle of a deserted road with her head thrown back, the truck's engine ticking as it cooled in the ditch. The sky is beautiful when it's just the sky, but it's terrible when it feels like the lid of the world has been lifted off and there's nothing between you and the staggering silence of outer space.

"It was just a fuzzy star," Alice says now, as if shaking off the chill of the memory of that night.

"That's just like you, Alice," Sara says.

"What's that mean?"

Sara stands up and stretches. She unbuttons her jacket and drops it in Alice's lap.

"Call Suzanne," she says. "If I were her and you were Paul I'd be worried about you."

"Thanks, Mom," Alice says.

"Mom's dead," Sara says, and goes back inside the house.

Alice puts on her sister's coat, but she doesn't call Suzanne. She imagines her lover sitting cross-legged on the hotel bed, a box of take-out in front of her, something mindless flickering on the television set. Alice doesn't know how long she's been considering leaving Suzanne, although she fears it might be years. Two weeks before they got the phone call from Sara, Suzanne had said, When you know what you want to talk about, let's talk. They were sitting at the breakfast counter in the kitchen having a supper of tomatoes and cheese on baguettes. Alice didn't say anything, and neither did Suzanne.

"Are you going to bed?" Sara asks.

She has been in the living room working on a cross-stitch. Alice has been sitting in the empty kitchen.

"Did you miss me when I went away to college?" Alice asks.

Sara sighs. Through all of their growing-up years, people remarked about how much Sara and Alice looked alike. Now, in their thirties, it seems to Alice that that family resemblance has all but faded away.

"Did you ever miss us?" Sara asks.

"You and Mom and Dad?" Alice asks.

"Yes."

"I didn't think to, Sara," Alice says.

Sara fills a glass of water at the sink. She checks the lock on the back door and then heads upstairs to go to bed.

"Shut the lights off when you come up," Sara calls down to her sister.

Alice rises and flips the light switch on the wall. She stands still, letting her eyes adjust to the sudden dark in the eerie quiet of a rural night. When she can make out the shape of the kitchen counter, she picks up the phone. She dials the number of Suzanne's hotel in town from memory. The phone rings three times before Suzanne picks up.

"Hi Suz," she says. "You asleep?"

"No," Suzanne says, although she is lying by the sound of her voice. "Hi Alice. How are you?"

"Tired," Alice says. "Can I tell you something I've been thinking about?"

"Sure," Suzanne says.

Alice can hear the rustle of sheets and blankets as Suzanne rolls onto her side. She imagines Suzanne curled up in an anonymous hotel room bed, her hair a tangled mess across her pillow, the phone pressed to her one available ear.

"I've been thinking about the time I was almost crushed under a hay bale. Do you want to hear about it?"

"Tell me, Alice," Suzanne says.

Alice stands and roams through the house as she talks. Curtains stand open at all of the windows letting in the strange, pale light of a waxing moon.

"I was playing in the barn," Alice says, "even though I wasn't supposed to. I climbed up to the top of this mountain of hay bales. Not the ones you're thinking of, though, Suzanne. Not those rectangular things. I'm talking about those massive rolls of hay. The ones that are six feet across. Literally. Do you know what I mean?"

"Yes," Suzanne says. "I know. Go ahead."

"I was all the way up to the top, nearly up to the rafters, when one of the bales shifted and tumbled forward. I could feel everything giving way beneath me, and I fell headfirst into this crevice between two bales. I was upside down, just one leg and a hand hooked over the side of a bale, choking on dust. I knew any minute, the whole thing was just going to topple and I'd be crushed to death in an instant. I remember wondering if it was going to hurt. So I'm coughing up dust and chaff, wondering if dying is going to hurt and thinking about how pissed my parents are going to be, when I realize that the bales have stopped shifting and if I climb out carefully, I might not get killed. I was scratched up from head to toe, but when I got inside I just told my mom I rode my bike into a sticker bush and no one ever knew. No big deal, right? I still think about that sometimes, though."

"Are you okay, Alice?" Suzanne asks. "Do you want me to come out there?"

"No," Alice says. "Don't come out here. I'm okay."

Alice has found herself in the laundry room. Sara has been stacking grocery bags and boxes full of the stuff she wants to keep from the house on the counter across from the washer and dryer.

"Alice," Suzanne says, "would you please tell me what you want me to do?"

Alice begins rifling through the contents of Sara's boxes.

"Nothing, Suzanne," Alice says. "Don't do anything. I just need to get through this and get the hell out of here. You just stay where you're at."

"Call me in the morning?"

"Yeah. I will," Alice says. "Good-night, Suz. Really, don't worry about me."

"Good-night," Suzanne says.

In the first of Sara's boxes, Alice finds a ceramic pencil-holder that Sara made for their father in art class, a number of old handkerchiefs, the stack of snapshots Alice had suggested they throw away, and their mother's large, teak jewelry box. Sara hadn't asked if Alice might want that, although she had offered Alice first choice of their mother's jewelry. Most of it was simple and inexpensive. Alice chose a strand of pearls that their father had given their mother as a Christmas gift when she and Sara were small girls. Beneath the jewelry box, Alice finds a manila file folder marked *From Sara* in their mother's careful script. Alice closes the door to the laundry room.

The folder is fat with letters addressed from her sister to her mother, a correspondence that goes back years. Some of the oldest ones, the ones from when Sara was away at college, look as if they've been folded and re-folded, carried around in a pocket, perhaps. The early letters are simple and thoughtful, an account of Sara's trials with a difficult math class, a description of her disappointment at not being chosen for the orchestra. They ask after the garden and the farm. They say she misses home very much. Shortly, the letters become more expressive, linger in detail, share fears and loneliness and hopes. The letters open with long responses to questions that must have been posed by their mother.

In the fifth letter Alice stumbles across her own name. No, I haven't heard from her either, not for several months. It's a funny thing to miss her, I suppose, since we were never very close. Alice. Her name its own sentence with a period placed after it. In the next letter she reads, Oh heavens, Mother, of course it's not your fault. Alice is Alice. That's all. She'd as soon talk to the man in the moon as say two words to me. Six months later Sara writes, You know, I've wondered that, too. She could be, I guess. We pray for her, Mom. Don't you think that's all we can do? Through fifteen years of letter writing, Sara and their mother hover around Alice's name like baffled moths around a lit porch light. There was a flurry of correspondence around the time that Alice moved in with Suzanne. It seems at one point their mother decided to come right out and ask Alice what was what, but nothing ever came of that resolve. Two years later, Sara reports, Paul asked me not long ago if I loved Alice and I said I hadn't the faintest clue. What kind of a thing is that for a sister to say?

The letters, of course, are not all about her. Sara and their mother have exchanged long meditations about their lives, their longings, their men. The letters chart the meeting, courtship, and marriage of Sara and Paul. Sara and their mother exchanged a tentative and shy correspondence about sex. The letters offer up in excruciating detail Sara's attempts at becoming pregnant—the excitement, the disappointment, the frustration, the fear. They cycle through a number of expensive and demoralizing fertility treatments. Alice can't remember ever being told about the two first-trimester miscarriages. The last letter is dated just a few weeks before their parents' death. The paper is still fresh and clean, neatly creased in a tri-fold. I think my thirties have changed me, Sara writes. I think I've learned to be happy with my lot. Maybe I just feel this way because it will soon be summer and the windows are open and Paul is out on the patio putting fish on the grill, but deep down, I think that it's true. Did you feel this way in your thirties? A new sort of peace about things? I don't know, though, because you had us running around in your thirties. Maybe you didn't have time the way I seem to. I was thinking just the other day that you were only five years older than I am now when Alice moved away. I can't imagine, Mom. I really can't. I no longer worry about Alice. Perhaps she's happy in her own way, but if that's true it's a happiness I can't recognize. Life's a mystery, sometimes, to me. The letter goes on to talk of the patio garden that Sara hopes to plant, how good she feels in the summer seeing tomatoes growing even if she has to grow them in a pot on a patio in the suburbs. This seems to be the last letter to their mother that Sara wrote.

In the bright light of morning, Sara and Alice move efficiently through the first floor of the house wiping down the remaining furniture with damp cloths. The air sparkles with kicked-up dust. Alice finds the empty pantry most disturbing of all the vacant and echoing rooms. How banal, Alice thinks, to only ever think of my mother in the pantry and kitchen. But still. Alice stands for a long time in the kitchen, gazing out the window over the sink. In her absence, her parents have expanded the side porch to wrap around into a back deck. They have dug elaborate flower gardens where her aluminum swing set used to be. Alice can't think when they chopped down the mulberry tree in the southeast corner of the property. She remembers how, playing in the backyard as a child, her mother's presence behind the screen of the kitchen window made her feel safe. This memory of her mother's silent watchfulness is what made Alice laugh when Suzanne had suggested the previous year that Alice would make a good mother. I'm just saying, sometimes I think about us. It's not that difficult to adopt, Suzanne had said. My god, Alice had said, you're serious. I think I'd be a train wreck of a mother. Do you know me? Have we met?

"What are you thinking?" Sara asks, coming to stand beside her sister at the sink.

"I was thinking about how Suzanne wants a baby," Alice says. "She wants to adopt. Probably something international, you know. If you can swing a plane ticket to China or Bangladesh, you can adopt in no time these days. How about you and Paul?" Alice asks.

"We don't have children," Sara says. There is a tinny sound to her voice.

"Yes, I know," Alice says, "but you and Paul could adopt if there's something wrong with you. You don't have to be a martyr if you don't want to, Sara. No one's impressed."

Alice feels her sister turn to stare at her, but she gives Sara nothing but her profile. Alice can hear her heart in her ears, a racing thrush, thrush, thrush. She doesn't know if her sister has yet missed the folder full of fifteen years of correspondence.

"What's that supposed to mean?" Sara asks.

"It means people only suffer if they want to nowadays," Alice says. "Now that Mom's gone, there's no one left to be impressed by your ability to rise above the rest of us."

Sara surprises Alice by failing to move. She stands quietly at the sink gazing out over their property. Hot thumbprint blotches rise up on Sara's neck and chest.

"I wouldn't expect you to understand, Alice," Sara says.

"No, I'm sure not. I couldn't possibly understand the way you feel, Sara. All that righteous stoicism involved in being a good wife, right? But you and Mom were thick as thieves trying to figure me out, huh? You don't get it, either, Sara. You people act like it's a goddamn mystery why I left."

"I don't know how many you read," Sara says, "but those were private letters. I'd like them back, please."

357

"Private, my ass. Private until they said word one about me."

"Oh, for crying out loud, Alice," Sara says. "You amaze me." She pivots to leave the kitchen, hands up in defeat, but snaps back around before she's taken a step. "You could have come home if you'd wanted to. You're the one who took the easy way out. You ran off as quick as you could to have your whole life somewhere else. You didn't even give us a chance." She bites her tongue the way she used to when they were girls and Alice would drive her to furious distraction in a fight. When she can speak without shouting, she says, "Life's not always easy, Alice. I don't think I'm entitled to something just because I want it. If that's how you think life's supposed to be, you're in for some serious disappointment. I'd always hoped some day you'd grow up."

"You think my life's easy?" Alice asks, her voice rising dangerously. She wants to be cruel. She wants to cut Sara to the quick. "Where have you been, Sara? You think I could have waltzed home with Suzanne and sat down for dinner with Mom and Dad? You think it doesn't bother me to drive past that church where we both grew up and see that god-awful sign out front—One Man, One Woman, Forever? That's where our Mom and Dad were three Sundays ago. I've been out there on my own for all these years trying to figure shit out, and you and Mom were sitting on your fat asses praying for me. You tell me how it would have been if I'd tried to come home."

The rage in Sara's face drains to nothing but exhaustion before she speaks.

"I don't know, Alice," Sara says. "I don't know how it would have been at first. All I know is that now you're fighting your own fight. You're in it alone."

"What's that supposed to mean?"

"You've never known how to treat people. If you're miserable, it's not my fault, or Mom's. It's not Dad's fault, and it certainly isn't Suzanne's."

Alice hits Sara before she even knows she's going to. She smacks Sara across the face hard enough to nearly knock her down. In the stunned silence after the crack of skin against skin, Alice stares at her hand. She doesn't see her sister's blow coming. Sara socks Alice straight in the face with a closed fist. Alice's head snaps back and an instant later, she is standing in her parents' kitchen, her hands cupped helplessly beneath a thick flow of blood from her broken nose. Sara doesn't seem startled by the force of her fist. She stands, blinking at Alice, flexing and relaxing her fingers. Her face hasn't a trace of remorse.

"Say you're sorry, Sara," Alice says, a command from their childhood.

"I'm only sorry if Suzanne loves you the way I tried to. That's who I feel sorry for here. We would have loved you if you'd let us, Mom and me. God help Suzanne."

A dust rag lies abandoned on the kitchen counter, and Sara tosses it at Alice as she crosses to the stairs. "Wipe the blood off the floor, Alice," she says. "The appraiser will be here by noon."

Alice blinks in the mid-day sun when she goes outside for a smoke, her left nostril stuffed with a tampon. Her left eye is swollen and bruised. She will tell people she got whacked in the face with a softball. It will take some doing to explain a softball game in conjunction with her parents' double funeral, but people believe almost anything if you say it with a straight face. She doesn't light her cigarette on the porch. Instead, she goes behind the garage where she used to hide sneaking cigarettes in her last year of high school.

Alice wonders what her father managed to get in the ground before he rolled his pickup truck. When Alice and Sara were girls, slightly too old for a babysitter but still too young to quite fend for themselves, Alice was given a walkie-talkie to use when her parents were out in these fields. When the harvest kept her parents out late into the night, raking through the soybeans with the combine, Alice would get out of bed and pad down to the kitchen to watch through the window. She would climb up on the counter, no lights on, and watch as the combine loomed close to the house, spun on pivoted wheels, and lumbered back down the field. Occasionally, she terrified herself by thinking the combine, with its ominous, high-voltage headlights, was really a space ship. When she was cold and clammy with fear, she would click on the walkie-talkie and summon her father's voice.

Breaker-breaker, this is the Little Lady, she would say in her best trucker voice. Looking for the Big Papa. You got your ears on, Dad? Over. She would lift her thumb and listen to the static, counting the seconds until her father's voice crackled through the handset.

This is the Big Papa, her father would say, the rumble of machinery beneath him forcing him to shout. What do you need, Little Lady? You okay? How's my big girl?

When he fell silent, Alice would click on to speak.

You have to say *over*, Dad. Over.

You okay? Over.

Yeah. Over.

Your sister asleep? Over.

Yeah. Last time I checked. Over.

How's about you get yourself back in bed? Over.

Okay, Alice would say. Over and out, Dad.

Back at you.

Dad.

Over and out, Alice, her father would say.

Alice squats, her back against the aluminum siding of the garage, and then drops to the ground. She and Suzanne have an apartment out there, somewhere. There is a city some seven hundred miles away, and in that city she has a MacArthur Foundation grant waiting for final revisions on her desk. She is thirty-five, and she is relatively certain that her girlfriend would like to stay with her for the rest of their lives. Alice takes a last drag on her cigarette, stubs it out in the damp dirt, and flicks the butt into the space between the garage and the empty chicken coop.

"I thought I'd find you out here," Sara says, coming around the corner of the garage.

"You know everything, don't you?" Alice asks.

"I know you."

Sara sits next to her sister in the dirt, apparently paying no mind to the seat of her clean and pressed slacks. She picks a foxtail and strips the fuzz from the stalk. She spins the smooth stalk in her fingers, then sticks the end between her lips.

Alice taps another cigarette from the pack.

"No one ever told me, you know?" Alice says.

"Told you what?" Sara asks.

"That life was like this. These brief moments together and then long lapses of silence." She waits, but Sara doesn't say anything. "Are we at the beginning or the end of something?"

"There are no beginnings," Sara says. "Just the middle, I think. I've been in the middle my whole life."

"What do you mean?"

"I'm not sure."

"I know," Alice says. She smokes while her sister rips up little patches of grass. "When I was about eight, I came home from school

360

one day all worked up with this idea that I wanted a big sister. Everyone at school seemed to have one. When Mom told me it was my job to be the big sister to you, I was shocked. I'd never thought of you like that. I couldn't comprehend our equivalency."

Sara laughs. "That sounds like you."

"I'm apologizing for a whole lot of things."

"Yeah, I know." Sara stands, dusts her hands, then swats at the dirt on her pants. "I'm going to go. I can't stick around to see this place sold. I've got what I need and the deed to the farm is on the counter in the kitchen. Their lawyer is coming over with the appraiser and all the rest, so you don't have to stay if you don't want to."

"Are we friends?" Alice asks.

"I don't think so." Sara shields her eyes with both hands. "I'm going to get home to Paul," she says at last.

"So without Mom and Dad we're just going to drift apart?"

"Did they hold us together?"

"No," Alice says.

"I'll write when everything's settled with the estate," Sara says.

"Fine. That's just fine."

Sara turns to go, but Alice reaches out and catches her by one pant leg.

"Tell Paul I said hello," Alice says.

"Yeah, okay." Sara looks down at her sister impatiently.

"Don't you want to say anything?" Alice asks. "Maybe give me some advice?"

"No."

"You could tell me to call Suzanne."

"Take care, Alice," Sara says. She extracts her leg from Alice's grip, and disappears around the corner of the garage.

"That's crappy advice," Alice calls, but her sister doesn't answer. Sara's car door slams and then the engine of her Honda roars to life. Alice listens to her sister pulling out of the drive, and then the sound of the Honda's engine fades down the empty country road.

Nominated by Threepenny Review

THE MEDICINE MAN

fiction by KEVIN MOFFETT

from MCSWEENEY'S

W<small>HEN I'M LOW</small>, I go to Bel-Air Plaza to look for the medicine man, Broom. He's not a medicine man in the exact sense, the ordained-by-his-fellow-tribesmen sense, but a generally wizened hard-looking Seminole Indian who works crushing boxes and sweeping. People call him Broom, which I figure is more nasty than honorary, like the old Russians in the building where I live call me Florida Power because sometimes I wear a hat that says Florida Power. Crushing boxes and sweeping is no proper vocation for a medicine man, even nonordained from a tribe that isn't officially recognized as a tribe. Early in school you're taught that Seminole is the only tribe to never officially surrender to the U.S. government and the only to help runaway slaves escape from crackers, which is whites with whips. My sister's husband says I'm manic depressant because sometimes I feel low and sometimes, like currently, high, and I think Indians are party to powerful secret forces even if they themselves aren't aware of it, like Broom isn't aware of it.

I didn't used to be so low-high. As a kid I played all the made-up games with my sister, Sally, games I can't recall now though I recall learning the rules, which varied from game to game, and now just to think about them, the rules, causes me, like it never used to, a certain quickness. Sally remembers the games and the rules to the games. Sally was a nice kid and is still nice. Maybe it's the games we played that made me low-high, or the rules to the games, which continued when the games ended, and often *became* the games, and continue now. Does anyone else feel a little pride to hear sirens and pull over to the roadside to let an ambulance or a police car pass by? It calms me.

Walking does too, especially mornings before the recycling truck comes, the blue bins curbed and filled with beer bottles, wine bottles, soup cans, leaflets, newspapers, antennas, half-and-half cartons, test tubes, magazines, cereal boxes, toothpastes. All this out in the open, this suggestion, to me it's like looking into people's secrets.

And visiting Sally, my sister, who lives in a condo at the beach with her husband, Steve, who teaches study skills at Flagler College. They're getting ready to have a baby, and what I really want to tell you about is the earphones and Sally's stomach, but I need to tell you first about Broom the medicine man, which I started to. He's who I was looking for before going to Sally's condo and seeing her with the conductant jelly on her stomach and the earphones which I put on while Steve said, *Do either of you have a goddamn*—but not yet, not yet.

Broom. Everyone knows you're supposed to bring a gift when you consult a medicine man, something valuable to you but not him so he can throw it away without regret. When I went to see Broom I had been low for almost six days. A thing happened at Indigo Pines, where I live with old people who're Russian Jews, escaped communists or escaped from the communists, they won't tell me which. These escaped Russians are old, old. I used to say I love all people, before these Russians, but now I can't. Now I love only most people and I've started to suspect that once you start decreasing a thing it's easy to keep going. I'm allowed to live at Indigo Pines even though I'm not old or Russian or sick or ready to be.

Indigo Pines prints the menus in both Russian and English and they're set in two stacks on a table in front of the cafeteria before it opens for dinner. I was early. I could smell it was zucchini latkes, that mossy smell zucchini latkes have, and I sat down and read the menu next to three Russians who are always sitting on the purple loveseat in front of the cafeteria, talking Russian or playing a Russian game with wooden pegs in a triangle, which is what they were doing tonight. The dinner menu said zucchini latkes with Provençal sauce, which is spaghetti sauce, and at the bottom of the menu inside the Dinner Events box I read, Tonight Is Indigo Pines Poetry Night! Between dinner and dessert, we will be passing out words and you will surprise us with your creativity! Should be fun!

When I read that, why didn't I leave and go to Hogan's Heros for an eight-inch number seven, no mustard, no lettuce, pressed, and watch them playing shuffleboard on that long tabletop with sawdust and spinny silver pucks, and eat alone but not lonesome with the noisy TV noise and eager-people-standing-around-the-shuffleboard-table noise? Hogan's serves mugs of beer and sandwiches called heros, which you order by number. I once overheard a woman there say she wanted no hot peckers on her hero and she meant, I've thought about it, hot peppers. Number seven means ham.

Being low-high causes bad decisions. I stayed at Indigo Pines for zucchini latkes with the thirty or so Russians who sat at the white-nylon-tableclothed tables in the same groups of five and six I'm familiar with and ate and talked Russian while I ate my latkes alone, and lonesome. Two Russians across the table from me gestured like weightlifters and laughed. I was wondering about *passing out words* by repeating it to myself while eating my latkes. The more I repeated *passing out words* the more it sounded like something I might want to stay around for and I started to get excited, high. Plus, dessert was fruit blintzes, which is like pancakes and good.

Passing out words meant being given a plastic Ziploc filled with white pieces of paper with words typed on them. The Russians in charge of Poetry Night were young Russians. They cleared away my plate, leaving a fork for the blintzes, and then handed me a Ziploc. One of them said, Take a few minutes and make a poem. Remember, one sentence is all it takes to surprise us with your creativity! And so on. The young Russians who work at Indigo Pines are pale and have bright blue eyes like huskies. They're a little nicer than the old Russians but still not nice.

My Ziploc was stapled shut and I opened it and put all my words on the white tablecloth in front of me with a few flower-formed stains from the Provençal sauce. My words were: On Some For Time The What And Mister Blew If. I was trying to figure out the rules of the game, what was expected of me to make this poem out of these words, who I would surprise with what, and why. I raised my hand to try to get the attention of one of the young Russians in charge of Poetry Night to tell them I wanted a new Ziploc of words, these are poor words I was going to tell them, but they, the Russians, the young Russians—all these Russians in Florida!—were gone. The quickness. Like being sped up and slowed down at the same time. These *words*.

I tried to piece together a poem out of On Some For Time The What And Mister Blew If, moving the words around on the white tablecloth, but I couldn't come up with anything that made sense. The two Russians across from me had pieced theirs together, and were gesturing and laughing again. I wanted to spill something steaming on them. The first cafeteria poem was read by a short old Russian who wears his silver apartment key, or some silver key, on a shoestring necklace around his neck. He stood up, two tables away from my table, cleared his throat, and read, Trees whine circles in thirsty eve-ninks, my dear only.

It sounded more Russiany than that, but I especially remember eve-ninks, which is evenings, thirsty eve-ninks, and I can understand cold eve-ninks and stormy eve-ninks and windy and happy eve-ninks, but *thirsty* eve-ninks? All the other Russians clapped for the thirsty eve-ninks and I clapped as well only because after the Russian read the poem he bowed to each side of the cafeteria and smiled and sat down. If this didn't entirely seem like a thing a Russian would do who wasn't nice, I asked myself while I clapped, why not? I didn't know and don't know.

The next few cafeteria poems were a lot like the trees whining in thirsty eve-ninks. Snakes rolling teeth and similar jigsawed poems spoken slow and formal like Russians speak. In front of and behind me, at the cafeteria's long picnic tables covered with white table-cloths, the Russians read their poems and clapped for other poems, and I started to panic. I was no closer to having a poem than when I took the words out of the bag, these poor words, and I decided to stand up. Actually, I didn't decide, I just stood up and when I did, decided it was a good idea. I left behind my fruit blintzes and walked toward the exit and before I could open the thick metal door with its square window trapping a grid of strings like tennis-racket strings, where you can't see outside until you're right against it, I heard one of the Russians say, Exit Florida Power.

I was starting to feel the quickness from the poem rules and thinking about rules from the made-up games I played with Sally and can't recall, and my poor Ziploc of words, then the thirsty eve-ninks, the Russians clapping, *Exit Florida Power.* By the time I climbed the eight sets of stairs to my apartment, which I do when I remember for exercise, I was, I knew, low. I knew because I went straight to the stove and put on water for hot tea. I had started shivering on the last few stairs, nothing seeming more true than the feeling of being trapped quick inside your body quick inside your body quick inside your body, which is the only way I know to say it.

And five days later—you don't want a sum-up of the five days which . . . the worst thing about low-highness is when you're high and most suitored by the unpredicted joys, you don't want anything to do with them, but when you're low, you beg for the unpredicted joys, and then where are they, you going through the old Tupperware of family photographs again like a punishment, and I can't call Sally because of Steve, alone and lonesome with nothing but time, nothing but time, and where are they?—I finally had my cafeteria poem:

Mister, and if some blew on, for the time what?

I was still low so I went to look for the medicine man.

Indigo Pines and Sally and the medicine man and I are all in Flagler, Florida, named after the man who built hotels a hundred years ago, and railroad bridges across the Keys. You learn this early in school in Florida along with De Soto and De Leon, who are Spaniard explorers, and the correct spelling of Florida cities with Indian names like Kissimmee, Sarasota, Palatka, Pensacola, and about the Seminoles helping runaway slaves escape from crackers (whites with whips). They don't teach you the railroad bridges aren't there anymore. You have to go see for yourself.

Everyone knows you should bring a gift when you consult a medicine man, so I looked around my apartment for something valuable to me and not him so he can throw it away without regret when I give it to him. I've been to the medicine man about a half-dozen times now, and I'm running out of gifts and the best I could do this time was my only pair of long underwear which you probably don't think you would need in Florida, the Sunshine State, but trust me.

Flagler is Old Florida, which means few tourists. Bel-Air Plaza is shaped like an opened-up box with the top off to the left side and the box opened up to the ocean right across Atlantic Avenue. Nobody much shops at Bel-Air Plaza which used to have a magic shop when I was a kid, where you could look at tricks and bins full of fake vomits and fake poohs, but now it has a Super Dollar store, Mister Video, and a wig store called An Affair For Hair. Broom is usually behind Super Dollar, which spans the whole bottom of Bel-Air Plaza's box shape and faces the beach, so that's where I looked for him, and where I found him, smoking a cigarette on the edge of the loading dock behind Super Dollar, where he works crushing boxes and sweeping. When he saw me approaching with the long underwear, Broom dropped his cigarette and hopped off the loading dock, pivoted the cigarette out, looked at me sideways like people do for effect not real study, and said, Is there a reason you're carrying around a pair of dirty britches, my man?

I saw that he had two oval bright-orange stickers stuck to his white Super Dollar apron, one that said BONELESS and beneath it one that said SKINLESS, like on packages of chicken.

It's a gift for you, I said. The medicine man.

He looked at me sideways a little more. This is just to unnerve you if someone ever tries it on you. The medicine man said, real slowly, A gift. For me. The medicine man. (He laughed, again for effect. Only when I'm low would I know this.) He said, Look, man, I told you: I'm just tan. I live with my grandparents across the street and cain't go anywhere because I cain't drive a car. (*Cain't*, the medicine man said, which means poor and Georgia. Only when I'm low.) He said, I'm no medicine man; I'm no Indian. I'm Dominican, Mexican, Hawaiian, I don't know what. My grandparents won't tell me. I been throwing away all that junk you give me.

We, Broom and I, do this routine every time I come to him. I don't care if he lives with his grandparents, cain't (Georgia) drive a car, and isn't full-on Seminole, which nearly no Seminoles are anymore. I said, I *know* you throw it away. It's what medicine men are supposed to do.

There's plenty of people in Flagler like Broom, people you meet who come off at first as mean and unagreeable but who are mostly, I think, afraid, and probably I'm talking about me, too. Looking for the medicine man doesn't make sense to anyone but me and it doesn't need to and I've been in in Flagler all my life and I don't want to leave. This isn't sad or heroic, really, but I think it's important. Broom wants to drive and cain't, my sister wanted to leave Flagler and cain't. We all have our illusions, I wanted to say to the medicine man, you thought you were telling me something I didn't know. Instead I said, I need some rest.

And as if he had already read my mind, as if he were keyed into my frequency, the medicine man was showing me pills.

Two of these, he said, and you'll sleep like a baby.

367

I looked at the pills, two liver-colored capsules in a roughened palm, roughened like oak bark or like he'd been messing with car engines. I don't want to sleep like a baby, I said.

The medicine man's hand closed quick on the pills, which he then shoved into the pocket of his light-green Super Dollar slacks, pressed neat with a sharp crease down the side, and I don't think I want to say much more about the medicine man. Think of me, in back of Super Dollar with him and his pills waiting for me to leave like I was at his front door and had handed him a package not addressed to him. I said *thanks* like a question and left, disappointed, like you, maybe.

What's wrong with me? Why aren't I normal? Walking toward Sally's condo from Bel-Air Plaza, I watched one of those single-person planes that fly over the beach towing a banner with an advertisement on it: BOOTHILL TAVERN: YOU'RE BETTER OFF HERE THAN ACROSS THE STREET and I frowned because across the street from the Boothill Tavern is an old cemetery. I frowned even though I'd seen the advertisement before.

We all have our illusions. When I'm low it's hard to think of anything except how I'm low, anything except me me me, which is like thinking of the rules to those made-up games instead of the game itself, being so concerned with how you are doing, or how you are supposed to be doing, that the *how* overwhelms the *you*, and the thinking about how I'm low becomes the reason I'm low. But often enough I find some unpredicted joy that calms me. Pulling over to let ambulances or police cars pass by, or walking around near the beach houses, especially mornings before the recycling truck comes, calms me. Walking to my sister's condo, I noticed a single blue recycling bin, likely left out too late for the recycling truck, curbed and open and filled entirely with about two dozen Mama and Papa Gus whipping-cream cartons. Secrets.

By the time I got to Sally's condo, I was feeling sluggish but anxious, like, have you seen the slowed-down footage of hummingbirds feeding over flowers, with the fastness of the hummingbirds residing in the slowness of the footage? The slower the footage the faster the hummingbird feeds. I felt poised for disappointment. I dialed Sally's condo and someone answered and buzzed me in by pushing seven on the other end of the line. They didn't even say hello. Sally would've said hello. There's a camera fixed above the phone in front of the condo which you can watch if you live at the Admiralty Club, seeing who comes and goes on channel 32. Steve (Sally would've said hello) must have been watching channel 32 and answered the phone and pushed seven on the telephone, which releases the lock on the front door to the condo, without saying hello, and this probably sounds paranoid, but it's true.

I walked the twelve flights to Sally's condo, which I do when I remember for exercise. She lives on the sixth floor, the top floor. I knocked on the front door with a brass knocker I'd never noticed before, and heard Sally yell, Back here. It didn't sound at the front door like a yell and she meant, I knew, back patio.

I went down the front hallway, through the dining room to the living room, where the television was turned to channel 32, and I watched the black-and-white footage of the phone in front of the condo, where I just was, no one coming or going right now, and the bare light above the phone turned on, which the mailman does when he comes so people in the building can turn to channel 32 to see if their mail has arrived, and I was dreading Steve, whose voice I could hear from where I stood, arguing with Sally about something. He is always arguing with Sally about something.

I know why I don't like Steve but that doesn't make me feel any better. On the back patio he was saying, Well, let's take it back then.

Sally says, I'm worried. Aren't you supposed to hear something?

Steve: It must be broken. Goddamnit. Where are the batteries? Let's take it back.

Sally: Aren't you worried?

Steve: Of course I'm not worried.

On channel 32 a man has picked up the phone in front of the condo and is dialing, looking at the camera, he must know the camera's there, and smiling and waving, whoever he's calling must be watching channel 32, and he hangs up the phone and goes inside.

Well, Charlie, Steve says. He has opened the patio door, a sliding screen door and is standing on the track, smiling with his teeth clenched. He says, What you got there?

The underwear. I forgot to give it to Broom and it's been gripped in my hand so long I've forgotten it's there, balled up and useless-feeling, who needs long underwear in Florida, but you do sometimes, trust me, and I say, They were for Broom.

Steve says, I see. The medicine man?

Me: That's him. He isn't official.

Steve: Of course. Listen, Sally's out back, but now's probably not a good time. You understand, I'm sure.

Sally says, Don't listen to him, Charlie. Come back here.

Steve walks past me, real close so I have to step forward out of his way so he can pass, and I walk out to the back patio and close the screen door, tossing the underwear behind a potted flower, a white potted flower that looks like an oleander which are poisonous. Sally is sitting in one of the reclining beach chairs with the white plastic straps and her shirt is pulled high over her stomach, which by now is swelled like a spider stomach and the sight of it, with clear jelly rubbed on her stomach so it shines, surprises me.

Please tell me what you're doing, I say.

She says, Where have you been, Charlie? I've been worried, I've been calling, I left messages with Mr. Sharova. (Mr. Sharova's the superintendent of Indigo Pines.)

I feel terrible, I say. There was poetry in the cafeteria and my words were like On Some If Blew What, Jesus. What's that box? What were those games we used to play? When's the baby coming?

Not for a while, she says. Relax, sit down.

I sit in one of the reclining beach chairs, which always makes me feel silly, and look at the ocean for the first time. I had forgotten there was such a pretty view from the back porch of Sally's condo, the sun going down and the sky is peach and clear, the ocean shining, shivering. I look at Sally who's looking at me, and I know I'm going to have a difficult time describing Sally. I've tried and it's like trying to pinpoint why certain smells are pleasing, or colors. She's tan, she wears wire-rimmed glasses, when she's not around she's a sensation I can't separate from the sensing. Here's Steve.

He says, Ginger ale for the mother-to-be, a beer for the uncle-to-be, and a g-and-t for the father-to-be.

G-and-t means gin-and-tonic. I say, I don't want beer, I don't drink beer. (This isn't true.)

Sally says, Do you think we should call the doctor?

Steve: Jesus, no. Calm down, it's Saturday.

Me: What doctor? What's wrong?

Steve: The earphones are broken and now Sally's panicking for no reason. Where'd your underwear go, Charlie?

Sally says something right after this, but I want to tell you the reason Steve keeps asking me about the underwear is not because he cares about the underwear but because he's an asshole.

370

Sally: I don't feel anything. My stomach's numb.

Steve: The earphones are broken.

Me: What earphones? What's wrong?

Sally pulls out a pair of earphones from the box next to her chair, which look like normal earphones but they're attached by a cord to a white plastic microphone, and says, We're listening for the baby's heartbeat.

Steve says, They're broken.

Sally puts the earphones back into the box and looks at Steve with a sort of relaxed anger I recognize from a long time ago, her looking at our parents that way, but too nice or something to yell at them and him, Steve, like I would, like I want to. Steve. I know he isn't doing anything particularly terrible, just asking about my underwear, which is annoying and not terrible, and saying the earphones are broken, which Sally doesn't seem to think is true, and drinking his g-and-t (gin-and-tonic), and saying things like *g-and-t for the father-to-be,* annoying not terrible, but trust me.

Sally says, So where have you been?

I say, Mostly in my apartment, going through old pictures.

Though it sounds like all this is happening right now, currently, it, this conversation, the earphones, already happened a few days ago and the reason I'm telling you about it is I feel high right now, and I think what did it was being with Sally on the back patio of her condo. Sally has brown hair which used to be curly and is still curly.

I say, Do you remember any of the games we used to play?

Sally laughs like letting a brief hiss out of a tire and says, Is it the games again, Charlie?

I guess it is, I think but don't say, and I remember I've asked her this before, gone through the old pictures before, but it feels good to ask it, to do it, like going to see the medicine man, and next time I'll probably ask it again. It feels good to have someone to ask questions you need the answers to. It feels good to give Broom a gift knowing he'll throw it away.

Sally says, He used to be such a good artist. (She's talking to Steve but to me really, if that makes sense.) I remember him going to the beach and coming home with like twenty drawings, birds, tourists, dunes. We used to have them hanging all over the house.

Sketches, I say.

They were *good,* Sally says.

Steve clink-clinks the g-and-t ice cubes in the glass, and I take a sip of the beer I've been holding, which I don't mean to do, but once I do, I take another.

I say, Where'd everybody we used to know go?

Sally says, It's okay.

I want to tell her about the Russians, Poetry Night, my poor words, Broom, talking to Sally always makes me feel better, not what's said but the saying it, the game not the rules. But there's Steve again, or still, clink-clinking his g-and-t, too lazy to get another one, maybe, leaning against the patio rail, waiting to stomp out anything I say.

I say, What's it like to have something alive inside you?

This sounds more philosophical than I intend it to, and I'm glad when Sally doesn't answer. Maybe I didn't ask it out loud. Sally wants a family. She used to have long conversations with her stuffed animals, which she collected, inventing personalities for each one of them, and feuds and marriages, and once she walked into the kitchen with a Ziggy doll and held it up to me where I was sitting. I remember the confused expression on Ziggy's face, and Sally said, she was maybe ten years old, she said, Ziggy's dead. Ziggy looked normal enough to me, maybe a little confused like wondering why nothing good ever happens to him, but we dug a hole and buried him anyway and that was that. I hope Sally didn't stay in Flagler to take care of me, but I suspect she did. If so, she married Steve because of me, she's unhappy because of me, my being attached to her is like an anchor being attached to her.

Steve looks like he's going to laugh. He says: So tell us, Charlie, can a medicine man marry you?

A medicine man is allowed to marry whoever he wants, I say, though I don't know if this is true.

Steve says, No, I mean, can a medicine man preside over a wedding, like a priest, or the captain of a cruise ship?

Sally looks at Steve with more relaxed anger, and when someone like Sally is angry at you, you should feel awful, awful. I say, Nothing funny about medicine men, Steve. They *help* people.

Steve says, So do I. He clink-clinks the g-and-t ice cubes again and I take another sip of beer, and I know why Steve thinks I'm manic depressant. It's because when I'm around Sally, who's the only person I'm not uncomfortable around—when I said before that I used to say I love all people until the Russians, that was a lie, not that I used to say it, I did, but that I meant it, I didn't. When Steve sees me around

Sally he thinks I act around Sally like I act all the time, and me hating Steve probably has little to do with him and a lot to do with Sally, whose stomach I've been looking at, the clear jelly shining sort of reddish in the peach light, and it surprises me again, once I realize what I'm looking at. Sally says, Conductant. It's for the sound. She saw me looking.

I say, I would like to listen to the baby's heartbeat.

I don't want to think I said this from meanness, knowing it would make Steve angry, though I might have. After saying it the idea seems like a decent-enough one. I'm the baby's uncle-to-be, why shouldn't I want to listen to its heartbeat?

Steve says, The earphones are broken.

Sally pulls the earphones out of the box again and unwraps the cord because it's tangled around itself and hands me the earphones while Steve repeats, They're broken.

One of the games we used to play involved running around and hiding, but it wasn't hide-and-go-seek. You had to switch hiding places every so often—this was outside at night—in the dark, and you counted to fifty, or a hundred, and switched hiding places, or yelled when you were yelled at, teasing the person who had to find you. It was called chase something-something. Sally hands me the earphones and I put them on as Steve's talking, saying, Do either of you have a goddamn—

Then they're on, the earphones, no more Steve, and when Sally turns on the machine, which I see says BabyBeat on the side and looks like a plastic microphone, a child's toy, I know right away that Steve's wrong, the earphones are not broken. He's still talking but I'm watching Sally who watches her stomach, the clear shiny reddish jelly, conductant, and I can hear a dead space sound on the earphones like the static sound in-between space transmissions, after an astronaut says *over*, that dead watery static sound, and I'm thinking there's something wrong with Sally, something terrible, and she's moving the microphone over the conductant, over her stomach which she's still watching, and I'm watching her, she looks so sad, and Steve's talking *rah-rah-rah-rah*, probably still clink-clinking his g-and-t, though I can't hear it over the dead space sound, unchanging as she moves the microphone over the conductant, and as I'm getting ready to take off the earphones, which are heavy and tight on my head, Sally moves the microphone under her belly button, pushed out of its socket, the belly button is, her stomach is so huge, and right before I take off the earphones, I hear a faint *buh-buh-buh-buh-buh*, faster than a normal heartbeat, but definitely a heartbeat, *buh-buh-buh-buh-buh*, fast and faint then louder as Sally slowly moves the microphone higher along her stomach, and I say, Hold it right there.

Sally stops and looks up from her stomach, at me, and Steve stops his *rah-rah-rah*, probably stops clink-clinking his g-and-t, though I can't hear anything but the *buh-buh-buh-buh-buh*, faster than a normal heartbeat and loud with the dead watery sound beneath it, but now something alive in the water. Sally is looking at me with obvious expectation holding the microphone on the conductant below her belly button, and there are wide tracks in the conductant from the microphone, and I don't want to say anything because of Steve. I want Sally to know by looking at me. I nod neutrally at Sally and Sally smiles, which means she knows and I know and Steve, who is moving toward me to take the earphones, doesn't know, and I'll end here after I tell you what Sally told Steve when he moved toward me to take the earphones and I held the earphones tight to my head, looked at Steve, and Sally said, loud enough for me to hear over the *buh-buh-buh-buh-buh* and the dead watery sound, Sally said, Don't move. I held the earphones tight to my head, already feeling better, and Sally said to Steve, Don't move a single goddamn muscle.

Nominated by McSweeney's

COOL THINGS

by BRIAN DOYLE

from OREGON HUMANITIES

As a fan's notes for grace, and quavery chant against the dark, and hoorah from the hustings, I sing a song of things that make us grin and bow, that just for an instant let us see sometimes the web and weave of merciful, the endless possible, the incomprehensible inexhaustible inexplicable *yes*,

Such as, for example, to name a few,

The way the sun crawls over the rim of the world every morning like a child's face rising beaming from a pool all fresh from the womb of the dark, and the way jays hop and damselflies do that geometric aeroamazing thing and bees inspect and birds probe and swifts chitter, and the way the young mother at the bus-stop has her infant swaddled and huddled against her chest like a blinking extra heart, and the way a very large woman wears the tiniest miniskirt with a careless airy pride that makes me so happy I can hardly squeak, and the way seals peer at me owlishly from the surf like rubbery grandfathers, and the way cormorants in the ocean never *ever* get caught by onrushing waves but disappear casually at the last possible second so you see their headlong black stories written on the wet walls of the sea like moist petroglyphs, and the way no pavement asphalt macadam concrete cement thing can ultimately defeat a tiny relentless green thing, and the way people sometimes lean eagerly facefirst into the future, and the way infants finally discover to their absolute agogishment that those fists swooping by like tiny fleshy comets are *theirs!*, and the way when my mom gets caught unawares by a joke she barks with laughter so infectious that people grin two towns over, and the way one of my sons sleeps every night with his right leg hanging over the side of his bed like an oar no matter how many times I fold him back into the boat of the bed, and the way the refrigerator hums to itself in two different keys, and the way the new puppy noses through hayfields like a headlong exuberant hairy tractor, and the way my daughter always makes one immense final cookie the size of a door when she makes cookies, and the way one son hasn't had a haircut since Napoleon was emperor, and the way crows arrange themselves sometimes on the fence like the notes of a song I don't know yet, and the way car engines sigh for a few minutes after you turn them off, and the way your arm goes all totally nonchalant when you are driving through summer with the window down, and the way people touch each other's forearms when they are scated, and the way every once in a while someone you hardly know says something so piercingly honest that you want to just kneel down right there in the grocery store near the pears, and the way little children fall asleep with their mouths open like fish, and the way sometimes just a sidelong glance from someone you love makes you all shaky for a second before you can get your mask back on, and the way some people when they laugh tilt their heads way back like they need more room for all the hilarity in their mouths, and the way hawks and eagles always look so *annoyed,* and the way people shuffle daintily on icy pavements, and the way churches smell dense with hope, and the way that men's pants bunch up at the knees when they stand after kneeling in church, and the way knees are gnarled, and the way faces curve around the mouth and eyes according to how many times you smiled over the years, and the way people fall asleep in chairs by the fire and snap awake startled and amazed, unsure, just for a second, what planet exactly they are on, which is a question we should probably all ask far more often than we do.

Look, I know very well that brooding misshapen evil is everywhere, in the brightest houses and the most cheerful denials, in what we do and what we have failed to do, and I know all too well that the story of the world is entropy, things fly apart we sicken, we fail, we grow weary, we divorce, we are hammered and hounded by loss and accidents and tragedies. But I also know, with all my hoary muddled heart, that we are carved of immense confusing holiness; that the whole point for us is grace under duress; and that you either take a flying leap at nonsensical illogical unreasonable ideas like marriage and marathons and democracy and divinity, or you huddle behind the wall. I believe that the coolest things there are cannot be measured, calibrated, calculated, gauged, weighed, or understood except sometimes by having a child patiently explain them to you, which is another thing that should happen far more often to us all.

In short I believe in believing, which doesn't make sense, which gives me hope.

Nominated by Genie Chipps

STAY

fiction by DAVID SCHUMAN

from THE MISSOURI REVIEW

WHEN THEY ASKED, I told them I wanted the dog that would take up the most space in my house. They opened a heavy door, went into the back and came out with a giant. He shambled. He was tall and hairy, and his head nodded on his long neck like a horse's. He swung his gaze in my direction. His expression was frank. It said, *Get me out of here*. One of the attendants said, "Do you know whose dog this was? That guy who set his wife on fire—his lawyer brought it in here and told us to put it down." I put the dog in my small car. Getting him home was like moving a sofa.

My only experience living with dogs up to this point had been a picture in my mother's house from the Victorian era depicting a hound mourning over the body of a young boy. It was one of several prints hanging staggered in the stairwell. The dead boy was propped up against a piled fishnet, and there was ocean in the background. The dog, with pearls of water rolling off its fur, cast its eyes up to a gaping hole in the clouds ready to receive its master's soul. Sometimes I couldn't bear to look at the picture and rushed past on my way upstairs to bed.

I named the dog Deli, from Fidelity and also because I learned that bologna really perked this animal up. We'd go out in the backyard and I'd throw discs of bologna—slices doubled up so they flew straight—and Deli would jump up and gobble them out of thin air. We did that every day, until the dog started getting fatty lumps the size of marbles under his coat and the vet told me to lay off. Anyway, it probably wasn't right to be throwing meat around like a toy.

I was happy with my dog, and he seemed happy with me. After a few years there was a story in the paper about how the man who'd set his wife on fire had been denied parole. I showed Deli the guy's grainy photo and searched for a glimmer of recognition—a catch in the dog's breath, a tremor in his tail—but there wasn't anything like that. As a matter of fact, he gave me a consoling lick across my entire face.

We lived together in a house next to the railroad tracks. Freight trains went by four or five times a day, and I put felt on the bottom of everything so it wouldn't rattle. Sometimes I'd be eating breakfast before work and Deli would put his chin down on the tabletop and give me a look like, *Why don't you go get a wife?* So I would try, and sometimes a woman would live with us for a while, and they loved us in different ways. One liked to put her underwear on the dog's thin hips. Later there was a woman who paused movies on the VCR if the dog left the room and wouldn't resume watching until he came back. After a few months it would always go back to being just the two of us in the house.

One night Deli didn't come in from the backyard, so I went to see what the matter was. It was just about winter, and the sky had a pinkness to it, the way it gets before snow. Deli was sitting like a sphinx in the dried-out grass, and there was a boy lying in front of him. This boy wasn't dead, but he was drunk. He'd been riding the train and hopped off and climbed over my fence when he saw Deli out in the yard. I didn't think you could ride freight trains anymore, and I tried to get some stories out of the kid, but he was too drunk to talk. I brought him inside and opened a can of soup and put on a pot of coffee and toasted some bread for him. When I brought the food out on a tray he said, "It's a rare dog that can make a person get off a moving train." The kid lived with us for a little while. I got him to go to AA meetings, and when he left he said he was going back to college. The night before he took off, he brushed Deli's coat until it shone.

Finally, Deli got old and stiff. It had been eight years since I had brought him home. His arthritis got so bad that a couple of times I had to lift his leg for him. The hair on his muzzle turned white. His nose was always dry and crusty, and his nostrils whistled. His eyes looked like they were filled with milk, and I couldn't tell what he was thinking anymore. One day he stopped being able to walk, and he looked at me, and this time, even with his cloudy eyes, I could see it was the same look he'd given me when I first met him.

The next morning I lifted him and brought him to the car. Either he was lighter than ever or I was as strong as I needed to be, but it was the first time I'd carried him in my arms. His chest felt fragile, like a birdcage covered with a blanket.

When I got to the vet's, Deli was barely breathing. The assistant took him out of my arms and into the back. The receptionist told me that the doctor would call me in when it was going to happen, and then I could say good-bye. I sat down on a bench covered with vinyl padding. I had never sat so straight in my life. There were magazines scattered on the table in front of me, and I wanted to banish them, with their catchy headlines and celebrity photos. I wanted the place to be a church.

Then something happened that I can't explain. The vet came out with Deli walking in front of her on the leash. It was a different vet than the one who'd told me to stop feeding the dog cold cuts. He must have retired. This vet was thin and had gray hair, but she wasn't old. She and the dog made a striking couple, very tall. Deli's glance was cast over his shoulder at her and his tail was going back and forth.

"This guy's all right," said the vet. "Nothing wrong with him that I can see."

I reached out, and Deli put his mouth around my hand softly, the way he always had. His eyes weren't entirely clear, but they were glossy. He breathed hard on my cheek when I leaned down to him. Little bubbles of excitement pulsed out of his nose. The vet placed the leash in my hand. Her fingertips were warm, and she smelled like birdseed.

"You ever need a dog sitter, you let me know," said the vet. "This one's a sweetie."

I didn't ask anything. I thanked her and hurried him out of there, fumbling with my car keys like someone might be after us.

I opened the windows on the way home to let in the spring air. For a while we rode along next to a freight train that would eventually pass our backyard with its cargo of grain. Deli stood in the backseat, and when I looked in the rearview mirror he was all I could see. Granted this reprieve, I thought about what we might do differently, but then I decided our best bet was to do everything exactly the same.

Nominated by Wally Lamb, Joyce Carol Oates, Missouri Review

THE FIRES

by PHILIP WHITE

from THE JOURNAL

1. *Lament*

My heart stopped,
but my body went on.
Love, have mercy on me.
The sky was ash,
the earth a cinder.
I don't know why I lived.
I walked up fifth street.
I walked up fifth street.
My face became a stranger.
I woke in dim chambers
with others around me.
I sat down amid joy
and ate without hunger.
My body went on,
my face a stranger.
The sky was ash.
I ate without hunger.
My love died,
but my heart went on.
I don't know why I lived.
Love, have mercy on me.

2. *Red Branch*

A terrible fidelity
held me. I had to move
to keep quiet. Limbs
plunging in the wind,
dark air hollowed, shot
through with the promise
of snow, I sought you.
Absence swept the fields.
At a bend, spiring
redcedar, cold, down-
licking brands of bared
sumac. Like you
they kept beckoning,
kept burning and not
burning, held their tongues.

3. *Baucis and Philemon*

As in the fable, linden and oak twining
together as one, yes; but before that
and after, two in pain who found themselves
up late, talking. So our portal of escape
became a language we could not talk
our way back through, our tongues, like limbs
and trunks, having fused in the passage:
nights in the nest, days, the bed made, unmade,
and memory growing thick around it, tangled
with dreams like flames driving streaks upward
through our leaves and veins. So when the gods
of endings came, we made a place even
for them inside, and when they asked, no need
to speak, we knew already what our wish was.
Never to grieve? Never to let suffer?
Impossible, then, to say who broke faith.
In the end we could not save the other:
there was one pain, one fraying braid, and two

tracing the snapped threads back, trying to mend.
Then there was one on the bed, up late, talking.

4. *The Fires*

Love, you took yourself from us, but why?
The part of me that knew your pain thought
it knew; now I founder. There was a fault
in me that shifted, the strata disaligned;
your lips, arms, eyes, the way you held your face
up to the wind in fierce concentration,
how do these pertain now? and to whom—
I have lived, as you wanted, loved again.
Yet feel the snow on one slope of the mountain
has slipped and all the trees I knew there
mangled, shorn—Wood for the new fires?
How terrible . . . these nights lying awake late
trying to explain what happens in this world
to our children, who were never born.

Nominated by Joshua Mehigan, The Journal

THE WAY OF IGNORANCE
by WENDELL BERRY
from NEW LETTERS

In order to arrive at what you do not know
You must go by a way which is the way of ignorance.

T. S. Eliot, "East Coker"

Our purpose here* is to worry about the predominance of the supposition, in a time of great technological power, that humans either know enough already, or can learn enough soon enough, to foresee and forestall any bad consequences of their use of that power. This supposition is typified by Richard Dawkins' assertion, in 2000, in an open letter to the Prince of Wales, that "our brains . . . are big enough to see into the future and plot long-term consequences."

When we consider how often and how recently our most advanced experts have been wrong about the future, and how often the future has shown up sooner than expected with bad news about our past, Mr. Dawkin's assessment of our ability to know is revealed as a superstition of the most primitive sort. We recognize it also as our old friend hubris, ungodly ignorance disguised as godly arrogance. Ignorance plus arrogance plus greed sponsors "better living with chemistry," and produces the ozone hole and the dead zone in the Gulf of Mexico. A modern science (chemistry or nuclear physics or molecular biology) "applied" by ignorant arrogance resembles much too closely an automobile being driven by a 6-year-old or a loaded pistol

*Written as a paper for delivery at The Land Institute, Matfield Green, Kansas.

in the hands of a monkey. Arrogant ignorance promotes a global economy, while ignoring the global exchange of pests and diseases that must inevitably accompany it. Arrogant ignorance makes war without a thought of peace.

We identify arrogant ignorance by its willingness to work on too big a scale, and thus to put too much at risk. It fails to foresee bad consequences not only because some of the consequences of all acts are inherently unforeseeable, but also because the arrogantly ignorant often are blinded by money invested; they cannot afford to foresee bad consequences.

Except to the arrogantly ignorant, ignorance is not a simple subject. It is perhaps as difficult for ignorance to be aware of itself as it is for awareness to be aware of itself. One can hardly begin to think about ignorance without seeing that it is available in several varieties, and so I will offer a brief taxonomy.

There is, to begin with, the kind of ignorance we may consider to be inherent. This is ignorance of all that we cannot know because of the kind of mind we have—which, I will note in passing, is neither a computer nor exclusively a brain, and which certainly is not omniscient. We cannot, for example, know the whole of which we and our minds are parts. The English poet and critic Kathleen Raine wrote that "we cannot imagine how the world might appear if we did not possess the groundwork of knowledge which we do possess; nor can we in the nature of things imagine how reality would appear in the light of knowledge which we do not possess."

A part of our inherent ignorance, and surely a most formidable encumbrance to those who presume to know the future, is our ignorance of the past. We know almost nothing of our history as it was actually lived. We know little of the lives even of our parents. We have forgotten almost everything that has happened to ourselves. The easy assumption that we have remembered the most important people and events and have preserved the most valuable evidence is immediately trumped by our inability to know what we have forgotten.

There are several other kinds of ignorance that are not inherent in our nature but come instead from weaknesses of character. Paramount among these is the willful ignorance that refuses to honor as knowledge anything not subject to empirical proof. We could just as well call it materialist ignorance. This ignorance rejects useful knowledge such as traditions of imagination and religion, and so it comes across as narrow-mindedness. We have the materialist culture that afflicts us now because a world exclusively material is the kind of world most readily used and abused by the kind of mind the materialists think they have. To this kind of mind, there is no longer a legitimate wonder. Wonder has been replaced by a research agenda, which is still a world away from demonstrating the impropriety of wonder. The materialist conservationists need to tell us how a materialist culture can justify its contempt and destructiveness of material goods.

A related kind of ignorance, also self-induced, is moral ignorance, the invariable excuse of which is objectivity. One of the purposes of objectivity, in practice, is to avoid coming to a moral conclusion. Objectivity, considered a mark of great learning and the highest enlightenment, loves to identify itself by such pronouncements as the following: "You may be right, but on the other hand so may your opponent," or "Everything is relative," or "Whatever is happening is inevitable," or "Let me be the devil's advocate." (The part of devil's advocate is surely one of the most sought after in all the precincts of the modern intellect. Anywhere you go to speak in defense of something worthwhile, you are apt to encounter a smiling savant writhing in the estrus of objectivity: "Let me play the devil's advocate for a moment." As if the devil's point of view will not otherwise be represented.)

There is also ignorance as false confidence, or polymathic ignorance. This is the ignorance of people who know "all about" history or its "long-term consequences" in the future. This is closely akin to self-righteous ignorance, which is the failure to know oneself. Ignorance of one's self and confident knowledge of the past and future often are the same thing.

Fearful ignorance is the opposite of confident ignorance. People keep themselves ignorant for fear of the strange or the different or the unknown, for fear of disproof or of unpleasant or tragic knowledge, for fear of stirring up suspicion and opposition, or for fear of fear itself. A good example is the United States Department of Agriculture's panic-stricken monopoly of inadequate meat inspections. And there is the related ignorance that comes from laziness, which is the fear of effort and difficulty. Learning often is not fun, and this is well-known to all the ignorant except for a few "educators."

Finally, there are for-profit ignorance, which is maintained by withholding knowledge, as in advertising, and for-power ignorance, which is maintained by government secrecy and public lies.

Kinds of ignorance (and there must be more than I have named) may thus be sorted out. But having sorted them out, one must scramble them back together again by acknowledging that all of them can be at work in the same mind at the same time, and in my opinion they frequently are.

I may be talking too much at large here, but I am going to say that a list of kinds of ignorance comprises half a description of a human mind. The other half, then, would be supplied by a list of kinds of knowledge.

At the head of that list let us put the empirical or provable knowledge of the materialists. This is the knowledge of dead certainty or dead facts, some of which at least are undoubtedly valuable, undoubtedly useful, but at best this is static, smallish knowledge that always is what it always was, and it is rather dull. A fact may thrill us once, but not twice. Once available, it is easy game; we might call it sitting-duck knowledge. This knowledge becomes interesting again when it enters experience by way of use.

And so, as second, let us put knowledge as experience. This is useful knowledge, but it involves uncertainty and risk. How do you know if it is going to rain, or when an animal is going to bolt or attack? Because the event has not yet happened, there is no empirical answer; you may not have time to calculate the statistical probability even on the fastest computer. You will have to rely on experience, which will increase your chance of being right. But then you also may be wrong.

The experience of many people over a long time is traditional knowledge. This is the common knowledge of a culture, which it seems that few of us any longer have. To have a culture, mostly the same people have to live mostly in the same place for a long time. Traditional knowledge is knowledge that has been remembered or recorded, handed down, pondered, corrected, practiced, and refined over a long time.

A related kind of knowledge is made available by the religious traditions and is not otherwise available. If you premise the falsehood of such knowledge, as the materialists do, then of course you don't have it, and your opinion of it is worthless.

There also are kinds of knowledge that seem to be more strictly inward. Instinct is inborn knowledge: how to suck, bite, and swallow; how to run away from danger instead of toward it. And perhaps the prepositions refer to knowledge that is more or less instinctive: up, down, in, out, etc.

Intuition is knowledge as recognition, a way of knowing without proof. We know the truth of the Book of Job by intuition.

What we call conscience is knowledge of the difference between right and wrong. Whether or not this is learned, most people have it, and they appear to get it early. Some of the worst malefactors and hypocrites have it in full; how else could they fake it so well? But we should remember that some worthy people have believed conscience to be innate, an "inner light."

Inspiration, I believe, is another kind of knowledge or way of knowing, though I don't know how this could be proved. One can say in support only that poets such as Homer, Dante, and Milton seriously believed in it, and that people do at times surpass themselves, performing better than all you know of them has led you to expect. Imagination, in the highest sense, is inspiration. Gifts arrive from sources that cannot be empirically located.

Sympathy gives us an intimate knowledge of other people and other creatures that can come in no other way. So does affection. The knowledge that comes by sympathy and affection is little noticed— the materialists, I assume, are unable to notice it—but in my opinion it cannot be overvalued.

Everybody who has done physical work or danced or played a game of skill is aware of the difference between knowing how and being able. This difference I would call bodily knowledge.

And finally, to be safe, we had better recognize that there is such a thing as counterfeit knowledge or plausible falsehood.

I would say that these taxonomies of mine are more or less reasonable; I certainly would not claim that they are scientific. My only assured claim is that any consideration of ignorance and knowledge ought to be at least as complex as this attempt of mine. We are a complex species—organisms surely, but also living souls—who are involved in a life-or-death negotiation, even more complex, with our earthly circumstances, which are complex beyond our ability to guess, let alone know. In dealing with those circumstances, in trying "to see into the future and plot long-term consequences," the human mind is neither capacious enough nor exact nor dependable. We are encumbered by an inherent ignorance perhaps not significantly reducible, as well as by proclivities to ignorance of other kinds, and our ways of knowing, though impressive within human limits, have the power to lead us beyond our limits, beyond foresight and precaution, and out of control.

What I have said so far characterizes the personal minds of individual humans. But because of a certain kind of arrogant ignorance, and because of the gigantic scale of work permitted and even required by powerful technologies, we are not safe in dealing merely with personal or human minds. We are obliged to deal also with a kind of mind that I will call corporate, although it is also political and institutional. This is a mind that is compound and abstract, materialist, reductionist, greedy, and radically utilitarian. Assuming as some of us sometimes do that two heads are better than one, it ought to be axiomatic that the corporate mind is better than any personal mind, but it can in fact be much worse—not least in its apparently limitless ability to cause problems that it cannot solve, and that may be unsolvable. The corporate mind is remarkably narrow. It claims to utilize only empirical knowledge—the preferred term is "sound science," reducible ultimately to the "bottom line" of profit or power—and because this rules out any explicit recourse to experience or tradition or any kind of inward knowledge such as conscience, this mind is readily susceptible to every kind of ignorance and is perhaps naturally predisposed to counterfeit knowledge. It comes to its work equipped with factual knowledge and perhaps also with knowledge skillfully counterfeited, but without recourse to any of those knowledges that enable us to deal appropriately with mystery or with human limits. It has no humbling knowledge. The corporate mind is arrogantly ignorant by definition.

Ignorance, arrogance, narrowness of mind, incomplete knowledge, and counterfeit knowledge are of concern to us because they are dangerous; they cause destruction. When united with great power, they cause great destruction. They have caused far too much destruction already, too often of irreplaceable things. Now, reasonably enough, we are asking if it is possible, if it is even thinkable, that the destruction can be stopped. To some people's surprise, we are again backed up against the fact that knowledge is not in any simple way good. We often have been a destructive species; we are more destructive now than we have ever been, and this, in perfect accordance with ancient warnings, is because of our ignorant and arrogant use of knowledge.

———

389

Before going further, we had better ask what it is that we humans need to know. We need to know many things, of course, and many kinds of things. Let us be merely practical for the time being and say that we need to know who we are, where we are, and what we must do to live. These questions do not refer to discreet categories of knowledge. We are not likely to be able to answer one of them without answering the other two. And all three must be well answered before we can answer well a further practical question that is now pressing urgently upon us: How can we work without doing irreparable damage to the world and its creatures, including ourselves? Or: How can we live without destroying the sources of our life?

These questions are perfectly honorable; we may even say that they are perfectly obvious, and yet we have much cause to believe that the corporate mind never asks any of them. It does not care who it is, for it is not anybody; it is a mind perfectly disembodied. It does not care where it is, as long as its present location yields a greater advantage than any other. It will do anything at all that is necessary, not merely to live, but to aggrandize itself. And it charges its damages indifferently to the public, to nature, and to the future.

The corporate mind at work overthrows all the virtues of the personal mind, or it throws them out of account. The corporate mind knows no affection, no desire that is not greedy, no local or personal loyalty, no sympathy or reverence or gratitude, no temperance or thrift or self-restraint. It does not observe the first responsibility of intelligence, which is to know when you don't know or when you are being unintelligent. Try to imagine an official standing up in the high councils of a global corporation or a great public institution to say, "We have grown too big," or "We now have more power than we can responsibly use," or "We must treat our employees as our neighbors," or "We must count ourselves as members of this community," or "We must preserve the ecological integrity of our work places," or "Let us do unto others as we would have them to do unto us"—and you will see what I mean.

The corporate mind, on the contrary, justifies and encourages the personal mind in its worst faults and weaknesses, such as greed and servility, and frees it of any need to worry about long-term consequences. For these reliefs, nowadays, the corporate mind is apt to express noisily its gratitude to God.

Now I must hasten to acknowledge that there are some corporations that do not simply incorporate what I am calling the corporate mind. Whether the number of these is increasing or not, I don't know. These organizations, I believe, tend to have hometowns and to count themselves as participants in the local economy and as members of the local community.

I would not apply to science any stricture that I would not apply to the arts, but science now calls for special attention because it has contributed so largely to modern abuses of the natural world, and because of its enormous prestige. Our concern here has to do immediately with the complacency of many scientists. It cannot be denied that science, in its inevitable applications, has given unprecedented extremes of scale to the technologies of land use, manufacturing, and war, and to their bad effects. One response to the manifest implication of science in certain kinds of destruction is to say that we need more science, or more and better science. I am inclined to honor this proposition, if I am allowed to add that we also need more than science.

But I am not at all inclined to honor the proposition that "science is self-correcting" when it implies that science is thus made somehow "safe." Science is no more safe than any other kind of knowledge. Especially it is not safe in the context of its gigantic applications by the corporate mind. Nor is it safe in the context of its own progressivist optimism. The idea, common enough among the universities and their ideological progeny, that one's work, whatever it is, will be beneficently disposed by the market or the hidden hand or evolution or some other obscure force is an example of counterfeit knowledge.

The obvious immediate question is, How *soon* can science correct itself? Can it correct itself soon enough to prevent or correct the real damage of its errors? The answer is that it cannot correct itself soon enough. Scientists who have made a plausible "breakthrough" hasten to tell the world, including, of course, the corporations. While science may have corrected itself, it is not necessarily able to correct its results or its influence.

We must grant, of course, that science in its laboratories may be well under control. Scientists in laboratories did not cause the ozone hole or the hypoxic zones or acid rain or Chernobyl or Bhopal or Love Canal. It is when knowledge is corporatized, commercialized, and applied that it goes out of control. Can science, then, make itself responsible by issuing appropriate warnings with its knowledge? No, because the users are under no obligation to heed or respect the warning. If the knowledge is conformable to the needs of profit or power, the warning will be ignored, as we know. We are not excused by the doctrine of scientific self-correction from worrying about the influence of science on the corporate mind, and about the influence of the corporate mind on the minds of consumers and users. Humans in general have got to worry about the origins of the permission we have given ourselves to do large-scale damage. That permission is our problem, for by it we have made our ignorance arrogant and given it immeasurable power to do harm. We are killing our world on the theory that it was never alive but is only an accidental concatenation of materials and mechanical processes. We are killing one another and ourselves on the same theory. If life has no standing as mystery or miracle or gift, then what signifies the difference between it and death?

Most of us would be inclined to say, perhaps instinctively, that nothing could be more ignorant than this killing, and my purpose here is to honor that impulse. But we have to recognize that this is not a moderate ignorance. It is a great ignorance making use, in a sort of self-induced delirium, of much knowledge. It is like the ignorance of the lawyer my brother heard about who was said to have been "educated beyond his comprehension."

To state the problem more practically, we can say that the ignorant use of knowledge allows power to override the question of scale, because it overrides respect for the integrity of local ecosystems, and only that respect can determine the appropriate scale of human work. Without propriety of scale, and the acceptance of limits which that implies, there can be no form—and here we reunite science and art. We live and prosper by form, which is the power of creatures and artifacts to be made whole within their proper limits. Without formal restraints, power necessarily becomes inordinate and destructive. This is why the poet David Jones wrote in the midst of World War II that "man as artist hungers and thirsts after form." Inordinate size has of itself the power to exclude much knowledge.

What can we do? Anybody who goes on so long about a problem is rightly expected to have something to say about a solution. One is expected to "end on a positive note," and I mean to do that. I also mean to be careful. The question, What can we do? especially when the problem is large, implies the expectation of a large solution.

I have no large solution to offer. There is, as maybe we all have noticed, a conspicuous shortage of large-scale corrections for problems that have large-scale causes. Our damages to watersheds and ecosystems will have to be corrected one farm, one forest, one acre at a time. The aftermath of a bombing has to be dealt with one corpse, one wound at a time. So the first temptation to avoid is the call for some sort of revolution. To imagine that destructive power might be made harmless by gathering enough power to destroy it is of course perfectly futile. William Butler Yeats said as much in his poem "The Great Day":

> Hurrah for revolution and more cannon shot!
> A beggar upon horseback lashes a beggar on foot.
> Hurrah for revolution and cannon come again!
> The beggars have changed places, but the lash goes on.

Arrogance cannot be cured by greater arrogance, or ignorance by greater ignorance. To counter the ignorant use of knowledge and power, we have, I am afraid, only a proper humility, and this is laughable. But it is only partly laughable. In his political pastoral "Build Soil," as if responding to Yeats, Robert Frost has one of his rustics say,

> I bid you to a one-man revolution—
> The only revolution that is coming.

If we find the consequences of our arrogant ignorance to be humbling, and we are humbled, then we have at hand the first fact of hope: We can change ourselves. We, each of us severally, can remove our minds from the corporate ignorance and arrogance that is leading the world to destruction; we can honestly confront our ignorance and our need; we can take guidance from the knowledge we most authentically possess, from experience, from tradition, and from the inward promptings of affection, conscience, decency, compassion, even inspiration.

This change can be called by several names—change of heart, rebirth, metanoia, enlightenment—and it belongs, I think, to all the religions, but I like the practical way it is defined in the Confucian *Great Digest*. This is from Ezra Pound's translation:

> The men of old wanting to clarify and diffuse throughout
> the empire that light which comes from looking straight
> into the heart and then acting, first set up good govern-

ment in their own states; wanting good government in their states, they first established order in their own families; wanting order in the home, they first disciplined themselves; desiring self-discipline, they rectified their own hearts; and wanting to rectify their hearts, they sought precise verbal definitions of their inarticulate thoughts [the tones given off by the heart]; wishing to attain precise verbal definitions, they set to extend their knowledge to the utmost.

This curriculum does not rule out science—it does not rule out knowledge of any kind—but it begins with the recognition of ignorance and of need, of being in a bad situation.

If the ability to change oneself is the first fact of hope, then the second surely must be an honest assessment of the badness of our situation. Our situation is extremely bad, as I have said, and optimism cannot either improve it or make it look better. But there is hope in seeing it as it is. Here I need to quote Kathleen Raine again. This is a passage written in the aftermath of World War II, and she is thinking of T. S. Eliot's poem *The Waste Land*, written in the aftermath of World War I. In *The Waste Land*, Eliot bears unflinching witness to the disease of our time: We are living the death of our culture and our world. The poem's ruling metaphor is that of a waterless land perishing for rain, an image that becomes more poignant as we pump down the aquifers and dry up or pollute the rivers.

But Eliot [Kathleen Raine said] has shown us what the world is very apt to forget, that the statement of a terrible truth has a kind of healing power. In his stern vision of the hell that lies about us, . . . there is a quality of grave consolation. In his statement of the worst, Eliot has always implied the whole extent of the reality of which that worst is only one part.

Honesty is good, then, not just because it is a virtue, but for a practical reason: It can give us an accurate description of our problem, and it can set the problem precisely in its context.

Honesty, of course, is not a solution. As I already have said, I don't think there are solutions commensurate with our problems. I think

394

the great problems call for many small solutions. But for that possibility to attain sufficient standing among us, we need not only to put the problems in context but also to learn to put our work in context. And here is where we turn back from our ambitions to consult both the local ecosystem and the cultural instructions conveyed to us by religion and the arts. All the arts and sciences need to be made answerable to standards higher than those of any art or science. Scientists and artists must understand that they can honor their gifts and fulfill their obligations only by living and working as human beings and community members rather than as specialists. What this may involve may not be predictable even by scientists. But the best advice may have been given by Hippocrates: "As to diseases, make a habit of two things—to help, or at least to do no harm."

The wish to help, especially if it is profitable to do so, may be in human nature, and everybody wants to be a hero. To help, or to try to help, requires only knowledge; one needs to know promising remedies and how to apply them. But to do no harm involves a whole culture, and a culture very different from industrialism. It involves, at the minimum, compassion and humility and caution. The person who will undertake to help without doing harm is going to be a person of some complexity, not easily pleased, probably not a hero, probably not a billionaire.

The corporate approach to agriculture or manufacturing or medicine or war increasingly undertakes to help at the risk of harm, sometimes of great harm. And once the risk of harm is appraised as "acceptable," the result often is absurdity: We destroy a village in order to save it; we destroy freedom in order to save it; we destroy the world in order to live in it.

The apostles of the corporate mind say, with a large implicit compliment to themselves, that you cannot succeed without risking failure. They allude to such examples as that of the Wright brothers. They don't see that the issue of risk raises directly the issue of scale. Risk, like everything else, has an appropriate scale. By propriety of scale we limit the possible damages of the risks we take. If we cannot control scale so as to limit the effects, then we should not take the risk. From this, it is clear that some risks simply should not be taken. Some experiments should not be made. If a Wright brother wishes to risk failure, then he observes a fundamental decency in risking it alone. If the Wright airplane had crashed into a house and killed a child, the corporate mind, considering the future profitability of aviation, would count that an "acceptable" risk and loss. One can only reply that the corporate mind does not have the householder's or the parent's point of view.

I am aware that invoking personal decency, personal humility, as the solution to a vast risk taken on our behalf by corporate industrialism is not going to suit everybody. Some will find it an insult to their sense of proportion, others to their sense of drama. I am offended by it myself, and I wish I could do better. Having looked about, I have been unable to convince myself that there is a better solution or one that has a better chance of working.

I am trying to follow what T. S. Eliot called "the way of ignorance," for I think that is the way that is appropriate for the ignorant. I think Eliot meant us to understand that the way of ignorance is the way recommended by all the great teachers. It certainly was the way recommended by Confucius, for who but the ignorant would set out to extend their knowledge to the utmost? Who but the knowingly ignorant would know there is an "utmost" to knowledge?

But we take the way of ignorance also as a courtesy toward reality. Eliot wrote in "East Coker":

> The knowledge imposes a pattern, and falsifies,
> For the pattern is new in every moment
> And every moment is a new and shocking
> Valuation of all we have been.

This certainly describes the ignorance inherent in the human condition, an ignorance we justly feel as tragic. But it also is a way of acknowledging the uniqueness of every individual creature, deserving respect, and the uniqueness of every moment, deserving wonder. Life in time involves a great freshness that is falsified by what we already know.

Of course, the way of ignorance is the way of faith. If enough of us will accept "the wisdom of humility," giving due honor to the ever-renewing pattern, accepting each moment's "new and shocking / Valuation of all we have been," then the corporate mind as we now have it will be shaken, and it will cease to exist, as its members dissent and withdraw from it.

Nominated by George Keithley, New Letters

HEARING NEWS FROM THE TEMPLE MOUNT IN SALT LAKE CITY

by JACQUELINE OSHEROW

from THE HOOPOE'S CROWN (BOA EDITIONS)

You know that conversation
in the elevator in the Catskills:
how one woman says, *Oy,*
the food here is so terrible
and the other *and the portions*
are so small? It's a variant
on Jacob's line to Pharaoh
when he gets to Egypt—*few*
and evil have been the days
of my life. Naturally, he's our
chosen namesake: this Israel
the Torah keeps forgetting and
calling Jacob, as if it doesn't
trust his cleaned-up name.

Obviously he's the perfect
guy for us—we're always
willing to take something
over nothing—hence
our lunatic attachment

to that miserable pinpoint
in the desert, where now,
whether it's Ishmael
or Isaac on the altar,
there's an earsplitting
crowd working to drown
out every angel until
Abraham fulfills his sacrifice.

It's none of my diaspora-
befuddled business, but
I'm not in the mood
to celebrate. Call me
thin-skinned, but I can't
get used to the idea that
all these hordes of people
wish me dead. You have
to remember: I'm Jacob's
offspring; I want as many
evil days as I can lay my
hands on. Thank God
I live in Salt Lake City. Who's
going to come looking for me
here? In this calm Zion,
where a bunch of blonde
meshugeners think *they're*
the chosen people of God.
Good luck to them is all
I have to say; let them
get the joy from it that I do.

Nominated by Judith Hall, Donald Platt, Alan Michael Parker, BOA Editions

VACATION

fiction by RICHARD BURGIN

from ONTARIO REVIEW

H E SHOULDN'T HAVE SAT next to a man in a bar at night, he knew that. He'd willfully broken one of his rules, so who else could he blame but himself? Yet it had happened so suddenly, he was looking up from his drink, surreptitiously scanning the room for women, when the man settled in. He was thin and average-looking, although there was something quasi-delirious about his eyes. Things were OK at first, though the man appeared to have been drinking already or (more likely) was high on something else. Then he began running his mouth about his mother. That was all right too—a little disconcerting but he could understand. Suddenly, out of nowhere, the man turned towards him, looking him right in the eye and said, "Do you think when you're old it's like being high all the time?"

He stared at him hard wanting to shout, "You're asking me? Why are you asking *me*, you stupid little snail?" Instead, he said, "Don't know," finished the rest of his drink quickly, then said, "I gotta roll."

That night in his apartment after reviewing the incident a number of times he decided he'd go to the salon the next day before playing ball at the playground. He watched TV and drank beer until it was past 2 a.m. but still felt preternaturally awake. When he finally did get to sleep, he once again dreamed of hurrying to a game he was late for.

He was in the salon the next morning by eleven. He figured he'd be done by lunchtime but would skip lunch so he could play with a light stomach. Then he could walk to the playground knowing he would in all likelihood be too early for a game but knowing it was much better to be early, even absurdly early, than to be late.

Besides the hairdressers, he was the only man in the salon. Sonny greeted him like he was a guest at his party, shaking hands and smiling. How was he? How were things going at the agency? He answered the questions as best he could, as he settled uneasily in the chair.

"So Gary, you want the usual today?"

"Yeah the usual, don't make it too dark."

"Would I do that to you?" Sonny said, putting his hand over his heart.

"Where's your assistant?" he wanted to say. "The one with the legs and the pop-up ass." Sonny always worked with good-looking women although he was actually straight and married. Once Sonny's wife had come into the salon and she was good-looking too. Had incredible legs. But Sonny himself was not much to look at although he was in pretty good shape, still young enough and had an appealing smile, he supposed.

In the salon women were walking by in black robes with different colored dyes and transparent plastic nets over their hair as they made their way to the dryers.

When Sonny asked him if he had a date tonight he lied and said he did.

"I've got a young one this time—that's why I have to color the hair."

"Hey when it comes to the ladies you gotta do what you gotta do."

"Exactly."

He'd colored his hair to increase his chances of getting picked for a game and not get passed over for being too old, but there were other benefits too. Maybe it was irrational but he felt stronger and certainly safer walking down the street (a few years ago he'd been mugged which he'd never forgotten, and since then he usually carried a knife with him, as he did today. He'd also bought two handguns, one of which he sometimes took with him in his car). He figured he looked five to ten years younger now—maybe more, why put a limit on it, and would once more appear to be in the age zone where he was less vulnerable to attack. More women would be available to him too, of course. That was the whole idea of his vacation, to play basketball in the daytime in early May when it still wasn't too hot in Philadelphia and to go after women at night. He knew it was ironic to be working at a travel agency and staying home on his vacation—especially with all the vacation perks the agency offered. He also knew he'd be teased and gossiped about if anyone at work found out that he was staying home, so he'd quickly decided to say he was going to Malibu. He even had a line ready in case he ran into anybody from the agency, which wasn't that far from the salon or from his walking route to the playground. If they said, "Gary, what are you doing here? I thought you were going to Malibu," he'd say, "You *believed* that?" like it had been a joke all along that they'd fallen for. Shift the emphasis to *them*, for once.

. . . All along he knew he was going to Taney Park. He could have gone to Fourth and Locust where there were better players and the baskets were in better shape, or 38th and Walnut near U Penn or even to Clark Park. But he'd lived near Taney Park for most of his Philadelphia years and a number of the players there knew him, so thinking about the other parks was just a game he was playing with himself—like a hopelessly faithful man fantasizing about cheating on his wife. Yet he couldn't deny that things had deteriorated at Taney— the nets kept getting torn down and the rims getting bent. It was all a racial thing. The largely Irish Catholic neighborhood didn't like the blacks invading "their park" although it was designated a "city park" open to everyone. They figured if they destroyed the baskets so no one could run full court, the blacks would stay away. But the players fought back by fixing the baskets, even buying and putting up new nets. The last few years you never knew the state the baskets would be in till you got there—it became part of the suspense of going to Taney. He thought of the neighborhood and clenched his teeth. He hated those bigots but loved their park, just because he'd played so many games there. So he blocked out the drug dealers that walked through the park and the smashed beer bottles and broken baskets because once something entered your permanent memory, you couldn't turn your back on it, could you?

Del was there shooting. Del was always there. His shirt was off; there wasn't a pound of fat on him. He had unusually sharp blue eyes too that seemed to see everything. He liked playing with or against him because Del tried so hard but wasn't quite as good as him. Besides himself, Del was one of the few white men who regularly came to Taney and he was liked and respected by the blacks. He had a menial job at Penn, something like a janitor—but he never complained

401

or acted embarrassed about it. The other odd thing was Del was gay, though he didn't act like it, much less flaunt it. At the same time he was open and completely unapologetic about it, which Gary found both mysterious and admirable for a basketball player. He always wondered how many of the black guys knew about Del. He knew that Del had once gotten into a fight with Barry, a tough black man with a very good physique and a big ego and that Barry had broken Del's jaw with a single punch. That was the only time Del hadn't been on the playground for a few weeks—while he was in the hospital recuperating—but as soon as his jaw healed he was back playing. It was Barry who stayed away for a while.

He was within talking distance now and knew Del had seen him but wouldn't say anything until he finished his jump shot. The ball went in, then Del turned his head a few degrees and nodded at him.

"Shot looks good," Gary said.

"Been working on the hitch in my delivery."

"Getting rid of it?"

"No, too late for that. Making it more fluid, know what I mean?"

"Sure. You been here long?"

"Half hour. Haven't seen you for a while."

"Been working. I'm on vacation now so I came here for a run. You staying?"

"No, I gotta go back to work in five minutes," Del said. "I'm on my lunch break."

Gary nodded, trying not to show his disappointment. Even just shooting with Del was soothing in a way. There was just the right amount of conversation. Half of it was about basketball—from players they knew at the park, to the N.B.A., but other times they talked about their relationships and he'd even told Del a few years back about his last serious girlfriend. Del also liked getting high and had turned him onto a pot dealer once—someone he still used.

After Del left, he took his ball out of the cloth bag he'd been carrying and shot for maybe twenty minutes—working on foul shots, his hook shot, his left hand, and his cross lane jumper. Then he'd sat on the wooden bench under a tree just behind the chainlink fence and rested, looking out every minute or so for players or for women who might be sunbathing. Every now and then a hooker might stroll through the park too. He repeated this pattern several times of shooting and resting until almost an hour and a half went by.

When the players arrived it was like a raid of soldiers. They came with basketballs and their talk and laughter from all directions. He took his ball and started shooting again so they could see his shot and couldn't ignore him. He was the only white person there and didn't know any of the players. Even a few years ago that wouldn't have happened—someone would have known him because he was playing four times a week then, but now his body couldn't take it, and he only played once a week at most.

It all happened so fast. After a few minutes of random shooting around, without any announcement, the players suddenly assembled just outside the three-point line. He was seventh in line and before he could shoot, two players made the shot and became captains. The good news was there were only 8 players to pick from so if no one else came in the next minute he'd get to play a full court five on five.

It was magical the way it worked out, especially since a half dozen new players arrived a few minutes after the game started. He realized that unless his team won, this would be his only game of the day because another team was already waiting to play.

Of course they underestimated him (this often happened the last few years) and put the slowest and shortest player on him defensively. But at least no one called him "veteran" or "old timer." The first time they passed to him he took his man into the low post and scored on a turn-around jump shot. He knew he had a step on him and could also shoot over him. It was a close game and he only got the ball a half dozen more times, making three more baskets the four times he shot. His team was ahead 13-11, in a game to sixteen, but froze him out at the end and lost 16-15.

As they were walking off the court Frankie, a tall black man who played center on his team, said to him, "We should have gone to you man, you had the match-up thing going . . . We should have gone to you." It was sweet music to hear and he played it over and over on his long walk home (he had left almost immediately, knowing he wouldn't get picked and not wanting to witness the injustice of it, the humiliation).

In his apartment he sat in his tub reviewing the shots he'd made; two drives, an outside shot, and the turn-around jumper that had given him his confidence. He reviewed them for a long time—it had been so vivid—until the beauty from it started to fade. Then he started to think about his hellish job and his woman situation—even worse—and the way his life was moving so fast like the game he'd just played, over almost before it began. He put some clothes on, swallowed a pill that he'd bought from the dealer Del had set him up with, and went out where it was already dark. It wasn't a difficult decision to make. He was too tired to walk so he took his car even though it was never easy to find parking spaces.

He was in a bar now in Center City. It was very dark and ornate. All the waiters and waitresses were dressed in black like vampires. There was gold on the tables and around the mirrors some form of gold that vampires probably liked. He was sitting down drinking at the gold and black bar talking to a woman in a black dress who had gold hair too. It was like the ending of *2001: A Space Odyssey* where the astronaut views himself passing through different phases of his life in a matter of seconds.

The next thing he knew he couldn't think anymore because the conversation with the woman required too much of his attention.

" 'Capish,' is that a foreign word? I don't know it," she said.

"It's Italian. It means 'do you understand?' "

"Are you Italian?" she asked. She had long fingers, which were a little disturbing, but overall was strangely appealing.

"No, but I've been in Europe a lot, especially Italy."

She raised her eyebrows and tilted her head in an odd way to show she was impressed. "My name is French, I think," she said.

"What is it?"

"Renee."

"Oh, oui oui. C'est Francais vraiment."

"Jeez, you know French too. What'd you just say?"

"Yes, your name is truly French."

"So what's yours?"

"Gary," he said, "my name is Gary."

"So are you really smart or something?"

"I do my best." He was trying to think of what college he should say he was from in case that was her next question.

"Are you a lawyer or a psychiatrist or something like that?"

"Something like that," he said, touching the tip of her nose for a second as if it were a baby's and making her smile. He thought his answer was probably too vague and decided on another one. "Actually, I only work occasionally at things I enjoy now, things that are philanthropic, that help people."

"How come?" she blurted.

"Because I'm in a financial position where I don't have to work full time anymore."

"Oh," she said, quickly straightening her hair and the next second reaching into her purse and withdrawing a hand mirror and lipstick. "So how come a smart, successful, good-looking guy like you is alone?"

"I could ask you the same question," he said, resting his free hand just above her knee. She looked a little flustered, and he thought again "shift the emphasis to *them*." It must have worked because she started talking while also letting his hand rest on her leg.

"This is the first time I've been out by myself in a long time," she said.

"Why's that?"

"I was with a guy for a couple of years. I thought we were gonna get married but it turned out he already was. You're not married, are you?"

"No, I'm definitely not married."

"But you like women, right?"

"I find they're a necessary evil," he said, laughing a little.

"I'm not evil."

"I hope not," he said, sliding his hand to her upper thigh and realizing then that he would score.

She laughed. He liked that she laughed a lot. It kept things light and entertaining.

He wished he'd drunk more. He was being overly careful, he knew that, but now he'd just have to wait till he got home to get high.

They were outside the bar walking towards his car in silence—just her heels against the sidewalk making a weird kind of music until she said, "Do you really think it's a good idea for me to get in your car?"

"Why not?"

"I'm pretty high."

Pretty high and pretty tall, he thought, figuring that she was almost as tall as he was, and in her heels about an inch taller. "I was thinking we both should drink more."

"No, no," she said, gesturing haphazardly with one of her long, surprisingly muscular arms. "I had too much already."

"Alright, here's my car," he said leaning her against the side door and kissing her with both hands on her face. He didn't like to do that, kiss someone by surprise—especially in public—but he felt he had to. It was as if she were demanding it in order to get inside the car.

"Wow," she said. "Did you learn to kiss in France too?"

He laughed and kissed her again, this time pressing against her and feeling her a little. She was getting hot quickly, actually moaning outside where anyone could walk by and hear her. He decided they should get in the car then, had to fish and fumble inside his pants pocket for a while to find the key next to his knife but then opened the door without asking her and helped her in. They continued making out immediately as if his opening the door and getting inside the car with her was merely a tiny interval between two kisses. She was making even more noise now. It was hard to tell in the half-dark but he thought her cheeks were turning red. When you were with a hot woman like that it was like being "in the zone" in basketball—you couldn't miss.

They continued kissing. She had her hands on his legs creeping up towards his crotch. He didn't like women to touch him there until he was ready (which created a kind of catch-22 situation, at times, he realized) but to his surprise, in spite of all the alcohol, he was erect.

"Let's go in back," she said.

"Why?"

"More room," she said, breathing heavily.

"I have a better idea. Let's go to my place," he said, putting his tongue inside her mouth, as if to answer for her.

"Where's that?" she finally said.

"Just a few minutes from here."

"Can't we just pull over some place and continue what we're doing?"

"We can get a drink there, we can get high. Don't you like to smoke? We can do that there too."

"I'm already high, seriously."

"Seriously," he said, laughing a little. "I really like you Renee."

"Then pull over some place and show me." In other words show her in the car why she should go inside his home.

He felt his heart race—feeling as much anger as excitement the way he was challenged, as if he were cut by a knife, which made him feel his own knife inside his pants pocket for a second. He told himself she was probably scared to go to his place—that it was one thing to make out or even have sex in a car and another to go to someone's home you'd only known for an hour. He drove a couple of blocks looking for the right kind of parking lot, then found a street with only one other car parked—the kind of side street that still occasionally existed in the city, pulled into a space and shut off the lights.

"Come on," he said, as he opened his door. But she waited till he came around the car and opened her door. "Let's get in back." He thought they'd make out for a little while, enough time to reassure her, and then she'd go to his place.

It was more cramped than he thought in the back seat because her body was so long. Still, he managed to get most of her down and began kissing her neck, and the tops of her (smaller than hoped for) breasts.

"Hey, slow down, will you?" she said.

"What?" he said. It was like another cut, and it stunned him for a moment.

"Can you just kiss me *slowly* for a while?"

He went slower, thinking that was women in a nutshell: *acting* so passionate and impulsive but then wanting it to be as slow as Chinese water torture and making sure to criticize you as much as they could get away with in the process. But he went along with it, even closing his eyes while they kissed. It was a strange feeling, like seeing dark inside dark as in a black Chinese box.

He opened his eyes as soon as he felt his erection fading and immediately stopped kissing her. At the same moment he thought he felt something strange, as if she had a tail somehow, near her bottom.

"Hey, don't stop now," she said. "What's the matter?"

"Jesus Christ," he hissed. "Are you a man?"

"What? Are you nuts?"

"Get out of the car."

"Are you crazy, calling me a man?"

"Just get out."

"I'm not getting out in the middle of nowhere."

"You *are* in the middle of nowhere and you *are* a goddamned man. I felt it."

"You *wish* I had a dick 'cause yours doesn't seem to be working."

"Get out! Get out!" he screamed, throwing her against the seat, then swinging at her face with his free hand but hitting the seat instead.

It was like the first time he was stung by a bee when he was a kid, the pain shocked him and for a moment he saw orange and was silent before he began to scream. It was like life had reversed itself and was suddenly upside down. Renee was trying to get out of the car but now he wanted to stop her, make her pay for this. He put his left (and weaker) arm around her waist but she slithered away like a snake. He reached out to grab her waist again but she elbowed him in the groin and he doubled over before he could get his knife.

He was screaming again as she ran out of the car leaving the door open. Then he suddenly stopped. He could feel the cool air as the world returned to black. His pain was manageable now and he could feel his other senses intensify. He could even hear the strange kind of music she made again while running in her heels across the parking lot.

He went into the front seat, opened the glove compartment and took out his handgun thinking that she wouldn't get far in her heels. He turned his lights on too, so he could see better, see something at all, then started to run after her, not even talking any more but just running after her as if any kind of speech, any kind of sound except the one his feet were making would slow him down. It was like the world had been reduced to speed alone, yet it wasn't that simple. It wasn't pure speed, it was more like hunting. He couldn't run in a straight line—it was too dark. It was more like chasing the dark in the dark, so he couldn't shoot either, couldn't risk hitting someone else who might be there—some sleeping vampire he didn't want to awaken or some stray zombie dreaming of a meal of dead flesh.

Then there was a flash—it might have been a pocket of orange exploding again, it might have been lightning—but he saw Renee running.

"Stop. Stop running," he hissed as if he were a snake talking. He raised his gun and fired into the dark but the running continued. He fired again until he realized that he was still running. Then he stopped and listened hard. A few seconds later he thought he heard someone running in the distance like an echo of the music he'd heard earlier—heels against cement. "Thank god," he thought. It was as if the world had reversed itself again, though he couldn't be sure it was Renee still running any more than he could now be certain that Renee was a man.

He was sitting in a bar again, this time at 8th and Market. Everyone around him was black. He'd reviewed the scene with Renee repeatedly like watching a video tape hundreds of times until he drank enough to finally get beyond it. People were watching him now, smiling at him—probably because of how much he'd drunk—but he was no longer worrying. He loved black people so why should he be worried? He was in the heart of Philly's hooker district and he wanted to

408

buy a woman to take home with him but given the shape he was in and the way the hookers looked, he was afraid to walk by his doorman (it was just his luck to have the one overly conscientious doorman in Center City!) so he'd probably have to spend the night with her in a nearby hotel.

Two or three had come in since he'd been here that he wouldn't have minded taking but he couldn't ask them in front of the black men in the bar who were watching him. How could he buy a black woman in front of a black man—though he was sure they'd seen it plenty of times. He thought he'd go out instead and get one on the street as soon as he finished his last drink. It was a much sounder plan.

He found a black hooker within a block of where he'd parked and she'd hustled inside his car as soon as he signaled to her.

"What're you doin'?" she said.

He had turned on the light inside the car and was staring at her.

"Why you checkin' me out? You already looked at me on the street. You already bought me mister—don't be changing your mind now."

"You wouldn't believe what happened to me earlier," he said, wondering if he would make sense when he spoke.

"Start the car mister, then tell me 'bout it. This ain't a good spot right here."

He shut off the light and drove slowly, for a few blocks. There were three or four hookers walking near his car, nearly colliding with his windshield like low-flying bats. He turned up a lightless alley and stopped, then turned the light on and looked at her again.

"Why you still lookin' me over? You already done that. You already made up your mind and bought me."

"Earlier tonight I was with a woman, at least I thought I was, and after we started fooling around I found out she was a man."

"So? What that got to do with me? You see my titties, they half out of my dress, ain't they? These ain't no man's titties," she said, cupping a hand under each of her breasts. "These are a woman's, see?" she said, finally taking them completely out of her bra and wiggling them in the air. Gary laughed. "O.K. you convinced me."

"You sure now?" she said, raising her eyebrows and looking at him seriously or mock seriously, he couldn't be sure which. "I don't want you tellin' me later I'm a man. I ain't no man but it gonna cost you to know that fo sure. What you wanna do with me mister?"

He saw a chipped front tooth now when he looked at her and then shut the light off.

"I want you for the night. I want to spend what's left of the night with you."

"That gonna cost you five hundred," she said, her voice wavering a little.

"Come on, don't bullshit me. You don't charge that much."

"You heard what I said."

"Anyway, that's way more than I can pay."

"What you got to pay?"

"Two hundred. There's only three or four hours of night left so you'll still be making fifty an hour," he said, feeling strangely proud of his logic and convinced now that he wasn't drunk at all.

"What you wanna do during those four hours?"

"Sleep mostly. Just sleep next to you."

"You wanna sleep next to mama?"

"I'm tired, really tired."

"O.K. I hear you. But after you wake up and see how nice I been, I hope you give me a little more 'for you leave."

"I will." He said, "What's your name? Mine's Gary."

"July."

"July?"

"Yah, you like it?"

"I love it."

"O.K. Gary. There's a place a couple of blocks from here."

"Is it safe?"

"Sure it's safe. You worry a lot, don't you?"

"How do I know it's safe?"

"I lay my ass those every night, so it must be pretty safe."

"So, it's your place?"

"Evidently," she said.

It was on a side street, a dark walk-up without a doorman but at least you needed a key to open the doors. July lived in one room with a queen-sized bed in the center, and not much else that he could see, not even a refrigerator or a desk. It was as if the bed were the whole purpose of the room. Certainly it received most of her attention with its red satin sheets and black pillows and its coverlet with a red heart in the middle. Facing the bed on a little stand of some kind was a small T.V.

"I'm glad you've got a nice bed," he said, taking off his shoes.

"I got a toilet, but if you wanna wash yourself you got to use the bathroom out in the hall."

"That's O.K."

"Hey, Gary 'for you lie down and get comfortable you wanna take care of me?"

"Sure, I was just going to," he said, reaching in his pants and withdrawing four fifties from his money clip. She took them, looking at them quickly but closely in the half-dark of the room (the only light coming from a red light bulb in a black floor lamp), then unzipped her boots and put them inside her boots in a kind of secret purse he hadn't noticed before.

"O.K., you lie down now if that's what you wanna do."

"What are you doing?"

"I'm gonna smoke me a number 'for I try to sleep. Wan' some?"

She turned her back to him and stood by the window while she smoked. She had a big bottom, visible behind her semi-transparent short skirt, and heavy thighs. She was probably the fattest prostitute he'd ever been with but she had a nice smile, and there was something about her that made him feel it would be safe to fall asleep with her.

Fear sneaked up and seized him like a Zombie with its hand around his throat. Maybe he shouldn't have smoked with July. Maybe what she gave him was cut with Angel Dust. He went out on the floor—it was like the bottom of a lake with strange fish and water snakes lying in wait—trying to find the lamp. Light was the first step, he tried to concentrate on it and forget about the water snakes on the lake floor.

When he finally found it and turned it on, the lake evaporated. The lamp was like a red god, silent but powerful enough to bring back the room in an instant. He stood up (not even aware that he'd been on his hands and knees while he was looking for the lamp) and saw her big bottom sticking up in the air. She was only wearing a thong and her enormous breasts (too flabby to be artificial) fanned out on either side of her. She was snoring too, every ten seconds or so. It was a mysterious sight, a mysterious presence and for what seemed like a long time he stared at and listened to her, wondering how her life allowed her to sleep like that.

Then he lay next to her, eventually even closed his eyes. But as soon as he closed them he saw an image of Renee's face when he first kissed her—saw her purple-streaked eyes just before they closed as she started moaning when they were outdoors. Then he remembered the way she slithered out of his car like a water moccasin, and the sound of her heels running on the parking lot like rattlesnake music.

He opened his eyes and began shaking July and when that did no good punched her (though not too hard) on her shoulder.

"What, what?" she said, turning on her side away from him.

"Get up, will you? Talk to me."

"What's the matter? Shit, I was sleeping."

"What's in the pot? Is it Angel Dust or just poison?"

"The weed? Shit, I didn't make you smoke it."

"I was seeing snakes and fish."

"Ain't none of either in this place, mister."

"Give me something to drink."

"You been drinkin' too much. That's why you're seein' things."

"No, no I need to pass out. I haven't been to sleep yet."

"You wanna grind for a while, that'll calm you down. See my titties, honey. Least you know I ain't no man."

"They're enormous," he said, glad to divert himself by staring at them. "Can I touch them?"

"You bought 'em, didn't you? You can do pull-ups with 'em if you want to."

He put his hands on them—they felt warm and comforting like putting on a pair of gloves in winter. She made a few soft moaning sounds though he wasn't trying to stimulate her. It was like a jukebox responding to a quarter.

"Why don't you grind with me for a while?"

He thought about it, but he couldn't feel himself, as if his dick had flown away like a bird to a distant island.

"I can't. I drank too much."

She laughed a little. "You got all kinds of problems, don't you. Shit."

"Just get me something to drink, I got some really bad stuff in my mind, and I need to pass out, O.K.? I'll pay you for it in the morning."

"Shit," she muttered as she stood up from the bed. "I got some whiskey. Ain't the best stuff in the world, but it'll knock you down. You gotta drink it warm though. I ain't going out to the hall, Gary. That's the only place where there's water, but I ain't goin out there."

412

"Sure, anything," he said. "I'll drink it straight."

"One more thing," she said, holding the bottle as she returned to him from across the room. "You feel like you're gonna heave go do it in the toilet over there," she said pointing in the dark. He pretended to look but even that pretend effort made him dizzy.

"Don't be puking on my bed, all right?"

Everything speeded up like the dam of his being could no longer hold back his words. It was broken, it was as if he could hear it break and the waterfall of words rushed forward no longer caring, simply needing to say themselves the way zombies simply need to move if only to feel themselves moving before they eat.

"That man/woman, I told you about, remember?"

"Sure I do."

"Something terrible happened."

"You sure you want to tell me this?"

He tried to think about what she was saying but the waterfall words kept on rushing through. "I might have killed her."

"Shit."

"She was running and I was chasing her in the dark and I shot a number of times. I don't know why I did it. I felt tricked but I shouldn't have shot at her."

"Where was you?"

"In a parking lot in the dark, as dark as this room so I couldn't be sure. I ordered her out of my car once I found out she was a man and at first he wouldn't leave and then he wanted to and I didn't want him to and that's when the chase began. But I couldn't see too well, could only see the actual body for a few seconds, maybe less. I was running and he was running, you listening?"

"Yeah, I'm listening."

"I was trying to see in the dark like a bat, but I couldn't. I'm not a bat, I'm not batman, you know what I'm saying? I could only go by the sound of his high heels on the ground. So I shot at a sound target, not even an image. And then I didn't hear the heels anymore and thought I'd hit him, that it was over but then I did hear something again. Not exactly the same sound but from a distance. It could have been Renee, it could have been someone else. I don't know. I'll never know. You understand? You listening? I've never killed anyone, I don't want to have killed him."

"You probably didn't. You heard the heels again, right?"

413

"Yah, but it sounded different."

"Course it did cause it was further away. Who else would it be? If someone else was there you woulda got your ass arrested."

"It was a miracle that no one else was there. A miracle." He started to shake.

"Where the gun now, Gary?"

"I got rid of it before I saw you. I got rid of it a long time ago."

"You ain't got no other do you?"

"Not with me, no."

"You ain't mad at me neither, right? I been nice to you, haven't I?"

"Yah, don't worry. I like you fine," he said with a little laugh. Then he thought of something else.

"You're not gonna tell anyone what I told you, are you?"

"Course not. I ain't dumb. I may be a whore but I ain't dumb."

"You sure?"

"Sure I'm sure. I don't blame you for what you did. You didn't want to have sex with no man. Shit—you didn't ask to be treated that way. You just relax about that. You want me to suck your dick now?"

"No, no. I'm too out of it. Just let me lie down on you, O.K.?"

"On my titties."

"Yes, they're warm," he said. "You don't think I killed anyone?"

"Course not. You would have heard it or seen it. You would've heard the body fall. You wouldn't have heard no heels neither."

He lay down then as if between two soft basketballs and felt he could sleep soon. That was the thing about basketball, you always knew if you made a basket or not. What kind of world was the rest of it when you couldn't even tell if you'd killed someone or not?

He closed his eyes. The videotape was finally gone. Instead he saw the playground coming into view as he was running towards it. Up ahead was Del shooting in the sunlight. Del turned and smiled at him and he looked at his eyes that were so beautiful—so wise and inviting—until he finally fell asleep.

Nominated by Josip Novakovich, Carolyn Alessio, Emily Fox Gordon, Susan Hahn, Floyd Skloot, Kevin Prufer, Ontario Review

THE ETERNAL IMMIGRANT

by SHARMILA VOORAKKARA

from NINTH LETTER

Some days, I find myself
just off the boat, bad English, no
papers,

and I think:
what New World is this?

The Old World limps along
with its epic bewilderments:

its toothless women
circle trashcans and spit;

its saintly winos
bless one doorway, then the next.

Here, the dervish
of a plastic bag or pigeon

is as close as one gets
to leaving.

~~~

I think of my father and his brothers,
kitted-up in their migrant disguises:

bellhop suit with epaulets,
headwaiter, dishwasher, cabbie,

who kept snakes in sock drawers,
and once, a meat-eating fish
in a black-lit tank.

It's the fish I recall best:
the whole of its exile spent
turning circles in glass,

each one narrower than the last—
forward and back, back and back,

to the mud-walls of the river
it remembered.
I know how a man can drown
on land, spend his life

in tiny, rented rooms,
and I   .

have gotten no further
than the alien that rows my blood.
In its little boat, it goes,

still immigrant, dumb
to the fast math, to the swindle
of fine print: beads, or magic beans

in lieu of cash. *America
is so beautiful country,
no?*

~~~

My uncle snapped off
slats of wood,

416

made a language,
stuttered, felt for.

Nailed together, make a boat,
make a

english:

America hard. America,
you alone. So no
body.

So am I heir
to the empty gaze
of legion deserters,

and such solitude as dreams up an ocean,
a zion, a fabled landfall
that eats the mind

and goads you faster, but no further
to a shore that never comes.

Nominated by Joan Connor

DAR HE

by R.T. SMITH

from PLOUGHSHARES

When I am the lone listener to the antiphony of crickets
and the two wild tribes of cicadas and let my mind
wander to its bogs, its sloughs where no endorphins fire,

I will think on occasion how all memory is longing
for the lost energies of innocence, and then one night—
whiskey and the Pleiades, itch from a wasp sting—

I realize it is nearly half a century since that nightmare
in Money, Mississippi, when Emmett Till was dragged
from his uncle Mose Wright's cabin by two strangers

because he might have wolf whistled at Carolyn Bryant,
a white woman from whom he had bought candy,
or maybe he just whispered "Bye," as the testimony

was confused and jangled by fear. The boy was not local,
and Chicago had taught him minor mischief, but what
he said hardly matters, and he never got to testify,

for the trial was for murder after his remains were dredged
from the Tallahatchie River, his smashed body with one
eye gouged out and a bullet in the brain and lashed

with barbed wire to a cotton gin fan whose vanes
might have seemed petals of some metal flower, had Bobo
—as friends at home called him—ever seen it. And why

this might matter to me tonight is that I was not yet eight
when the news hit and can remember my parents at dinner—
maybe glazed ham, probably hand-whipped potatoes,

iced tea sweeter than candy, as it was high summer—
shaking their heads in passing and saying it was a shame,
but the boy should have been smarter and known never

to step out of his place, especially that far South. Did I
even guess, did I ask how a word or stray note could give birth
to murder? He was fourteen, and on our flickering new TV

sober anchormen from Atlanta registered their shock,
while we ate our fine dinner and listened to details
from the trial in Summer, though later everyone learned

the crime occurred in Sunflower County, and snoopy
reporters from up north had also discovered that missing
witnesses—Too Tight Collins among them—could

finger the husband Roy Bryant and his stepbrother
named Milam as the men in the truck who asked, "Where
the boy done the talking?" and dragged Emmett Till

into the darkness. His mother, Mamie, without whom
it would have all passed in the usual secrecy, requested
an open-casket funeral, so the mourners all saw the body

maimed beyond recognition—his uncle had known
the boy only by a signet ring—and *Jet* magazine
then showed photos, working up the general rage

and indignation, so the trial was speedy, five days
with a white jury, which acquitted, the foreman
reporting that the state had not adequately established

the identity of the victim, and I don't know how
my father the Cop or his petite wife the Den Mother
took it all, though in their eighties they have no love

for any race darker than a tanned Caucasian. I need
a revelation to lift me from the misery of remembering,
as I get the stigma of such personal history twisted

into the itch of that wasp sting. Milam later told *Life*
he and Bryant were "guilty as sin," and there is some
relief in knowing their town shunned them and drove

Bryant out of business, but what keeps haunting me—
glass empty, the insect chorus fiercer, more shrill—
is the drama played out in my mind like a scene

from some reverse *To Kill a Mockingbird*—or worse,
a courtroom fiasco from a Faulkner novel—when
the prosecutor asked Mr. Wright if he could find

in the room the intruder who snatched his nephew
out of bed that night, and the old man—a great uncle,
really—fought back his sobs and pointed at the accused,

his finger like a pistol aimed for the heart. "Dar he,"
he said, and the syllables yet echo into this raw night
like a poem that won't be silenced, like the choir

of seventeen-year insects, their voices riddling strange
as sleigh bells through the summer air, the horrors
of injustice still simmering, and I now wonder what

that innocence I miss might have been made of—
smoke? rhinestones? gravied potatoes followed
by yellow cake and milk? Back then we called

the insect infestation *ferros*, thinking of Hebrew
captivity in Egypt and believing they were chanting
free us, instead of the *come hither* new science

420

insists on, but who can dismiss the thought
that forty-nine years back their ancestors dinned
a river of sound all night extending lament

to lamentation, and I am shaken by the thought
of how easy it is for me to sit here under sharp
stars which could mark in heaven the graves

of tortured boys and inhale the dregs of expensive
whiskey the color of a fox, how convenient
to admit where no light shows my safe face

that I have been less than innocent this entire
life and never gave a second thought to this:
even the window fan cooling my bedroom

stirs the air with *blades*, and how could anyone
in a civilized nation ever be condemned for
narrowing breath to melody between the teeth,

and if this is an exercise in sham shame I am
feeling, some wish for absolution, then I have to
understand the wave of nausea crossing me,

this conviction that it is not simple irony
making the whir of voices from the pine trees
now seem to be saying *Dar he, Dar he, Dar he.*

Nominated by Robert Wrigley

FORMATION

fiction by KIM CHINQUEE

from NOON

THE TECHNICAL INSTRUCTOR sang a cadence: *uu, oo, ee, our.* Little consonants were needed. The airmen had been in training for three days, and they could march, swing their arms, and turn when they heard a column right.

The tallest airman was the front and right of the formation. The shortest was the back and left. The others were between. They were all in order. They almost looked alike, except for their sizes.

There was Minnie, Ruby, Scarlet. Sara, Betsy, Janet. Jill and Kit and Penny. They were all there for some reason.

The instructor commanded them to halt. They did, but not in unison. It was like a football game, the wave, which a girl named Stacy knew about so well. Her brother was a Packer.

The instructor yelled for them to get it right.

Last night, in their beds they lay, the beds aligned in perfect rows. The blankets were green and the pillows were small and some pillows were wet. Some of the airmen had been crying. Some of them stared up at the walls, listening to the dripping of the sink, ready to jump up.

Now they stood in formation. Trying to act.

Nominated by Jean Thompson, Noon

SOME TERPSICHORE

fiction by ELIZABETH MCCRACKEN

from ZOETROPE: ALL-STORY

1.

THERE'S A SAW HANGING on the wall of my living room, a house key for a giant's pocket. It's been there a long time. "What's your saw for?" people ask, and I say, "It's not my saw. I never owned a saw."

"But what's it *for?*"

"Hanging," I answer.

By now if you took it down you'd see the ghost of the saw behind. Or—no, not the ghost, because the blue wallpaper would be dark where the saw had protected it from the sun. Ghosts are pale. So the room is the ghost. The saw is the only thing that's real.

These days, though it grieves me to say it, that sounds about right.

2.

Here's how I became a singer. Forty years ago I walked past the Washington Monument in Baltimore and thought, *I'll climb that.* It was first thing in the morning. They'd just opened up. As I climbed I sang with my eyes closed—"Summertime," I think it was. I kept my hand on the iron banister. My feet found the stairs. In my head I saw myself at a party, leaning on a piano, singing in front of a small audience. I climbed, I sang. I never could remember the words to "Summertime," largely because of a spoonerized version my friend Fred liked to sing—*Tummersime, and the ivin' is leazy / jifh are fumpin', and the hotten is cigh . . .*

Then a man's voice said, "Wow."

In my memory, he leans against the wall two steps from the top, shouldering a saw like a rifle. But of course he didn't bring his saw to the Washington Monument. He was a big-boned, raw-faced blond man with a smashed Parker House roll of a nose. His slacks were dark synthetic, snagged. His orange cardigan looked like it'd been used to scrub out pots then left to rust. A tiny felt hat hung off the back of his head. He was so big you wondered how he could have got up there—had the tower been built around him? Had he arrived in pieces and been assembled on the spot? "Wow," he said again, and clasped his hands in front of himself, bouncing on his knees with the syncopated jollification of a love-struck 1930s cartoon character. I expected to see querulous lines of excitement coming off his head, punctuated by exclamation marks. He plucked off his hat. His hair looked like it had been combed with a piece of buttered toast.

"That was you?" he asked.

I nodded. Maybe he was some municipal employee, charged with keeping the noise down.

"You sound like a saw," he said. His voice was soft. I thought he might be from the South, like me, though later I found out he just had one of those voices that picked up accents through static electricity. Really he was from Paterson, New Jersey.

"A saw?" I asked.

He nodded.

I put my hand to my throat. "I don't know what that means."

He held up his big hands, one still palming his hat. "*Beautiful*," he said. "Not of this earth. Come with me. I'll show you. Boy, you sure taught George Gershwin a lesson. Where do you sing?"

"Nowhere," I said.

I couldn't sing, according to my friends. The only person who'd ever said anything nice about my voice was my friend Fred Tibbets, who claimed that when I was drunk I sometimes managed to carry a tune. But we drank a lot in those days, and when I was drunk Fred was drunk, too, and sentimental. Still, I secretly believed I could sing. My only evidence was the pleasure singing brought me. Most common mistake in the world: believing that physical pleasure and virtue are in any way related, inversely or directly.

He shook his head. "No good," he said very seriously. "That's rotten. We'll change that." He went to take my hand and instead hung his hat upon it. Then I felt his hand squeeze mine through the felt.

424

"You'll sing for me, okay? Would you sing for me? You'll sing for me."
He led me back down the monument, the hat on my hand, his hand behind it. My wrist began to sweat but I didn't mind. "Of course you'll sing," he said. He went ahead of me but kept stopping, so I'd half tumble onto the point of his elbow. "I know people. I'm from New York. Well, I live there. I came to Baltimore because a buddy of mine, part of a trio, he broke his arm and needed a guitar player, so there you go. There are 228 steps on this thing. I read it on the plaque. Also I counted. God, you're a skinny girl, you're like *nothing*, you're so lovely, no, you are, don't disagree, I know what I'm talking about. Well, not all the time, but right now I do. I'll play you my saw. Not everyone appreciates it but you will. What's your name? Once more? Oof. We'll change that, have to, you need something short and to the point. Take me, I used to be Gabriel McClonna-hashem, there's a moniker, huh? Now I'm Gabe Mack. For you I don't know, let me think: Miss Porth. Because you're a chanteuse, that's why the Miss. And Porthkiss, I don't know. And Miss Kiss is just silly. Look at you blush! The human musical saw. There are all sorts of places you can sing, you don't know your own worth, that's your problem. I've known singers and I've known singers. I heard you and I thought, *There's a voice I could listen to for the rest of my life.* I'm not kidding. I don't kid about things like that. I don't kid about music. I was frozen to the spot. Look, still: goose bumps. You rescued me from the tower, Rapunzel: I climbed down on your voice. I'll talk to my friend Jake. I'll talk to this other guy I know. I have a feeling about you. I have a *feeling* about you. Are you getting as dizzy as me? Maybe it's not the stairs. Do you believe in love at first sight? That's not a line, it's a question. I do, of course I do, would I ask if I didn't? Because I believe in luck, that's why. We're almost at the bottom. Poor kid, you never even got to the top. Come on. For ten cents it's strictly an all-you-can-climb monument. We'll go back up. Come on. Come on."
"I can sing?" I asked him.
He looked at me. His eyes were green, with gears of darker green around the pupils.
"Trust me," he said.

I wasn't the sort of girl who'd climb a monument with a strange man. Or go back to his hotel room with him. Or agree to move to New York the next day.

But I did.

His room was on the top floor of the Elite Hotel, the kind of room you might check into to commit suicide: toilet down the hall, a sink in the corner of the room, a view of another building with windows exactly across from the Elite's windows.

"Musical saw," said Gabe Mack. He opened a cardboard suitcase that sat at the end of the single bed. First he took out a long item wrapped in a sheet—a violin bow. Then a piece of rosin.

"You hit it with that?" I asked.

"Hit it? What hit?" Gabe said.

"I thought—"

"Look," he said. The saw he'd hung in the closet with his shirts, an ordinary wood saw. I'd thought a musical saw would be a percussion instrument. A xylophone, maybe. A marimba. He rosined the bow and sat on a chair in the corner. The saw was just a regular wood saw. He clamped his feet on the end of it and then pulled the bow across the dull side of the blade. You could hardly see the saw, the handle snagged on one toe, his left hand folded over the bare end: he was a pile of man with a blade at the heart, a man doing violence to something with an unlikely weapon.

It was the voice of a beautiful toothache. It was the sound of every enchanted harp, flute, princess turned into a tree in every fairy tale ever written.

"I sound like that?" I said.

He nodded, kept playing.

I sound like that. It was humiliating, alarming, ugly, exciting. It was like looking at a flattering picture of yourself doing something you wished you hadn't been photographed doing. *That's me.* He was playing "Fly Me to the Moon."

He finished and looked at me with those Rube Goldberg eyes. "That's you," he said. He flexed the saw back and forth and then dropped it to the ground. I knelt to look at it and saw my garbled reflection in the metal.

I picked it up. "You don't take the points off?"

"Nope," he said. "This is my second saw. Here. Give me." I lifted it by the blade and he caught it through the honey-colored handle. "First one I bought was too good. Short, expensive. Wouldn't bend. You need something cheap and with a good length to it. Eight points to an inch, this one. Teeth, I mean." He flexed it. The metal made that backstage thunder noise I'd imagined when he'd first said I sounded like a saw. "This one, though. It's right." He flipped it around and caught it again between his brown shoes and drew the bow against it. He'd turned on just one light by the bed when we'd come into the hotel room. Now it was dark out. I listened to the saw while I watched the corner sink. A spider came to the edge, tapping one leg ahead like a blind man with a cane before clambering out, its shadow enormous. The saw sighed. Me too. He reached over to me with the bow. I flinched. The horsehair touched my shoulder, and he played me: I mean, he drew the bow across the cap sleeve of my shirt, then adjusted the angle and drew it across my collarbone.

"That's you," he said again.

Maybe I loved Gabe already. What's love at first sight but a bucket of something thrown over you that smoothes out all your previous self-loathing, so that you can see yourself slick and matted down and audacious and capable of nearly anything? Anyhow, I believed for the first time that I was capable of being loved. Or maybe I just loved the saw.

4.

We left for New York the next day. The story of our success, and it wasn't much success, is pretty boring, as all success is. A lot of waiting by the phone. A lot of bad talent nights. One great talent night, at which I won a box of dishes. Walking home that evening, Gabe carried the box and smashed the plates into the gutter one by one. "Don't do that," I said, "those are mine—"

He held one dish to my forehead, then lifted it up, then touched it down again, the way you do with a hammer to a nail before you drive it in.

Then he stroked my forehead with the plate edge.

"Don't tell me what to do," he said.

He wrote songs. Before I met him I had no idea of how anyone wrote a song. His apartment on Elizabeth Street smelled of burnt tomato sauce and had in the kitchen, in place of a stove, a piano that looked as though it had been through a house fire. Sometimes he played it. Sometimes he sat at it with his hands twitching over the keys like leashed dogs. "The Land Beyond the Land We Know." "A Pocketful of Pennies." "Your Second-Biggest Regret." "Keep Your Eyes Out for Me." He was such a sly mimic, such a sneaky thief, that people thought these were obscure standards, if such a thing exists, songs they'd heard many times long ago and were only now remembering. He wrote a song every day. He got mad that sometimes I couldn't keep them straight. "That's a Hanging Offense." "Don't You Care at All." "Till the End of Us."

We played them together. He bought me a green Grecian-draped dress that itched, and matching gloves that were too long, and lipstick, and false eyelashes—all haunted, especially the eyelashes. History is full of the sad stories of foolish women. What was terrible was that I was not foolish. Ask anyone. Ask Fred Tibbets, who lied and said I could sing.

We cut a record called *Miss Porth Sings!* For a long time you could still find it in bins in record shops under VOCALS or OTHER or NOVELTY. Me on the sleeve, my head tipped back. I wore red lipstick that made my complexion orange, and tiny saw-shaped earrings. My hair was cashew-colored. That was a fault of the printing. In real life, in those days, my hair was the color of sandpaper: diamond, garnet, ruby.

I was on the radio. I was on *The Gypsy Rose Lee Show*. Miss Porth, the Human Musical Saw! But the whole point was that Gabe's saw sounded human. Why be a human who only sounds like an inanimate object that sounds human?

6

In the world we were what we'd always been: two cripplingly shy, witheringly judgmental misfits who fell in love in private, away from the conversation and caution of other people, and then left town before anyone could warn us.

He began to throw things at me—silly, embarrassing, lighter-than-air things: a bowl full of egg whites I was about to whip for a soufflé, my brother's birthday card, the entire contents of a newly opened bottle of talcum powder. For days I left white fingerprints behind. Then he said it was an accident, he hadn't meant to throw it at all.

And then he began to threaten me with the saw. I don't think he could have explained it himself. He didn't drink, but he would seem drunk. The drunkenness, or whatever it was, moved his limbs. Picked up the saw. Brought it to my throat, and just held it there. He never moved the blade as he spoke to the terrible things he would do to himself.

"I'm going to kill myself," he said. "I will. Don't leave me. Tell me you won't."

I couldn't shake my head or speak, and so I tried to look at him with love. I couldn't stand the way he hated himself. I wanted to kill the person who made him feel this way. Our apartment was bright at the front, by the windows, and black and airless at the back, where the bed was, where we were then, lying on a quilt that looked like a classroom map: orange, blue, green, yellow.

"My life is over," said Gabe. His summer freckles were fading. He had the burnt-tomato smell of the whole apartment. "I'm old. I'm old. I'm talentless. I can see it, but you know, at the same time. I listen to the radio all day and I don't understand. Why will you break everyone's hearts the way you do? Why do you do it? You're crazy. Probably you're not capable of love. You need help. I will kill myself. I've thought about it ever since I was a little kid."

The saw blade took a bite of me, eight teeth per inch. Cheap steel, the kind that bent easily. I had my hands on the dull side. *How did we get here,* I wondered, but I'd had the same disoriented thought when I'd believed I'd fallen in love with him at first sight, lying in another bed: *How did this happen?*

"I could jump," he said. "What do you think I was doing up that tower when you found me? Windows were too small, I didn't realize. I'd gotten my nerve up. But then there you were, and you were so little. And your voice. And I guess I changed my mind. Will you say something? You've broken my heart. One of these days I'll kill myself."

I knew everything about him. He weighed exactly twice what I did, to the pound. He was ambitious and doubtful: he wanted to be famous, and he wanted no one to look at him, ever, which is probably the human condition: in him it was merely amplified. That was nearly

429

all I knew about him. Sometimes we still told the story of our life together to each other: Why had I climbed the tower *that* day? Why had he? He'd almost stayed in New York. I'd almost gone back home for the weekend, but then my Great-Aunt Marian died and my folks went to her funeral. If he'd been five minutes slower he wouldn't have caught me singing. If I'd been ten minutes later, I would have smiled at him as he left.

We were lucky, we told each other, blind pure luck.

7.

One night we were at our standing gig, at a cabaret called Maxie's. It hurt to sing, with the pearls sticking to the saw cuts. The owner was named Marco Bell. He loved me. Marco's face was so wrinkled, when he smoked you could see every line tense and then slacken.

> *There's a land beyond the land we know,*
> *Where time is green and men are slow.*
> *Follow me and soon you'll know,*
> *Blue happiness.*

My green dress was too big and I kept having to hitch it up. It hadn't been too big a month before. At the break, I sat down next to Marco. "How are you?" I asked.

"My heart is broken," he answered. He leaned into the hand with the cigarette. I thought he might light his pomaded hair on fire.

"I'm sorry," I said.

"*You* break it, Miss Porth. With your—" He waved at the spot where I'd been standing.

I laughed. "They're not all sad songs."

"Yes," he said. He had a great Russian head with bullying eyebrows. Three years earlier his wife had had a stroke, and sometimes she came into the club in a chevron-patterned dress, sitting in her wheelchair and patting the tabletop in time with the music or looking for something she'd put down there. "You're wrong. They are."

I said, "Sometimes I don't think I'm doing anyone any favors."

Then Gabe was behind me. He touched my shoulder lovingly. Listen: Don't tell me otherwise. It was not nice love, it was not good love, but you cannot tell me that it wasn't love. Love is not oxygen, though many songwriters will tell you that it is; it is not a chemical

430

substance that is either definitively present or absent; it cannot be re-
duced to its parts. It is not like a flower, or an animal, or anything
that you will ever be able to recognize when you see it. Love is food.
That's all. Neither better nor worse. Sometimes very good. Some-
times terrible. However to say—as people will—*That wasn't love.* As
though that would make you feel better! Well, it might have been un-
nourishing, but it sustained me for a while. Once I'd left I'd be as
bad as any reformed sinner, amazed at my old self, but even with the
blade against my neck, I loved him, his worries about the future, his
reliable black moods, his reliable affection—that was still there, too,
though sullied by remorse.

I stayed for the saw, too. Not the threat of it. I stayed because of
those minutes on stage when I could understand it. Gabe bent it
back and it called out. *Oh, no, honey, help.* It wanted comfort. It
wanted to comfort me. We were in trouble together, the two of us:
the honey-throated saw, the saw-voiced girl. *Help, help, we're still
alive*, the saw sang, though mostly its songs were just pronouns all
stuck together: *I, we, mine, you, you, we, mine.*

Yes, that's right. I was going to tell you about the saw.

Gabe touched my shoulder and said, "Let's go."

Marco said, "In a minute. Miss Porth, let's have a drink."

"Marya," said Gabe.

"I'd love one," I said.

Maxie's was a popular place—no sign on the front door, a private
joke. There was a crowd. Gabe punched me. He punched me in the
breast. A very strange place to take a punch, not the worst place. I
thought that as it happened: *Not the worst place to take a punch.* The
chairs at Maxie's had backs carved like bamboo. He punched me. I'd
never been punched before. He said, "See how it feels, when some-
one breaks your heart?" and I thought, *Yes, as it happens, I think
I do.*

I was on my back. Marco had his arms around Gabe's arms and
was whispering things in his ear. A crowd had formed. People were
touching me. I wanted them not to.

Here is what I want to tell you: I knew something was ending, and
I was grateful, and I missed it.

431

8

About five years ago in a restaurant near my apartment someone recognized me. "You're—are you Miss Porth?" he said. "You're Miss Porth." Man about my own age, tweed blazer, bald with a crinkly snub-nosed, puppyish face, the kind that always looks like it's about to sneeze. "I used to see you at Maxie's," he said. "All the time. Well, lots. I was in grad school at Penn. Miss Porth! Good god! I always wondered what happened to you!"

I was sitting at the bar, waiting for a friend, and I wanted to end the conversation before he arrived. The man took a bar stool next to me. We talked for a while about Philadelphia. He still lived there, he was just in town for a conference. He shook the ice in his emptied drink into his mouth, and I knew he was back there—not listening to me, exactly, just remembering who was at his elbow, and did she want another drink, and did he have enough money for another drink for both of them. All the good things he believed about himself then: by now he'd know whether he'd been right—and right or wrong, knowing was dull. I didn't like being his time-travel device.

"I have your album," he said. "I'm a fan. Seriously. It's my field, music. I—Some guy hit you," he said suddenly. His puppy face looked over-sneezish. "I can't remember. Was he a drunk? Some guy in love with you? That's right. A crazy."

"Random thing," I said. "What were you studying?"

"Folklore," he said absentmindedly. "I always wondered something about you. Can I ask something? Do you mind?"

Oh, I thought, *slide down that rabbit hole if you have to, just let go of my hem, don't take me with you.*

"I loved to hear you," he said. Puppy tilt to his head, too. "You were like nothing else. But I always wondered—I mean, you seem like an intelligent woman. I never spoke to you back then." One piece of ice clung to the bottom of his glass and he fished it out with his fingers. "Did you realize then that people were laughing at you?"

Then he said, "Oh my God."

"I'm sorry," he said.

"Not me," he said, "I swear, you were wonderful."

I turned to him. "Of course I knew," I said. "How could I miss it?"

The line between pride and a lack of it is thin and brittle and thrilling as new ice. Only when you're young are you able to skate out onto it, to not care which side you end up on. That was me. I was innocent. Later, when you're old, when you know things, well, it takes all sorts of effort, and ropes and pulleys, and all kinds of tricks, to keep you from crashing through, if you're even willing to risk it.

Though maybe I did know back then that some people didn't take me seriously. But still: maybe the first time they came to laugh. Not the second. I could hear the audience. I could hear how still they were when I sang with my eyes closed. Oh, maybe some of them thought, *Who does she think she's fooling? Who does she think she is, with that old green gown, with those made-up songs?* But then they'd listen. It was those people, I think, the ones who thought at first they were above me, who got the wind knocked out of them. Who brought their friends the next week. Who bought my records. Who thought: *Me. No more, no less, she's fooling me.*

Later I got a letter asking for the right to put two songs from *Miss Porth Sings!* on a record called *Songs from Mars: Eccentrics and Their Music*. The note read "Do you know what happened to G. Mack? I need his permission too."

9.

The night he punched me, I went home with Gabe for the last time. "Of course don't call the police," I told Marco. Gabe was exhausted, repentant. I led him to the bed, to the faded quilt, and he fell asleep. From the kitchen I called his sister in Paterson, whom I never met, and told her Gabe Mack was in trouble and alone and needed help. Then I climbed into bed next to him. Gabe had an archipelago of moles on his neck I'd never noticed, and a few faint acne scars on his nose. His eyebrows were knit in dreamy thought. I loved that nose. He hated it. "Do I really look like that?" he'd ask, seeing a picture of himself. He'd cover his nose with his hand.

I didn't know what would become of him. I had to quit caring. It wasn't love and it wasn't the saw and it wasn't a fear of being alone that kept me there: it was wanting to know the end of the story, and wanting the end to be happy.

At 5:00 AM I left with a small bag, the saw, bamboo-patterned bruises on my back, and a fist-shaped bruise on my left breast. Soon enough I was amazed at how little I cared for him. Maybe that was worse than anything.

10.

Still, no matter what, I can't shake my first impression. Even now, miles and years away, the saw in my living room to remind me, when I think of Gabe, I see a 1930s animated character: the black pie-cut eyes; white gloved hands held flat against the background; dark long limbs, without elbows or knees, that do not bend but undulate. The cheap jazzy glorious music that, despite your better self, puts you in a good mood. Fills you with cheap, jazzy hope. And it seems you're making big strides across the country on your spring-operated limbs, in your spring-loaded open car, in your jazzy pneumatic existence. You don't even notice that behind you, over and over in the same order, is the same tree, shack, street corner, mouse hole, table set for dinner, blown-back curtains.

Nominated by Zoetrope, Joyce Carol Oates, Valerie Sayers, Zoetrope

LAMENT FOR A STONE

by W.S. MERWIN

from THE YALE REVIEW

The bay where I found you faced the long light
of the west glowing under the cold sky

there Columba as the story goes looked
back and could not see Ireland any more

therefore he could stay he made up his mind
in that slur of the sea on the shingle

shaped in a fan around the broad crescent
formed all of green pebbles found nowhere else

flecked with red held in blue depths and polished
smooth as water by rolling like water

along each other rocking as they were
rocking at his feet it is said that they

are proof against drowning and I saw you
had the shape of the long heart of a bird

and when I took you in my palm we flew
through the years hearing them rush under us

where have you flown now leaving me to hear
that sound alone without you in my hand

Nominated by Tony Quagliano

GASSED

by STEVE GEHRKE

from MICHIGAN QUARTERLY REVIEW

after John Singer Sargent

They might as well be walking toward a firing squad, blind-
folded, single file, a guide wire strung between them, each man
a wounded Theseus crawling back up from the underworld,

though this thread leads only to the infirmary, where the gas
will shut their bodies down, will move between the bodies' rooms
and snuff each lantern out. The dying grasp at their pant-legs

as they pass, as they wobble along the duckboards just above
the mud gasping at their feet, the steaming trash heaps
of the dead, the battlefield sloppy as a butcher's floor, all blood

and aftermath, the dusk-glint of God turning to put his knives
away. Looking out through the insect eyes of his mask,
fatigued, Sargent can't quite believe he's not imagined them,

called them up from the foxholes of a torched and rubbled mind,
a mind battered by three weeks at the front, burrowed into itself
and paranoid. At home, he worked slowly, sitting for days

with his models, spoonfuls of pigment tapped onto the scales,
working the empathetic muscles until he could roll the stone
of each face away. He painted through the nights when the black-

out curtains fell, Paris, light-starved and feverish with sirens,
the newsstands charred, the smoldering grill-pits of bombed-
out cars, the city blown back, in scraps, through his memory.

Now when a flock of poisoned birds begins to fall,
one by one, into No Man's Land, like descending souls,
he sees them as cathedral stones, Saint Gervais collapsing

again with his niece inside, Sargent, astonished, absorbed,
but not quite there, brushing the air-borne plaster from his coat
like snow, watching the wheelbarrows teeter under the rubble-

weight, the stretchers hauling off the faithful dead, one man
mouthing, for eternity, a final hymnal note, and the girl's face
erased but everywhere, in the rag-pile of the church, reflected

in the cobblestone, his mind, in pain, unable to see her death
except in metaphor. Even here, where the bodies are given
a brief skeletal radiance in the shell light, as if he really might see

into them, he edits the horror out, no vomit, no severed limbs,
the faces a touch too bright, each man with his hand
on the shoulder of the one in front of him, like elephants

hooked snout to tail, the men washed and strung along
the line, as if he might make our soiled history clean again.
Or is it just another drop of poison stirred into the wine,

he thinks, a way to make the wretched tolerable? What else
could he do, an old man who knew by now this war
would be the end of him, who knew even if he could paint

the blistered, naked bodies, the shit streaking down the inside
of a man's thigh as he walks, the white angel-maggots burrowing
into a face, his mind, at its core, could not help making things

beautiful. With the night turning purple as the gas disperses
through the atmosphere, Sargent works with his mask slung
across his shoulder like an extra face, letting his inspiration

filter all doubts away as he sutures the men back together
with a pencil tip, as he feels them moving through his thoughts
like a line of text, written a century later by a man

with a book of paintings open on his desk, who sits and watches
the rain fall into the empty flowerpots outside his window,
which he can't help seeing as the upturned helmets of the dead.

Nominated by Sherod Santos, John Allman, Dan Masterson

ESCAPE FROM HOG HEAVEN

by DINA BEN-LEV

from FIVE POINTS

DURING THE SUMMER OF 1978, New York City garbage bags leaked and oozed in front of every building. The waist-high trash blocked access to the parked cars, and dogs were forced to urinate and worse against the stench-filled bags. After coming in from outside, I needed a few minutes of lying prone on the couch to regain a regular breathing pattern. One evening my parents suggested that I might benefit from a couple of months out of Manhattan. As the son and daughter of poor immigrants, they'd never had the chance to escape the odoriferous city heat. Perhaps, they said, I should breathe in fresh air, see some nature, and possibly learn French.

My high school required that I take several years of either French or Spanish. At thirteen I'd just finished my first year of French, and I'd barely squeaked by—my New York accent kept the teacher continually shaking his head. It was gibberish to me, and I kept failing the listening part of our exams. A friend of the family had suggested a program called "The Experiment in International Living," and we excitedly filled out the application.

The concept was that for a fee a teenager could be sent to spend the summer with a family in a foreign country. As I was only thirteen, I wasn't considered mature enough for France or Switzerland or any of the more exotic options. I was eligible for a rural town in Quebec.

There were fifteen of us and a program director arranged our living situations. I was to live with a family who owned a pork farm. They fattened up a little over a thousand pigs, eventually selling them to a rendering plant that turned them into neatly-sliced Canadian bacon. The family, consisting of Monsieur and Madame LeDuque, their three daughters, aged eight, ten, and seventeen, and a son, fifteen, knew not a word of English. I would be forced to speak French.

When I heard there would be a fifteen-year-old son, I began daydreaming about the love affair that would ensue. We would use our hands to say all that we couldn't manage with words. When I arrived and saw that Pierre was a skulking sort of fellow with mud in his hair and a permanent sneer, I let that daydream drop to my feet.

The daughters seemed happy enough to see me, and the parents, clearly up to their elbows in the tasks that keep a large farm running, tried to be solicitous and polite. I carried my pocket dictionary with me everywhere. I would point and one of the girls would tell me the word in French. I did a great deal of pointing, but *Couchon*—pig, was by far the most spoken word that summer.

It became clear to me by day two that this family, in allowing me to join them, expected great labor on my part. I didn't disappoint them. Pigs that weigh around seven hundred pounds will produce prodigious amounts of fecal matter. Day after day the trampled turds oozed up and covered the ill-fitting work boots the family had lent me. I hated tying those crap-splattered laces each morning.

Raking out and spraying down the pigpens wasn't difficult, but it took time and effort. Even the New York City garbage strikes hadn't quite prepared me for these overwhelming odors. Afterwards, we filled the troughs with grain, cakes, and pies. The LeDuque family had a deal with the nearby Vachon Factory, a Little Debbie kind of establishment, to buy up all the returned or stale baked goods. It was a tedious effort, tearing open hundreds of little snack-sized packages of cupcakes and pies. I felt like a host at a birthday party for the phenomenally pushy and obese.

The two younger girls and I would wake up just before sunrise and work in the pigpens until lunch time. We washed our hands, of course, but ate our enormous hot meals wearing our splattered and smelly outfits. Our crap-caked shoes waited on a mat in the garage.

Lunch was the main meal of the day. We drank pitchers of fresh milk Madame LeDuque had just retrieved from one of the several cows. It was warm, but deliciously thick and frothy like a vanilla shake. We gobbled down slabs of ham and sausages. An assortment of fresh pies and cookies always awaited us for dessert.

In the afternoons the girls and I did laundry, peeled potatoes, picked vegetables from the garden, and acted as beer and coffee fetchers for Monsieur LeDuque, his son, and several young men who were building a new barn on the far side of the property.

In the evenings the parents and the two older siblings sat around smoking cigarettes and drinking Molson Golden Ale. An old television set was tucked away in a corner of the living room, but they rarely turned it on because only one station came in, and it was in English. Mostly evenings were filled with card games and Elvis' greatest hits, the only record they played that entire summer.

The most striking thing was the fact that there were no books in the house, not even school texts, which they must've borrowed during the year and returned at the end of the term. The only book I ever saw was a little red Bible on the coffee table in the living room, but it was so yellowed, I was afraid to touch it, certain that it would crumble in my hands. And maybe it would have, for I never saw anybody attempt to pick it up.

Aside from my pocket-sized *Cassell's*, I'd brought only two books with me, assuming that all my free moments would be spent chatting happily in French. Well, during my month with the LeDuques, I read *Picture of Dorian Gray* and *The Good Earth*, three times each. When you spend all day working until the veins in your arms ache, apparently you don't feel like talking. You feel like sitting and looking into space or playing a hand of cards. Still, I was learning French at a furious pace, even if it was a Quebeçois dialect.

After a month I had begun to dream in French, and I lost that heavy New York City intonation. In all respects, the "Experiment in International Living" seemed to be a success. I hadn't made life-long friends, but the girls and I spent time amiably side by side. I'd conquered my fear of French and gained an appreciation for the physically consuming life of a farmer. In fact, up until my last week with the LeDuque family, there'd been only one thing that had, well, made my stomach do flip-flops: their attitude towards death.

When you have a large farm with over a thousand animals, it's inevitable that some will die. Piglets were sometimes born malformed, chickens fell ill, and Monsieur LeDuque routinely drowned litters of kittens as there were more than enough cats around the property.

But for some reason the dead animals weren't buried. Maybe that would've been too time-consuming, or they thought bacteria would leach into the shallow ground water; I'm not sure. Instead, feathered, furry, and pink-colored corpses were piled up on top of each other where they rotted in the sun. Every few days new corpses were added to the pile. The smell of decomposing flesh is like no other in the world; it makes the most vomitive fecal odors seem palatable. It pushes you to the darkest dungeon of your mind. It pulls at the trap door of your throat. God forbid, if you had even one screw loose and were forced to stand in the breeze of rotting corpses, you might seriously try to tear off your nose.

The pile of dead animals was about four feet high and about three hundred feet from the house, which was way too close, if you asked me, but nobody did, and I learned to hold my breath and walk by with my hands over my ears. The buzzing of what sounded like a billion-some flies was more than I could bear.

I was also poorly prepared for the way human deaths were discussed. On the two occasions we visited some neighbors, photo albums of the deceased and their funerals were brought out for me to see. One family had a white satin album that covered their son's fatal motorcycle accident—pictures of the bloody scene, the boy's broken body. A leg had been severed and was lying in a bloody pool twenty feet from the bike. The mother slowly turned the pages, to make sure I didn't miss anything.

There were pictures of the funeral, the open casket, and finally, pictures of her son's gravestone. Although it must have been incredibly painful for this mother to be reliving this event, especially with a stranger, she chatted happily with Madame LeDuque while I did the best I could to mask my horror. Later, another neighbor showed me an identical album, this time of her son's car accident. The pictures from the accident scene were no less gruesome than those I'd viewed previously. I'd told both mothers how sorry I was, and both had answered that their sons were "better off up there with God." The LeDuque family explained that it was customary to have Death Albums; they were a tribute to the deceased.

If the two popes hadn't died that summer, one right after the other, I don't think we would've gone to church. As it was, one Sunday Madame LeDuque handed me one of her skirts and told me we were going to visit the basilica Sainte-Anne-de-Beaupré. I welcomed a change in the routine. Monsieur LeDuque had unveiled and washed a raspberry-colored Cadillac. Up till that point, I had only seen their muddy, sputtering old truck. We were certainly on our way to something special.

In a vague way I knew the family was religious. There were crucifixes nailed in corners all over the house. Sometimes Madame LeDuque would cross herself as she passed one of these, but that was the extent of the family's religious practice as far as I saw.

Madame LeDuque and the two older daughters cried during the newscast about the first pope's death, and they had looked at me and said, "*C'est triste, c'est triste, non?*"

Oh yes, I assured them, being the diplomat, so very, very sad. For days the TV was kept on, and each evening the family continued to watch those crowds of mourners at the Vatican, crying under umbrellas. Given their belief, I couldn't figure out why everyone was so devastated; didn't they think that a pope would be sitting up in heaven's version of a La-Z-Boy, bathed in the happy glow of God?

I went back to reading *The Good Earth* with its starving Chinese peasants. I wondered whether Pearl S. Buck made herself ravenous, writing about those who were grateful to suck on strands of grass.

But here we were, all of us bathed and wearing our so-called Sunday best. Raised an atheist Jew, I'd never been inside a church before. Since there were only two hundred people living in that region and the nearest general store, a mom-and-pop kind of establishment, was a half hour away, I expected to see a small, frail wooden structure, one like I'd seen in a documentary.

When we pulled into the parking lot, I was completely unprepared for the breathtaking stone cathedral that stood before me. Twin spires soared several hundred feet into the sky.

On entering the building, the LeDuques dabbed themselves with water from a wide stone bowl. I followed suit. The church could easily have seated three thousand people, but there were only about a hundred of us. There was kneeling, some silent praying with eyes closed, and then the service began. Several men wore long robes, and one spoke into a microphone—in Latin. We listened for what seemed like an eternity, not understanding, kneeling, standing, sitting, and waiting for it to end.

Then we rose and did something I later learned was called communion. That was where my trouble started. I drank my wine and chewed my cracker as soon as it was given to me. I didn't know I was supposed to wait for some kind of signal in order that we could all do it together. Glares came from several members of the family. Apparently, you were supposed to let the wafer sit on your tongue for a while, and loudly crunching it between your teeth was bad form.

When we got home, Madame questioned me. "Do you go to church at home?" she asked as we set the table for lunch.

"No," I stated matter-of-factly. "Today was my first time."

Madame and Monsieur looked at each other.

"Your parents don't go to church?" she asked.

The three daughters and the scowling son were silent, awaiting my answer.

"No, we're Jewish," I said. I might've have said "non-practicing Jews," but that was too much of a leap for my limited French. When I said the word *Jewish*, all eyes fixed upon me like I'd just coughed up a cup of phlegm.

Immediately, Monsieur rushed out of the room with his son. The three girls continued to stare at me in a state of disbelief while Madame questioned me further.

"What about your nose?" she asked. "You had an operation to change it?"

"No," I said.

"Jews have big noses. You fixed yours so you could fool people, so they couldn't tell?"

I began laughing. She couldn't be serious.

"Not all Jews have big noses," I said. "None of my Jewish relatives do." I thought that would be the end of the discussion. These farmers didn't read books, and they never met Jews or anyone other than the two hundred folks who lived in their town. I wouldn't judge them for thinking all Jews fit a physical stereotype. After all, I'd assumed they belonged to a little, rickety run-down church, not a glorious architectural wonder. I certainly didn't think of complicating matters by telling them I was adopted. At that time I assumed (as it turned out half-correctly) that I came from Jewish stock.

But this wasn't the end of the questioning; the interrogation had just begun. The eight-year-old daughter, Lisette, started sobbing and ran from the room. I was left with Madame and the two older daughters.

"So where's the money?" Madame asked.

"What money?" Now I was confused.

"The money you stole from us!" She hissed, her face trembling

445

and red. Monsieur and Pierre came back into the kitchen. They spoke to Madame at a break-neck speed. I didn't catch many of the words. However, I heard the word *voleur*, "thief," several times.

Madame turned back to me. "Money's been missing from our room—now we know you stole it!"

I'd only been in their bedroom the first day I'd arrived, as part of the tour of their home. Since there'd been no place to spend money while on the farm, my hundred dollars' worth of American Express traveler's checks remained neatly tucked away in their paper envelope. I told them the truth. "I didn't steal any money," I said. "And I don't know what you're talking about."

"Jews *always* steal money!" Monsieur growled.

Madame grabbed me by the arm and pulled me up the flight of stairs to the room I shared with her daughters. She dragged my suitcase out from under the bed and yelled at me to open it.

The son and daughters came in and stood in the doorway.

"You open it!" I cried. The accusation, the simple hatred in their eyes, the boredom and frustration I'd talked myself out of on a daily basis all welled up in me, and suddenly tears began slipping down my cheeks.

"Open it!" I yelled. "I don't have your money!"

Madame dumped my clothes on the floor. Monsieur kneeled and pawed through them. He opened the envelope with my traveler's checks and threw them down.

They looked up at me, confused.

Madame spoke next, yelling something I didn't quite understand. "*Dis-moi, où as-tu caché tes cornes?*"

"Tell me," she had said. "Where have you hidden your . . ."

"*Cornes?*" I wondered. What are "*cornes?*" I knew she didn't think I'd stolen corn. I knew the word was plural. I searched my mind and came up blank. Apparently, that word hadn't been pointed to during the past month.

I told Madame I had to check my dictionary. I flipped quickly through the pages. There it was, "*Cornes*" translated as "horns." Where had I hidden my horns? My mind raced—horns? Why would I hide horns?

And then it hit me, and I held my hands up to my head, like make-believe antlers.

Instantly, the lot of them stepped back. Madame began praying under her breath. Now it was clear, this family truly believed I was a devil, that all Jews were devils, and as such, I would, by right, have a pair of horns.

I wanted to laugh. Nothing in my New York City upbringing had prepared me for this. I'd run from muggers, flashers, sounds of gunshots, but here was an entire family stepping back in fear of a thirteen-year-old me!

I spoke in English for the first time that summer. I told them they could all go to hell with their pigs and cigarettes and stupid pile of corpses. I'm sure my unfamiliar English sounded like the devil's own language.

They stared at me with hatred, and I stared back with anger. We were at a stand-off.

I began to wonder just how one supposedly dealt with a devil. Was Monsieur ready to club me with a crucifix? Would I be photographed for a so-called satanic death album?

"Please call the Program Director," I hastened to say in French.

And that's what Madame did. As she went into the hall to dial the phone, I ran past the rest of the family, down the stairs, and out of the house. I proceeded to run down the dirt road, hoping I could get to the next neighbor's house where I could wait until I was driven away from this nightmare.

I hadn't run more than a quarter mile before Monsieur drove up in his battered truck.

"Get in!" he yelled.

"Screw yourself!" I answered in English. I kept running, but eventually he got out of the truck, held my arms behind me, prisoner-style, pushed me inside, and drove me back to the house.

I sat sullenly on a plastic lawn chair for two hours until Shelly, the Program Director, arrived.

Madame had packed my suitcase for me. Shelly, the Program Director who'd assigned me to this family, was a Jewish woman in her late twenties. Soon after we'd met, she'd confessed that she was still recovering from a breast-reduction job. "Back-breaking boobs are a Jewish woman's burden," she had said, obviously not looking at me.

I have no idea what transpired between Shelly and the LeDuque family, and I didn't care. When she and I drove off in her Volkswagen bug, I took my last glance at that farm, at the enormous barn where the pigs were happily resting, having snorted down cakes and pies, and I, who had yet to believe in God, silently thanked the heavens for saving me.

I don't remember anything else that happened that summer. I know my parents shook their heads when I told them the story. My dad said something about the "idiocy of the countryside" and that civilization outside of New York City was iffy at best.

Back at school, I began getting A's in French, and the language would follow me to college and then to universities where, in order to earn advanced degrees, I had penciled in irrefutable answers to prove proficiency. So French and I were clapped together from time to time like ambivalent relatives waiting for the occasion to end. And as I sit here typing, I know how ludicrous it is to blame an entire language for the bad aftertaste of one unfortunate summer. I have long ago forgiven the LeDuques, but I may never forget those French words accusing me of hiding my horns.

What I also remember are some of the last words my grandmother said before her heart gave out. She sat me down on her bed in Brighton Beach and handed me yellowed pictures of friends and relatives who'd been incinerated in the ovens of World War II. She said, "Sometimes when I'm walking up to the subway and the wind blows a little soot in my mouth, I think I can taste them."

Nominated by Five Points

FIGHT

fiction by MICHAEL CZYZNIEJEWSKI

from NEW ORLEANS REVIEW

IN THE END, it was animals fighting that turned us on. S&M had run its course, swinging and swapping a step down from there; combining the two harvested few responses to our personal ad. The kids kept us from divorcing, but even their feelings were wearing thin: neither was very good in school, or at sports.

When the squirrel snuck through the doggie door and dropped gloves with Ichiro, our three-legged Siamese, we called the babysitter and checked into the Comfort Suites by the airport. We talked a lot beforehand, too, mostly about Ichiro's comeback victory, then invoked the missionary position for the first time since the first time. We stayed two nights, turning down maid service, not even bothering to eat.

The woman at the shelter looked at us with suspicion, but the trapper from up north asked no questions. Raccoons, we soon found out, were more than a match for any dog, and opossum, despite our predictions, fought better during the day, except against foxes. Foxes had the most fight in them, that was clear. Once, when the babysitter bailed, we rented that cartoon where the mongoose battles the cobras, but felt guilty when the kids wanted to watch with us. That, we quickly agreed, held no interest whatsoever.

Like the rough stuff and the orgies, one species duking it out with another lost its luster. The combinations became less imaginative, a collie versus an Airedale, a mouse versus a shrew. Even the trapper from up north stopped returning our calls. Our last gasp pitted a gerbil against a hamster, but to tell you the truth, going in, we didn't know which was which. Expectations were at an all-time low.

What happened next, though, reignited the flame, at least for a day. Instead of tearing at each other's flesh, the gerbil initiated what would be called, by any witness, sexual assault. The hamster, a miniature Cowardly Lion, ran for the safety of the wheel, but relented, we hypothesized, just to get it over with. Later, we wondered if the hamster was female and the gerbil male, or vice versa, and what would become of this union. The possibilities were endless. We moved closer and grasped hands, squeezing tight, fighting off the rolling eyes of the kids who, when they were old enough, would, if they were lucky, one day understand.

Nominated by New Orleans Review, Jean Thompson

SPARROW TRAPPED IN THE AIRPORT

by AVERILL CURDY

from POETRY

Never the bark and abalone mask
cracked by storms of a mastering god,
never the gods' favored glamour, never
the pelagic messenger bearing orchards
in its beak, never allegory, not wisdom
or valor or cunning, much less hunger
demanding vigilance, industry, invention,
or the instinct to claim some small rise
above the plain and from there to assert
the song of another day ending;
lentil brown, uncounted, overlooked
in the clamorous public of the flock
so unlikely to be noticed here by arrivals,
faces shining with oils of their many miles,
where it hops and scratches below
the baggage carousel and lights too high,
too bright for any real illumination,
looking more like a fumbled punch line
than a stowaway whose revelation
recalls how lightly we once traveled.

Nominated by Reginald Gibbons, Edward Hirsch, Poetry

CHART

by KAY RYAN

from THREEPENNY REVIEW

There is a big
figure, your age,
crawling, then
standing, now
beginning to bend
as he crosses
the stage. Or
she. A blurred
and generalized
projection of you
and me. For a
long time it seems
as remote
from the self
as the ape chart
where they rise up
and walk into man.
And then it seems
the realer part.

Nominated by Joshua Mehigan, Jane Hirshfield

SHELTER

fiction by NAMI MUN

from WITNESS

I'D BEEN AT THE SHELTER for two weeks and there was nothing to do but go to counseling or lie on my cot and count the rows of empty cots nailed to the floor or watch TV in the rec room where the girls sat cornrowing each other's hair and went on about how they'd like to pull a date with Reggie the counselor because he looked like Billy Dee Williams and had a rump roast ass. I didn't see a way to join in but I didn't feel like being alone either. It was cold. Outside the lobby doors the thick snow falling made it hard to see the diner across the street. The walls in this place were too bright, too lit up in a peppermint light. I wandered down the long green hallway, walked past the cafeteria and the nurse's station without saying hi to anyone, and looked for Knowledge.

I liked Knowledge. She stood up for me my first night—whacked a huge girl named Kecia with a dinner tray across her face, then sat right down on top of her. With a hand choking Kecia's neck, Knowledge told her to give back the sneakers to their rightful owner. Actually I hated those sneakers, was glad when Kecia took them so the counselors could give me a new pair, but that really wasn't the point. Nobody's ever stuck up for me before.

I saw her at the end of the hall, jumping rope.

"OK, how about this," she said, as I walked up. "What if I was to pull off something incredible, something that'll change our lives forever but I needed your help. You gonna be there?" The rope buzzed over her face as her eyes focused on some point down the hallway.

"Depends, I guess." I hopped an imaginary hopscotch. "You want to go play cards?"

"*Depends?* On what?" She stopped jumping. The white beads in her hair stopped jumping too. Clenching the rope she said, "You either trust me or you don't. We're either partners or we ain't, and believe me, you can't make it on the street without a partner covering your flat ass." She yanked up her gloves, which were really tube socks with ten finger holes. "So. You'd watch my back or what?"

"If I say OK, can we go play cards?"

"Good. That's what I'm talking about. Here, take this."

I took the rope from her and she dropped to the floor. Between each push-up, she bubbled her cheeks and exhaled real loud. "Gotta get in shape so we can bust out tonight," she said. I coiled the rope around my wrist to make an African tribal bracelet. I didn't know what she was talking about, and plus, the shelter doors were always open—we could leave whenever we wanted. Over the speakers, dinner was being announced.

"C'mon. Let's go," I said. "I'll let you teach me blackjack."

"At a time like this?" She shot up and began running fast in place, slowing down only to deliver uppercuts. "You have *got* to be out of your mind."

My mom turned crazy the night my dad left us for good. I was ten then, it was winter. As soon as his car turned the corner she ordered me to grab all his things and pile them in our yard. Like his socks, underwear, toothbrush, the basement TV, his leather Bible, the briefcase I'd gotten him for his birthday which he never used, pictures of him, pictures of him and me, his half-empty jar of Sanka. While I made runs back and forth into the house my mom lay flat on the dead grass, the moon shining down on her tears and the small pile of Dad I'd created next to her. "What do you think God does to people like you?" she rolled over and asked the grass. And then, "I'm so close to empty."

Across the street our neighbor's light came on.

"Did you hear me?" She sat up.

I told her that I did.

She slapped something off her knees. "Did you forget anything?" she asked, staring past me and into the house.

I whispered No and looked down at my slippers he'd bought me, wondering if they were supposed to go into the pile. But before I could ask she walked off into the garage, coming out seconds later carrying a small can in each hand. With all the lighter fluid the pile lit up fast, the flash instantly warming my face. I stayed and watched because I couldn't see anything else, and I loved her too much then. I knew it wasn't good to burn all of Dad's things but how can you not love someone who lets you see them in all that pain? For the first time I saw her clearly, as if I was standing inside a dream of hers, watching all her thoughts. There was no act. She wasn't being a nurse, she wasn't being a mother or a wife or a good Christian. She was just dropping to her knees, inches from the fire, and sliding her thin arms into the flames. If I screamed I didn't hear it, but I did pull her back, grabbing a fistful of her pajama top and fully understanding that I was now playing a part in that dream.

When the fire trucks and the ambulance came I left her and ran into the house. I shut all the doors, turned off all the lights. Crouching under a window that faced the yard, I heard two neighbors talking, saying how they'd never seen such a thing. A man's voice asked my mom how she felt.

She said, "I've never been so hungry."

In the cafeteria Knowledge said to me, "Life's only as bad as you make it out to be. It's got nothing to do with the way it is." After three quick shovels of mashed potatoes, she mumbled, "You get me?" Her knees rattled under our table. I folded, then unfolded the paper napkin on my lap and drank my milk before telling her that I didn't, and that I didn't understand most of what she said.

"Here, for your bones." She pulled out a half-pint of milk from under her sweatshirt, sneaking it onto my lap. "I like your honesty. I do. I demand it actually." Then, after a few minutes of quiet: "You know, I never knew a Chink before."

"That's OK." I packed the potatoes and the Salisbury steak inside my dinner roll.

"I didn't even know Chinks ran away from home."

"I know. We can do a lot of neat things," I said, swallowing.

I liked hearing her laugh. And I didn't care that she called me a Chink, though I wanted to say that Chinks were for Chinese and that Koreans had their own special name. But that was another subject, and I liked the way we were talking right then.

"Hello, ladies."

I'd seen Wink walk up to us—strutting past the tables, looking to

455

see who was checking him out. He could've been Chachi's younger brother, dressed in tight jeans with a red bandana tied around his thigh.

"Step away, meatball." Knowledge aimed her plastic fork at him. She didn't like boys talking to me, but especially Wink. To her, boys were either weak or evil—he was both.

"You're the boss," he said, but sat down next to me anyway. I liked that about him. He could really annoy people but at least he was stubborn about it. He didn't seem to care what anyone said behind his back, even after the whole counseling incident. I only got it from Knowledge but during Wink's first rap session, some guys I guess sobbed and told their stories, and when it was Wink's turn, he admitted that he'd been on the streets for almost a year because his mom used to heat up coat hangers to beat him when he was little, and she was sent to Bellevue for trying to hang herself *and* him. Anyway, he cried too. After the session was over and the counselor left, the boys cornered Wink and pushed him down, stepping on him and laughing. They told him they'd all made up their stories, and how they rolled queers like him for kicks. Knowledge then told me that Wink was a prostitute, that he was whoring before he came to the shelter and he sure as hell was gonna be whoring after he left. I didn't even know they had boy prostitutes.

But you couldn't tell any of this by looking at him. Always in his shiny Member's Only jacket with the sleeves scrunched up, Wink walked around the place like he was the president of money.

"Hey there." He sat down, took out his baseball from his jacket pocket and started tossing it up and snatching it out from the air.

I was about to say hi back when Knowledge elbowed me. "Don't tell him about tonight," she whispered.

"What about tonight?" I whispered back but she waved her hand and shushed me.

Then Wink said something.

"What?" I turned to him.

"It's autographed, see?"

He held up the baseball. In big capital letters it read WILLIE MAYS, each letter stringed together like some penmanship exercise.

"Hey, you gonna be here on Christmas?" he asked.

"I don't know. I guess." I went back to my dinner, mashing my mashed potatoes.

"That's cool because," now he rolled the ball back and forth on the table, "because I got you a gift."

"Oh." I bit into my sandwich.

"And I'm telling you so you have time to get me one," he said, laughing a little.

"Don't you know it's rude to whisper?" Knowledge smacked the back of his head.

"Get your hands off me, you crazy dyke." He knocked her hand away and jumped up. "Why can't you act like a girl for once?"

I slipped under the table to get out of the way while Knowledge stood up and bumped her chest into his, staring him down.

"A fight, a fight, a nigga and a white," some girl sang but we all knew Wink would back down. Beat up a girl or get beaten by a girl, either way it didn't look good.

"This is bunk, man. I'm outta here." He tucked the baseball back into his pocket. "I'll see you later my Empress," he said, giving me a wink. As he walked out of the cafeteria, practically all the girls booed him, calling him a white ass honky trick baby and things like that.

That night, after the sirens left and the neighbors went back into their homes, I went through our house all over again, this time to see if Dad had left me a note, or maybe a phone number. Nothing turned up. I dragged my blanket into the living room and watched TV, but mostly I kept thinking somebody would call—the cops or the hospital, or even a neighbor. But no one did. I didn't feel sad or lonely. The house was quiet for the first time in months. I ate a package of dry instant noodles, dipping it in peanut butter, and stayed up late to watch Midnight Kung Fu Theater.

Knowledge slept in the cot next to mine, and as usual, she cried in her sleep. I got to know her best during these times. Most nights she called out to someone, and by the way her lips trembled you could tell the person never came, or maybe was never there to begin with. I turned on my side to look at her—her short thick lashes upcurled so tight and eyebrows scrunched close together. I sort of liked watching her like this—I liked that there was nothing between me and her. Not even her.

"Hey," I said, nudging her arm.

She woke up, opened her eyes real big and didn't blink.

457

"Did it seem real?" I lay back down, ready to hear out her dream. The light on the ceiling hung on two chains and I imagined the links snapping off, the long glass tubes falling, slicing into my face.

"Get up," she said, getting up herself.

"What?"

"It's time." She sat up on the cot and launched her legs into her pants. "You trust me?"

"Not really," I said, but she didn't laugh.

"OK, this is what's gonna happen." She put on her T-shirt like a kid—her head going in first, then the arms sprouting one at a time. "Hurry up."

"Hurry up what?"

She rolled her eyes. "Just look around the room."

Four walls. A piano that nobody touched. Green cots, each with a lump of a girl.

"Do I gotta say more?" She started making her bed.

"If you want me to understand you."

"Exactly." She shot a look at the door. "I'll cause a distraction. You gotta get past the Pigs by yourself, alright?"

"What pigs?" I asked, but she didn't hear. Her eyes were working so hard solving some geometry problem in her head, it seemed more dangerous to stop her.

"I'll wait for you at the Greek's across the street. You got until the count of five." Then she sprinted out of the room, screaming, "One! Two! Three! Four! Five!"

Outside, I could hear her running up and down the hall, yelling, "Deck the halls with boughs of holly!" like she was demanding you to do it.

"Crazy ass motherfucker," a voice said in the dark.

I got dressed.

In the lobby, Reggie sat with his feet up on the counter, sucking on a toothpick and mumbling on the phone. I thought about waving bye to him but decided to just go. He probably didn't even know who I was.

"Your bed ain't gonna be here when you come back," he said, covering the mouthpiece. He really did look like Billy Dee Williams.

I pushed opened the door, tucked my sweatshirt into my pants and crossed the street. The snow hadn't let up. I'd forgotten about the bed policy but who cared. That's what Knowledge would've said, or something more fortune cookie-like, like, *The bed belongs to no one.*

I didn't have money to go into the diner so I waited outside, watching people walk by in their long black coats, hats over ears, their lips blowing smoke. Some people rushed and ducked into cabs, their bodies eaten up whole. Other bodies disappeared in sections, inch by inch, as they stepped down the subway stairs. Then there were the people up the block whose bodies turned to black strings until they thinned out of sight. All these people, rushing through the streets like something good was waiting for them at every corner. Inside the coffee shop, President Reagan was on TV until an old waiter crawled up onto the counter and clicked him off. Then he went around flicking off lights with the tip of his cane. Somehow, the diner going dark made the sidewalk seem colder.

A few minutes later he came out. In a thick accent he said he was closing up.

I didn't know why he was telling me this but I said OK.

Then he told me to get out of the way so he can pull the gate shut.

I apologized and moved aside. "She'll be here any second," I assured him.

"I'm very happy for you," he said, yanking on the padlock to make sure it had fastened.

That's when I saw Wink. Snap-buttoning his jacket collar, he casually walked out the shelter doors and jogged across the street toward me. I stopped myself from running to him. For that long second he was my best friend.

"I thought you weren't gonna leave," he said, giving me a hug. I was surprised by the hugging thing, but it felt OK. We let go quick.

"I know," I said. "Knowledge." That was all I could think to say.

"Man, she stinks of trouble," he said, already shivering, blowing into his cupped hands. "She doesn't care about nothing but herself, and—Excuse me! Excuse me, sir! Can you spare some change so me and my little sister could get something to eat?"

The man stopped and handed over some coins.

"Thank you, sir. My sister thanks you too." As soon as the man turned his back, Wink counted the money. "Twelve cents!" he shouted. "You fucking dick!"

He seemed different on the outside, older maybe, even his eyes looked darker. I wondered about Knowledge, if she would look different too.

"We made it!"

459

Knowledge sprang out from the shelter and charged the street as if she'd just barely escaped an explosion. Behind her, Reggie swiveled in his chair with his back to us, still on the phone.

"We made it!" she screamed again, putting her hand on my arm. I thought she wanted to lean on me so she could catch her breath, but instead she pulled me across the street and down into the subway.

The wheels grinding on the tracks made a dry whistling sound.

"Who the fuck invited you?"

"Ah, shut up. You're just pissed 'cause you ain't got a dick."

"I'm still more man than you, you skanky fag."

"Hey guys?" I said, mostly to myself but they both stopped shouting to look at me. I hadn't expected it. "Do we know where we're going?"

"You leave that up to me." Knowledge propped up her legs on the seat in front of her. Wink stood by the doors with his arms folded and feet apart. "I ain't a queer," was all he said.

The train rocked us from side to side.

"Give me your laces." Knowledge started untying hers.

Wink and I looked at each other.

"Do you even know what a freak you are? I ain't giving you my laces or anything like my laces." He looked to me. "What're you doing?"

"Taking off my laces."

"Why?"

Because I always ended up doing what she wanted—thought I'd speed things up. But I didn't say any of that to Wink. I just shrugged.

A few stops later a black man carrying a crumpled McDonald's bag came on and our car instantly smelled of fries. He had the saddest eyes, the lights behind them had been turned off for good. Sitting in the middle of the car he bit into his burger, stared at it while chewing, then looked out the window that only gave back a darker version of his face. Behind him, at the end of the car, another man sat by himself too, but him I didn't like. His bony face was too shiny, like you could peel off the Elmer's glue, and when we'd first hopped on the train he'd given us a snotty look and cinched up his overcoat as if we were looking to steal his kidneys.

I wouldn't have noticed this man again except that Wink was now walking up to him, dragging his sneakers a little since having given up his laces. Grabbing the top rail he loosely dangled his body near the man's face, pretending to read an ad while the man slowly patted his moustache, pretending not to see him.

"You watching this? What did I say?" Knowledge plopped down next to me. She shook her head and gave a few tut tuts while braiding our laces into rope. Green gems of light streaked by the windows as our train went through what seemed like an endless tunnel, and Knowledge went on about sex being a weakness and how all men were sick with this disease. The man stood up. Without looking at each other, they both headed for the next car. "When you can't control yourself, then something else will," Knowledge said, as Wink jerked open the doors and walked on through without looking back.

We shot out of the tunnel and all the sounds of the train turned loose in the air. I took a breath. The train had turned into an El and the shaky tracks reminded me of a tired roller coaster. Down below, small dark bodies in fat hooded jackets walked by tenements. Some buildings were empty, some burnt black, one had pretty flower planters on every window sill, with a little white boy or a little black girl looking out, smiling stupidly. But everyone knew those weren't real—they were the fake window posters the city'd pasted up.

The front of the train curved into an S and just like that, the streets disappeared and the apartments were now only inches away. We moved slow and each family's window clicked by like View Master frames. They were so close. I could've touched every one of them—the man and his kids watching TV, the big-breasted aproned mother tying up a garbage bag, then a girl my age talking on the phone. It was too cold to pull down the window but I did it anyway. I wanted to put my face out there and smell every home.

My mom came back the next morning and wouldn't speak to me, wouldn't even look at me. After a few days of silence I tried shocking her into talking—I chopped my hair off, played MeatLoaf real loud in the middle of the night, stared at her without blinking while she prayed by her bed, but nothing. She eventually took on more double shifts at the hospital, I stayed later at school, and we only saw each other once in a while in the kitchen or the hallway. We ate alone, cried alone, we never answered the door. My dad never called, so pretty soon we stopped answering the phone too. One night I found her reading her Bible on the sofa. I sat next to her and begged her to say one word, just one. I even gave her suggestions: Apple. Lotion.

461

Jesus. Rice. She didn't look up from the pages. This lasted three years. This lasted until the day I left.

A long car without headlights drove by. I looked up at the subway stairs and thought I'd seen Wink standing with the man but I wasn't sure and Knowledge was losing her patience. "We got things to do," she shouted, grabbing my arm and marching us down the street.

The sky was blue-black. It was colder here than in the city, not enough tall buildings blocking the wind. We walked along a row of cars double parked, passing windows draped with bed sheets and bicycle wheels chained to fire escapes. Across the street a small dog raised its leg and the wind blew its pee onto a liquor store sign that read Chicken Liver & Hot Chocolate, $2.35.

"Do you think you'll ever tell me where we're going?" I asked.

"Sure," she said, but we were already there.

We'd stopped under a fire-escape ladder. Knowledge whipped out the rope she'd made from our shoelaces and tossed it up so that it lassoed the bottom rung. She tugged on the rope, pulling down the ladder.

"C'mon. I wanna show you something," she said, starting to climb.

I looked down the street, in both directions, looking for something to decide for me. But it was dark and empty, except for pieces of trash rolling toward me with the wind.

"Pssst!" Knowledge waved me up.

By the time I caught up to her, she was on the third floor, trying to open a window.

"It's unlocked. Help me get it open."

I got next to her and the two of us looked like weightlifters—our knees bent, our hands by our ears, trying to lift up a window that wouldn't budge. "Can you please tell me what we're doing?" Somewhere far away, a siren went by.

"You'll see," she said, and the window burst open. A gust of snowflakes rushed inside and before I could say a word, she went in.

I stepped onto a table, a chair, then the floor that squeaked when I landed. The kitchen smelled of fish grease. It was dark but not so black that I couldn't see Knowledge opening the refrigerator. It made a suction sound, and its light didn't come on. She poked her head in, then turned to me, pinching her nose and shaking her head No. How she could even think about food I didn't understand. I was sick to my stomach, my whole body felt different sneaking around someone else's home. Heavier, muddier. I heard every sound I made as I followed her across the hallway and into a room that was blinking red, white, red, white.

And then I saw it. What Knowledge wanted to see. A humongous white Christmas tree that was as tall as the room, as big as the tree at Alexander's. Knowledge stood with her hands on her hips, studying every Santa head, every string of lights, and every strand of silver tinsel that was clumped to the plastic branches. The color of her face changed with the flashing lights and she smiled up at the tree as if the black angel perched on top was singing secrets. I didn't see any presents, though, and the rest of the room was crowded with a deflated couch and a coffee table, which was really a slab of wood on top of two, back-to-back TVs. Above the couch hung a poster-sized photo of a black couple. The woman had thick pretty lashes and sat with her hands folded. Behind her stood a stocky man with tinted glasses and Jeri curls, wearing a velvet suit, and the picture made him look as though he had only one hand—a fat one, with a gold pinky ring, resting on the woman's thin shoulder.

"OK, we saw it. Now let's go." I checked behind me.

"Don't worry," she said, "It's lighter than you think."

She was bent over, picking the tree up by the stand and telling me to grab the top.

"Are you crazy?"

"Shut up. You're gonna get us busted!"

"Me?"

A light came on from down the hall. I didn't even think—I ran. And for some reason I thought Knowledge would too. But with one foot out the window I turned back and saw her entering the kitchen, dragging the tree behind her, stand and all. I told her to drop it but knew it was useless as I was saying it. I stepped down to help, and we had the tree almost halfway out when the kitchen light came on.

It was the man from the photo but much thicker. I hadn't expected him to come out wearing a velvet suit or anything but I was surprised to see him in his tiny underwear and black socks, his stomach so big it could've housed the woman standing next to him. With a pink curler in her bangs the woman stood with her hands covering her nose and mouth, like she was going to cough.

"Knowledge," the woman finally said.

The three of them stood frozen—the man with his arms folded, staring fiercely at the tree and at Knowledge, who would not look at the woman. Me: I couldn't believe Knowledge was her real name.

"Let's go," she said, pulling the rest of the tree through. She didn't care about the ornaments anymore. The angel had fallen off by the fridge.

We tossed the tree over the railing, watched it land in the middle of the street, and climbed down the fire escape. The man stuck his head out the window.

"She'll be back. You'll be back!" he shouted.

I kept waiting to hear the woman's voice but it never came. We jumped down to the sidewalk.

"And what. You think, I'm just gonna give you my damn tree!" the man said.

"You didn't give it to me, asshole." Knowledge looked up and gave him the finger. "I took it from you." Propping up the tree she started skipping around it, saying, "I took it, I took it, I took it, and I ain't gonna take it any more!"

An old lady on the second floor stuck her head out her window, telling us how she'd come down and wring our necks with her own bare hands, so help her God.

"You know why you'll be back?" the man started again. "Who the hell would want you? You're too damn ugly to get anyone else. Look at her, she don't even look like a—"

Right then a baseball flew over the man's head, shattering his window. The sound of glass breaking was so clear, almost cartoonish. Knowledge and I both turned to find Wink standing across the street, admiring his aim before running toward us, carrying a paper bag in hand.

"Shermaine, call the police," the man yelled, and as if we were of one body, the three of us grabbed the tree at the exact same time— Knowledge in front, me in the middle, and Wink with a free hand holding up the stand, and we ran as if a gun had gone off and a race had started. The cold air stung my nose and my sneakers felt like they'd slip off any second but by the end of the block we were laughing. Wink hollered, "Merry Christmas, I love you all," over and over again while Knowledge shouted, "Fuck you barber shop, Fuck you, you butcher, Fuck you basketball court and playground," just fuck you to every place we ran past. Leaving a trail of Santa heads behind us Knowledge sped us through the neighborhood. "Look at them fools, running with a damn tree," a skinny old man said as he stepped out from the liquor store. "Fuck you old man," she shouted. And

464

with the snow hitting my eyes, my fingers almost numb, I suddenly felt like one of those people who walked the streets like something good was waiting for them.

We turned a corner and came to a whole square block that looked to have been bombed. I'd seen it from the El. Piles and piles of rubble, broken buildings. We trampled over bricks, cement blocks, toilet bowls and tire rims until we finally ran into a tall, burnt-out building. "Up here," Knowledge said, tugging on the tree, and we ran with her up to the third floor and into a room.

The room was big. We dropped the tree in the center. We didn't know what to do first—laugh or catch our breath but we did both, and hugged and gave each other high fives, saying, "Aw man, that was the fucking best," and things like that, then looked up at the tall empty tree that seemed so different in this room. The floor was covered in newspapers, cereal boxes, a shower cap, dried shit, a burnt mattress with springs poking through. The wall had a hole the size of a small car that let us see where we'd come from. Wink opened up his soggy paper bag and handed out Styrofoam cups, to our surprise. Knowledge peeled the tab off and took a sip. It was hot chocolate. And not even Ovaltine, but the real thing, with whip cream and sprinkles. "Goddamn! This is good, isn't it?" Wink shouted, almost scaring me. He paced back and forth, taking another sip, nodding his head. "You know what it tastes like?" He stopped to place a hand over his chest and scrunched his jacket right where his heart was. "It tastes like love," he said and dropped to the ground, pretending to have been shot. I laughed and sat down next to him, then Knowledge next to me. "Shit. Tastes like love, my ass," she said.

We heard the El crawling by, the sound reminding me of Wink and that man, and it wasn't until the train left us for good that we realized Wink was crying. He wiped his nose across his arm and took a long sip from his cup. I imagined a lump in his throat being washed over. I drank too, wanting to taste whatever he tasted, and soon our breathing slowed and we sat there, our numbness wearing off, not really knowing what else to say and not seeing the room or the walls or the sky outside or even each other, but only seeing the tree in front of us, for exactly what it was.

Nominated by Witness

GOLDFISH: A DIPTYCH

by SUSAN TERRIS

from FIELD

—Science has proven the goldfish has a memory of a second and a half.

1. Tale of the Goldfish

Look, there's a castle,
submerged so its world magnifies
in water hazed with algae,
but I see willow, sun, a dragonfly.

Look, a castle—
rays of sunlight through its doorway,
a mermaid on a rock
amid roots and burnished shells.

Look, there's a castle,
and I angle through the door, out the window,
everything static,
yet behind I sense a shadow.

Look—
its distorted world is pooling,
until I see a rock with no mermaid,
sense jaws of darkness.

Look, there's . . .

2. A Man Is a Goldfish with Legs

Look, there's a castle,
where Circe turns seamen to swimming pigs
while the universe expands,
so watch out for solar glare.

Look, there's . . .
and at its hearth, a clockwise flame,
but below continents of ice,
stress lines.

Look, a castle—
and a pearl at my throat to keep me alive,
yet if there's heat lightning,
Venus will wink at daybreak.

Look—
how Circe takes up the pearl,
and Venus, in morning sun, floats fire and ice,
and may her lightning give you pause.

Some days—it's less than a second.

Nominated by Andrea Hollander Budy, Michael Waters

ZION

by DONALD REVELL

from PENNYWEIGHT WINDOWS: NEW AND SELECTED POEMS
(ALICE JAMES BOOKS)

Suddenly copper roses glow on the deadwood.
I am these because I see them and also see
Abolition, the white smock on a girl
Eating an apple, looking down into
The valley, a small train steaming there.
I go to the uplands to join death,
And death welcomes me, shows me a trailhead,
Foot-tracks overfilled with standing water.
Man has never owned another man here.
Aglow in the shade hang apples free for the taking.
I'm saying that death is a little girl. The apple
There in her hand is God Almighty where the skin
Breaks to her teeth and spills my freedom all over
Sunlight turning deadwood coppery rose.

Nominated by Mark Irwin, Reginald Shepherd, Alice James Books

WHY BUGSY SIEGEL WAS A FRIEND OF MINE

fiction by JAMES LEE BURKE

from THE SOUTHERN REVIEW

In 1947 NICK HAUSER AND I had only two loves in this world—baseball and Cheerio yo-yo contests. That's how we met Benny, one spring night after a doubleheader out at Buffalo Stadium on the Galveston Freeway. His brand new Ford convertible, a gleaming maroon job with a starch-white top, whitewall tires, and blue-dot taillights, was stuck in a sodden field behind the bleachers. Benny was trying to lift the bumper while his girlfriend floored the accelerator, spinning the tires and blowing streams of muddy water and torn grass back in his face.

He wore a checkered sports coat, lavender shirt, hand-painted necktie, and two-tone shoes, all of it now whipsawed with mud. But it was his eyes, not his clothes, that you remembered. They were a radiant blue and literally sparkled.

"You punks want to earn two bucks each?" he said.

"Who you calling a punk?" Nick said.

Before Benny could answer, his girlfriend shifted into reverse, caught traction, and backed over his foot.

He hopped up and down, holding one shin, trying to bite down on his pain, his eyes lifted heavenward, his lips moving silently.

"Get in the fucking car before it sinks in this slop again!" his girlfriend yelled.

He limped to the passenger side. A moment later they fishtailed across the grass past us. Her hair was long, blowing out the window,

469

the pinkish red of a flamingo. She thumbed a hot cigarette into the darkness.

"Boy, did you check out that babe's bongos? Wow!" Nick said.

But our evening encounter with Benny and his girlfriend was not over. We were on the shoulder of the freeway, trying to hitch a ride downtown, flicking our Cheerios under a streetlamp, doing a whole range of upper-level yo-yo tricks—Round the World, Shoot the Moon, Rock the Cradle, and the Atomic Bomb—when the maroon convertible roared past us, blowing dust and newspaper in our faces.

Suddenly the convertible cut across two lanes of traffic, made a U-turn, then a second U-turn, horns blowing all over the freeway, and braked to a stop abreast of us.

"You know who I am?" Benny said.

"No," I replied.

"My name is Benjamin Siegel."

"You're a gangster," Nick said.

"He's got you, Benny," the woman behind the wheel said.

"How you know that?" Benny said.

"We heard your name on *Gangbusters*. Nick and me listen every Saturday night," I said.

"Can you do the Chinese Star?" he asked.

"We do Chinese Stars in our sleep," Nick said.

"Get in," Benny said, pulling back the leather seat.

"We got to get home," I said.

"We'll take you there. Get in," he said.

We drove out South Main, past Rice University and parklike vistas dense with live oak trees, some of them hung with Spanish moss. To the south, heat lightning flickered over the Gulf of Mexico. Benny bought us fried chicken and ice cream at Bill Williams Drive-In, and while we ate, his girlfriend smoked cigarettes behind the wheel and listened to the radio, her thoughts known only to herself, her face so soft and lovely in the dash light I felt something drop inside me when I stole a look at it.

Benny popped open the glove box and removed a top-of-the-line chartreuse Cheerio yo-yo. Behind the yo-yo I could see the steel surfaces of a semiautomatic pistol. "Now show me the Chinese Star," he said.

He stood with us in the middle of the drive-in parking lot, watching Nick and me demonstrate the intricate patterns of the most difficult of all the Cheerio competition tricks. Then he tried it himself.

470

His yo-yo tilted sideways, its inner surfaces brushing against the string, then twisted on itself and went dead.

"The key is candle wax," I said.

"Candle wax?" he said.

"Yeah, you wrap the string around a candle and saw it back and forth. That gives you the spin and the time you need to make the pattern for the star," I said.

"I never thought of that," he said.

"It's a breeze," Nick said.

"Benny, give it a rest," his girlfriend said from inside the car.

Fifteen minutes later we dropped off Nick at his house on the dead-end street where I used to be his neighbor. It was a wonderful street, one of trees and flowers and old brick homes, and a horse pasture dotted with live oaks beyond the cane-brake that enclosed the cul-du-sac. But when my father died my mother and I were evicted, and we moved across Westheimer and took up residence in a neighborhood where every sunrise broke on the horizon like a testimony to personal failure.

Benny's girlfriend pulled to a stop in front of my house. Benny looked at the broken porch and orange rust on the screens. "This is where you live?" he asked.

"Yeah," I said, my eyes leaving his.

He nodded. "You need to study hard, make something of yourself. Go out to California, maybe. It's the place to be," he said.

Our next-door neighbors were the Dunlops. They had skin like pig hide and heads with the knobbed ridges of coconuts. The oldest of the five boys was executed in Huntsville Pen; one did time on Sugarland Farm. The patriarch of the family was a security guard at the Southern Pacific train yards. He covered all the exterior surfaces of his house, garage, and tool shed with the yellow paint he stole from his employer. The Dunlops even painted their car with it. Then, through a fluke no one could have anticipated, they became rich.

One of the girls had married a morphine addict who came from an oil family in River Oaks. The girl and her husband drove their Austin Healey head on into a bus outside San Antonio, and the Dunlops inherited two hundred thousand dollars and a huge chunk of rental property in their own neighborhood. It was like giving a tribe of pygmies a nuclear weapon.

I thought the Dunlops would move out of their dilapidated two-story frame house, with its piles of dog shit all over the backyard, but instead they bought a used Cadillac from a mortuary, covered their front porch with glitter-encrusted chalk animals and icons from an amusement park, and continued each morning to piss out the attic window onto my mother's car, which looked like it had contracted scabies.

As newly empowered landlords, the Dunlops cut no one any slack, did no repairs on their properties, and evicted a Mexican family who had lived in the neighborhood since the middle of the Depression. Mr. Dunlop also seized upon an opportunity to repay the parochial school Nick and I attended for expelling two of his sons.

Maybe it was due to the emotional deprivation and the severity of the strictures imposed upon them, or the black habits they wore in ninety-degree humidity, but a significant number of the nuns at school were inept and cruel. Sister Felicie, however, was not one of these. She was tall, and wore steel-rimmed glasses and small black shoes that didn't seem adequate to support her height. When I spent almost a year in bed with rheumatic fever, she came every other day to the house with my lessons, walking a mile, sometimes in the hottest of weather, her habit powdered with ash from a burned field she had to cross.

But things went south for Sister Felicie. We heard that her father, a senior army officer, was killed on Okinawa. Some said the soldier was not her father but the fiancé she had given up when she entered the convent. Regardless, at the close of the war a great sadness seemed to descend upon her.

In the spring of '47 she would take her science class on walks through the neighborhood, identifying trees, plants, and flowers along the way. Then, just before 3 P.M., we would end up at Costen's Drug Store, and she would let everyone take a rest break on the benches under the awning. It was a grand way to end the school day because on some afternoons the Cheerio yo-yo man would arrive at exactly 3:05 and hold competitions on the corner.

But one day, just after the dismissal bell had rung across the street, I saw Sister Felicie walk into the alleyway between the drug store and Cobb's Liquors and give money to a black man who had an empty eye socket. A few minutes later I saw her upend a small bottle of fortified wine, what hobos used to call short-dogs, then drop it surreptitiously into a trash can.

She turned and realized I had been watching her. She walked toward me, between the old brick walls of the buildings, her small shoes clicking on pieces of gravel and bottle caps and broken glass, her face stippled with color inside her wimple. "Why aren't you waxing your string for the Cheerio contest?" she said.

"It hasn't started yet, Sister," I replied, avoiding her look, trying to smile.

"Better run on now," she said.

"Are you all right, Sister?" I said, then wanted to bite off my tongue.

"Of course I'm all right. Why do you ask?"

"No reason. None. I just don't think too good sometimes, Sister. You know me. I was just—"

But she wasn't listening now. She walked past me toward the red light at the corner, her habit and beads swishing against my arm. She smelled like camphor and booze and the lichen in the alley she had bruised under her small shoes.

Two days later the same ritual repeated itself. Except this time Sister Felicie didn't empty just one short-dog and head for the convent. I saw her send the black man back to Cobb's for two more bottles, then she sat down on a rusted metal chair at the back of the alley, a book spread on her knees as though she were reading, the bottles on the ground barely hidden by the hem of her habit.

That's when Mr. Dunlop and his son Vernon showed up. Vernon was seventeen and by law could not be made to attend school. That fact was a gift from God to the educational system of southwest Houston. Vernon had half-moon scars on his knuckles, biceps the size of small muskmelons, and deep-set simian eyes that focused on other kids with the moral sympathies of an electric drill.

Mr. Dunlop was thoroughly enjoying himself. First, he announced to everyone within earshot he was the owner of the entire corner, including the drug store. He told the Cheerio yo-yo man to beat it and not come back, then told the kids to either buy something inside the store or get off the benches they were loitering on.

His face lit like a jack-o'-lantern's when he saw Sister Felicie emerge from the alley. She was trying to stand straight, and not doing a very good job of it, one hand touching the brick wall of the drug store, a drop of sweat running from the top edge of her wimple down the side of her nose.

"Looks like you got a little bit of the grog in you, Sister," Mr. Dunlop said.

"What were you saying to the children?" she asked.

"Oh, her ladyship wants to know that, does she? Why don't we have a conference with the pastor and hash it out?" Mr. Dunlop said.

"Do as you wish," Sister replied, then walked to the red light with the cautious steps of someone aboard a pitching ship.

Mr. Dunlop dropped a buffalo nickel into a pay phone, an unlit cigarette in the corner of his mouth. His head was shaved bald, his brow knurled, one eye recessed and glistening with pleasure when someone picked up on the other end. "Father?" Mr. Dunlop said.

His son Vernon squeezed his scrotum and shot us the bone.

The Cheerio yo-yo man did not come back to the corner and Sister Felicie disappeared from school for a week. Then one Monday morning she was back in class, looking joyless and glazed, as though she had just walked out of an ice storm.

That afternoon Benny and his girlfriend pulled into my driveway while I was picking up the trash Vernon and his brothers had thrown out of their attic window into the yard. "I can't get the Atomic Bomb right. Get in the car. We'll pick up your friend on the way out," he said.

"Way where?" I said.

"The Shamrock. You want to go swimming and have some eats, don't you?" he said.

"I'll leave my mom a note," I said.

"Tell her to come out and join us."

That definitely will not flush, I thought, but did not say it.

Benny had said he couldn't pull off the yo-yo trick called the Atomic Bomb. The truth was he couldn't even master Walk the Dog. In fact, I couldn't figure why a man with his wealth and criminal reputation would involve himself so intensely with children's games. After Nick and I went swimming, we sat on the balcony of Benny's suite, high above the clover-shaped pool of the Shamrock Hotel, and tried to show him the configurations of the Atomic Bomb. It was a disaster. He would spread the string between his fingers, then drop the yo-yo through the wrong spaces, knotting the string, rendering it useless. He danced up and down on the balls of his feet in frustration.

"There's something wrong with this yo-yo. I'm gonna go back to the guy who sold it to me and stuff it down his throat," he said.

474

"He's full of shit, kids," his girlfriend said through the open bathroom door.

"Don't listen to that. You're looking at the guy who almost blew up Mussolini," he said to us. Then he yelled through the French doors into the suite, "Tell me I'm full of shit one more time."

"You're full of shit," she yelled back.

"That's what you got to put up with," he said to us. "Now, teach me the Atomic Bomb."

Blue black clouds were piled from the horizon all the way to the top of the sky, blooming with trees of lightning that made no sound. Across the street we could see oil rigs pumping in an emerald green pasture and a half dozen horses starting to spook at the weather. Benny's girlfriend came out of the bathroom, dressed in new jeans and a black and maroon cowboy shirt with a silver stallion on the pocket. She drank from a vodka collins, and her mouth looked cold and hard and beautiful when she lowered the glass.

"Anybody hungry?" she said.

I felt myself swallow. Then, for reasons I didn't understand, I told her and Benny what Mr. Dunlop had done to Sister Felicie. Benny listened attentively, his handsome face clouding, his fingers splaying his knotted yo-yo string in different directions. "Say all that again? This guy Dunlop ran off the Cheerio man?" he said.

It was almost Easter and at school that meant the Stations of the Cross and a daily catechism reminder about the nature of disloyalty and human failure. When he needed them most, Christ's men bagged it down the road and let him take the weight on his own. I came to appreciate the meaning of betrayal a little better that spring.

I thought my account of Mr. Dunlop's abuse of Sister Felicie and the Cheerio man had made Benny our ally. He'd said he would come by my house the next night and straighten out Mr. Dunlop and anyone else who was pushing around kids and nuns and yo-yo instructors. He said these kinds of guys were Nazis and should be boiled into lard and poured into soap molds. He said, "Don't worry, kid. I owe you guys. You taught me the Atomic Bomb and the Chinese Star."

The next day, after school, when I was raking leaves in the yard, Vernon used his slingshot to shoot me in the back with a marble. I felt the pain go into the bone like a cold chisel.

"Got a crick?" he said.

"Yeah," I said, mindlessly, squeezing my shoulders back, my eyes shut.

"How about some hair of the dog that bit you?" he said, fishing another marble out of his shirt pocket.

"You screwed with Benny Siegel, Vernon. He's going to stuff you in a toilet bowl," I said.

"Yeah? Who is Benny Sea Gull?"

"Ask your old man. Oh, I forgot. He can't read, either."

Vernon's fist came out of the sky and knocked me to the ground. I felt the breath go out of my chest as though it were being sucked into a giant vacuum cleaner. Through the kitchen window, I could see my mother washing dishes, her face bent down toward the sink. Vernon unbuckled my belt, worked the top button loose on my jeans, and pulled them off my legs, dragging me through the dust. The clouds, trees, garage, alleyway, even the dog dumps, spun in circles around me. Vernon pulled one of my pants legs inside out and used it to blow his nose.

Benny and his girlfriend did not show up at my house that night. I called the Shamrock Hotel and asked for his room.

"There's no one registered here by that name," the clerk said.

"Has he checked out?"

There was a pause. "We have no record of a guest with that name. I'm sorry. Thank you for calling the Shamrock," the clerk said, and hung up.

The next day at recess I saw Sister Felicie sitting on a stone bench under a live oak in a garden behind the church. Her black habit was spangled with sunlight, and her beads lay across her open palm as though the wind had robbed her of her concentration. Her face looked like ceramic, polished, faintly pink, not quite real. She smelled of soap or perhaps shampoo in her close-cropped hair, which was covered with a skull cap and veil that must have been unbearable in the summer months.

"You're supposed to be on the playground, Charlie," she said.

"I told Benny Siegel what Mr. Dunlop did to you. He promised to help. But he didn't show up last night," I said.

"What are you talking about?"

"Benny is a gangster. Nick and I have been teaching him yo-yo tricks. He built a casino in Nevada."

476

"I'm convinced you'll be a great writer one day," she said, and for the first time in weeks she smiled. "You're a good boy, Charlie. I may not see you again, at least for a while. But you'll be in my prayers."

"Not see you?"

"Run along now. Don't hang out with too many gangsters."

She patted me on top of the head, then touched my cheek.

Benny had shown Nick and me color photographs of the resort hotel and gambling casino he had built in the desert. He also showed us a picture of him and his girlfriend building a snowman in front of a log cabin in west Montana. In the photograph she was smiling and looked much younger, somehow innocent among evergreens that rang with winter light. She wore a fluffy pink sweater and knee-length boots stitched with Christmas designs.

I kept wanting to believe Benny would call or come by, but he didn't. I dreamed about a building in a desert, its exterior scrolled with neon, a grassy pond on one side of it where flamingos stood in the water, arching their necks, pecking at the insects in their feathers.

I put away my Cheerio yo-yo and no longer listened to ballgames at Buffalo Stadium. I refused to eat, without understanding why, threw my lunch in a garbage can on the way to school, and fantasized about hurting Vernon Dunlop.

"We'll set fire to his house," Nick said.

"Serious?" I said, looking up from the box of shoes we were shining in his garage.

"It's a thought," he replied.

"What if somebody gets killed?"

"That's the breaks when you're white trash," Nick said. He grinned, his face full of play. He had a burr haircut and the overhead light reflected on his scalp. Nick was a good boxer, swallowed his blood in a fight, and never let anyone know when he was hurt. Secretly I always wished I was as tough as he was.

He and I had a shoe-shine route. We collected shoes from all over the neighborhood and shined them for ten cents a pair, using only one color polish—brown; home delivery was free. Nick peeled open a Milky Way and bit into it. He chewed thoughtfully, then offered the candy bar to me. I shook my head.

"You got to eat," he said.

477

"Who says?" I replied.

"You make me sad, Charlie," he said.

My father was an old-time pipeline man whose best friend was killed by his side on the last day of World War I. He read classical literature, refused to mow the lawn under any circumstances, spent more days than he should have in the beer joint, attended church irregularly, and contended there were only two facts you had to remember about the nature of God: that He had a sense of humor and, as a gentleman, He never broke His word.

The last part always stuck with me.

Benny had proved himself a liar and a bum. My sense of having been used by him seemed to grow daily. My mother could not make me eat, even when my hunger was eating its way through my insides like a starving organism that had to consume its host in order to survive. I had bed spins when I woke in the morning and vertigo when I rode my bike to school, wobbling between automobiles while the sky, trees, and buildings around me dissolved into a vortex of atomic particles.

My mother tried to tempt me from my abstinence with a cake she baked and the following day with a codfish dinner she brought from the cafeteria, wrapped in foil, butter oozing from an Irish potato that was still hot from the oven.

I rushed from the house and pedaled my bike to Nick's. We sat inside the canebrake at the end of our old street, while the day cooled and the evening star twinkled in the west. There was a bitter taste in my mouth, like the taste of zinc pennies.

"You miss your dad?" Nick asked.

"I don't think about it much anymore. It was an accident. Why go around feeling bad about an accident?" I replied, turning my face from his, looking at the turquoise rim along the bottom of the sky.

"My old man always says your dad was stand-up."

"Benny Siegel treated us like jerks, Nick," I said.

"Who cares about Benny Siegel?"

I didn't have an answer for him, nor could I explain why I felt the way I did.

I rode my bike home in the dusk, then found a heavy rock in the alley and threw it against the side of the Dunlops' house. It struck the wood so hard the glass in the windows rattled. Vernon came out

478

on the back porch, eating a piece of fried chicken, his body silhouetted in the kitchen light. He wore a strap undershirt and his belt was unbuckled, hanging loosely over his fly.

"You're lucky, dick wipe. I got a date tonight. But wait till tomorrow," he said. He shook his chicken bone at me.

I couldn't sleep that night. I had terrible dreams about facing Vernon in the morning. How could I have been so foolish as to actually assault his house? I wished I had taken the pounding right then, when I was in hot blood and not trembling with fear. I woke at 2 A.M. and threw up in the toilet, then went into the dry heaves. I lay in bed, my head under the pillow. I prayed an asteroid would crash into our neighborhood so I wouldn't have to see the sunrise.

At around five o'clock I fell asleep. Later I heard wind rattle the roof, then a loud knocking sound like a door slamming repeatedly on a doorjamb. When I looked out my window screen I could see fog on the street and a maroon convertible with whitewall tires parked in front of the Dunlops' house. An olive-skinned man with patent leather hair parted down the middle, wearing a clip-on bow tie and crinkling white shirt, sat in the passenger seat. I rubbed my eyes. It was the Cheerio man Mr. Dunlop had run off from the parking lot in front of Costen's Drug Store. Then I heard Benny's voice on the Dunlops' porch.

"See, you can't treat people like that. This is the United States, not Mussoliniville. So we need to walk out here and apologize to this guy and invite him back to the corner by the school. You're good with that, aren't you?"

There was a gap in the monologue. Then Benny's voice resumed. "You're not? You're gonna deny kids the right to enter Cheerio yo-yo contests? You think all those soldiers died in the war for nothing? That's what you're saying? You some kind of Nazi pushing around little people? Look at me when I'm talking, here."

Then Benny and Mr. Dunlop walked out to the convertible and talked to the Cheerio man. A moment later Benny got behind the wheel and the convertible disappeared in the fog.

I fell sound asleep in the deep blue coolness of the room, with a sense of confidence in the world I had not felt since the day the war ended and Kate Smith's voice sang "God Bless America" from every radio in the neighborhood.

When I woke, it was hot and bright outside, the wind touched with dust and the stench of melted tar. I told my mother of Benny Siegel's visit to the Dunlops.

"You must have had a dream, Charlie. I was up early. I would have heard," she said.

"No, it was Benny. His girlfriend wasn't with him, but the Cheerio man was."

She smiled wanly, her eyes full of pity. "You've starved yourself and you break my heart. Nobody was out there, Charlie. *Nobody*," she said.

I went out to the curb. No one ever parked in front of the Dunlop's house, and because the sewer drain was clogged, a patina of mud always dried along the edge of the gutter after each rain. I walked out in the street so I wouldn't be on the Dunlops' property, my eyes searching along the seam between the asphalt and the gutter. But I could see no tire imprint in the gray film left over from the last rain. I knelt down and touched the dust with my fingers.

Vernon opened his front door and held it back on the spring. He was bare chested, a pair of sweat pants hanging below his navel. "Losing your marbles, frump?" he asked.

By noon my skin was crawling with anxiety and fear. Worse, I felt an abiding shame that once again I had been betrayed by my own vanity and foolish trust in others. I didn't care anymore whether Vernon beat me up or not. In fact, I wanted to see myself injured. Through the kitchen window I could see him pounding dust out of a rug on the clothesline with a broken tennis racquet. I walked down the back steps and crossed into his yard. "Vernon?" I said.

"Your butt-kicking appointment is after lunch. I'm busy right now. In the meantime, entertain yourself by giving a blowjob to a door-knob," he replied.

"This won't take long," I said.

He turned around, exasperated. I hit him, hard, on the corner of the mouth, with a right cross that Nick Hauser would have been proud of. It broke Vernon's lip against his teeth, whipping his face sideways, causing him to drop the racquet. He stared at me in disbelief, a string of spittle and blood on his cheek. Before he could raise his hands, I hit him again, this time square on the nose. I felt it flatten and blood fly under my knuckles, then I caught him in the eye and throat. I took one in the side of the head and felt another slide off my shoulder, but I was under his reach now and I got him again

480

in the mouth, this time hurting him more than he was willing to live with.

He stepped back from me, blood draining from his split lip, his teeth red, his face twitching with shock. Out of the corner of my eye, I saw his father appear on the back porch.

"Get in here, boy, before I whup your ass worse than it already is," Mr. Dunlop said.

That afternoon Nick Hauser and I went to a baseball game at Buffalo Stadium. When I came home my mother told me I had received a long-distance telephone call. This was in an era when people only called long-distance to inform family members that a loved one had died. I called the operator and was soon connected to Sister Felicie. She told me she was back at Our Lady of the Lake, the college in San Antonio where she had trained to become a teacher.

"I appreciate what your friend has tried to do, but would you tell him everything is fine now, that he doesn't need to act on my behalf anymore?" she said.

"Which friend?" I asked.

"Mr. Siegel. He's called the archdiocese twice." I heard her laugh, then clear her throat. "Can you do that for me, Charlie?"

But I never saw Benny or his girlfriend again. In late June I read in the newspaper that Benny had been at her cottage in Beverly Hills, reading the *L. A. Times*, when someone outside propped an M-1 carbine across the fork of a tree and fired directly into Benny's face, blowing one eye fifteen feet from his head.

Years later I would read a news story about his girlfriend, whose nickname was the Flamingo, and how she died by suicide in a snow-bank in Austria. I sometimes wondered if in those last moments of her life she tried to return to that winter-time photograph of her and Benny building a snowman in west Montana.

Vernon Dunlop never bothered me again. In fact, I came to have a sad kind of respect for the type of life that had been imposed upon him. Vernon was killed at the Battle of Inchon during the Korean War. Nick Hauser and I became school-teachers. The era in which we grew up was a poem and Bugsy Siegel was a friend of mine.

Nominated by David Jauss, The Southern Review

PORTRAIT OF HER MOTHER AS THE 19TH CENTURY

by KEITH RATZLAFF

from THE COLORADO REVIEW

She's holding a rabbit,
wearing a flowered dress
that melts into a background of flowers.
I mean, a woman wears a dress
and lies on a bed sheet
printed with flowers
so busy and Victorian
we almost can't see how tight
she's holding the rabbit—
who looks at us over his shoulder,
ears spread in a little V
at her neck like a collar,
like birds going somewhere.

The dress is printed zinnias,
a 1970s pattern meant to fool us
into thinking it's not an idea
left over from the 19th century,
like flowered wallpaper,
like the language of flowers—

china rose for beauty,
chrysanthemum for truth,
zinnia the old maid flower—
like photography,
like the working class
and the working class portrait,
like the idea that art can save your life.

She's 10, the daughter I mean,
in Guatemala. Someone's given
her a camera to save her life.
She's sure this is the best photograph
she's ever taken—the illusion
of floating above her mother
like an airship, cutting her
off at the knees, off at the forehead
the rabbit's black fur
echoing her mother's storm of hair,
the animal small, her mother's hands
large and muscular like the hands
Leonardo and Picasso gave women.
But she can't know that,
about the hands and Leonardo,
or that next year this photograph
will make the Times and make her famous.
She's 10, she doesn't know anything
about art, or love, or her mother—
a woman who would never pose like this
for anyone else, who is holding a rabbit
over her heart to keep it from running away.
Her heart, I mean, the rabbit.

Nominated by Philip Appleman

SPECIAL MENTION

(The editors also wish to mention the following important works published by small presses last year. Listings are in no particular order.)

NONFICTION

A Weekend At Montauk—Sven Birkerts (Virginia Quarterly)
The Bottle of Words—Tina Bennett-Kastor (Vocabula Bound)
The Green Fairy—Elissa Schappell (Tin House)
Zoroaster's Children—Marius Kociejowski (Parnassus)
The Nuptial Flight of the Ants—Kimberly Meyer (Fourth Genre)
Getting Yourself Home—Brenda Miller (On The Page)
Flow Versus Hoard—Brian Evenson (Marginalia)
Angels & Engines: Culture of the Apocalypse—Marina Warner (Raritan)
The Space Between—Rick Bass (Open Spaces)
"The Piano Has Been Drinking": On the Art of the Rant—Robert Cohen (Georgia Review)
From Outbound—Charlie Geer (River City Publishing)
A Starbucks State of Mind—Jan Koenen (Fourth Genre)
On Why the Fact Needs Fun: An Essay in Response to Nonfiction's Police—John D'Agata (Columbia)
Relief—Kim Dana Kupperman (Hotal Amerika)
Why Does It Always Have To Be A Boy Baby?—David Kirby (Southwest Review)
Desiring By Myself—Adam Phillips (Raritan)
Crisis Line—Dorene O'Brien (Connecticut Review)
Robert Bly and James Wright: A Correspondence—(Virginia Quarterly)
Running After My Father—Floyd Skloot (Witness)

Make Me A Picture—W.S. DiPiero (Threepenny Review)
from Exist to Kiss You—Howard Norman (Conjunctions)
I've Been Told: A Story's Story—John Barth (Conjunctions)
The Flight to Newark—Arthur Miller (Michigan Quarterly)
Meditations On An Old Love, Enshrouded in Prayer—Michael Sandoval (*Topography of War*, Asian American Writers' Workshop)
The Trouble With Postmortality—Elizabeth Tallent (Threepenny Review)
Celia—Peter Gordon (Ploughshares)
Moonface and Charlie—Angela M. Balcita (Iowa Review)
The Bald and the Beautiful—William Bradley (Bellevue Literary Review)
The Death of A Red Guard—Xujun Eberlein (*Topography of War*, Asian American Writers' Workshop)
Disappearances—Prisilla Long (Ontario Review)
Precious Things—Albert Goldbarth (Bellingham Review)
from Paul—Michelle Latiolais (Santa Monica Review)
The Sorrows—Gary Fincke (Santa Monica Review)
You Can't Even Remember What I'm Trying To Forget—Rebecca Brock (Threepenny Review)
Digesting The Father—Kellie Wells (Kenyon Review)
Manners of Speech—Philip J. Cunningham (Kyoto Journal)
Joint Custody—Elizabeth Rollins (New England Review)
She, Under The Umbrella, Went—Melissa Haley (Post Road)
The Reality of Reality Television—Mark Greif (N + 1)
Burying The Dead—Paul Christensen (Antioch Review)
John Dos Passos In Provincetown—Townsend Ludington (Provincetown Arts)
Return To Sender—Mark Doty (Writer's Chronicle)
Back—Rebecca McClanahan (Gettysburg Review)
Teaching the N-Word—Emily Bernard (American Scholar)
Goodbye to All That—Eula Biss (North American Review)
Vanished—Jennifer Mattern (Brain, Child)
The Great Wheel—Bill Holm (Speakeasy)
At Home And Away—Evelyn Shakir (Another Chicago Magazine)
Faith And Heresy—Karen Hering (Speakeasy)
The Fanatic Heart—James Nolan (Boulevard)
Letter To A German Friend—C.K. Williams (Salmagundi)
Romancing The Dankerts—Ben Miller (Agni)
Group Grief—Lily Tuck (Hudson Review)

John Berryman—David Wojahn (Blackbird)

An Old Home, Who'll Stay?—Brandon R. Schrand (River Teeth)

Yom Kippur Night Dance—Susan Hahn (Kenyon Review)

Sam At the Gun Show—Greg Bottoms (Creative Nonfiction)

They Are Feeding Those Kids Something That They Didn't Feed
Us—Abigail Hanlon (Gettysburg Review)

Slaughter—Bonnie J. Rough (Bellingham Review)

16 Postcards From Terra Incognita—Michael Martone (Prism)

The Bicycle and The Soul—Michael Waters (New Letters)

American Mazl: Yiddish Poets In the New World—Jacqueline Os-
herow (Western Humanties Review)

FICTION

Drawing The Line—Meredith Hall (Five Points)

Reservations—Dan Pope (Crazyhorse)

Get It One Last Time—Peter Nathaniel Malae (ZYZZYVA)

Fishing—Margaret Kaufman (Kenyon Review)

St. Helene—Alice Hoffman (Ploughshares)

The Proper Words For Sin—Gary Fincke (Black Warrior Review)

Local Time—Robin Hemley (Southern Review)

Good Samaritan Points—Susanne Rivecca (Blackbird)

Centrally Isolated—Alice Fulton (Epoch)

This Way Uncle, Into The Palace—Paul Eggers (Missouri Review)

Heart Shaped Rock—Antonya Nelson (Cincinnati Review

Sir John Paper Returns to Honah Lee—Robert Coover (Conjunc-
tions)

On The Decline of Sparrows—Willima J. Cobb (Antioch Review)

The Napoleon of Champagne—Charlie Smith (Five Points)

The Raft—Bob Hicok (Southern Review)

This Is Why I'm Thinking of You—Callie Wright (Southern Review)

The Proprietress—Yiyun Li (Zoetrope)

Dominion—Mark Slouka (TriQuarterly)

Why I Sold My Baby At The Wal-Mark—Elizabeth Orndorff (Boule-
vard)

Creep—Sarah Shun-lien Bynum (TriQuarterly)

Coulrophobia—Jacob M. Appel (Bellevue Literary Review)

Her Gorgeous Grief—Catherine Harnett (Hudson Review)

Great Men And Famous Deeds—Janet Peery (Kenyon Review)

My Mouth, Her Sex, The Night, My Heart—Steve Almond (Missouri Review)
Good To Go—Frederick Busch (Threepenny Review)
Living In The Trees—Paul Zimmer (Shenandoah)
Sleepwalk—Valerie Sayers (Ploughshares)
A Friend of Dr. Reis—Robert Boyers (Michigan Quarterly)
The Cold Just Does Things To You—Jolie Lewis (Tin House)
The Lives of Rocks—Rick Bass (Zoetrope)
Growing Up Drug Free In America—Terry Dubow (Paper Street)
High Lonesome—Joyce Carol Oates (Zoetrope)
Open Up and Say Ow—Steve Almond (New England Review)
Mudder Tongue—Brian Evenson (McSweeney's)
Jimmie Fitz, Bette Davis and A Chirsty Mathewson Episode—Don Fredd (Underground Voices)
Up—Randy DeVita (Third Coast)
Through The Water of the Clouds—Sharon May (StoryQuarterly)
Amphibious Life—Lee Ann Roripaugh (North American Review)
Solos—Christopher Coake (Five Points)
The Agriculture Hall of Fame—Andrew Malan Milward (Crazyhorse)
The Man With The Hairy Back—Shahan Sanossian (Speakeasy)
Next In Line—Jessica Francis Kane (Brain, Child)
John McEnroe Visits Seven Months—Sean Aden Lovelace (Crazyhorse)
The Magic Box—Robert Anthony Siegel (Post Road)
The Guild of Thieves, Lost Woman, and Sunrise Palms—Nic Pizzolato (Quarterly West)
Held At Gunpoint—Ellen Morris Prewitt (Image)
Skyglass Bastard—Kari Strutt (Event)
Interference—Richard Hoffman (Witness)
The Driest Season—Meghan Kenny (Iowa Review)
Pioneer—Anne Sanow (Shenandoah)
Indivisualized Altimetry of Stripes—Charles McLeod (Iowa Review)
Portions—Jodi Angel (Zoetrope)
The Boston Globe Personal Line—Champa Bilwakesh (Kenyon Review)
Q & A—Stephanie Dickinson (Water-Stone Review)
Thorazine—Scott Schrader (Gettysburg Review)
The Dog—Jack Livings (Paris Review)

Jamestown, N.Y.—Thomas Bonfiglio (Northwest Review)
The Magic Box—Robert Anthony Siegel (Post Road)
Nadia—Judy Budnitz (One Story)
A More Perfect Union—Jessamyn Smyth (American Letters & Commentary)
A Dove On Top of the Tower—Yan Lianke (Turnrow)
The Brief—Oliver Broudy (Glimmer Train)
All Or Nothing At The Faberge—Peter Grandbois (Post Road)
Is Your Figure Less Than Greek?—Stephen Taylor (Antioch Review)
Girl Reporter—Stephanie Harrell (One Story)
Tending Something—Ann Beattie (TriQuarterly)
Fragile: This Side Up—Melodie Edwards (Michigan Quarterly)
from Chasing The Sun—Christopher Fahy (Puckerbrush Press)
A Drowning Accident—Brian Booker (One Story)
So Now Sorrow—Mary Kuryla (Pleiades)
My Uncle's Poor French—Robert Day (New Letters)
The Silent Men—Peter Rock (Western Humanities Review)
The Animal Girl—John Fulton (Alaska Quarterly Review)
You Love That Dog—Mary Helen Stefaniak (Epoch)
Road of Five Churches—Stephanie Dickinson (Pearl)
Sleeping Baby—Glori Simmons (Chelsea)
Weekend In Alexandria—Maria Golia (Fiction International)
Such Fun—James Salter (Tin House)
A More Perfect Union—Jessamyn Smyth (American Letters & Commentary)
A Purple Story—Josip Novakovich (Boulevard)
Mudman—Pinckney Benedict (Tin House)
Paradise In A Cup—Keith Scribner (TriQuarterly)
The Price of A Haircut—Brock Clarke (Agni)
The Tinker's Bairn—Ellen Grehan (Ontario Review)
La Golandrina—Tom Filer (Artful Dodge)
Good Girl—Holly Goddard Jones (Southern Review)
Shipwrecks—Jerry D. Mathes II (Dos Passos Review)
The Dead In Paradise—Lee Martin (Shenandoah)
His Own Time—John Thompson (Bellevue Literary Review)
The Casual Car Pool—Katherine Bell (Ploughshares)
What She Learned In Sears Charm School—Barbara Hamby (Bamboo Ridge)
Conservation—Christopher Torockio (Laurel Review)
Border—Alyson Hagy (Ploughshares)

A Bad Egg—Kathleen Lee (Colorado Review)
Gone—Glen Pourciau (Ontario Review)
Homework—Susan McCarthy (Northwest Review)
Any Landlord's Dream—Gregory Spatz (New England Review)
Gravity—Lee K. Abbott (Georgia Review)
Secret—Maxine Swann (Ploughshares)
Thunderbird—Mark Poirier (Conjunctions)
Aliens—Robert Cohen (Virginia Quarterly)
The Daily Willa—Philip Graham (Crab Orchard Review)
Riverside—Rus Bradburd (Southern Review)
The Briefcase Of The Pregnant Spylady—Jeff Parker (Columbia)
Escape—Susan Kenney (Epoch)
Betting on Men—Joan Frank (Antioch Review)
Respect-the-Aged Week—Kenzaburō Ōe (Threepenny Review)

POETRY

Rare—Betty Adcock (Smartish Pace)
Why The Marriage Failed—Adrian Blevins (Beloit Poetry Journal)
Snabbt Jagar Stormen Våra År—Ann Fisher-Wirth (Drunken Boat)
Fines Doubled In Work Zone—Richard Jackson (Georgia Review)
Weltschmerz—Rita Dove (Callaloo)
Father Merc, Mother Tongue—Linda Gregerson (Poetry)
If They Don't Have Ritalin In Heaven—Roy Jacobstein (Gettysburg
    Review)
Vermont Barn—Lynne Knight (American Poetry Journal)
Yard Work—James Longenbach (Yale Review)
Why Coal Companies Favor Mountaintop Removal—Maurice Man-
    ning (*Missing Mountains*, Kentuckians for the Commonwealth)
The River Scrapes Against Night—Wendy Mnookin (Runes)
Breaking The Spell—Carl Phillips (Ploughshares)
You've Got It Made—J. Allyn Rosser (Poetry)
First Sight—Ellen Doré Watson (*Never Before*, Four Way Books)
Officer, I Saw The Whole Thing—Eric Paul Shaffer (*Lahaina Noon*,
    Leaping Dog Press)
The Meadow—Kate Knapp Johnson (Poetry 180)
To a Chameleon—Michael Collier (Georgia Review)
Ovid in Tears—Jack Gilbert (The Paris Review)
A Marriage in Belmont—D. Nurkse (Poetry)
The Hook—Nadine Myer (New Letters)

from Girls' School—Claudia Emerson (The Greensboro Review)
Tired—Christopher Michel (Free Lunch)
The Past as Obsolete Gesture—Mark Svenvold (Frostproof Review)
The Happy Friend—David Mason (Southwest Review)
Grille—Sarah Maclay (Field)
First Lesson: Winter Trees—Michael Waters (Four Way Books)
The Word from His Mouth . . .—Brian Teare (Crowd)
Paradelle: Prayer—Daniel Tobin (Image: Art, Faith, Mystery)
Hush—Erin Malone (Field)
The Mist Netters—Davis McCombs (Poetry)

PRESSES FEATURED IN THE PUSHCART PRIZE EDITIONS SINCE 1976

Acts
Agni
Ahsahta Press
Ailanthus Press
Alaska Quarterly Review
Alcheringa/Ethnopoetics
Alice James Books
Ambergris
Amelia
American Letters and Commentary
American Literature
American PEN
American Poetry Review
American Scholar
American Short Fiction
The American Voice
Amicus Journal
Amnesty International
Anaesthesia Review
Another Chicago Magazine
Antaeus
Antietam Review
Antioch Review
Apalachee Quarterly
Aphra
Aralia Press
The Ark

Art and Understanding
Arts and Letters
Artword Quarterly
Ascensius Press
Ascent
Aspen Leaves
Aspen Poetry Anthology
Assembling
Atlanta Review
Autonomedia
Avocet Press
The Baffler
Bakunin
Bamboo Ridge
Barlenmir House
Barnwood Press
Barrow Street
Bellevue Literary Review
The Bellingham Review
Bellowing Ark
Beloit Poetry Journal
Bennington Review
Bilingual Review
Black American Literature Forum
Blackbird
Black Rooster
Black Scholar

Black Sparrow
Black Warrior Review
Blackwells Press
Bloom
Bloomsbury Review
Blue Cloud Quarterly
Blue Unicorn
Blue Wind Press
Bluefish
BOA Editions
Bomb
Bookslinger Editions
Boston Review
Boulevard
Boxspring
Bridge
Bridges
Brown Journal of Arts
Burning Deck Press
Caliban
California Quarterly
Callaloo
Calliope
Calliopea Press
Calyx
Canto
Capra Press
Caribbean Writer
Carolina Quarterly
Cedar Rock
Center
Chariton Review
Charnel House
Chattahoochee Review
Chautauqua Literary Journal
Chelsea
Chicago Review
Chouteau Review
Chowder Review
Cimarron Review
Cincinnati Poetry Review
City Lights Books
Cleveland State Univ. Poetry Ctr.

Clown War
CoEvolution Quarterly
Cold Mountain Press
Colorado Review
Columbia: A Magazine of Poetry and
    Prose
Confluence Press
Confrontation
Conjunctions
Connecticut Review
Copper Canyon Press
Cosmic Information Agency
Countermeasures
Counterpoint
Crawl Out Your Window
Crazyhorse
Crescent Review
Cross Cultural Communications
Cross Currents
Crosstown Books
Crowd
Cue
Cumberland Poetry Review
Curbstone Press
Cutbank
Dacotah Territory
Daedalus
Dalkey Archive Press
Decatur House
December
Denver Quarterly
Desperation Press
Dogwood
Domestic Crude
Doubletake
Dragon Gate Inc.
Dreamworks
Dryad Press
Duck Down Press
Durak
East River Anthology
Eastern Washington University Press
Ellis Press

Empty Bowl
Epoch
Ergo!
Evansville Review
Exquisite Corpse
Faultline
Fence
Fiction
Fiction Collective
Fiction International
Field
Fine Madness
Firebrand Books
Firelands Art Review
First Intensity
Five Fingers Review
Five Points Press
Five Trees Press
The Formalist
Fourth Genre
Frontiers: A Journal of Women Studies
Fugue
Gallimaufry
Genre
The Georgia Review
Gettysburg Review
Ghost Dance
Gibbs-Smith
Glimmer Train
Goddard Journal
David Godine, Publisher
Graham House Press
Grand Street
Granta
Graywolf Press
Great River Review
Green Mountains Review
Greenfield Review
Greensboro Review
Guardian Press
Gulf Coast
Hanging Loose
Hard Pressed

Harvard Review
Hayden's Ferry Review
Hermitage Press
Heyday
Hills
Hollyridge Press
Holmgangers Press
Holy Cow!
Home Planet News
Hudson Review
Hungry Mind Review
Icarus
Icon
Idaho Review
Iguana Press
Image
Indiana Review
Indiana Writes
Intermedia
Intro
Invisible City
Inwood Press
Iowa Review
Ironwood
Jam To-day
The Journal
Jubilat
The Kanchenjuga Press
Kansas Quarterly
Kayak
Kelsey Street Press
Kenyon Review
Kestrel
Latitudes Press
Laughing Waters Press
Laurel Review
L'Epervier Press
Liberation
Linquis
Literal Latté
Literary Imagination
The Literary Review
The Little Magazine

Living Hand Press
Living Poets Press
Logbridge-Rhodes
Louisville Review
Lowlands Review
Lucille
Lynx House Press
Lyric
The MacGuffin
Magic Circle Press
Malahat Review
Mānoa
Manroot
Many Mountains Moving
Marlboro Review
Massachusetts Review
McSweeney's
Meridian
Mho & Mho Works
Micah Publications
Michigan Quarterly
Mid-American Review
Milkweed Editions
Milkweed Quarterly
The Minnesota Review
Mississippi Review
Mississippi Valley Review
Missouri Review
Montana Gothic
Montana Review
Montemora
Moon Pony Press
Mount Voices
Mr. Cogito Press
MSS
Mudfish
Mulch Press
Nada Press
National Poetry Review
Nebraska Review
New America
New American Review
New American Writing

The New Criterion
New Delta Review
New Directions
New England Review
New England Review and Bread Loaf
    Quarterly
New Issues
New Letters
New Orleans Review
New Virginia Review
New York Quarterly
New York University Press
News from The Republic of Letters
Nimrod
9 × 9 Industries
Ninth Letter
Noon
North American Review
North Atlantic Books
North Dakota Quarterly
North Point Press
Northeastern University Press
Northern Lights
Northwest Review
Notre Dame Review
O. ARS
O. Blēk
Obsidian
Obsidian II
Oconee Review
October
Ohio Review
Old Crow Review
Ontario Review
Open City
Open Places
Orca Press
Orchises Press
Oregon Humanities
Orion
Other Voices
Oxford American
Oxford Press

Oyez Press
Oyster Boy Review
Painted Bride Quarterly
Painted Hills Review
Palo Alto Review
Paris Press
Paris Review
Parkett
Parnassus: Poetry in Review
Partisan Review
Passages North
Pebble Lake Review
Penca Books
Pentagram
Penumbra Press
Pequod
Persea: An International Review
Perugià Press
Pipedream Press
Pitcairn Press
Pitt Magazine
Pleiades
Ploughshares
Poet and Critic
Poet Lore
Poetry
Poetry East
Poetry Ireland Review
Poetry Northwest
Poetry Now
Post Road
Prairie Schooner
Prescott Street Press
Press
Promise of Learnings
Provincetown Arts
Puerto Del Sol
Quaderni Di Yip
Quarry West
The Quarterly
Quarterly West
Raccoon
Rainbow Press

Raritan: A Quarterly Review
Red Cedar Review
Red Clay Books
Red Dust Press
Red Earth Press
Red Hen Press
Release Press
Review of Contemporary Fiction
Revista Chicano-Riquena
Rhetoric Review
Rivendell
River Styx
River Teeth
Rowan Tree Press
Runes
Russian *Samizdat*
Salmagundi
San Marcos Press
Sarabande Books
Sea Pen Press and Paper Mill
Seal Press
Seamark Press
Seattle Review
Second Coming Press
Semiotext(e)
Seneca Review
Seven Days
The Seventies Press
Sewanee Review
Shankpainter
Shantih
Shearsman
Sheep Meadow Press
Shenandoah
A Shout In the Street
Sibyl-Child Press
Side Show
Small Moon
The Smith
Solo
Solo 2
Some
The Sonora Review

Southern Poetry Review
Southern Review
Southwest Review
Speakeasy
Spectrum
Spillway
The Spirit That Moves Us
St. Andrews Press
Story
Story Quarterly
Streetfare Journal
Stuart Wright, Publisher
Sulfur
The Sun
Sun & Moon Press
Sun Press
Sunstone
Sycamore Review
Tamagwa
Tar River Poetry
Teal Press
Telephone Books
Telescope
Temblor
The Temple
Tendril
Texas Slough
Third Coast
13th Moon
THIS
Thorp Springs Press
Three Rivers Press
Threepenny Review
Thunder City Press
Thunder's Mouth Press
Tia Chucha Press
Tikkun
Tin House
Tombouctou Books
Toothpaste Press
Transatlantic Review
Triplopia
TriQuarterly

Truck Press
Tupelo Press
Turnrow
Undine
Unicorn Press
University of Georgia Press
University of Illinois Press
University of Iowa Press
University of Massachusetts Press
University of North Texas Press
University of Pittsburgh Press
University of Wisconsin Press
University Press of New England
Unmuzzled Ox
Unspeakable Visions of the Individual
Vagabond
Verse
Vignette
Virginia Quarterly
Volt
Wampeter Press
Washington Writers Workshop
Water-Stone
Water Table
Western Humanities Review
Westigan Review
White Pine Press
Wickwire Press
Willow Springs
Wilmore City
Witness
Word Beat Press
Word-Smith
Wormwood Review
Writers Forum
Xanadu
Yale Review
Yardbird Reader
Yarrow
Y'Bird
Zeitgeist Press
Zoetrope: All-Story
ZYZZYVA

CONTRIBUTING SMALL PRESSES FOR PUSHCART PRIZE XXXI

A

Abyss & Apex, 7635 Jefferson Hwy., Baton Rouge, LA 70809
The Adirondack Review, 305 Keyes Ave., Watertown, NY 13601
Agni, Boston Univ., 236 Bay State Rd., Boston, MA 02215
Akashic Books, P.O. Box 1456, New York, NY 10009
Alaska Quarterly Review, Univ. of Alaska, 3211 Providence Dr., Anchorage, AK 99508
Alice James Books, 238 Main St., Farmington, ME 04938
All Nations Press, P.O. Box 601, White Marsh, VA 23183
The American Journal of Poetry, P.O. Box 250, Chesterfield, MO 63006
American Letters & Commentary, 850 Park Ave., Ste. 5B, New York, NY 10021
American Poetry Journal, P.O. Box 4041, Felton, CA 95108
The American Scholar, 1606 New Hampshire Ave., NW, Washington, DC 20009
Ancient Paths, P.O. Box 7505, Fairfax Station, VA 22039
Anhinga Press, P.O. Box 10595, Tallahassee, FL 32302
Another Chicago Magazine, 3709 N. Kenmore, Chicago, IL 60613
Antietam Review, 14 W. Washington St., Hagerstown, MD 21740
Antioch Review, P.O. Box 148, Yellow Springs, OH 45387
Antrim House, 21 Goodrich Rd., Simsbury, CT 06070
Apex Publications, 4629 Riverman Way, Lexington, KY 40515
Apogee Press, P.O. Box 8177, Berkeley, CA 94707
Arctos Press, P.O. Box 401, Sausalito, CA 94966
Arizona Literary Magazine, P.O. Box 89857, Phoenix, AZ 85080
Arkansas Literary Forum, Henderson State Univ., Box 7601, Arkadelphia, AR 71999
Arkansas Review, P.O. Box 1890, Arkansas State Univ., State University, AR 72467
Arriviste Press, Inc., 2193 Commonwealth Ave., Boston, MA 02135
Arsenic Lobster, 1608 S. Paulina St., Chicago, IL 60608
Artemesia Publishing, P.O. Box 6508, Rocky Mount, NC 27802
Artful Dodge, English Dept., College of Wooster, Wooster, OH 44691
Arts & Letters, Georgia College & State Univ., Campus Box 89, Milledgeville, GA 31061
Asian American Writers' Workshop, 16 West 32nd St., Ste. 10A, New York, NY 10001
The Aurorean, P.O. Box 187, Farmington, ME 04938
Autumn House Press, 87 1/2 Westwood St., Pittsburgh, PA 15211

B

Backwards City Review, P.O. Box 41317, Greensboro, NC 27404
Backwater Press, 3502 N. 52nd St., Omaha, NE 68104
Ballyhoo Stories, 18 Willoughby Ave., #3. Brooklyn, NY 11205
The Baltimore Review, P.O. Box 36418, Towson, MD 21286
Barbaric Yawp, 3700 County Route 24, Russell, NY 13684
Barrelhouse, 3500 Woodridge Ave., Wheaton, MD 20902
Barrow Street, P.O. Box 1831. New York, NY 10156
Bayeux Arts, 4712 Bayard St., Pittsburgh, PA 15213
Bellevue Literary Review, Dept. of Medicine, NYU School of Medicine, 550 First Ave., OBV-612, NY, NY 10016
Bellowing Ark Press, P.O. Box 55564, Shoreline, WA 98155
Beloit Poetry Journal, P.O. Box 151, Farmington, ME 04938
Birch Book Press, P.O. Box 81, Delhi, NY 13753
BkMk Press, Univ. of Missouri, 5101 Rockhill Rd., Kansas City, MO 64110
Black Clock Magazine, 24700 McBean Pkwy, Valencia, CA 91355
Black Warrior Review, Box 870170, Tuscaloosa, AL 35487
Blackbird, Virginia Commonwealth Univ., Eng. Dept., Richmond, VA 23284
Blue Fifth Review, 267 Lark Meadow Ct., Bluff City, TN 37618
Blue Mesa Review, 1108 Calle del Solne, Albuquerque, NM 87106
Blue Tiger Press, 2016 Hwy 67, Dousman, WI 53118
BOA Editions, Ltd., 260 East Ave., Rochester, NY 14604
Boston Review, Bldg. E53. Rm. 407, MIT, Cambridge, MA 02139
Boulevard, 7545 Cromwell Dr., Apt. 2N, St. Louis, MO 63105
Box Turtle Press, 184 Franklin St., New York, NY 10013
Brain, Child, P.O. Box 714, Lexington, VA 24450
Branches, P.O. Box 85394, Seattle, WA 98145
The Briar Cliff Review, P.O. Box 2100, Sioux City, IA 51104
Bridge, 119 N. Peoria, #3d, Chicago, IL 60607
Brilliant Corners, Lycoming College, Williamsport, PA 17701
Bullfight Review, P.O. Box 362, Walnut Creek, CA 94597
The Bunny and the Crocodile Press, 1821 Glade Ct., Annapolis, MD 21403
Byline, P.O. Box 5240, Edmond, OK 73083

C

Caduceus, P.O. Box 9805, New Haven, CT 06536
Cake Train, 174 Carriage Dr., North Huntingdon, PA 15642
Callaloo, Texas A&M Univ., 249 Blocker Bldg., College Station, TX 77843
Calyx, P.O. Box B, 216 SW Madison, Corvallis, OR 97339
The Canary, 512 Clear Lake Rd., Kemah, TX 77565
The Caribbean Writer, Univ. of the Virgin Islands, RR2-10000 Kingshill, St. Croix, U.S. Virgin Islands, 00850
Carve Magazine, P.O. Box 1573, Tallahassee, FL. 32302
Cellar Roots, EMU, Goddard Hall, Ypsilanti, MI 48197
Centennial Press, P.O. Box 170322, Milwaukee, WI 53217
Center, 107 Tate Hall, Columbia, MO 65211
Central Avenue Press, 2132A Central St., #144, Albuquerque, NM 87106
Cezanne's Carrot, P.O. Box 6037, Santa Fe, NM 87502
Chaffin Journal, Eastern Kentucky Univ., 521 Lancaster Ave., Richmond, KY 40475
The Chattahoochee Review, Georgia Perimeter College, 2101 Womack Rd. Dunwoody, GA 30338
Chautauqua Literary Journal, P.O. Box 2039, York Beach, ME 03910
Chelsea, Box 773, Cooper Sta., New York, NY 10276
Chick Flicks, 3108-B Westbury Lake Dr., Charlotte, NC 28269

Chicory Blue Press, Inc., 795 East St., North, Goshen, CT 06756
Cider Press Review, 777 Braddock Lane, Halifax, PA 17032
Cimarron Review, 205 Morrill Hall, Eng. Dept., Oklahoma State Univ., Stillwater, OK 74078
Cincinnati Review, English Dept., Univ. of Cincinnati, P.O. Box 210069, Cincinnati, OH 45221
City Lights Books, 261 Columbus Ave., San Francisco, CA 94133
Cleveland State University Poetry Center, 2121 Euclid Ave., Cleveland, OH 44115
Cloverfield Press, 429 N. Ogden Dr., #1, Los Angeles, CA 90036
Coal City Review. Univ. of Kansas, Lawrence, KS 66045
Coconut Poetry, 2331 Eastway Rd., Decatur, GA 30033
Colorado Review, English Dept., Colorado State Univ., Fort Collins, CO 80523
Concrete Wolf, P.O. Box 730, Amherst, NH 03031
Conjunctions, Bard College, Annandale-on-Hudson, NY 12504
Connecticut Review, English Dept., WCSU, Danbury, CT 06810
Cottonwood, Univ. of Kansas, Rm. 400, Kansas Union, Lawrence, KS 66045
Crab Creek Review, P.O. Box 840, Vashon Island, WA 98070
Crackpot Press, 10915 Bluffside Dr., #132, Studio City, CA 91604
Cranky Literary Journal, 322 10th Ave. E, #C-5, Seattle, WA 98102
Crazyhorse, English Dept., Univ. of Charleston, 66 George St., Charleston, SC 29424
Cream City Review, English Dept., Univ. of Milwaukee, Milwaukee, WI 53201
Crowd, 341 42nd St., #4, Oakland, CA 94609
Crumpled Press, 477 West 142nd St., #5, New York, NY 10031
Cue, P.O. Box 200, 2509 N. Campbell Ave., Tucson, AZ 85719
The Culture Star Reader, 45 Hudson Ave., #743, Albany, NY 12207
Curbstone Press, 321 Jackson St., Willimantic, CT 06226
Cynic Press, P.O. Box 40691, Philadelphia, PA 19107

D

Dana Literary Society, P.O. Box 3362, Dana Point, CA 92629
DC Books, Box 662, 950 Decarie, Montreal, Que., CANADA H4L 4V9
Diner, Box 60676, Greendale Sta., Worcester, MA 01606
The DMQ Review, 16393 Bonnie Lane, Los Gatos, CA 95032
Dogwood, English Dept., Fairfield Univ., Fairfield, CT 06824
Donatello Press, 2508 Stoner Ave., Los Angeles, CA 90025
Dragonfire, 3210 Cherry St., 2nd fl., Philadelphia, PA 19104
The Duck & Herring Co., 279 Josephine St., Atlanta, GA 30307
Dunhill Publishing, 18340 Sonoma Highway, Sonoma, CA 95476

E

Ecotone, 622 Waynich Blvd., #102, Wrightsville Beach, NC 28480
Edgar Magazine, RD Box 5776, San Leon, TX 77539
Edge Publications, P.O. Box 799, Ocean Park, WA 98640
elimae, 1420 R.V., El Paso, TX 79928
Elkhound, Box 1453, Gracie Sta., New York, NY 10028
Emergency Press, 531 West 25th St., New York, NY 10001
Epiphany, 244 East 3rd, New York, NY 10009
Epoch, 251 Goldwin Smith Hall, Cornell Univ., Ithaca, NY 14853
Esopus, 532 LaGuardia Pl., #485, New York, NY 10012
Eureka Literary Magazine, 300 E. College Ave., Eureka, IL 61530
The Evansville Review, 1800 Lincoln Ave., Evansville, IN 47722
Event, Douglas College, P.O. Box 2503, New Westminster, B.C. CANADA V3L 5B2

F

F Magazine, Columbia College, 600 S. Michigan Ave., Chicago, IL 60605
Facets: A Literary Magazine, P.O. Box 380915, Cambridge, MA 02238
Failbetter, 40 Montgomery Pl., #2, Brooklyn, NY 11215
Fairy Tale Review, English Dept., Univ. of Alabama, Tuscaloosa, AL 35487
Fiction International, San Diego State Univ., San Diego, CA 92182
Field, Oberlin College, 50 N. Professor St., Oberlin, OH 44074
Finishing Line Press, P.O. Box 1626, Georgetown, KY 40324
Firewheel Editions, 181 White St., Danbury, CT 06810
The First Line, P.O. Box 250382, Plano, TX 75025
Fithian Press, P.O. Box 2790, McKinleyville, CA 95519
5 AM, Box 205, Spring Church, PA 15686
Five Points, Georgia State Univ., P.O. Box 3999, Atlanta, GA 30302
flashquake, P.O. Box 2154, Albany, NY 12220
Floating Bridge Press, P.O. Box 18814, Seattle, WA 98118
Florida Review, UCF, P.O. Box 161400, Orlando, FL 32816
Flume Press, English Dept., California State Univ., Chico, CA 95929
Focus, English Dept., Spelman College, 350 Spelman La., SW, Atlanta, GA 30314
Fourteen Hills, San Francisco State Univ., 1600 Holloway Ave., San Francisco, CA 94132
Fourth Genre, 285 Bessey Hall, Michigan State Univ., East Lansing, MI 48825
Free Lunch, P.O. Box 717, Glenview, IL 60025
Free Verse, M233 Marsh Rd., Marshfield, WI 54449
Fresh Boiled Peanuts, P.O. Box 43194, Cincinnati, OH 45243
Frigg, 9036 Evanston Ave., N, Seattle, WA 98103
Frith Press, P.O. Box 161236, Sacramento, CA 95816
Frostproof Review, 3190 NW Blvd., Columbus, OH 43221

G

Gargoyle, 3819 13th St., W, Arlington, VA 22201
Garrett County Press, 614 S. 8th St., #373, Philadelphia, PA 19147
A Gathering of the Tribes, P.O. Box 20693, New York, NY 10009
The Gettysburg Review, Gettysburg College, Gettysburg, PA 17325
Ghost Road Press, 5303 E. Evans Ave., #309, Denver, CO 80222
Gin Bender, P.O. Box 150932, Lufkin, TX 75915
Givall Press, LLC, P.O. Box 3812, Arlington, VA 22203
Gloucester Spoken Art, 2066 Kings Grove Crescent, Gloucester, Ont., *CANADA* K1J 6G1
Gobshite Quarterly, P.O. Box 11346, Portland, OR 97211
Grayson Books, P.O. Box 270549, West Hartford, CT 06127
The Great American Poetry Show, P.O. Box 69506, West Hollywood, CA 90069
Great River Review, Anderson Center, P.O. Box 406, Red Wing, MN 55066
Green Hills Literary Lantern, 100 E. Normal, Truman State Univ., Kirksville, MO 63501
Green Mountains Review, Johnson State College, Johnson, VT 05656
The Greensboro Review, UNCG, P.O. Box 26170, Greensboro, NC 27402
The Grove Review, 1631 NE Broadway, PMB#137, Portland, OR 97232
Gulf Coast, English Dept., Univ. of Houston, Houston, TX 77204

H

Hanging Loose Press, 231 Wyckoff St., Brooklyn, NY 11217
Harp-String Poetry Journal, Box 640387, Beverly Hills, FL 14464

Harper's Ferry Review, Arizona State Univ., P.O. Box 87502, Tempe, AZ 85287
Harpur Palate, English Dept., Binghamton Univ., Binghamton, NY 13902
Harvard Review, Lamont Library, Level 5, Harvard Univ., Cambridge, MA 02138
Haunted Rowboat Press, 162 Longley Rd., Madison, ME 04950
The Healing Muse, Upstate Medical Univ., 750 E. Adams St., Syracuse, NY 13210
Heliotrope, P.O. Box 456, Shady, NY 12409
Historical Society of Ocean Grove, P.O. Box 446, Ocean Grove, NJ 07756
H-NGM-N Press, Northwestern State Univ., Natchitoches, LA 71497
Hobart: A Literary Journal, P.O. Box 1658, Ann Arbor, MI 48103
Hollins Critic, Hollins Univ., Roanoke, VA 24020
Home Planet News, P.O. Box 455, High Falls, NY 12440
Hopewell Publications, LLC, P.O. Box 11, Titusville, NJ 08560
Hotel Amerika, Ohio Univ., 360 Ellis Hall, Athens, OH 45701
The Hudson Review, 684 Park Ave., New York, NY 10021
Hunger Mountain, Vermont College, 36 College St., Montpelier, VT 05602

I

Ibbetson Street, 25 School St., Somerville, MA 02143
The Iconoclast, 165 Amazon Rd., Mohegan Lake, NY 10547
Illuminations, English Dept., College of Charleston, 66 George St., Charleston, SC 29424
Illya's Honey, P.O. Box 700865, Dallas, TX 75370
Image, 3307 Third Ave., W, Seattle, WA 98119
Indiana Review, 1020 E. Kirkwood Ave., Bloomington, IN 47405
Inkwell, Manhattanville College, 2900 Purchase St., Purchase, NY 10577
Invisible Insurrection, 925 NW Hoyt St., #231, Portland, OR 97209
The Iowa Review, Univ. of Iowa, Iowa City, IA 52242

J

Jabberwock Review, English Dept., Drawer E, Mississippi State, MS 39763
Jewish Women's Literary Annual, 820 2nd Ave., New York, NY 10017
The Journal, English Dept., Ohio State Univ., Columbus, OH 43210
Journal of New Jersey Poets, CO. College of Morris, 214 Center Grove Rd., Randplph, NJ 07869
Jubilat, English Dept., Univ. of Massachusetts, Amherst, MA 01003

K

Karamu, English Dept., Eastern Illinois Univ., 600 Lincoln Ave., Charleston, IL 61920
Kelsey Review, P.O. Box B, Trenton, NJ 08690
The Kenyon Review, 104 College Dr., Gambier, OH 43022
Killing the Buddha, 1986 McAfee Rd., Decatur, GA 30032
The King's English, 3114 NE 47th Ave., Portland, OR 97213
Kitchen Sink Magazine, 5245 College Ave, #301, Oakland, CA 94618
Knock, Antioch Univ., 2326 Sixth Ave., Seattle, WA 98121
Kyoto Journal, Minamigoshomachi, Okazaki-Ku, Kyoto 606-8334, JAPAN

L

Lake Effect, 5091 Station Rd., Erie, PA 16563
Land-Grant College Review, P.O. Box 1164, New York, NY 10159
Laurel Poetry Collective, 1168 Laurel Ave., St. Paul, MN 55104
Licking River Review, Nunn Dr., Highland Heights, KY 41099
Like Water Burning Press, 109 Mira Mar Ave., #301, Long Beach, CA 90803
Lillies and Cannonballs Review, P.O. Box 702, Bowling Green Sta., New York, NY 10274
Lily Literary Review, P.O. Box 76, Nucla, CO 81424
LIT Magazine, 66 West 12th St., Rm. 514, New York, NY 10011
Lorraine & James, 3727 W. Magnolia Blvd., Box 406, Burbank, CA 91505
Louisiana State University Press, P.O. Box 25053, Baton Rouge, LA 70894
The Louisville Review, Spalding Univ., 851 S. Fourth St., Louisville, KY 40203
Lyric Poetry Review, P.O. Box 2494, Bloomington, IN 47402

M

Mad Hatter's Review, 105 West 13th St., New York, NY 10011
The Malahat Review, Univ. of Victoria, P.O. Box 1700, Sta. CSC, Victoria BC V8W 2Y2 *CANADA*
Mandorla, Illinois State Univ., Campus Box 4241, Normal, IL 61790
The Manhattan Review, 440 Riverside Dr., #38, New York, NY 10027
Manic D Press, 250 Banks St., San Francisco, CA 94110
Manoa, English Dept., Univ. of Hawaii, Honolulu, HI 96822
Margin, 321 High School Rd., NE, PMB #204, Bainbridge Island, WA 98110
Marsh Hawk Press, P.O. Box 206, East Rockaway, NY 11518
Marsh River Editions, M233 Marsh Rd., Marshfield, WI 54449
The Massachusetts Review, Univ. of Massachusetts, South College, A103770, Amherst, MA 01003
The Means, P.O. Box 183246, Shelby Township, MI 48318
Memorious. Org, 60 Winslow Ave., Somerville, MA 02144
Mercer University Press, 1400 Coleman Ave., Macon, GA 31207
Me Three Literary Journal, 101 Lafayette Ave., Brooklyn, NY 11217
Micah Publications, Inc., 255 Humphrey St., Marblehead, MA 01945
Michigan Quarterly Review, 915 E. Washington St., Ann Arbor, MI 48109
Michigan State University Press, 1405 S. Harrison Rd., Ste. 25, East Lansing, MI 48823
Mid-American Review, English Dept., Bowling Green State Univ., Bowling Green, OH 43403
Mindfire Renewed, 2518 Fruitland Dr., Bremerton, WA 98310
Mind Prints, 800 S. College Dr., Santa Maria, CA 93454
The Minnesota Review, English Dept., Carnegie Mellon Univ., Pittsburgh, PA 15213
MiPOesias Magazine, 4601 SW 94 Ct., Miami, FL 33165
Mississippi Review, Univ. of So. Mississippi, Box 5144, Hattiesburg, MS 39406
Missouri Review, Univ. of Missouri, 1507 Hillcrest Hall, Columbia, MO 65211
The Modern Review, RPO P.O. Box 32659, Richmond Hill, Ont. L4C OA2 *CANADA*
Moon in Blue Water, 430 M St., SW-N600, Washington, DC 20024
Moondance, P.O. Box 92-3713, Sylmar, CA 91342
Multicultural Books, 6311 Gilbert Rd., Richmond, BC V7C 3V7 *CANADA*

N

N + 1, PO Box 20688, Park West Station, NY 10025
Nassau Review, Nassau Community College, 2 Education Dr., Garden City, NY 11596
The National Poetry Review, P.O. Box 4041, Felton, CA 95018

Natural Bridge, English Dept., Univ. of Missouri, St. Louis, MO 63121
New England Review, Middlebury College, Middlebury, VT 05753
The New Hampshire Review, P.O. Box 322, Nashua, NH 03061
New Issues Poetry & Prose, WMU, 1903 W. Michigan Ave., Kalamazoo, MI 49008
New Letters, see BkMk Press
New Orleans Review, Box 195, Loyola Univ., New Orleans, LA 70118
New Orphic Review, 706 Mill St., Nelson, B.C., V1L 4S5, CANADA
The New Renaissance, 26 Heath Rd., #11, Arlington, MA 02474
New York Stories, 218 Gale Hill Rd., East Chatham, NY 12060
Night Train, 212 Bellingham Ave., #2, Revere, MA 02151
Ninth Letter, English Dept., Univ. of Illinois, 608 S. Wright St., Urbana, IL 61801
Noon, 1369 Madison Ave., PMB 298, New York, NY 10128
North American Review, Univ. of Northern Iowa, Cedar Falls, IA 50614
North Dakota Quarterly, P.O. Box 7209, Univ. of North Dakota, Grand Forks, ND 58202
Northwest Review, 369 PLC, Univ. of Oregon, Eugene, OR 97403
No Tell Motel, 11436 Fairway Dr., Reston, VA 20150
Not One of Us, 12 Curtis Rd., Natick, MA 01760
Notre Dame Review, English Dept., Univ. of Notre Dame, Notre Dame, IN 46556

O

OFF the Coast, P.O. Box 205, Bristol, ME 04539
Old Mountain Press, 2542 S. Edgewater Dr., Fayetteville, NC 28303
Onearth, 40 West 20th St., New York, NY 10011
One Story, 425 3rd St., Apt. 2, Brooklyn, NY 11215
One Trick Pony, P.O. Box 11186, Philadelphia, PA 19136
Ontario Review, 9 Honey Brook Dr., Princeton, NJ 08540
Open Minds Quarterly, 630 Kirkwood Dr., Bldg. 1, Sudbury, Ont. P3E 1X3 CANADA
Open Spaces Publications, Inc., PMB 134, 6327-C SW Capitol Hwy., Portland, OR 97239
Opium Magazine, 40 East Third St., Ste. #8, New York, NY 10003
Order and Decorum, P.O. Box 1051, Carlisle, PA 17013
Osiris, P.O. Box 297, Deerfield, MA 01342
Other, 584 Castro St., #674, San Francisco, CA 94114
Other Voices, English Dept., Univ. of Illinois, 601 S. Morgan St., Chicago, IL 60607
Owen Wister Review, 302 Carthell Rd., Laramie, WY 82070
Oyez Review, Roosevelt Univ., 430 S. Michigan Ave., Chicago, IL 60605

P

Palo Alto Review, Palo Alto College, 1400 W. Villaret Blvd., San Antonio, TX 78224
The Paper Journey, P.O. Box 1575, Wake Forest, NC 27588
Paper Street Press, P.O. Box 14786, Pittsburgh, PA 15234
Paradox, P.O. Box 22897, Brooklyn, NY 11202
Parakeet, 115 Roosevelt Ave, Syracuse, NY 13210
The Paris Review, 62 White St., New York, NY 10013
Parlor Press, 816 Robinson St., West Lafayette, IN 47906
Parnassus: Poetry in Review, 205 W. 89th St, #8F, New York, NY 10024
Pathwise Press, P.O. Box 178, Erie, PA 16512
P.A.W. Magazine, 2720 St. Paul St., 2F, Baltimore, MD 21218
Pearl, 3030 E. Second St., Long Beach, CA 90803
Pebble Lake Review, 15318 Pebble Lake Dr., Houston, TX 77095
Penumbra, P.O. Box 15995, Tallahassee, FL 32317
Perugia Press, P.O. Box 60364, Florence, MA 01063

Phantasmagoria, 3300 Century Ave. North, White Bear Lake, MN 55110
Phoebe, George Mason Univ., 4400 Univ. Dr., Fairfax, VA 22030
Plan B Press, 3412 Terrace Dr., #1731, Alexandria, VA 22302
Pleiades, English Dept., Central Missouri State Univ., Warrensburg, MO 64093
Ploughshares, Emerson College, 120 Boylston St., Boston, MA 02116
PMS, 1530 3rd Ave. S, Birmingham, AL 35294
Poems and Plays, English Dept., Middle Tennessee State Univ., Murfreesboro, TN 37132
poetic diversity, 6028 Comey Ave., Los Angeles, CA 90034
Poetry, 1030 N. Clark St., Ste. 420, Chicago, IL 60610
Poetry Midwest, Johnson Co. Community College, 12345 College Blvd., Overland Park, KS 66210
Poetry Miscellany, English Dept., Univ. of Tennessee, Chattanooga, TN 37403
Poetry Project, St. Mark's Church in-the-Bowery, 131 E. 10th St., New York, NY 10003
Poetry West, P.O. Box 2413, Colorado Springs, CO 80901
Pool, P.O. Box 49738, Los Angeles, CA 98849
Post Road, P.O. Box 400951, Cambridge, MA 02140
Prairie Schooner, Univ. of Nebraska, P.O. Box 880334, Lincoln, NE 68588
Press 53, P.O. Box 30314, Winston Salem, NC 27180
Pretty Things Press, P.O. Box 55, Point Reyes, CA 94956
Prism International, Univ. of British Columbia, 1866 Main Mall, Vancouver, B.C., *CANADA* V6T 1Z1
Provincetown Arts, 650 Commercial St., Provincetown, MA 02657
A Public Space, 323 Dean St., Brooklyn, NY 11217
Puckerbrush Press, 76 Main St., Orono, ME 04473
Puerto del Sol, English Dept., New Mexico State Univ., Las Cruces, NM 88003

Q

Quarterly West, 255 S. Central Campus Dr., Salt Lake City, UT 84112

R

Raritan, 31 Mine St., New Brunswick, NJ 08903
Rattle, 12411 Ventura Blvd., Studio City, CA 91604
Red Hen Press, P.O. Box 3537, Granada Hills, CA 91394
Redactions: Poetry & Poetics, 24 College St., Apt. 1, Brooklyn, NY 14420
Redivider, Emerson College, 120 Boylston St., Boston, MA 02116
Releasing Times, 6077 Far Hills Ave., Centerville, OH 45459
Rhapsoidia, 6570 Jewel St., Riverside, CA 92509
Rhino, P.O. Box 591, Evanston, IL 60204
Rio Nuevo Publishers, 451 N. Bonita Ave. Tucson, AZ 85745
River City, English Dept., Univ. of Memphis, Memphis, TN 38152
River City Publishing, 1719 Mulberry St., Montgomery, AL 36106
River Teeth, English Dept., Ashland Univ., Ashland, OH 44805
Rogue Scholars Press, 228 East 25th St., New York, NY 10010
The Rose & Thorn, 3 Diamond Ct., Montebello, NY 10901

S

Salamander, English Dept., Suffolk Univ., 41 Temple St., Boston, MA 02215
Salmagundi, Skidmore College, Saratoga Springs, NY 12866
Salt Flats Annual, P.O. Box 2381, Layton, UT 84041

Salt Hill, English Dept., Syracuse Univ., Syracuse, NY 13244
Santa Monica Review, Santa Monica College, 1900 Pico Blvd., Santa Monica, CA 90405
Sarabande Books, Inc., 2234 Dundee Rd., Ste. 200, Louisville, KY 40205
Saranac Review, 101 Broad St., Plattsburgh, NY 12901
Schuylkill Valley Journal, 240 Golf Hills Rd., Havertown, PA 19083
Scissor Press, P.O. Box 382, Ludlow, VT 05149
Seems, Lakeland College, P.O. Box 359, Sheboygan, WI 53082
Sensations Magazine, P.O. Box 90, Glen Ridge, NJ 07028
Shenandoah, Mattingly House, Washington & Lee Univ., Lexington, VA 24450
Silk Label Books, P.O. Box 700, Unionville, NY 10988
Skidrow Penthouse, 44 Corners Rd., Blairstown, NJ 07825
Slipstream, P.O. Box 2071, Niagara Falls, NY 14301
Small Beer Press, 176 Prospect Ave., Northampton, MA 01060
Small Spiral Notebook, 172 5th Ave., #104, Brooklyn, NY 11217
Smokelong Quarterly, 239 Corby Pl., Castle Rock, CO 80108
Somerset Hall Press, 416 Commonwealth Ave., Ste. 117, Boston, MA 02215
So To Speak, George Mason Univ., 4400 Univ. Dr., MSN 206, Fairfax, VA 22030
Soundings East, English Dept., Salem State College, Salem, MA 01970
The Southeast Review, English Dept., Florida State Univ., Tallahassee, FL 32306
Southern Arts Journal, P.O. Box 13739, Greensboro, NC 27415
Southern Poetry Review, 11935 Abercorn St., Savannah, GA 31419
The Southern Review, Louisiana State Univ., Baton Rouge, LA 70803
Southwest Review, Southern Methodist Univ., P.O. Box 750374, Dallas, TX 75275
Speakeasy, 1011 Washington Ave. S, Ste. 200, Minneapolis, MN 55415
Spoon River Poetry Review, Illinois State Univ., Campus Box 4241, Normal, IL 61790
Spuytenduyvil, 42 St. John's Place, Brooklyn, NY 11217
Starcherone Books, P.O. Box 303, Buffalo, NY 14201
Stirring, 501 S. Elm St., #1, Champaign, IL 61820
Story Circle Journal, 5802 Wynona Ave., Austin, TX 78756
Story Quarterly, 431 Sheridan Rd., Kenilworth, IL 60043
Story South, 898 Chelsea Ave., Bexley OH 43209
The Storyteller Magazine, 2441 Washington Rd., Maynard, AR 72444
The Strange Fruit, 300 Lenora St., #250, Seattle, WA 98121
Streetlight, P.O. Box 259, Charlottesville, VA 22902
The Summerset Review, 25 Summerset Dr., Smithtown, NY 11787
The Sun, 107 N. Roberson St., Chapel Hill, NC 27516
Sun Rising Books, 724 Felix St., St. Joseph, MO 64501
Swan Scythe Press, 2052 Calaveras Ave., Davis, CA 95616
Sweet Annie Press, 7750 Hwy F-24W, Baxter, IA 50028
Swivel Magazine, P.O. Box 17958, Seattle, WA 98107

T

Tampa Review, 401 Kennedy Blvd., Tampa, FL 33606
Texas Poetry Journal, P.O. Box 90635, Austin, TX 78709
Third Coast, English Dept., WMU, Kalamazoo, MI 49008
32 Poems, P.O. Box 5824, Hyattsville, MD 20782
three candles, 5470 132nd Ln, Savage, MN 55378
Threepenny Review, P.O. Box 9131, Berkeley, CA 94709
Timber Creek Review, 8969 UNCG Sta., Greensboro, NC 27413
Tin House, 2601 NW Thurman St., Portland, OR 97210
Toadlily Press, Box 2, Chappaqua, NY 10514
Traprock Books, 1330 E. 25th Ave., Eugene, OR 97403
Travelers' Tales, 350 Stonegate Lane, Front Royal, VA 22630
Triple Tree Publishing, P.O. Box 5684, Eugene, OR 97405

Triplopia, 6816 Mt. Vernon Ave., Salisbury, MD 21804
TriQuarterly, Northwestern Univ. Press, 629 Noyes St., Evanston, IL 60208
Tryst Poetry, 3521 Longfellow Ave., Minneapolis, MN 55407
Tupelo Press, P.O. Box 539, Dorset, VT 05251
Turnrow, English Dept., Univ. of Louisiana, Monroe, LA 71209

U

Underground Voices Magazine, P.O. Box 931671, Los Angeles, CA 90093
University of Georgia Press, 330 Research Dr., Athens, GA 30602
University of Nevada Press, Reno, NV 89557
University of New Mexico Press, 1601 Randolph Rd, SE, Ste. 2005, Albuquerque, NM 87106
U.S.1 Poets' Cooperative, P.O. Box 127, Kingston, NJ 08528

V

Valley Contemporary Poets, P.O. Box 661614, Los Angeles, CA 90066
Vallum Magazine, P.O. Box 48003, Montreal, Que., H2V 4S8, CANADA
Val Verde Press, 30163 Lexington Dr., Val Verde, CA 91384
Velvet Mafia/Outsider Ink, 201 W. 11th St, Ste. 6E, New York, NY 10014
Verse Libre Quarterly, Box 185, Falls Church, VA 22040
Verse Press, 221 Pine St., #258, Florence, MA 01062
Vestal Review, 2609 Dartmouth Dr., Vestal, NY 13850
The Vocabula Review, 5A Holbrook Ct., Rockport, MA 01966
The Voice, 8906 Aubrey L. Pkwy, Nine Mile Falls, WA 99026
Vox, P.O. Box 4936, University, MS 38677

W

Water-Stone Review, Hamline Univ., 1536 Hewitt Ave., St. Paul, MN 55104
Wayne State University Press, 4809 Woodward Ave., Detroit, MI 48201
We Press, P.O. Box 436, Allamuchy, NJ 07820
West Branch, Bucknell Univ., Lewisburg, PA 17837
West Wind Review, 1250 Siskiyou Blvd., Ashland, OR 97520
Western Humanities Review, English Dept., Univ. of Utah, Salt Lake City, UT 84112
Whispering Prairie Press, P.O. Box 8342, Prairie Village, KS 66208
Whistling Shade, P.O. Box 7084, St. Paul, MN 55107
White Pelican Review, P.O. Box 7833, Lakeland, FL 33813
White Whiskers Books, 726 Portola Terrace, Los Angeles, CA 90042
Wild Embers Press, 155 Seventh St., Portland, OR 97520
Wildside Press, LLC, 9710 Traville Gateway Dr., #234, Rockville, MD 20850
Willow Review, College of Lake Co., 19351 W. Washington St., Grayslake, IL 60030
Willow Springs, 705 W. First Ave., Spokane, WA 99201
Winged Victory Press, P.O. Box 16730, Chicago, IL 60616
Wings Press, 627 E. Guenther, San Antonio, TX 78210
Witness, Oakland Community College, 27055 Orchard Lake Rd., Farmington Hills, MI 48334
Wolverine Farm Publishing, P.O. Box 814, Fort Collins, CO 80522
Women in the Arts, P.O. Box 2907, Decatur, IL 62524
The Worcester Review, 1 Elkman St., Worcester, MA 01607
The Word Works, Inc., P.O. Box 42164, Washington, DC 20015

Words of Wisdom, P.O. Box 16542, Greensboro, NC 27416
Words on Walls, 18348 Coral Chase Dr., Boca Raton, FL 33498
Writer's Chronicle, George Mason Univ., Fairfax, VA 22030

X

Xantippe, P.O. Box 20997, Oakland, CA 94620

Y

Yalobusha Review, Bondurant Hall, Box 1848, University, MS 38677

Z

Zahir Publishing, 315 S. Coast Hwy. 101, Ste. U8, Encinitas, CA 92024
Zoetrope, 916 Kearny St., San Francisco, CA 94133
ZYZZYVA, P.O. Box 590069, San Francisco, CA 94159

FOUNDING MEMBERS OF THE PUSHCART PRIZE FELLOWSHIPS

Betty Adcock
Agni
Carolyn Alessio
Dick Allen
Henry H. Allen
Lisa Alvarez
Jan Lee Ande
Ralph Angel
Antietam Review
Ruth Appelhof
Philip Appleman
Linda Aschbrenner
Renee Ashley
Ausable Press
David Baker
Jim Barnes
Catherine Barnett
Dorothy Barresi
Barrow Street Press
Jill Bart
Ellen Bass
Judith Baumel
Ann Beattie
Madison Smartt Bell
Beloit Poetry Journal
Pinckney Benedict
Andre Bernard
Christopher Bernard
Wendell Berry
Linda Bierds
Stacy Bierlein
Bitter Oleander Press
Mark Blaeuer
Blue Lights Press
Carol Bly
BOA Editions
Deborah Bogen
Susan Bono
Anthony Brandt
James Breeden
Rosellen Brown
Jane Brox
Andrea Hollander Budy
L. S. Bumas
Richard Burgin
Skylar H. Burris
David Caliguiuri
Kathy Callaway
Janine Canan
Henry Carlile
Fran Castan
Chelsea Associates
Marianne Cherry
Phillis M. Choyke
Suzanne Cleary

Joan Connor
John Copenhaven
Dan Corrie
Tricia Currans-Sheehan
Jim Daniels
Thadious Davis
Maija Devine
Sharon Dilworth
Edward J. DiMaio
Kent Dixon
John Duncklee
Elaine Edelman
Renee Edison & Don Kaplan
Nancy Edwards
M.D. Elevitch
Failbetter.com
Irvin Faust
Tom Filer
Susan Firer
Nick Flynn
Stakey Flythe Jr.
Peter Fogo
Linda N. Foster
Fugue
Alice Fulton
Eugene K. Garber
Frank X. Gaspar
A Gathering of the Tribes
Reginald Gibbons
Emily Fox Gordon
Philip Graham
Eamon Grennan
Lee Meitzen Grue
Habit of Rainy Nights
Rachel Hadas
Susan Hahn
Meredith Hall
Harp Strings
Jeffrey Harrison
Lois Marie Harrod
Healing Muse
Lily Henderson
Daniel Henry
Neva Herington
Lou Hertz
William Heyen
Bob Hicok
R. C. Hildebrandt
Kathleen Hill
Edward Hoagland
Daniel Hoffman
Doug Holder
Richard Holinger
Rochelle L. Holt
Richard M. Huber

511

Brigid Hughes
Lynne Hugo
Illya's Honey
Susan Indigo
Mark Irwin
Beverly A. Jackson
Richard Jackson
David Jauss
Marilyn Johnston
Alice Jones
Journal of New Jersey Poets
Robert Kalich
Julia Kasdorf
Miriam Poli Katsikis
Meg Kearney
Celine Keating
Brigit Kelly
John Kistner
Judith Kitchen
Stephen Kopel
David Kresh
Maxine Kumin
Valerie Laken
Babs Lakey
Maxine Landis
Lane Larson
Dorianne Laux & Joseph Millar
Sydney Lea
Donald Lev
Dana Levin
Gerald Locklin
Rachel Lodin
Radomir Luza, Jr.
Annette Lynch
Elzabeth MacKierman
Elizabeth Macklin
Leah Maines
Mark Manalang
Norma Marder
Jack Marshall
Michael Martone
Tara L. Masih
Dan Masterson
Peter Matthiessen
Alice Mattison
Tracy Mayor
Robert McBrearty
Jane McCafferty
Bob McCrane
Jo McDougall
Sandy McIntosh
James McKean
Roberta Mendel
Didi Menendez
Barbara Milton
Alexander Mindt
Mississippi Review

Martin Mitchell
Roger Mitchell
Jewell Mogan
Patricia Monaghan
Jim Moore
James Morse
William Mulvihill
Carol Muske-Dukes
Edward Mycue
W. Dale Nelson
Daniel Orozco
Other Voices
Pamela Painter
Paris Review
Alan Michael Parker
Ellen Parker
Veronica Patterson
David Pearce
Robert Phillips
Donald Platt
Valerie Polichar
Pool
Jeffrey & Priscilla Potter
Marcia Preston
Eric Puchner
Barbara Quinn
Belle Randall
Martha Rhodes
Nancy Richard
Stacey Richter
Katrina Roberts
Judith R. Robinson
Jessica Roeder
Martin Rosner
Kay Ryan
Sy Safransky
Brian Salchert
James Salter
Sherod Santos
R.A. Sasaki
Valerie Sayers
Alice Schell
Dennis & Loretta Schmitz
Helen Schulman
Philip Schultz
Shenandoah
Peggy Shinner
Vivian Shipley
Joan Silver
John E. Smelcer
Raymond J. Smith
Philip St. Clair
Lorraine Standish
Michael Steinberg
Barbara Stone
Storyteller Magazine
Bill & Pat Strachan

Julie Suk
Sweet Annie Press
Katherine Taylor
Pamela Taylor
Marcelle Thiébaux
Robert Thomas
Andrew Tonkovich
Juanita Torrence-Thompson
William Trowbridge
Martin Tucker
Victoria Valentine
Tino Villanueva
William & Jeanne Wagner
BJ Ward
Susan Oard Warner
Rosanna Warren
Margareta Waterman
Michael Waters

Sandi Weinberg
Andrew Weinstein
Jason Wesco
West Meadow Press
Susan Wheeler
Dara Wier
Ellen Wilbur
Galen Williams
Marie Sheppard Williams
Irene K. Wilson
Steven Wingate
Wings Press
Robert W. Witt
Margo Wizansky
Matt Yurdana
Christina Zawadiwsky
Sander Zulauf
ZYZZYVA

SUSTAINING MEMBERS FOR THIS EDITION

Agni
Carolyn Alessio
Henry Alley
Anonymous
Jacob M. Appel
Philip Appleman
Marjorie Appleman
Renee Ashley
Ausable Press
David Baker
Catherine Barnett
Dorothy Barresi
Charles Baxter
Ann Beattie
Joe David Bellamy
Beloit Poetry Journal
Linda Bierds
Carol Bly
BOA Editions
Bridgeworks Press
Ethan Burmas
Steve Cannon
Fran Castan
Siv Cedering
Dan Chaon
Chelsea Editions
Suzanne Cleary
Martha Collins
Joan Connor
Bernard Connors
Tricia Currans-Sheehan
Ben Davidson
Kent Dixon
Dan Dolgin
Nancy Edwards

Dallas Ernst
Finishing Line Press
Sharon & Ben Fountain
Gina Frangello
Alan Furst
Eugene Garber
Loraine Gardner
Meredith Hall
Hamptons Shorts
Jeffrey Harrison
Gwen Head
Neva Herrington
Kathleen Hill
Jane Hirshfield
Edward Hoagland
Daniel Hoffman
Doug Holder
Richard M. Huber
Mark Irwin
David Jauss
Renee & Don Kaplan
Miriam P. Katsikis
Edmund Keeley
Thomas Kennedy
Judith Kitchen
David Kresh
Maxine Kumin
Valerie Laken
Dorianne Laux
Sydney Lea
Gerry Locklin
Annette Lynch
Elizabeth Macklin
Norma Marder
Michael Martone

The Pushcart Prize Fellowships Inc., a 501 (c) (3) nonprofit corporation, is the endowment for The Pushcart Prize. We also make grants to promising new writers. "Members" donated up to $249 each, "Sponsors" gave between $250 and $999. "Benefactors" donated from $1000 to $4,999. "Patrons" donated $5,000 and more. We are very grateful for these donations. Gifts of any amount are welcome. For information write to the Fellowships at PO Box 380, Wainscott, NY 11975.

514

CONTRIBUTORS' NOTES

LINSEY ABRAMS teaches at CCNY in New York. She is editor of *Global City Review*.

TONY BARNSTONE teaches at Whittier College in California. His books have been published by Sheep Meadow Press, University Press of Florida, Anchor Books and Prentice Hall.

BRUCE BEASLEY is the author of six poetry collections, most recently *Signs and Abominations* (Wesleyan). He lives in Bellingham, Washington.

KAREN BENDER is the author of the novel *Like Normal People* (Houghton Mifflin). Her fiction has appeared in the *New Yorker*, *Granta*, *Zoetrope*, and other magazines. She is at work on new stories and a novel and teaches at the University of North Carolina.

RICHARD BURGIN is the author of eleven books, including the novel *Ghost Quartet*. He edits the journal *Boulevard*.

WENDELL BERRY is a poet, novelist, essayist and philosopher who has written dozens of books of poetry, fiction and essays. He is the recipient of Wallace Stegner and Guggenheim Fellowships. He lives and farms in rural Kentucky.

KATE BRAVERMAN has won numerous awards for her fiction. She lives in San Francisco. This is her first appearance in the Pushcart Prize.

JAMES LEE BURKE has authored a short story collection and many books of fiction for which he has twice won the Edgar Award. His most recent novel is *Pegasus Descending* (Simon & Schuster, 2006).

JONATHAN CARROLL lives in Vienna, Austria. He is the author of fourteen volumes available from Orb Books and Tor Books.

KIM CHINQUEE's fiction has appeared in *Denver Quarterly*, *Fiction International*, *Cottonwood*, *North Dakota Quarterly* and other journals. She lives in Michigan.

JOHN CLAYTON's stories have been published in many periodicals and have been anthologized in O. Henry, Best American and Pushcart Prize collections. His third novel is *Kuperman's Fire*.

AVERILL CURDY lives in Chicago and teaches at Northwestern University. Her poems have appeared in *Raritan*, *The Paris Review*, *32 Poems* and elsewhere.

MICHAEL CZYZNEIJEWSKI lives in Bowling Green, Ohio and teaches at Bowling Green State University. He is editor of *Mid-American Review* and his stories have appeared in *Witness*, *Bat City Review*, *StoryQuarterly* and elsewhere.

BRIAN DOYLE is the editor of *Portland Magazine* and the author of seven books, most recently *The Wet Engine* and *The Grail*. He lives in Portland, Oregon.

DAVID JAMES DUNCAN lives in Lolo, Montana. This is his second appearance in the Pushcart Prize.

STEPHEN DUNN won the 2001 Pulitzer Prize. He is the author of fourteen poetry collections including *Everything Else In The World* (Norton 2006).

PAM DURBIN is the author of a short story collection and two novels. She is a recipient of an NEA Fellowship and Whiting Writers Award. She teaches at the University of North Carolina at Chapel Hill.

BEN FOUNTAIN is the author of the short story collection *Brief Encounters With Che Guevara* and the forthcoming novel *The Texas Inch*, both from Echo. He lives in Dallas.

STEVE GEHRKE's third book was selected for the National Poetry Series and will be soon published by the University of Illinois Press.

SCOTT GEIGER is a member of the Architecture Research Office. His short fiction has appeared in *Lady Churchhill's Rosebud Wristlet* and *Conjunctions*.

LOUISE GLÜCK is the author of numerous books of poetry including most recently *The Seven Ages* (Echo

2001). She has received the Pulitzer Prize, the William Carlos Williams Award and the National Book Critics Circle Award. In 2003 she was named Poet Laureate of the United States.

MARK HALLIDAY's books are *Little Star* (1987), *Tasker Street* (1992), *Selfwroth* (1999) and *Jab* (2002). He teaches at Ohio University.

TONY HOAGLAND's most recent collection of poems is *Hard Rain* (Hollyridge Press). His book of essays about poetry is just out from Graywolf Press. In 2003 he was a finalist for the National Book Critics Circle Award.

MARK IRWIN is the author of five poetry collections including most recently *Bright Hunger* (2004). He teaches at the University of Southern California.

KATHERINE KARLIN is a doctoral candidate at the University of Southern California. Her fictions appear in numerous journals and she is at work on a novel.

MARY KARR's new book of poems is *Sinners Welcome* (Harper Collins 2006). She has written two memoirs, *The Liars' Club* (1995) and *Cherry* (2000).

LAURA KASISCHKE's most recent novel is the *Life Before Her Eyes* (Harcourt 2002). She has also published six collections of poetry and teaches at the University of Michigan.

SALLY KEITH's first book, *Designed*, won the 2000 Colorado Prize. Her second book, *Dwelling Song*, was published from the University of Georgia Contemporary Poetry Series.

KRISTIN KOVACIC is co-editor of *Birth: A Literary Companion*(University of Iowa Press). Her work has appeared in many magazines and she teaches writing in Pittsburgh.

LAURA KRUGHOFF lives, writes and teaches in Chicago. Her short stories have appeared in several literary journals.

JULIE LARIOS lives in Seattle. This is her first appearance in The Pushcart Prize.

PHILIP LEVINE's most recent book is *Breath* (Knopf 2004). He lives in Fresno and New York City.

E. J. LEVY's essays and stories have appeared in the *Missouri Review*, *Orion*, *The Paris Review*, *Gettysburg Review*, and *North American Review* and have been recognized with numerous awards.

CLEOPATRA MATHIS directs the creative writing department at Dartmouth College. Her sixth book of poems, *White Sea*, is just out from Sarabande Books.

ALICE MATTISON's *In Case We're Separated: Collected Stories* was published in 2005, her eighth book. She teaches at the Bennington Writing Seminars.

ELIZABETH McCRACKEN was a finalist for the National Book Award and won the Pen/Winship Award, plus grants from the NEA and the Guggenheim Foundation.

W. S. MERWIN is the recipient of the Pulitzer, Bollingen, Tanning, and Lenora Marshal poetry prizes. His *Migration: New and Selected Poems* (Copper Canyon Press) won the National Book Award.

KEVIN MOFETT won the Iowa Short Fiction Award in 2006 for his story collection *Permanent Visitors*. He lives in Gettysburg, Pennsylvania.

NAMI MUN lives in Ann Arbor and has published in *Tin House*, *Iowa Review* and *Evergreen Review*.

JEAN NORDHAUS is the author of *Innocence*, just out from Ohio State University Press. Her other poetry books are available from Milkweed Editions.

RISTEARD O'KEITINN is an engineer, inventor, painter and novelist who has published in both the US and the UK. He presently lives in Illinois.

DZVINIA ORLOWSKY is the author of three poetry collections from Carnegie Mellon University. She is founding editor of Four Way Books.

LISA OLSTEIN's first collection of poems, *Radio Crackling, Radio Gone*, won 2005 Hayden Carruth Award and will soon be published by Copper Canyon Press.

JACQUELINE OSHEROW is the author of four previous poetry collections. Her poems have appeared in collections from W. W. Norton and Penguin.

BENJAMIN PERCY is the author of *The Language of Elk*. His stories have appeared in *Swink*, *The Greensboro Review*, *Amazing Stories* and elsewhere.

KEVIN PRUFER's newest book is *National Anthem* (Four Way). He is an editor of *Pleiades* and lives in rural Missouri.

MARY ANN SAMYN lives in Morgantown, West Virginia. This is her first appearance in the Pushcart Prize.

KEITH RATZLAFF's poems and reviews have appeared in *New England Review*, *Arts and Letters*, *Colorado Review*, *The North American Review* and elsewhere. He teaches at Central College, Pella, Iowa.

DONALD REVELL is the author of nine previous collections of poetry, most recently *Pennyweight Window: New and Selected Poems* (Alice James Books 2005). He is the poetry editor of *The Colorado Review*.

STACY RICHTER is the author of *My Date With Satan*, a collection of stories. She lives in Tucson, Arizona. Her next book will be out soon from Counterpoint.

KAY RYAN's most recent book is *The Niagara River*. She is the author of six books of poetry.

DAVID SCHUMAN lives in St. Louis and teaches at Washington University. He is associate editor of *The Land-Grant College Review*.

REGINALD SHEPHERD is the author of four books of poetry, all from the University of Pittsburgh Press. His next book, *Fatima Orgama*, is forthcoming from Pittsburgh next year.

FLOYD SKLOTT is the author of several books of poetry, memoir and fiction. He lives in Amity, Oregon.

R. T. SMITH is the author of three collections of poetry including most recently *The Hollow Log Lounge* (University of Illinois 2003). A new collection is due out next year from the University of Arkansas Press.

MAUREEN STANTON lives in Georgetown, Maine. Her essays have appeared in *Fourth Genre*, *The Sun*, *Iowa Review* and other journals. She has received numerous fellowships, including a 2006 NEA grant.

SUSAN TERRIS' third book is *Natural Defenses* (Marsh Hawk Press 2004). Her next book, *Contrari Wise*, will be published by Time Being Books next year. She is co-editor of *Runes*.

NATASHA TRETHEWEY is recipient of fellowships from the Guggenheim Foundation, the NEA, the Bunting Fellowship Program at Radcliffe and the Rockefeller Foundation. She is the author most recently of *Native Guard* (Houghton Mifflin 2006) plus two books from Graywolf.

BRIAN TURNER lives in Fresno. This is his first appearance in the Pushcart Prize.

DINA BEN-LEV is the author of three poetry collections. She lives in Dalton, Georgia.

SHARMILA VOORAKKARA teaches at Ohio University. Her first book, *Fire Wheel*, was published in 2005 at the University of Akron Press.

PHILIP WHITE teaches at Centre College in Danville, Kentucky. His poems have appeared in *The New Republic*, *Southwest Review*, *Literary Imagination* and elsewhere.

INDEX

The following is a listing in alphabetical order by author's last name of works reprinted in the *Pushcart Prize* editions since 1976.

519

520

521

524

526

527

528

531

532

533

535

536

543

545

547

548

549